RANDOM
HOUSE

LARGE
PRINT

THIS STORM

JAMES ELLROY

THIS STORM

A NOVEL

RANDOM HOUSE
LARGE PRINT

Copyright © 2019 by James Ellroy

All rights reserved.
Published in the United States of America by Random House Large Print in association with Alfred A. Knopf, a division of Penguin Random House LLC, New York.

Cover design by Chip Kidd
Cover photograph: Hollywood, California. Old Visuals / Alamy

Title pages and part opening pages: Rain over black background by sirtravelalot / Shutterstock

The Library of Congress has established a Cataloging-in-Publication record for this title.

ISBN: 978-0-593-16437-2

www.penguinrandomhouse.com/large-print-format-books

FIRST LARGE PRINT EDITION

Printed in the United States of America

10 9 8 7 6 5 4 3 2 1

This Large Print edition published in accord with the standards of the N.A.V.H.

To **HELEN KNODE**

Blood alone moves the wheels of history.

—Benito "Il Duce" Mussolini

THIS STORM

Reminiscenza.

I remain spellbound. That then-to-now fever still consumes me. I am very old and the sole living witness. The Maestro willed me his piano and the score we smuggled from Russia. I retain faultless vision and memory. Long bouts of practice keep my hands strong.

I compose at the keyboard. Improvisation spawns recollection. Words and music sustain me and forge my repudiation of death.

The war.

The rain.

The gold.

Los Angeles and Mexico, the Fifth Column.

I will not die as long as I live this story.

THE THUNDERBOLT BROADCAST/FATHER CHARLES COUGHLIN/XERB RADIO, LOS ANGELES. BOOTLEG TRANSMITTER: TIJUANA, MEXICO. TUESDAY, DECEMBER 30, 1941

Good evening and **bienvenidos,** a belated **Feliz Navidad,** and let's not forget **próspero año y felicidad**—which means "Happy New Year" in English and serves to introduce the Mexico-at-war theme of tonight's broadcast. And at war we are, my fellow American listeners—even though we sure as shooting didn't want to be in the first place.

Let's talk turkey here. **Es la verdad,** as our Mex cousins say. We've been in this Jew-inspired boondoggle a mere twenty-three days, and we've been forced to stand with the rape-happy Russian Reds against the more sincerely simpatico Nazis. That's a shattering shame, but our Jew-pawn president, Franklin "Double-Cross" Rosenfeld, has deliriously decreed that we must fight **der Führer,** so fight that heroic **jefe** we regretfully must. It's a ways off, though—because we've got our hands full with the Japs right now.

So, let's meander down Mexico way—where the **señoritas** sizzle and more HELL-bent **jefes** hold sway.

Mexico connotes **"PROUDLY CATHOLIC,"** does it not, friends? Add **THEOCRATIC REPUBLIC, ANTI-RED,** and **DUTIFULLY RELIGIOUS** to that. It paints a picture, doesn't it? Yes—but the picture is wholly inaccurate and sorrowfully seditious, dating back to the tempestuous '20s and the repugnant Red reign of **Presidente** Plutarco Calles.

Item: Calles instituted a Six-Year Plan for social and political reform, patterned after Red Russia's Five-Year Plan.

Item: Calles set out to eradicate the influence of the Catholic Church, barred religious festivals and processions, and created "workers' collectives" to counter the alleged excesses of industrial capitalism and further secularize the Mexican body politic, despite the stubborn opposition of the **CATHOLIC** Mexican people.

Item: Catholic bishops were forced to suspend public worship.

Item: Calles's "Redshirt" goon squads shuttered churches across Mexico.

Item: priests were murdered, nuns were raped, bishops sought South American asylum, and the Holy Mass was performed as a secret sacrament.

Item: cancerous Calles was succeeded by limp leftist Lázaro Cárdenas. He was a motley mollycoddler of a less malicious sort. His anticlerical policies bore a still Stalinist, but less overt stink. Priests were still murdered, nuns were still raped, provincial despots still shuttered churches and satanically forbade Mass.

Item: these practices continue under current **Presidente** Manuel Ávila Camacho—a purported "leftist-centrist"—read that as one mealymouthed **muchacho.**

This brings us to the Cristeros—the ripsnorting, righteous, **CATHOLIC** resistance.

The Goldshirts—not the **Red**shirts of the Calles/Cárdenas/Communist ilk. The armed home guard that fought fire with fire, killed Redshirts, lynched Communist commissars and apoplectic apparatchiks, and burned more than a few Red reptiles alive.

The Cristeros flourished under Calles and were forced into hiding under Cárdenas. In '37 they majestically metamorphosed into the Unión Nacional Sinarquista.

Synarchism means "without anarchy." Sinarquismo represents a full-fledged assault on the anti-Catholic Left. Underground **Üntermenschen** now enforce **Presidente** Camacho's atheistic agenda; the Sinarquistas magnificently mount a Catholic counterattack. The Sinarquistas are growing in number. They proselytize for a merged Catholic-secular state. They've been called **fascistas** and Nazis—but that's all Red hoo-ha. Yes, but they surely grew out of the Spanish Falange and **Generalissimo** Francisco Franco's valiant victory in the Spanish Civil War. And, now—with the United States embroiled in a consuming world conflict, and with Mexico situated at our southernmost tip—will the Greenshirt Sinarquistas serve our best interests as the emergent world power both anti-Axis and nationalistically non-Red?

Item: Mexico has remained "neutral" in this world conflict so far.

Item: **Presidente** Camacho closed the German consulate in August '41 but has let a great many pro-Axis Krauts and Japs linger down May-hee-co way.

Enter Baja California.

Baja's that lurid lick of Mexican land south of our own San Diego. It's a hellish hotbed of fascist-**comunista** intrigue. There's a great many resident Japs. The Mex State Police suspect the presence of a great many Jap submarine berths along Baja's Pacific coastline. There's talk of secret Jap air bases being readied for raids on U.S. naval installations and defense plants near Los Angeles.

Enter Sinarquista boss man Salvador Abascal.

Señor Abascal **es muy católico.** He's the Sinarquista's spiritual and intellectual leader, and wears Sinarquismo's Greenshirt proudly. Like most male adherents to Sinarquismo, he wears a small "SQ" with a coiled snake encircling it, tattooed in the web of his right forefinger and thumb. He's a handsome man of thirty-one—and **Presidente** Camacho seems to fear him.

Item: the Sinarquista membership is growing in Mexico and the U.S.

Item: punk patriarch Camacho has granted them land for an encampment at Magdalena Bay in

Southern Baja. Is he isolating the Sinarquistas or readying them for some task?

U.S. Army Intelligence officers are mobilizing in Baja. They will sort out the political gestalt and round up Japs, in a replication of our own Jap-internment efforts. What's the upshot here? Will Mexico end its neutered neutral stance and throw in with Uncle Sam? America is now alarmingly aligned with the repugnant Russian Reds, and allied against the nifty but nefarious Nazis. Will the Mexican peso and the U.S. dollar plummet and will a new gold standard arise? What about those ripe rumors—Nazis and Russkies melting gold bars into swastika and hammer-and-sickle artifacts?

Mexico, my American **hermanos** and Christian countrymen. It's the southern gateway to our cherished shores. Will waterlogged wetbacks breach our borders and sap us with sabotage? Will the Sinarquistas come to our aid as a heroic home guard?

Part One
RAIN

(December 31, 1941–
January 23, 1942)

1

(LOS ANGELES, 9:30 P.M., 12/31/41)

Stakeout.

It's a sit-and-wait job. Some hot-prowl burglar/rape-o's out creeping. He's Tommy Glennon, recent Quentin grad. He's notched five 459/sodomies since Pearl Harbor.

Happy fucking New Year.

Three-man stakeout. Two parked cars. 24th and Normandie. Sit and wait. Endure bugs-up-your-ass ennui.

The rain. Plus war-blackout regulations. Drawn shades, doused streetlamps. Bum visibility.

It's a stag hunt. The PD worked that way. Four victims mugshot-ID'd Tommy. The Chief and Dudley Smith conferred. They called it. Per always: perv shit on women mandates **DEATH.**

Elmer gargled Old Crow. He had the front-house car. Mike Breuning and Dick Carlisle had the alley.

Tommy had the crib cased. Two leggy sisters lived there. Lockstep surveillance locked down the gestalt.

Central Burglary tailed Tommy a week running. Elmer moved the sisters out and moved his leggy girl-friend in. She had the legs and the stones for the job.

Ellen Drew. His **part**-time girlfriend and **part**-time Paramount starlet. Ellen glommed raves in **If I Were King** and went **pffft.** She **part**-time whored for Elmer and his **full**-time girlfriend.

Brenda Allen. **Part**-time squeeze of Chief Jack Horrall. It's who you know and who you blow. Call-Me-Jack set up the bait gig.

Elmer scoped the house. Upstairs lights gleamed. Ellen cracked the shades to spotlight her gams. It violated blackout regs and lit her legs **gooooood.** Tommy G. was a leg man. Elmer read his Quentin file and glommed the gestalt.

Thomas Malcolm Glennon/white male American/ DOB 8/19/16. Preston Reform School and Quentin. Tight with pachucos and Four Families tong men.

Fireworks popped somewhere north. The rain drenched the sparks and killed the effect.

"It's who you know."

Elmer knew Dudley and Call-Me-Jack. Thus, this shit job. Mike B. and Dick C. were Dudley's strong-arm goons. Dud got the night off. Some unknown geek shivved him three days ago.

Elmer yawned. Elmer futzed with his two-way radio. Police calls spritzed.

Niggertown 211/Happytime Liquor/prowl cars at

scene. Dope roust at Club Zombie. Mexi**coon** rumble, 84th and Avalon. Zoot-suit beaners **ex**-cape.

Elmer yawned. Elmer skimmed the dial. He hit a civilian band and got lucky. The PD's New Year's bash warbled.

It's live from City Hall. It features Count Basie's Band. The Detective Bureau muster room's rigged with radio mikes. The Count's at the keyboard. There's Lester Young's sax.

Here's the inside tattle. Two bluesuits popped the Count with reefers. Jack Horrall caught wind and tossed the pitch. Your call, Count. Six months honor farm or a one-night engagement?

Rain slammed the car. Said rain outslammed Count Basie. Elmer skimmed to Band 3. He caught an open line to Breuning and Carlisle.

"Know" and "blow." Maladroit Mike and Dipshit Dick. This jive New Year's Eve. What good's your insider-cop status?

He loved Headquarters Vice. It dispensed yuks and served to scotch his call-biz competition. Then the fucking Japs bombed fucking Pearl Harbor and fucked the white world up the brown trail.

He got detached to the Alien Squad. It was Japs twelve days a week. Japs, Japs, **JAPS.** Foreign-born, native-born, for sure and alleged Fifth Column. Raid their pads. Confiscate their goods. Transport them to ritzy horse stalls at Santa Anita.

Band 3 popped sound. Breuning and Carlisle bullshitted. Who shivved the Dudster? Their rambunctious kids. This meter maid with jugs out to here.

Breuning and Carlisle gassed. They hashed out the Fed's phone-tap probe. The PD was knee-deep in shit. It's a nail-biter.

City Hall was bugged and tapped, floor-to-rafters. Rival cop factions spied on each other. Grifter cops, tonged-up cops, cop strikebreakers. The Feds took note and launched a probe.

Cop fiefdoms. Cop thieves. Cops in the Silver Shirts and German-American Bund. Calls to the DA's Office. Calls to Mayor Fletch Bowron. Detective Bureau cops be **scaaared.**

Elmer was **scared.** He ran a call-girl ring. He peddled flesh to the L.A. elite. He made biz calls from the Vice squadroom.

The radio browned out. Shit—line crackle, static, hiss. Elmer twirled the dial. He caught some luck there. Good Lord—it's Cliffie Stone's **Hometown Jamboree.**

It was auld lang syne for displaced crackers. That was him, defined. Cliffie connoted hayrides and moonshine. Cliffie brought back Wisharts, North Carolina.

Wisharts was Klan Kountry. Geography is destiny. Klan life fucked up his daddy and big brother, Wayne Frank. That hate-the-jigs diet stuck in young Elmer's craw. He hit eighteen in '30. He joined the Marine Corps. Semper Fi: Parris Island, Camp Lejeune, Nicaragua.

Man-o-Man Managua. The Marine detachment

backstops puppet **Führer** Somoza. Jarheads snuff his political rivals and stand embassy guard. They're bellhops and part-time assassins. **El Jefe** loves Lance Corporal E. V. Jackson. Hence a plum job: run **Jefe**'s favorite whorehouse.

He learned the biz that way. It spawned his notion of call-service-to-your-door girls. **Jefe** shot him Plum Job #2. He watchdogged the L.A. police chief.

James Edgar "Two-Gun" Davis. One vivid lunatic. Davis and **Jefe** were sordid soul mates. They boozed and whored together. Davis loved Lance Corporal E. V. Jackson. Here's why:

A leftist zealot charged Davis with a machete. Lance Corporal Jackson shot and killed him. Davis shot Lance Corporal Jackson a police department appointment.

Goodbye, Marine Corps. Hello, Los Angeles.

Elmer liked police work. Davis set him up with a cooze pusher named Brenda Allen. Elmer and Brenda clicked. They concocted their phone-exchange biz and saw it flourish. The L.A. grand jury sacked Two-Gun Davis. He poked one Jailbait Jill too many and took it up the dirt road.

Call-Me-Jack's in now. He's got 7% of the call biz. Sergeant E. V. Jackson is twenty-nine. He's one lucky white man.

Cliffie Stone laid down hick ballads. That was Wayne Frank's mawkish meter. Wayne Frank was a hate dog and nativist nabob. Kid brother Elmer notched opportunities. Wayne Frank harvested shit.

Wayne Frank goes Klan, goes rumdum, goes hobo. He habituates the West Coast and clocks an untimely end.

Elmer gargled Old Crow. He was half-tanked. It was 10:18. Tommy G. always hit between 10:00 and midnight.

The hick music rubbed him raw. He doused the radio and gassed on the rain. His prowl car was sunk fender-deep.

He checked the house. Cracked blinds gave him a look-see. Ellen was upstairs. She was pacing and smoking. She provided a Leg Show De-luxe. Smoke plumes plumed out a transom slot.

Elmer tuned in Band 3. Mike B. groused to Dick C. Dudster this, Dudster that. More drift per their rambunctious kids.

More line fuzz and static. Elmer killed his jug and tossed it out the window. "Whoa, Junior" fuzzed in.

Elmer grabbed the receiver and flipped the talk switch. The fuzz-static cleared.

"Yeah, Mike."

"Our boy's coming south. He hopped the next-door fence. You take the front. Let him sniff Ellen and start upstairs before you sh—"

Elmer jumped.

He shoved out the door. He puddle-leaped and lunged for the curb. His shoes squished and leaked. He pulled his piece and chambered a round.

His hat flew off. The rain stung his eyes and ratched

up his vision. He made the lawn/the front porch/ the front door.

It's unlocked. Go in slow now. You oiled the hinges and jambs. Tommy won't hear shit.

He got inside. He smelled Ellen's cigarette smoke and perfume. He made for the stairway. He squished all over the living room rug.

Mike and Dick squished toward him. They hit the stairway. Everybody went **sssssshhh.**

They scoped Tommy's muddy footprints. They heard floorboard creaks and foot scuffs upstairs.

Mike winked. Dick did that slice-the-throat thing. Elmer gulped—**mother dog, holy shit—**

Ellen screamed.

Mike whooped. Dick whooped. They ran upstairs and raised a ruckus. They bumped each other off the walls and hit the landing. Elmer heard front-window glass shatter. Tommy pulled some human-fly stunt.

Elmer ran back out the door. There's that black sky and sluice rain, there's half a glimpse. There's Human Fly Tommy, running northbound—

He's two front yards up. He's cutting toward the sidewalk. There's no soaked grass and more traction there.

Elmer cut crossways and hit asphalt. His flapping raincoat slowed him down. He gained ground, lost ground, gained ground. He aimed at Tommy's back and popped three rounds. Muzzle flash turned the rain red.

Tommy gained ground. Mike and Dick fired—back there, long-distance. Shots ricocheted off front porches.

Tommy ran east on 26th. Elmer caught a sideways look and emptied his clip. The flare messed with his eyes and made little halos.

Elmer ran east. He reloaded and sprinted. His raincoat slipped off. Window shades went up. He got some sight-in light.

He gained ground. His wind faltered. Something dropped from Tommy's pants pocket. He stopped and aimed tight. He had him, he had him, something said **DON'T.** He squeezed three shots wide on purpose.

Tommy cut north. He's a Human Fly. He's a fleet-foot rape-o. Watch him vamoose.

Elmer heard Mike and Dick, way back there. Shots bounced off the street. Them dumbfucks blasted will-o'-the-wisps.

Elmer stopped and caught some breath. He walked east and checked the sidewalk.

Tommy dropped something. Elmer saw it and picked it up. Well, now. Tommy dropped a red leather address book.

Ellen said, "Swell New Year's."

Elmer said, "I had that same thought."

"I guess you're not much of a shot."

"Come **on.** At night, in the rain?"

They drove through Hollywood. Ellen flopped at the Green Gables Apartments. It adjoined Paramount and lubed early cast calls. Ellen had a second marriage going. Two husbands and a kid at age twenty-seven. Her hubby was off with the Air Corps. She serviced Elmer's clients out of ennui. She serviced Elmer, likewise.

Elmer hit Melrose, westbound. Call it Aquacade by Night. Muted streetlamps. The blackout and curb-high floodwater.

Ellen lit a cigarette. "He pulled out his pecker and waved it. That's when I screamed."

Elmer yocked. Ellen wagged a pinkie. Tommy Glennon—hung like a cashew.

Elmer yocked anew. Ellen groped his trouser pockets and extracted his roll. She peeled off a fifty and stuffed the roll back.

"That felt nice."

"Not tonight. The weekend, maybe."

"I've got late duty. My bodyguard gig with Hideo Ashida."

Ellen said, "He's cute, for a Jap. Do you think he's queer?"

"Come on. He's the best forensic chemist in this white man's PD."

Ellen tossed her cigarette. "Tell Jack Horrall thanks for the fifty, and tell him no more bait jobs for this little black duck."

"Anything else?"

"Tell him I said you should go back in the Marines. There's a war on, and you should be fighting it, like my husband."

Elmer said, "Do you love me?"

Ellen said, "No. You're just my wartime diversion."

Ellen scrammed at the Gables. Elmer U-turned and booked east. This nutty brainstorm percolated. His short hairs prickled on overdrive.

Tommy G. lived at the Gordon Hotel. Breuning and Carlisle were too lazy to go toss it. The Gordon was straight up Melrose.

Let's prowl Tommy's room. Let's sniff leads. Let's get some buy-back on that fuckup. Let's mess with Dudley Smith.

The Dudster gored his goat. Hey, Elmer—toast this guy. That don't sit right. He ain't no black-robe killer.

The goddamn rain. Backed-up sewers. Mud slides. No hot toddies, no swell women.

Elmer parked upside the Gordon and puddle-jumped in. The lobby was threadbare. A clerk dozed by the switchboard. He wore a green felt leprechaun hat.

Tommy rented 216. Elmer walked upstairs and braced the door. He caught zero voices and no radio warble. He pulled his piece and shoulder-popped the jamb.

No Tommy. No nobody. Just this flop. Just this twelve-by-twelve den of despair.

No bathroom. One closet. A milk-bottle pissoir by the bed. No chairs. One closet, one chest of drawers.

Elmer locked himself in. Thunder shook the whole building. Geeks yelled "Happy New Year!" out on Melrose.

He checked the closet. It contained nada. That meant Tommy lammed. He had a car or stole a car. He traded shots with three cops and vamoosed. Farewell, you rape-o cocksucker.

Elmer tossed the drawers. He caught some provocative shit.

A teach-yourself-Spanish book. A smut-photo book. Spicy donkey-show pix, à la Tijuana. Note the porkpie hat on **El Burro.**

Nazi armbands. Jap flags. One tattoo stencil. Note the excised parts:

Outlines for swastikas. Outlines for an "SQ" circumscribed by coiled snakes.

Elmer thumbed Tommy's address book. More odd shit accrued. Look—there's no addresses and no full names.

Look—a "J.S." and a Hollywood exchange. "St. Vib's" and a downtown exchange. It's probably St. Vibiana's catholic church.

Look—RE-8761. No names or initials. Republic's a south-of-downtown exchange.

Look—MA-4993. That number's familiar. He scoured his brain and snagged it.

Eddie Leng's Kowloon. A Chinatown slop chute. It's open-all-nite. It features tasty shark-fin soup.

Eddie Leng was a Four Families tong geek. Tommy G. was a known tong associate.

Plus: three more no name/no initial numbers.

Elmer grabbed the wall phone and roused the switchboard geek. Get me MA-6884, pronto.

The Detective Bureau. The Vice Squad night line. It was manned round the clock.

He got four rings and a pickup. He heard noise-maker squeal. The clerk came off blotto.

"Uh . . . yeah?"

"Rise and shine, dipshit. You got phone numbers to run."

The clerk yawned. "That you, Elmer?"

"It's me, so grab your pencil."

"I got it here someplace."

Elmer said, "HO-4612. The subscriber's got the initials J.S."

"Okay, I got—"

"The number for St. Vibiana's Church, and the subscriber name for RE-8761."

The clerk perked up. "I know that last number. It's a hot-box pay phone, and them **farkakte** phone-probe Feds been looking at it. A lot of hinky City Hall guys make their hinky calls from there."

Elmer said, "Don't stop now."

"Who's stopping? I was just pausing."

"Come on. Don't string this—"

"It used to be a bookie's hot-box, and the drift is it still is. It's over on 11th and Broadway, by the **Herald.** That **farkakte** reporter Sid Hudgens stiffs his unkosher calls from it."

Sid the Yid. Scandal scribe, putz provocateur. St. Vib's—**the** papist hot spot. Eddie Leng's eatery. **Tommy, what does this shit portend?**

2

(LOS ANGELES, 11:30 P.M., 12/31/41)

Surging brass. Soaring reeds. Driving rain in syncopation.

The muster room jumped. The Count and his boys cranked it. "Annie Laurie" now. Up-tempo and grandly Gaelic.

The room broiled. Steam heat fights cold L.A. winter. Dance-once-a-year cops danced tonight and overdid it. They quaffed table booze and tossed their dates, willy-nilly. The Count observed. White folks were circus clowns. This confirmed it.

Dudley watched. He had a side table and a cracked-for-air window. He wore his Army dress uniform. Claire wore a kelly green frock.

The Archbishop played to her. J. J. Cantwell liked women. He observed his vows and properly abstained.

Monsignor Joe Hayes ignored Claire. She converted. It proved her inauthentic. He reluctantly served as her confessor.

Women repulsed Monsignor Joe. He liked boys. He contravened his vows and indulged his bent.

Father Coughlin liked raw discourse. His trinity was booze, slander, and foment. He loathed the Reds and the kikes. He played to the nuns at St. Vib's and sundered them with hate tracts. He lived to sway souls and spawn discontent.

A waiter restocked the table. He bowed and laid out scotch, gin, and ice. The waiters were county jail trusties. This lad was a weenie waver. He habituated schoolyards and slammed his ham.

Claire freshened drinks. The clerics lit cigarettes and imbibed. The Archbishop ogled Claire. Monsignor Joe ogled the waiter. Father Charles doodled up a napkin. He drew swastikas dripping blood.

Dudley adjusted his sling. His left arm had sustained multiple shiv wounds. A pesky Chink, surely. Tong intrigue, most likely. He was allied with Uncle Ace Kwan and Hop Sing. Said alliance might have spawned rival-tong enmity. Said shiv man would soon be sternly rebuked.

Claire shared her morphine. It facilitated his rapid recovery. Her love for him outweighed her habit. The drug salved pain and rendered the world elegiac. It granted noblesse oblige.

It deadened his recent failures. Pearl Harbor and the Jap roundups as one big botched business deal.

He hatched war-profit schemes. Ace Kwan assisted him. They all went blooey. He chased a heroin stash in Baja. Mike Breuning, Dick Carlisle, and Hideo Ashida assisted. That went blooey. It was Captain Carlos Madrano's stash. Madrano and the Mex Staties interdicted the Smith cartel. A Jap sub fiasco played in. He planted nitro in Madrano's car and blew up **El Capitán.** It was small recompense.

Father Coughlin knew Madrano's replacement. José Vasquez-Cruz was anti-Red and anti-Jew, but less overtly **Fascista.** Baja bodes again now. Police Sergeant Smith as Army Captain Smith. He'll meet Vasquez-Cruz and perhaps seek to suborn him. Baja bodes as opportunity reborn.

Count Basie kicked off a Latin-tinged ballad. Claire squeezed his good arm. Let's dance, **mi corazon.**

The sling curtailed movement. Dudley let Claire help him up and lead him. She cradled his bad arm. They danced close. Claire laid her head on his shoulder.

She said, "We'll be there in two weeks. We'll get tired of this music."

"Major Melnick has secured us a grand hotel suite. We'll have our own terrace, with a lovely ocean view."

Claire nuzzled up. "We'll go to Mass and observe all the saints' days. We'll be taller and better-looking than everyone else, and they won't believe how well we speak Spanish."

Dudley laughed. "The hoi polloi will adore you. They'll call you **'La Gringa'** behind your back, and wonder how this mick thug got so lucky."

"Don't deride yourself, dear. Never forget that I've civilized you more than you've corrupted me."

"It's a toss-up, isn't it? It's a determination that time and fate will reveal."

Claire said, "Yes, darling. It is all of that."

The dance floor was packed. Revelers bumped and tangled up their feet. Dudley swapped grins with his fellow policemen.

There's Lieutenant Thad Brown. He's jawing with a high-yellow songstress. There's ex-Chief Davis, spiking the punchbowl. There's Captain Bill Parker and Kay Lake. They comprise a dashed romance. There's a full room between them. They shoot sparks across it, nonetheless. Parker's a persistent burr in his tail. Miss Lake's comely, if fatuous.

Parker's in uniform. Note his soggy blues and drooping gunbelt. He's been clocking traffic grief in the rain. He's hiding out from his wife. He's here to ogle comely Kay Lake.

Many men find La Lake brilliant and alluring. Parker surely does. He himself does not. She's a dilettante and a round-heeled police buff. She's non-conjugally shacked with surly Officer Lee Blanchard. Parker is pious and dangerous. He may ascend to Chief one day.

Bill Parker. The Watanabe case. Roadblocks on his sprint, post–Pearl Harbor.

Fujio Shudo. The Werewolf psychopath. He was Sergeant D. L. Smith's proffered slayer. Bill Parker worked for a true solve. Bill Parker failed. Hideo

Ashida assisted Sergeant Smith. It cinched the whole deal.

Claire swayed close. Dudley felt her tremors. She'd excuse herself soon. She'd retrieve her hypodermic.

He steadied her. She steadied him. It was a new love affair and a most tender pact.

His arm ached. He'd lost weight. The attack climaxed his post–Pearl Harbor sprint.

He vowed vengeance. Mike and Dick were meeting him later. They recruited some Alien Squad muscle. A grand tong sweep loomed.

The Count segued to "Adios." Soft reeds with low-brass punctuation. A Mexican motif.

Claire said, "Good-byes are never that beautiful."

Dudley kissed her neck. She was damp there. He knew her body and her dope habit already.

"It's our song, for the war's duration. It prohibits all farewells."

Claire shuddered. He eased her back to their table. Father Charles launched a raw joke. "Have you heard it, Your Eminence? It's the swell tale of Come-San-Chin, the Chinese cocksucker."

J. J. Cantwell roared. Joe Hayes glowered. Claire snatched her clutch and made for the loo.

She cuts a swath. Drunken cops step aside. She betrays no haste and smiles at each one.

Dudley checked his watch. It's 11:51. Where's Mike and Dick? Where's dim bulb Elmer Jackson?

Quo vadis, Tommy Glennon?

Tommy self-decreed his extinction. A three-count

indictment levied charges. Count One: Tommy raped women and thus annulled the civil contract. Count Two: Tommy was Sergeant D. L. Smith's ex-snitch and pal of current-snitch Huey Cressmeyer. Count Three: Tommy ran wetbacks for ex–Baja kingpin Carlos Madrano.

Count Three, subordinate clause:

He visited Tommy at Quentin, mid-November. Tommy pumped him per Madrano and his own Mexican plans. He has **grand** Mexican plans. He will exploit his Army SIS status to implement them. He will push heroin and run wetbacks. He will sell jailed Japs into slavery. Tommy could fuck it all up. Thus, Tommy must die.

Dudley chased pills with club soda. Two for knife-wound pain. Three bennies for late-night woo-woo.

Cantwell, Hayes, and Coughlin were shit-faced. They defamed the coons and Red scourge Joe Stalin. The English prottys concocted this war and brought in the Jew bankers. They fixed the '36 Olympics. That shine Jesse Owens? He runs slow as me old Irish granny.

Ten seconds to midnight. Count Basie rolled the trumpets—9, 8, 7, 6—

Dudley stood up. Cops waved table flags. Dudley waved the Stars and Stripes and Irish Republican green.

—5, 4, 3, 2—

Mike and Dick walked in. Dudley saw them. Such grand goons they were. They saw Dudley and cringed.

Dudley waved and went **Tommy?** Mike and Dick shook their heads **no.**

—1, zero, **HAPPY NEW YEAR**—

Shouts, back slaps, popped corks galore. Noisemaker blare and flags on sticks—

The Count kicked off "Auld Lang Syne." Dudley reeled. The mock ballroom went hothouse hot and spun topsy-turvy.

His arm throbbed. He thought he'd faint. Claire sailed up to him.

She steadied him and kissed him.

She said, "It's our time, love."

3

JOAN CONVILLE

(SAN DIEGO, 12:15 A.M., 1/1/42)

Should auld acquaintance be—

Yells and hoots. Noisemaker shriek. Shouted toasts and **Remember Pearl Harbor!!!**

Revelers crammed up the Sky Room. You've got Navy brass on a toot. There's grabbing and groping. There's full-length necking on the dance floor.

Stan Kenton presents "Artistry in Rhythm." The Misty June Christy purrs select vocals. The Sky Room was glass-walled and umpteen floors high. You got wide views of battle-dressed beachfront. You got storm clouds and the world's darkest sky.

Joan dodged gropes. She clutched her purse and made for the door. She was half-gassed. L.A. was three hours north. Army checkpoints would stall traffic. The shoreline blackout would drop shroudlike.

She dodged last-ditch gropes and escaped. She made the elevator and pushed 1. Mirrored walls hemmed her in. They were too good to pass up.

She winked. She whistled. She was too proud to falter and too tall and good-looking to lose.

Her red hair. Her green eyes. Her bold six-foot sway. Her trim winter uniform. Gold buttons and braid. **Lieutenant Junior Grade J. W. Conville, USNR. You shitbird Japs better watch out.**

She enlisted in L.A. on Pearl Harbor day. It was pure impulse. She kicked out her one-night lover and drove downtown. The Fed building was deluged. She stood in line six hours straight.

Anchors aweigh.

She was a registered nurse and graduate biologist. Her jazzy CV got her a rank jump at the gate. Nurse Corps training camp loomed. She put in for battleship duty. Point Loma, here I come.

The elevator jarred and stopped. There's the lobby. Joan pushed her way through swarms of rich stiffs.

The famous El Cortez Hotel. Dowagers and old

guys in tuxedos. Walls festooned with tricolored bunting. THWAP THE JAP! signs. Fat Wallace Beery, signing autographs.

Joan ducked out to the parking lot. Short men google-eyed her. Holy moly—**the rain.**

She got soaked. She found her car and huddled in. She kicked the heater and ran the wipers. She lit a cigarette. She popped over to the coast road, northbound.

She observed blackout regs and rode her low beams, exclusive. They lit up this **looooong** rain sluice. Beach waves crashed off to her left.

She chain-smoked. She knew the sober-up drill, inside out. Fix on task and quash those dozen highballs.

She blew out of Dago proper. Traffic thinned. She hit a clear stretch and goosed up more speed.

Barrel through. It's the Conville family code.

It was Earle Everett Conville's code. It's his elder daughter's now. It's not the kid sister's. She married a papist and smeared Big Earle's legacy.

That clear stretch telescoped. It formed one black hole, here to always. Joan floored the gas. Her low beams hit rain smashing down.

Wind slashed it horizontal. Just like Tomah, Wisconsin.

The wind played tricks. Snow flew horizontal. Uprooted trees flew likewise. Big Earle was the Monroe County game warden. He made Joan blast felled trees with a 10-gauge shotgun. Five trees supplied all-winter kindling.

Her hometown curriculum. Dead, like her parents. Absent, like her sister and inbred cousins in Bilgewater, Scotland. Usurped by nursing school and grad work at Northwestern. Gone, like her numerous men.

Holy moly—this rain.

She barreled through. It's what Convilles do. She chain-smoked. It fought her booze load. She slowed for an Army checkpoint. Saboteur Alert. She slowed for a cop checkpoint. Wetback Alert. White thugs smuggled wets in car trunks and flatbed trucks.

The cops wore blue serge and fat gun belts. They brought back this L.A. police captain. He all but swooned for her.

Northwestern. Spring 1940. This skinny sad sack with glasses. He followed her everywhere. He watched her shoot skeet off Lake Michigan. He eyeballed her at sock hops. She almost asked him to dance.

Nobody knew his name. He was in for some traffic cops' seminar. He peeped Joan Woodard Conville in his spare time.

The seminar ended. The captain vanished. Here's the weird epilogue. She saw him in L.A., three nights back.

Hollywood Boulevard. A war-bond rally. The Ritz Brothers grovel for laughs. **Poof**—she sees him. **Poof**—he sees her. **Poof**—he's gone again.

The checkpoint cops waved her through. One cop whistled. Joan blew him a kiss and floored the gas.

Rain came down vertical. Wind kicked it horizontal. Rain brought back Big Earle—a forest fire casualty.

Big Earle, firefighter. Big Earle, shitkicker and drunk. Big Earle, friend and foe of migrant Indians hooked on bathtub juice.

He hired them to fight forest fires. They blew their pay on hooch and started more fires for more wampum. A big blaze hits—April 9, '38. Maybe it's the Indians. Maybe it's not. Maybe it's premeditated arson.

E. E. Conville, dead at forty-nine. Her father, burned alive. The U.S. Forest Service investigates. Their call: "No evidence of arson extant."

Joan disagreed. She switched grad-school majors. She dropped premed for biology. She studied **forensic** biology. She haunted the blaze site. She studied soil and tree-wood samples. She interviewed Indians and compiled a suspect list. A soused Indian fondled her. She blew his left foot off with her shotgun.

She shredded her suspect list. It wasn't liquored-up redskins. The fire felt deliberate—not haphazard.

She discovered an airplane-fuel spill. It was near the fire's flash point. She examined fuel-laced soil. She determined the molecular content and the fuel's brand name. She traced the fuel to a charter-airplane service in Duluth, Minnesota. The service pointed her to Mitchell A. Kupp.

Kupp called himself an inventor. He lived off of family money. He was pals with Charles Lindbergh.

Kupp chartered a small aircraft on 4/9/38 and flew it over Monroe County.

She learned all that. Her case fizzled, then. Her fuel-spill evidence was erratically collected and logged. She could not attribute motive. She could not connect E. E. Conville to Mitchell A. Kupp in any discernible way.

Barrel through. It's what Convilles do. Big Earle expects it.

She held down night-nurse jobs. She crash-coursed her master's degree. She read extensively. She devoured monographs by L.A. coroner Norton Layman and police chemist Hideo Ashida. She took her degree and moved to L.A. She got a lab job and applied to the doctorate program at Cal Tech.

Joan barreled through. It's what Convilles do. She'll return to Wisconsin and avenge Big Earle's death. Vengeance is **thine.**

Banzai. Pearl Harbor preempts her. She's a sucker for hot dates. It's her hot date with History.

Rain battered her car. Visibility decreased. Pooled water doused her low beams and cut sight lines down to zero.

Thunder boomed. Joan sighted in off lightning flare. She hit close-to-L.A. traffic. She chained cigarettes. She downshifted, fishtailed, swerved. She saw a sign for Venice Boulevard.

She pulled right. She went woozy and white-knuckled the wheel. She got light-headed. It's that booze-catching-up feel—

Lights hit the windshield. Big full-on **head**lights. They violated blackout reg—

Joan went glare-blind. She rubbed her eyes and lost the wheel. She smashed the lights and this great big something.

4

(LOS ANGELES, 2:30 A.M., 1/1/42)

The Werewolf sleeps. He's fetal-curled and looks pacified. Oblivion becomes him.

He has a one-man/vacant-tier cell. Jailers keep him penned up and sedated. Fujio Shudo/age thirty-eight/male Japanese. He's bought and paid for. He's down for four counts of Murder One.

A sanity hearing pends. It's strictly rubber stamp. He allegedly killed the four Watanabes. It was a sex lust/pro-fascist caper. He's green room–bound. He'll be dead inside six months. Police chemist Hideo Ashida stands complicit.

Ashida watched the Werewolf sleep. Lee Blanchard watched and kibitzed. Big Lee. Kay Lake's faux lover, ex–heavyweight contender.

"The Werewolf and the Wolfman. I don't know the difference. Maybe it's the actors who play them."

They stood in the vacant-tier catwalk. Thunder echoed. Barred windowpanes shook.

Ashida said, "It's one symbolic character, with differing narratives."

Blanchard yawned. "I don't mind bodyguarding you, Hideo. But the Central Station jail ain't my idea of New Year's Eve kicks."

The Werewolf snored. The Werewolf twitched and sucked his thumb.

Blanchard said, "Talk to me, Wolf. Tell me something I don't know."

Ashida ventriloquized the creature. He kept the spiel internal. He mimicked the Werewolf's pidgin-English/Japanese stew.

Dudley Smith framed me. Sensei Ashida assisted. Dudley Smith coerced him. Dudley Smith applied pressure and made the frame stand. Sensei Ashida fawns for Sergeant Smith.

Blanchard nipped off his flask. "Here's to you, Werewolf. You want my opinion? You deserve the loony bin more than the gas chamber."

Ashida grabbed the flask. "We should go upstairs. I'm on call to Traffic. Captain Parker might call in."

"He was at the City Hall bash. Him and Kay were making with the big eyes."

Ashida sipped brandy. He rarely drank. This small dose induced a small glow.

"I'm sure she makes you uncomfortable. She must be difficult to live with."

Blanchard grinned. "My shack job's 'difficult,' but my shack job's Kay Lake, which has its compensations. She's always off to something new. You want the latest? She's fallen in with these classical-music types, out in Brentwood. Mostly Reds and Jews, on the run from **der Führer.** I don't know how much time she's got for Bill Parker."

Ashida passed the flask. His eyes burned. The cold jail went warm. Ashida felt antsy. He was backlogged. Pearl Harbor put the lab in arrears. The Japanese roundups spawned massive confiscations. Evidence log-ins stood un-logged, back to mid-December.

He stood un-jailed. His family stood free. The roundups would resume, tomorrow. Dudley Smith's patronage vouched his freedom. He lived in a Biltmore Hotel suite. His mother and brother had their own rooms. Dudley's patronage carried a price. Call the Werewolf frame part and parcel.

Blanchard said, "You're in a trance, Hideo. Maybe it's all that caustic shit you been sniffing."

Ashida smiled. They walked out to the jailside hallway. Ashida heard snores.

Blanchard went **sssshh.** He pointed to the Alien Squad cot room. They walked over and peeked in.

Confiscated swag covered the floor. Radios, flags, Nazi Lugers. Kanji script and English-language hate tracts. Hate the Chinks, hate the Jews, hate all Americans.

Plus three plainclothesmen, sprawled out on cots. They were stripped to their skivvies. Their sidearms and belt gear were piled adjacent. Brass knucks, leather truncheons, beavertail saps.

Three big guys. Cop heavies. On-call strike-breaker types.

Blanchard said, "Lunceford, Rice, and Kapek. You've got the Silver Shirts and the Thunderbolt Legion represented here. These dinks chasing down Fifth Column Japs? Don't tell me I don't know what's ironic."

A bluesuit walked up. He was blitzed. He wore a dumb party hat and a WELCOME 1942 button.

"Captain Parker called, Ashida. He needs you in Venice. It's a vehicular homicide. There's four dead wetbacks and some Navy woman in custody."

Pole-mounted tarps held the rain back. A sawhorse barricade held off the looky-loos. It's a Car-Crash Inferno and Car-Crash Holocaust.

Head-on collision: '36 Dodge coupe hits jalopy. No visible skidmarks. Eastbound Dodge, westbound heap. Two front ends accordion-pressed.

The Dodge: minus the driver's-side door. The heap: compressed to the rear seats and trunk ledge.

Flares marked the crash site. Prowl cars stood close. Two morgue sleds were parked snout-to-snout. There's four sheet-draped stretchers, out in the wet.

Blanchard pulled up to the flare line. Ashida got

out and eyeballed the site. He deployed Man Camera. **Click, click**—a wide-lens shot.

Click—no skid marks. **Click**—the rain erased them. **Click**—the blown door saved the Navy woman's life. **Click**—there's more damage to the heap. **Click**—the Navy woman was speeding. **Click**—the jalopy driver was slowing down.

Ashida walked up to the stretchers. Wind tugged at his hat. Rain stung his eyes.

All four sheets were blood-soaked. Ashida pulled them halfway down. Four clicks clicked. Let's extrapolate.

Four male Mexicans. All dead. Two men in the front seat, two men in the back.

Head-on impact. The frontseat men sustain massive chest wounds. Their hearts explode. The backseat men sustain downward-thrust trauma and are thus disemboweled.

Ashida looked up. Bill Parker stepped out of his prowl car. An empty pint jug fell from his lap.

It clattered and rolled. Ashida looked away. He heard a muffled shriek.

He tracked it. He walked up to the jalopy. He flashed his Man Camera, in tight. The trunk lid's ajar. Something's in there.

He jammed up the lid. He saw a little boy. The boy was crushed dead under a spare tire. A little girl murmured and coughed blood.

She tried to say something. Ashida picked her up and held her close. She clawed at his face and died in his arms.

5

(LOS ANGELES, 3:15 A.M., 1/1/42)

Kwan's Chinese Pagoda. It's open-all-nite. It's a cop haunt. It's Hop Sing Tong HQ and **the** Chinatown hot spot.

Here's Uncle Ace Kwan. He's a PD puppet. He's your warlord-restauranteur.

The rain killed business. Local Chinks and night owls stayed home. The boys hogged a prime table.

The Dudster held court. Ace laid on pupu platters and mai tais. He was sixty-six years old and too thin. He switchblade-skewered fried dumplings and snarfed them.

Oooga-booga. All-cop summit. It's that botched stakeout. There's this fugitive rape-o at large.

The boys noshed and boozed. Elmer chased two bennies with Bromo Seltzer and went **aaahh!** Mike Breuning and Dick Carlisle sulked. Also present: Catbox Cal Lunceford, Wendell Rice, and George Kapek. Tag them shithead goons roused from sleep.

All eyes on Dudley. Elmer's the most. This mick fuck sends him out to kill a man. That don't sit right.

The Dudster played off-key. His voice fluttered. His arm sling seeped. His Army threads fit slack. Elmer eyed him surreptitious and tried to look contrite.

Dud passed out roust sheets. Tommy Glennon's KAs and known haunts. Chink-o-phile Tommy. He perched in C-town. The sheet tagged juke joints, whore cribs, and dope dens.

The boys skimmed the sheets. Dudley tapped his fork. **Achtung, meine kameraden!**

"We're here to redress tactical errors committed earlier this evening, and perhaps accrue collateral leads on the man who shanked me in the basement here three days ago. He was a slight man, well within the bodily range one expects to see in the Chinese. He also wore a lacquered-wood mask, one depicting Oriental features, such as the masks worn by Japanese actors in the Japs' more arcane theatrical productions. I sense a baroque and oddly playful sensibility at work. You would honor me by bringing in this rare bird alive, as you would by shooting Tommy Glennon on sight."

Mike and Dick fawned. They went **Yeah, boss** and dispensed grins. Catbox Cal cracked his knuckles. Rice and Kapek glared. Elmer scoped their belt shit. Per always—they packed saps and throw-down guns.

Elmer reskimmed his roust sheet. One column tagged locations. He noted boocoo spots nearby. Yeah—but where's Eddie Leng's Kowloon?

He'd memorized Tommy's address book. It held damn few listings. Eddie's joint stood out.

Rice said, "We should take these guys to the Bureau? Put the boots to them there?"

Dudley lit a cigarette. "Brace them where you find them. Bring your likely suspects here."

Ace knifed a fried shrimp. "You bring to basement. We put balls in vise and burn with cigarettes."

Elmer gulped. His windpipe bobbed. Dudley clocked it. Elmer clocked his clock.

Kapek said, "Say we get us a whole shitload. Call for a whore wagon then?"

Dudley said, "Shackle chains. Hook them up and march them down Broadway. Create a stir. Make a statement. The PD stands with Hop Sing. Four Families **chingasos y putasos.**"

Lunceford said, "Dud's practicing. He's Mexico-bound."

Ace knifed a rumaki. "Viva the Chinaman and white man! Kill all jigaboos and Japs!"

Elmer yukked. Ace was a moondog psycho. He ran afield sometimes.

Breuning drained his mai tai. "Tommy's tonged up the ying-yang. Him and Four Families go way back."

Elmer unwrapped a cigar. "We should issue an APB and call the Immigration cops. Tommy used to run wetbacks. He'll have a green sheet, sure as shit."

Dudley smiled. "No. You precipitated this fuckup, Elmer. Now, go forth with your grand colleagues and remedy that."

Two squads swamped C-town. They wore rain slickers and packed shackle chains and belt gear. Lunceford went with Breuning and Carlisle. Elmer went with Kapek and Rice.

North Broadway was all bars and slop chutes. Local Chinks and white stiffs hobknobbed. New Year's increased foot trade. The big rain **de**creased it. Both squads trekked north.

Elmer's squad took the west flank. Elmer packed his .45 and a buckshot-stitched sap. He walked point and carried the billy club. It was Chink sweep de rigeur.

Rice and Kapek lugged the shackle chains. They were six-two beefcake types and well suited. They shoulder-draped the chains and went hunchback. It pissed them off.

The PD was Hop Sing–allied. Uncle Ace was Jack Horrall's #1 Chink. Hop Sing joints were sacrosanct, Four Families the converse. Fuck last month's tong truce.

Elmer walked point. He smashed front windows and galvanized attention. He went in the door first. Rice and Kapek fanned out behind him. They ignored eeeeks, shrieks, and flustered women. They braced blue-kerchief tong guys and went in tough.

Elmer took the bar-stool guys. He sap-smashed hands on bartops and broke bones. He kicked over bar stools. He logged bilingual eeeeks and shrieks.

Rice and Kapek took the booths and tables. They donned sap gloves and broke faces. They dunked said mugs in tureens of shark-fin soup.

The boys hovered close and tossed questions. They pushed past eeeek and shriek. They got **Don't know**

nothing, don't know nothing! They got **Nobody know who slice Dudster—not us, not us!**

Elmer stood by. He posed tough. He looked **untough** upside Kapek and Rice. He leaned close. He logged gibberish laced with rat-outs.

Tommy Glennon know Huey Cressmeyer! Tommy go queer up at Preston!

It was pidgin English. Elmer called it "**Chink**lish." Sputters and nonsense talk. Some enticing tattle. Huey C. was a known Dudster snitch.

That's it for bars and slop chutes. That's it for North Broadway. It's all lackluster leads. There's no shackle bait yet.

The boys cut west on Ord. Elmer smashed clubhouse windows. Rice and Kapek kicked in doors. They tore down to basements and stormed opium dens.

They encountered noxious smoke and hopheads on pallets. Coolies packed pipes and lugged water bowls. **You know Chiang Kai-shek, papa-san? You know famous sleuth Charlie Chan?**

The dens served a Chink clientele. Some white swells made the scene. There's a city council hump. There's Ellen's studio rival—ice-blond Veronica Lake.

Rice and Kapek thumped blue-kerchief guys. They imitated Jap Zeros. They knocked tong punks off pallets and hauled them down from Cloud 9. Elmer water-doused them. The noxious fumes messed with his gourd.

He clubbed "O" fiends. Ankle and wrist shots.

Eeeek-and-shriek inducers. Rice and Kapek lobbed queries. Gibberish and half-baked leads accrued.

Tommy G. run wets from T.J.! Tommy G. supply truck farms in Imperial Valley! Don't know who slice Dudster—don't know, don't know, don't know!

Elmer laid on the hurt. Rice and Kapek worked their sap gloves. They got more eeeek and more shriek, and more **Chink**lish.

Tommy nancy boy! Don't know where he is! Tommy poking some priest!

Elmer caught **that** one. It brought back Tommy's address book. It underlined the St. Vib's listing.

Rice and Kapek went pure rogue. They lifted wallets and plucked cash rolls. The fumes got to Elmer. "O" plus bennies induced all this weird wispy shit.

He went **eeek** his own self. He upchucked on some Chinaman's shoes and made for the door. He bumped into Veronica Lake. She said, "Whoa, sailor."

The rain felt good. It cleared his skull somewhat. All those colored raindrops went neutral again.

He lost his billy club. He still had his hat, badge, and roscoe. His watch said 4:35. It was still dark. It was still Chinatown and still Ord Street.

He recalled Tommy's address book. He recalled that number for Eddie Leng's Kowloon.

Kantonese Kuisine. Ord & Hill. Your gracious host, Eddie Leng.

It's a block up. Why not? Maybe Veronica's there. Maybe she'll smile at you. Maybe she'll sleep with you. You won't know till you try.

He walked over. The rain felt good. There's Eddie's place. It looks dark. That plays wrong. It's a 24-hour dive.

Elmer pressed up to the window. He left nose prints on the glass. Okay—the kitchen doorway's lit up.

He shook the doorknob. The door was ajar. He walked in and shut the door behind him. His eyeballs adjusted. He popped through the dining room. He smelled something all scorched up.

He knew from scorched. He'd flamethrowered Nicaraguan insurgents. It dispersed crowds good. Those humps got their tail feathers singed.

Elmer weaved toward the kitchen. He bumped tables and chairs. He made the doorway and saw all the stoves and deep-dip fryers. Well, shit—it's **fried** flesh, not scorched.

Eddie Leng was rope-cinched to a four-burner stove. He was barefoot. Charred anklebones extended from two fryer thingamajigs. Residual grease and blood bubbled. Eddie's feet got deep-fried.

Elmer reeled and caught himself. He double-scanned the stiff. Eddie wore reet-pleat pants and a Hawaiian shirt. Some fuck folded his hands on his chest.

Note the tattoo. It's there on the right forefinger-thumb web. It's an "SQ" circled by snakes. Remember

Tommy Glennon's tattoo stencil? It's flat out just like that.

6

(LOS ANGELES, 4:45 A.M., 1/1/42)

Opium.

His private room at Kwan's. The tar, the match, the pipe. It's a tainted locale now. He was knifed in this selfsame spot.

Dudley smoked opium. It stamped his travel visa and whooshed him off to wispy locales. Stopover, Baja. Seaside Ensenada appears.

There's shoreline coves. There's Jap subs stashed out of sight. Nitroglycerin explodes. There's Carlos Madrano—now particulate waste.

There's Tommy Glennon. He's wearing a sombrero and bullfighter chaps. Mike Breuning and Dick Carlisle mewl. They've been transmogrified to **dos perros.** There's no dead prey for their master. There's Elmer Jackson, bad shot and bumptious trash.

Dudley smoked opium. He succumbed to pictures and colors. His mind still logically tracked.

Stopover, Beverly Hills. Claire De Haven's Colonial manse. The Red Queen spars with the Cop Arriviste.

They express inimical views. They walk upstairs. There's the too-bright bedroom sun. He counts the freckles on Claire's back.

Stopover, Dublin.

His trek to the New World. Joe Kennedy and Father Coughlin wave. Uncle Joe donates gun money. J. J. Cantwell funnels it to Republican causes. It's 1921. Dudley Liam Smith's a schoolboy killer. Uncle Joe says he'll sponsor American citizenship.

There's a Grafton Street skirmish. Schoolboy Smith shoots three Black-and-Tans. Their faces explode.

Dudley trembled. He dropped the pipe, the pallet shook, the colors and pictures dispersed. He saw Tommy Glennon as he looks today.

Another wayward Irish lad. A Coughlinite, a rape-o, a snitch.

Tommy at that costume party. Brentwood, winter '39. The Jewish Maestro's home, sublet. Nazi antics reenacted. Orgiastic overtones. **Sturmbannführer** D. L. Smith injudiciously attends.

Dudley fought back jitters. He reached for his pipe. He saw an envelope on the floor.

Popped through a door crack. A colored envelope. A Western Union telegram.

Dudley slit the envelope and read it. The tone was brusque. The gist was **this:**

It's an active-duty summons. We're calling you in, early. Report to the Special Intelligence Service command post in Ensenada, **NOW.**

7

(LOS ANGELES, 6:30 A.M., 1/1/42)

Thumps. Muted squeals. Dream fade—you're half in, half out.

Murmurs now. Singsong voices. You're more out than in.

They're foreign voices. They're all female and all Jap. It's a movie encore. It's that film they show Navy recruits.

Know Your Foe. Loose Lips Sink Ships. Jap Women Report to Jap Men.

Joan woke up. She assessed it all, quicksville.

Booze blackout. You're driving up the coast road. Then something happens. Now you're **HERE.**

A jail cell. A hard bunk. Her scuffed palms. Her rumpled uniform.

She heard real voices. She distinguished them and counted five altogether. There were five Jap matrons, crammed in a cell down the tier.

Joan stood up and stretched. The Jap ladies stared at her. Joan stared right back.

They looked down and went **I'm so humble.** Joan looked past them. She saw dawn out a window and more goddamn rain.

No purse, no cigarettes. This goddamn cell. Odd aches and pains.

Joan tucked her blouse in. She flexed her hands and smoothed out her coat and skirt. She stood by the front bars and willed panache.

A door clanged. A uniformed cop walked up. He was midsized and slight. Joan loomed over him.

Captain's bars and three hashmarks. Wire-rim glasses. They magnified his dark brown eyes. He'd never be handsome. He'd always be unnerving.

So, it's you. Northwestern—spring 1940.

He said, "Lieutenant Conville."

A prairie drawl. The Dakotas, maybe.

Joan said, "We haven't met, but I've seen you before."

"My name's Parker. I'm with the Los Angeles Police Department. I command the Traffic Division."

"Acknowledge me, will you? 'I've seen you before.'"

Parker gripped the bars. "You might well have. I checked your enlistment file. We attended Northwestern concurrently."

Joan gripped the bars. Their hands were close. Joan moved hers away.

"Can you be more emphatic? You seemed to be surveilling me then."

Parker got out his cigarettes and offered the pack. Joan took one. Parker lit it.

Joan tossed her head and exhaled. It telegraphed vamp move. She felt stupid and out of her league.

"What happened? Why am I here?"

Parker lit a cigarette. "You've been arrested for four counts of vehicular manslaughter. Four men are dead because you drove inebriated in a heavy rainstorm. If you're lucky, you'll do five years at Tehachapi."

Joan stepped back. She grazed the bunk ledge and almost tripped. She caught herself and stepped back up to the bars.

"I need a lawyer. I'll be charged and arraigned, and there'll be a trial."

Parker said, "I've had some experience with this sort of matter. Most inebriate killers evince regret or remorse and ask questions about the people they killed. You went to your own survival immediately. I don't know whether to be impressed or appalled."

Joan gripped the bars. Her hands brushed Parker's. She kept them there.

"Tell me about the people I killed. I'll react, and you can decide whether to be impressed or appalled then."

Parker said, "They were Mexican illegals. They were transporting marijuana, and had extensive criminal records. Their offenses included strongarm robbery, aggravated assault, kidnapping, white slavery, and first-degree extortion."

Joan dropped her cigarette and crushed it. "I'm evincing regret now. I can't quite embrace remorse."

Parker grinned a tad. "You're a cum laude forensic biologist. A prison sentence would scotch whatever degree of success you might ultimately achieve."

"You're leading me, Captain. There's something going on here."

"Oh, **really**? And what would that be?"

Joan winked. "**Really,** sir? It wasn't that long ago."

"Lieutenant, now **you're** lead—"

"I was shooting skeet off the Evanston Bridge. You were watching me. I thought, That man should go home and be nice to his wife, because his attention has surely strayed."

Parker blushed. It was almost but not quite endearing.

"You rid the world of four vicious thugs. I'll extend muted bravos, and add that all opportunities carry a price. If you resign your Navy commission, I'll see to a dismissal of all charges against you. I'll secure you a position with the PD's Central Crime Lab and personally vouch your wartime employment."

Booze blackouts, skeet guns, cop voyeurs—

"Is this your métier, Captain? Have you made a career out of entrapping young women?"

Parker said, "I've only done it once before."

"And when was that?"

Parker said, "Last month."

Joan laughed. "I've read monographs by your Dr. Ashida. I greatly admire them."

"Would you like to meet Dr. Ashida?"

Joan said, "When?"

Parker said, "Now."

8

(LOS ANGELES, 7:45 A.M., 1/1/42)

The bash felt stale now. '41 was old news. '42 was au courant.

Nobody danced. Count Basie's boys dozed in their chairs. A few cops and dates schmoozed. A buffet dispensed Bloody Marys and stale bagels.

Lee Blanchard was out cold. He topped out his bodyguard shift. The dead kids got to him. He hit the party and drank himself insensate.

The day-shift man was due. Elmer J. always ran late. Blanchard said he had late work with the Dudster.

Thad Brown circulated. He ran the Homicide Squad. Kay Lake circulated. She was the PD's favored seductress. Brenda Allen table-hopped. She ran call girls with Elmer. Jack Horrall and Fletch Bowron dozed on a couch. The Count dozed with them. His head brushed the mayor's shoulder.

The dead kids.

Ashida teethed on it. He teethed each and every split second. He sipped coffee and stayed alert.

Bill Parker issued a gag order. No reporters, no public exposure. Four male wetbacks, **muerto.** It stands at **THAT.** The Navy woman must not know.

Parker called Catholic Charities. He had oomph there. A private hearse hauled the kids off.

Parker admonished Blanchard and Ashida. **I demand silence. Do not talk about this.**

Ashida trawled the room. The Count was up and bleary-eyed. He chatted with Kay. La Grande Katherine looked up-all-night fetching.

Brenda Allen blew a kiss. Ashida waved back. Colored sax men fish-eyed him. Yeah—we ain't white, but you're a **JAP.**

Elmer walked over. He straddled a chair and drained Blanchard's highball.

"Sorry I'm late. Dud had us hopping."

Ashida sipped coffee. "You tend to be overextended."

Elmer said, "It'll get worse, starting tomorrow. The roundups'll kick in again, and your few remaining countrymen on the loose'll be headed for the pokey."

"We're backlogged on your confiscations. You're bringing in more than we can process."

Elmer relit a cigar. "You're lucky we got thieves on the squad. Georgie Kapek and Wendell Rice got your swag appropriated."

Ashida laughed. Elmer eyeballed the room. He said, "Kay looks swell, don't she?"

"Are you in love with her?"

"I'm entranced. That's worse. You acknowledge that you ain't got a chance, so you act even dumber than you usually do."

Ashida jumped topics. Romantic intrigue bored and vexed him.

"I read a Teletype from Fourth Interceptor. There's

allegedly hidden air bases out in Indio and Brawley. The command picked up coded pay-phone calls from here to Baja."

Elmer shrugged. "Dud's headed south. He'll nip that grief in the bud. 'Knock, knock, who's there? Dudley Smith, so spies beware.'"

Ashida smiled. Elmer scoped the doorway. Ashida tracked his gaze.

Bill Parker walked in. He wore a fresh uniform and looked all spruced up. He brought a date.

A Navy lieutenant. Rumpled blues, red hair, quite tall and statuesque. Vehicular manslaughter/six counts/two counts unacknowledged.

Elmer waggled his eyebrows. Elmer wolf-growled.

Ashida deployed Man Camera. He framed Parker and the redhead. He panned to Kay Lake and caught her reaction. He zoomed in for a close-up. Kay and Parker shared This Big Freighted Look.

Parker and the redhead hit the buffet. They ignored the food and mixed high-test Bloody Marys.

They clicked glasses. Their hands brushed. Kay saw it all.

Thad Brown walked up. He ignored dozed-out Blanchard. He braced Ashida and Elmer.

"Let's go. We've got mud slides in Griffith Park. They've dislodged a body by the golf course."

9

(LOS ANGELES, 8:30 A.M., 1/1/42)

They ran Code Three/red lights and siren. It goosed squarejohn drivers curbside. Thad Brown hauled. Ashida rode shotgun. Elmer hogged the backseat.

First reports state **this:**

The stiff is a long-term decomp. That means all bones. It washed up on the par-3 golf course. Said course adjoined Mineral Canyon—i.e., the spot where Wayne Frank Jackson died.

Elmer agitated it. Elmer segued to more pressing shit. Eddie Leng's deep-fried feet. Tommy Glennon's address book.

He'd dropped the book on the day-watch Vice clerk. He'd slipped him a yard and told him to run a phone-number check. Chop, chop. I need results, pronto. And don't blab on this.

Brown hauled up Vermont. Rainwater jammed the wheel wells. The car belly-flopped and drifted. Brown veered right and caught a flat surface. They shimmied down a golf course access road.

Elmer saw two black-and-whites and a prowl sled. Plus a snack hut. Plus green fairways and the dump site.

There's two harness blues and two plainclothesmen. They've got arc lights and a rain tarp set up. They've got a steep hillside all lit.

Brown fishtailed over and yanked the brake. They all went **whew.** Elmer bundled into his hat and trench coat. They all got out and ran.

Elmer got there first. He saw Al Goossen and Colin Forbes—Hollywood Squad hard-ons.

Nods circulated. The tarp fluttered and dripped rain. Brown and Ashida caught up. The arc lights lit **this:**

Soaked grass up the fairway. The mud spill and all this loose soil. A big dirt hole. Exhumed mud sluicing down to this flat spot.

The spill dislodged a box. It tumbled down the hillside. It's a pine box—six-six by two feet.

It's charred black. They're char marks, for sure. Intermittent marks—mud-and-root-matted.

The lid was warped and soil-eroded. The mud slide sprung it off, clean. It's a jig-rigged casket. There's green goo caked inside. There's skeletal remains.

Ashida pointed to the goo. "That's congealed quicklime. It serves to speed decomposition."

Elmer relit his cigar. Forbes and Goossen lit cigarettes. Brown spit tobacco juice.

"That tags it Murder One."

Ashida leaned in close. Elmer said, "Genius at work."

Bluesuit #1 rolled his eyes. Bluesuit #2 said, "Like Charlie Chan." Elmer said, "Charlie Chan's a Chinaman, dipshit."

Bluesuit #2 blanched. Ashida foot-tapped the box. "Note the width of the pelvis and the overall length and breadth of the remains. The victim was male, tall, and heavyset."

Brown said, "Talk to me, dead man."

Forbes said, "Who killed you, boss?"

Ashida futzed with the stiff's jawbones. They went **creak.** He pulled them loose.

"The killer knocked his teeth out. Note the mandible fractures. The uppers and lowers are unidentifiable stubs."

Elmer studied the box. The fire aspect gouged him. October 3, '33—the Griffith Park blaze.

Ashida tapped a shattered rib bone. "It's a knife-thrust homicide. The killer hit hard, went in deep, and twisted the knife."

Brown leaned low. He studied the skull. He pointed out a hole and faint cracks adjacent.

"He was shot once. You'll find a spent round embedded."

Elmer looked up the hill. Lightning backlit the whole golf course.

"You remember that big fire, back in '33? I'm thinking it could have whooshed over the box and caused all the charring."

Ashida said, "I don't think so. There's too much mud for the fire to have gone that deep."

Brown poked at some rags. They were quicklime-caked and bore singe marks.

"That green shit dissolved the clothes off the body."

Forbes said, "Who killed you, dead man?"

Goossen said, "It's a missing-person job. That stuff puts me to sleep. Give me a nigger homicide any day."

Brown said, "You're out of luck there. Get the box and the stiff to Doc Layman at the morgue."

Forbes and Goossen sulked. Elmer chewed his cigar. He recollected Wayne Frank. He felt all razzle-dazzle.

"Here's what gets me. Some of the box is burned, but some ain't. I don't see no special flame pattern on the wood."

Forbes said, "Elmer's brother died in that fire. He's got fires on the noggin."

Goossen said, "I remember that day. Fire trucks were backed up all the way down Los Feliz."

Forbes said, "It was the Reds. They never proved arson, but some Red cell was supposed to be good for it."

Ashida studied the box. Genius at work. All eyes on Ashida now.

He said, "Elmer could be right. I think the box was burned concurrent with an aboveground fire. 1933 might be a good guess."

The rain let up. Black clouds hovered. Thad B. drove Elmer and Ashida back downtown. L.A. was hungover. Shops closed, nil traffic, local yokels sleeping it off.

Ashida hopped out at the Biltmore. Elmer snagged his civilian sled at City Hall. That Vice clerk delivered. He'd stuck the phone-call list under the wiper blades.

Elmer had a bachelor flop at 1st and Saint Andrews. He drove by and fed his tropical fish. Brenda had a house up Laurel Canyon. He part-time shacked there. Brenda might be home. She might toss him some New Year's woof-woof.

He drove over and let himself in. The place was done up Spanish Hacienda. Brenda scrounged used sets from **The Sword of Zorro.** Some homo art director went nuts.

Elmer built a highball and buzzed the call-service switchboard. The dispatch girl delivered the dish. She knew Elmer was het up and voyeurizized.

Dig tonight's roster:

Fletch Bowron booked a threesky. DA Bill McPherson booked a colored cooze. Sheriff Gene Biscailuz booked a tall blonde.

The service featured house calls, plus three fuck flops. Apartment-building tryst spots. Replete with hidden wall peeks and cameras. Folks paid to peep bedroom action. The camera shit doubled as potential shakedown gear.

The Chapman Park flop was booked tonight. Cary Grant, Butch Stanwyck, and Ruth Mildred Cressmeyer were tricking with "Ten-Inch" Tony Mangano.

Tony tricked switcheroosky. He turned Ruth Mildred straight in one-night allotments. Ruthie was a disbarred physician and scrape doc. Ruthie was tight with Dudley Smith. Ruthie recruited lez girls for Brenda.

Fourteen peepers had booked seats for the show. The peepers peeped anonymous. They paid fifty scoots a head. Butch and Tony commanded top dollar.

Also, on tonight's roster:

Mickey Rooney booked a girl. Likewise John "Cricket Dick" Huston. Eight girls for a USC frat bash. Six boys for a Brentwood hen party.

Elmer signed off the call. The phone rang and startled him. He snagged the new call.

"Talk to me."

"It's Kay, Elmer."

"Well, then. Some weather, huh? It's like the flood in the Bible. You think it'll ever stop?"

Kay laughed. "I didn't call to discuss the weather."

Elmer laughed. "Well, it sure ain't the war, because we hashed all that out the last time we talked."

"Don't be a C.T. You know what I'm angling for."

"Oh, yeah? And what's that, pray tell?"

Kay stage-sighed. "Come on, Elmer. Give."

Elmer stage-sighed. "The party? The big redhead with Bill Parker? That catch your eye?"

"Now, he gets to it."

"Hard not to notice, huh?"

Kay laughed. "I've known William Henry Parker the Third for twenty-seven days, and during that time he has repeatedly cast his eyes about for tall, red-haired, naval-officer women."

Elmer said, "You're counting the days since you've met him. What's that tell you about yourself?"

Kay said, "You're deliberately tweaking me."

Elmer said, "I don't know no more than you do, except how much you love that man."

Kay blew him a kiss and hung up. The ten-second phone call was her standard MO.

Elmer yawned and kicked his shoes off. He got out the Vice clerk's list. He studied Tommy G.'s address book and put shit together.

St. Vibiana's Church. He decoded that one already. It's the home of papal poobah J. J. Cantwell. He's the Dudster's old pal.

The Deutsches Haus. 15th and Union. Pro-Nazi hot spot. Kraut regalia for sale.

Let's backtrack. We're in Tommy's hotel room. There's that tattoo stencil. It features swastikas and an "SQ" circled by snakes. The "SQ" snake job was embroidered on the late Eddie Leng.

More names, more phone numbers. Huey Cressmeyer. A Hollywood phone exchange. That's no surprise. He's Ruth Mildred's perv-o son and a Dudster informant. C-town tattle: Huey and Tommy were reform-school chums.

Monsignor Joseph Hayes. A West L.A. exchange. More C-town drift: Tommy and "some priest" travel the Hershey Highway.

Jean Clarice Staley. A Hollywood exchange. That rates a **Huh?** She's a woman—but Tommy runs Greek. He **rapes** women—he don't **call** them.

That hot-box pay phone. It's right upside the **Herald.** It's drilled for slug calls. Plus **this** head-scratcher. It rates a big **Huh?**

Fourteen pay phones. All down in Baja. All in Ensenada. All eighty miles south of T.J.

Let's backtrack. Tommy ran wetbacks for Carlos Madrano. That Spanish-language book in Tommy's room.

Head-scratchers. Brain-broilers. Code 3 Alert. Look out, son. You're brushing upside Dudley Smith.

Rain kicked up hard. Elmer walked to the front window and looked out. He saw fresh mud slides. He saw storm crews on Crescent Heights.

Let's backtrack. The Griffith Park slide, the old-new DOA. Let's backtrack. The 1933 fire.

It's October 3. It's 103 degrees in L.A. Santa Ana winds change course. CCC workers are out cutting brush. Wayne Frank's among them.

Thirty-four men die. It gets ambiguous here. There's sloppy rosters and files and fly-by-night work crews. Who died and who didn't? There's un-ID'd bodies. There's Wayne Frank—ID'd off old dental charts.

Arson or not? It gets ambiguous here. It's the Depression. There's Red revolt in the vox populi. Garment workers agitating. Labor marches. Kreepy Kremlin prophecies. Fires, tidal waves, storms.

Elmer dug out his scrapbook. Wayne Frank pix consumed four pages. Wayne Frank in a boxer's pose, 1924. Wayne Frank in a Klan sheet, 1926. Elmer V. in Marine green, 1930. Wayne Frank giving him the horns.

Wayne Frank was taller and handsomer. Wayne

Frank was smarter and meaner. Elmer V. was slow to rile. He could kick big brother's hate-dog ass all day long.

What made Wayne Frank tick? Nobody knew. Wayne Frank was whimsical. Wayne Frank imagined impossible shit and convinced himself that it was true. Wayne Frank developed this big gold-heist fixation.

May '31. A mint-train job. A Frisco-to-L.A. gold-transfer run. Gold bars. A small number. Triple-locked in a cage. Shackled passengers under guard. San Quentin convicts bound for retrials in L.A.

Chaos attends a track switch in Monterey County. All eight cons escape. Seven men are hunted down. They're shot on sight **faaaaast.** One man remains at large still.

More grief. A downed-track snafu two hours south. Chaos atop chaos. Guards and crew succumb to frayed nerves. The heist occurs then. The heister or heisters are smart. Just one box's worth of bars leaves the train.

The train treks south. Santa Barbara's a coal stop. The theft is discovered then. Suspicion falls on Leander Frechette. He's the train's odd-job man. He's dim-witted, Negro, fucking-A strong. The Santa Barbara cops posit a single-o heister. He walked the bars off the train two or three at a clip. It had to be Frechette. Nobody else had the strength. **Some**body bossed him. He was too dumb to concoct the plan himself.

The Santa Barbara cops beat Frechette **baaaaad.**

He refused to confess. A colored preacher with cop clout intervened. Frechette was released. The case fizzled out. It went to open-file status, stale bread.

Wayne Frank hoarded news clips and treasure-magazine pieces. He studied the heist and worked himself up to fever pitch. Wayne Frank, the dreamer. Wayne Frank, the fantasist. What makes Wayne Frank tick? He's a news-clip hoarder and treasure-magazine collector. He's an all-time fabulist.

"Oh, Lord. He's in a fugue state. He's got his scrapbook out, and he's gone stir-crazy from the rain."

Elmer flinched and spilled his highball. Brenda walked soft. She snuck into her own house. It was some trick on high heels.

"You know what Kay says. 'Keep referring to me in the third person. It sends me.'"

Brenda shut the door. "Katherine Ann. She's the first thing out of your mouth. She's the only one you'll ever love, in case you ain't figured it out."

Elmer checked his watch. "It's almost noon. The party must have run long."

"I spent some time with Jack. I'll tell you, so you won't ask. It was a paid date, and Jack said he wants you to run bag to some city councilmen. Him and Fletch got worries on that phone-tap probe. They're buying forgiveness in advance."

Elmer smiled. "Let's hit the kip. We ain't spent time there in a coon's age."

Brenda said, "The weekend, maybe. You know I do my best work by appointment."

Elmer scoped the world at large. Hard rain hit, palm trees wiggled, palm fronds flew.

"There's too much going on out there. God's telling us something."

Brenda said, "You're at loose ends, Citizen. You're looking to louse something up and put yourself in a jam. Go see Ellen and get your ashes hauled. You'll do us both a favor."

Ellen tapped his forehead. "You're broody. Something's going on in there. And don't tell me it's the Fate of Mankind, because you're not that deep."

They were naked. Ellen's mattress sagged. Her baby boy dozed one room over.

Elmer said, "It's too warm in here. You get that with these big buildings. They don't leave you no choice with the heat."

Ellen lit a cigarette. She sat up crossways and blew smoke rings. Their sweat was all mingled up.

"That's not a real answer. I could turn down the heat if I wanted to, but I keep it warm for the baby."

Elmer said, "We've got this rule, remember? We're not supposed to talk about him."

"You're broody. Give me a hint. There's the war, the draft, and you blew that stakeout, so maybe Dudley Smith's peeved at you. You don't like harassing these so-called innocent Japs, and you wish you could go back to Vice. Give me a little clue."

Elmer relit his cigar. Smoke fumes fumed the room up good.

"One little clue. I'll hold you captive here until you tell me."

Elmer said, "That's a swell inducement not to talk."

Ellen said, "And that's a swell compliment. But tell me something, or I'll start brooding on adultery and kick you out."

Elmer touched her hair and kissed her. Ellen nuzzled his hand.

"My life's too easy. I got the world by the dick, but it don't sit right with me."

Loose ends. The New Year's blahs. Elmer hit the road.

He drove to City Hall and prowled corridors. The Hall was holiday dead. The PD ran a light crew. The Air Patrol guys stuck to the basement. The mayor's office and City Council chambers were dark.

Elmer had keys and a briefcase. He hit Call-Me-Jack's office and unlocked his desk drawers. Jack left four envelopes. They were marked with initials. They were probably five-yard payoffs.

The mayor's office ran swank. Walnut panels and a Mussolini-size desk. Elmer unlocked Fletch Bowron's drawers. He grabbed four more envelopes. He saw that familiar green binder.

His binder. Brenda's. Their merchandise book. Nude pix of their girls.

He leafed through it. He got titillated and broody, simultaneous.

He replaced the binder. He hit the Council chambers and divvied up the gelt. The 4th District guy kept a desk jug. Elmer helped himself. He sat in the guy's green leather chair and put his feet up.

Loose ends. The New Year's blahs. Elmer hit the road.

The hard rain subsided. A drizzle held in. Central Station was close. Elmer walked over.

The crime lab was locked. The main squadroom was locked. The Alien Squad pen was lit bright. Elmer poked his head in. He saw Wendell Rice and George Kapek. They were in their skivvies. They were tossing dice and snarfing pizza pie.

Elmer said, "Happy New Year."

Rice said, "You up and took off last night. Dud wondered what happened to you."

"You and George started lifting wallets. I got a burr in my tail."

Kapek said, "You're pious, Jackson. That, and you don't need the money. You got your girl racket, and you're Jack Horrall's favorite Okie."

Elmer waved his cigar. "I'm a cracker, not an Okie. There's a distinction."

Rice raised his hands. "Peace, brother. We're all white men, and we're going back to rousting Japs first thing tomorrow."

Elmer made the jack-off sign. Kapek said, "Last night was a bust. We got no good drift on who sliced Dud, and nothing ripe on Tommy Glennon."

Rice said, "Dud's hipped on Tommy. Something's going on there that I don't comprehend."

Kapek said, "Dud's right hand don't know what his left hand is doing."

Elmer gauged the chitchat. Nothing gored him. Fucking Eddie Leng gored him. There was no dead-body call. These humps would have heard. There was no **Herald** headline: DEEP-FRIED CHINAMAN FOUND! COPS SIFT CLUES!

Kapek rolled snake eyes. He crapped out and moaned. Rice snatched the dice. His undershirt hiked and exposed his left arm. Note the thunderbolt armband.

Still life. Geek cops at play. Exiled from home and hearth. Jap hunters in repose.

Elmer fought off the New Year's blues. Elmer hit the road.

The hard rain revived. He drove through swamped intersections and sewer floods. Who snuffed Eddie Leng? Who's the dead man in the box?

Elmer drove to the Gordon Hotel. Tommy's "SQ" tattoo stencil tweaked him. He braced the desk clerk. Let me retoss Tommy's room. Tommy's a fugitive rape-o.

The clerk went **Nyet, sahib.** He said two cops just

tore through here. They tossed Tommy's room. I'm not repeating that grief with you.

The clerk described Mike Breuning and Dick Carlisle. They **re**tossed his first toss. That scotched toss #3.

Elmer drove back downtown. He hit 11th and Broadway and parked. He recharged with bennies and Old Crow. He got electricized.

He eyeballed that hot-box phone for no damn good reason. It stood outside the **Herald.** It was just some coin booth.

But:

Tommy called it. Maybe **mucho** times. Tommy's address book. Think fast, now. Tommy called **fourteen** Baja pay phones.

Elmer glanced across the street. He spotted a Fed sedan. Ed Satterlee was tucked in. He was eyeballing the booth.

Cop life. Circle jerk. Who you know, who you blow. Satterlee bossed the Fed probe. Satterlee tricked with the Brenda-Elmer service. Satterlee was tonged up.

Elmer stared at the hot-box. Baja calls. That's a head-scratcher. Ain't the Dudster Baja-bound now?

10

(TIJUANA, 3:30 P.M., 1/1/42)

Border cops saluted and waved them through. **Bienvenidos, señor y señora.**

They were Falangista thugs. They were Francoesque in dress and demeanor. They saw the staff car and Army **jefe.** They noted the comely **mujer.** They fawned and clicked their heels.

Mexico. Our grand, if raucous, neighbor. A properly subservient hello.

Dudley and Claire breezed into T.J. Claire drove. Dudley's arm sling precluded. A late sun lit rain clouds.

They cut inland and south. The coast road detoured through T.J. proper. It's **muy feo.** Let's see how Claire reacts.

The child-beggar swarms. The cat-meat taco vendors. The women-fuck-donkey clubs. The open-air **farmacias.** Voodoo health cures and sub-rosa dope.

Liquor stores. Niteklubs. Prowling sailors and Marines. Strolling **putas.** He-she's in bullfighter garb.

The cops wore mismatched uniforms and drove mismatched cars. Jackboots, jodhpurs, tunics— all Nazi black. **Der Führer**—style purveyor to the world's great unwashed.

Chevy prowl cars, Ford prowl cars. U.S. confiscations. Wait, there's a Packard. Note the coyote-pelt seats.

Claire said, "I left Beverly Hills for this. It must mean that I love you."

Dudley laughed and squeezed her knee. His bad arm ached. Claire caught a lane back to the coast road. To the east: scrub hills and abandoned-car encampments. To the west: cliffside coves and sea swells.

Claire hit the gas. Dudley read her. She wanted to get there and dose herself. She wanted to craft her rich-leftist-among-the-peons persona.

She brooded her way down from L.A. He brooded in inimical sync. He concentrated on Tommy Glennon.

Mike and Dick tossed Tommy's room. A clerk told them that another cop had already tossed it. The clerk described the doltish Elmer Jackson.

He caught a noon radio broadcast. It stressed "Chinese restauranteur slain." There was no "victim Leng tong affiliate." There was no "close pal of Thomas Malcolm Glennon." Both facts should have been stressed.

Tommy's missing now. Mike and Dick saw a Spanish-language text in his room.

Dudley scoped the terrain. Eyes left: hills and Jap fishing towns. He'd raid them. He'd roust Fifth Column Japs and plain old Japs set for internment. Eyes right: the cliffs, the coves, the sea.

Storm-tossed now. Like last month. Shallow beachfront/glide-in spots/perfect sub concealment.

Like last month. Like the botched dope raid. Like the Jap sub and blown-to-shit Carlos Madrano.

Claire said, "You're clenching, dear. Your jaw is trembling."

Dudley lit a cigarette. "I'm considering failure and the means not to repeat it. Mexico redefines opportunity, and I must not stumble here."

Claire smiled. "You're a war profiteer."

Dudley winked. "Bright lass. I knew you'd figure it out."

Ensenada.

Fishing spot, tourist trap, lovers' hideout. Cliffside hotels and sportfishing piers. Slum piers crammed with tuna boats and bait shops. Streets named for saints and notable despots.

Claire turned off the coast road. Avenida Costera hugged low cliffs and offered up jazzy views. The Army usurped the Hotel Pacifico del Norte. The third floor was all SIS.

Officers billeted in sea-motif suites. Enlisted men lived in off-site barracks. They were jerry-rigged, post–Pearl Harbor. Convict laborers toiled, posthaste.

The hotel was Moorish-mosque adobe. Eight stories, thick walls, tile roofs. The front entrance was sandbagged. Howitzers and tripod Brownings flanked the doors. Mex Staties stood guard. They held tommy guns at port arms.

Claire pulled into the porte cochere. Greedy valets swooped. Beaners in movie-usher attire. Coolie hats à la Grauman's Chinese.

A full-dress major broached the car. He was forty-five, short, and porcine. He leaned in on Dudley's side. He expelled booze fumes.

"Captain Smith, Mrs. Smith. I'm Ralph Melnick, and I'll escort you to your quarters, and show you around before you can say **'más rápido.'**"

Dudley grinned and stuck out his hand. Melnick bone-crushed him. Claire saw something. She ignored the exchange and glanced streetside. Dudley tracked her eyes.

It's a waif girl. About fifteen, tattered coat and skirt, scuffed Army boots. Dark hair, glasses, feral élan.

Dudley touched Claire's arm. She turned back and smiled—a dazzler.

"I'm not Mrs. Smith, Major. I'm Miss De Haven."

The tour, then.

The gringo was king here. Army personnel and swank turistas capered. Statie drones worked the desk and switchboard. They wore starched fatigues and packed sidearms. Mix-blood mestizos fetched drinks and scrounged tips. Dark **indios** slaved.

Three restaurants. Seaside lounge. Private fishing pier and Rose Bowl–sized lobby. Dolores del Rio, engulfed by fawning fans.

Captain Smith's billet: the Plutarco Calles Suite. Dudley roared—the Red priest-killer, **conmemorativo.**

Two bedrooms, living room, dining room/kitchen.

Ocean-view balcony, mounted trophy fish through-out. Bathrooms with five-foot-deep tubs.

Claire decamped to explore the suite and geez morphine. Major Melnick blushed and curtsied good-bye. He walked Dudley down to 3. The floor had been wartime-gutted. **Arriba,** SIS. The U.S. Army has arrived.

One massive squadroom. Forty-odd cubicles and desks. Floor-to-ceiling corkboards and file banks. U.S./Baja wall maps.

Switchboard. Forty phone lines. Eight Teletypes. All-new photostat. Coding room and armory. Two dozen men on duty. Twenty-four-hour work shifts.

Captain Smith got a full office. He got a large desk and green leather chairs. The FDR wall pic had to go.

Melnick produced a flask. They traded pops. Dudley turned the FDR pic facedown. Melnick yuk-yukked.

"So, right now Mexico's 'neutral,' but it's just a pose, because **El Presidente** Camacho's a dick tease, and he wants to extract all the U.S. aid he can get his mitts on before he comes onboard with the Allies. Baja's full of Japs, with a sprinkling of Krauts, and Camacho's been dragging his heels on that, while he keeps up his neutrality pose. We've got to get these Jap boogers detained and interrogated. We've got eight hundred and fifty miles of coastline here, beach coves up the ying-yang, and Jap fishermen with Fifth

Column sympathies and the wherewithal to guide a goddamn armada of subs in."

Dudley passed the flask. "My special duties, sir?"

Melnick said, "You're my executive officer, with all corresponding authority. You'll serve as liaison to the Mexican State Police and the California-based police and civilian authorities. You'll supervise inland airplane searches and shoreline sub checks. You'll round up Japs and see to their U.S. deportation and internment, because the spic powers that be haven't got the manpower and facilities to intern the fuckers here, and the Mexican government's out to steal all the Jap money it can. The Baja governor is a Kraut-Mex breed named Juan Lazaro-Schmidt. He's another heel-dragger. He kind of likes Hitler and Tojo, and thinks they just might win the war. So, we try to work around this guy. Our big asset in north Baja's the new boss of the Statie boys here. José Vasquez-Cruz. He's coming by to see you at 1800. He's an honorary white man in my book."

Dudley swiveled his desk chair. He took two full spins. The office went **wheeee.**

Melnick said, "Miss De Haven sort of bushwhacked me. Your personnel file said you were married."

Dudley said, "Miss De Haven bushwhacked **me.** She wasn't the first woman to contravene my vows, but she may well be the last."

———

Dusk hit early. They kept the terrace doors open and the bedroom lights low. Storm clouds brewed just past the harbor. More rain was due.

Claire sat up in bed. Dudley cradled his bad arm. The sling tanked their lovemaking. They laughed it off.

Claire scootched down and got their eyes level. Dudley plumped pillows and drew her in close.

"We're here now. Are you aware of how much things have changed?"

Claire kissed him. "We of the Left see our lives as History. I find myself counting the days since Pearl Harbor, and chalking all change up to the novelty of the war."

Dudley kissed her. "We're both unruly. The war will serve as our justification until we tire of the falsehood. We've both endured failures of late. I failed in business, but it has not derailed my resolve. You succumbed to the infiltration efforts of William H. Parker and Kay Lake. They succumbed to war fever and a desire to hunt Reds, and took it out on you. You succumbed to your idealism and susceptibility to fetching waifs, as evinced by Miss Lake. This war will advance our individual and often antithetical agendas. If we remain candid and strong, we will not derail ourselves."

Claire hooked a leg over him. They were **this** close.

"Grant me a concession, darling. Merge our agendas just a little bit."

Dudley laughed. "Hitler is every bit as bad as Stalin. That's as far as I'll go tonight."

Claire laughed. "Quid pro quo, then. Stalin is every bit as bad as Hitler, and in case you're wondering, it was Kay Lake who first got me to concede that."

"Then concede this. It's **our** war."

"Yes, love. It is surely our war. And it's Kay's war, as much as I dislike her."

Rain drummed the terrace. Lightning flashed. Claire lit a cigarette and blew smoke rings.

"I'm in the market for a new waif. I might go looking for that girl we saw."

The coast road, southbound. It's a rain sieve and slalom course. There's thunder. There's wave smash. It's eerie-beautiful in the dark.

Captain Vasquez-Cruz drove. He proposed the excursion. Here's his windup and pitch:

"Captain Smith, I have something to show you. It is on the beach a fair way from here. I think it will amuse and confound you."

They drove due south. Vasquez-Cruz wheeled a Cadillac impound. He called it a "Jew canoe." He expressed regard for Adolf Hitler and defamed nun-raping Reds. He knew El Dudster's rep and toiled at rapport.

He was snazzy. He was thirty-two or -three and ever bemused. He wore Statie blacks and spit-shined jackboots.

They comported in a merry monsoon. Vasquez-Cruz sped through it. Dudley futzed with the radio.

He tuned in XERB and Father Coughlin. The pulsing padre praised the Sinarquistas and Salvador Abascal. Static ditzed the broadcast. Dudley skimmed the dial. He caught more static and a coon jazz quartet.

Vasquez-Cruz doused the sound. "I'm glad that you killed Carlos Madrano. It secured me his position."

Dudley said, "And how did you secure this information?"

"I tortured his **ichiban.** Scorpions attacked his small dick. He revealed that you and your policeman colleagues attempted to steal Madrano's heroin cache. You blew up Madrano with nitroglycerin you uncovered at the cache site, but failed to get the heroin."

"Because **you** got it?"

"Yes. **You** killed Madrano, but **I** commandeered his soul. I assumed his State Police command and appropriated his dope racket. If he had a woman, I would have fucked her or killed her."

Dudley laughed. "You embody the beating heart of machismo."

Vasquez-Cruz went **tee-hee.** He embodied the vicious-bantamweight aesthetic. He tittered in the near-soprano range.

"You and your policeman friends discovered a Jap sub at the Colonet Inlet. You interrogated members of the crew and determined their Fifth Column intent. They were going to pass themselves off as Chinese and perform sabotage in Los Angeles."

Dudley popped his holster flap. His raincoat featured fast-draw pockets.

"Madrano's **ichiban** told you that?"

"Yes, just before I killed him."

Dudley smiled. Vasquez-Cruz swung a hard right and hit a beach-access road. The Jew canoe brodied on loose mud and sand. He skidded up to the shoreline. His headlights strafed ocean swells.

He set the brake. "We are near the Colonet Inlet. This must seem familiar to you."

Dudley popped the glove box. He saw two flashlights, straight off.

He grabbed one. Vasquez-Cruz grabbed one. He stepped out of the car and walked ahead. Dudley lagged five yards back. He unbuttoned his raincoat and unholstered his piece.

Low cliffs deflected the rain. They kicked through wet sand and skirted the wave line. Dudley reholstered. Vasquez-Cruz turned on his flashlight. He aimed it at a rock cove. It was shallow—about eight feet deep.

Dudley smelled it and saw it. Dudley noted the drag marks and counted the stiffs.

Sixteen Jap sailors. Not yet decomposed. Close-range gunshot wounds. Shots to the head. Probable close-range ambush.

Tangled bodies. Facial powder burns and jawline stippling. Exploded bridgework and shattered teeth.

Vasquez-Cruz flashed his flashlight ten yards north. There's the beached sub.

Dudley said, "The Colonet Inlet Japs were a first wave of saboteurs. I would call this a second wave. They were killed by rival Fifth Columnists or rogue State Police. I'll need to interrogate any and all men you might suspect."

Vasquez-Cruz bowed. **Sí, mi capitán.**

Dudley said, "The contact man for the Colonet saboteurs was a Chinese plastic surgeon named Lin Chung. He lives in Los Angeles. The rest of the cabal are wealthy white men, too powerful to touch. Please permit me to work the Los Angeles end of this. I have thoughts already."

Vasquez-Cruz bowed. **¿Qué, mi capitán?**

Dudley lit a cigarette. It smothered the death stink.

"A Chink restauranteur was murdered in Los Angeles last night. He was a tong affiliate, and I'm sure he knew Lin Chung. They were both Jap-haters and committed rightists. This war of ours is breeding some rare birds."

Vasquez-Cruz said, "Yes. You and I among them."

Dudley bowed. **Sí, mi hermano.**

"Do you have access to a capable crime lab? I would like all of this assessed."

Vasquez-Cruz shook his head. Dudley said, "I know a man in L.A. It may amuse you to know that he's Japanese."

11

(LOS ANGELES, 8:30 P.M., 1/1/42)

Captain Parker was late. Joan nursed a highball and killed time. She felt bushwacked and adrenalized.

She wore a clean uniform. Last night's blues were a mess. She'd go back to civvies tomorrow. Navy commission, adieu. She'd unpack her lab smock and white shoes.

Pinch me.

The party in Dago. The smash-up and dead men. "Cholos" and "wetbacks" in cop parlance. The City Hall party. All those politicos and policemen.

She meets ex-Chief "Two-Gun" Davis. She meets the L.A. mayor and the current chief, "Call-Me-Jack" Horrall. Count Basie says, "Hi there, Red."

Now she's here. Mike Lyman's Grill, 8th and Hill streets. A long oak bar and red leather booths.

Parker chose the spot. The PD had its own private room. Parker laid out the gist.

You had couches, chairs, and a Murphy bed. A police Teletype and phone line were laid in. Mike Lyman supplied free cold cuts and liquor. Married cops "poked" their girlfriends there. "Famous madam" Brenda Allen supplied high-class prostitutes.

Pinch me.

Joan lit a cigarette. Her booth faced the bar and the front door. Lyman's was packed. War chat bubbled.

Jap atrocities. FDR's draft quota. **I heard Hitler's really Jewish. The Jews started this boondoggle, if you ask me.**

Joan sipped scotch and bitters. The Navy bash faded out, the cop bash faded in.

She almost met Hideo Ashida. He went out on a dead-body call as she arrived. She talked to a cop named Lee Blanchard. His girlfriend Kay something hovered. Blanchard ran down the Captain Parker gestalt.

He was "Whiskey Bill" and "The Man Who Would Be Chief." He was a hotshot lawyer, juicehound, and devout Catholic. He was impervious, tough, and commanding. He was somewhat slovenly.

He's married. He hides out from his wife and sleeps in his prowl car. The capper: "You're too tall for him, Red."

Men always called her "Red." They thought it was hep. Said men were dinks and buffoons.

I ain't jiving you, cousin. Hitler's a lox jockey from way back. My wife's cousin's a full-blood Kraut. He knows whereof he speaks.

Parker walked in. He wore a fresh uniform. He'd trimmed his hair. He primped and slid into the booth.

He wore piss-poor lime cologne. He sucked a hide-the-hooch lozenge.

He tossed his cigarettes on the table. A waiter

materialized. Parker pointed to Joan's glass and held up two fingers.

Joan slid the ashtray over. "Am I officially employed by the Los Angeles Police Department?"

Parker lit a cigarette. "Forty-two hundred dollars a year. You'll work Central Station, under Ray Pinker and beside Hideo Ashida. Learn what you can, while you can. Pinker's looking at an indictment in this Fed-probe megillah, and Ashida will probably be interned next month. You'll be logging property, as well as processing evidence."

Joan snapped her fingers. "Just like that?"

Parker snapped his fingers. "I called in a favor. We don't have to discuss it. You're in means you're in."

"Yes, but you've got me at a disadvantage. You've placed me in your debt, and you know a great deal about me, while I know virtually nothing about you."

Their drinks arrived. Joan let hers sit. Parker bolted his.

"You're being disingenuous, Lieutenant. You read men like you read chemical tables. You met Lee Blanchard and Jim Davis at the party and solicited information. You gauged their bias and arrived at conclusions. You're as up to speed on me as I am on you. I'll concede my crush on the lithe Northwestern coed, if you won't labor the point."

"I'll concede the scope of my debt, then, and refrain from judging your motives."

Parker said, "Let's go see Nort Layman and Dr. Ashida. They're working late at the morgue."

Dr. Nort **lived** at the morgue. Dr. Nort lived for his work.

Corpse gurneys flanked clothes racks. Formaldehyde bottles lined bookshelves. A cot and booze cabinet covered one wall. A charred box lolled on an autopsy table. A skeleton was jammed within.

Parker played emcee. The drift was meet your new colleague. She's credentialed. She's qualified. She swapped her Navy commission for a crime-lab gig.

Dr. Nort blushed. Dr. Ashida bowed Oriental. They stood by the table. The box deterred small talk.

Dr. Nort said, "These damn mud slides dislodged this box on the Griffith Park golf course. Our late friend here was stabbed, shot, and put to rest. We're trying to determine the source of the fire and when it occurred."

Joan studied a dirt clod jammed under the rib cage. She saw desiccated roots and granular ash.

"The box has been suspended in dirt for a very long time. I would posit that the killer or killers dumped the man in the box with that dirt mound stuck to his upper posterior, while he was still clothed. Those rags rotted off the cadaver, and the passage of time was accelerated by the application of the quicklime that remains visible on those cloth fragments. I think the box has been covered by heavily rooted soil for close to ten years."

Ashida said, "A fatal brush fire in '33 most likely caused that charring."

Joan examined the box. "Look at the flame pattern. The box was surely buried on a hillside, and the flames leapt irregularly and scorched through to dry, freshly excavated dirt, at some point in time before the seeding that produced grass on that hillside. I would conclude that the box was buried immediately before the 1933 fire that Dr. Ashida mentioned, or at the time of the fire itself."

Dr. Nort gawked. Ashida half-grinned. Joan tickled the dead man's chin.

"Run molecular-compound tests on the charred wood, and check the grain markings against the photographic records kept at local lumberyards. You might be able to match the grain to a presold lot."

Parker weaved a tad. Joan caught his booze breath. She reached in his pants pocket and tossed him a lozenge. Ashida slack-jawed the move.

12

(LOS ANGELES, 6:00 A.M., 1/2/42)

Man Camera. Attach your reverse lens. Become the object you observe. Deploy this Hans Maslick technique.

Maslick the Mystic. At one with nature and the material world. Organic specimens and objects live. You must assume their perspective.

Ashida rigged a microscope and dialed it in tight. He examined old dirt particles. He saw Miss Conville's stripped roots.

He one-upped Miss Conville then. He added ionized water and bonded the particles. He dialed down and caught **petrified** ash. It theoretically confirmed the nine-year-old-fire assessment.

Maslick propounded time-travel theories. Place yourself in immediate context. You were there and you saw it. You observed and/or committed the crime.

He was alone. He beat the day-shift chemists in. He savored early-morning work. Juxtaposition. Bright lab lights and a black sky outside.

He time-traveled. He buckled into his time machine. It's 10/3/33 now. It's that very hot day.

He was at Belmont High. He was watching Bucky Bleichert toss a football. He indulged daydreams. Bucky needs a postpractice shower. You can kibitz and throw him a towel.

He watched Bucky dry off. A radio blared: **BIG GRIFFITH PARK BLAZE!!!** They got in Bucky's car and drove over. Fire trucks stopped them short at Riverside Drive.

Ashida shut his eyes. It shuttered his Man Camera. He placed himself in Griffith Park. It's still that very hot day.

Mineral Canyon. Dry dirt and scrub. It's undeveloped. There's no par-3 golf course yet.

The dead man. The killer or killers. The pine box, stashed. A hillside hole, at least partially dug.

Spontaneous blaze or covert arson. One gunshot. One stab wound. A hasty burial as the flames spread.

Thirty-four dead. The killer or killers might have survived. The killer or killers might have perished.

Ashida opened his eyes. His time machine lurched. His recollection lurched in sync.

He read Maslick in high school. He invented his own Man Camera. It was a trip-wire photo device. He shamefully deployed it. He snapped pictures of Bucky in the Belmont High locker room.

He updated the device. He deployed it at a robbery scene late last year. The forensic application backfired.

Dudley coveted the device. Dudley broke into his apartment and covertly studied it. He found the picture stash. Dudley ran the Watanabe job. Dudley blackmailed him and co-opted him to the Werewolf frame.

Ashida rubbed his eyes and cracked a window. Cold air rushed in. He felt wind-deflected rain.

Thad Brown put two detectives on the boxed-dead-man job. It was perfunctory. Here's a postscript: Elmer Jackson's brother died in that fire.

A radio blared down the hallway. Sid Hudgens blared his a.m. **Herald** piece.

Chinatown torture snuff. Jap-hater Eddie Leng. Fifth Column Japs on Chinatown rampage?

Ashida shut the door and muzzled the Sidster. Miss Conville was due. She seemed competent. Dr. Nort and Captain Parker were dazzled. Parker quashed Manslaughter Two and got Miss Conville a job. She knew she killed four Mexicans. Parker quashed her knowledge of the dead kids in the trunk. Lustful men and corrupt women. It was ghastly business.

The phone rang. The noise startled him. Ashida snatched the call.

"Crime lab. Dr. Ashida speaking."

Dudley said, "Good morning, lad. It has been entirely too long."

13

(LOS ANGELES, 8:45 A.M., 1/2/42)

Today's B-Squad roust sheet. It's all J-town and nearby. There's three likely Tojoites.

The squad pen was drafty. The day-watch guys honked their snouts and skimmed their roust summaries. Elmer unwrapped a cigar and crib-noted his sheet.

Yanigahara, Willy J. Age 47/tavern employee. Rat-off by: Agent Ed Satterlee. Noted Chink-hater. Spotted at bund rallies. Has white girlfriend.

Yamazaki, Robert/AKA "Bad Bobby." Age 34/ railroad employee. On Federal rat list. Deutsches Haus habitué. Has Negro girlfriend. Frequents jazz clubs and tokes maryjane.

Matsura, Donald L. Age 41/metallurgist/gold broker/imports samurai swords. Rat-off by: Agent Ed Satterlee. Has Jap Navy KAs. Wears zoot suits. Has Mexican girlfriend.

Per above suspects:

No wants/no warrants/no parole holds. Inventory domiciles and transport to Lincoln Heights Jail. Today's B-Squad pair off: Kapek, Jackson, Rice.

Elmer lit his cigar. He got unlucky today. Kapek and Rice gored his gourd. Lee Blanchard got A-Squad/ Lunceford and Moss. He notched the relative luck.

The boss took the lectern. Noted nosebleed Lew Collier. The squad humps straddled chairs and snapped to.

Collier said, "Go easy on your confiscations. The lab's overloaded. Inventory the flops and tape-seal them. This squadroom is not a pawnshop. Don't bring stuff in, thinking you can hock it later on."

Lunceford said, "No tickee, no washee."

Kapek said, "That's what you call a mixed metaphor. The Chinks say that, not the Japs."

Blanchard pulled his cheeks taut. He did the squint-eyed Chinaman—always good for laughs.

Ha-has rose and subsided. Elmer said, "What about plain old stealing, boss? You might direct your answer to Kapek and Rice."

Kapek sput-sputtered. Spit bubbles popped.

Rice said, "Jackson's a Bolshevik."

Lunceford said, "He's a Jap-lover, you mean."

Blanchard said, "How come we're not rousting the dagos and the Krauts?"

Moss said, "They're in this here war, the last time I heard."

Collier rolled his eyes and held up the **Herald.** "You all know this, right? Eddie Leng bought it New Year's Eve. Safe to say you also know the Japs hate the Chinks. The Chief wants you guys to keep your ears down in J-town."

Blanchard said, "Who's working it for the Bureau?"

Collier said, "Nobody. The Chief's kicked it over to Ace Kwan. Let the Chinks police the Chinks, he always says."

Elmer said, "Eddie Leng was Four Families, and Ace runs Hop Sing. You see a certain hypocrisy there?"

Rice said, "Jackson's a Bolshevik."

They walked to J-town. Unjailed Japs voodoo-eyed them. **Oooga-booga.** It's B-Squad, on the hoof.

They wore civvies and carried pump shotguns. Rock-salt rounds replaced buckshot. Rock salt knocked you down and pocked your ass bloody. It stopped short of instant death.

Kapek and Rice dwarfed Elmer. They hoofed three abreast and dwarfed all known Japs. Yanigahara lived on East 2nd. Yamazaki lived on East 1st. Kapek hit a call-box phone and summoned a whore wagon. The wagon met them outside the Yamazaki crib.

Bad Bobby went peaceful. Elmer wrote the inventory and gave him a cigar. There was no evil swag extant. Bad Bobby owned boocoo jazz records and zoot suits. Plus pulp westerns and a Packard-Bell radio. Nix on hate tracts and guns.

They tape-sealed the door and dumped Bobby in the wagon. They hit East 2nd Street. Willy J. Yanigahara went peaceful.

Elmer wrote the inventory and gave him a cigar. There was no evil swag extant. Racy swag, though.

Kapek found a stack of girlie mags. Rice bootjacked them. Elmer found a locket stuffed with blond pubic hair. A note was jammed in. It read "To Willy, love always, Lorene."

Elmer bootjacked it. They tape-sealed the door and dumped Willy in the wagon. The wagon trailed them south on San Pedro.

Donald Matsura lived at 219 3rd. His pad was upstairs rear. There was no elevator. B-Squad hoofed it up and back.

Rice banged the door. Music snapped off inside. A skinny Jap opened up.

He was TB-ward thin. He had gassed hair topped by a jigaboo hairnet. He had pinned-out, darty eyes.

Oooga-booga. He put out dat fear stink.

Elmer said, "Son, don't you rabbit."

Matsura squealed words, Jap-talk falsetto.

Rice and Kapek grabbed him. They smashed him against the door and cuffed his hands behind his back.

Matsura squealed squeal words. They verged on crazy-man squeaks. Rice grabbed his hair and smashed his face into the doorjamb. Matsura screeched falsetto. Elmer ran through the crib and eyeball-tossed it.

He saw ratty furniture and a fly-swarmed kitchen.

He saw a console radio and smelled burned-out tubes.

He dumped a hamper full of sock-padded jockstraps.

He dumped a nightstand full of gold swastika paperweights and **Goldlover** magazines.

He saw a terpin hydrate still. It was hooked up to a four-burner hot plate. It featured feeder vats and four yeast spouts.

He saw a take-out menu for Eddie Leng's Kowloon.

He opened a closet. He saw samurai swords up the wazoo.

He ran back to the front room. Rice and Kapek had Matsura pinned to that wall.

They wheeled and saw Elmer. They stopped rabbit-punching Matsura. They dropped their mitts and went **Well?**

Matsura squirmed loose and ran out the doorway. Kapek gave him a ten-yard lead and raised his shotgun.

He let three rounds fly. Rock salt shredded the shirt off Matsura's back and scalped off most of his hair.

14

(ENSENADA, 8:00 A.M., 1/3/42)

Dudley said, "I've issued a blanket arrest order. All Japs registered in the '40 census. Noncoms and State Police have been dispatched."

Coffee klatch. Strict dress code. Olive drabs for SIS. Statie fasco black.

They perched in Ralph Melnick's office. The boss served coffee and sweet rolls. His ODs were crumb-flecked.

"Captain Smith lets no moss grow under his feet. Isn't that right, José?"

Vasquez-Cruz winked. Dudley winked back. They sat in Chinese lacquered chairs. Melnick worked the Asia desk back in the Ming dynasty.

"No, Major. He does not. Captain Smith is not here to coddle Fifth Columnists or view the notorious donkey show at the Blue Fox."

Melnick slapped his knees. Almond flecks flew. Desk knickknacks rattled.

Dudley said, "I've reserved cells and interrogation rooms at the Statie barracks. The coastal site has been sealed and is now under guard. My police chemist will be driving down later today. He'll forensic the sailors and the submarine itself."

Melnick said, "**¿Qué pasa, amigo?** What did you make of it all?"

"I think Mexican leftists killed the sailors, sir. I'll investigate with that in mind."

Vasquez-Cruz smirked. He knew the truth. Or thought he did.

Melnick slurped coffee. "We've got sixteen dead saboteurs. You could say we got lucky, and let it go at that."

"They were Fifth Column, sir. That's undeniable. I'll be grilling our in-custody Japs, with an eye toward turning leads along those lines."

Melnick checked his watch and went **Shit-I'm-late.** He saluted and booked out the door.

Vasquez-Cruz smirked anew. Smug little shit. His mother cavorts with **El Burro.** He was **born** at the Blue Fox.

"'Mexican leftists,' hardly. You told me something quite different."

Dudley lit a cigarette. "Let's discuss money first."

"We should begin with Carlos Madrano. You blew up his car, and a great many burned U.S. dollars were found amid the wreckage. Madrano had just left the Colonet Inlet, where the first sub had berthed. Now we have a second beached submarine. I'm thinking there may be additional monies hidden onboard."

Dudley said, "I searched the Colonet sub and found ten thousand dollars U.S. My friend Hideo Ashida did the bulk of the work. We gave the money to Madrano, in exchange for our safety. I think we will find a similar amount in this newly beached craft. We will split the money, of course."

Vasquez-Cruz pulled his chair up. "There is more to tell me, I'm sure."

Dudley pulled his chair up. Their knees bumped. Burro Junior winced.

"There's a fugitive at large in Los Angeles. His name is Tommy Glennon, and I know him rather well. I think Tommy killed a Chinese restauranteur, Eddie Leng, that I told you about. He disappeared the night Leng was killed, and they were both known to be jungled up in the Four Families tong. I also consider it likely that Tommy knows Lin Chung, a dubious physician who is surely privy to both sub berthings and sabotage plots. Tommy ran wets for Carlos Madrano and was dunning me for information about the man, when I last saw him. I think Tommy is part of all this, but he had to have had considerable help here in Baja."

Vasquez-Cruz oozed delight. He fluffed his cravat and tee-heed.

"Such strategic insight. You are Robespierre, reborn."

Dudley laughed. "Our mandate is to foil sabotage and make money."

Vasquez-Cruz stuck his hand out. Dudley bone-crushed it. Vasquez-Cruz went **Caramba**—such strength.

———

Claire was out. Dudley patched switchboard calls straight from the suite.

He got Mike Breuning. They bypassed amenities. Mike reported **this:**

Drift per Tommy Glennon. Tommy owed Eddie Leng money. Eddie was crowding him. Jack Horrall palmed the Leng snuff off on Uncle Ace. Jack hated Chink snuffs. Their heathen customs fucked things up. Chinks should arbitrate Chinks.

The Alien Squad popped a Jap named Donald Matsura. He was a terp man and renaissance lowlife. He showed up in dead Eddie's KA file. Matsura knew Tommy and Chink sawbones Lin Chung.

The phone rang. Dudley jiggled the receiver. The switchboard patched out Mike B. and patched in Uncle Ace.

Ace gibbered. English and Chinese overlapped. He talked himself dry. He pooped out and coughed himself hoarse.

Dudley said, "Good morning, my brother."

"My Irish brother. I have missed you."

"Eddie Leng, my brother. Jack Horrall has appointed you judge and jury."

Ace said, "No leads, Dudster. I make piss-poor Charlie Chan. That why white man play him in movies."

Dudley laughed. "There's a Jap named Donald

Matsura at Lincoln Heights. Lean on him, and confirm or eliminate him. I think Tommy Glennon killed Eddie, but I could be wrong. Put this matter to rest, my brother. We should seek to avoid a tong war as we pave our way to the money."

Phone static hit. Ace talked over it: "Fuck"/"shit"/ "money, how?"

The line cleared. Dudley said, "We run wetbacks. We smuggle heroin in Army vehicles transporting Baja Japs to U.S. internment camps. There's a sell-Japs-as-slaves scheme I'm pondering."

More line hiss. More garbled Ace: "Fuck"/"shit"/ "cocksucker." The line cleared. Ace said, "Jap beast must die." It was his boffo signature close.

15

(LOS ANGELES, 9:00 A.M., 1/3/42)

The lab smock clashed with her hair. Her sensible shoes lacked panache. Navy blue and gold, farewell.

She waltzed on the war. She served notice at the Fed Building and cabbed to Central Station. She lugged her gear by the muster room. Short cops ogled her.

Anchors aweigh.

Joan schlepped two suitcases. They contained her

microscope and textbooks. She trudged the stairs. The lab was unlocked and unoccupied.

She surveyed it. She smelled luminol and gun oil. The ballistics chute leaked asbestos.

PD chemists worked sardine tight. Her desk adjoined Dr. Ashida's. They shared bookshelves and burner plates. Joan unpacked and stashed her suitcases in a closet.

Dr. Ashida kept his desk tidy. The charred box was propped up against it. Dirt-packed jars sat three across.

They were evidence-tagged. Mineral Canyon/ Griffith Park/1-1-42.

The case intrigued her. It merged human passion with elemental forces. The rain, the mud slide, a precipitant fire. Possible-probable arson. Her specific métier.

She went by the **L.A. Times** yesterday. She flashed her police ID and wheedled a set of page scrapbooks. They detailed the Griffith Park blaze. Santa Ana winds and scorcher heat. A firebug arrested and released. A Communist cell scrutinized. No arrests. No firm forensic determination.

She should reread and annotate the scrapbooks. She should discuss the case with Dr. Ashida. Catastrophic fire was **her** métier. Dr. Ashida was prissy and domineering. She should establish crime-lab parity.

Joan unscrewed a dirt jar. She sniffed the dirt and placed a small clod in a beaker. She filled a stopper with liquid ammonia and squeezed in eight drops.

She added sink water and placed the beaker on a hot plate.

She brought up a flash boil. The heat induced blue coloration. She checked her organic chemistry text and found a color chart. She got a perfect match.

She studied the charred box. She memorized the wood grain and consulted her woodlot text. There's one more perf—

Hideo Ashida walked in.

He glared. He stomped one foot. Joan preempted him.

"This batch of wood derives from late summer '33. It was cut by the Anawalt Lumber Company. My book lists Anawalt's key 1933 customer as Los Angeles City Parks and Recreation. The dirt I tested contains traces of a four-to-one solution of oil-diluted kerosene, which has been known to be employed as a secondary accelerant to spread already-lit fires. I talked to Dr. Layman and did some newspaper research. Accordingly, I would surmise that the killer had knowledge of an impending arson in Griffith Park, or started the overall fire himself. The box was unearthed in a canyon that was then nearly invisible from the warren of canyons at the apex of the blaze. I would surmise that the killer knew his victim would be in that nearly invisible canyon or lured him there, then killed him, boxed him, covered him in deep, soft earth, and then set the secondary fire."

Ashida slack-jawed it. Mr. Brain was struck dumb. Bill Parker lounged right behind him. Joan smelled his dumb lime cologne.

16

(TIJUANA, 2:00 P.M., 1/3/42)

He knew the look. It said **YOU'RE A JAP.** It vexed him in L.A. This border variant **scared** him.

Mexican cops. With their hate glares. With their soiled uniforms and hand-tooled gun belts. Swastikas and coiled snakes carved in.

Dudley wrangled him an Army pass. A slew of border guards perused it. They hemmed and hawed. Cars piled up behind him.

Horns blared. A man yelled, "Goddamn Jap!" Time stuttered and stalled flat.

A guard returned his pass. A guard pointed south. A guard grabbed his crotch. A guard spit on his windshield.

Ashida floored the gas. He detoured through T.J. and hit the coast road. He counted days backward. He stopped Christmas Day.

It was his first Baja visit. He joined Dudley, Mike B., and Dick C. He survived the botched dope raid. He survived the Statie jail and **mucho** torture. He caught the first beached-sub incursion. He questioned captured sailors and beat them with sap gloves. A fat sailor called him a swish.

He searched the sub. Dudley assisted. They found a cash stash and bought their freedom. They hogtied the sailors and dumped them in the sub. He started the engines and got the sub out to sea.

It was explosive-rigged. Twenty-four men fired shotguns and tore out the hull. The sub detonated. The sailors burned alive.

They drove back to L.A. then. He sat in the backseat. Dudley sat beside him. Their legs brushed. He fluttered, all over.

Ashida drove south. Rain clouds gathered off the coast. He brought an evidence kit. He left notes for Elmer Jackson and Lee Blanchard.

He called off their bodyguard schifts. He fed Elmer a P.S. It laid out Joan Conville's charred-box diagnosis. "I know about your brother. This new wrinkle's a non sequitur. It shouldn't bother you."

Ashida drove south. He played the radio and caught a news broadcast. "Recent Jap aggressions" blared. He turned the radio off.

Ensenada came and went. Low clouds seeped rain. He saw Statie goons perched on a beach bluff.

He pulled over. The goons came on servile. They pointed him down a steep roadway. He skidded on hard dirt and sand.

The beachfront was right there. He brodied in tight. He hit his headlights and framed the scene.

Low tide. A beached sub. Dead sailors stacked on wood pallets. A cove entry right behind them.

Rain tarps at the ready. Two generators. Dry ice, dumped in wire-mesh buckets. It foils decomposition. We've got fans rigged. They'll blow cold air on the stiffs.

And there's Dudley. He's dashing in his olive drabs. He's with a Statie captain. Note the jodhpurs and peaked Nazi hat.

Ashida walked over. **El Fascisto** clicked his heels.

Dudley embraced him. Dudley said, "Hello, my dear friend."

He surveyed the scene and went in close. Statie goons held spotlights. The tarps deflected light rain.

High tides eradicated drag marks. Storm tides hit the cove and wrecked his trace-element search. A Statie van backed down to the tide line. The tailgate gave him a flat place to work.

Ashida examined the bodies. He saw the facial powder burns that Dudley saw first. He studied a rock outcropping. He found three dead flashbulbs. He restudied the dead men and examined their tunics and exposed upper chests.

The goons held their spotlights tight-close. Ashida saw silencer threads and noted varied formations.

He tweezer-plucked three representative batches and placed them on slides. He carried them to the tailgate and dialed his microscope tight-tight.

Dudley hovered. Ashida studied the threads. He saw three individuated formations. He looked at Dudley. He smiled and bowed.

"There were three gunmen. They stood at that near outcropping and hit the sailors with flashbulb glare. They ran up and shot them while they were blinded, and they used silencer-fitted guns."

Dudley smiled and bowed. Ashida walked back to the pallets. The goons snapped to. He pointed to the sailors' heads. He said, **"Se siente todos."**

The goons flashed their spotlights. Ashida went in with a surgeon's ax and knife.

He cracked skulls. Eyeball sockets collapsed. He scooped brain tissue and dropped it in the sand. He dug out forty-eight spent bullets, **todos.**

The goons looked ill. They murmured prayers. Ashida was blood-spattered, blood-smeared, blood-flecked.

He walked back to the van. Dudley and Vasquez-Cruz hovered. Ashida sprayed his hands with 100-proof alcohol. He dipped the spents in gasoline and blotter-dried them.

He clamped sixteen spents to microscope slides. He dialed the scope close and passed the slides under his lens. He studied fragmentary striations.

Dudley and Vasquez-Cruz hovered. They chain-smoked and eyed the process. Ashida ran through said process three times.

"The lands and grooves are obliterated, but I can state that the bullets themselves are surely of U.S. manufacture. Based on what I can see of circumference, my best guess would be Smith & Wesson Police .38s."

Dudley said, "Ambush. Three capable men, identically armed."

Vasquez-Cruz went **tee-hee.** He spoke baritone and tittered soprano.

Dudley winked at Ashida. "The submarine, lad. We're looking for money, of course."

Ashida worked straight through. He felt energized. Dudley worked beside him. Vasquez-Cruz supplied tools. They replicated their first inch-by-inch search.

They unscrewed bolts and looked behind panels. They unwired instrument clusters. They disassembled the periscope mount. They scuffed their knuckles and gouged their arms. They pulled up loose floor plates and found **MONEY.**

It was duffel-bagged the first time. It was attaché-cased tonight. Vasquez-Cruz tee-heed and cut through the locks. The yield: twenty grand, U.S.

Dudley grabbed half. **El Fascisto** grabbed half. A fat goon grabbed the attaché.

———

On to photographs. Let's capture the dead and shoot for long-shot IDs.

El Fascisto tipped his goons. He was one high-stepping **jefe.** He dispensed C-notes. The goons genuflected. They went **Sieg Heil** and called Vasquez-Cruz **"Führer."** Dudley dog-bayed and laughed himself hoarse.

It was full dark now. The goons erected arc lights. Ashida loaded his lab camera and close-up shot the stiffs.

He went through sixteen flashbulbs. He dumped bulbs and duplicated the pix. He shot two full sets. One for the Staties, one for SIS.

On to fingerprints. That was a long shot. The sailors were surely native-born Japanese. Their prints were filed in Tokyo and nowhere else.

Ashida hustled up the goons. They were half-tanked on mescal. They **weeeaved** through more arc-light work.

Ashida numbered sixteen print cards and inked thirty-two hands. Rigor mortis worked against him. The goons supplied weavy light. He placed the cards on a wood plank and maneuvered stiff fingertips.

Some were too stiff. He knife-severed those fingers and rolled them free and clear.

Dudley's staff car stood cliffside. Ashida washed his hands and walked up. Dudley and Vasquez-Cruz worked in the backseat.

They dug through file carbons. Resident-alien files. Baja-resident Japanese/pickup orders issued. They trawled for Japanese Navy KAs.

Ashida sat up front. Dudley passed him a file stack. Ashida trawled for KAs. He trawled twelve files and tapped out. He hit on file #13.

The file tapped one Kyoho Hanamaka. He was an "Imperial Navy attaché."

Ashida said, "I've got a man named Hanamaka here. He's tagged as a naval attaché, but he's got very few KAs, and none in the Navy."

Vasquez-Cruz said, "He's one slippery eel. He's quite the friend of Juan Lazaro-Schmidt, the Baja governor."

Supper at the Hotel del Norte. The beach-view dining room served late. Picture windows and wave crash. Your host, Dudley Smith.

In civvies now. Blue blazer, gray slacks. Claire De Haven sat to his left. She satirized this arrangement and tossed barbs at **El Fascisto.** Vasquez-Cruz indulged her and laughed.

He wore his black uniform. He came off sinister. Ashida cleaned up and changed in his room. He showered off brain matter. He scrubbed off fingerprint ink.

Pacific lobster and champagne. Convivial Dudley. No man should be so handsome. Ashida tried not to stare.

Talk flowed. Ashida sipped club soda and ignored his food. He counted days back to Pearl Harbor. He hit the Bill Parker/Kay Lake pogrom.

His role was Kay's lover. He failed at it. Claire threw

a party. Leftist Los Angeles bickered and preened. Kay caused a scene. She deployed her Jap paramour and overplayed the pose. Claire saw through Kay. Claire teethed on her nonetheless.

Dudley dropped a bon mot. Vasquez-Cruz laughed. No **El Fascisto** titter. He laughed deep baritone.

He played to Claire. He moved his chair close and leaned in.

"You must not judge neutral Mexico too harshly, Miss De Haven. This dinner conclave proves my point. We have a Latin man and a Japanese man. We have an Irish-Catholic immigrant and a landed Protestant lady."

Claire lit a cigarette. "I converted to the Roman Church, Captain. I'm an apostate in my faith as well as my politics. You'll have to cite pithier examples if you wish to make time with me."

Vasquez-Cruz went **Salud.** "Perhaps I should cite Mr. Leon Trotsky. He fled Stalin's death squads and found asylum nowhere but here. President Cárdenas provided him with a home when no one else would."

"Only as a means to counter accusations that he was a Stalinist, Captain. And, of course, Trotsky was assassinated in your selfsame country, under that self-same **capitalista** poseur."

Vasquez-Cruz smiled. "Spanish and French in one sentence. Aaay, **caramba.**"

Claire blushed. Ashida caught her dope-pinned eyes. Dudley winked at him. It conveyed subtext. If **El Fascisto** gets too frisky, I'll kill him.

Ashida laughed. It verged on a squeal. He covered his mouth and muzzled himself.

Claire said, "Is something amusing, Dr. Ashida? Something you forgot to tell me when you were a much-welcome but finally intrusive guest in my home last month?"

Ashida said, "I'm quite tired, Miss De Haven. I've spent a busy day in Captain Smith's employ."

Claire glanced away. She looked out the window and stood up. Ashida clocked the window. He saw a raggedy girl on the beach. The girl picked up a starfish and cradled it to herself.

Vasquez-Cruz stood for Claire. Call him Señor Decorum. She touched his hand—**un momento.**

She walked out. **El Fascisto** watched her go. He clicked his heels and bowed to Dudley. He pivoted and walked off.

Ashida said, "He's going to check on Claire. He must have police friends in Los Angeles."

Dudley said, "You're a very bright penny tonight."

Ashida blushed. He looked out the window. Claire engaged the raggedy girl. They fussed over the starfish and had quite a chat.

Dudley rocked his chair back. "My Claire has an enormous and impetuous heart."

Ashida went dizzy. The dining room tilted. Spots popped in front of his eyes.

"What **is** this? Why am I here?"

Dudley tapped his knee. "There's my ex-snitch Tommy Glennon, and a dead Chinaman named Eddie

Leng. There's our old friend Lin Chung, and the scent of money."

"Yes, but what's in it for me?"

Dudley said, "I intend to rescue you and your family from the internment. Would a U.S. Army commission and a posting here suit you?"

17

(LOS ANGELES, 10:00 P.M., 1/3/42)

Elmer doodled. It soothed his gourd and vitalized his brain cells.

Lyman's was jam-packed. He nursed a highball and worked at his table. He scribbled up napkins. He drew pit dogs with sharp fangs and big dicks.

He wrote, **"DUDLEY SMITH EATS SHIT!!!!!"** He laughed. He scoped the bar and saw Thad Brown and Two-Gun Davis. The highball kicked in. He quit futzing around and got to it.

He wrote, **"D.S. & T.G."** He underlined it and added question marks. He wrote, **"T.G. to E.L. (murder vict)"** and underlined it.

He wrote, **"Donald Matsura & E.L.—???"** He wrote, **"Can't talk to Breuning & Carlisle—D.S.'s goons."** He wrote, **"Kapek & Rice—too corrupt."**

He circled. He underlined. He drew arrows and **X**s and stitched all this shit up. He got bored and periscoped Lyman's.

He saw Kay in a back booth. He saw Bill Parker's redhead at the bar. She wore civilian vines now. Jim Davis crowded her. He blathered and sprayed pretzel gack.

Elmer wrote, **"E.J. & J.C."** and drew a heart around it. He added Cupid's arrow and got back to work.

He wrote, **"T.G.'s address book—???"** He wrote, **"Hot-box phone calls—???"** He wrote, **"Calls to 14 Baja pay phones—???"**

He drew an SQ circled by snakes. He drew more question marks. He drew Eddie Leng's death rictus and french-fried feet.

Kay hopped in his booth. There she is, her all-time self.

Elmer scooped up his doodles. Kay laid down her Manhattan. Elmer plucked out the cherry and ate it.

"Tell me something I don't know. And make it interesting, because it's Saturday night, and the world's got me batshit."

Kay laughed. "Thad told me about the DB call New Year's morning. I thought, Uh-**oh**, Elmer's brother died close by there. That's the chickens come home to roost."

Elmer spit the cherry pit in an ashtray. Elmer jiggled Kay's hands.

"I got no dish on this one. It's '42 now, and Wayne

Frank cashed out back in '33. I don't see no hook between him and this here DB. And if I **did,** I wouldn't know what to do, because I'm really just a whore-peddler, a bagman, and a strongarm thug. I **might** be the world's luckiest white man, but I sure as shit am not much of a detective."

Kay lit a cigarette. "There's a look you get. Your jaw sets a certain way, and your eyes go flat. It's like you're saying, 'The comedy hour's over.'"

Elmer snatched her drink. He plucked an orange rind and waved the swizzle stick.

"The Dudster sent me out to kill a man, but I couldn't do it. I been reading some C-town files, and it looks to me like that selfsame geek killed himself a tonged-up Chinaman."

Kay looked him over. She had well-known X-ray eyes. Elmer squirmed and relit his cigar.

Bar chat escalated. Elmer caught threads. Jim Davis called FDR "Double-Cross Rosenfeld." Joan Conville took offense.

Kay caught the kerfuffle. She X-ray-eyed Joan. Elmer said, "There's your gossip."

"If you mean vehicular manslaughter, I've already heard it. Lee told me. He said it's worse than the dead Mexicans, but he wouldn't say why."

Elmer shrugged. "You know everything that I know. If there's more to it, you could ask Bill Parker."

Kay jiggled his hands. Elmer laced up their fingers.

"Kick Lee out. You don't sleep with him, anyway. Tell Parker to leave his wife and marry you. If he nixes it,

I'll marry you. I'll get a cop job in Bumfuck, Indiana. We'll live fat and sassy on a farm someplace."

Kay laughed and **un**laced their fingers. She scanned the bar and X-ray-eyed Big Joan.

He got itchy. He stayed batshit. He fought the Saturday Night Blues.

Elmer drove to his place and fed his tropical fish. Said fish ignored him. Itchy feet pushed him back out. L.A. was blackout black. He drove straight to Brenda's place.

He almost walked in. **Oooh-baby** grunts stopped him dead at the door. He peeped the front window. **Shit**—Brenda's shtupping Jack Horrall on the floor.

Elmer drove to Ellen's place. He parked outside her building and reconnoitered. He elevatored up to her floor. He climbed out on a fire escape and peeped the front room. **Shit**—Ellen's shtupping her husband on the couch.

More loose ends. More fucking rain. Mama, dem blues gots me **baaaaaad.**

Elmer drove to Chapman Park. Brenda's fuck flop overlooked the Ambassador Hotel. Tonight, at the Coconut Grove: Glenn Miller and the Modernaires.

He parked and elevatored up. He let himself in and stormed the kitchen. He built a ham sandwich and a highball. He pondered dumb moves.

Send Kay flowers. Send Big Joan flowers. Take her to the Coconut Grove. Mess with Bill Parker.

Elmer guzzled his highball. He unlocked the wall peek and checked the camera gear. He skimmed the play-for-pay girl book.

Charlotte, French expert. Dirty Diane, striptease. Call the switchboard. You're the boss. You get the woof-woof for free.

Or—

Hit the Lincoln Heights Jail. Brace Crazy Don Matsura. Remember? He had that menu for Eddie Leng's Kowloon.

The rain got worse. He snail-trailed up the Parkway to 19th Avenue. The jail stood upside the off-ramp. He hooked right and sluiced up to a PD space. He got out and ran in.

The entrance hall was bare bones/all gray cement. Elmer brushed off his raincoat and shook himself dry. A night cop lounged by the gate racks. He wore that I-hate-this-job look. He beady-eyed a cheese-cake book.

Elmer walked up and badged him. The night cop said, "So?"

Elmer said, "I'm with the Alien Squad. You've got a frisky Jap named Donald Matsura here. I know, because I brought him in."

The night cop said, "He ain't so frisky now. **Banzai,** if you know what I mean."

"Why don't you explain what you mean?"

"I mean, Chief Horrall called the watch commander. He said Ace Kwan would like a few words with your boy. As in, 'Put him in a sweatbox and then walk away.'"

Elmer slipped the dink twenty. "Ace and I go way back. Call-Me-Jack, likewise. If Ace is still at it, I'd like to watch the show."

"Well . . ."

Elmer doubled up the bribe. The night cop went **Mum's the word** and racked the front gate. Elmer took the main catwalk back. Crisscrossed catwalks extended. Japs were packed in six and eight to a cell.

He hit a bisecting hall. He saw recessed doorways. Oh, yeah—it's sweatbox row.

Four twelve-by-twelve rooms. All the same. Look-see mirrors/floor-bolted tables/two screwed-down chairs.

Elmer cut straight left. He peeped three mirrored doors and got bupkes. He peeped room #4 and got the real shit.

There's Demon Don. There's Uncle Ace. It's the well-known third degree.

Ace was a known rubber-hose man. His hose looked heavy-duty. It was friction-taped. It stood straight up. It had to be ball bearing–packed.

Matsura was chair-cuffed. Ace swung the hose. He threw tight shots—arms, rib cage, legs.

Elmer popped the door. A shit and piss stink hit him. Matsura screamed. He bucked his chair. The floor bolts shimmied. One bolt pulled loose.

Ace saw Elmer. Ace said, "Jack H. give okay."

Elmer said, "You mean Dudley did."

Matsura dribbled blood on the table. Ace threw a head shot. Matsura screamed. Gold bridgework flew.

Ace gibbered. Matsura dribbled blood. Elmer saw gum flaps laced in.

Ace shrieked, trilingual. He went Chink/English/**Chink**lish. Elmer caught **this:**

You Jap fucker/you tonged up/Four Families/sell terp/winos and dope fiends. You sell pharmacy hop/with Lin Chung/you know Tommy Glenn—

Ace stopped. Ace went **Oops.** Ace shut his fat fucking mouth.

Elmer went **Oh shit.**

Ace swung the hose. He threw rib shots and leg shots. Elmer heard bones break. Matsura dribbled blood. The hose cracked down the middle. Ball bearings flew—

Elmer grabbed Ace by the neck and hard-shoved him. Ace bounced off the back wall and hit the floor flat on his ass. Matsura bucked his chair and tore out all the floor bolts. The chair capsized.

Ace keened and screeched. It was some heathen curse. He got to his knees and pulled out his dick. He piss-polluted this big pool of Jap blood.

18

(ENSENADA, 9:15 A.M., 1/4/42)

That cretinous redneck. That Klan-klique bumpkin. That maladroit buffoon.

The telephone exploded. Dudley dropped the receiver. It cut Mike Breuning off.

Bad news. Elmer Jackson muscled Ace Kwan and caused a big upscut. Tough tiff at the Lincoln Heights Jail.

Dudley lit a cigarette. His office spun. Squadroom noise went cacophonous. The temperature zoomed.

He wiped his face and roused the switchboard. He got more bad news. All Baja-to-L.A. circuits—full up.

He should call Jack Horrall and demand reprisals. That could boomerang. Jack was thick with Brenda Allen. That fact mandated circumspection.

Dudley rubbed his bad arm. The sling came off yesterday. An Army doc checked him out and pronounced him okay.

Minor aches persisted. They induced flutters and sweats. They derailed his concentration. His mind wandered. He teethed on the inconsequential. Little things set him off.

His wife called. She wanted to chat. He forgot his eldest daughter's name. Claire eavesdropped on the bedroom phone. It enraged him.

Claire missed Mass this morning. It vexed him. Claire was off with her fetching, if feral, new waif. The girl vexed him no end.

Joan Klein was age fifteen. She was a New York runaway and a Zionist Jew. Her immigrant kin veered hard left. Claire found the girl **très** enchanting.

She bought the girl clothes. She got her a room down the hall. The girl told tall tales. Labor agitators clash with Fed thugs. Mayhem results.

He humored Claire. He said, "You're under-employed, darling. You're picking up strays and grasping at straws."

Claire lashed out. She defamed the "effete" Hideo Ashida. She excoriated the harmless dilettante Kay Lake. Young Kay shivved him in Kwan's basement. Claire fell prey to her most fleeting whims. The charge was preposterous.

José Vasquez-Cruz gored Claire. She thought she gored him. That was **très** Claire. She confused enmity with mild contempt. She said, "I think I've seen him before. Somewhere—perhaps a demonstration."

That felt spot-on. Vasquez-Cruz was a chameleon. He tee-heed to his Army pals. He low-growled to pro-vocative women.

Dudley flexed his bad arm. He made a fist and squeezed it tight. He tore through the pain—and laughed.

Statie HQ:

Three dank buildings inland and south. Slave labor

built them. Jail, trooper barracks, administration. They were plopped down beside an arroyo. Lettuce fields stood close by.

Shackled inmates toiled there. Stoop labor. Lift that barge, tote that bale. The jail featured sweat rooms and torture dens. Scorpions nested there. They ate bugs and stung recalcitrant spics.

Admin featured file vaults and cramped office suites. Dudley called ahead. He talked to a lieutenant named Juan Pimentel. They gabbed at length. Lieutenant Juan reported **this:**

He braced their in-custody Japs. They possessed nada knowledge of the beached sub and dead sailors. He developed Hideo Ashida's film. He cross-checked it against mug-shot files and resident-alien sheets. He got more nada there. He got no fingerprint matches. Sixteen dead Jap sailors? **Es mucho mierda.**

Juan Pimentel was **muy bueno.** He jumped on all the small shit.

He head-counted jail Japs. He got 44 in custody/ 182 still loose. He prepped admin suite 214. He stacked the custody files and made a pot of coffee.

Dudley drove over and parked outside. Prowl cars hemmed him in. Statie bossmen custom-fitted them. Note the hood-mounted flamethrowers. Note the hand-painted saints and giant rodents emitting death rays.

Dudley entered the building and found 214. Lieutenant Juan delivered. He had the homey touch.

The desk, the chair, the coffee. The ashtray and

ceiling fan. The worm-in-the-jug mescal. Forty-four files laid out.

Dudley read through them. He chain-smoked. He read from this spark point:

Kyoho Hanamaka. He's a naval attaché. Hideo skimmed his file and nailed a big inconsistency.

There were very few KAs. There were no naval KAs. It startled Hideo. Hanamaka was still on the loose. That fact troubled him.

Dudley reread the file and studied the clipped photograph. Hanamaka looked psychopathic.

Born in Kyoto, 1898. Career Navy man. Intel background. Toured Europe, '35-'36. Toured Russia, likewise. Brilliant student at the German Naval Warfare School.

There were three male KAs listed. They were all fishermen. That was enticing. Jap Navy man, the Baja coast, beached submarines.

Three KAs. Hiroshi Takai, Hector Obregon-Hodaka, Akira Minamura. All coastal fishermen.

Dudley thumbed custody files. He checked name tabs and hit Obregon-Hodaka.

He read the file. The man was a Jap-Mex half-breed. He spoke English. His moniker was "Big Tuna." He had a valid U.S. travel visa.

Dudley snatched the desk phone and dialed double ought. A jail noncom picked up. Dudley said, "Inmate Obregon-Hodaka. Room 214, please."

———

"I know I'm headed for the shithouse, boss. What I'm angling for is a nice internment berth up near L.A. The Chino work farm, maybe. Dexter Gordon's there. He blows tenor. You've got to gas on his chord changes for 'Ol' Man River.'"

Hector the hepcat. More Mex than Jap. He knew the type. They bred like rats in L.A.

"Quite the jazzman, are you?"

"You ain't lyin', daddy. I know L.A. niggertown like I know the coast here. All the coons on Central Avenue call me 'El Tojo,' 'cause of my mixed blood-line. I'm the Big Tuna here, and El Tojo in L.A."

They sipped mescal. Dudley got a glow on. 160-proof. Satanic worms afloat in the jug. No drink for nancy boys.

"Do you possess strong political convictions, sir?"

"Well, I'm not Fifth Column, if that's what you're getting at. I'm a live-and-let-live, hold-for-the-downbeat sort of cat. I'm looking to get interned at some amenable spot, sit out the war and go home."

Dudley smiled. "I wish you well in that regard, sir."

Hector sipped mescal. His eyes buzzed. He looked halfway blitzed.

"I've got a colored girlfriend in L.A. She's a waitress at the Club Alabam. They'll let me out once Uncle Sambo wraps this war up. I'll marry her and have some whelps with her, even though she's got four pups with Coleman Hawkins already."

Dudley bowed. "You have convinced me of your political solvency and your allegiance to the Allied cause, sir. Now, please describe your relationship with the Japanese naval attaché, Kyoho Hanamaka."

Hector made the jack-off sign. "That cocksucker owes me money."

"Sir?"

"I'd been supplying him with prime tuna for over a year—and by that I mean boatloads. He skipped town owing me **mucho dinero.**"

"So, your relationship with Hanamaka was entirely professional?"

Hector plucked a worm from his glass and ate it. Hector evinced great style.

"We'd bat the breeze sometimes. I knew he was pals with the governor, Juan Lazaro-Schmidt, who's a Nazi sympathizer and a big Jew-hater. So what? World conflicts breed strange bedfellows. I could live with that, but not with him stiffing me for three big boatloads of fish."

Dudley said, "Did the quantities that he purchased in any way arouse your suspicions?"

"Yeah, they did. After Pearl Harbor, I started thinking, What's he want all that fish for? You follow me, boss? Fish, submarine crews, sailors with hearty appetites?"

Dudley lit a cigarette. "We are having parallel thoughts, sir."

"Okay, so I'll wrap it up, then. I was having these suspicious thoughts, and Hanamaka owed me money. He lives up in the Baja hills, so I drove up there to collect. It was December 18—I remember because it's my birthday. I drove up there, but the house had been cleaned out."

Dudley said, "Take me there. We'll leave now."

Hector said, "This jungle juice has got me hopped up. I might try to escape."

Dudley said, "I'm prone to whim, sir. I'll either shoot you dead or bid you sayonara."

They cut inland. They hit half-paved roads and breezed through lettuce fields and scrub hills. Bugs bombed the windshield. Dudley tapped his wipers and scraped them to pulp.

They hit low mountain ranges. Low clouds blurred the view. Hector was blitzed. He blathered out his hopes and dreams and extolled jigtown L.A.

He'd get a soft internment berth. He'd deflower Jap virgins and learn to play the bass sax. He'd teach the virgins to play skin flute. He'd rent his boat out to full-blood cholos while he was inside.

Central Avenue. **Está** the most. Ivy Anderson's chicken shack. Minnie Roberts' Casbah—the best spook gash in the West. Club Alabam, Club Zombie. Stan Kenton, mud shark. He's got twenty-eight Congo cuties on the string.

Jam sessions. Back-to-Africa mosques. Political clubhouses. Zoot-suit pachucos, zorched on Sinarquismo. These two rogue cops and their **craaaaaazy** crib on

East 46th. Crap games and cooked terpin hydrate. Cole Porter's "Anything Goes."

Maybe he'll learn the bass clarinet. Maybe he'll open a seafood dive—Hector's Hacienda. Bring **la familia.** He'll import that Cuban guy with the two-foot dick. **El Cubano** will poke your **mujer** while you watch and jack off.

Dudley half-heard it. He took rickety bridges across arroyos and climbed more scrub hills. Hector switched gears and jabbered: right there, it's right **there**!

Dudley swung a tight left turn. Dudley braked and saw it:

A mock ski chalet. Two stories/pitched frame/big glassed-in view. Front carport and no cars extant.

Dudley pulled into the carport. Hector smiled at him. So, **Ichiban**? What have we got here?

Dudley winked. Dudley slipped him a border pass and a ten-dollar bill.

Hector took off. He amscrayed, vamoosed, and vanished in five seconds flat.

Dudley stepped from the car. He sniffed the air. He felt raindrops. He pulled his piece and walked up to the door.

It was locked. He stepped back and threw his weight. He slammed hard and shouldered the door in.

He looked right and saw dumped furniture. He looked left and saw a blood-spattered wall.

19

(LOS ANGELES, 4:30 P.M., 1/4/42)

Morgue Powwow. One forensic agenda. ID the Charred-Box Man.

Morgue personnel: Joan, Dr. Nort, Hideo Ashida.

They measured Box Man. Joan stifled a yawn. She'd indulged a late night at Lyman's. She'd hit the sack at 5:00 a.m.

Ashida placed the bones on a gurney. Dr. Nort unrolled his tape. Joan steadied Box Man. Dr. Nort marked the height at seventy-five inches.

Joan said, "He was six-three. If we factor in erosion at the joints and the compression of the spine that comes with age, we can posit that he was as tall as six-four and a half in his youth."

Dr. Nort poked odd bones. "He was tall, and heavyset. Note the pelvic width."

Ashida measured the back-to-front rib cage. He got a fifty-two-inch circumference.

Joan said, "Big man."

Dr. Nort said, "He must have gone two forty-five. His spine's crunched. Note the socket frays. You carry that much weight, you pay a price. I'll go out on a limb. He went DOA in his early forties."

Joan jiggled the foot bones. "Hey there, cutie."

Ashida flushed. He balled his fists and glared.

"We're having a scholars' lark here, Miss Conville. I should add that our late friend in no way constitutes a breaking case, while the lab is currently backlogged with breaking-case evidence, which demands our more immediate attention."

Joan flushed. She balled her fists and glared back.

"We're backlogged with Japanese-property confiscations, Dr. Ashida. I think you might feel a certain ambivalence about that aspect of our work. I deem that understandable, and I can hardly condemn you for dragging your feet and exploiting our late friend's reappearance, so that you might abstain from facilitating your own countrymen's misfortune."

Oooh—hear that pin-drop silence? Now, hear it **streeetch.**

Joan glared at Ashida.

Ashida glared at the floor.

Dr. Nort said, "Children, enough."

Joan lit a cigarette. Dr. Nort, ditto. Ashida looked up. Joan blew smoke in Box Man's face. Dr. Nort laughed.

They all stretched and unclenched. They put out some small talk. Safe topics—the weather, the war, the '42 congressionals. The PD's Fed-probe travails.

Ashida coughed. "We can check CCC worker lists and DB lists in the newspapers. We've got report carbons stored somewhere, and the fire department Arson Squad must have a comprehensive file."

Dr. Nort said, "That's assuming our late friend was a CCC worker."

Joan said, "We can cross-check the death lists to height listings on California drivers' licenses and CCC registration cards. We can cross-check **those** names against missing-persons reports."

Dr. Nort tapped Box Man's skull. He'd extraction-bored the bullet hole last night.

"I dug out the spent. It's flattened and badly decomposed."

Ashida said, "I'll examine it at the lab. I might determine a partial make on the lands and grooves."

Joan said, "We could try for a match to ballistics bulletins from '33. We could run test fires with old custody guns."

Dr. Nort slow-cruised Joan. She knew the drill. The cruise ran head to toe. It was half-leer comprehensive.

"How did you get this job anyway?"

Joan laughed. "I was drunk New Year's Eve. I hit a car and killed four Mexicans. Bill Parker goes for me, and I'm sure you can fill in the rest."

Dr. Nort went **oooh-la-la.** Ashida balled his fists and **glaaaared.**

Oooh-la-la? Well, not quite.

Joan walked to Lyman's. She was cash-flush. She'd hit an Alien Squad crap game and won forty scoots.

The game ran most Sunday nights. Wendell Rice and George Kapek draped the squadroom floor and steered the show. Bluesuits and Bureau men rolled.

Lee Blanchard and Elmer Jackson rolled hot. Joan

put five on the pass line and let it ride. She cashed out right on cue. Forty clams—Man-O-Manischewitz!

The boys called her "Red." **That's** a new one. Elmer slipped her a mash note. She ruffled his hair and laid one on him. Rice and Kapek wolf-howled. Catbox Cal Lunceford roared.

Joan cut south on Hill. She counted back to New Year's Eve and ran highlights. Her Navy life then, her PD life now. The show ran four days, door-to-door.

She liked the PD. She liked Mike Lyman's Grill. She perched there and eavesdropped most nights. She rebuffed passes and logged scuttlebutt. She learned the personnel.

There's Two-Gun Davis. He's tonged up. He speaks Chinese and drills underage slash. There's Lee Blanchard—shacked with PD siren Kay Lake.

Big Lee did not drill Kay. His abstinence stemmed from old grief. La Kay scorched for Bill Parker. Whiskey Bill scorched back. He refused to pounce. His abstinence stemmed from his dead-dog marriage and prim Catholic guilt.

Rumors. Barroom scuttlebutt. The skinny, the dish, the drift.

Lyman's back room. The PD's haven and redoubt. Here's how it commenced:

A beaner exposed himself to Mike Lyman's niece. Sensitive Mike was distraught. Sergeant Buzz Meeks shot Whipout Juan dead. Grateful Mike bestowed the back room.

She joked with Buzz at Lyman's. They had a running shtick. "I'm too tall for you, sweetie." "Yeah, but I know how to climb."

Joan hit 8th Street and breezed into Lyman's. She clocked tableside traffic and breezed to the back room.

There's Oooh-La-La Bill. He's Two-Fisted Bill now. He's wolfing a highball and a club sandwich. His uniform's a mess.

Joan said, "Don't spoil your dinner."

"That can't be an invitation."

"I'm rich tonight. You should take advantage."

Parker tossed his sandwich and brushed off stray crumbs. The wastebasket thunked.

"You've got me thinking there's a catch."

" 'Catch'? **Me?** As catches go, you're the master."

"Well . . ."

"Come on. I owe you dinner, **at least.**"

Parker blushed. It was almost endearing. Joan almost swooned.

They ate at the Biltmore. It was swank meets plush de-luxe. Joan had roast sirloin. Parker had apricot duck. Their table overlooked Pershing Square.

Soapbox pundits declaimed. Partisan crowds egged them on. Fistfights ensued. White winos shrieked at colored winos and vice versa.

A bar waiter brought cognacs. Parker lit their cigarettes. Joan said, "Tell me what you're thinking."

Parker warmed his snifter. "That I should be fighting this war."

"I've heard the stories. Chief Horrall won't let you enlist, despite your stated intention to steal his job and enact reforms that might well land him in jail, if the Fed probe fails to do so first."

Parker smiled. "You're a quick study."

"I am, yes."

"What else have you heard?"

"Tales of your feud with Dudley Smith. Intimations that then-Sergeant Smith clashed with you on the Watanabe case, and perhaps rigged a convenient solution, abetted by Dr. Hideo Ashida."

Parker sipped cognac. "Policemen run their goddamn mouths, with no sense of consequence."

Joan crushed her cigarette. "I clashed with Dr. Ashida today."

"He's uncomfortable with women. I've observed it with . . ."

"With **Kay Lake**? The PD's favorite round heels and all-around provocatress?"

Parker slugged cognac. "Can it, will you? I realize that you've had a heady few days, but you're being quite indiscreet."

Joan scanned the dining room. It was dinner-rush packed. She read faces. She sensed outrage and furious intent.

"It's America's moment, isn't it?"

Parker said, "Yes, it is."

"We're going to win, aren't we?"

Parker said, "Yes, we are."

"We're going to lay out the Japs and the Nazis, and woe be to the Russians if they try to crowd us then."

Parker said, "Yes, you're right."

Joan got goose bumps. She felt all torn up. A cloudburst hit. Rain banged the picture window right beside her.

"This war is the shit, isn't it? Doesn't it make you want to get lost, make love, and go crazy?"

Parker said, "Miss Conville, you go from zero to sixty faster than any—"

Joan grabbed his face and kissed him. Water glasses capsized. Parker kissed her back. He leaned in and pinned her arms to the table.

He trembled. She felt it. It went all the way through her.

20

(LOS ANGELES, 10:15 A.M., 1/5/42)

The rain let up. The sky gleamed. The Central Station roof supplied views.

Ashida took advantage. He brought binoculars and trained them due east. He caught a roust at 1st and San Pedro.

He zoomed his lens and played Man Camera. The roust's Alien Squad. There's Wendell Rice and George Kapek. Catbox Cal Lunceford's running backup. They've got four Japanese men, shackle-chained.

Rice waved a red-sun flag. Ashida supplied a thought balloon. "Say! This would make a swell crap-game blanket!"

Ashida swiveled south and scanned upward. Sun framed the Biltmore Hotel. He caught his mother's bedroom window. He saw Mariko looking out.

Their elegant suite. Dudley Smith bestows gifts. His pending Army commission. Lieutenant Hideo Ashida.

Shakespeare, revised. **I owe this bad man more tears than you shall see me pay.**

Joan Conville was a briefly tenured Navy lieutenant. Bill Parker bestows gifts. He entraps comely women. The silly girl works with **him** now.

Parker bestows gifts and abrogates justice. **Do you see the children in your dreams, sir? The reckless girl killed them. I see them every night.**

Ashida turned northeast. He saw a foot procession. It was all male and mostly Chinese.

Tong thugs. Jap-haters astroll. They waved casket pix of Eddie Leng. The bigwigs marched up front. Uncle Ace Kwan, Two-Gun Davis, Dr. Lin Chung.

Ashida dialed a close-up. He caught Chung gesticulating. He knew Chung, secondhand. He's the butcher plastic surgeon. He's the mad eugenicist. He's the bagman for last month's sub approach.

This new approach feels somewhat different. It's like the first approach, refined and revised. The first approach was oddball inclusive. The new approach could be much more or much less of that.

Right is Left and Left is Right. Dr. Chung is tight with a leftist eugenicist named Saul Lesnick. Dr. Lesnick is a psychiatrist and FBI informant. He is Claire De Haven's analyst. Kay Lake knows Dr. Lesnick. He figured in Bill Parker's anti-Red crusade.

Inclusion. Confluence. Wartime folly. The Fifth Column is everyone.

Ashida walked back down to the lab. Two chemists logged evidence. Ray Pinker and Joan Conville were out.

He caught something.

His photo device. He'd been oiling the parts. It was placed just so on his desk. He left the lab for twenty minutes. The device was set off-kilter now.

Mr. Pinker. **He** handled it. The device confounded and thrilled him. Japanese inventors can't secure patents. Mr. Pinker wants to front the device. He wants half the money. This war spawns opportunities. Fair-minded men turn unfair.

A ruckus bubbled up, streetside. Ashida heard shouts and shrieks. He checked the window. Two cops wrestled Fujio Shudo into a van.

The Werewolf wore a straitjacket and jail khakis. A sanity hearing beckons. His gas-chamber trek begins. He's a ready-made Jap. He's been handpicked for prosecution. Dudley Smith, inquisitor. Hideo Ashida, forged-document man.

The chemists walked out. Ashida locked himself in. Gossip spritzed through a wall vent. The lab shared vents with the Alien Squad. Lee Blanchard and Cal Lunceford groused. **The fucking phone-tap probe. What a crock of shit.**

Ashida walked to his desk. Joan Conville had compiled reports. She supplied study stacks. They were squared off and pencil-marked.

Missing-persons bulletins. A tight geographic spread. Southern California, all police agencies. L.A. County, Orange County, San Diego County. Ventura and Santa Barbara counties. San Bernardino, Riverside.

A tight date spread. Late summer '33 to early winter '34. Tall men only. Heavyset men only. A tight age spread. Mid-thirties to mid-forties.

Plus CCC survivor lists. Grist for their thesis. Box Man died concurrent with the Griffith Park fire.

Miss Conville oversupplied paper. He didn't need the dead-and-identified lists. He read through them anyway. He saw a morgue pic. It displayed Wayne Frank Jackson's charred corpse.

Ashida scanned lists. He looked for matched names and compatible descriptions. He sifted reports. He eyeball-clicked. He got zero, zero, zero, and **this:**

A CCC living survivor. Karl Frederick Tullock/ 6'4"/235. Born 6/14/93. Forty in October '33. A Santa Barbara County missing person.

An ex-cop. On the S.B. County Sheriff's Department. Wife reports Tullock missing—1/12/34.

It fits circumstantially. It's a hot one. It's a possible match.

Zealous Miss Conville. She oversupplies paper and supplies a possible match. And—she's stuffed a box under his desk.

Ashida went through it. He saw off-the-corpse clothing patches. He studied them. He noted quicklime saturation and seed husks.

He saw a white cotton swatch. He identified collar points. The swatch tweaked him. It was hand-stitched Egyptian cotton. He placed the swatch under his fluoroscope and brought up a blurred laundry mark.

He got goose bumps. Box Man's a CCC wage slave. Wage slaves don't wear high-quality shirts. They don't send them out to be laundered.

Ashida went through the box. He sifted cloth fragments. He pulled pieces. He grabbed a folded-over trouser cuff. It felt weighted down.

He dug into the fold. He pulled this out:

A small piece of gold. One-inch by one-inch. Small but hefty. Irregular-shaped.

It felt substantial. It felt pure-gold dense. It was mid-range nugget-sized.

It was bored through. A metal chain and key were attached. The key was stamped "648." It looked like a locker stamp.

Ashida got goose bumps and flushed hot and cold.

He rigged a microscope. He hook-clamped the gold chunk and dialed his lens close. He saw faint markings. "U.S." and "023" stood out.

Mint marks. They had to be that. He was locked-in, dialed-in sure.

21

(LOS ANGELES, 11:45 A.M., 1/5/42)

Oooga-booga. Vile voodoo ascends. Eddie Leng goes out in style.

Pit dogs pulled Eddie's casket. They wore tong kerchiefs and spiked breastplates. The casket was tiger-striped and rolled on tricycle wheels.

Spectators lined North Broadway. Car traffic was verboten. Boocoo Chinks trailed the casket. They waved REMEMBER PEARL HARBOR! and KILL THE JAPS! signs.

Elmer stood at Alpine and Broadway. Street vendors hawked ptomaine tacos and egg foo young. Elmer reeled. It was all of it—plus **this** shit:

Deep-fried Eddie Leng. These suffocation dreams. It's really Wayne Frank and him in that charred box.

All **that** shit. Plus his fool stunt with Ace Kwan.

Said stunt got him cogitating. Ace blathered that

night. He said Lin Chung and Don Matsura crossed hate lines and hobknobbed. They sold pharmacy dope. Matsura was tonged up. He peddled terp to winos and dope fiends. He knew Tommy Glennon. Lin Chung knew Tommy, likewise.

Cut to the Matsura roust. It's him, Rice, and Kapek. There's the terp still in Matsura's dump. There's the Leng's Kowloon menu.

It got him cogitating. So, he did **this:**

He read Chinktown intel files at the Bureau. Thus, he learned **this:**

Lin Chung peddled opiate compounds. He supplied "O" dens in the San Gabriel Valley. He pushed pharmacy hop to herb quacks.

And, he saw **this:**

Fed routing stamps on Chung's file. That was provocative. That meant **this:**

The Feds had Chung pegged as hinky and suspect. Thus, he did **this:**

He staked out Chung's house. He saw Ed Satterlee staked likewise. He tailed Ed the Fed to the phone-probe stake spot by the **Herald.** The hot-box phone outside: listed in Tommy G.'s address book.

The hot-box was a bookie-call phone. Sid Hudgens purportedly used it. Sid scribed at the **Herald.** It all felt popcorn-fart tight.

Elmer watched the parade. He pondered a ptomaine-taco lunch. The casket rolled out of sight.

He felt something behind him. Some lurking beast. His fellow spectators veered, lurched, and scrammed.

Something/someone grabbed him. He got all smothered up. It was an octopus snatch. Six arms clamped him tight.

He squirmed and orbed the octopus. Tentacles became arms. It was Jim Davis and two Hop Sing shits. Our ex–police chief and two heathen slants.

They snatched him and scissor-walked him. Sidewalk geeks gawked. Yellow folks went **White men claaaaazy!** They gassed on the show. Jim Davis tossed them Chink bon mots.

They scissor-walked down Broadway. They hit Kwan's and scissored through the dining room. **Shit**—it's packed.

White stiffs quaffed mai tais and slurped pork fried rice. **Shit**—there's Fletch Bowron, there's Wallace Jamie, there's fucked-up Father Coughlin.

They scissor-walked downstairs. They hit the basement. They pushed through the "O" den and Chinks reposed on Cloud 9. They hit a small office. **Bam!**—the tong shits depart.

Davis unwrapped him and plopped him down in a chair. The fat cocksucker was red-faced and all sweated up.

Elmer dredged savoir faire. "You don't look too good, Chief. You look like a man in need of medical care."

Davis caught his breath. "You're still a pup to me. You're still this lance corporal I befriended."

Elmer said, "That was '35, and this here's '42. And

I'm recalling that I shot this loopy beaner trying to kill you."

The office was smother-cramped. Desk, chairs, **claaaazy** wall art. Velour-flocked pictures. Fire-spitting dragons roasting Jap dragoons.

Elmer stood up. He smoothed out his coat and tie and redredged savoir faire. Davis said, "You're still a pup. And pups require a rap on the snout when they misbehave."

"It's starting to dawn on me, Chief."

"Okay, then you listen close. Jack Horrall's pissed because the Dudster's pissed, because you muscled Ace. You've got to desist on whatever it is that's goring you and got you acting dumb. That means the Leng snuff, Tommy Glennon, and Donald Matsura—who just happened to hang himself in his cell last night. **¿Tú comprende, muchacho?** The Chinks police the Chinks, and that's straight from Jack H. Ace makes Matsura for the Leng job, and that's the way it stands. Tommy G.'s long gone, and nobody cares."

Uncle Ace walked in. He wore that steam-pops-out-the-ears look. He resembled the aggrieved Donald Duck.

Elmer said, "Hey, pappy."

Davis said, "Jack Horrall wants you to apologize."

Elmer said, "I apologize, Ace."

Uncle Ace shrieked curses. Elmer feigned deep remorse. Ace whipped out his dick and pissed on his shoes.

Stakeout.

11th and Broadway. Upside the **Herald** building. Upside that hot-box phone.

Elmer sprawled in his prowl sled. He felt revivified. He went by the Biltmore first. He got a double-fine shoe shine and quaffed two Rob Roys. He lunched on salted peanuts and bought a one-dollar cigar.

Stakeout.

Elmer lit the cigar and eyeballed due south. Ed Satterlee sat in a Fed sled and eyeballed the hot-box. Elmer scratched his balls and kicked the seat back.

He eyeball-clicked. Click to the phone booth. Click to the Fed sled. Click to the **Herald**'s front door.

Stiffs fed the phone nickels. Nobody aroused suspicion. They made brief phone calls and scrammed.

Elmer savored the cigar. It was El Supremo Cuban. He watched the booth, the Fed car, the door.

He stuck at it two hours. Sid Hudgens walked out at 3:32.

He strolled to the hot-box. He waved to Ed Satterlee. He consulted a racing form and fed the coin slot. A four-minute confab ensued.

Sid hung up and waltzed. Elmer vacated his sled and hoofed back around to the alley. He popped a storm door and hit the lobby. He caught Sid at the elevator. They indulged some unfunny shtick.

Sid went **I surrender.** Elmer went **Kid, you're a sketch.** Sid went **¿Qué pasa?** Elmer flashed his hip flask and fed him two twenties. Sid walked to a mop closet and went **After you.**

Elmer stepped in. Sid joined him. The fit was tight. Sid cracked the door for air.

"Elmer the J. It's been too long, **bubi.**"

Elmer passed the flask. "Let's start with Eddie Leng. I've been reading your columns."

Sid yodeled Old Crow. "All right, and here's what's **un**fit to print. Mike Breuning braced me, and said the Dudster would appreciate it if I killed the Leng series, which I summarily did."

Elmer took a pop. "Don't stop there."

"Dud's up to something, which don't surprise me, and shouldn't surprise you—but I don't know what it is."

Elmer went **Give—don't dick-tease me here.**

Sid said, "About a week back, Mike and Dick Carlisle told me that Dud wanted his ex-snitch Tommy Glennon clipped, allegedly because he's a rape-o, which don't sit right with Dud and Jack Horrall. You were supposed to be part of that—but you, Mike, and Dick blew that stakeout New Year's Eve. So, Eddie Leng gets clipped that same night, and Eddie was tight with Tommy. Conventional wisdom would have it that Tommy clipped Eddie for some **farkakte** reason, after he escaped **your** dubious clutches—but I heard that Eddie was low-rent Fifth Column, and tangled up with some unholy mélange of right-wing Chinks and Japs. I also heard that Ace the K. clipped this Jap fucker Donald Matsura, who allegedly killed himself at Lincoln Heights. And that's as far as I can think it through."

Elmer sucked on the flask. "Leng was a Jap-hater. It feels like a race job to me."

Sid said, "Nix. I heard that Leng and Matsura were tight, and that Matsura manufactured terp, and Leng and Four Families peddled it to the Chinks, along with drugstore hop."

"A doctor named Lin Chung. Ring any bells?"

Sid yocked. "Yeah. He's a plastic surgeon, and he peddles nose jobs to all the Jew girls trying to pass for **goyishe.** Lin, the snout doctor. Strictly cut-rate."

Elmer switched gears. "Leng had a tattoo on his right hand. A little 'SQ' with snakes curled around it. Tommy G. had stencils for that selfsame tattoo in his hotel room."

Sid fingered his Jew star. "The 'SQ' means Sinarquista. It's some kind of batshit Catholic, pro-Nazi movement in Mexico. Like Father Coughlin, only worse. I'm a hebe, so I don't feature that shit."

"I saw you wave to Ed Satterlee. What's with that?"

"Open secret, **bubi.** Fey Edgar Hoover concocted this phone-tap schmear before the Japs tapped Pearl and put our great country in a tizzy, so now he's obliged to see it through, but he don't wet his pink lace undies for it. Some good-sized fish will get indicted, but only a few minnows will burn. This Wallace Jamie kid's tight with some hotshot Republicans who want to run him for office, and his dad's close pals with

Fletch Bowron. The inside pitch is that Fletch, Jack Horrall, the Jamie putz, Ray Pinker, and a few DAs will get indicted and acquitted. Jamie will be revealed to be a secret Fed informer. He'll turn State's on some Hollywood Reds that Fey Edgar wants to fuck with, and goose his own career."

Elmer went **Oh, my cabeza.** Sid yock-yocked.

"Why would Tommy Glennon have this hotbox number?"

"Why **wouldn't** he? Everybody's got this number. It's a former bookie-drop call-in phone that used to take slugs, and for all I know, it still does."

Elmer cogitated. "Why would Tommy G. have the numbers of fourteen Baja pay phones in his address book?"

Sid shrugged. "Why wouldn't he? He's a perv. Baja's the Perv Capital of North America. Tommy's pals with the Dudster's snitch, Huey Cressmeyer, who ranks with Leopold and Loeb in the Perv Hall of Fame. Don't be naïve, **bubelah.** Tommy pokes boys in the keester and rapes women. That spells P, E, R, V in my book."

Elmer recogitated. "Can pay phones be tapped?"

"Supposedly, yes—at least the incoming calls. Some Mexican cop supposedly devised a plan."

The closet shot heat waves. Warm, hot, too hot. Elmer wiped his forehead.

"There's Fed routing stamps on Lin Chung's DB file. Recent, with your boy Satterlee as the agent requesting."

"Well, it don't sound phone probe, so maybe the snout doctor runs Fifth Column."

Elmer cracked the door wide. Cool air vitalized him. Lobby noise whooshed in.

"I don't get where all this is going."

"What's not to get? God's telling you not to fuck with Dudley Smith."

22

(BAJA, 4:15 P.M., 1/5/42)

Chez Hanamaka. It's a magnetizing force. It mandates a second visit.

Drudge work ate up yesterday. Paper piles and phone calls deluged him. The bloodstained wall summoned him today.

Dudley studied the wall. He quadrant-scanned it. He made two eyeball circuits. Something felt wrong.

He saw three bullet holes. He pegged the tight spread and upper-right-side wall placement. He pulled his pocketknife and dug out the spents.

He studied them. He saw dried blood and dark-hair fragments on all three. The bullets were embedded per a left-to-right trajectory.

But:

The **full** wall was bloodstained. That was wrong. Only the upper-right quadrant should be spattered.

Late sun hit the living room. Picture windows threw glare. It enhanced magnification. That wall gleamed—bright, bright, bright.

Dudley brainstormed. Dudley got it. It had to be **this:**

There's Mr. X. It's probably Kyoho Hanamaka. He needs to paint a picture. It's an urgent need. This wall provides a canvas and picture frame.

Mr. X gulps. The job entails self-mutilation. It puts him in a squeamish state. He must create a slaughter scene.

Mr. X holds his left arm up and out. He's angled toward the right side of the wall. He holds the gun in his right hand. He employs an upward-right trajectory. He aims very closely and fires three flesh-grazing shots.

Thus:

The dark hair on the spents.

Thus:

The upper-right-wall slug placement.

But:

The entire wall was bloodstained. That surely resulted from **this:**

Mr. X squeezed blood from his superficial flesh wounds and flung it randomly. Thus, the wide spatters. Why did he do this? Here's a theory:

Mr. X fakes his own death. He's a Jap Navy man prone to Fifth Column mischief. He wants to vanish. His blood type is police-filed. He knows the **estúpido** Staties will peruse this wall and scrape samples. They will compare them to their file. They will thus conclude:

Hanamaka was killed here. His body was removed and most likely dumped in the sea.

No suspects present themselves. Case closed, finito.

Where's Kyoho Hanamaka? Hector Obregon-Hodaka saw him here. That was December 18. It's now January 5. The Staties have not been here. There's no evidence tags or signs of a toss.

Think. Expand your theory. Layer in Hepcat Hector. He plays in here.

This hilltop home connotes hideaway. Hanamaka probably lives in Ensenada. His resident-alien file might list the address. The Staties would look for Hanamaka there first.

He's scared. He's afraid he'll be interned soon. His friendship with Governor Lazaro-Schmidt will be rudely breached. He needs to vanish. He has Fifth Column duties. He needs this hideaway to be discovered inadvertently.

Enter Hector Obregon-Hodaka.

He's a cat's paw. Hanamaka brought him up here. He knew that Hector would be interned. Hector would suck up to his Statie captors and reveal that this place exists.

Hector was a patsy. Hanamaka rigged the faked-death scene all by himself. Hector got lucky. Captain D. L. Smith set him free.

It's virgin turf. No tags, no tape seals. It's a fresh toss.

Dudley checked the kitchen. He found a toilet plunger and plunged the two commodes. He brought up gauze strips and adhesive-bandage snips. The gauze showed water-bleached bloodstains. It confirmed his wall-tableau theory.

He emptied cupboards. He opened canned food-stuffs and dumped the contents. He dumped drawers and examined innocuous glut. He unscrewed sink drains and plunged standing water. He ripped apart stuffed furniture. He unscrewed light fixtures. The net yield was zilch.

The walls now.

He brought a stethoscope. He attached the earpieces and began downstairs. He walked room-to-room. He tapped the walls and listened. He got all solid thunks. He worked downstairs to upstairs and wall-tapped. He got all solid thunks.

He walked back downstairs. He retapped the walls, higher up. He turned down a side hallway and tapped the right-side wall. He got solid, solid, solid, solid, and—

Hollow thunks. Pitch-perfect—tap, tap.

He brought a pry bar. He ran to the living room and grabbed it. He ran back to the hallway and swung.

The wall was wood-reinforced plaster. Two hits crumbled it. The boards snapped. Plaster grit swirled. Twelve hits ripped a floor-to-ceiling hole.

A hidey-hole. Rendered inaccessible. There was no latch entry, no wall-panel hinges and slides.

The hole ran twelve by twelve. It was carpeted. There were light fixtures, clothes racks, and shelves.

Dudley brushed off grit and sawdust. He stepped in and tapped a light switch. Well, now. What's this?

Mahogany walls. Well buffed and gleaming. A flag spray at the rear. Pole-mounted banners, elegantly fringed and draped.

Dudley unfurled them. They were smooth silk. They proclaimed stark alliance and devilish intent.

A swastika flag, a rising-sun flag, a hammer-and-sickle banner. Flags for Franco's Falange. Ku Klux Klan flags. Redshirt Battalion flags. Flags ablaze with "SQ"s and coiled snakes.

Lovely silk twill. Bright yellow fringe. Lurid emblems, ablaze.

Dudley smelled mothballs. They hung from gauze sachets. They protected haute-**KKK**outure threads.

Nazi uniforms. Winter- and summer-weight wool. Gray Wehrmacht tunics and breeches. Black SS dress kit.

Collar and shoulder insignia. All field-grade rank. Creased trousers and puffed jodhpurs. Jackboots on foot racks. Peaked hats on a shelf.

Dudley time-machined. Brentwood, north of Sunset. It's winter '39 again.

That costume party. The Jewish Maestro's house, sublet. It's done up Bauhaus-moderne. He's an SS Sturmbannführer. The party replicates a Nazi purge. The party swirls out of sync.

More uniforms. Jap Army and Navy issue. Cut small. Hanamaka is small. The yellow peril boys run tiny and shrill.

Soviet uniforms. Coarse olive wool. Drab beside Herr Hitler's couture.

The People's Army. Drab comrades. Godless Bolsheviks hooked on dead-Jew Marx and stiff potato brew.

Dudley plucked a Nazi hat and tried it on. It was too small for him. He saw a leather-bound diary, stuffed behind the foot rack. He grabbed it and leafed through.

Kyoho Hanamaka wrote in English. He introduced his historical memory book and stated that he saw it all firsthand. "Please be credulous. I witnessed the following events."

He ignored chronology. He hopped locale sans explanation. He did not justify his presence at moments of pitiless terror. He remained mutely complicit then and broke his silence on these pages.

He witnesses the Rape of Nanking. Jap soldiers make Chinese fathers fuck their own daughters. Those soldiers behead one thousand Chinamen a day. Jap flyers toss Chinese children from airplanes at five thousand feet.

Witness Hanamaka heads northwest. He visits Hermann Goering. The **Reichsführer** drinks the morphine-laced blood of Aryan virgins.

El Jefe Franco needs help. He calls **El Supremo Jefe** Hitler and requests air support. Witness Hanamaka cozies up to the Condor Legion. He joins the bombing runs over Guernica. He describes the firestorm and Basque civilians burned alive.

Witness Hanamaka heads east. He drinks vodka with Joe Stalin and tours Red Square. Uncle Joe predicts the Nazi pact back in '36. He murders the army brass and Party apparatchiks he deems potential refuseniks.

He kills 100,000 men. Witness Hanamaka views mass murder. NKVD death squads burst into homes and blast perceived traitors. Wives and children scream. The death squads blast them point-blank.

Hanamaka views Stalin's booze-blitzed rages. Uncle Joe issues five hundred death decrees a day. Hanamaka views torture sessions at the Lubyanka prison. He's there for the Moscow show trials. They couch all loose talk as sedition.

Stalin orders up slaughter. He's the psychopathic god to rival Auden's Hitler. Show-trial defendants stand mute. They are condemned and shot in their cells. Their last words are often "What for?"

Witness Hanamaka hops back to Deutschland. It's now summer '34. It's the Night of the Long Knives.

Hitler's purges are small scale beside Stalin's. They are intimately conceived and plotted on the q.t. Brownshirt boss Ernst Röhm is a boy-buggering bully. He's holed up in a spa hotel outside Munich. He's there for an all-boy bacchanal. Witness Hanamaka and some SS lads fly down.

They tear through the hotel. It's a rude disruption. It's sodomy and **soixante-neuf interruptus.** There's death shots to the head. There's slashed genitalia.

Dudley stopped there. Winter '39 tore through him. The party reprised the Night of the Long Knives. Tommy Glennon witnessed **Sturmbannführer** Smith's nadir.

Maestro Klemperer's house. The Maestro's recording of **Tristan und Isolde.** The prelude soars. The costumed guests caper.

Dudley fondled Nazi uniforms. He touched silver thunderbolts and death's-heads. He kissed stiff black wool. He loved beautiful clothing. Claire joshed him about it.

He'd sweated through his clothes. He felt dizzy. He reached behind the foot rack and pulled out an oak box.

It was two feet long and weighty. It looked ceremonial. A hinged lid lifted up.

Dudley opened the box. A bayonet had been placed on black velvet. Swastikas were carved on the handle. The bayonet glowed.

Dudley picked it up and cradled it. He gauged the weight as eight pounds. The bayonet was pure gold.

23

(SANTA BARBARA, 12:30 P.M., 1/6/42)

Dissemble now. You're here ex officio. It's just a scholar's lark.

The probable widow played slow. Joan played off of that. Dr. Ashida authored the text. Joan improvised.

I'm with the L.A. Police. This is strictly routine. Your missing-persons report. I'm compiling a lab-file update.

Ellen Marie Tullock. Fifty-five and too thin. The wife of Karl Frederick. He's on the CCC survivor list. He's the probable Box Man.

"I don't quite understand what you do, young lady."

"I'm a biologist. I work in the crime lab, and we're reviewing our missing-persons files. We're up to January 1934, the month you submitted the query on your husband."

Mrs. Tullock frowned. "Are you a policewoman? I don't understand why they didn't send a man."

Joan smiled. "My immediate superior is Japanese. Given the times, he thought you'd rather speak with me."

Mrs. Tullock blinked. Joan plainly vexed her. The front parlor broiled. Heating vents audibly hissed.

The house induced claustrophobia. It ran hot **and** overfurnished. Doilies and tchotchkes abundant. Too many too-stiff chairs.

"Did you know that your husband was present at the Griffith Park fire of 1933? Many men died, but he survived."

Mrs. Tullock tugged at her skirt. "No, I didn't know that. What month was this fire?"

Joan said, "October."

"Well, Karl took off in August of '33, and I've never heard from him since."

"You waited five months to report him missing. Was there a reason for that?"

"Well, Karl just took off, and it took a while for me to start to miss him."

"Do you know why he took off?"

Mrs. Tullock smirked. "He took off to pursue buried treasure, which was the onliest thing he ever did when the Sheriff's Department canned him."

Joan said, "Could you explain that?"

"Well, Karl was a treasure seeker. If you don't know the type already, you should take heed. Brazilian diamonds and pearls in Jamaica. That gold robbery off that train, back in '31. Karl worked that one for a little bit, which is why it had such legs for him."

A memory popped. Joan recalled bar chat. Lee Blanchard talks to Wendell Rice. They discuss Elmer Jackson's dead brother.

He was torched in Griffith Park. He was this nutty rumdum. He was torqued by that big mint-train heist.

"Young lady, are you all right?"

Joan smiled. "Mrs. Tullock, are you saying that

your husband was a wanderer? And that he had an untoward interest in that mint-train robbery?"

Mrs. Tullock tugged at her skirt. She wore tennis shoes with threadbare tweeds.

"I'm saying he read treasure magazines written for bums with big dreams, and he believed everything he ever read. The amazing thing is that he only got in trouble the one time—but it up and cost him his job."

"Would you explain, please?"

"That gold robbery. Karl worked on the Santa Barbara end, and he got this fool notion that this dimwit colored boy was the thief. He did some beating on that boy, but some colored preacher with police friends in L.A. went to bat for the boy and got him released, and Karl got the ax for the whomping he did."

Joan sifted it. "Did Karl ever mention any friends he might have had with the CCC in Los Angeles?"

Mrs. Tullock sneered. "Karl didn't have friends. He had treasure magazines."

Hot potato. The old girl tossed it. Catch it—don't drop it.

Joan left the Tullock house and reparked down the street. Some sidewalk boys showed off for her. They chugged sneaky pete. They strutted and posed.

A cloudburst drove them indoors. Joan sat it out. She chain-smoked and fumed up the car.

She reprised the conversation. It ran circuitous. She sat in Lyman's, two nights back. Lee Blanchard and Wendell Rice shot the shit.

Kay's in with these Jew exiles. Longhair-music types. Otto Klemperer. She dotes on him.

Elmer the J. His dipshit brother died in the Griffith Park fire. This alky drifter. Always the big dreams. This big hard-on for that gold-train heist.

We have proximity. We have Karl Tullock and Wayne Frank Jackson. We have two men and one fire. One dead man has been ID'd. One dead man has been unearthed. We have a probable identification.

One ex-cop, one drifter, one idiot dream. Two violent deaths in concurrence. The ex-cop worked the gold heist. That event preceded and might have precipitated catastrophic arson.

And she kissed Bill Parker. And Bill Parker kissed her back.

I blew my shot at the war. Who cares? My new life's aswirl.

24

(LOS ANGELES, 9:30 A.M., 1/7/42)

A college kid approached. He glared and flashed his fangs. His intent beamed.

He closed in. He leaned down. He said, "Filthy Jap."

The library was dead still. The kid employed stealth. He made like a Jap Zero. No one else heard.

The kid strolled off. Ashida scanned his page book. He'd ordered up the **L.A. Times.** A clerk brought him bound photostats.

From May 19–23, 1931. From October 4–12, 1933.

Joan Conville called him last night. She described her talk with Ellen Tullock. They discussed death-by-fire and death-by-knife-and-gun proximity. Was it design or coincidence?

He told her not to talk to Elmer Jackson. Elmer might go off half-cocked. He described his lab findings. He omitted just **this:**

I found a gold nugget in that box you left me.

He found it. **He's** hoarding the lead. **He's** studied under Dudley Smith. **He's** learned to lie. **He's** a Jap. **He's** shifty and stealthy.

He called Thad Brown last night. Thad was brusque. The dislodged-body job's a dog. Chief Horrall wants it reburied. It puts a stink on the PD.

He withheld from Thad. He omitted the gold nugget and two-dead speculation. Karl Tullock and Wayne Frank Jackson died at the same time and place. Both were gold heist–fixated. He knew the full Wayne Frank story. Joan had picked up bar scuttlebutt.

The library was dead still. College kids studied and evil-eyed the Jap. Winos dozed in rock-hard chairs.

Ashida skimmed news stories. He read the heist accounts first. The stat sheets printed out white on black. The coverage ran threadbare.

The Frisco-to-L.A. mint train. Eight Quentin cons on board. There's a track-switch snafu. Four masked men swarm the train. They overpower the crew. The cons escape en masse. The escape precedes the robbery. Seven men are hunted down and shot and killed that day. The unwritten law holds sway. Escape mandates death.

One man eludes the dragnet. He's still at large. Fritz Wilhelm Eckelkamp. DOB 10/12/98.

He's German-born. He's a Great War stalwart. He wins the Iron Cross. He goes bad in '20s Berlin. He toes the Sparticist line and skirmishes with Brownshirt thugs. He robs banks and jewelry stores. He stows away on a steamship and comes here. It's '27 now. He migrates to California and settles in Oakland. He reverts to armed robbery.

Liquor-store jobs. There's always cash on hand. It's high risk for low yield. Fritz falls behind multiple counts. He gets twenty-five to life at Big Q.

Fritz becomes a virtuoso jailhouse lawyer. He learns to write Federal writs. He secures a retrial. The Federal court's in L.A.

Fritz Wilhelm Eckelkamp. Missing since 5/18/31. Karl Frederick Tullock. Reported missing 1/12/34.

Ashida chalked brain notes. He reviewed his stat sheets and compiled a checklist.

Secure Eckelkamp's Oakland police file. Secure his Quentin file. Secure Tullock's Santa Barbara Sheriff's personnel file.

The mint train resumes its southbound journey. There's a second track snafu. The heist occurs then. The theft is discovered at the Santa Barbara stop. Leander Frechette is grabbed for it. Karl Tullock "beats on him." A Negro preacher intercedes and greases Frechette's release. The preacher has "cop friends in L.A."

Frechette drops from sight. Where is he now? Who's the preacher? What cop friends in L.A.?

Ashida switched page books. He jumped from gold to fire. He logged more sketchy coverage.

It's late September '33. We're into Indian summer. It's hot in L.A. The heat provokes unrest. There's leftist agitation and a garment workers' strike.

It's now October 3. The blaze occurs. The death toll mounts. It may or may not be arson. A pro forma query goes down. The Young Socialist Alliance proves suspect. The leader's one Meyer Gelb.

YSA sloganeers "prophesied apocalypse." Their

rants ran from mid-September to the blaze. Meyer Gelb urged "a workers' revolt." "One line burned memorably at a Pershing Square stump speech."

Gelb railed. He called out, "This storm, this savaging disaster."

The line drew oohs and aahs. The **Times** got pissy here. "The flowery sentence might have been lifted from a noted British poet of the homosexual ilk."

Ashida flipped pages. The fire was initially tagged "a spontaneous conflagration." The death toll fluctuated daily. CCC workers tagged dead showed up alive. They'd been on booze binges and deserted their wives for a spell.

A well-dressed man was glimpsed in Mineral Canyon. Eyewits described him as "Chinese or Japanese." He vanished as the blaze whooshed. A studio carpenter got popped the same night. He set a blaze in Fern Dell Park. Eyewits nailed his car's license plate.

His name was Ralph D. Barr. He was a known firebug and public jack-off man. He was alibied up for the big blaze. He worked at Paramount all day.

That was it. The PD tapped out. The fire department tapped out. Nobody proved arson or **dis**proved it. Local leftists were grilled and released. News coverage fizzled.

Ashida restacked his books. He stood up and stretched. He chalked more brain notes.

Get more on the YSA. Get more on Meyer Gelb.

Track the gold chunk. What does "648" mean? Does the attached key correspond to a storage locker someplace?

He walked to the drop-off desk. A college boy waltzed by. He said, "Stinking Jap."

Dark clouds blew in. They unzipped and leaked rain. Ashida drove to Griffith Park and trekked the golf course.

He was killing time. He needed privacy at the lab. The day-shift chemists clocked out at 6:00.

Gale winds hit. Cloudbursts followed. Fairways and sand traps flooded. It occurred just like that.

Ashida walked into it. He sketched brain pictures and transposed newspaper maps. He crafted a then-to-now terrain.

He noted incipient mud slides. Hillsides with thin turf planes and exposed roots. He employed Man Camera and assumed killer and victim perspectives.

It's four-burner hot and dry. A Santa Ana wind fans flames. He set the fire/a cohort set the fire/the fire started itself. It's deliberate arson or crime of opportunity. The box stands ready, either way.

He lures the probable Karl Tullock someplace secluded. He shoots him and stabs him and dumps him in the box. He buries the box. He chokes on thick smoke. Approaching flames singe his eyebrows. He runs. He gets away or burns to death.

The converse now.

He's lured. He's stabbed and shot. He's the probable Karl Tullock. He's dead in the box. He did or did not know Wayne Frank Jackson. Rest in peace. The two men die the same day.

Ashida walked back to the parking lot. The wind pushed him along. He saw a phone booth by the snack hut.

He ducked in and went through the Yellow Pages. He tore out all the storage-locker ads.

There was still time to kill. He had two hours to clock-out and assured privacy.

Ashida drove to Central Station. He went down to the cellblocks and watched the Werewolf sleep.

The jailer brought his son's Scout troop down. They goofed on Fujio Shudo. They finger-poked him through the bars and squealed. A boy stared at Ashida. He read the kid's mind. Hey, mister—aren't you a Jap?

He walked up to 3. A crap game whooped and hollered. It was Alien Squad SRO.

The players rolled on rising-sun flags. Wendell Rice and George Kapek wore Wehrmacht helmets and green eyeshades. Lee Blanchard and Cal Lunceford rolled.

Chief Horrall stopped by. He chatted up the boys and dropped off pizza pies and beer. The boys whoop-whooped and cheered.

Call-Me-Jack winked at Ashida. He said, "Chin up, kid."

Rice passed Ashida the dice. He told him to roll once, for grins. Ashida rolled a big six. The boys stomped and cheered.

He rolled again. He came up seven and crapped out. The boys stomped and booed.

6:05 p.m. The lab was off-shift dark. Ashida walked over and locked himself in. Miss Conville had left ballistics bulletins on his desk. He slugged cold coffee and got to it.

He worked the gold first. He got out the nugget and naked-eyed it. The mint marks went naked-eye unseen. The chunk was rough-cut. Buff swirls were present. The chunk felt talismanic. It was pure brag. **Look what I've got, look what I did.**

Ashida boiled an acid-phosphate solution. It would create faint abrasions and scrub the buff swirls.

He dropped the gold in the beaker. The solution fizzed and turned the liquid black. He timed the dunk at three minutes. He turned off the burner and scooped the gold out.

He'd preset his microscope. He put the chunk on a clamp slide and studied it. The swirls had abraded and sloughed off.

He studied the chunk. He moved it around on the slide. He hit four separate angles. A fifth angle gave him **this:**

The letters **L.U.S.**

It was scratched on. It was **diamond**-scratched. The scratcher scratched the letters below-the-surface deep. He bought a rough diamond and carved, assiduously. The abrasive dip raised the letters. It had to be that.

He had the gold chunk/the L.U.S./the key fob marked "648." He had storage-locker listings. He'd pulled two pages' worth.

The pages were half wet and crimped. Ashida smoothed them out on his desk. He started at A and eye-scanned.

A-1 Storage, Albright Storage, All-Nite Storage. He read subheads and caught the gist.

Store your belongings. Safety and privacy assured. Your key unlocks your locker. Front-door key provided. We're open-all-nite. There's no questions asked.

He knew these places. He'd read Burglary and Robbery reports. They were extra-legal stash holes. You had lockers rented short-term, long-term, and lifetime.

You had transient renters. You had come-and-go traffic. You rent 648 in '31. You rent it lifetime. There's no-questions-asked. It's still your locker today.

Ashida scanned listings.

Bring-Your-Key Storage. Capitol Storage. Carthage Storage/open-all-nite. He jumped to page two. He quick-skimmed to the L's. He hit Larry's Lockers, Len's Lockers, Lucky Lon's Locker Vault. Wait, now—

Lock-Ur-Self Storage. 829 North Glendale Boulevard. "U Store, U Karry the Key."

Lock-Ur-Self. L.U.S. Open-all-nite. Locker 648.

Ashida burned hot and cold. Sweat ran into his eyes. He flexed his hands and steadied them. He grabbed a lab towel and wiped his face.

It's 8:06 p.m. It's still too early. Folks are still out and about. Lock-Ur-Self might be packed.

The bullet now.

It was skull-smash/up-close flattened. He naked-eyed six impact crimps. He attached bullet forceps to both ends and pulled.

The clamps held. He got a half stretch. Four crimps flattened out. He naked-eyed very faint lands and grooves.

The microscope now.

He studied the bullet. He eyeball-measured millimeters between the stretched crimps. He slide-clamped the bullet and dialed his lens deep.

Magnification meets imagination. It's forensically haphazard. Yes—but sound guesswork sometimes results.

He imagined his way to full lands and grooves. He memorized the fragmented patterns. He imposed a crimp-point differential.

The bulletins now.

Ignore the crime summaries. Go straight to the microscope pix. Juxtapose your imagination and extrapolate.

Miss Conville had arranged the stack chronologically. Ashida went to January '32 and quick-skimmed.

He got through '32. No full land-and-groove reads
tweaked him. He skimmed into '33. Winter, spring,
summer—

Wait—

The bulletin was dated 8/12/33. It summarized four
liquor-store heists. **"UNSOLVED"** was stamped on
four bulletins. **"STILL UNSOLVED"** was stamped
on 8/12/36. The summary brief detailed **this:**

Wilshire Division. Four near-southside locations.
No gunshot wounds. Shots fired into wood-plank
ceilings.

Flat, flatter, flattened. Like his skull-flattened spent.
Brainwork now.

Take your skull-flat spent. Compare it to your plank-
flat-spent photos. Add your imagined differential.

Ashida did it. Ashida brainworked **this:**

Five spents. All time and sheer-impact degraded.
Four from the liquor-store planks. One from Karl
Tullock's skull. Consider all angles. Stir it all up, you
get **this:**

Almost three-to-one identical markings. Call it
72%. It's a possible, if not probable, match.

He knew the block. It was just north of Belmont
High. He brought a celluloid shim. He possessed B
and E skills. Dudley Smith taught him well.

It was 1:00 a.m. He parked a block down and walked over. The building was two-story stucco. The parking lot was empty. He heard thunder and felt light rain.

He approached the front door. It was glass-paneled and wood-jambed. The interior was full-lit. He peered inside. He clocked an entryway and bisecting hallway.

Open-all-nite. U-keep-the-key. Make-like-you-belong-here.

Ashida stood at the door. He patted his pockets. Where's my key? I'm Mr. Flustered. I'm Mr. Jap in disguise.

He shimmed the lock-jamb juncture. The door wiggled and popped wide. He stepped inside and shut himself in. He walked back out of sight.

There were no first-floor lockers. They were all upstairs.

Ashida walked up. The steps creaked. He almost shrieked. He clamped his mouth and held it in. Shrieks made him sound effete.

There's the lockers. There's rows and rows. It reprised Bucky at Belmont. The boys gym, the showers, the locker room.

He walked the rows. He pegged 648. He strolled the rows and saw no one. He walked back to 648.

The boy's gym, redux. The same gray metal locker, the same padlock.

He slid the key in the keyhole and turned it. The padlock snapped.

He opened the door. It was right there on the shelf.

May '31, redux. Memo to Karl Tullock and Wayne Frank Jackson.

You're dead and I'm not. I've got what you don't. It's solid gold and weighs thirty pounds. You died for this.

25

(LOS ANGELES, 1:30 A.M., 1/8/42)

Late cocktails at Brenda's. Three old pals and inveterate nite owls. Comfy chairs and ticker-tape dish.

The Japs take the Malay Peninsula. The Japs eye the Dutch East Indies. The PD slams local Japs. The Feds slam local cops.

Brenda said, "Jack Horrall's scared, Citizens. The probe's got his dick in a twist."

Elmer said, "The probe's a shuck. That's straight from Sid Hudgens. Ed Satterlee's J. Edgar's straw man. They'll let the probe fizzle out and put it to some Hollywood Reds."

Kay said, "Satterlee's in with Hop Sing. I picked that up when I was deep off in Bill Parker's incursion. Bill told me he was selling leads on Japanese confiscations."

Brenda said, "Katherine Ann reveals herself. She's gone from 'Captain Parker' to 'Bill' in a hot tick. 'Sweetie Pie's' warming up in the bull pen."

Kay laughed. Brenda stirred the fireplace. Elmer relit his cigar.

"Ed Satterlee's a drip. He wouldn't cut it in our white man's PD."

Brenda lit a cigarette. "Elmer's jealous. Ed's spent notable time with his pal Ellen Drew, which I will readily concede that he pays for."

Elmer said, "Let's change the subject."

Brenda sipped Cointreau. "It's Citizen Kay's turn to yak. As long as she don't start extolling Maestro what's-his-name and those Stalin lovers out in Brentwood."

Kay lit a cigarette. "The Maestro's name is Klemperer, and most of his friends are Trotskyites. There's quite a rabid distinction."

Elmer blew smoke rings. "The Reds are all rabid dogs. So's Kay's friend Bill. But he don't hold with Roosevelt, much less the Russkies."

Kay said, "I'm worried about him."

Brenda said, "You're **jealous,** Citizen."

Kay bristled. "Tell me why I should be."

Elmer said, "You're front row at Lyman's, so you've seen the big redhead. That's one damn good 'why' in my book."

Kay doused her butt in Elmer's highball. Elmer woofed. There she is—Katherine Ann Lake, hopping mad.

"I know the rumor, Elmer. 502 PC and vehicular homicide. She's working at the lab now."

Elmer looked at Kay. Lamplight torched her eyes. Why euphemize? He loved her past all hoo-ha and hurt.

"I shouldn't have said what I said. I know how you feel about Captain Bill."

Brenda said, "Look at you two. You'll be spooning there on the couch sometime soon."

Elmer laughed. Kay rolled her eyes. Brenda tossed an ice cube and missed her.

"Here's a ripe rumor, Citizens. I saw Bill Parker kissing a big redhead outside City Hall, and he had to stand on his tiptoes to do it."

Ellen said, "You keep forgetting our rules. 'No shop talk in bed,' 'no talk about my husband or the baby.' "

The bed sagged. The headboard drooped. Elmer smelled cheap pomade on the sheets.

"He's Elmer Jr. You can't tell me he don't resemble me."

"You weren't in play at the moment of conception."

Nite-owl serenade. A 4:00 a.m. quickie. Elmer Jr. messed with Ellen's sleep. Elmer Sr. capitalized.

"Toss me a little one. How dirty's Ed Satterlee? I know you trick with him, and I'm not jealous."

Ellen twisted up two fingers. "He's like that with the Chinks."

"Stale bread. Give me something hot off the griddle."

Ellen mulled it. Thunder slammed the windows. Junior squalled one room over.

"He's bragging about all this Fifth Column work he's doing. Mr. Hoover wants to extort some key guys, and he wants Ed to run sex shakedowns."

Lyman's ran round the clock. They served select pols and cops after hours. Elmer cruised the bar. It was wee-hours packed. Select nite owls waved.

Lee Blanchard. Joan Conville. Thad Brown. Two-Gun Davis and Mike Breuning, Buzz Meeks from Robbery.

Elmer hit the back room. He evicted Catbox Cal Lunceford. He called chez Satterlee. He woke up Ed the Fed. He told him **this:**

"If this probe of yours is a shuck, why are you working it so hard?"

Ed said, "Shit." Ed said, "I'll meet you at Lyman's in ten minutes."

Elmer hung up and fixed breakfast. He chugged one ginger ale and gobbled three bennies. Ed showed in six minutes flat.

He snarled. You-redneck-fucker-you-fucked-with-my-sleep. He fixed himself a Bromo and drained it.

"Who told you it's a shuck?"

"A little birdie."

"A little birdie named Ellen Drew?"

"Talk circulates, Ed."

Satterlee flopped on the couch. Elmer flopped beside him.

"Okay, it's a shuck. Mr. Hoover's putting a sheep dip on that punk Wallace Jamie. He'll be off to Congress before you know it."

Elmer tossed a curveball. It swerved low and inside.

"There's a doctor named Lin Chung. Your name's on his intel file. The routing stamp's recent."

Satterlee lit a cigarette. "If there's something in this for me, let me know. If it's we're brothers under the sheets, fuck off and let me go home."

Elmer relit his cigar. "You've got carte blanche with the service. One full month. I've already cleared it with Brenda."

Satterlee held up two fingers. Elmer went **Shucks** and **Okay.**

"All right, here's what this is. A, we're picking up code intercepts from Baja. We think it's some kind of subtle Jap-Chink Fifth Column gang, and we're trying to separate the tract pushers and **Sieg Heil** boys from the real menace. B, I'm not naming names, not for two months' or ten years' worth of the best gash on the planet. C, Chung knows lots of well-heeled rightwingers, and he's got a communist doctor pal that he talks eugenics with. D, I don't care that he was jungled up with that dead Chink Eddie Leng, or that guy Don Matsura, who stretched his neck at Lincoln Heights."

Elmer waved his cigar. "Have you got a file on a punk named Tommy Glennon?"

Satterlee shook his head. "No dice. Tommy goes back with Dudley Smith, and my policy with Dud is 'hands-off.'"

"Tommy used to run wets. I'm thinking he ran them with Carlos Madrano."

"He did, so I'll issue a warning here. Tommy was very loyal to Captain Carlos, and I have it on good authority that it was Dud who blew up Carlos last month. I also heard that Ace Kwan warned you away from Tommy—which was very sound advice. Let Dud, Ace, and the Staties take charge of Tommy. You're not equipped for it."

Elmer blew smoke rings. "Does Dud think Tommy will come after him for clipping Madrano?"

"Well, there's that. But mostly I think Dud's afraid that Tommy will try to ingratiate himself with whoever took over Madrano's wetback biz, which I bet Dud's got his eye on himself."

Elmer said, "That little birdie told me something else."

Satterlee sighed. "You confide to a woman in the sack, and it's on the Teletype within twenty-four hours."

"Sex shakes. You want to put the squeeze on some Fifth Column geeks."

Es la verdad, daddy."

Elmer said, "I've got a fuck spot, all wired up.

Right on Wilshire, upside the tar pits. Wall peek—the whole deal."

"I'll take it. It puts you in contention for White Man of the Week honors."

Elmer smiled. "Give me more on Tommy."

Satterlee shrugged. "I don't consider him a traitor, or a saboteur, or any kind of hot-blood seditionist. To me, he's just a **Sieg Heil** boy, looking for giggles. He's a Coughlinite, and he's in with these Mex right-wingers called the Sinarquistas. They're righteous Catholics and anti-Reds, and their boss is some cholo lawyer named Salvador Abascal. Tommy's in with them, and he's been poking Dud's snitch, Huey Cressmeyer, in the keester since the year one. They called him 'the Sheriff of the Brown Trail' up at Quentin."

Elmer slapped his knees. Satterlee said, "I'm ahead on this deal so far. What can I do to even things up?"

"Pick up Huey C. and rattle him. I'll give you a script, so it don't come back to me."

"I'll consider it. And, while I've got you, should I issue a formal warning on the Dudster?"

Elmer said, "I'd just ignore it."

Harem hideaway. Lovers' lair. Rendezvous redoubt. The spot radiated S-E-X.

Two rooms. One poontang parlor, one bootie bandits' boudoir. Brocade walls and French postcard art.

Fake panels hid the peek. Stashed microphones caught the **FUCK ME!** and pillow-talk sound tracks. A spy mirror framed the bed.

Wall baffles soundproofed the crawl space. The camera guys worked with impunity. The fuckers and fuckees couldn't hear shit. Special film lit in-the-dark ruts.

RKO hotshots rigged the place. Ed Satterlee would love it. His Fifth Column fuckers and fuck-ees were fucked.

Elmer hooked up a piggyback camera. He laced wires to the camera already aimed at the bed.

He'd see everything Ed the Fed saw. That meant Ed the Fed was fucked.

26

(ENSENADA, 8:00 P.M., 1/8/42)

Polyglot. That said it. We're this strange new alliance. We're strange bedfellows all.

Joan Klein—Jewish waif extraordinaire. Red dress and Red Youthbund dialectic. **Dos fascistas**—José Vasquez-Cruz and Juan Pimentel. His dear Claire. Besotted by her new daughter. Kyoho Hanamaka—present but unseen.

The restaurant stood on the Malecon. Waves smashed below. Table talk flew polyglot.

In English and Spanish. Plus Claire and the Klein girl's French.

Dudley ignored it. He was back at the hidey-hole. He revisited it at whim. Hanamaka cached his secret life there. That meant he'd be coming back. He might send a trusted stooge in his stead. Captain D. L. Smith crashed his secret life. Hanamaka must not know.

He found a second-floor trapdoor. It supplied quick access and was well devised and disguised. He refitted the boards and replastered the wall he broke in through. He celebrated his seamless job. He stole the gold bayonet.

Table talk droned on. It was trilingual and smug. Vasquez-Cruz flirted with Claire. Pimentel flirted with Joan. The girl found a big sister. Claire found a kid sister. Let's discuss the war and sing the "Internationale."

He weighed the bayonet. It ran 8.2 pounds. The swastika was stunningly embossed. He issued an APB. Kyoho Hanamaka/all Mexican states/hold and detain. He studied the photos in his Statie file. Hanamaka's hands were burn-scarred. It was not explained.

He studied the file. No Baja address was listed. Hanamaka lived at the hideaway. That seemed certain now.

Hanamaka.

Fifth Column warlord. **Es la verdad.** Embroiled

in two sub fiascos. Allied with leftists and rightists abroad. **Es la verdad,** as well.

The Fatherland and Mother Russia greet him. They present their indigenous horror. He crafts his memory book.

Hanamaka.

He might be in the U.S. His Jap visage would endanger him there. Someone abetted his flight. Governor Juan Lazaro-Schmidt might have pitched in.

The wall-panel cache lies intact. Lieutenant Pimentel is his watchdog. He's ensconced in a nearby house. He's got chez Hanamaka surveilled.

Lieutenant Juan's a technical whiz. He developed a plan to tap incoming calls to Baja pay phones. SIS has shot him a hot work assignment. Decode suspect slug calls from the U.S.

Table talk droned. Young Joan spun tales. Garment strikes and Uncle Shmuel of the **Yiddish Tagelblatt.** The Jews proclaim their woes and boo-hoo the world's vexation.

Vasquez-Cruz said, "Captain Smith appears to be bored."

Pimentel said, "His women are ignoring him. Captain Smith requires their constant attention."

Vasquez-Cruz twirled an ashtray. "Miss Klein's regard for Leon Trotsky gets his goat."

Dudley winked at the lads. "At least he was killed in Mexico. You'll always have bragging rights there."

"Trotsky" tweaked Young Joan. She raised her seltzer glass and pinged Claire's wineglass.

"Comrade Trotsky, lady and gentlemen. The antidote to Fascism at home and abroad."

Dudley raised his glass. **Los fascistas** went **tut-tut.** The whole gang imbibed. Musicians table-hopped and scrounged tips. They wore pink floral shirts and plaid cummerbunds. They carried trumpets and jiggled maracas.

Vasquez-Cruz ordered a rhumba and slipped the maraca man chump change. He bowed to Claire. She stood up and offered her hand. They walked to the dance floor and found their hip-popping fit.

Dudley watched. It sent him back. This spic's hands on Claire. He recalled a precedent.

That dance in London. 1922. The Irish Citizens Army sent him in to plant bombs. A protty boy asked his date to dance. He said, "You don't mind, do you, Paddy?"

The boy danced with her. He encircled her waist. Dudley Liam Smith, age sixteen. Here's a dilemma.

The dance crowd dwindled. His date drifted off with her sister. He followed the boy down a dark road and blew his brains out.

Vasquez-Cruz held Claire's hips and steered her. Pimentel watched Dudley watch. Young Joan watched it all.

She had small brown eyes. She wore glasses. She spoke Yiddish and French. She had long black hair with gray swirls. Gray hair at fifteen. Your call— benighted or possessed.

Pimentel said, "My captain has abridged the social

code. I would not ask another man's woman to dance without first seeking permission."

Dudley lit a cigarette. "You abridge the officers' code of conduct, Lieutenant. Your comment was impolitic, however well put and well taken."

Pimentel smiled. "My captain appears to have misjudged you. You demand diffidence from your fellows. You offer loyalty and camaraderie in return."

Young Joan walked out on the dance floor. She tapped Claire on the shoulder and cut in. Claire bowed and deferred. Vasquez-Cruz and Young Joan took up the beat. His hands went straight to her hips.

Claire walked back to the table. Pimentel excused himself and walked off. Good lad—such decorum.

Claire pointed to Vasquez-Cruz. "I've seen him before. I know it."

Dudley pointed to Young Joan. She danced a mean rhumba.

"How does she get by?"

"She steals out of stores. She hasn't asked me for anything, but she appreciates the clothes I buy her."

Dudley said, "I'm going to have her tailed."

They walked back to the hotel. Harbor lights blinked. Young Joan took Claire's arm. They mimicked nineteenth-century daguerreotypes. Faux Parisians stroll Saint-Germain.

The Malecon cut inland. Shoreline hostelries loomed. They bucked a sea wind, three abreast. Alleyways bisected the sidewalk. Gaslamps lit narrow footpaths.

They walked single file. Claire said something. Young Joan slid on wet asphalt and went **whee!**

A man stepped in front of them. He moved alleyway to lamplight. He was unkempt and looked dissolute. He verged on raggedy-ass.

He's got a revolver. He's aiming it. It's a hand cannon. The hammer's cocked.

He yelled slogans. They were nonsensical. He braced his gun arm and aimed straight ahead. Dudley pulled his piece. His arm fluttered, his aim fluttered, he fired two shots wide.

A second man stepped out. He moved alleyway to lamplight. He's young and sleek. Note the twill shirt and armband. He's got a sawed-off shotgun.

He tripped two triggers. Muzzle flare lit the load:

Steel scraps/tight-packed/trench-warfare-slaughter weaponry—

The Slogan Man blew up. Such blood you've never seen. The scraps disemboweled him. His gun arm severed and flew.

Claire and Young Joan fell back. Dudley body-blocked them and covered their eyes. The Sleek Man dipped his fingers in the Slogan Man's blood.

He said, **"Comunista."** He spat on the corpse. He saluted Dudley and ran off.

Opium.

Kwan's basement. His private den. The tar, the match, the pipe. His body anesthetized, his mind relinquished and adrift.

He drove to L.A., impromptu. He wanted to see Mike and Dick. He wanted to see Jim Davis. He wanted to conspire with Ace and cultivate Hideo Ashida.

Dudley smoked opium. He dipped elsewhere. He leaped time and rewrote History. He went with the tar and the pipe.

Stopover, Ensenada. All-too-recent History. Bleak moments, last night.

Statie Blackshirts arrived. They cased the stiff and called for a morgue van. He walked down that bisecting alley. He saw wet-blood artwork on a wall.

A garland of swastikas. An "SQ" wrapped in coiled snakes.

The Slogan Man remains unidentified. The Sleek Man, likewise. The attack might be premeditated. The attack might be happenstance.

His uniform denotes random target. The D. L. Smith persona denotes something else. Last month's knife attack. Last night's attack. Dudley Liam Smith attracts **HATE.**

Stopover, Europe and the eastern steppes. Here, you become someone else.

You've touched his uniforms and gold bayonet.

You've read his diary. Don the attire, now. Live the History and wield the bayonet.

You're Kyoho Hanamaka. You're a little Jap with burn-scarred hands and a consuming appetite. You feast on horror as it disillusions you. Your diary ex-posits one great theme. Ideology is solely a means of entrapment and thus a barbaric shuck.

The Fascist Right. The Communist Left. Divergent in rhetoric. Identical at their core.

The Reds embrace wretchedness and promise peasants tasty gruel and a warm place to shit. They scapegoat capital and hoard it to build prison camps and tanks. The Nazis embrace Norse gods and exalt art. They extoll civilization as the Reds defame it as bourgeois. They scapegoat Jews because Jews contra-vene the all-is-beautiful Nazi aesthetic. The Nazis and Reds tell the selfsame lie in boldly diverse guise. Both lies indict the democratic West and defame it as naïve and effete.

Totalitarianism will win. The rabble will opt for conformed identity over chaos. Which lie will you accede to? Which hidey-hole uniform will you don?

Dudley Liam Smith, **Sturmbannführer.**

You donned the uniform at that party. You enacted the Night of the Long Knives. Now, wield your gold bayonet.

Stopover, Baja. Your Army duties summon you.

He read a Fed Teletype this morning. Agent Ed Satterlee wrote it. Now, hear **this:**

The rumors persist. Coded phone calls have been

received. There's been L.A. pay-phone to Baja pay-phone traffic. The Baja pay phone was tapped and thence transcribed. This was revealed:

There are hidden Jap airfields in San Berdoo County. No exact locations have been determined. Indio and Brawley are both rumored. He should talk to Juan Pimentel. Juan developed the phone-tap technique.

Opium.

The tar, the match, the pipe. His mind untethered, his imagination adrift.

He pictured a lineup stage. The lights remain bright. The height strips extend. The dead and the missing stand tall.

Eddie Leng and Donald Matsura. Tommy Glennon and Kyoho Hanamaka. They burn under stage lights. He interrogates them. They reveal their interconnectedness and tell him nothing else.

Ex-Chief Jim Davis. He's vivid—if in decline.

He's sclerotic and obese. He's half-mad and ravaged by aphasia. He still packs two belt guns. He was a Great War doughboy. He's tight with spic dictators and nativist hucksters. He's volatile and sentimental. He's mentored Elmer Jackson and Whiskey Bill Parker.

They dined at Kwan's. Jim slurped shark-fin soup. His color was off. Malaria yellow meets dead-man gray.

"I was hoping I could ask a few favors, Chief."

"For you the world, Dud. You say 'Jump,' I say 'How high?' "

Dudley sipped tea. "Keep your snout down. There appears to be a Chink and Jap Fifth Column play afoot."

Jim slurped soup. He dribbled up his suit coat. Dudley tossed him a napkin.

"And, I'd be grateful if you'd continue to watchdog Elmer Jackson. I realize that you and Ace leaned on him, but the warning might not have held."

"I taught Elmer the whore business. He was a wet-behind-the-ears jarhead when I met him. I made him the man he is today."

Dudley said, "He bears your imprimatur, Chief. He's suave in the Jim Davis manner."

Jim fidgeted. He blotted his necktie and pushed his soup bowl away.

"I'm going batshit, Dud. I'll blow a gasket if I don't tell someone."

"Tell them what, Jim?"

"That Werewolf creep's no killer. I killed the Watanabes."

27

(LOS ANGELES, 1/9–1/23/42)

Fire and gold.

Scholar's lark.

Ex officio quest.

Her father burned to death. It taught her to fight and think. That fire drove her to this riddle of two intertwined deaths. The possible-probable arson and the mint-train heist merged there. The gold symbolized her blown shot at the war.

She's a treasure hunter. She's the female Karl Tullock and Wayne Frank Jackson. She broods on gold. She's bought books and done library research. She's studied gold like she once studied fire.

She bought herself solid-gold cuff links. They cost half a week's pay. She found treasure magazines in a used bookshop. She fell prey to Congolese diamonds and man-eating pygmies. She succumbed to gold artifacts in Malaysian caves. She's a scientist. She stood outside her fixation and watched herself swirl. She's a sensationalist. She fell prey because it felt good.

She's studied PD and FD Arson Squad reports. She's read up on the dead CCC men. No leads surfaced there. She's logged morgue time with Dr. Nort Layman. No further leads surfaced. Dr. Nort formalized it. Karl Tullock **is** the man in the box.

The downtown library's her refuge. It's a brooder's perch. Newspaper rolls report the gold and the fire. She's gone from ignorant to expert. She's a scientist trained to hypothesize.

Just like Hideo Ashida. He's her scholar's-lark confrere.

She hit the library late one night. She looked up and saw Ashida. He was studying her. The moment unnerved her. She realized **this:**

He's omitting and dissembling. He's withholding. He knows things that he will not reveal.

The gold consumes him. He craves it as substance and money. He may see it as the means to abrogate wartime injustice. He may crave it out of pure greed.

Gold is money. It would buy her a cabin in lakebound Wisconsin. It would buy British shotguns and hunting dogs. She could shoot quail and sleep with her dogs. Provocative men might appear.

Scholar's lark.

Treasure hunt.

Potent riddle.

The drudge work that pays her rent and counterweights her lust for the gold.

She works confiscations. The Alien Squad raids Japanese homes and impounds property. Appliances, guns, shortwave radios. Flags and political hate tracts. Ashida translates the tracts. She transcribes the dreary content.

They run ballistics tests on impounded guns and compare the results to custody pieces. They dismantle appliances and look for hidden explosives. They've found none to date.

The squad rousts are overzealous and waged against passive foes. The U.S. government has instituted full-scale internment. She's observed brutal rousts and has a sense of the boys.

There's Lieutenant Collier. He's the permissive boss. Elmer Jackson and Lee Blanchard are the sweethearts. There's Wendell Rice, George Kapek, and Catbox Cal Lunceford. They're the Rodent Squad. They man-handle their prisoners and steal what they can.

Her work entails Lincoln Heights Jail runs. Ashida goes with her. They inspect the property of already-jailed Japs. Rank-and-file Japs hate Ashida. They hiss and spit at him. They curse him in Japanese. It started with Pearl Harbor and the Watanabe case.

He's the white man's slave. He's the PD's toady. He's a tong shitheel. He sucked the big white dick and sidestepped internment. He's a traitor and the real fascist. The big white woman is his whore.

She feels kinship with Ashida then. It dissolves fast. She's always been good with men. Ashida's the one man she can't touch.

She's assumed a role. She's the handmaid to a cloistered patriarchy. She's met Jack Horrall and Mayor Fletch Bowron. They radiate good cheer and casual corruption. The PD is rankly corrupt and headed toward rank incompetence. Good men go off to the war. Unfit "war hires" replace them. Cops fear the draft and the phone-tap probe.

She understands men. They're seducible. Hideo Ashida is not.

She faked an excuse and dropped by his hotel suite. It was her sole visit. She angled her way in. Ashida's living quarters impressed her.

The Biltmore. A large parlor and three bedrooms. Dudley Smith's patronage and largesse.

She met Ashida's affable brother and boozed-up mama-san. She went through Ashida's bedroom en route to the john. She rifled drawers and found a boxed photo stash.

Candid pix. A boys' locker room backdrop. A lanky boy in the foreground. He's naked and toweling his hair.

She recognized him. He was Dwight "Bucky" Bleichert. She saw him fight in Milwaukee. He headlined a big card and knocked out a stumblebum.

The photos saddened and repulsed her. They force-fed her Hideo Ashida's sickness and corruption. They backlit his complicitous bond with Dudley Smith.

Lyman's. The all-night rumor mill. Here's the tattle on Sergeant/now Army Captain Smith.

His blithe expediency. His axman-to-Jack-Horrall status. His rivalry with Captain Bill Parker. Their Watanabe-case clash.

She's seen him at Lyman's and Kwan's. He's a ravishing man. Hideo Ashida must be in love with him.

Which gives her pause. Which tells her to dissemble.

Which tells her to withhold fire and gold leads. She knows that he's omitted. He's most likely up on her there.

Ashida underestimates women. He cannot **see** them. Let him underestimate you as he seems to underestimate Kay Lake.

They costar in the Male PD Drama. Joan Conville's the handmaid. She's PD-employed and has professional cachet. Kay Lake's a specious seductress and brainy bawd. And William H. Parker stands between them.

Rumor: Kay Lake tears through men. Ask the long-aggrieved Lee Blanchard. Rumor: Kay and Whiskey Bill are yet to consummate. Rumor: Kay Lake shivved a bull dyke cop named Dot Rothstein. Dot's pal Dudley Smith nixed reprisals. Rumor: Bill Parker and "Big Red" are madly enjoined.

No, it's not true.

He's an alcoholic voyeur. He abbreviates his marital vows. He does not trash them. They've kissed three times. Twice at the Biltmore. Once outside City Hall. Brenda Allen witnessed that last kiss.

He isn't tall and handsome. His Catholicism gores her Protestant core. His wild grit mirrors her own and almost makes her love him.

Bill Parker knows from sin. It's a shared papist-protty trait. Bill Parker revealed his great sin of omission.

They were half-gassed at Lyman's. He told her that

Two-Gun Davis killed the four Watanabes. Davis sat at the bar, a few feet away.

Parker solved the crime himself. Davis confessed to him. Parker withheld the solution from the at-large PD. The crime derived from Fifth Column intrigue.

Davis acted alone. His lunatic cohort did not participate. Rich America Firsters roamed the periphery. Japanese and Chinese saboteurs joined them. The band redefined Treasonous Alliance.

There was a Chinese physician. He was a plastic surgeon/eugenicist and very **right**-wing. There was a Beverly Hills psychiatrist. He was very **left**-wing. He pandered to film stars and socialites and snitched them off to the Feds.

Parker devastated her. She told him to reveal Two-Gun's guilt and exonerate Werewolf Shudo. Parker refused. He cited Shudo's sex-assault priors. He stressed this fact: Jim Davis indicted would destroy the PD.

She relented. Her protty guilt pushed her back. She got drunk and plowed the Mexicans. That meant two four-count indictments. Four dead wetbacks and four dead Watanabes.

It was her sin omitted. Bill Parker covered it up. Their shared complicity ran breathless deep.

She went to the library. She read Sid Hudgens' series on the Watanabe case. Hudgens fawningly praised Dudley Smith. Equal praise went to Hideo Ashida.

Parker and Smith chat at Lyman's and Kwan's. She's observed their brusque civility and the hatred underneath. They attend the same church. They drink with Archbishop Cantwell and confess to Monsignor Joe Hayes. They worship God, to the detriment of God's law.

She drinks and jousts with Bill Parker. They drink, to their equal detriment. She worked a property-confiscation string with Hideo Ashida. They bagged a terpin hydrate still. The owner killed himself at the Lincoln Heights Jail.

She filched a dozen terp vials from Don Matsura's apartment. She wanted to experience the effect. She consumed two vials in the back room at Lyman's. She entered a vivid dream state.

She saw forest fires near Tomah, Wisconsin. She shotgunned a drunken Indian. She woke up on the couch. Dudley Smith looked down at her.

He said, "Hello, lass. You were extolling the wonders of gold in your sleep."

28

(LOS ANGELES, 1/9–1/23/42)

Gold.

He stole the bar and stashed it in his hotel suite.

He kept the key and called Lock-Ur-Self Storage. He learned the provenance of locker 648.

It was a permanent rental. A "John Jones" paid the full fee in June '31. A file card listed John Jones' address. It was a fake.

Dead end.

He reprowled Lock-Ur-Self and brought his evidence kit. He print-dusted 648 and got smudges and rubber-glove prints.

Dead end.

He wants the gold. Joan Conville wants the gold. He saw Joan at the library. She was reading old newspapers and jotting notes. He cruised the reference desk and scanned Joan's request slip. The words **fire** and **gold** jumped out.

Joan knows most of what he knows. He's certain of that. She knows nothing of Lock-Ur-Self. She has not **seen** the gold. He's far ahead of her there.

The gold.

It's Joan's idée fixe. She wears gold cuff links. She works in the lab and fondles them constantly. She's clocked him clocking her. Their omissions and suspicions reverberate both ways. She's seen all the reports and news clips that he's seen. She queried him per his ballistics tests. He laid out the liquor-store spree. Joan extrapolated. She said, "Fritz Eckelkamp. Liquor stores were his métier."

She's a natural detective. She knows how to cull facts and think. They have not discussed fire or gold since.

He subtly pumped Elmer Jackson. He quizzed him per Wayne Frank's death and gold idée fixe. He curve-balled "Karl Frederick Tullock." Elmer deadpanned the name.

Wayne Frank and Karl Tullock. This simple conclusion. They converged in Griffith Park that day. This less simple question perplexed him. The gold nugget in Tullock's trouser cuff. How did it get there?

He sought to buttress his fire-case logic. He set out to establish a **certain** Box Man ID. He recalled gossip. The Santa Barbara Sheriff's Bertillon-charted their deputies.

The men were comprehensively measured. Hand spans/arm and leg lengths/twelve phrenological marks. He could measure Box Man. He would measure up or he would not.

He called the SB Personnel Office and stiffed the request. He said it pertained to a missing-persons job. The photostat arrived the next day.

He went by the morgue. Nort Layman was out. He consulted the Bertillon chart and duplicated the measurement regime.

He measured hand spans/arm lengths/distances between toes. He tape-wrapped the skull and plumbed the occipital sockets. Box Man and Chart Man measured up exactly.

October 3, '33. The two gold seekers converge in Griffith Park and die there that day. Those are facts. The rest is conjecture.

He tracked conjectural logic. It led him back to the ballistics bulletins. He'd studied the spent lodged in Karl Tullock's skull. He got that partial lands-and-grooves read. It partially matched the liquor-store spents.

He walked over to the DB and pored through Robbery files. He snagged a file for the '33 liquor-store spree. He saw an eyeball-witness sketch. It vaguely resembled Elmer's Wayne Frank wallet pic.

He walked back to Central Station. A basement storeroom housed misdemeanor files. He breathed dust and mold and tore his hands bloody. He wagered on **this:**

Alky Wayne Frank. At loose in L.A., summer '33. It's logical. He would have been popped for plain drunk or vagrancy.

He dumped file boxes and went through them. It was pure shitwork. He hit a July '33 box. He caught a "Jackson, Wayne Frank" file tab.

Wayne Frank sustained a vag roust. Note the attached mug shot. It's a more than vague/half-ass-good match. It veers toward the liquor-store sketch.

Tell Joan Conville none of this. She wants the gold, to your exclusion. Your probity exceeds hers. The gold will buy her a man-trap wardrobe and front-row nightclub seats. The gold is your racial bargaining chip.

You diverge in moral intent. She's a round-heeled

girl out for kicks. You're out to ensure your family's freedom. You converge as scientists. You both love gold as an entity.

He went to a jeweler's. He bought two solid-gold second lieutenant's bars. They brought Dudley Smith to mind. They warned him of Joan Conville. They told him not to underestimate her.

She's gifted but erratic. She's conjoined with the gifted but erratic Bill Parker. Their union comes off deluded. It may play out effective. It mirrors his own union with Dudley Smith.

Ever-gracious Dudley. His proffered Army commission. It carries a price. He'll abet evil designs. He'll enter the man trap that is Dudley Smith.

Dudley has usurped Bucky Bleichert. Dudley is now the naked man in his dreams. Dudley calls him twice a week. He always issues directives.

Brace Elmer J. Find out what he's doing. Bring up Tommy Glennon. Mention Eddie Leng and Donald Matsura. Don't forget the sketchy Lin Chung.

He quizzed Elmer. He was subtle. Elmer sloughed him off. He told Dudley that Elmer felt clean. He said the Glennon/Leng/Matsura/Chung alliance felt Fifth Column.

Dudley told him to scour J-town for Kyoho Hanamaka. He's dubbed Hanamaka Baja's spy king. Hanamaka runs Baja's boss saboteur cell. Dudley wants to extort the cell and limit the extent of their damage.

Baja suits Dudley. He's created a second family

there. He's got Claire and her street-urchin daughter. Dudley's screen sleuth Charlie Chan. **He's** Dudley's #1 son.

He loves Dudley's egalitarianism. He loves Dudley's realpolitik. Dudley sees the internment as fear-spawned race hate. The Manzanar camp opens March 25. The Owens Valley broils in the summer and sustains winter's deep freeze.

Dudley, the Irish arriviste. Dudley, ever strategic. Dudley, most chilling here:

"I've heard that Bill Parker and your colleague Joan Conville make quite the pair. I met lovely Joan at Lyman's recently, and became somewhat entranced. Any friend of Bill Parker's merits my attention. Please keep me apprised of Miss Conville's activities."

Dudley denotes equal measure. You love him and fear him proportionately. You submit to him because it delights him and proves your utility.

Lieutenant Hideo Ashida, Army SIS.

You will survive and exploit this war by Dudley Smith's sole decree.

29

(LOS ANGELES, 1/9–1/23/42)

He's scared. It crept up, belated. **Oooga-booga.** Dem demons done launched demselves his way.

He's scared of the war. He's scared of the draft. He's scared of Jap infantry. He's ex–Marine Corps. They'll resnag his cracker ass and get his cracker ass slayed quick.

That's surefire terror. It's regulation issue. It's standard for this shitstorm time and place. It pales before his fear of Dudley Smith.

Oooga-booga. It's like he back in de ole south. He done **ex**-caped Parchman. De hellhound's on his trail.

Dud won't kill him. He's too tight with Brenda and Jack H. Dud's too savvy for Murder One. He'll just nullify his redneck ass in some cagey way.

The hellhound's got him pinned. The beast's baying baleful. Elmer, why'd you pull all this meddlesome shit?

Well, it's my case, hound. It's my very own big-deal investigation. That means Glennon/Leng/Matsura/Chung et al. I've got to wrap it up for some special woman—and Dud just got in the way.

Who's the woman, shithead?

I don't know—but L.A.'s full of candidates.

He's scared. He's restless. Diverse shit's coming and going. The Box Man job went **pffft.** Dr. Nort, Big Joan, and Hideo did what they could. He retooled memory lane and jawed with Wayne Frank in his dreams. But Wayne Frank's still dead and buried. Who's the Box Man? Who gives a shimmering shit?

There's still his case. It's breaking wide. Where will it go?

He's got address-book names. Tommy G.'s oddball KAs. We'll start with Monsignor Joe Hayes. He's a mick priest and Dudster KA. That tong rumor: "Tommy's poking some priest."

There's this Jean Staley twist. He ran her through R & I. File checks revealed **this:**

She's thirty-three. She's a carhop. She fell behind maryjane, back in '36. She did six months honor farm and thenceforth kept her snout clean.

He might brace her. She might tattle Tommy for some scurvy misdeeds. She might be bored and het up and sleep with him.

Ed Satterlee might roust Huey Cressmeyer. Ed's considering it. He'll write Ed's script and peep the sweatbox mirror. Ed's a phone-book man. Huey'll be hurtin' for certain.

Huey might hold his mud. Huey might break. Huey might reveal Tommy's whereabouts or some extraneous dish. Here's for sure—Dud will get wind of it quick.

Ed hasn't utilized Brenda's trick spot. He's checked

the piggyback camera four times to date. Ed's on some trap-spies crusade. He's out to honey-bait Fifth Columnists. The wall peek could yield roundabout leads on his case.

Ed's played out as a white man. It rebuts his nose-bleed rep. Ed's evinced high class per the phone-tap hullabaloo.

"You're afraid we've got wires on you, right? Okay, I'll give you the chance to listen to any calls you might be on. You can erase them, if we keep it on the q.t."

Wartime camaraderie. Spy chasers afield. Plus, new folks orbiting through.

There's Hideo Ashida. He's all-time tight with El Dudley. There's Big Joan. She allegedly scares Hideo. Joan haunts Lyman's and trades looks with Kay Lake. **Oooga-booga**—she de hellhound on Kay's trail.

The war's shifting things. The draft's depleting the PD. The phone probe's an undulating under-current. Jack Horrall wants to ride the war and probe out and retire. Let Thad Brown or Bill Parker take over then.

He braced Jack at Kwan's. Rotate me back to Vice, boss. I hate the Alien Squad. Most of these Japs were sandbagged. They ain't pulled no ruinous shit.

Jack said, "The Squad rates you war-essential. Stick it out, son. If you rotate back to Vice, you're draft bait."

Sage fucking advice.

The war's got folks calculating. Brenda's pulling away from him. Ellen's veering back to her husband. Hideo's running off to Baja. The Dudster's got his hooks in deep.

Hideo's feeling his oats. He blows off his bodyguards. Him and Lee Blanchard got pink-slipped there. The crime lab's fielding a Jap-woman team. The goddamn rain won't stop.

The Box Man job worked some hoodoo on him. He's had all these Wayne Frank dreams. Plus dreams of tall redheads in gold lamé gowns.

The war's a moneymaker. His call biz has gone gold post–Pearl Harbor. Everybody's scared and fucking willy-nilly. He got plastered and tried to kiss Kay. She pushed him away and said **this:**

"The war's got us all by the scruff of the neck. That doesn't mean we should succumb."

Sage fucking advice.

He wants to succumb. He's more hopped up than scared. That's his dilemma here.

30

(BAJA AND LOS ANGELES, 1/9–1/23/42)

He can't shake the thought. He can't exploit it for profit. The revelation bodes **CATASTROPHE.**

Jim Davis slaughters four Japs. He tells his ex-adjutant. Bill Parker keeps mum, so far as we know. Parker is a grandiose drunk. He's remorseful and suffused with blind ambition. He probably won't blab. Jim Davis has blabbed twice already.

A gaudy psychopath seeks absolution. Father D. L. Smith grants it. He now knows **this:**

Lin Chung was privy to the Watanabe snuffs. Ditto Claire's doctor chum, Saul Lesnick. Jim Davis runs amok. The local Fifth Column bodes, crazily diffuse and politically inclusive.

He's scared. He's hamstrung. He can't kill Jim Davis or Bill Parker. He ran the Watanabe job. Widespread knowledge of Jim Davis' guilt would create widespread panic. It would keelhaul Jack Horrall and Hideo Ashida. It would ruin one D. L. Smith.

He'd face criminal indictment. He'd forfeit his Army commission. His dear Claire would disavow him. He'd stand condemned.

He's scared. He's hamstrung and stalemated there. His Baja work compensates.

He discussed the pay-phone taps with Juan Pimentel. The deciphered codes suggest Jap air bases in San Berdoo County. The specific wording suggests rumor more than hard fact. He forwarded the allegation to Fourth Interceptor. They knew the rumor already. They considered it hogwash.

José Vasquez-Cruz considers it hogwash. He's got a brand-new hobbyhorse. He wants to infiltrate U.S. diplomatic junkets. The notion consumes him. It's his #1 intel priority.

El Capitán is politically savvy. He hates FDR. FDR's Latin American stance is "One Big Red Ruse." Franklin "Double-Cross" Rosenfeld has seduced film folk en masse. He's sending them out to hawk the Jew Deal and the Allied war effort.

Captain D. L. Smith has blackmailed numerous film stars. Vasquez-Cruz wants him to recruit junketeering informants. Claire finds Vasquez-Cruz suspicious and attractive. They danced, hands on hips. Captain D. L. Smith noticed it then.

Claire lives within herself. He feels her slipping away. She's a capable woman, underemployed. She pervs on odd beaners and boots morphine. She communes with Joan Klein. Young Joan steals from stores. He's spot-tailed her and observed her thefts.

She consigns junk jewelry to street vendors and takes a quarter cut. She's a petty thief and seasoned prevaricator. He was killing British soldiers at her age. He likes the girl nonetheless.

He likes Juan Pimentel. Lieutenant Juan is competent and adroit. He watchdogs Kyoho Hanamaka's hideaway. He sees Captain Smith visit the premises. Captain Smith locks himself in and lingers **loooooong.**

He visits the wall cache. He brings the gold bayonet. He poses with it.

He found a discreet tailor in T.J. The man altered wall-cache uniforms to fit him. He's bypassed the Russian garb. He poses in Wehrmacht gray and SS black.

A cobbler fitted him with jackboots. He bought a sheath for the gold bayonet. His fascist trousseau stands complete.

The bayonet consoles and confounds him. He's run a magnifying glass down the whole length. He picked up the probable remnants of U.S. mint marks. Buff-out marks also appear.

The provenance. That's what confounds him. FDR banned gold hoarding back in '33. The dictate was widely ignored. Let's indulge fantasy here.

There's a wealthy U.S. fascist. He employs an artisan. A gold bar is cut into bayonet shape. It makes its way to the Fatherland and Kyoho Hanamaka. Fetishistic horror ensues.

Provenance. A fantasy rendition. Fantasy as necessity and a firewall against chaos.

A man tried to kill him. That made two attempts in two months. He scanned Statie mug-shot books. He ID'd his second would-be assassin.

The Slogan Man. Victor Trejo Caiz. Born Calexico,

1901. Priest killer under Kommisar Calles. Commandant of a Redshirt Battalion. In disfavor under Lázaro Cárdenas. Suspected wheelman for the Leon Trotsky snuff.

Caiz was the Slogan Man. **Está muerto** now. The Sleek Man killed him. He mug-shot ID'd the Sleek Man. He's one Salvador Abascal.

The Sinarquista **Führer.** Born 1910. Blood foe of all Reds and anticlerical slime. Devout Catholic hegemonist. Fiery supporter of the Irish Republican cause.

A man to honor. A man to covet. A man to scrutinize.

He drove south on a whim. He hit Magdalena Bay and surveilled the Sinarquista encampment. He watched a priest perform outdoor Mass for six hundred Greenshirts.

Abascal gave a rip-roaring speech. He stood too far off to hear. He admired the **Führer**'s fluent gestures and delivery.

He drove back to Ensenada. Joe Hayes called. He was in town with Charlie Coughlin and the Archbishop. They came to fish and drink. "And, you owe us dinner, Dud."

He made good. They dined at the Hotel del Norte. He steered talk to the Sinarquistas. His pals praised Salvador Abascal. **Es un hombre magnifico.**

Father Charles brought up Tommy Glennon. You know Tommy, don't you, Joe? Monsignor Hayes blushed and blanched.

Tommy tops the still-missing list. Elmer Jackson

seems to have curtailed his rogue antics. The Baja Jap roundups proceed. Two more L.A.-to-Baja pay-phone calls have hit.

They were decoded. Sub berths were abstractly discussed. No exact locations or coordinates were mentioned. It was just abstract chat.

Human voices spieled code words. Said voices were muffled and barely audible. They might have been prerecorded. Pay-phone stakeouts were the logical next step.

He discussed it with José Vasquez-Cruz. **El Fascisto** was bored. They discussed their racket plans. **That** perked him up.

Running wetbacks. Running heroin. Moving wets and "H." Their Utopian vision, shared.

It's all grand, but—

Jim Davis and Bill Parker still trouble him. Jim's blabbed twice already. Parker might blab.

Beth Short will visit Baja soon. She'll be eighteen this summer. She's his favorite bastard spawn. She wants to quit school and roam. He'll play stern dad and dissuade her.

It's all grand, but—

He's due in L.A. The county grand jury has summoned him. He's set to testify. He'll be resolute. Werewolf Shudo killed the four Watanabes. He'll concede that he may be insane.

It's all grand, but—

Jim Davis and Bill Parker remain meddlesome.

A recent snapshot blinded him. The bulb glare slowly cleared. He saw lovely Joan Conville at Lyman's.

She stirs and mutters in her sleep. Her skirt's hiked. She's red-haired and rangy. She's got midwestern je ne sais quoi.

She woke up. They spoke briefly. Now she's back and blinding him. Dear girl, what took you so long?

Part Two

TERPINHYDRATE

(January 24–
February 25, 1942)

31

(LOS ANGELES, 9:00 A.M., 1/24/42)

Collusion.

City Hall. Room 546. Today's Monster Matinee. Werewolf Shudo versus the L.A. County grand jury.

The jurors perched at desks. They faced the room. Eight old men and eight old ladies. They were rich-stiff pedigreed. They radiated high-end Pasadena and Hancock Park.

A witness box stood adjacent. Counsel tables faced the perch. DA Bill McPherson repped the county. Note the Werewolf's seedy lawyer. Check the racing form in his hip pocket.

The Werewolf dozed in his seat. He wore a strait-jacket and jail denims. PD men sat behind the DA. Officer Lee Blanchard and police chemist Hideo Ashida.

Dudley Smith sat with the DA. He wore his Army dress uniform. Note the flap-holstered sidearm.

Handsome devil.

Two chair rows faced the show. Joan sat there. Bill Parker got her in. He'd said, "Consider what you know now. You don't get a deal like this every day."

Parker supplied drift. The DA liked colored girls. Shudo's lawyer was ex-PD. He had a night-school diploma and serviced a Negro pimp clientele. He procured for the DA.

Joan doodled up a scratch pad. She'd done research. She knew gold-per-ounce prices in '31 and today. She teethed on the upswing.

$20.67 then. $35.50 now.

Mint bars weighed 33.3 pounds. She calculated then-to-now prices. $8,268 a bar then. $14,200 now. The heist men clouted thirty-odd bars. Take it from there.

Lee Blanchard testified. It felt pro forma. Joan suppressed yawns.

It's December 6. There's a loud-party squawk. Him and Sergeant D. L. Smith check it out and find the stiffs. He called the Watanabes "Japs" and went **Oops.** The jurors laughed.

Blanchard concluded. Hideo Ashida took the stand. The DA lobbed softballs. The Werewolf dozed. His lawyer skimmed the racing form.

Ashida breezed through the forensics. He described various documents and their evidential value. He forged those documents. Bill Parker told her that.

Persuasive Ashida. Submissive dog Ashida. Fetch, running dog.

Ashida concluded. He walked to the door and passed right by Joan. She looked at him. He stared straight ahead.

Dudley Smith took the stand. The lady jurors swooned. Joan read their minds. Now, **that's** a witness.

The Dublin brogue. The idiomatic flair. The wild charm and sheer language.

He ran down the case. He glowed warm and lied with blithe assurance. He noticed Joan. He gave her a bolt-from-the-blue look.

Their eyes snagged and held. Dudley smiled. Joan tried not to smile back. Dudley glitched his testimony and glanced away. It might have been seductively feigned/it might have been real.

Joan observed Dudley. She believed each lie and caught herself duped within seconds. He threw nods and smiles. She nodded and smiled back and caught herself duped again.

Her face burned. She looked away/shit, I'm mortified/she looked back again.

Dudley concluded. He left the witness box and walked to the door. He winked at Joan en route.

The Werewolf jury adjourned. The Fed-probe jury convened. Joan kept her seat.

New jurors heard evidence. More rich stiffs perched. A U.S. attorney replaced "Mud-Shark" Bill McPherson.

Joan fidgeted. She fretted her gold cuff links. She wanted a cigarette, she wanted two highballs, she wanted a steak sandwich.

Jack Horrall testified. He was disingenuous. Phone taps and bugged squadrooms? That's the first I've heard of it.

Mayor Fletch testified. He grandstanded and burnished his crimebuster credentials. He failed to understand all this hoo-ha. He was a lawyer himself. "Frankly, I know whereof I speak."

Wallace N. Jamie testified. He extolled his noted uncle. Eliot Ness was a T-man and certified hotshot. He bragged up his electronics know-how. He laid out his dirty-cops probe in Saint Paul, Minnesota. Fletch B. hired him. Mayor Fletch wants the truth. Mayor Fletch don't know bupkes per wall bugs. "The truth will out here."

Joan yawned and stretched. A shadow hit her. She split-second knew.

"It's what we call the 'rubber-stamp' grand jury. True-bill indictments are ever assured."

Joan smoothed her skirt. She shot her blouse cuffs and displayed her gold cuff links.

"You framed that man Shudo. It's as much an open secret as the phone taps."

Dudley sat beside her. They brushed arms. He kept his voice low.

"I'll concede the possibility. But I could hardly have accomplished it without the brilliant assistance of your Dr. Ashida."

Her face burned. Shit, there's the blush.

Joan blinked. She suppressed a full primp. She thought fast and dredged up a punch line.

Shit—one split-second blink, and he's gone.

She got her highballs and steak sandwich. Lyman's was Saturday-packed. She bridged the lunch crowd and the early bar crowd. The grand jury crowd bled in.

Wallace Jamie schmoozed Eliot Ness. Uncle Eliot cruised the bar and glad-handed Fletch Bowron. Big Earle Conville hated Ness. Big Earle had a beef. Ness raped the Monroe County Forest Service on extraditions. Big Earle called Ness "that preening cocksucker."

Kay Lake walked in. She saw Joan and waved her little snoot wave. Joan snoot-waved her back.

They never spoke. They hadn't been introduced. They knew each other secondhand. Cops supplied two-way drift and tantalized them.

Joan sipped highball #3. Kay bootjacked Elmer Jackson's stool and eased him down the bar. Lee Blanchard pulled his stool close. Kay leaned into him. They discussed household hoo-ha. Kay made her voice carry.

Kay always did that. Kay wanted her to hear. Kay telegraphed her moves. Kay Lake, grandstander and ham actress.

The backed-up sink. Otto Klemperer's party, next

Wednesday night. Name-dropper Kay. Bertolt Brecht and Orson Welles. Spy-mistress Kay. A symphonic score, smuggled from Russia.

Joan hexed Kay Lake. Shut up or drop dead, you poseur. She killed off her highball. Bill Parker walked in.

He passed by the bar. He wore leave-me-the-fuck-alone blinders. He spotted Kay and dumped them. Kay saw him. Their hands laced up for one second.

Parker weaved to the back room. Joan stood up and shoved her way over. She hit a waiter. His drink tray flew.

Some Shriners got booze-doused. A whole table, spritzed. A fat man **eeked** and wiped his face with his fez. Joan hit the door at a sprint. The hinges shook.

Parker stood by the Teletype. He held a photostat and a cold beer. He saw Joan and blinked.

Joan slapped the beer out of his hand and ripped up the photostat. She got **this** close to him. Parker just stood there.

They were **this** close. Joan said, "Whose man are you? Are you your wife's, mine, or Kay Lake's?"

They were **this** close. Joan said, "How dare you tell me that Jim Davis killed those people, and you refuse to reveal it? How dare you lay that burden on me?"

They were **this** close. Joan said, "Or, did you dream it all up? Does that make Dudley Smith and Hideo Ashida credible? Is Fujio Shudo's life worth saving, given his established transgressions?"

This close:

"Whose man are you?"

"How many women do you plan to entrap before this war is over?"

"Why haven't we made love?"

"How can you live with what you know and do nothing?"

"What do you think you're doing with me?"

Parker swerved out of the room. Joan slammed the door and threw the bolt and locked herself in.

She dug in her purse. She pulled out a terp vial. She drank the terp and shuddered. The terp burned going down.

There's the heat and the **whoosh.** There's the gleaming gold bars right behind.

32

(LOS ANGELES, 8:30 P.M., 1/24/42)

His photostat popped from the tube. The PD and FD shot him paperwork. The Griffith Park fire. Two agencies weigh in.

He'd forged the stat request. He signed Ray Pinker's name. Mr. Pinker was off somewhere. He was Fed bait. He was scrounging lawyer money. He shined his lab duties on.

Ashida unrolled the photostat and read at his desk. He saw a Fed-routing code. He jumped on the text.

Two agencies weighed in. Two agencies zeroed in on the Young Socialist Alliance.

The YSA was a Red front. The membership fluctuated. College kids came and went. The state AG's Office deemed the group harmless. One fact bothered them.

The YSA cloaked a Communist cell. It was live-wire CP. It was cloistered and clandestine. A nameless Fed snitch finked it out.

Ashida recalled an **L.A. Times** piece. The YSA boss man was one Meyer Gelb. He was a Pershing Square slogan shouter and didactical creep.

Gelb's really **Comrade** Gelb. The Comintern bankrolled the cell and presumably issued directives. Bold obfuscation spawns bold cover.

Gelb, the florid buffoon. Gelb, the cell **Führer.** Kommisar Gelb, the Red cell master of:

Jorge Villareal-Caiz. A Mexican national. No further facts.

Jean Clarice Staley. No further facts.

Saul Lesnick, M.D. No further facts.

Andrea Lesnick. No further facts.

Ashida broke a sweat. He got the mean megrims and the shakes.

He knew the Lesnicks. He'd observed them at a Claire De Haven party. Saul Lesnick was a Beverly Hills psychiatrist. He was a left-wing eugenicist. He was a pal of right-wing race man Lin Chung. Andrea

Lesnick was Dr. Saul's daughter. She'd been convicted of vehicular manslaughter. She served a brief term at Tehachapi.

Ashida wiped his face. He fought off the mean megrims and stifled some shakes. He went through the L.A. phone books. The lab kept a full set.

There was no Meyer Gelb listed. There was no Jean Staley and no Villareal-Caiz. Dr. Saul's office was listed. There was no Andrea Lesnick listing.

The cell names felt seductive. They confirmed the pervasive presence of the 1930s Left. Police-file names were police-file names and most often no more. They lived in the non sequitur void of snitch-out information. This new lead felt seductive and inconsequential. It was more than trivial and less than germane.

Ashida plumbed the lead. He vowed to withhold it from Joan Conville. She craved the gold to his exclusion. He held the upper hand there. He possessed a gold bar and she didn't.

The bar troubled him. It was casually but expertly stashed. The heist occurred almost eleven years ago. The bar remained unutilized.

He'd checked '31 and '42 gold prices. The bar had nearly doubled in value. Heist men ran long on impulse and short on circumspection. He saw circumspection here. He sensed motives that contravened pure greed.

"Hello, lad."

Ashida wiped his face. His hands jumped. He

squared his shoulders and patted his hair. Stop it—
you're primping.

He checked the doorway. Dudley wore a tweed
suit now. His uniform flattered him more. He turned
heads at the grand jury.

Ashida kicked his chair back. I'm nonchalant
and indifferent. What's your name again?

Dudley held a suit coat on a hanger. Dark cellophane covered it.

"I couldn't go back without dropping this off. It's a
moment to celebrate."

Ashida stood up. His legs held. He said, "Dare
I ask?"

Dudley unveiled the coat. It was Army OD. Second
lieutenant's bars gleamed.

"Fourth Interceptor has approved your commission, and there's a great many papers to sign. Your
mother and brother have been granted Mexican am-
nesty for the war's duration. You will serve as my adjutant in Baja. You will interpret the Japanese language,
assist in the roundup of resident Japanese, and work
to further our antisabotage mandate."

Ashida walked over. Dudley unbuttoned the coat
and held it open. Ashida slipped it on.

It fit perfectly. The lieutenant's bars were pure gold.

Dudley said, "My Japanese brother."

Ashida said, "My Irish brother."

33

(LOS ANGELES, 11:00 P.M., 1/24/42)

J. Kurakami/DR #8619641/one console radio, one snubnose .38.

Check.

D. Matsushima/DR #8619642/one spring-loaded sap, twelve Nazi armbands, one lead-filled baseball bat.

Check.

H. "Hophead" Hayamasu/DR #8619643/one hypodermic syringe, one rising-sun flag, twelve Mr. Moto novels, twenty-nine vials of terpin hydrate.

Check.

Elmer prelogged confiscations. He called out the juicy bits. Rice and Kapek ran their mouths. Catbox Cal Lunceford picked his nose and watched.

They slogged through a late duty stint. The fucking squad pen froze. The fucking janitor fucked with the heat vents. Rice and Kapek habituated the squadroom. Their fucking wives tossed them out like the fucking shitheels they were.

A. Takamina/DR #8619644/one vial of Spanish fly, fourteen smut books, 142 Japs-kill-Chinks atrocity pix.

Check.

Rice said, "That Takamina guy's a beast. I pondered killing him for a minute there."

Kapek said, "You should have. I know this Chink's selling Jap shrunken heads."

Lunceford said, "I heard about that. Frisco PD put out a bulletin. They found twenty-one decapitated Japs in the bay."

Rice said, "Remember Pearl Harbor."

Kapek said, "I remember—but don't tell my draft board that."

The squadroom was jammed floor-to-rafters. Elmer tagged boxes and logged shit. Hey, check **this:**

R. "Banzai Bob" Yoshida/DR #8619645/nine spike-studded dick sheaths, four blood-flecked samurai swords.

Lunceford said, "Ouch."

Rice said, "The guy told me he used the swords to kill chickens. Some Jap voodoo ritual. He supplies the rice bowls on Alameda."

Kapek said, "Yeah, and them riceheads feed the slop they cook to white cops."

Ed Satterlee walked in. Elmer clocked him. The kibitzers flashed fuck-the-Fed looks.

Satterlee hooked a finger. Elmer dumped his confiscation box and trailed him out to the hall.

"I'm in a bind tonight, Elmer. I figured you could help me out."

Elmer said, "Short notice, but okay."

"I've got a mark set up with one of Brenda's girls,

but I've got nobody to work the camera. The gig just fell in my lap."

"And the girl's all primed to pump him?"

Satterlee lit a cigarette. "That's right. Annie Staples. She could get the sphinx to cut loose."

College Girl Annie. The bobby-sox type. **Woof!!! Woof!!!** Ivy League threads and long blond hair.

"Who's the mark?"

"An informant of mine. A geezer named Saul Lesnick."

The name reverberated. It reprised some Kay Lake dish. La Kay worked old Saul for Bill Parker. She'd mentioned some upcoming soirée. Old Saul was sure to attend.

Elmer said, "Okay, Ed. I'd be happy to help out."

The lovebirds showed at midnite. Elmer crouched in the wall peek. Annie winked at the two-way mirror. Elmer yocked and rolled film.

The birds peeled and hit the sheets. Doc Saul looked cancer-cough consumptive. Annie vibrated Viking Vixen Supreme.

Perfunctory woo-woo ensued. Annie rode old Saul. She straddled him and found the fit. She faced the mirror and went mock **craaaaazy.**

Elmer timed the ride. It ran 4.8 minutes and felt practiced. Elmer nailed the gestalt.

Annie's Ed the Fed's mock girlfriend. She's a

shakedown pro. Fey Edgar Hoover **looooves** this shit. He watches it and slams the ham. It justifies his political agenda. He thus entraps Red slime.

Annie disengaged. She patted Saul's pecker and walked to a sideboard. She poured two Drambuies and spritzed in seltzer. Saul lit cigarettes.

The lovebirds cozied in. Annie sipped her drink and blew smoke rings. She basked nude. Old Saul covered himself.

Talk hit the wall mikes. Elmer goosed the volume. Saul said, ". . . and Hitler's not what people think he is. He's more subtle than that."

Annie patted her mouth. It expressed big ennui. Elmer yuk-yukked.

"The war's a yawn. I've had it up to here. My sister joined the Wacs, because she's a lezbo, and it's full of young tail. She looks like the Bride of Frankenstein, and she got fired from her gym-teacher job for honking this girl on the volleyball team."

Old Saul chained cigarettes. "That confirms my point about Hitler. He places a premium on physical culture. His Aryan breeding program impresses me. He subsidizes good Nordic stock and pays the females a breeding bonus. He's convinced that the selective breeding of superior specimens can eliminate the specter of congenital disease."

Annie rolled her eyes. "Okay, but what about good looks? I look good, and so do my mom and dad. But my sister looks like something the cat dragged in."

Saul coughed into his handkerchief. Elmer yocked. The old hebe dug the Nazis. It was unrequited love.

"Racial science is still in its infancy. Comrade Stalin should put his people to work. We can't let the Right ace out the Left here. Stalin's designs are humane. He'll implement compulsory breeding from a workers' perspective."

Annie patted her mouth. "You're putting me to sleep."

"What shall we talk about? You're eager to learn. It's what I like most about you."

Annie tickled old Saul. Old Saul giggled. She swatted him with a pillow. Old Saul evinced glee.

"You like my big breasts and long legs, and these collegiate outfits that Brenda makes me wear. Do you know how many pairs of saddle shoes I've got now?"

Saul went **Oy vey.** "All right, then. What shall we talk about?"

"That party you mentioned last time. You said all these music exiles and movie stars would be there."

"Oh, yes. At Otto Klemperer's. I saved his life, you know. I diagnosed his brain tumor and got him into surgery, jack flash."

"You're heroic, sweetie. They should put you on the cover of **Time** magazine."

Old Saul went **tut-tut.** "Comrade Stalin deserves it more than I do."

"Will **he** be at the party?"

"No, but Orson Welles will be. I know you, Annie. Orson's your favorite. You can't fool me."

Annie crushed her cigarette. "He should lose weight. I like my men lean."

Old Saul laughed. "Like me?"

"You're too lean, sweetie. I saw a newsreel at the Wiltern last night. The Japs captured these prisoners somewhere. They looked emaciated, like you sort of do."

Old Saul glared. Elmer mind-read him. **You dumb goyishe twat.**

Annie said, "Come on, baby. Let's get back to Mr. Welles."

Old Saul sighed. "All right, Comrade Welles. He's going out on one of FDR's diplomatic missions, to Latin America, so that he can shtup Dolores del Rio and espouse the Red cause with all the gifted-dilettante fervor he's capable of, which is considerable. He's been my analysand dating back to his radio days, and his best work isn't **Citizen Kane,** believe me. It's the smut films he makes with big-name movie stars. You wouldn't believe the names."

Annie put out big eyes. The mike volume glitched. Elmer caught "Kurt Weill," "Bertolt Brecht," "Spanish Civil War." He goosed the knob and replugged a wire. He caught "Meyer Gelb," "analysand," "incendiary whiz." He caught "badly burned" and "battle with Franco's Falange."

The glitch unglitched. Full volume kicked on. Old Saul said, "I saved his life, too. I've got a Chinaman pal. He's a plastic surgeon, and he performed skin grafts on Meyer."

Elmer snagged it. The surgeon was Lin Chung. Who else but? It's who you know and who you blow—

Annie said, "I thought Terry Lux was the big plastic surgeon. I tricked with him once. He told me he was America First, and the world's greatest plastics man. He said he could turn my ugly sister into Betty Grable."

Old Saul shrugged. "Terry's Terry. He's as right as I'm left, and sometimes the twain shall meet. The war's created odd alliances. The left and right converge to acknowledge the shuck of democracy. My analysand Claire De Haven and her cop lover underline that perception."

Elmer snagged it. **Wooo**—Claire the D. and El Dudster Alert.

Annie lit a cigarette. "You told me about her. She's a socialite, but she's Communist up the wazoo."

Old Saul sipped Drambuie. "I'd call her a morphine-addicted dilettante before I even addressed her speciously reasoned politics. And, I'd add that her cop lover is an evil brute, and that Claire's out for thrills, plain and simple. They're in Mexico now, and Claire and I have phone sessions twice a week. She's behaving paranoically, I'm afraid. She thinks that a transplanted prairie tart named Kay something stabbed her lover last month, and I can in no way dissuade her."

Wooo—that's a hot one. It's a Code 3 Alert.

Annie patted her mouth. "Claire what's-her-name bores me. Tell me more about Mr. Welles."

She was **goooooooooood.** She neon-beamed **SHAKEDOWN.** Ed the Fed was out to jack Reds. Fey Edgar Hoover loathed Orson Welles. It was common-knowledge drift.

Old Saul popped a boner. Annie google-eyed the event. The bedsheet stretched and held taut.

"That ogre William Randolph Hearst is out to fuck Orson for **Citizen Kane.** Conversely, I would add that Orson would surely love to fuck you."

34

(LOS ANGELES, 3:00 A.M., 1/25/42)

Pub crawl. Movie shitbirds slumming. We're at Kwan's "O" den. It's open-all-nite.

Amateur pipe fiends hold sway. Orson Welles and Ann Sheridan. Plus froufrou hairdressers and prop boys. They're film geeks hot to restage **Fantasia.**

They settled on pallets. Seasoned Chinks ignored them. They sucked smoke and coughed a great deal.

Dudley and Uncle Ace watched. They rode chairs upside a back wall. Ace wore a KILL THE JAPS T-shirt and an I AM NOT A JAP armband.

Fumes drifted over. Dudley breathed deep.

"I would summarize as follows, my brother. The

plan entails corrupting, usurping, and co-opting the Ensenada contingent of the Mexican State Police, under Captain José Vasquez-Cruz. Once accomplished, we would create a mass exodus of wetback workers, to pick crops at San Joaquin Valley farms."

Ace said, "I listen raptly, my Irish brother. Please tell me more."

Dudley clocked Orson Welles. Fat Boy purportedly fucked Claire. They coupled at Terry Lux's clinic. Rumors persist.

"Mexico will ditch its neutral stance in May, and throw in with the Allies. A guest-worker program will go into effect in August. It will be signed into law by our Governor Olsen, and Baja's governor, Juan Lazaro-Schmidt. It will effectively legalize slave immigration, and all attendant profits will bypass us. We need to preempt and supersede the program with our own wetback exports."

Ace pissed in a drainage sluice. He was earthy. He exemplified the hearty-peasant aesthetic. He possessed a cashew-sized dick.

"I still listen raptly. Please tell me more."

Dudley lit a cigarette. "We'll take handsome kickbacks from the farmers and attach our wets' wages. We'll house the more educated wets in the dwellings of interned Japs and grab a percentage of the rent they pay, along with a percentage of their wages from the better jobs they secure. Conversely, we will reduce the Jap population of Baja through a concerted internment effort, and will seek U.S. government assistance in housing Mexican Japs in U.S. internment centers. We will house **rich** Mexican Japs here in Los Angeles, under your Chinese protection. The reduced Jap population in Baja will alleviate the specter of coastal sabotage and infiltration, which will fulfill my Army mandate."

Ace said, "Kill the Japs."

"A hearty and well-informed sentiment, my brother."

Ace laughed. Dudley clocked a peep show. Ann Sheridan hopped on Fat Boy's pallet. She tossed her hair and went for his fly.

"I find Captain Vasquez-Cruz problematic, and Claire agrees with me. He's inherited Carlos Madrano's heroin business, and we've struck an alliance of sorts. **El Capitán** has welcomed me to Baja, but I suspect that he has designs on my designs. This brings us to our long-lost pal, Kyoho Hanamaka."

"I keep eye down here. No Hanamaka. No tickee, no washee."

"O" fumes circulated. Dudley caught wisps. He drifted a bit. He dream-caressed the gold bayonet.

"Hanamaka disappeared on December 18. He should have been detained on Pearl Harbor day, which leads me to believe that he was allowed to remain at large. It now appears as though he's faked his own death. He's the logical man to run sabotage operations in Baja, and I'm determined to capture

him. Our ventures in Baja will succeed in direct proportion to my success in interdicting the Baja Fifth
Column."

Ace said, "You interdict, we make money. Good
tickee-washee there."

Dudley said, "We've picked up code calls from here
to Baja. There's allegedly hidden air bases in Indio
and Brawley. It may or may not be credible innuendo.
Should the former be true, I would tag Hanamaka
my number-one suspect."

Ace squinted. The dope fumes stung his eyes.

"You think Staties help Hanamaka escape? Maybe
Vasquez-Cruz help? You get proof and extort his
greaseball ass? We take over 'H' trade then?"

Dudley smiled. "Great minds think alike, my
Chinese brother."

Ace bowed. "Tommy Glennon. He remain at
large also?"

"Yes, and vexingly so. He was Carlos Madrano's boy,
and he's a long-standing Mex-o-phile. He could very
well fall prey to the charms of José Vasquez-Cruz."

"Tommy kill Eddie Leng. You think so, Dudster?"

"Yes. It's likely, but I don't know why."

"I rubber-hose Don Matsura. He don't know shit.
I fake suicide. Hang that Jap fucker in his cell."

Dudley whooped. Ace was a good dog. Ace always
fetched.

"Tommy's been out in the vapors since New
Year's. I don't see how he could have done it without

professional help. My instincts tell me that he's in Baja, and that Hanamaka's here."

Ace said, "Tommy Fifth Column. Crazy fuckers jungled up in strange ways."

Dudley said, "He's Catholic Fifth Column, my brother. Sadly, I see more sinister forces at play."

Fat Boy's pallet shook. He squealed and bit his pillow. Lovely Ann wiped her chin and zipped him up.

Whiskey Bill fought the booze. He had one drink. Then one more drink. His thirst persisted. Dudley watched him dither and succumb.

Stag dinner at St. Vib's. Archbishop Cantwell hosted. Joe Hayes slurred the kikes and the prods. Father Coughlin slurred the frogs and the coons. Every man jack slurred the Japs.

The Archbishop's study. Packed with golf-themed artwork. Golf as holy sacrament. Heretical horseshit.

Deep chairs bid sleep. Parker bid scrutiny. Dudley yawned. He took bennies yesterday. He charged thirty-six hours straight.

He read Alien Squad files and trawled for notes on Hanamaka. No mentions popped up. He walked J-town and flashed his Baja file pic. **Hanamaka? Me no see him.** He logged that response, ceaselessly.

He issued a U.S. APB. All points/hold and detain. His mind churned. He teethed on the gold bayonet.

It's provenance. The who/the why/the upscut. He

indulged fantasy. He merged reality. Who first possessed the gold? Who forged the bayonet? He recalled a mint-train job. It went down in the spring of '31. The job stood unsolved. It felt non sequitur. Impecunious heist men and gold fenced down in value. Gold now long gone.

Cantwell said, "Dud's tired. He's been yawning since he walked in the door."

Hayes said, "He's got one eye fixed on Bill, though. Those two share a history."

Cantwell said, "Like Scylla and Charybdis. Evenly matched apparitions in the Old Testament."

Hayes said, "Greek mythology, Your Eminence."

Coughlin said, "Lay off the 'Greek,' Joe. You'll get all fluttered."

Hayes blanched and gulped. Coughlin winked at Cantwell. Dudley tweaked Whiskey Bill.

"Are the refreshments to your liking, Captain?"

"Yes, Captain."

"I thought you might appear at the grand jury. The Watanabe job was your overall command."

"My testimony would have proved redundant. You were the lead investigator."

"Yes, but I thought you might have felt compelled to present an alternative solution."

"Your solution was expedient and stunningly crafted—if speciously reasoned and fallacious in your presumption of guilt."

Dudley laughed. "Aaahh, there's our impasse."

Cantwell coughed. "You boys quell your differences. We're five good Catholic men here to get shit-faced."

Hayes said, "Hear! Hear!"

Coughlin said, "Let the Japs kill the Japs with impunity, then fry the Jap who killed the Japs in the first place."

Cantwell said, "Dud's spoiling for a tiff. The Mexican sun's broiling that grand brain of his."

Dudley lit a cigarette. "Mexico's an opportunity in search of a solution, Your Eminence. On that note, I should add that Father Coughlin's friend Salvador Abascal did me quite the favor recently."

Coughlin said, "Salvador's quite the lad. An honorary mick, that one. I'll set up a feed the next time I'm in T.J."

Nuns wheeled in a steam tray. Dinner is served. It was god-awful corned beef and cabbage. It smelled like canned dog food.

The clerics dug in. Dudley cracked a window. Cabbage fumes dispersed.

Parker flashed the **malocchio.** He was half-tanked. Dudley evil-eyed him back. Parker blinked first.

Frat-boy antics. Such cheap diversion. Wholly indecorous and undignified.

Joan Conville wisped by. Dudley caught her musk and savored it. She crashed his dreams most nights.

Bill Parker entraps young women. It's one per month now. His patronage carries a price. It creates exploitable rage.

Joe Hayes ignored his food. He checked his watch once per second. Monsignor Joe possessed family money. He kept a beachfront apartment. He held all-male retreats there.

Hayes stood up and murmured good-byes. The gang waved and laced back to their grub. Dudley ticked off thirty seconds and excused himself.

He walked outside. He caught Hayes in the rectory lot. Family money. Such a smart roadster. Wire wheels and red leather seats.

The engine throbbed. Hayes looked up and fluttered. Dudley reached in and cut back the key. The engine coughed and died.

"Hot date, Monsignor?"

"I don't care for your tone, Dud."

"Where's Tommy Glennon, Monsignor? I won't comment on your relationship, but I do need to see him."

Hayes wore driving gloves and a puce muffler. They clashed with his penguin suit.

"Tommy comes and goes as he pleases. I'm his confessor, not his nursemaid. I haven't seen him since he left San Quentin."

Blunt lies. This sacrosanct fairy. Not some thug you rubber-hose.

"You're Bill Parker and my Claire's confessor, as well. I'd pay good money to hear their confessions."

Hayes smoothed his muffler. His clan assimilated. He left his brogue in Galway, 1919.

"I'm your confessor, to boot. You surely have much to tell me, if Bill Parker is to be believed."

"I'm beyond sin, Monsignor. I was killing Black-and-Tans when you were in the seminary. I'm bucking for Pope Pius' job. Do you think the Vatican Council will grant me a dispensation to fuck women?"

Hayes laughed. "Check the rightist mailing lists. Tommy's quite the avid reader. You might get a line on him that way."

Dudley flicked the key. The engine purred.

Hayes donned a tweed cap. " 'Pride goeth before a fall,' Dudley. Not everyone fears you. Men like you tend to trip and fall in the shit."

35

(LOS ANGELES, 9:30 P.M., 1/26/42)

Joan walked home. She felt dream-smacked and wispy.

She cut west on 1st Street. She crossed Bunker Hill and bypassed Belmont High. She caught wisps of Hideo Ashida. He ran track at Belmont. Gold dust wisped by.

She floated. She drank two terp vials back at the lab. It was blackout dark and cool-evening still.

Faces popped here and there. She saw Dudley

Smith and Bill Parker. Terp had that effect. It unlocked doors and let you peek in.

Joan cut north on Carondelet. Her courtyard was
blackout black/shades drawn/we do our part. She got
out her keys. She heard, "Hello, lass."

She dropped her purse. He caught it and stood up.
He'd camped out on her steps and popped up in the
dark.

Tall. The trim-cut Army uniform. The cross-
draw .45.

Joan mimicked his brogue. " 'Lass,' is it? Not 'Miss
Conville'? How long have you been in America?
Shouldn't you have lost your accent by now?"

"That's a great many questions. I'll note that you
didn't ask, 'What are you doing here?' "

Joan unlocked the door and turned on the lights.
Dudley followed her in. She tracked his eyes. She saw
him catch **this:**

Her framed diplomas. Her mounted shotguns. Her
sepia prints of Big Earle. Her microscope and chemistry texts.

"Policeman's daughter, are you? That man in the
photographs is wearing a badge."

"You've dimmed the brogue, Captain. And, yes,
my father was the game warden of Monroe County,
Wisconsin."

Dudley singled out the diplomas. "I admire scientists. I know nothing of science, so I stand naïve and
admiring before those of your stripe."

Joan smiled. "Call **me** naïve, Captain. I can't see you as a supplicant outside of church, and even then I'd have doubts."

Dudley said, "And I'm sure you doubt the probity of this visit."

Joan said, "I've narrowed it down. You were in the neighborhood, so you thought you'd drop by. You're monitoring your longtime nemesis, Bill Parker, and you'd like a hand with that task. Lastly, you'd like to screw me, which is a motive that I've encountered before."

Dudley bowed. He mimed Hideo Ashida. The little Jap taught the big Irishman style.

"One drink, then. That's my motive. Before you ask, I'll concede that I called the lab for your address."

Joan walked to the kitchen. She took some deep breaths and poured two double scotches. Her hands shook.

She carried the drinks back. Dudley sat on the couch. He skimmed a typed manuscript. Lee Blanchard leaked it to her. "Beethoven and Luther," by Katherine Lake.

"Reading up on a rival, are you?"

Joan sat beside Dudley. She tossed Kay's manuscript on the floor and handed him his drink. She caught his fine French cologne.

"Kay's deft. She's mad to attribute meaning, which is a trait that good scientists share."

They lit cigarettes. They sipped scotch. Her float intensified. A thunderstorm kicked in. A window breeze tossed her hair.

"Your father looks like a bold lad. You used 'was' to describe him. Has he left us?"

Joan said, "He died in a fire, back in '38. I've spent some time investigating it. I need to go back and reassess my notes. I'm not giving up."

Dudley said, "I've heard reports of the charred box unearthed in Griffith Park. The genesis of your great interest comes into focus now."

"Hideo Ashida reports to you. It doesn't surprise me."

Dudley went **Tu salud.** "I live to attribute meaning. By your lights, it makes me as one with scientists and unschooled essayists."

Joan crushed her cigarette. "Should I bluntly note the genesis of **that**? Your dirt-poor childhood in Dublin? The gun money you funneled to then-Monsignor Cantwell? The Ulster Constabulary men you've killed?"

Dudley said, "Bill Parker reports to you. It doesn't surprise me."

Joan laughed. "Sometimes I don't want the war to end. If it ends, people will fall back into their old circumspect ways. They won't talk as much and delight me as much and give me all this crazy drift to attribute meaning to. We're the end result of our curiosities and the extent to which they're sated. Has that ever occurred to you?"

Dudley said, "Yes, it has."

"I've begun to see the war as an opportunity. The realization confounds me."

Dudley said, "I understand."

"I'm starting to see how far I'll go to get what I want. It's exhilarating beyond anything that I've ever experienced."

Dudley said, "I know."

Joan touched his captain's bars. She held on his eyes. She said, "I was a Navy lieutenant for ten seconds."

Dudley smiled. Joan leaned in and kissed him.

They kept the light off and the windowpanes up. Rain hit frayed screens and sprayed them. The breeze cooled their sweat.

It rained all night. They made love all night. They talked in between.

Don't you have a wife and kids somewhere?

In Van Nuys, I think. I forget my daughters' names sometimes.

Those scars on your back. What happened there?

Some Ulstermen hooked me up to a truck battery. I broke free and killed them.

My sister married a Catholic. It caused a big uproar in Tunnel City, Wisconsin.

Your father. Do you think it was arson?

I lean that way. I've sworn vengeance, but the war's hexed me. I don't think of my father as much as I should.

In the first war, was he?

He killed Germans in the Ardennes. Not enough, he always said. It looks like history has proved him right there.

I prefer them to the Reds.

We should sic them on each other and bow out. Bill Parker always says that.

Aaah, our friend Bill.

The first time you sleep with someone, all these other people hop in the bed.

Who were you thinking of here?

Bill, Claire what's-her-name, and Hideo Ashida. Kay Lake, most of all.

Aaah, La Belle Kay. The poor man's Kirsten Flagstad and Eleanora Duse. I've never seen the allure, but my Claire credits her with a wide array of mischief.

I think she's capable of anything.

36

(LOS ANGELES 12:00 P.M., 1/27/42)

Boomerang.

Ashida trudged the Biltmore lobby. He wore blinders. They scotched **You're a Jap** looks.

He was pissed off. He tried to shuck the FBI. He forged Ray Pinker's name to a file request. He marked it **"Urgent."** All mint-train-heist paper/ please expedite.

He stressed a collateral case. Forensic evidence has surfaced. Please expedite ASAP.

He hovered by the stat tube. A reply arrived fast. It read **"Request Denied."**

Ashida trudged up to his floor. He was past mortified. He lived at the Biltmore. Elmer said, "You're shitting in tall cotton, son."

A colored maid dipped by. She sneered at him. The slave class revolts. You're the slant-eyed Jim Crow. That means **You're a Jap.**

Ashida unlocked the door. The lights were off. Somebody flipped a wall switch. Somebody yelled, "Surprise!"

The parlor was SRO. Somebody'd hung red-white-and-blue bunting. People stood and clapped. Somebody hummed **for spacious skies and amber waves of grain.**

People. Dudley, Jack Horrall, an Army major. Dr. Nort, Ray Pinker, Lee Blanchard.

People. Elmer Jackson, Joan Conville, Kay Lake. Note the full bar and buffet. Note the tipsy Mariko and Akira.

They swarmed him, they pumped his hand, they clapped his back. Ashida went slaphappy. They circled up and enclosed him. It all felt rehearsed.

Call-Me-Jack raised a glass. "Our very own enemy alien. A thorn in my side on the Watanabe case, but he delivered in the end."

Some people laughed. Some people cringed. Some

people rolled their eyes. They all raised their goblets and went **L'chaim.**

The major stepped close and held out a Bible. Ashida placed his left hand atop it and raised his right hand high.

"Repeat this, son. 'I, Hideo Ashida, do swear the following oath. I will observe the rules and regulations of the Army Officer Corps and will defend the United States Constitution against all enemies foreign and domestic, at home and abroad.'"

Ashida said the words. The major shook his hand. The crowd whistled and clapped. Dudley stepped up.

He said, "Lieutenant Ashida." He pinned gold bars on his suit coat. People cheered and whistled. Lee Blanchard handed him champagne.

A conga line formed. Dudley steered Ashida through. People shook his hand and tossed congratulations. Dudley swapped looks with Joan Conville. Ashida caught a two-way surge.

Dudley went **Hush.** The hubbub subsided. Dudley picked up a long leather case. He held it out, presentation-style.

The crowd circled tight. Dudley opened the case. It was black velvet–lined. Black velvet cradled a gold bayonet.

It was two feet long. It was blood-guttered and swastika-embossed. Ashida saw faint blade etchings. They might be mint marks.

The crowd ooohed and aaahed. Dudley said, "The spoils of war you'll encounter in Mexico, lad."

Ashida went **eyes right.** Joan went **eyes left.** Their eyes met and held. Ashida trembled. They orbed back to the bayonet.

Dudley said, "It's solid gold."

Ashida said, "I'd like to commemorate the moment. May I take some photographs?"

37

(LOS ANGELES, 2:00 P.M., 1/27/42)

Fucking Hideo Ashida. The brilliant little hump transcends.

Or exploits.

Or steps from shit to clover.

Or sells his soul to Dudley Smith.

The party throbbed. Elmer circulated. Hideo donned his full uniform. Dig the tight-creased trousers and holstered .45.

Jack Horrall was blotto. Hideo's mom and brother, likewise. Lee Blanchard jawed with Doc Layman. Dudley slow-cruised by.

He said, "Are you behaving, lad?"

Elmer said, "You bet I am, boss."

Dudley slow-cruised Big Joan. He caressed her shoulder. Big Joan went **Oooh, baby.**

Elmer caught it. Kay caught it. Elmer caught her rebound catch. He grabbed a bottle of champagne. Kay scoped the grab and pointed straight up. Elmer winked assent. Kay blew a kiss back.

Elmer strolled.

He sidled out of the suite. He hit the corridor and tapped an elevator. He whooshed to the penthouse floor and jogged up to the roof.

Downtown L.A. sparkled. Storm clouds brewed, north and east. The San Gabriels were all snowflake white.

Kay stood by a storage shed. She wore a black beret and a jazzy wool suit. She looked **très** swell.

Elmer walked over. Kay popped the champagne. They bottle-chugged. It was bargain-basement swill. Elmer gulped and tossed a flare.

"Tell true, now. Did you shank Dudley Smith?"

Kay gulped. "Elmer, come **on.**"

"Come on, yourself. You shivved Dot Rothstein."

Kay lit a cigarette. It took three match swipes. Her hands shook that bad.

"All right, I'll bite. Who told you I shanked Dudley?"

Elmer chugged champagne. "I was working the peek in one of Brenda's trick spots. This Commo doctor blabbed on Claire De Haven. He was poking a college-girl pro. He blabbed, and I picked up on what the De Haven bint said about you."

Kay blew smoke rings. They trailed sky-high. Kay pulled herself together, quick.

"You tell true, now. What's with you and Dudley?"

Elmer said, "He's crowding me. I've got a bug up my ass to crowd back."

"Was the doctor Saul Lesnick?"

Elmer relit his cigar. "He's a Fed snitch. His handler's keeping tabs on him, and he needed me to fill in with the camera. He thinks Lesnick's prone to blab to young tail."

Kay mulled it. Elmer heard her gears click. She played classical piano and wrote highbrow hoo-ha. She was the smartest—

"The Fed's right. I met Lesnick during Bill Parker's incursion. He's very susceptible to young women, but Claire's giving me more credit than I deserve. What you're telling me dovetails."

Elmer reset Kay's beret. He set it farther back on her hair and pulled up the stem.

"Can I sleep with you tonight?"

Kay laughed. "No, Brenda would kill me. Sleep with the college girl. It's not like you're not susceptible."

Elmer laughed. "Who are you holding out for?"

"Bill—once he gets free of the redhead."

"She gets around, that one."

Kay said, "Dudley. All roads lead back."

Elmer said, "I'm gathering information. Shit could play out a half dozen ways."

Kay sipped champagne. "Operate the college girl.

I'd be curious to know what Dudley and Claire are saying about me."

Elmer said, "You've got the darkest brown eyes I've ever seen. They hide what you're really thinking."

Annie Staples had green eyes. She ran 5'10"/150. She induced **looooooooow** growls.

They coupled at Brenda's fuck flop. Elmer made it **laaaaast.** They basked naked afterward. Elmer lay supine. Annie sat cross-legged on the sheets.

She sipped Cointreau, neat. Elmer dug in his trousers and plucked his flash roll.

He peeled off ten C-notes. He dropped them in Annie's lap. Annie went google-eyed.

"That can't be a tip. Brenda says we're supposed to take care of you for free. 'You keep Sergeant Jackson well supplied, Citizens. That way, he won't be demanding on those rare nights he sleeps over.'"

Elmer haw-hawed. "You've got Brenda down, and I sure would like to make this a regular thing."

"I see what you're saying. There's something else going on here."

Elmer said, "There's a certain FBI man that I think you know pretty well. He's got you prompting old Doc Lesnick, who I also think you know pretty well."

Annie pointed to the wall peek. "Ed Satterlee's filming us. You've seen the prints. Ed probably screens them at FBI smokers. All these G-men eat popcorn and pull their puds."

Elmer said, "There you go—but I wouldn't say Ed's all that crass."

Annie lit a cigarette. "All right. I'll concede that Ed's got me working Saul. He's a Fed snitch, and I'm snitching him to Ed. Filming us is something else, which I think Ed should pay me for more than he's paying me now."

Elmer jiggled Annie's feet. "Whoa, now. I'm not going to film you or us, and I promise I'll get your film back from Ed, and dissuade him from letting his pals take a look-see."

Annie sighed. "Sergeant Elmer's a sweetie pie. All the girls know that. He never asks for anything perverted, and he always tips."

Elmer blushed. "Does Lesnick always blab so much about his patients?"

"Always. We screw for two minutes, then he talks for two hours."

Elmer zeroed in. He stroked Annie's hair. He dialed their eyes tight.

"I want to know whatever that woman Claire De Haven and her cop boyfriend say about me, a woman named Kay Lake, and possibly a kid named Tommy Glennon. Old Saul spiels to you, and you spiel to me. There's a party in Brentwood tomorrow night. You're going to work old Saul, and I'm hooking you up to a microphone gizmo."

38

(TIJUANA, 2:00 P.M., 1/28/42)

"Hirohito's hellions rape Rabaul and pound pitiful Palau. The jungle-bred Japs parse peril throughout the Pacific. They cornhole the Carolines and savage the Solomon Isles. Ripsnorting Rommel lashes Libya and causes camel caravans to flee. Here in **mucho magnifico** Mexico, a furtive Fifth Column keesters coastal inlets. This quivering question remains—"

Father Coughlin cranked it. Dudley sat in the waiting room. Wall speakers popped the padre's pitch. Glass walls showcased his gesticulations.

XERB Radio. 500,000 watts. It broadcast from Baja to Bangladesh. The whole world heard Charles Coughlin's shit.

Coughlin cranked it. He threw sweat. His microphone melted. He'd promised a "special guest." He said, "You'll love this lad, Dud."

". . . as the lachrymose Left bemoans justified Jap roundups, and Mexico's cucumber-cool cognoscenti wonders if Prez Camacho has turned righteously right, as evinced by his land grant to the sizzling Sinarquistas. And, since there's no business like show business, are those ripe rumors about Eleanor Roosevelt and Colored Commissar Paul Robeson true?"

Charging Charlie Coughlin. Uproarious in short doses. T.J. by way of his Detroit parish and the Emerald Isle. Pope Pius pulled his U.S. show. The padre ran rogue and popped south. The Mex right wing loved him.

Dudley tuned him out. He daydreamed. He donned fascist garb and swung the gold bayonet.

He eviscerated priest-killers and nun-rapers. He butchered the British House of Commons. He speared Winston Churchill and noted royals. He decapitated FDR and all the men who'd fucked Claire.

He recalled Joan, two nights back. She tossed her hair just so. She wore gold cuff links. He watched her unfasten them.

He didn't crave gold as gold or money. The bayonet's provenance now bored him. He wanted to know who it killed. Only Herr Hanamaka could tell him that.

Joan was six feet tall. She'd be his height in heels. He wanted to dress her in black SS kit.

Her father burned to death. It might have been arson. He wanted to find the killer and offer him to Joan. She'd wield the gold bayonet.

Father Coughlin went reverential. His voice dropped. There's his trademark pulpit hush.

Dudley watched. Coughlin bowed his head and hosanna'd. A man walked up to him. The two embraced.

Aaay, caramba. Es El Flaco Explosivo. It's the Sleek Man himself.

He dressed pure Greenshirt. He wore jackboots and the coiled-snake armband. He looked through the glass wall and saluted El Dudster. Dudley stood and saluted him back.

Salvador Abascal. Why equivocate? He's Saint Ignatius of Loyola, reborn.

Abascal straddled a hair and grabbed the microphone. He spoke perfect English. He addressed the World Grand Jury and laid down indictments. He demanded true bills penned in blood.

He defamed President **Puta**rco Calles and his Red regime. He ridiculed Lázaro Cárdenas and his "godlessly gutless" reforms. He maimed modernism. It was "perversion perpetrated by the Jewish/atheist/nihilist Left." He quoted the **Protocols of the Learned Elders of Zion.** He critiqued communism as Jew-derived. He lashed Uncle Sam's **imperialista** forays in Latin America. He urged the U.S to embrace the Catholic Church and reform from within.

He spoke straight to Dudley. Their eyes held through the glass.

Abascal cranked it. His spiel borrowed from Huey Long and Gerald L. K. Smith. He pumped his fist à la Conde McGinley and wailed like Klan preachers and **El Führer** himself. His voice rose and fell. He'd studied the soapbox orators of Weimar-era Berlin. He knew when to purr and when to **SHRIEK.**

The Protestant Reformation? "Wholly genocidal"

and "the Christian Diaspora." Martin Luther? "A tyrant to rival Josef Stalin." Adolf Hitler? "A great, if unruly, leader, and a beatific beacon to the Western world at large."

Abascal cranked it.

He mourned the martyred Cristeros. He described the Redshirt tortures inflicted upon them. He detailed a Sinarquista death list. The torturers would be slaughtered, one by one.

Dudley walked up to the glass. He placed his hands on it. The glass vibrated. The Sleek Man's words did that.

Abascal walked to the glass. He placed his hands even with Dudley's. The glass seemed to melt.

They were **this** close. Abascal spoke to a ceiling mike. Abascal said **this:**

"I vigorously condemn the British-Protestant imperialism levied against the sovereign Catholic people of Ireland. I call for all-out Irish revolt against the British beast."

Dudley wept then.

39

(LOS ANGELES, 7:00 P.M., 1/28/42)

Star-studded bash meets field study. Know your foe. Observe her habitat. You're a scientist and a thrill seeker. This could be fun.

She read up on Klemperer and his guests. The **Herald** previewed the party. She had the address and the pedigrees. The piece featured pix and boxed bios. It's a slick study guide.

Pretend it's a frat bash. You're the new girl on campus. Breeze in and blend in. Crash the party.

Joan surveilled the Lake-Blanchard house. It was streamline moderne and just north of the Strip. It was turned out, **c'est bon.**

The house intensified rumors. Ex-boxer Lee took dives and reaped big payoffs. He was a name heavyweight. He raked it in for a spell. The cop rumor mill stamped it true.

Joan sat in her car. Her beat-to-shit '36 Dodge. It still bore New Year's Eve dents. She'd had the cracked windshield replaced.

Kay Lake drove a '41 Packard. It sparkled and gleamed up her driveway.

Joan lit a cigarette. Her thoughts tumbled. She tossed words and characterized the excursion. Words came and went. **Voyeuristic** and **Inconsequential** stuck.

She watched Kay's front door. She wore a green cocktail dress and high heels. She felt too tall/gawky girl at the prom. She went sleeveless. She missed her gold cuff links.

Her thoughts retumbled. They went party-to-party. She jumped back to the Biltmore. New-Captain Smith and new-Lieutenant Ashida. Behold the gold bayonet.

Possible mint marks. A raised swastika. She studies Ashida as he studies her. It's a **holy shit** moment. Ashida photographs the bayonet. It's evidence now.

Joan stretched and kicked off her shoes. Kay Lake stepped out on her porch. Kay, you're a knockout. That black cashmere dress really works.

Kay walked to the Packard. She pulled out and swung down to the Strip. Joan U-turned and caught her at Doheny.

It's a two-car caravan. It's heading west through Beverly Hills. It's all voyeuristic and inconsequential.

Joan reviewed her study guide. She respooled that **Herald** piece. Sid Hudgens penned it. He laid in a sidebar on Claire De Haven.

Dudley's screwball lover. A "former Las Madrinas Ball debutante." "Scrupulously scrutinized in 1940. State HUAC reads Red Claire the ripe riot act."

Claire looked highborn and haughty. Buzz Meeks dished her at Lyman's. He said she was snooty goods and rode the white horse.

Westbound on Sunset. Two women/two cars/one schoolgirl prank.

Joan lagged back. They passed the Bel-Air gates and UCLA. They swung through Brentwood and cut north on Mandeville Canyon. The terrain went posh rural. Recessed lawns and topiary. These rich folks had spreads.

Spanish haciendas. French châteaux. All-glass-cube moderns. Tall eucalyptus trees and terraced backyards.

Kay cut west. Joan followed her. Kay slowed and braked. There—that's the spot.

A massive adobe. The Sidster's "Maestro Manse." Bright windows and lantern-lit yard. Blackout-reg violations up the ying-yang.

A wide porte cochere. Mexican valets. Loudspeaker music—gloomy and dissonant.

Kay swung in. Joan hung back and let a Coupe de Ville pass her. Kay ditched the Packard. She tossed her keys. A Mexican kid snagged them.

Joan swung in. She stepped into her shoes and out of the car. A little Mex gawked **La Gringa Grande.**

She gave him her keys and a dollar bill. He said, "It's free." She said, "It's a tip."

The porte cochere was spiffed up. Three flagpole banners rotated in sequence and supplied a drape effect. Stars and Stripes/Loyalist Spain/hammer and sickle. Red guardsmen flanked the front door. They looked like winos hired off skid row.

The front door stood open. Joan breezed inside.

Kay played whirling dervish. She whooshed and disappeared.

Now, the looks. They're all standard-issue. Who's that? Check the big redhead.

Joan rebuffed looks. She checked the Maestro Manse. Holy moly. Somebody **lives** here.

There's a foyer. It's stark Deco and Nuremberg-sized. Living room, **nein.** It's a Bauhaus beer hall. It's all pillared and bas-reliefed.

Brass statuary. Backlit and floodlit. Beethoven and Wagner, splashed in workers' red. It's all distinctly modernist. Note the Picassos and Mirós on the walls.

Black leather couches and chairs. Silk tapestried carpets. Cut-crystal tables. A forty-foot fireplace. Mounted polar bears standing guard.

Joan just stood there. Guests mingled in clumps. War blah-blah bombarded her.

Hitler was wicked. Stalin was swell. Their recent pact was all rightist ruse. Hear those piano chords? That's Otto's sneak peek. He got V-mail from Shostakovich. It's his new symphony. Nazi tanks attack Leningrad. Listen close—you can tell.

A waiter swooped by. Joan snatched a champagne flute. She imbibed Pernod and absinthe. It went straight to her head.

She stood her ground. She looked around. She matched faces to newspaper pix.

There's the Maestro. That's easy. Talk about tall. He suffered a brain tumor, circa '39. He's got a half-frozen face.

There's Thomas Mann, Kurt Weill, and Bertolt Brecht. There's Lotte Lenya and Arnold Schoenberg.

Sid Hudgens defamed them all. He wrote a private-PD dirt sheet. It covered his poker losses to Jack Horrall.

Lenya was a loin-lapping lezbo. Weill traveled Estrada Chocolato with George Cukor. Mann and Schoenberg ran Red. Brazen Brecht brought the bratwurst to Leni Riefenstahl.

Joan laughed. She snagged another Pernod and absinthe and quaffed it. Short men dipped by and gawked her. She looked left and saw José Iturbi. She looked right and saw Claire De Haven.

She's patrician and near-translucent. She's got hophead eyes. She's Edna St. Vincent Millay, in Dudley Smith's bed.

Claire evinced screechy nerves. She fretted a handkerchief. Her eyes darted. Guests swirled by her. Joan saw her eyes land.

On a small old man. Playing courtier. Perched on a black leather couch.

He sported a Sigmund Freud beard. He held a doctor's bag. He pontificated on overdrive. A big blond girl cleaved close to him. She wore a tweed skirt and a brown crewneck sweater. She wore prep-school saddle shoes.

Joan sidled over. She perched in eavesdrop range. The old man gasbagged. Partygoers dropped by and said hi. They called pops "Saul" and "Dr. Lesnick."

The blonde oozed adoration. She looked parodistic/

he talked parodistic. Joan caught "Comrade Stalin" and "noble Red Army."

Claire beelined up. Party fools swelled and crushed against her. She pointed to the doctor's bag. Lesnick nodded. Lesnick went **There, there.**

Joan hovered. Claire fidgeted. A Chinese man pushed his way over. He plopped on the couch. The blonde went **eeek** and spilled half her cocktail.

She blotted her skirt. Lesnick patted her knee. He copped a leg feel and went **Oy vey.** The Chinaman gasbagged.

Joan heard "Hitler"/"Waffen-SS"/"racial science." Words devolved to jabber. Lesnick said, "Slow down, Lin. I know some French, but I don't know Chinese."

Lin laughed. "Two-Gun Davis speak Chinese. Not you. Chinese new master race. They fix your Jew wagon."

Lesnick laughed. The Davis crack ditzed Joan. The whole exchange warped in weird. Someone told her something pertinent. Some Lyman's barfly. The exact source eluded her.

Claire leaned in and whispered to Lesnick. Chinaman Lin jabbered on. Joan caught movement, stage right.

Kay Lake hovered. She stood within voyeur range and eyed Lesnick and Claire. Guest swarms covered Joan. Lin's blather drowned out Lesnick and Claire.

Kay drifted off. Lesnick and Claire stood up. The

blonde pouted—Don't leave me, lover. Lesnick mollified her. He laid out **There, there**'s.

Joan voyeurized. Pops bid deference. Moses parts the Red Sea. Guests step aside and hosanna. Lesnick hooks Claire's arm and leads her off.

Joan followed them. They walked outside. Pole-fixed lanterns lit the backyard. Guests mingled by a barbecue pit. Negro chefs in Red Army tunics dished out spareribs and slaw.

A guesthouse stood by the back fence. Lesnick led Claire over and in. Joan caught up and peeped a side window. She caught an eye track inside and saw **this:**

Lesnick opens his bag. He pulls out a hypo and jabs a vial of morphine sulfate. Claire rolls up her left sleeve. Lesnick ties a silk-sash tourniquet. Claire shuts her eyes. Lesnick dips a cotton swab in rubbing alcohol. Claire trembles. Lesnick swabs her arm and injects her.

Joan walked off. She got the Sad-as-Shit Blues and traipsed back to the house. The triad concept ditzed her. It applied to chemistry. She applied it right here and right now.

Kay Lake/Dudley Smith/Claire De Haven. Unknown quotients abound. Smith/Parker/Conville. The same applies. Claire thinks Kay knifed Dudley. I'm a Wisconsin farm girl. What am I doing here?

Bombs away:

She caught more war talk. More guests talked it.

More guests shouted it. More guests shouted over other guests and poked at their chests.

More spilled drinks. More cigarette-burned furniture and dumped ashtrays. No more sit-down space. More guests tripping and sprawling flat on their ass.

Joan detoured. She traipsed up a back stairway and hit the second floor. She heard a piano. Somebody played soft Chopin or Liszt.

She walked toward it. She stopped short at a doorway. She tucked herself out of sight and peeped.

Kay Lake and the Maestro played four-handed. Kay played the easy parts, the Maestro carried the weight. They sat close together. They wore symphony black. Kay was half the Maestro's size. He had that half-frozen face.

They played to a crescendo. Klemperer's hands trembled. Kay improvised one-handed chords and steadied them.

The piece built to an off-key finish. Klemperer laughed. Kay said, "Please tell me I'm not all that bad."

Klemperer half-slurred. He pushed words and made himself understood.

"Your formal sense exceeds that of most amateurs. You learn very quickly. You interpret passionately, and you will give a successful recital before the end of this decade."

Kay said, "I'm honored." Klemperer banged chords. **Boom, boom, boom.** They were ominous and bluntly repetitive.

261

"German tanks descend upon Leningrad. Dimitri errs on the side of the descriptive and polemical here. He hates Hitler and Stalin equally, you know."

"You should conduct the American premiere. I'm sure Maestro Toscanini would disagree, but you—"

"But I shall preempt him, dear Katherine. The finished score will reach me in advance. Smuggling plans now proceed. I will put together a vast assembly of film-studio musicians. Exorbitant ticket prices will assure vast sums for European war relief."

Kay said, "Don't price out my Police Department friends."

Klemperer laughed. His whole face contorted.

"I will give your suitor Lee Blanchard a free ticket. That is because I saw him beat the piss out of Irish Eddie Gilroy in 1935. Did you know that I enjoy boxing? I will give your Lee a free ticket, because I fear him."

Kay said, "The fight was fixed, **Liebchen.**"

"Then I hereby retract the offer."

Joan waltzed. She felt overmatched. The Sad-as-Shit Blues reappeared. She traipsed back to the yard. A standing bar was set up. She ordered a double scotch mist.

Orson Welles whizzed by and vamped her on the fly. He tapped his wristwatch and mimed **We'll talk later.**

Joan blinked. The Welles vignette consumed .5 seconds. She pulled up a lawn chair. A young woman materialized.

Frizzy-haired. Saul Lesnick's distaff double. Her white gown trailed the ground. The hemline had been trampled. Joan saw footprints.

"I saw you watching my father. He was talking to that Nazi Chink."

"It's Miss Lesnick, is it?"

"It's Andrea, or 19832040. That was my booking number at Tehachapi. I married a butch while I was inside, so that would have made me Mrs. Cahill. It wasn't a real marriage, but it kept the really bad girls off of me."

The Sad-as-Shit Blues, redefined and—

"I was in for vehicular manslaughter, but my daddy turned FBI snitch, and got me sprung as part of the deal."

Too-real reprised.

"Do you always unburden yourself to total strangers at parties?"

Andrea said, "Yes. That's what parties are for. I always come with my daddy. I keep him company while he writes dubious prescriptions for his numerous hophead patients—especially the ones he has qualms about finking off to the Feds."

"Does your daddy supply his patients with liquid morphine?"

Andrea nicked a cigarette. Joan slid the pack over. Andrea dropped it in her purse.

"He supplies a Communist lady named Claire. She throws the best parties, because she's really rich, and a faux Communist. He tattles her to the Feds, and shares it with me. He showed me a naughty film she was in. She had a scene with an actor named 'Captain Hook.' He had this big you know what, shaped like a dousing rod."

Kay walked by. She bypassed Andrea's floor show. Andrea glared at her and made claws.

"I met that girl at Claire's house. Claire hates her. My daddy says she's a police snitch. I always say it takes one to know one."

Joan killed her drink. "Who was that blond girl sitting with your daddy?"

"That's a whore he's fucking. He fucks her and tattles his patients to her. He showed me a lock of her snatch hair."

The Sad-as-Shit Blues. Revised and regurgitated— Joan waltzed.

She ducked back inside. She snagged a Pernod and absinthe and downed it. She saw Doc Lesnick write scripts for Orson Welles and the Maestro. She saw the Chinese quack hobknob with a famous clinician. She made him. It was Terry Lux—"Plastic Surgeon to the Stars." Sid Hudgens called him "Herr Eugenics."

Joan circulated. The weird drinks had her weavy. Lesnick's blond dipped by. Joan followed her outside. The blond ducked behind the guesthouse. Joan crouched behind a banyan tree and peeped her.

The blond pulled off her sweater and blouse. The blond went **Oh shit** and futzed with a microphone taped to her bra.

Bombs away:

Joan walked back to the house. Loudspeakers blared **Tannhäuser.** The ten thousand guests went rouge-cheek opera buffa. Kurt Weill and Lotte Lenya bushwhacked her.

They German-jabbered. They dragged her to a book nook. A projector and movie screen were set up. Opera buffa ghouls whistled and cheered.

Shucks. No Claire De Haven, no Captain Hook. Too bad, but:

Barbara Stanwyck fellated Walter Pidgeon. Carole Lombard and Anna May Wong went 69. Fredric March keestered Norma Shearer. A German shepherd scoped the two-bed action. He looked like Rin Tin Tin and wore a foil leprechaun hat.

Bombs away:

Joan waltzed. Lotte Lenya yelped good-bye. Joan pushed through yet more ghoul swarms and made it back outside.

She caught some air. War-chat cliques mingled. She glanced around. She looked for Kay and didn't see her. She felt voyeuristic and inconsequential.

It was cold. The car valets lugged out coil heaters. Joan hit the stand-up bar and ordered black coffee.

It diluted the oddball drinks and revived her. A bar-side clique formed. Joan heard Spanish and Russian yak-yak.

Saul Lesnick plus two. One man and one woman. They dragged lawn chairs up to a heater and warmed themselves.

Joan pulled up a chair. The woman was dark-haired

and wore klutzy glasses. The man was tall and gone to fat. He wore a Spanish Loyalist greatcoat and tuxedo pants.

Supplicants buzzed the clique. Lesnick played emcee. He introduced the woman. Her name was Jean Staley. The man got no intros. His coat did the job. The supplicants fawned. He was "our Meyer" and "Comrade Gelb."

He stood up and embraced his fans. He employed the Spanish-style **abrazo.** Joan saw his burn-scarred hands. She nailed the full gist then.

The fire. **L.A. Times** coverage. Meyer Gelb fronts the Young Socialist Alliance. The Pershing Square orator. His public rants precede the blaze.

Joan pulled her chair close. Doc Lesnick schmoozed Jean Staley. They came off as old pals.

Jean updated him. She said she flogged real estate. She specialized in ritzy sublets. So many rich people traveled.

Lesnick said, "Don't shit a shitter, Jean. You're a carhop. Your house gig's strictly part-time."

Joan tuned them out. She brushed her chair up against Comrade Gelb's. He turned and looked straight at her.

She said, "It's a pleasure to meet you, Mr. Gelb. I heard you give a speech many years ago. I've never forgotten it."

He appraised her. He did that slow head-to-toe cruise.

"You're very tall. Are you a lesbian volleyball player? It's a shame there's no money in it."

"I was quite young when I heard that speech. High school girls are impressionable, and it was very hot that day. I'll chalk this chance meeting up to disillusionment. You were someone aflame with purpose then, and you're someone bitter now."

Gelb lit a cigarette. He blew smoke too close to her face.

"You've never been to a political rally, and you're not from L.A. Your drawl denotes the northern Midwest. Don't try to jive me, I've been jived by the best."

Joan lit a cigarette. She blew smoke too close to his face.

"It was '33, Comrade. I remember the time vividly. The Griffith Park fire occurred a few days after your speech. My father was a greenskeeper on the golf course. He was lucky to escape with his life."

Gelb twitched and flicked his cigarette. It hit damp grass and fizzled.

Joan said, "It was 'a low, dishonest decade.' That's another line you could have stolen from Auden. 'This storm, this savaging disaster' has got more punch, but the former acknowledges History, which I know you Red shitheels deem essential."

Gelb balled his fists. Joan opened her purse and went for a hat pin.

He spoke soft now. "Who are you?"

She spoke soft now. "I'm a forensic biologist. I work for the Los Angeles Police Department, and I've extensively studied the causal factors of arson and spontaneous wildfires. Which was it in your case? Or did you burn your hands in Spain, where you valiantly battled the fascist beast?"

Gelb bolted. Pure bluff torqued him. He jumped up. He kicked his chair and kicked the coil heater. Joan went **What did I do?** Jean Staley went **Sweetie, that's just Meyer.**

Lesnick chased after Gelb. Joan chased to the bar and chugged scotch. Her pulse dipped to 300-plus.

She walked back to the party proper. The Bauhaus beer hall throbbed. **Parsifal** replaced **Tannhäuser.** That Wagner cat came to work.

Where's Kay? Let's find her. Let's get it over with.

The Maestro Manse ran labyrinthine. Joan cut down hallways and got lost. She traipsed downstairs and upstairs. She hit a third-floor corridor. Steam seeped out a door crack.

She saw Orson Welles and Claire De Haven. They huddled tight and missed her. They wore white cotton robes. They exited a dressing room and entered the steam room. Steam billowed out.

Joan debated it. She plumbed the when-in-Rome concept. She just filleted a Red shitbird. In for a penny, in for—

She stepped into the dressing room. She stripped and hung her clothes beside Claire's. She donned a robe and walked straight to the steam room. The steam was all-the-way hot.

They sat on a top ledge, buck naked. She dropped her robe and sat across from them.

Welles said, "Hi, Red."

Joan said, "Hello, Mr. Welles."

He stage-laughed. It was Falstaff's ho-ho-ho. He said, "This is Claire De Haven."

Joan said, "I'm Joan Conville."

Steam mist covered Claire. Joan squinted. She wanted to see Claire stark nude.

Claire said, "Are you a friend of Otto's, dear?"

Joan gouted sweat. She smelled purged absinthe and scotch.

"I worked at a research lab, up until Pearl Harbor. A doctor I knew there invited me."

Welles said, "Red's a physician. I knew it. Hey, Red—write me a script for pharmaceutical cocaine. I need to curb my appetite and lose weight."

Joan laughed. "You look fine, Mr. Welles."

"Orson, please."

"We're fishing for your occupation, dear. What you currently do for a living."

Catch this, dear. "I work for the L.A. Police Department. I'm a biologist."

Welles said, "Red's a brain. I knew it."

Claire toweled off. Joan caught a look. Her rib cage showed. Her breasts flared unevenly. Her legs were too thin. She was all translucence and veins.

"I know people there. Do the names Hideo Ashida, William Parker, Dudley Smith, and Katherine Lake ring any bells with you?"

A steam vent clicked off. The haze dissipated. Everybody caught looks.

"I work with Dr. Ashida, so I know him rather well.

I know of Captain Parker and Sergeant Smith, but I haven't met them. I don't know Miss Lake at all."

Welles said, "Smith's Claire's new flame. They're shacked up in Mexico now. He's an Irish hothead. He'd shoot me if he knew I'd seen Claire in the buff."

Claire caressed Welles. She ran a hand between his legs. Welles bit his lips and stifled a gasp. Claire eyed Joan throughout.

"Be careful of Dr. Ashida, dear. He's duplicitous and unmanly."

The steam vent kicked back on. The peep show clicked off. Welles coughed out vapors.

"Hey, I'm feeling ignored here."

Joan said, "You'll never be ignored, Orson."

"Are you kidding? In **this** town?"

Claire said, "Orson's set to tour Latin America. Our faux-left president has him eating out of the palm of his hand. It's a cultural mission. Orson's been told to brownnose fascist despots to shore up the Allied cause."

Welles mock-whispered, "This from the lady shacked with a cop who gets his kicks beating up Negroes."

Claire caressed Welles. He moaned and bit his lips. Claire full-on grabbed him. She eyed Joan throughout.

Joan stood up and put her robe on. Welles said, "So long, Red. See you in church."

Claire said, "Are you a police informant, Joan? Did Kay Lake recruit you when I got wise to her?"

Joan stepped outside. She went light-headed and hugged the wall. She stepped into the dressing room and dressed in two seconds flat.

Her pulse dipped crazy high and low. She walked downstairs and got lost. She caught **Lohengrin** blare and cut down a side hallway. She ran straight into Kay Lake.

Kay said, "Isn't this party the most?"

They two-car'd back to the Strip. Kay trailed Joan this time. Dave's Blue Room stayed open late. They rendezvoused there. They noshed steak sandwiches and quaffed gin fizzes.

Joan kept mum per Dudley and Claire. Meyer Gelb, likewise. They wolfed their food. They juiced. Andrea Lesnick had nicked Joan's cigarettes. She smoked out of Kay's pack.

A barman whipped up refills. Brenda A. and Elmer J. owned a house percentage. Kay dined and boozed gratis. They dished the dish and unfurled the hot ticker tape.

Kay said, "I'm wondering what you know that I don't."

Joan said, "I credit everything I hear—because I'm the new girl in town, and I haven't developed a knack for discernment."

"Run one by me. I'll confirm or refute."

"The Fed probe's a shuck. J. Edgar Hoover's a secret fairy. He goes for beefcake types like Ed Satterlee, and they both get their real jollies entrapping Reds."

Kay lit a cigarette. "Don't stop there."

Joan played kamikaze. Her drift featured Dudley and Hideo Ashida.

"The Watanabe job's a frame. The Werewolf looked convenient, so they nailed him. I'll quote your chum Lee Blanchard. 'The PD was running a fever on Pearl Harbor and the internment, so Jack Horrall told the boys to come up with a Jap-kills-Japs solve.'"

Kay whistled and went **woo-woo.** She said, "Here's one you don't know, because Jack H. can hold his mud, and it concerns you. Are you listening?"

Joan said, "Give."

Kay said, "Jack dates Brenda once a week, at her place. It goes back to when Brenda was a line girl. She's his confidante, and he tells her everything. The dish is he goes for you, and he wants you to run the lab and the whole Scientific Division. Ray Pinker's taking a teaching post at Cal Tech in '44. Mind your p's and q's, and the job's yours. You'll be the highest-ranking woman on the PD, and you'll be sworn in as a full-boat police officer. Are you ready? You'll attend the Academy and come out a captain."

The room rolled cockeyed. Joan went breathless. Obscure psalms passed through—

Kay pushed her water glass over. Joan took big gulps.

"He likes my legs. I know that."

"He told Brenda they go on forever."

"I'm better qualified than that."

"Jack's soft on odd people. It's an endearing trait for a crooked police chief."

"I saw that with Hideo Ashida."

Kay said, "Hideo's a twisted little pansy. He framed the Werewolf to get next to Dudley Smith. They put Bill Parker in the middle, and devastated him."

Joan said, "He was devastated, and he did nothing. Bill put his career and the PD's reputation before an innocent man's life, and what will it do to his soul when Shudo goes to the gas chamber?"

Kay crossed herself. She formed the protty cross. She's a prairie Lutheran.

"I know. **Es la verdad, muchacha.**"

Joan squeezed Kay's hands. "So, who tells him? Who holds him when he's terrified and the world veers away from him? Who tells him that certain principles supersede his idiotic ambition?"

Kay laced up their fingers. "You're saying, 'Who gets him?'"

"Yes, I am."

"There's something that Lee used to tell his opponents, before the first-round bell."

"Which was?"

"'Luck, short of winning.'"

Joan drove home. She kept saying it. Captain J. W. Conville, Los Angeles PD.

She kept seeing it. The blue uniform. The silver bars. The rank parity with Dudley and Bill.

Two years from now. 1944. The war might well be over. America would win. She'd be twenty-nine then.

Joan pulled up to her courtyard. A prowl car was parked right in front of her. The driver's window was down.

She walked over and looked in. Bill Parker was passed out in the front seat. A photograph was taped to the dashboard. It was sun-yellowed and bleached.

Winter, '38. Bowler, Wisconsin. Big Earle Conville, shutterbug.

She's sitting on a split-rail fence. She's wearing a plaid shirt, jodhpurs, and lace-up boots. Her shotgun's there in the frame.

Joan looked at Parker. She squared up his glasses and kissed the top of his head. He can't weigh much. He's not tall. He's cumbersome at worst.

She pulled him out of the car and slung him over one shoulder. His gun belt bumped her. She tottered on her stupid high heels.

She lugged him inside her bungalow and laid him down on the bed. She unhooked his gun belt and took off his shoes.

A fresh rainstorm hit. She closed windows and kicked off her shoes. She sat at her desk and crossed herself like Kay did. She opened her lab notebook and wrote **this:**

"For better or worse, I am as one with this man."

40

(LOS ANGELES, 6:00 A.M., 1/29/42)

He came in early. He locked the door. He had the lab free and clear.

He developed photo prints. He enhanced his snapshots of Dudley's bayonet. He close-up shot his gold bar and microphotographed them both. Eureka. The mint marks matched.

Ashida clamped two photo slides and prepped his two-lens microscope. He'd prepared for this. He read gold textbooks and monographs. He gained metallurgical knowledge. He studied forge componentry and learned how gold spun and knit.

The **L.A. Times** supplied facts. Gold-heist sidebars laid out mining data. The stolen bars were forged from one Alaskan lode. He bet on knit bonds identically fused.

Dudley knew nothing of the gold heist and subsequent fire. He determined that at his swearing-in bash. The bayonet was stashed in Kyoho Hanamaka's stash hole. It was the fetishistic apex of his Red/fascist cache.

Ashida dialed the two lenses. They maximum-magnified. He studied knit lines and melt marks and noted flaw patterns. He sifted them through his new knowledge. He concluded **this:**

His bar and Dudley's bayonet. Separate-source items. They comprise a perfect match. They're both gold-heist contraband.

Perfect symmetry. Dudley Smith. All roads intersect.

Ashida heard key-in-lock sounds. Ray Pinker opened the door. He said, "Hello, Lieutenant." He shuffled his feet. He looked mortified.

Ashida said, "Is something wrong, sir?"

Pinker said, "I'm what's wrong. I'm short on lawyer money, so I back-doored you. The Feds have got me cornholed, so I sold the plans for your photo device to the Mexican Staties. A Baja officer named Juan Pimentel brokered the sale."

Ashida sighed. "You didn't have to do that. I'll be stationed in Ensenada. If the Staties require assistance, I'll be happy to provide it."

Pinker sighed. "God bless you, Hideo. And, before you say it, I'll concede that I'm a shitheel. And, before you ask, I'll kick back half the gelt."

Joan Conville walked in. She sidestepped Pinker and Ashida. Pinker skulked back out the door. He dragged his feet. He looked hangdog.

Joan stood at Ashida's desk. She looked in his microscope and adjusted the right- and left-side eyepieces. She dialed tight and saw the two photo blowups. She glimpsed the gold bar that he'd hid from her.

Ashida shut his eyes. He shut out Reckless Girl and Cunning Girl. He braced for her voice.

She said, "Well?"

Ashida opened his eyes. Reckless Girl and Cunning Girl stared him down. **Shameless** Girl. He saw suck marks on her neck.

"We both want the gold. You've withheld from me. That might be a good place to start."

He stammered. His hands twitched. He fought back chills and nausea. He laid out what he'd withheld.

Joan said, "Half the gold's mine. Don't trifle with me. I'll ruin you with Dudley Smith if you do."

41

(LOS ANGELES, 11:00 A.M., 1/29/42)

Annie was **goooooood.** She laid on the gee-whiz. Her tell-me-more, sweetie? The cream de la cream.

Elmer adjusted his headphones. The wire gizmo covered his desk. He kicked his chair back and put his feet up.

The Vice squadroom was yawnsville. Elmer's cubicle cocooned him. He heard party sounds and extraneous voices. Annie laid dat voodoo on old Saul.

She said, "That was Red Claire you were talking to, right? I'll tell you this. She looks like a hophead. I know from hopheads, 'cause my kid brother's one."

Old Saul said, "I'll credit Claire with a certain

courage. She took that Parker and Lake pogrom that I told you about in her stride. Did I tell you that she converted to Catholicism a while back? It softened her regard for Parker, I'm afraid. They attend the same church and confess their specious woes to the same priest. I met the man at one of Claire's tedious mixers. He impressed me as a fruitcake."

Go, Annie, go! You gots me all voyeurizized!

Old Saul hacking-coughed. It fritzed up Elmer's headphones. He said, ". . . and she's prone to grandiose whim. To wit—this brutal cop-beast she's shtupping. Her soul veers right as she poses left, and she thinks I don't notice. To wit—she critiques my friendship with the esteemed racial scientist Lin Chung, who's more politically savvy than ten Claire De Havens at their dilettante best."

Annie lobbed a soft one. Gee-whiz meets sugar pie. "Racial science. It's the same thing as 'eugenics,' right?"

Old Saul harrumphed. "Yes, and in that regard, I must concede that Hitler really does stand as the vanguard of a new world order. Who can fail to applaud his stand on euthanasia and the sterilization of mental misfits? Are we seriously to believe these idiot claims that he's slaughtering Jews en masse? I pose that question as an informed Jew myself, and I'll go on to add that all enlightened people must be ready to accommodate Hitler, should he win the war."

Annie said, "Gee, Saul. You've really given this some serious thought."

Elmer haw-hawed. Go, Annie! Skewer that bug-fucker!

Old Saul said, "Claire accedes to none of this, of course. She accedes to her cop-brute lover and passively condones his horrid beliefs, but she can't comprehend the simple truth as far as Hitler is concerned."

Party noise escalated. Elmer heard strange music. Annie came through, skunked.

"Welles . . . oh, dear . . . he's put on weight."

Old Saul said, "Orson was coddled in his crib and improperly toilet-trained. He wet his bed into his teens and still sucks his thumb when nobody's looking. He eats too much, drinks too much, fucks too much, and sniffs too much cocaine. He's a sucker for flattery and a shill for the OIACC—and every other acronym shuck that FDR's ever dreamed up. Claire's been known to orally copulate him in steam rooms—"

Mike Breuning and Dick Carlisle popped in the door. They looked hot-fevered. Elmer dumped his headphones.

Mike said, "There's a callout. We've got three down at 46th and Central. Thad Brown wants you there."

It was niggertown. It was Code 3, lights and siren. Jack Horrall decreed a hot rush.

Eight vehicles rolled. Lab car/foto car/morgue vans. Newton Station sleds ran escort.

Thad Brown ran the pole car. Breuning and Carlisle

dogged him. Elmer bumper-locked them. Sirens blared god-awful loud.

It was one fucking big cop armada. It rolled east-bound and south. It magnetized street fools. They bug-eyed the white man's hurried-up shit.

Call-Me-Jack was due later. He told Thad to tight-seal the location. It can't be some triple shine killing. Shine killings drew zero heat.

Cop cars made like bumper cars. They siren-blared and snout-bashed civilian cars out of the way. The caravan strafed the jazz-club strip. Elmer gassed on the marquees.

Club Zamboanga, Port Afrique, Club Alabam. Pasteboard music clefs two stories high. Club Zombie, Ivy's Chicken Shack, Mumar's Mosque #3. The Church of the Living Dead and Congregation of the Congo. Rae's Rugburn Room—**the** darktown dyke den.

There's 46th. It's a sharp left turn. Newton blues have got the crib cordoned off.

It's a two-story backhouse. It's dilapidated. The in-front house looks gutted. Note the surrounding crab-grass and discarded short dogs.

The caravan screeched up and braked all in sync. Fenders smashed and locked eight in a row. The blues stepped aside. Plainclothesmen hauled ass straight over and in.

Elmer elbowed up to the front. He got there first. He saw **this:**

It's some jazz fiend/dope fiend/right-wing-geek

klub**haus.** There's two pool tables. There's ratty furniture. There's a terp still. There's a dry bar stocked with Mex mescal and tequila.

There's a phonograph. There's a sax, trombone, and trumpet dumped on a chair. There's smut mags piled beside them. There's Hitler pix taped to the walls. There's Sinarquista flags interspersed.

Thad Brown ran in. Breuning and Carlisle crowded up. It got real hushed inside and real noisy out.

Sirens whooped and cut off. Car doors slammed. Doc Layman ran in. Hideo Ashida and Joan Conville followed. Everybody eyeballed the death crib. Everybody cased the stiffs.

Three dead men. All clothed. Perched upright on one couch. They've got upraised heads and wide open mouths. They're sucking in last gasps of breath.

A low-life Mex.

Officer George Kapek.

Officer Wendell Rice.

42

(ENSENADA, 12:30 P.M., 1/29/42)

Dudley said adios. Long-distance fuzz skunked the call. He got the gist but no context.

Mike called from the Club Alabam. There's three dead in some coontown shithole. Two Alien Squad humps and a Mex rumdum. It might be homicide. It might be terp ODs. Thad Brown's got the command.

Thad formed a crash squad. Mike and Dick from Homicide. Hideo and Joan from the lab. Lee Blanchard and Elmer Jackson from the Alien Squad.

Blanchard was lackluster. Jackson was meddlesome. Elmer's proximity troubled him. It recalled Chinatown, New Year's Eve.

The botched stakeout. Tommy Glennon escapes. He forms a posse. Mike and Dick suit up. Ditto Jackson. Ditto dead cops Kapek and Rice. Add on Catbox Cal Lunceford.

Eddie Leng is snuffed that night. Proximity as destiny. Design within the chaotic.

Dudley spun his desk chair. He orbited his office and applied the brakes. He brooded up the coontown job. Two options appeared.

Possible ODs. That meant cover-up. Dope-fiend cops just would not do. Possible homicide. That meant showcase. It's the PD's first double cop killing. Pull out the stops. Whitewash the victims. Enact justice at all costs.

Sound recent and familiar? It should.

The Watanabe job consumed December. It's late January now. Two-Gun Davis remains volatile and perhaps talkative. He should choose a propitious moment and inform Jack Horrall.

Dudley spun a reorbit. It cleared his head. Juan Pimentel walked in. He clicked his heels and saluted. He placed a grand object on the desk.

Hideo Ashida's photo device. A contraption suffused with true dash.

"You've succeeded in delighting me, Lieutenant. Dr. Ashida's invention has served to revolutionize policework in Los Angeles."

Pimentel reclicked his heels. "Mr. Ray Pinker sold the plans to Captain Vasquez-Cruz, who promptly had the design duplicated. He has already installed three devices at the Tijuana border. We can now photograph license plates as vehicles enter and leave our country."

Dudley pondered the sale. One conclusion popped. Pinker sold the plans covertly. Hideo would have told him otherwise.

"I've had a grand brainstorm, Lieutenant. I would like you to place one of these alongside Kyoho Hanamaka's carport. Stretch the trip wire across the entire circumference and affix three wide-angle lenses. I'm going up there now. I'll bring you back a dimensional drawing."

Pimentel clicked his heels. He clicked elegantly and often. Heel clicks punctuated his dutiful young life.

"A question before you go, Lieutenant."

"Sir?"

"I would call your dislike and distrust of Captain Vasquez-Cruz plainly apparent. Am I correct here?"

Pimentel clicked. "Sir, you are vastly correct."

He brought the bayonet. He undressed in the hidey-hole and donned Nazi black. The gold shaft caught lamplight and threw his image back. He rewrote History a tad.

The Blitz. Evil London burns. Irish Republicans light bonfires to guide Luftwaffe bombers. He's there to watch.

Salvy Abascal joins him. They're dressed in Sinarquista green. Joan Conville's their consort. She's green-clad. She wears her Scottish clan's tartan sash.

They've had one night together. He's learned a few things. The scientist-empiricist shares his mystical streak. She's as death-derived as he is. He told her of the Wolf he met on the British moors. She did not doubt the Wolf's occasional visitations. He touched her clothing while she slept. He became the Wolf chasing her scent.

She's as man-bound and father-bound as he's bound to his mother and women. She rages to kill the man who burned her father dead. She's told him some things. He's made a few queries. He shares her suspicions of mad inventor Mitchell Kupp.

Burned Londoners run toward them. They resemble Joan's father felled by scorched trees. Joan wields the gold bayonet. It's both merciful and brutally just.

She's his sister-lover now. Her conduit-to-Bill Parker status may or may not play out. He will help her take a man's life. Salvy Abascal saved his own life. He's Joan's half brother and his own full one. He demands respect and commands scrutiny.

Salvy killed Victor Trejo Caiz. It was an act performed with bold premeditation. They spoke briefly after Father Coughlin's broadcast. Their touchstone is shared ideology. Salvy wants something from him. This seductive dimension will soon be revealed. There's a Sinarquista rally in Ensenada tonight.

Lover-sisters/brothers/daughters/sons—

Beth is due for a visit. He'll pair her off with Joan Klein and commend them to mischief. Young Joan pilfers from stores. She's pilfered bland SIS memos and cabled them to her "Comrades" in New York. She asked him to teach her how to shoot a gun. They had a father-daughter jaunt on the beach.

Young Joan blasted driftwood with his .45. A sidearm vanished from the armory the next day.

Young Joan to Young Juan. The snappy heel clicker and pay phone–tap whiz. The tireless surveiller of this selfsame hideaway.

He read Juan Pimentel's personnel file. He noted Class A fitness reports and a pithy biographical aside.

Pimentel resigned a war college posting. He defamed President Cárdenas' anti-Church policies. Lieutenant Juan is devoutly Catholic and pro-Sinarquista.

Salvy will address a large crowd tonight. **El Flaco Explosivo** will surely explode.

Dudley swung the gold bayonet.

Where's Kyoho Hanamaka?

A nice heart attack would rectify the Two-Gun Davis glitch.

Joan must miss him. He'll send the Wolf by to sleep at the foot of her bed.

Young Joan showed off her pin map. The Russian campaign wowed her. Her people hailed from that neck of the woods.

They sat on Dudley's terrace. Claire was off at afternoon Mass. Young Joan had nicked an atlas and tore out the Russian spread. She nicked the pins from the SIS squadroom.

Little swastikas for the Nazis. Hammer and sickles for the martyred USSR.

A grand child. Perhaps psychopathic. Only time would tell.

She said, "The green swastikas represent armored battalions. The blue ones represent troop movements, and the penciled-in **X**s represent the Germans' retreat from Moscow. The red pins show the Home Guard dug in."

"You get your war news from the radio, do you?"

"XERB. I know some Spanish now, but I base my troop movements on the English-language broadcasts."

Dudley lit a cigarette. Young Joan nicked one just to nick one. She didn't smoke.

"No more stealing memorandums to impress your chums back home. Keep the gun you stole, but don't steal any others. Since you know damn well how softhearted I am, I'm offering you a job as a consolation prize."

Young Joan said, "That sounds intriguing."

She mimicked Claire's inflections. She invaded Claire's closets and tried on her clothes. He'd caught her at it.

"Your Aunt Claire finds Captain Vasquez-Cruz suspicious, and I must say I agree. I've requisitioned a great many police files, and I don't have time to go through them. I'd like you to. Study them and look for pictures and notations pertaining to the captain. I'll pay you, of course."

Young Joan said, "You're a pal, Uncle Dud."

They shook hands on the deal. She pinned a green swastika to his necktie. Dudley roared.

Avenida Ruiz was blocked off and torch-lit. Blackshirt Staties and Greenshirt Sinarquistas mingled. The crowd numbered some six hundred. Dudley stood at the back.

He wore his Class A uniform. He retained the swastika tiepin for giggles and grins. He stood near men with coiled-snake armbands and women in green twill frocks.

He caught a nap at the hotel. A dream placed him in the Maestro Manse, among gargoyles. Beethoven and Wagner busts sprang to life.

A long-distance call roused him. Mike Breuning reports:

The darktown crib remains chaotic. It's still undetermined—homicide or terp ODs. Mike braced Thad Brown on Elmer Jackson. Thad said, "He worked the Alien Squad with Kapek and Rice. I want him in on this."

The call disconnected. Something vague tweaked him. He'd heard of the death crib. He can't recall where or when.

Cheers went up. Salvy Abascal took the stage. It was built from tin cans and lashed-up orange crates.

El Flaco held a microphone. It was hooked up to a '32 Ford. A Statie sergeant ran the engine and sparked the battery. **Flaco** let loose.

He spoke Spanish. The microphone cut in and out. Dudley quick-translated and still lost bursts of text. The shrieking crowd further blitzed comprehension. Nobody heard a thing the man said.

Dudley gave up sound for sight. Salvy gave the crowd Weimar Berlin, reborn. His gestures urged them to listen to their one united voice and imagine what it was saying. He swayed on rickety orange crates and held a dead microphone. He spoke the truth in the crowd's one voice.

It extended. It remained vitalist. Salvy swayed and made the crowd speak in his voice. Dudley supplied his own words. He began with the Book of Revelation and worked backward. Salvy stopped and he stopped with **this:**

God gave Noah the rainbow sign. No more water—the fire next time.

43

(LOS ANGELES, 9:00 P.M., 1/29/42)

They stood nine hours in. Thad Brown ran the Crash Squad. Nobody sleeps till I give the word.

Newsmen swarmed outside. Brown nixed them inside. It's the PD's first double cop snuff. That's the urgent gist and newsprint hook here.

Arc lights glared outside. Cops and lab folk swarmed inside. Doc Layman left to testify in court. He was Crash Squad–adjunct. Hideo Ashida ran the lab slot. Joan backed him up.

Newton blues roped off 46th Street. They cordoned Central to the west and Hooper to the east. Newsmen hopped backyard fences and got though regardless. Radio scribes spieled right there in the yard. Said yard was trampled past all forensic hope.

Joan stepped outside. She gobbled aspirin and dosed a solvent-fume headache. Breuning and Carlisle ducked past her. They ran in and out. Ashida and Brown stuck inside. Lee Blanchard was canvassing. Elmer Jackson booked off somewhere. He'd redubbed the "death crib" the "klub**haus**." The news fools lapped it up.

Joan lit a cigarette. Arc light glare torqued her headache. She caught newshound jabber. Dumb comments overlapped.

It's a shine caper. Coons off the jazz strip. You've got a skirt and a Jap on the job. The Dudster and Whiskey Bill should have a piece of this. They scored good on them Watanabe snuffs.

"The Skirt and the Jap." The news ghouls loved it. She ran her own Skirt-and-Jap riff. The punch line reverb'd.

Half the gold's mine. Don't trifle with me. I'll ruin you with Dudley Smith if you do.

Ashida trembled then. She acted then. She typed a note to the Santa Barbara Sheriff's. She forged Ray Pinker's signature and demanded **this:**

"Photostat the gold-heist file. Do it now. Priority expedite."

Then, this callout. Then, all this grief.

They'd worked nine straight hours. She dusted touch-and-grab surfaces and got all smudges and smears. She elimination-printed all the blues and detectives. Ashida photographed the klub**haus** interior. The bodies remained on the couch. The Mex remained un-ID'd.

She combed a two-block radius. She jotted vehicle descriptions and plate numbers. She brushed up against jazz-club habitués. Negroes and Mexicans with big conks and hairnets. They made faces and coochie-coo'd her. She blew that Indian's foot off for less.

Joan tossed her cigarette. She was hungry. Thad Brown just called Kwan's. He ordered eight pupu platters and four fifths of hooch.

Jumped-up jazz echoed. The Club Zombie and Club Alabam stood forty yards off. A big sedan bucked the west cordon and bumped up on the curb. The driver leaned on the horn. Jack Horrall got out.

The newshounds cheered. A radio man held his mike up to catch the kerfuffle. Call-Me-Jack hopped the gate. He tried to look somber and tanked. He was a huckster. He lived for this.

He held up his hands. He went **Thank you, thank you.** He almost but not quite grinned.

The newsmen simmered down. Call-Me-Jack shook fifty hands in ten seconds. Joan pushed in close. Jack saw her and went **woo-woo!**

He pushed two flat palms down and got instant **ssshhh.** He looked up at God and down at his feet. He tried to look humble and tanked. He looked straight at the newsmen and launched his spiel.

"It's a sad occasion any way you slice it, but we don't know if it's homicide or not. We haven't ID'd the Mex yet, but our two late policemen are Officer Wendell D. Rice, age thirty-four, and Officer George B. Kapek, age thirty-six. Officer Rice came on in '28, and Officer Kapek came on in '30. They are survived by their lovely wives, Mrs. Vera Rice and Mrs. Dorothea Kapek. They've got a whole brood of kids between them, but I'm not sure how many. Our prayers go out to the bereaved families of these two fine young policemen, and to the Mexican's family, if he had one."

The newsmen clap-clapped. Call-Me-Jack re-launched his spiel.

"Here's a tidbit you boys will enjoy. We're reviving the all-league team that solved the baffling Watanabe murders last month, with a few exceptions and one addition. Sergeant Dudley Smith's battling the Fifth Column in Mexico now, but he's sure as you know what here in spirit. We've got Captain Bill Parker to ride herd, Lieutenant Thad Brown to run the show, Sergeants Mike Breuning and Dick Carlisle from Homicide, and two close pals of the dead men— Officer Lee Blanchard and Sergeant Elmer Jackson— from the Alien Squad. Big Lee was once a ranked heavyweight contender, so you reporters better be nice to this white man's PD."

Haw-haws rose and fell. Call-Me-Jack did the flat-palms bit.

"Last but not least, we've got Sergeant Turner Meeks, detached from Robbery. All you Western-movie fans know Buzz. He's played in a lot of those oaters they shoot out in the Valley. He never gets the girl, but he always gets the horse. Maybe one day he'll get lucky."

The Meeks jive drew laughs. It cued Meeks his own self. He jumped out of the Chief's sedan and jumped through the gate. That drew more laughs. He saw Joan and jumped straight her way.

He said, "Will you go to Acapulco with me?"

Joan looked down at him. She patted his head. She said, "No, you're too short."

That drew the **biiiiiig** laughs. Meeks doubled over. Newsmen pulled their notebooks and wrote up the shtick.

44

(LOS ANGELES, 10:30 P.M., 1/29/42)

Dr. Nort shooed the cops out. They hit the yard and mingled with the press. Sid Hudgens made a liquor-store run and juiced the whole gang.

Breuning and Carlisle dished out stale rumaki. Thad Brown sloshed bourbon in coffee cups. Buzz Meeks snoozed on the grass. Lee Blanchard was off canvassing. Elmer Jackson plain vanished.

Ashida walked back inside and cased the dead men. He'd photographed them at 1:00 p.m. and re-shot them at 8:00. They were rigor-locked and lightly livid the first time. They were full stiff now. Blood expanded their ankle and foot tissues. That meant they died sitting down.

Dr. Nort wheeled up an arc light. He strapped a surgeon's lamp around his forehead.

"We're not here to strictly determine cause of death, unless something jumps up and bites us. I'll do the formal autopsies at the morgue. This is a triple the likes of which I've never seen. I'd like to examine them within the context of this equally unique place we have here."

Joan said, "I haven't even begun the inventory."

Ashida said, "You have three men, near-identically posed. That suggests that the killer or killers rearranged their bodies postmortem."

Dr. Nort shook his head. "Yes, to an indeterminate degree. But the first thing that comes to mind for me is that they all appear to have died while struggling for breath, which suggests three men, insensate from the ingestion of narcotics, who died of toxic exsanguination within short intervals of one another."

Joan said, "They would have flailed then, Doctor. There's a certain symmetry in the way they're posed on the couch."

Ashida tugged the Mexican's left biceps. He got no flex and no give.

"The approximate time of death, sir?"

Dr. Nort said, "I took rectal temperatures the moment I got here. I'm calling it 2:00 to 4:00 a.m."

Ashida deployed Man Camera. He panned the couch and framed the three men. He studied their clothes first.

The Mexican wore slit-bottom khakis and black leather oxfords with crepe soles. Plus a white undershirt and striped zoot coat. Crepe-sole oxfords were burglars' shoes.

Rice wore brown wingtips and gray flannel slacks.

He wore a cross-draw belt gun on his left hip. Plus a blue sport coat and loud Hawaiian shirt.

Ashida extrapolated. The Man Camera revealed **this:**

No wedding ring on Rice's left-ring finger. An indentation where wedding rings normally sit. Rice was married. Rice removed his ring to hide the fact. Rice was a tomcat.

Kapek wore a green cardigan and navy dungarees. His footwear seemed anomalous. He wore patent-leather pumps.

Ashida extrapolated. The Man Camera revealed **this:**

They were dancing shoes. The klub**haus** adjoined a jazz strip. Officer George B. Kapek was a jitterbug.

Dr. Nort said, "Our Hideo's worked himself into a trance."

Joan said, "It's a study technique. I learned it in grad school."

Ashida stepped back and aimed off the couch. He framed a coffee table and strafed a glass ashtray. It was filled with spent matches and cigarette stubs.

Ashida extrapolated. The Man Camera revealed **this:**

There are more matches than stubs. The ashtray appears freshly wiped.

Ashida said, "I've spotted an inconsistency. We have a freshly washed-out ashtray, filled with cigarette butts. I've counted twenty-four butts and twenty-seven expended matches. That's three more than we have butts for, and we have three potential homicide victims."

Joan examined the ashtray. "I'll extrapolate. The killer wants to remove incriminating evidence, yet retain what I'll call 'forensic normalcy' here in the klub**haus.** He removes the three butts and washes the ashtray. Now, I'll hazard a guess. Our victims, who might not **be** victims, but just inadvertent bunglers, smoked liquid terp in hand-rolled cigarettes. It's the butts themselves that appear anomalous. The killer removed the hand-rolled butts and wiped the ashtray to eliminate all traces of liquid terpin hydrate."

Dr. Nort cracked a smile. Ashida balled his fists. Reckless Girl usurped his thesis.

"There's a terp still here on the premises. We should determine the molecular makeup of the drug that remains in the feeder vats. Dr. Layman can check it against any terpin hydrate he might find in the victims' bloodstreams."

Dr. Nort whistled. He went **Whoa, now.**

"Let's not jump the gun. We don't know for sure that they're victims. And we don't know that smoked terpin hydrate killed them."

Joan approached the couch. She reached down and turned out Wendell Rice's front pants pockets. They were empty. Imperious Girl. Ashida balled his fists.

Dr. Nort said, "You're looking for rolling papers."

Joan nodded. She turned out the Mexican's front pants pockets. They were empty. She turned out George Kapek's front pants pockets. She pulled out a cigarette-paper deck.

Dr. Nort went all gaga. Reckless Girl did that to men.

Ashida rearranged the corpses. He turned out their back pockets and got lint balls and nothing else.

Joan said, "We confiscated a still from that man Don Matsura's apartment. Remember, Dr. Ashida? He committed suicide at the Lincoln Heights Jail."

Dr. Nort shook his head. "We're getting ahead of ourselves. They could have bought terp at any one of the clubs half a block from here. Let's have this discussion after my postmortem."

Ashida leaned over the couch. He worked three across. He grabbed the dead men by the hair and looked in their wide-open mouths. The room light was just right. He saw inflamed lesions.

Dr. Nort leaned down. He adjusted his headband light. He close-up lit the mouth cavities. He stepped back and stretched.

"Precancerous lesions. All three men. Similar levels of inflammation, of a type common to habitual terp smokers."

Thad Brown and Buzz Meeks walked over. They'd huddled up to watch.

Meeks said, "What about maryjane? They spray the crops with chemicals down in Mexico, then the grasshoppers up here got to contend with all kinds of medical grief."

Brown said, "Toss the place, Buzz. Look for mary-jane, and tag any contraband you find."

Meeks clumped upstairs. Brown poked around. He had well-known eagle eyes.

He scoped a pile of hate tracts and the Hitler wall pix. He touched the sax and trombone on the chair. He went through phonograph records. He ran his hands under the couch and pulled out a matchbook.

Ashida stepped close. Brown opened the matchbook. Half the matches were gone. They'd been removed left to right.

Brown held the matchbook out. Joan stepped close. Ditto Dr. Nort.

Brown said, "Southpaw. It's something or it's nothing, but it's not a bad elimination lead."

Ashida aimed his Man Camera. He framed the dead men. He close-up shot their hands. He caught your standard size discrepancy.

"They were all right-handed. Their right hands are larger and more muscularly developed."

Dr. Nort said, "Kapek and Rice wore their belt guns on the left. That connotes a right-hander's cross-draw."

Brown checked out the matchbook. Club Zamboanga/yellow-and-black type/a snarling panther motif.

"Blanchard's out canvassing. He's supposed to meet up with Elmer. They'll check the Zamboanga, for sure."

Meeks banged on the upstairs floorboards. He sent up a racket. His voice boomed down.

"No maryjane! Nothing but a whole shitload of disarray!"

Ashida pointed to the ashtray. "I'm positing a fourth man. I understand that it's precipitous, but please indulge me. I'm thinking that he fashioned hand-rolled cigarettes but did not partake."

Dr. Nort shrugged. "All right, I'll play. Maybe it's terp, maybe it's not. It could have been a toxic level of some other inebriant that I'll determine at autopsy."

Joan braced the couch. She leaned close and circled it. She worked three across.

She clamped heads, three across. She studied them. She came up behind the couch. She reverse-angled the process and said, "There's something here."

Ashida leaned in. Dr. Nort and Thad Brown watched. Joan pointed to **this:**

A blood dot below George Kapek's left ear.

Ashida look-see'd. It was less than a puncture/more than a pinprick.

Joan slid man to man. Showy Girl struts and poses. She pointed below Wendell Rice's left ear. The Mexican, likewise. She nailed identical dots. They were less than punctures/more than pinpricks.

Thad Brown said, "Mother dog."

Dr. Nort said, "If he came at them from behind, he had to have been left-handed."

Joan said, "These are in no way killing wounds. They barely penetrate the skin, and they don't correspond to visible veins at all."

Ashida pointed three across. "It could be a coerced

ingestion of a lethal substance. The killer per-
suaded them by the means of a sharp instrument at
their necks."

Brown wiped his glasses on his necktie. He put
them back on and peered extra close.

"Here's a guess. They were partially debilitated already. That's the only way I can see one man taking
out three. And there's no dust on that matchbook,
smack in the middle of this shitty little dust hole.
That means it was shoved under the chair recently."

Dr. Nort shrugged. "Maybe the killer had accom-
plices. Maybe we should concede that all of this is
suppositional and may have no bearing on the matter
at hand."

Joan smiled. "Dr. Nort's being a killjoy, so I'll add
that those dots look like icepick markings I've seen in
Crim One texts."

Ashida got bristles and chills. Watch this, colleagues. Brilliant Boy shows off.

He pulled down George Kapek's shirt collar. Ditto
for the Mexican and Wendell Rice. He laid their
necks bare. It revealed **this:**

Single hand-span bruises. All right-handed/all applied from behind. Thumb marks on the left side of
their necks. Finger-grab marks on the right.

"I don't know how they died, but he held them
steady with his right hand and held the ice pick with
his left. A left-hander would favor that hand for such
a task."

Joan said, "Single-hand strangulations are very rare.

It might have been two men applying force from both the front and the back."

Dr. Nort said, "All right, I concede. Call the Chief, Thad. It's homicide."

45

(LOS ANGELES, 11:00 P.M., 1/29/42)

Local jazzcats made him. They sniffed grief and gave him dat **wiiiiiiiiiiiiiide** berth. He magnetized resentment. He percolated fear and hate.

Elmer walked the strip. He felt underdressed. His squarejohn suit clashed with all the full-drape zoots. Lots of cats and kittens, lots of saucy dash. Coloreds, beaners, whites. The Dark Continent jumps tonite!!!

Peace, my dusky brethren. I'm as hopped up as you are. It started New Year's Eve—but it be exploding HERE.

The Sinarquista flag at the klub**haus.** The Sinarquista stencil in Tommy G.'s room. The Sinarquista tattoo on Eddie Leng. The terp still in the klub**haus.** The terp still in Don Matsura's apartment. Matsura's jail "suicide." Matsura's KA'd up with Eddie Leng and Lin Chung. Two Alien Squad hard-ons. Said hard-ons now **muerto.** Don't dis shit read Fifth Column to you?

Elmer loitered at 47th and Central. Kool kats and kittens skunk-eyed him. He caught blare-blasted music. He smelled whorehouse perfume and spattered grease.

Lee Blanchard was due. They had late-nite canvass duty. Elmer loitered and brain-broiled His Big Case.

He blew out of the klub**haus.** He went AWOL. He got this wild bug up his ass. Let's detonate this whole fucker. He drove to his place and got to work.

He called the Vice clerk he braced New Year's Eve. He told him to keep mum and promised him five yards. He said, "You never ran them phone numbers I troubled you with." The clerk pledged **silencio.**

Oooga-booga. Let's blow this klub**haus** job straight to shit.

Elmer studied Tommy G.'s address book. He got Tommy's block-print style down pat. He spiced up the book. He drew swastikas and Sinarquista snakes. He added right-wing thunderbolts. He skimmed phone books and got some choice numbers. PC Bell shot him unlisteds. He forged and spawned chaos then.

Tommy's book ran provocative from jump street. It listed St. Vib's, the Deutsches Haus, Dudster snitch Huey Cressmeyer. You had unknown cooze Jean Staley and homo priest Joe Hayes. You had the hotbox phone by the **Herald.** You had fourteen Baja pay phones. Now, let's add **this:**

Lin Chung. Low-rent plastic surgeon/dope peddler/ Fifth Column shitbird.

Orson Welles. Hotshot actor-director/quasi-Red flotsam/finked-out patient of Dr. Saul Lesnick.

Dr. Saul himself. Red tool/Fed snitch/Annie Staples' fatmouth trick. Headshrink and morph pusher to Claire De Haven.

Wallace N. Jamie. Nosebleed PI/Fletch Bowron confrere/rumored Fed-probe indictee.

He spiced up Huey Cressmeyer's listing. He drew swastikas and coiled snakes beside it. Huey was Tommy's bun boy at Preston. He wrote "Big Dick!!!!!" and drew Cupid's heart and arrow. He printed "T.G. & H.C." inside it. The whole address-book fantasia was some unholy shit.

He drove back to the klub**haus.** The joint was abuzz. Dr. Nort tagged the job Murder One.

He walked upstairs. He planted Tommy's address book under a carpet strip. He hoofed out to meet Blanchard. He got the I'm-fucking-with-Dudley Smith chills.

Elmer loitered. A floor show unfolded upside him. Kolored kats bopped into a hair-process joint. Eight barbers worked the late shift. The kats slipped into chairs and donned hair-suction gizmos. They sat down kinky and stood up straight.

Blanchard showed. They walked the strip and tossed queries. That backhouse on 46th? Who owns it/who rents it/what's the secret story here?

They braced street strollers and ducked into nitespots. They got **Huh?/Beats me/Say what?** They got rebop per Jew landlords raping the black man. They hit jazz joints and rib cribs. They hit liquor stores and pool halls and Minnie Roberts' Casbah. They got more, more, and more of the same.

They witnessed a shiv show at Port Afrique. Two jigs swapped swipes. A he-she whore watched and shrieked. A jazz trio laid down knife-fight riffs. Elmer dug the sax wails that mimicked screams. Blanchard told the barman to call an ambulance.

They ducked out and ducked into Club Zombie. Note the rhinestone-studded walls. The stones depicted the solar system and rocket ships zooming. They were open-cockpit. Spooks with red lightbulb eyes jockeyed them.

Small tables fronted a bandstand. Mixed-race lovebirds spooned. High-yellow girls served drinks. They wore tiger-striped leotards.

Elmer glimpsed Mud-Shark Bill McPherson. The DA hosted two bronze cuties. He saw Elmer and waved. Elmer waved back. Blanchard pulled him up to the bar.

A tall jig tended it. A jumbo conk put him up at six-ten. A wall sign extolled the Baron Samedi cocktail. "One sip leaves you zombified."

Elmer and Blanchard grabbed stools. The jig ambled up. He once-over'd Blanchard and smirked.

"I saw you fight Andre McCoover. He punked your white ass, but you got the decision. I hope you ain't here for information on no one near and dear to me."

Blanchard grabbed the jig's conk and jammed his face into the bar. The jig flailed and knocked over ashtrays and drinks. Bar patrons scrammed. Elmer snatched the jig's left hand and bent his fingers back.

"There's a shitty little backhouse on 46th, just east of Central. We want to know who owns it, who rents it, and who owns the vacant house in front. You got two choices here. Give us something we can work with, or get zombified."

The jig squirmed. He blubbered and dug for façade. Blanchard smashed his head on the bartop. Nose bones broke audible. Blood burst and pooled.

Elmer said, "We're listening."

The jig screeched. Elmer bent his fingers. The jig coughed blood and coughed up **this:**

"Jew landlords own most of them cribs. . . ."

"But not that one."

"This preacher, Martin Luther Mimms . . ."

"This back-to-Africa con . . ."

"Congregation of the Congo—47th, down the strip."

It's a storefront church. There's big plate-glass windows. There's pews from here to Mozambique. It's lit bright at 1:30 a.m.

The door's wide open. Some dink artist muraled the walls.

Pygmies spear-hunting lions. Hunchbacked Jews in skullcaps lugging money sacks. L.A. in flames. White folks roasted alive. Colored folks butt-fucking them with hot pokers. A flotilla of back-to-Africa seacraft. The destroyer USS **Negro.** The battleship **Colored Man's Triumph.** PT 69—replete with colored folk engaged in that selfsame act.

Elmer looked at Blanchard. Blanchard looked at Elmer. They went **Holy shit** in sync.

They bopped in and bopped up to the altar. A colored man and white man counted collection-plate cash.

The colored man was heavyset and cleaved close to fifty. The white man was twenty-three, tops. He was tall and fit. He wore a Navy ensign's uniform, with flyboy wings. He smoked a corncob pipe.

Elmer badged them. The screwy duo made nice-nice. They dropped their cash count and laid down handshakes. It settled everyone's hash.

The colored man said, "I'm Martin Luther Mimms. You can call me 'Reverend' or 'Rev.' "

The white boy said, "Link Rockwell."

Mimms chided him. "George **Lincoln** Rockwell. Be proud of that. Your namesake freed the slaves."

Rockwell pipe-jabbed the Rev. It came off re-hearsed. They worked their salt-and-pepper act.

"A dubious distinction, sir—especially coming from a well-known slave driver like yourself."

Mimms took the cue. "Link thinks I'll reinstate the Dred Scott decision over on African soil. Colored folk as chattel, to do with as I wish. I'll have them excavating gold from secret mines in Zimbabwe. I'll be putting the boots to the best-looking yellows and putting the horns on their men."

Blanchard jiggled a cash plate. "Business is good. Huh, Rev?"

Mimms cued Rockwell. "This is Officer Lee Blanchard. He was once billed as 'the Southland's good but not great white hope.'"

Rockwell tapped his pipe on the pulpit. "You should fight Joe Louis, Officer Blanchard. A white man deserves a shot at the crown."

Elmer harrumphed. "We had some questions, Rev."

Mimms grinned. "I'll be pleased to answer them, in my sanctum sanctorum. If you'll follow me."

Elmer and Blanchard swapped looks. Link Rockwell resumed his cash count. Mimms played pontiff and strode on ahead. Elmer gassed on his act. He sucker punched the white man and called all the shots.

Mimms waked to a side door and swung it open. Elmer and Blanchard caught up. The room was knotty pine–paneled. The walls were foto-festooned. The Rev's desk was eight feet long and all knick-knacked. It featured big-dick crocodiles and pygmy-goddess statuettes.

Mimms said, "My people will be knee-deep in zebra shit by this time next year. The USS **Negro** will be sailing about then. We've got to be watchful, though. Hitler's U-boats pervade the Atlantic, and are ever alert to torpedo Allied shipping. Let me state for the police record that I've got no beef with the **Führer,** and that I admire his subjugation of the Jews, the colored man's traditional foe."

Blanchard cleared his throat. "We appreciate your hospitality, daddy—but there's still some questions we've got to ask."

Elmer orbed the wall pix. Oh, yeah. They explicate some shit.

There's the young Mimms. He's standing with the young Jack Horrall. They're doughboys. Jack's a major. Mimms wears captain's bars.

There's colored cops in formation. There's Mimms with Fletch Bowron. There's Mimms with our mud-shark DA.

Blanchard scoped the wall pix. He went **Man-O-Manischewitz.**

Mimms said, "As you can see, Jack Horrall and I go back. He commanded a colored battalion, and I was his staff adjutant. I might add that we've stayed in touch, and that I get my people on your police department—for prudent remuneration, of course."

Blanchard cracked his knuckles. "Sounds like a sweet deal."

Mimms said, "Let colored police colored. Keep colored south of Slauson until the pilgrimage begins. Keep your colored cops south of Slauson, where they know the turf."

Elmer winked. "That's white of you."

Mimms guffawed. Blanchard said, "We've got these questions. We know you own that backhouse on 46th, and you must have got the word by now."

Elmer flashed his foto spray. PD pix of Rice and Kapek. The Mex, DOA.

Mimms studied them. Mimms went **nix.**

Elmer said, "Tell us about the backhouse. Two cops were killed there."

Mimms popped his suspender straps and pulled himself tall. Hold for a sermonette.

"I own fourteen houses in these parts, and half of them have backhouses that have come to be utilized as playpens by unruly elements. Over the years, the backhouses have been taken over by my acolytes, all of whom live squeaky-clean. The only exception is my backhouse on East 46th. It's a place where coloreds, spics, and ofay hepcats congregate, hold jam sessions, and are assured of the privacy they require to drink and fuck in peace. That particular clubhouse took on a political bent—but as long as it isn't the Reds or the Klan, I don't give a rat's ass. The front house has been empty for a while—but I'll find a new tenant sooner or later."

Elmer said, "Let me guess. All your tenants pay in cash, and you don't keep written records."

Mimms said, "That is correct."

Blanchard said, "Let me guess. You'll beef us to Jack Horrall if we start poking too deep into your financial shit."

Mimms said, "That is correct."

Elmer relit his cigar. "Who specifically rents this backhouse? Who pays the rent every month?"

Mimms snapped his suspenders. "As stated, I keep no records and recall no specific names. The clubhouse denizens pay in cash, and anonymous cholos drop off the gelt on the first of the month. I would guess that the habitués take up a collection."

Blanchard said, "There's a terp still on the premises. That's illegal."

Mimms resnapped his suspenders. "I don't condone terp. I exhort my people to live clean."

Blanchard lit a cigarette. "The dump's full of Nazi regalia."

"You had best check with the fearsome Gestapo and the illustrious SS about that. And, once again, let me state that I bear no grudge against the Nazis— but the Reds and the Klan bear the full brunt of my enmity."

Elmer blew smoke rings. "What about the Sinarquistas?"

Mimms said, "Tacoheads and fools from the gate. Just another copycat movement trying to piggyback Adolf Hitler and make hay while the zeitgeist bends their way. I would advise them to refine their wardrobe, though. Green doesn't cut it. You've got to go with basic black, and snazzy armbands."

46

(ENSENADA, 10:00 A.M., 1/30/42)

Green twill and black leather. The green connotes Ireland and Mexico. The black boldly stamps Sinarquismo. It's a right-wing affront.

Starched green twill. Cut to fit him. Shirt, necktie, pants. Stiff black leather. Boots, holster, belt. A red-white-and-black armband. It stamps resurgent realpolitik.

Dudley sat in his office. The squad bay buzzed bilingual. Army noncoms and Staties shared desk space. Anti-Jap fever raged.

He just missed **El Flaco.** He found this grand ensemble placed on his desk. Salvy came and went, **rápidamente.**

The courtship continues. Salvy bears gifts. There's still unanswered questions. They're couched in unstinting rapport.

Victor Trejo Caiz planned to kill him. How did Salvy know? Salvy **understands** him. How much does Salvy know and where did he learn it?

The squad bay bustled. Japs, Japs, Japs. The internment push roared. Dudley shut his door and muzzled the blare.

He touched green twill and black leather. He rolled the armband on and off his left sleeve. He decided to stage a dress rehearsal. He'd don Salvy's gift and pose in K. Hanamaka's lair.

He'd utilize his secret fashion runway. He'd wear Sinarquista green and black SS kit. He'd swing the gold bayonet.

The Teletype clacked and popped a page into his tray. Dudley snatched it and skimmed it. Fourth Interceptor blared cautionary drift.

L.A. defense plants targeted/Red Alert imposed. Secret air bases in San Berdoo County/Red Alert imposed. Jap sub berthings in Baja/Red Alert imposed. L.A. pay-phone communiqués decoded. Jap air attack on L.A. predicted. Red Alert: hold for late February.

Dudley teethed on it. Red Alert/Jap Alert/alarmist rhetoric. He was Japped to the gills. The Statie jail was Japped, floor-to-rafters. Jap overflow was Japped up in slum cribs Baja-wide. Statie goons tortured Japs for hot leads and kicks.

He called the Ventura County Sheriff. He offered him bribe cash and proposed a sub-rosa deal. House Baja Japs on county work farms. Bunk them in horse stalls. Rent them out as stoop labor. We'll split the money.

The Sheriff agreed. Dudley called José Vasquez-Cruz and cut him in on the deal. José said he'd oversee the inmate transfer. Their racket front now bears fruit.

Japs, Japs, Japs.

Slant-eyed intruders. They haunt his dreams. The Wolf stalks them across the Baja plains. Where's

Kyoho Hanamaka? No one has visited his mountain hideaway. Juan Pimentel surveills it. Hideo Ashida's photo device has snapped no license plates. Lieutenant Juan tortures Japs. Where's Kyoho Hanamaka? None of the Japs knows shit.

Japs, Japs, Japs.

Fourth Interceptor's besieging SIS. Major Melnick's crawling up his ass. Interdict coastal sabotage without further delay.

Juan Pimentel has chartered a twin-engine plane. They'll cruise the coastline later today. They'll scan for sub berths and dip south to Magdalena Bay. They'll swoop by the Sinarquista encampment.

Japs, Japs, Japs.

The Wolf hunts Japs in his dreams. The Wolf rips them and eats them and shits them out, postmortem. Last night's dream dissolved a memory glitch.

The Wolf cornered an unruly Jap. The Wolf said something's troubling my old pal Dudley Smith. There's a backhouse/klub**haus** on East 46th. Herr Dudley thinks someone's mentioned it before. He can't dredge the memory. What say ye to this?

The Jap feared the Wolf. The Jap had the inside dirt. The Jap revealed **this:**

Hector Obregon-Hodaka blabbed to the Dudster. **He** mentioned the klub**haus** and wild goings-on there. **He** said two rogue cops ruled the roost.

All hail the Wolf. The Wolf retrieved that lost memory.

Mike Breuning called him. He bore hot news.

Nort Layman tagged the klub**haus** job Murder One. Hector's rogue cops? Surely Wendell Rice and George Kapek.

Hector's a Kyoho Hanamaka KA. He'll photostat Hector's Statie print card. He'll get it to Hideo Ashida. Hideo will redust the klub**haus** and try to fix Hector's presence there.

Mike B. updated Dudley. Mike B. reported **this:**

There's that dead Mex. El Dudster's Spanish-fluent. Jack Horrall thinks the klub**haus** job could dip south. He wants Dudley to consult, long-distance. Bill Parker's set to oversee. It's their Watanabe-case assignments, grandly reprised.

With attendant sidebars. Werewolf Shudo's innocence and Jim Davis' guilt. Sinarquista flags at the klub**haus.** Elmer Jackson on the job. Hideo's Baja posting on hold.

Dudley touched green twill and black leather. He should buy the Wolf a black leather harness and spiked collar. The Wolf retrieved that memory. He deserves a treat.

Lieutenant Juan flew low. The Army supplied a twin Beechcraft and all-purpose weaponry. Flamethrowers, tommy guns, grenades.

They hugged the coastline. Dudley binocular-scanned.

The cockpit was sun bright and altitude cold. Dudley sat behind the pilot's seat and peered out. He marked latitudes on a relief map. He **X**'d coves and inlets and saw no signs of life.

They flew south. Dudley scanned fishing boats. They featured all-Mex crews and came off kosher. Lieutenant Juan refueled the plane in Puerto Romulo. They swung back south and cruised Magdalena Bay.

Lieutenant Juan swooped low and dipped toward the Sinarquista encampment. He'd prepped a leaflet drop. Hate tracts **en español.** He got them at the Deutsches Haus in L.A. They featured German death-camp photos with humorous captions. Lieutenant Juan found them **howl**arious.

Dudley saw men tilling soil and women dunking clothes in a stream. Lieutenant Juan dipped to three hundred feet. **Los cameradas** looked up and waved. Lieutenant Juan dropped the cargo hatch. Hate tracts hit blue sky.

The **kameraden** whooped en masse. They jumped up and down. The tracts caught air streams and flew. The sky went **craaaazy**-paper white and eclipsed all sunlight.

Lieutenant Juan U-turned and gained altitude. They flew northbound and low. Lieutenant Juan dropped down to two hundred feet and air-trekked the coastline. Dudley binocular-scanned.

It got boring. Rocks, waves, and sand. Time stands still. Rocks, waves, sand shoals. The same shit—**por vida** and beyond.

Then—**bip!**—there's this lone Jap.

He's just outside an inlet. He's tossing a fishing net. He's not looking up.

Dudley jabbed Lieutenant Juan. Lieutenant Juan looked down and went **Caramba.**

He dipsy-doodled up and east. He cut past the coast road and nosed the plane down. There's a flat dirt patch/mock runway.

The ground came up **faaaaaast.** Dudley braced himself against the seat back. Lieutenant Juan hopscotched around rocks and dumped trash. He found a clear stretch. He cut the flaps and put the wheels on the ground. The plane fishtailed and pulled two full doughnuts.

The engine thumped and stalled dead. The propellers tapped out. Dudley went **whew!** They jumped out and indulged **abrazos.** They armed themselves.

Dudley grabbed a tommy gun. Lieutenant Juan grabbed a flamethrower. They ran across the dirt patch and dodged cars across the coast road. They hit an embankment. A carved path led down to the beach.

Dudley saw an outcropping due north. That was his landmark. He spotted that Jap forty yards up.

He pointed north. Lieutenant Juan gripped the flamethrower and fell in beside him. They trekked down to the beachfront. The sand was wet-wet. Wavelets doused them knee-high.

They walked north. Wet sand sucked at their feet.

They approached the inlet. It fronted a cove cave. Dudley saw fishing-net drag marks. Dudley heard jabber: Mex, Jap, Mex.

They hugged the rocks and crept close. The jabber escalated. Dudley craned and looked into the cave. A Jap flag hung off a two-by-four. Voices jabbered— men, women, kids.

Lieutenant Juan went **So, Jefe?** Dudley went **Of course.** They wheeled and walked right in.

The cave was **muy** deep. They hit a left fork and veered toward the voices. Dudley saw them then.

Thirty-odd souls. Fifth Column **familia.** Half Jap and half Mex. Right there in front:

Hector Obregon-Hodaka, himself.

Lieutenant Juan kicked a rock, inadvertent. The noise echo-chambered. **La familia** turned and looked. Hector looked straight at Dudley and pulled a waist-band piece.

Lieutenant Juan aimed and cut loose. Flames shot up and out. They hit Hector. He screamed and went all bugshit on fire. Lieutenant Juan hit the kill switch. The barrel whoosh died. **La familia** ran, **todos.** They reached the back of the cave and hit a dead end.

Lieutenant Juan walked up and cornered them there. Dudley followed him. He read their fear, close-up. Lieutenant Juan got blast-oven close. Each and every one of them screamed.

Lieutenant Juan hit the on switch. Flames shot up and out. He fried each and every one of them alive.

47

(LOS ANGELES, 8:00 A.M., 1/31/42)

Crash Squad confab. Jack Horrall's office. It's a double cop snuff. There's fanfare and razzmatazz.

The squad ran ten strong. Folding chairs fanned the Chief's desk. Dudley Smith was down in Baja. He pledged daily call-ins and/or Teletypes.

They signed a check-in log. It was big-job de rigueur. The duty roster ran thus:

Captain W. H. Parker: Traffic Division/commanding officer.

Captain D. L. Smith (Army SIS): executive officer/Spanish-speaking consultant.

Lieutenant T. B. Brown: Homicide Division/squad whip.

Sergeant M. D. Breuning: Homicide Division.

Sergeant R. S. Carlisle: Homicide Division.

Norton Layman, M.D.: medical consultant.

Lieutenant H. J. Ashida (Army SIS): crime lab supervisor/on-leave consultant.

Miss J. W. Conville: crime lab/forensic biologist.

Sergeant E. V. Jackson: Vice Division/Alien Squad.

Officer L. C. Blanchard: Central Division Detectives/Alien Squad.

Sergeant T. R. Meeks: Robbery Division/detached for current duty.

They sat ten across. They smoked and sipped coffee. They wore that down-for-the-count look. They were forty-four hours in.

Joan glanced at Parker. He glanced back. She smelled his dumb lime cologne. She was antsy. The Santa Barbara Sheriff's file arrived. She wanted to jump on it.

She stroked her gold cuff links. She was distracted. The Chief said something. She missed the lead-in.

". . . and if you're wondering why you don't see Ray Pinker, it's because he's in Dutch with the Fed probe, and he's running raw these days. That means Lieutenant Ashida's our top lab dog, until Dud S. pulls some strings and hauls him back to Mexico. There's a war on, you know. Things like that tend to supersede."

The gang laughed. Breuning and Carlisle smirked. They hated Ashida. Dud loved him more than them.

Call-Me-Jack drummed his desk. "We all know why we're here, so let's get to it. Will someone please tell me something I don't know?"

Dr. Nort raised his hand. "I found large quantities of carbolic acid in the three victims' livers. This indicates that the terp they were smoking just prior to their deaths had been spiked. They were deliberately poisoned—but organ saturation indicates that all three men were habitual terp smokers."

Call-Me-Jack rolled his eyes. "We can't defame our fallen colleagues as terp fiends. Let's keep that fact away from any and all reporters you might be talking to. As far as reporters go, this is gospel. The inside dirt goes exclusively to Sid Hudgens and his legman Jack Webb, and that's it. They've done us proud before, and they'll do us proud here. Given the state of the klub**haus,** I'd say we're looking at a Fifth Column job. I want Sid and Jack to play up that angle, because Fifth Column hoo-ha's the rage now, and that sort of emphasis will make us look good with Fourth Interceptor and the Feds."

Elmer waved his cigar. "What about a command post, boss? There's no room at Central, and there's no room here at the Hall."

Call-Me-Jack sipped coffee. He spiked it with schnapps. It's PD-certified dish.

"You got lucky here. I'm giving you Lyman's back room, until we clear this thing. You'll all have keys, and it'll be off-limits to rank-and-file PD. I'm putting cots in, and you'll have food and booze twenty-four hours."

Carlisle said, "Suppose we have to . . ."

Elmer woofed him. "Put some hurt on a suspect or witness, Dick? That what you're thinking?"

Breuning said, "You've got shit for brains and shit for tact, Jackson. And it's not like people don't know it."

Elmer woofed him. Here's your fucking tact.

"**People?** You mean like a certain Irishman, well known to folks in this room?"

Joan held her breath. Buzz blew Elmer an Okie-redneck kiss. Hideo Ashida gasped.

Call-Me-Jack banged his ashtray. Desk clutter hopped.

"Not in my office, and not on my time card. You're policemen investigating a double cop killing, and I've got no time for pique from any of you. To the point of Dick's question, I'll add this. There's a storeroom two floors up from Lyman's, and I'm having a chair bolted to the floor. It's nice and quiet. If you need to stretch someone, do it up there."

Breuning and Carlisle smirked. Elmer winked at Meeks. Thad Brown coughed.

"What about the victims' families? At the very least, we should interview the wives."

Call-Me-Jack made the cutoff sign. "I paid condolence calls, and unless something pertinent comes up, I want them left alone. I don't want to aggravate them and get them thinking they should slap a wrongful death suit on the PD. There's that, and there's the undisputed fact that their dutiful hubbies were skirt chasers and God knows what else, given a certain klub**haus** on East 46th."

Parker said, "We've got to ID the Mexican. That's our first priority."

Blanchard said, "I'll be checking mug books against the DB pix."

Ashida said, "I'll start checking print cards immediately."

Joan said, "I want to redust, resweep, and rephotograph the premises. There has to be something there."

Ashida shot his shirt cuffs. Joan saw his new gold watch. He evinced drag-queen taste.

"I found a series of semen stains on the bedsheets upstairs, and I've already typed them. All four of the men were secretors. I'll be checking my samples against blood samples from our victims."

Elmer whooped. "That's the sort of bed traffic you see in your everyday whorehouse."

Parker said, "Elmer's speaking as an expert witness here."

Buzz said, "I found an address book under a piece of carpet upstairs. Ray Pinker swooped by and dusted it for me. He turned up two latents. They match to a hot-prowl hump named Tommy Glennon."

Breuning and Carlisle went lockjawed. Elmer woof-woofed them.

"Tommy the G. Does it get you all nostalgic for New Year's Eve?"

Call-Me-Jack said, "Tommy G. That Irish cocksucker has been a thorn in my side since God was a pup."

Buzz said, "The Chief knows from Irish cocksuckers, given his long-standing friendship with Dudley Smith."

Call-Me-Jack went **tut-tut.** Breuning and Carlisle trembled. Elmer blew Buzz an Okie-redneck kiss.

Joan laughed outright. **Pinch me. What am I doing—**

Thad Brown said, "Jackson, Blanchard, Meeks. You

take the address book. Jump on the names, jump on Glennon, and jump on all of it now."

Call-Me-Jack yawned. I'm half-gassed, I need a nap, you're wearing me thin.

"Get out of here. All of you. Find the guy who killed our pals Wendell and George, and try not to kill him until he's confessed."

Parker dashed for the door. He detoured and slipped Joan a note. It read "Tonight?"

Joan whistled and brought him up short. Parker turned and faced her. Heads shot their way. Joan spoke full vibrato. Damn circumspection. Let the world know.

"Yes, Bill. I'd love to see you tonight."

The all-clear horn blew. The Army searchlights kept swirling. They lit up clouds you just never saw. False-alarm nights moved her. The war had its upsides.

Joan said, "When peace comes, we'll lose this."

Parker said, "They magnify the moon. That's the part I like best."

They sat on Joan's back steps. Joan sat one step down. His feet were right there. Joan held an ankle just so she could touch him.

"You've been detached to work this job. I thought you'd be more displeased than you are."

Parker touched her shoulder. "We're skirting that topic we weren't going to discuss."

"You're saying Jack Horrall's pining for a certain

case last month, so he's assembled a near-identical Crash Squad."

"You understand this police department very damn well. You wouldn't have learned the ins and outs of the Navy anywhere near as fast."

"I dreamt about the Mexicans last night. I was being tried for vehicular manslaughter, and the DA asked me if I knew the names of the victims. I said, 'Well, my policeman colleagues call them wetbacks and cholos.'"

Parker touched her hair. "Don't do that. Don't derail yourself when things start going your way."

Joan kissed his hand and placed it back on his knee. A searchlight beam crossed the moon. Joan saw little craters.

She left City Hall and drove back to the klub**haus.** She redusted and rephotographed all day. She hadn't seen the Santa Barbara file. Ashida was there all day. He hadn't seen it, either.

Parker tapped her shoulder. "You've developed a particular habit. You keep worrying those gold cuff links, like you're checking for signs of stigmata."

Joan smiled. "There's a story behind it, but I'm not going to tell it to you."

"I'll quote Jack Horrall, then. 'Tell me something I don't know.'"

Joan looked up at him. His dumb sport coat complemented his dumb cologne. His trousers drooped. He wore a cross-draw belt gun.

"I went to a wild party, just to observe Kay Lake. I

took a steam bath with a famous actor and your old nemesis Claire De Haven. I kept thinking, Why am I naked with people I don't even know? and They don't do this in Tomah, Wisconsin."

Parker looked down at her. "What are you saying? You're a scientist, and you never speak elliptically. I admire that about you. I never have to strain myself to grasp your intent."

Joan touched his leg. "I'm saying, 'Darling Bill, you've given me a life that I never could have imagined, and I will remain forever grateful, however this thing of ours plays out."

Parker tripped down two steps instead of just one. Joan grabbed his arm and pulled him back up. She brought him in close. They kissed. His glasses snagged in her hair. They stumbled inside and into the bedroom. They knocked over a wobbly lamp as they fell.

48

(LOS ANGELES, 5:00 A.M., 2/1/42)

Ashida dawdled. He felt gob-smacked. It felt indolent and all wrong.

He made beaker-brew coffee. It salved his

drinks-with-Dudley hangover. He ran checklists. He cleaned his lab gear. He replayed last night.

They met at the Windsor and sat at the bar. They wore their uniforms and turned heads. It felt like a hot date.

Dudley ordered stingers. Ashida felt like a girl plied with booze. Dudley brought a Statie print card. Hector Obregon-Hodaka/Kyoho Hanamaka's KA.

The klub**haus** job dips south. It melds with Hanamaka and his gold bayonet. The bayonet's mint marks match the marks on his gold bar. The mint-train heist and Griffith Park fire further intersect.

Ashida cracked windows. Cold air fanned a lab-solvent stink. He sipped coffee. He tallied case points. What he knew and Joan Conville knew. What Dudley knew nothing of.

He lost track of his falsehoods. He realized **this:**

He was Dudley's idolatrous accomplice. Joan was Dudley's lover. He saw them together and sensed it. They had to disclose everything. They had to share the gold, three ways.

Rain bounced off window screens. The coffee induced cold sweats.

Dudley loved the bayonet. Its utility superseded 8.2 pounds of gold. The bayonet accessorized his fascist aesthetic. Captain D. L. Smith killed people and communed with a fantasy wolf. Lieutenant H. J. Ashida's fantasy lover was quite insane.

The bayonet was History. The bayonet was Dudley's beloved Wagner and Norse myth. Dudley would accede to gold as money. The Myth of This Gold would gob-smack him and inspire him to possess it.

Ashida checked his watch. He was due at the klub**haus.** He had three lab tasks first.

Test the semen-stained sheets. Run the Mexican's prints. Study the Santa Barbara Sheriff's heist file. Hope that Reckless Girl hasn't studied it first.

He'd blood-typed the ejaculate and ID'd four secretors. Two O-positive/one A-negative/one rare RH-positive. Dr. Nort would comparison-type the victims' blood types. **He** was set to run foreign-substance tests himself.

He prepped a burner and preheated an acid-phosphate solution. He added purified water and brought up a boil. He placed sheet swatch #1 in the liquid. The semen stain eroded in two seconds flat.

Ashida noted swirling particles. One type was dark and granular. One type was viscous and near-transparent.

He naked-eyed them. They were forensically compatible and easily ID'd.

Human fecal matter. A glycerin-based lubricant. Most likely K-Y jelly.

Ashida flinched. He turned off the burner and set the other swatches aside. He wide-cracked windows. A wet breeze raised goose bumps. He pulled the Unknown Mexican print card.

Drudgework now. The print-card index. Card drawers subdivided by gender and race. Twelve drawers for "Mexican, Male."

Ashida microphotographed the Unknown Mex card. He got all ten digits and hit the photo lab. He locked himself in the darkroom. He worked with scissors, dip solvents, and a magnifying camera. He shot ten six-by-eight prints.

A heater fan dried them inside twenty minutes. They developed white on black. He taped them to the wall above the print-card bank. He pencil-marked significant ridges and whorls. He pulled out the **A** drawer and worked standing up.

He started at Abrevaya, George and Acosta, Ramon. He noted inconsistent whorl patterns and moved on. He went through Alvarez, Alvaro/Alvarez, José and Alvarez, Juan. Alvarez was a dirt-common name.

He studied nine more Alvarez cards. He hit Archuleta, Arturo, aka "Archie."

There's a tweaker. Check the left-forefinger print. Look—the top ridge patterns match.

Ashida snatched his eyepiece scope. He went up/down, up/down, up/down. He studied Archuleta's left-hand prints. He eyeball-skimmed the unknown Mex fotos.

He counted comparison points. He got ten points, fourteen points, a big twenty-one. That cinched it. **Bam!**—Archie Archuleta was klub**haus** stiff #3.

The lab went sauna hot. Ashida cracked all the windows. A breeze blew loose papers off desks.

He hit the green-sheet index. He yanked the **A** to **B** file drawer and finger-walked. He pulled Archuleta's green sheet. It revealed **this:**

THIS STORM

Born: Tijuana, Mexico—8/19/89. Narco jolts back to '15. Two years at the dope hospital in Lexington, Kentucky. Two Chino terms here. Popped for plain drunk/drunk 502/forging doctors' scripts. 27 dope rousts, total. LKA: 841 Wabash, Boyle Heights. No KAs listed. Last bounce: drunk 502/3-6-39. Popped in '35 Ford/59th and Central.

Ashida wrote up his findings. He'd call Thad Brown and inform him. He'd paper-post his reports at Lyman's.

He got out the heist file. The page stack felt heavy. He checked the bottom of the pile and saw loose paperwork. It pertained to the '33 liquor-store jobs. Robbery Division weighs in.

Reckless Girl forged a file-request slip. She was Sloppy Girl here. **His** forgeries surpassed hers. **Her** "Ray Pinker" sigs looked like tomb hieroglyphs.

Ashida skimmed the heist file. It detailed the mint train's Santa Barbara stop. It featured Leander Frechette and Deputy Karl Tullock.

Negro youth Frechette. He's six-eight and weighs 340. He's mentally dim and inhumanely strong. The Santa Barbara cops posit **this:**

The gold-cage lock was removed. A look-alike lock was cosmetically affixed. **Just enough gold** was clouted. The low bar count ensured that the cache would not appear ransacked.

The bars were wheeled off, walked off, or tossed off the train. Waiting confederates grabbed them. The cops canned the toss-off theory. It entailed

confederates in moving surveillance. Said confederates could not know **this:**

When the gold-cage walkway would stand unob-
served. When the theft and toss-off would occur.

The cops canned the wheel-off theory. Somebody
would have seen it. The walk-off theory remained.
The bulk weight of the bars meant **this:**

The thief is exceptionally large and strong. He
hides the bars on his person and obfuscates the load.
He walks on and off the train. His confederates grab
the gold.

It's a stop-for-coal stop. The eight convicts escape
precedingly. The overall atmosphere remains chaotically charged. It obscures the thief's actions.

One train worker possesses just such strength and
bulk. It's Leander Frechette. Deputy Karl Tullock has
at him.

Tullock badgers and beats on Frechette. Leander
holds firm. I didn't do it/I don't know who did it/
I don't know nothing.

Frechette remains in stir. A Negro man named
Martin Luther Mimms secures his release. Mimms is
tight with L.A. Police high-ups. Frechette is released
to his custody.

Ashida kicked it around. **This** seemed certain now:

The mass escape and train heist comprised one
event. The two repair stops were caused by staged
mechanical glitches. It all cohered behind Fritz
Eckelkamp.

He escapes and remains at large. He was a career

heist man. The other escaped cons are shot on sight. It feels like preengendered chaos.

Cut to the klub**haus** job. Hector Obregon-Hodaka laid the **haus** gestalt out to Dudley. Hector knew Kyoho Hanamaka. Hanamaka's gold bayonet: cast from the same ore as the bars on the train. This seems certain now:

Eckelkamp, the German Marxist. Hanamaka, the left-right horror connoisseur. The klub**haus** as haunt of debauched politicos. There's a stench here. It's Fifth Column mischief couched in criminal greed.

Two mug shots were clipped to the file. Fritz Eckelkamp looked Teutonic fierce. Leander Frechette looked bewildered.

Ashida jumped files. He went gold heist to liquor-store jobs in one heartbeat. He saw the witness-composite sketch. He saw a list of look-alike vagrants. They were detained, un-ID'd, released for lack of proof.

The fourth name down: Jackson, Wayne Frank.

49

(LOS ANGELES, 10:00 A.M., 2/1/42)

The boys are back in town.
That bluegrass ditty nailed them. The **KKK**lan

outkast and Okie shitkicker. Sergeants E. V. Jackson and T. R. Meeks their own selves.

With their own prowl sled. On this big case. Fuck struck with bitching intent.

Elmer drove. Buzz kibitzed. They got pigshit lucky. Hotdog Ashida notched a print make. The dead Mex now stood ID'd.

Boyle Heights was Baja north. Shack rows on flat streets and hillsides. Tacofied taverns and pachucoized pool halls. Lots of Catholic churches. Sinarquista decals on souped-up cars.

Elmer said, "Wabash. It's around here somewhere."

Buzz said, "She'll take it rough. Her Archie treated her raw, but he gave her the big chorizo like nobody else."

Elmer went **nyet.** "What did our first two widows give us? Nothing but relief that their hubbies were dead, and 'Where's my survivors' pension check?'"

"Twenty says you're wrong."

"Twenty says I'm right."

They shook on it. It sealed their Pax Redneckiana. They'd breached Jack Horrall's orders already. They braced the Personnel Division boss and the two widows. It revealed **this:**

Call-Me-Jack pulled Rice's and Kapek's Personnel files. Them boys were just **toooooooo** dirty. Dirt leaks might besmirch the PD. Their bust lists were in those files. The Crash Squad needed a look-see. Maybe some crazed felon was fresh out of stir and hot for revenge.

The widows pissed on Rice and Kapek, postmortem. You want baleful bile? Gas on **this:**

Rice pimped his wife to cover his poker debts. Rice fathered Kapek's three kids, and vice versa. The widows were lezbo lovers and turned dyke tricks out of Linda's Little Log Cabin. Rice and Kapek filmed their antics and peddled the lez epics down in T.J.

The widows evicted their hubbies at least once a week. They had a hideout somewhere. The widows knew zilch per the klub**haus** and hubbies' KAs. They knew their hubbies veered far right. Rice and Kapek made them wear dirndl skirts and Nazi armbands. Their kids wore lederhosen and Tyrolean beanies to school. They frolicked at German-American Bund summer camp.

Elmer and Buzz eyeball-tossed their two domiciles. Rice possessed some **farkakte** fly-ur-self/build-from-scratch model-airplane kit. The fucking thing consumed half his garage. It had rivet-attached wings. It had Luftwaffe insignia and a cockpit-mounted machine gun. The Widow Rice said he bought it from some right-wing geek in Minnesota.

Georgie Kapek possessed twenty-six incendiary bombs. The Widow Kapek called him a "Secret Firebug." Georgie possessed two terp stills and thirty-four back issues of **Goldlover Magazine.**

Georgie's swag gored Elmer's gourd. He knew he'd seen similar shit somewhere. It hit him belated:

The late Don Matsura owned that selfsame shit. Terp stills and **Goldlover Magazine.**

Elmer and Buzz logged man-hours. They quizzed the Alien Squad guys per Kapek and Rice. Nobody coughed up good drift. They said Georgie and Wendell were bent. So what? We all are. We're bent in the ways of this bent PD in this bent and fucked-up town.

That approach tanked. They braced the watch boss at Newton Station then. They pressed on complaints levied against the klub**haus.** Nope—there were none. That approach tanked, likewise.

Buzz said, "That's the address."

Elmer pulled to the curb. Said address: a cinder-block and wood firetrap. Note the fat **mamacita** ensconced on the porch.

The boys piled out and drifted over. Mama-san sniffed bad news. She had good feelers. Her snout twitch-twitched.

"You've got him downtown, right? He topped out his parole, but you still got him for some dumb law he shouldn't have broke."

Buzz doffed his hat. "Archie's dead, ma'am. It took a few days to identify him, but it's him. He was killed, along with two policemen. It occurred in a little club-house down in the colored side of town."

Mama shrugged. "Live by the sword, die by the sword. Adios, Arturo. With him you always knew the other shoe would drop."

Elmer said, "How so, ma'am?"

Mama said, "Archie ran with lower companions. Water seeks its own level. He was a **pendejo** and a

borracho. He snitched to the police and mainlined the white horse. You pay the piper, the piper calls the tune. You buy trouble, you get what you pay for."

Buzz spit tobacco juice. He doused the porch steps good.

"Did he snitch to any particular policemen?"

Mama shook her head. "I always told him 'Don't name me no names, 'cause what I don't know can't hurt me.' I know he snitched to these two fools on the Alien Squad, but I made sure he didn't name no names."

Elmer relit his cigar. "You're saying you didn't know Archie's running partners, and you only had a general sense that he was out in the world, causing trouble."

"That's right. Archie was a snake in the grass, but I told him 'Don't you bring no mice home to me.'"

Elmer said, "Archie must have had himself a parole officer. He'd have known Archie's associates."

"He always topped out his parole, so there'd be no strings attached. He said that way, he'd have the world on a string."

Buzz said, "How many **niños** you got, ma'am? You think they'd have more details on their daddy's pals and activities?"

Mama snorted. "Arturo was a back-door man. You don't conceive no **niños** that way."

Elmer whooped. Ashida posted a lab report. **Oooga-booga.** Jizz stains, K-Y jelly, shit traces.

"Here's a question, ma'am. You're the late Archie

Archuleta. You've got time on your hands and a penchant for trouble. How do you spend your days?"

Mama picked her nose. "Arturo knew his way around C-town and J-town. He sought most of his trouble there. 'Seek and ye shall find.' He sold his dope and bought his dope there, and he snitched to these two Alien Squad bulls who worked around there. He knew lots of tong men, crooked Japs, and these Jap Fifth Column types. He bought these Nazi-type trinkets from some Jap, and he sold them to the zoot-suit **pendejos** here in the Heights."

Elmer said, "Is that the Sinarquistas you're talking about?"

Mama crossed herself. Mama whipped out some voodoo amulet and hexed the world at large.

"Evil **fascistas.** May they boil in a vat of nigger pus and potato-chip lard."

Buzz winked at Elmer. "What about that clubhouse, ma'am? 46th and Central, off the jazz strip?"

Mama went **¿Qué?/Who cares?/So what?**

Elmer said, "These two Alien Squad cops. Do the names Wendell Rice and George Kapek sound familiar?"

Mama went **Huh?/¿Qué?/So what?**

Buzz spritzed tobacco juice. He nailed Mama's mailbox **gooooood.**

"Give us some names, mama. Feed these two weary dogs a bone."

"I don't got no names. I know Arturo went back with them Alien Squad bulls, to when they worked the Narco Detail. Arturo said, 'Better to snitch to the devil you know than the devil you don't know.'"

Rice and Kapek worked Narco. They allegedly grafted there. It was pre-established drift.

Elmer teethed his cigar. "What else can you tell us about these nameless Narco guys?"

Mama waved her amulet. "They were **dos fascistas.** They loved Hitler, Tojo, and Father Coughlin. Arturo mostly finked out these Jap pharmacists who wouldn't sell him no morphine."

Buzz said, "Names, ma'am?"

A rat zipped across the porch. A big cat-sized fucker. Mama hexed him.

"Arturo said he only snitched off one real Fifth Column fool. Some fool white boy named Huey Cressmeyer. The Alien Squad bulls said, 'Huey's sacrosanct. He's got high-up friends, and he's our pal.'"

50

(LOS ANGELES, 5:00 P.M., 2/1/42)

Call-Me-Jack shagged phone calls. He lived to wheedle, bully, and schmooze. Dudley shagged the chair by his desk.

Jack blah-blahed and yeah-yeahed. He bloviated

with Fletch Bowron and Fourth Interceptor. Dudley
lit a cigarette. Jack went **Un momento.**

His phone-light blinked. He winked at El Dudster.
He coo-coo'd and oh-baby'd now.

It was surely Brenda Allen. The two shared a history. It predated Brenda's liaison with doltish Elmer
Jackson.

Dudley wore civvies and a belt piece. He drove up
rápido. Mike B. called him in Baja. Mike reported **this:**

Tommy Glennon's address book appeared at the
klub**haus.** It contained Huey Cressmeyer's name.
Ditto Lin Chung's name and Saul Lesnick's name. Plus
more provocative listings.

Chung and Lesnick were Watanabe-case adjunct.
That mandated discretion. Huey was a glue ad-
dict and plainly psychopathic. That mandated a
T.J. retreat.

Jack coo-coo'd good-byes and hung up. He stared
across his desk. He read the Dudster's dire look.

"Lay it out. Bypass the blarney and get to it."

"Jim Davis killed the Watanabes. Bill Parker put
it together. Jim confessed to him in late December,
and unburdened himself to me more recently. I'm assuming that no one else knows. That stated, I should
add that we now have peripheral names crossing over
to the klub**haus** job. Dare I say that we need to be
careful here?"

Jack went deep-vein sclerotic. He chugged digitalis straight from the vial. He chased it with desk-
jug scotch.

"Parker won't blab. He goes way back with Jim, and Jim's got dirt on him that could sink his career."

Dudley said, "Yes, but our Bill is nothing if not capricious. He'll do anything to appease God and impress young women."

The desk phone rang. Jack squelched the call.

"Adjudicate this thing with Parker, Dud. Make whatever concessions you deem necessary. Brace Jim D. and tell that lunatic cocksucker in no uncertain terms to keep his fucking mouth shut. As for the klub**haus** job, I'll state this. We need a clean solve and dead suspects who'll never enter a courtroom. Keep that in mind, along with this. Do whatever you deem necessary to put the quietus on those 'peripheral names' you just mentioned. **¿Tú comprende, muchacho?**"

Dudley chained cigarettes. "You pulled Rice's and Kapek's Personnel files. That severely restricts our access to their arrest records. I'll hazard a guess here, sir. They ran bag for you when they worked the Narco Squad back in the Davis regime."

Call-Me-Jack tipped scotch. The pills kicked in. His color receded.

"They covered niggertown for Jim D. and yours truly. Envelopes changed hands. My old Army pal the Reverend Mimms greased the skids south of Slauson. That's the drift, and here's the upscut. I burned the Personnel files and the Narco files. Leave Mimms alone, and get me a clean solve despite those restrictions. Elmer Jackson and Buzz Meeks are playing gadfly with you, but I'm disinclined to cut them loose. As our pal Sid Hudgens says, 'That's all the news that's **un**fit to print.'"

The phone rang. Jack squelched it. He slurped scotch and wagged his eyebrows.

"You're working angles in Baja. My best guess is that Ace the K. is covering you here. By my calculations, I should be in for 8%."

Dudley smiled. "12%, sir. With a codicil attached."

"Would that be latitude on everything we've just discussed?"

"Yes, and I would like you to detach Lieutenant Ashida, effective immediately."

"Yes to the former, no to the latter. I need Ashida here."

Dudley stood up. Jack said, "I met Jim Davis in 1919. He's always been good to me. Here's **my** codicil. I positively forbid you to kill him."

Whiskey Bill dozed in his prowl sled. Long naps served to revive him. Dudley tagged him in the City Hall lot.

Herr Bill snored. He was unkempt and looked stale overall. Note the photograph taped to the dashboard.

Joan Conville, hometown seductress. She's posed on a split-rail fence. Note her fetching huntress ensemble.

Fierce Joan. Note the shotgun. She blew a randy redskin's foot off with it.

The passenger door stood ajar. Dudley slid in

beside Parker. He rattled him awake. Parker flinched and went for his gun.

Dudley pinned his hand. "Wake up, Captain. We've a serious matter to discuss."

Parker blinked and rubbed his eyes. He had booze-hound breath. Dudley passed him a mint lozenge.

"You woke me up."

"Yes, and with good cause. Jim Davis told me that he killed the Watanabes. He told you in December, and I'm wondering who else he might have told."

Parker crossed himself. His eyes zipped to the dashboard.

"There's the issue of who you've told, Captain. Have you confessed to Monsignor Hayes? Have you told your wife or the twin sirens, Miss Conville and Miss Lake?"

Parker recrossed himself and reogled the dashboard. Of course—the sodden shit told Joan.

Sea winds bore down. Bad rain threatened. Wave chop doused his boots. It rendered the beach trek unpleasant.

He drove back last night. He left pressing biz in L.A. A deal with Bill Parker. A bedroom chat with fair Joan.

The Wolf urged his return. The Wolf told him to check the other caves near the death cave. The Wolf wondered **this:**

Juan Pimentel. Did he torch those saboteurs with undue haste? Herr Juan was the slow-torture type. French-fried Japs and spics played out of character. The Wolf was most emphatic here.

Dudley trekked north. He carried a flashlight and a tommy gun. He saw the death cave and smelled it concurrent.

The scorched flesh. The stale stomach gas and burst entrails.

He entered the cave. The Wolf growled. They walked back and viewed the charred-corpse mound. The Wolf wagged his tail and gnawed flame-bleached bones. Dudley counted thirty-four dead.

They walked back to the beach and turned north. Dudley spotted a cave cove fifty yards up. They walked over. Dudley racked his tommy gun and stepped in. The Wolf walked point ahead of him.

Yes. It's the same setup. A deep cave. Numerous forks. Beachfront recessed. Wave-free access.

They explored the cave. The Wolf chased enticing scents. They saw **this:**

Empty food cans. Two dozen bedrolls. A smashed and thus useless shortwave radio set.

Plus **this:**

Charred airplane parts. Oddly flimsy. Rivet perforations. Incongruous construction.

The wings snapped onto the fuselage. Flimsy wires secured them. They resembled model-airplane parts.

The engine compartment laid there, exposed. Four

small cylinders leaked gas. There's a flywheel and an automotive gear train attached. There's hammer-and-sickle decals on a wing plate.

The Wolf cocked his head and perked his ears. Dudley said, "Yes, I know—it's quite the mad contraption."

They left the cave and trekked farther north. The Wolf frolicked and chased beach rats. They found four more saboteur nests.

All abandoned. Smashed radios/empty cans/dumped bedrolls. No more jig-rigged airplane parts.

The Wolf possessed a keen intellect and sharp fangs. He gnawed on **this:**

Did Herr Juan torch those shits judiciously? Did he torch them to warn off other cave dwellers?

Dudley had sharp fangs. He gnawed on it.

A thunderstorm blew in. The Wolf stayed home with Claire and the Klein girl. Dudley teethed and drove back out in the rain.

He gnawed on the Jim Davis snafu. He gnawed on the klub**haus** job. He gnawed on his nascent Baja rackets and José Vasquez-Cruz. He gnawed on his L.A. versus Mexico duties and his Army mandate. He gnawed on Kyoho Hanamaka and the gold bayonet.

He took Benzedrine and gnawed with revived gusto. He drove to T.J. and bootjacked a Border Patrol office. The Benzedrine induced brainstorms. It said do **this:**

Study photo-device footage. Check the north-bound passages only. Look for covered vehicles and exposed license plates. Test the efficacy of Hideo Ashida's grand creation.

The Staties had stockpiled eight photo boxes. Trip wires caught approaching and departing bumper plates. They'd rigged a viewfinder thingamajig in the office. It was crank-scroll operated. Plate numbers appeared on a bubble screen. Date markings ran below them.

Let's look for suspect vehicles. Let's study upward-jerking pix and nail suspect **trucks.**

Overpacked trucks. Trucks riding low on their axles. Fleeing Japs. Internment-dodging Japs. Saboteur Japs.

Dudley scrolled and rescrolled. His mind scrolled and unscrolled as he descrolled license plates. He saw Joan Conville naked. He saw her dressed in SS black. She swung the gold bayonet. She killed the man who killed her father.

License plates abundant. License plates redundant. Front plates, rear plates. Car plates, truck plates, all heading-adios plates.

Dudley got eyestrain. He went through two full boxes. He scrolled up to 1/25/42. He kept seeing Jap goblins who weren't really there. He kept seeing Joan naked and the Wolf abed with naked Claire.

He fed in the 1/25 pix. He scrolled through boring turistas waving good-bye and leering jarheads sated from the Blue Fox. His brain scrolled/**un**scrolled/**re**scrolled/**de**scrolled.

He kept seeing Joan naked/Joan naked/JOAN NAKED. He blinked to **re**scroll reality. He **re**installed the imposition of boring license plates. He plate-scrolled up to 10:14 p.m., 1/25/42.

He caught a northbound bumper plate and truck grill. The camera lens jerked upward. He caught an up-to-the-windshield shot and caught **this:**

Wendell Rice and George Kapek—right there in the cab. They've got three fucking nights left to live.

51

(LOS ANGELES, 9:00 A.M., 2/3/42)

Cramped quarters. They verged on SRO. Lyman's back room as Crash Squad HQ.

The crammed-in chairs. The food table and coffee urn. The Teletype and phone lines. The corkboard-hung walls.

The booze table. The sweat room upstairs. A bolted-down chair for recalcitrant suspects. Rubber hose and phone-book-thumping tools, on call.

Joan sat between Elmer and Buzz. Ashida sat beside Dr. Nort. Breuning, Carlisle, and Blanchard hogged the back row. Bill Parker and Thad Brown stood and faced their crew. Brown summarized.

We're six days in. We've ID'd the Mex. He long-term snitched for Kapek and Rice. Jack Horrall dumped their Personnel and Narco files. The Mex topped out his paroles. We've got no leads there.

We've got two rogue cops. They're embroiled in a secret life deal. We've got Tommy Glennon's address book and jizz-stained sheets. We've established a unique cause of death. The lab folks are still at the klub**haus.** We need names. We've got to stretch this goddamn thing.

Joan ignored the spiel. She jotted gold-heist notes and snuck looks at Bill Parker. Call him lover #1. Dudley was here in L.A. She was seeing him tonight. Call him lover #2.

Brown haggled with Breuning and Carlisle. They wanted to haul in "jazz-club niggers" and "put the boots to them." Brown told them to pipe down. Joan tuned most of it out.

She doodled. Her thoughts scattergunned. She had breakfast with Kay. They discussed Kay's diary. She started it the day before Pearl Harbor. Bill Parker knocked on her door that night.

They discussed Joan's diary. She started it right after the Maestro's party. Bill Parker lay insensate in her bedroom. Bill Parker, ubiquitous. La Conville and La Lake—now screwball friends.

Lee Blanchard squawked. He canvassed ninety-one houses and didn't learn shit. Joan tuned him out. She fretted her gold cuff links and rehashed the Santa Barbara file.

Ashida got to it first. He'd thumbed it. She saw that. She'd dog-eared random pages. He undid them. She set a trap for him. He fell into it.

She left the file out for him. He hadn't mentioned it. He was starting to omit and dissemble again. She simply knew it.

She'd included some liquor-store 211 reports. She'd skimmed that paperwork first. There's "Jackson, Wayne Frank" on a detain-and-release slip.

Ashida had thumbed that file. Ashida did not mention the Wayne Frank Jackson lead.

It was Bingo #1. Bingo #2 surpassed it.

Martin Luther Mimms sprung Leander Frechette. That was 5/31. Now jump to 1/42. Martin Luther Mimms owns the klub**haus.** Elmer Jackson and Lee Blanchard turned up the lead.

Mimms: purportedly tight with high PD brass. Mimms: southside slumlord and bilk-the-poor preacher. Mimms: there for the gold-heist aftermath.

The room trapped cigarette smoke. Ashida fanned it away and made faces. Elmer and Buzz winked at Joan. Joan smiled and winked at Bill Parker. Lover #1 blushed.

Thad Brown said, "Breuning and Carlisle. Check DB files and see if you turn any paper submitted by Kapek and Rice. Blanchard, you recanvass the same radius, whether you like it or not. Jackson and Meeks, shake the names in Tommy Glennon's address book, and put your snouts down for Tommy himself."

Get it? We're finished here. Go to work. This fucking job's going nowhere so far.

Chairs scraped. The room thinned out. Parker shot
Joan a look. It meant **Tonight?** Joan shot a look back.
It meant **Sweetie, I can't.**

Parker slunk off. A bottleneck hit the door to
Lyman's proper. The room thinned all-the-way out.

The smoke clouds dispersed. Ashida hit the doorway. Joan grabbed his arm and pulled him back in.
She slammed the door and leaned against it. Talk to
me, you prissy queen.

"You've seen all the paperwork, and you haven't
said a word. We need to follow up on Mimms and
see what we can get on Wayne Frank Jackson."

Ashida shook his head. "I'll be called down to Baja
soon. The gold bayonet derives from there. I'll un-
cover leads in Mexico. That's how I can best serve this
venture."

"That's not an answer. It's an evasion. And 'this
venture' does not begin to describe all of this."

"Yes, and 'all of this' means that 'half of this' is
down in Mexico. I told you about Kyoho Hanamaka
and Dudley's fixation with him, and we're not going
to turn leads on him here in Los Angeles."

Joan shook her head. "That's not what you're saying. You're leading me and playing me blithe, and
you're withholding the punch line."

Ashida shook his head. "All right. Here's your
denouement. Dudley's in Mexico, and we don't

stand a chance without cutting him in. He uncovered the Mexican lead, but I know he hasn't connected the bayonet to the heist. We can't work around him, not with leads crossing over to the klub**haus** job. He has to be told, and he has to share in whatever gold we take possession of."

The room spun off-kilter. Joan got ground-floor vertigo. The prim little shit—

"Who tells him?"

"You do. You're his lover."

Joan said, "Yes, I am—however much you'd like to be."

Ashida hurled his coffee cup across the room. It hit a file cabinet and shattered.

52

(LOS ANGELES, 11:00 A.M., 2/3/42)

He hid from Reckless Girl. The klub**haus** as hideout. He worked upstairs. She worked downstairs. The klub**haus** as haunted house. He felt her through the floorboards and walls.

Reckless Girl. Brutal Girl. Hausfrau and Harlot. Consort of two brutal cops.

Ashida rephotographed the upstairs bedroom. He

wanted to re-create the full-scale **haus** and run forensic reconstructions. He cracked the front window.
Full-scale chatter chattered up.

Patrol cops and press. They crowded the yard and
spritzed rumors. "It's a coon caper" persisted. "It's a
jealous-wife job" ran second. "Nazis and Sinarquista
humps" ran third.

Gossip persisted. Sid Hudgens said he got a tip.
There's a big powwow brewing. It's a face-off. Whiskey
Bill versus Dudley Smith.

It pertains to Rice-Kapek. It pertains to Watanabe.
My lips are sealed past that. It's all **very** hush-hush.

Jack Webb bird-dogged Sid. Jack was a Belmont
alum. He bird-dogged Ashida and Bucky Bleichert in
high school. He bird-dogged cops now. He was the
PD's favored stooge-mascot.

A hot dog vendor worked the front yard. Cops and
reporters swarmed him. Ashida shut the window and
rephotographed.

He deployed a Man Camera variant. It merged
Man Camera and Camera Camera and created a
merged tableau. His goal was full depiction. Capture
the klub**haus**-death**haus** full on.

Ashida shot baseboards and closet corners. He
worked with and without flashbulbs and lights.
He got the walls. He got stacks of **Thunderbolt**
and **Stormtrooper Magazine.** He should print-
dust them. They hadn't been dusted. There was no
powder residue.

He shot every page. **Thunderbolt** featured hate

diatribes and cheesecake pix. Ashida saw Wendell Rice's wife in fishnet stockings. He recognized a contributor's name. George Lincoln Rockwell penned a back-to-Africa screed. He praised "Ebony **Führer**" M. L. Mimms at great length. Elmer Jackson and Lee Blanchard braced Mimms and Rockwell. They'd posted their report.

Rockwell, Navy pilot. Mimms, gold-heist periphery.

Ashida shot wall cracks and warped floorboards. He saw shoe scuffs on both sides of the bed. The bed engaged heavy traffic. He knew that.

The floor creaked behind him. The bedroom door creaked.

"I brought you some lunch, Hideo. Worker bees have to eat sometime."

Ashida wheeled. Jack Webb tossed him a hot dog. Ashida tossed his camera on the bed and snagged it.

Jack said, "I'd call you the world's hardest-working white man, except you're not white."

Ashida laughed and unwrapped the hot dog. Jack lounged in the doorway.

"I'm chasing leads for Sid's private dish sheet. Like, 'Call-Me-Jack's dragging his heels on cutting old Hideo loose for the Army.' Like, 'Jack wants to build a new crime lab before he retires, and Bill Parker or Thad Brown ascends to the throne.' Like, 'Jack's got it bad for the Conville cooze, and he's sending her to the Academy and swearing her in as a captain.' She'll command the division, and you'll jump to civilian chief chemist. How do them apples sound?"

Ashida ate half the hot dog and wiped his hands. Jack smirked. He was Mr. Insider's scent dog. He sniffed out the dirt.

"Tell me about the Reverend Mimms. He owns this property, and he impresses me as someone you and Sid would have the lowdown on."

Jack chortled. "Hideo Ashida says 'lowdown.' Coontown's getting to him. He'll be wearing zoot suits and poking colored girls before you know it."

"Come on, Jack. Mimms. You and Sid must know something."

Jack ticked points on his fingers. Jack aped the Sidster's gruff growl.

"Okay, boychik. He's the white sheep of a prominent Negro family. He bilks his own people with that return-to-our-homeland shuck. He's got a southside network of snitches reporting to him, and he reports to Jack the H. exclusive, because they're pals from 'The War to End All Wars.' As a snitch himself, he always bypasses the Dudster and goes straight to Jack. He's got his minions pushing maryjane, in corrosive counterpoint to these Armenian shits who push white horse under Jack's aegis, with Dud as the middleman. Both these factions service an all-jig clientele, which is the way Jack H. and his **un**illustrious predecessor, Two-Gun Davis, think narcotics should play out in our town."

Ashida said, "And that's all the news that's unfit to print?"

"Well, you got your costar in this Mimms drama.

He's this Navy flyboy named Link Rockwell. He's the white Abbott to Mimms' Costello. He passes through L.A. when he's on leave, and he's a bagman for these rich white guys who back the Rev's deport-the-spooks agenda."

Ashida sifted it. His brain gears clicked and meshed. Mimms was sacrosanct. That scotched an approach.

Jack said, "Mimms has got darktown hot-wired. He could help the PD out with this job, but you'd have to bypass Chief Jack. He don't like to be reminded that he's asshole tight with the Rev."

Reckless Girl went to lunch. He hid upstairs and watched her walk to Central Avenue. He deployed Man Camera. He close-up shot photo trails.

He began downstairs and worked upstairs. He detail-shot the stairway to the landing and the bedroom door. He was a camera lens and shutter. He went objective and subjective. He posited **this:**

He's a left-handed killer. He walks Rice, Kapek, and Archuleta downstairs. He walks them individually. His victims are terped to the gills. He's got his ice pick pressed to their necks.

His victims flail and bounce off the walls. Note the wall pictures knocked to the floor.

Man Camera. Let's shoot reverse-angle snapshots downstairs.

Ashida walked back down. He's the killer. His victims have ingested carbolic acid. All three are near death. He positions them on the couch. He's got his ice pick to their necks. He steadies them with it. He one-hand strangles them. **Or—he has help.**

Ashida went back upstairs. He reversed field and walked from the bedroom door to the stairway. He Man Camera'd the right-side hallway wall and the floor-juncture points. He snapped the downed pictures. Palm trees and seascapes. Pix that came with the crib.

Let's shoot close-ups now. Let's shoot those floor-juncture points.

He did it. He snapped scuff-mark indentations. They were low on the wall. They were sharp-point indentations. They're in with the dumped pictures. Dent, dent, dent—here to there:

Straight across from the bedroom doorway. Dent, dent, dent—all along the right-side wall. Dent, dent, dent—terminating at the steps leading downstairs.

Man Camera. Let's hypothesize. Let's hazard a guess.

They're scuff-mark indentations. They're sharply pointed. They connote a woman wearing high-heeled shoes.

It's all theoretical. It's inconclusive and unprovable at this point.

Ashida walked into the bedroom. He dumped his Man Camera and opened his evidence kit. He studied photos of the semen-stained sheets.

Four semen stains. Four differentiated blood types. Two O-positives. One O-negative. One rare

RH-positive. Dr. Nort blood-tested the dead men. Archuleta was AB-neg/not applicable. Rice and Kapek were O-positive secretors. It was odds-on NA. O-positive was the most common white-European blood type.

Whorehouse. Fuck flop. Acey-ducey antics. Differentiated jizz stains. Perverted acts performed. Performed with men, performed with women. There's no way to tell.

Did sex acts precede the murders? Did the victims or their killer or killers watch/abstain/perform? There's no way to determine that.

Ashida donned his headband light. He bent over the bed and went in close. He quadrant-scanned and saw five small hairs. He'd run two prior scans and missed them.

Dark hairs, curled hairs. Surely pubic hairs. The three victims were dark-haired men.

He tweezed the hairs and prepped his kit microscope. He dialed tight and scoped the hairs, one-off and collectively. He determined **this:**

Three hairs are male. Two hairs are female. The maxilla circumference indicates gender. He's not a physician. It's Dr. Nort's final call.

Ashida walked downstairs. He grabbed the PD's callout phone and buzzed Dr. Nort. He described the hair samples and said he'd bring them in. Dr. Nort said he'd compare them to the stiffs' pubic hair.

Reckless Girl was due back. Ashida walked upstairs and went back to work.

He stifled shrieks. He quashed effete exhalations. It came on belatedly. He knew what it meant.

The stains. The shit traces. Inverted sex acts. He ran from Reckless Girl. She understood inversion and called him an invert. He should have fought back.

Ashida wiped his face and caught his breath. He redusted. He redid touch-and-grab planes. He hit one dresser, two nightstands, the closet door and shelves. He got smudges, smears, distressed latents. He pulled a stack of phonograph records. The grooved plastic would thwart lifts. The covers would sustain.

Jazz records. Duke Ellington and Count Basie. Obscure Negro ensembles. The klub**haus** rolls heterodox.

Ashida dusted. He powdered twenty-one album covers. He got smudges, smears, badly distressed latents. He dusted cover #22. Erskine Hawkins and his 'Bama State Collegians. **The White Dog Blues.**

He got more smudges and smears, more badly distressed latents. He got one partial latent—a top-half fingertip.

Ashida tape-lifted it and rolled it on blank cardboard. The partial looked near-familiar. He checked it against his elimination prints. No loops, whorls, and ridges matched. He saw the two Statie print cards that Dudley supplied. Hector Obregon-Hodaka and Kyoho Hanamaka.

He instantly nixed Hanamaka. All his fingertips bore burn scars. He ran eye clicks. He clicked the partial to the Obregon-Hodaka card. He matched three comparison points. He fell short of a conclusive ID.

He dusted four more album covers. He got smudges and glossy-surface smears.

He got out Tommy Glennon's address book. Ray Pinker pulled two Glennon latents off the front cover. He didn't dust the pages. They were semigloss paper. They might sustain prints.

Ashida flipped through the book. He got hackle bumps. Something seemed wrong. He noted four names. All four played **wrong.**

Dr. Lin Chung.

Dr. Saul Lesnick.

Orson Welles.

Wallace N. Jamie.

Tommy Glennon's a rape-o. Lesnick and Chung are dubious physicians. He knows their reputations himself. Jamie and Welles. A private eye and a film **wunderkind.** Those names, this address book. It does not logically track.

The address book was pocket-sized. Page dusts were difficult work.

Ashida adjusted his headband light. He placed the book atop the dresser and opened it flat. His car keys held it steady. He arrayed his powder and brushes and jumped—

He got thumb-ruffle smears on page one. He got straight smears on page two. He got zero on pages three, four, and five. He got something on page six.

It looked familiar. I've seen you before. You look like a smooth-glove print, but—

You lie flat below the top-digit line. Glove prints

don't do that. I've got a hunch that I know what you are.

Man Camera now. Strike an all-objective pose. Observe yourself as you do this.

It's auspicious. You're trembling. Open your evidence kit. Pull that print card Dudley sent you. There it is. You willed it. Yes—it's a perfect match.

Kyoho Hanamaka. His burn-scarred right forefinger. The ghoul touched Tommy Glennon's address book.

53

(LOS ANGELES, 2:30 P.M., 2/3/42)

The boys are back in—

Elmer and Buzz hit the Gordon Hotel. They parked their prowl sled on the sidewalk and opened strong. They pinned their badges to their sport coats and tornado'd the lobby. The desk clerk went **Oh shit.**

Elmer went **Oh shit.** That selfsame guy worked the desk New Year's Eve. He'd tossed Tommy G.'s room then. Buzz knew shit per all that.

Rumdum tenants snoozed in chairs. A radio spieled war news. The fucking Japs stormed the Pacific. They barbecued white missionaries and keestered stray cats.

The clerk said, "Gentlemen?"

Buzz said, "We're looking for Tommy Glennon. This is his last known address. We figure he might have come by for old times' sake, or he might have had folks coming by to say hi."

The clerk eyeballed Elmer. Buzz retrieved the look. Elmer gulp-gulped.

The clerk picked his nose. "Tommy skedaddled New Year's Eve. He said, **'Adios, muchacho,'** so I figured he was Mexico-bound. He gave me ten clams to store his boxes, which I summarily did."

Buzz slid him a ten-spot. " 'Summarily,' huh? That's fine for then, but now's now, which means you should show us Tommy's shit."

The clerk unlocked a door upside his switchboard. He pulled a light cord, all nice-nice.

Elmer and Buzz stepped behind the desk and scoped the doorway. Elmer gulp-gulped. Buzz woo-woo'd Tommy's shit.

It was old news to Elmer and new news to Buzz. There's Tommy's New Year's Eve gear.

The smut books. The Jap flags and Nazi armbands. The tattoo stencils—swastikas and Sinarquista snakes.

The clerk futzed with the switchboard. Buzz pulled Elmer in tight.

"You seen all this before. How's New Year's Eve sound? You, Breuning, and Carlisle fluffed that stakeout on Tommy. You got this dimwit notion to go out rogue."

Elmer smiled and zipped his lips. Buzz said, "Who put that burr in your tail?"

"I wasn't about to shoot some fucker in cold blood. It all came down to the Dudster messing with me."

Buzz winked. "This partnership is starting to gel. We're looking at some big fun."

Big fun, huh?

Buzz tattled his own Dudley tale. It's the Watanabe job, post–Pearl Harbor. Dud's working a land grab. He's out to snatch Jap property and promote boocoo gelt. Buzz extorts the mick fucker. He gets cash plus a **biiiiiiiiiiig** bonus.

Buzz had three pregnant girlfriends. Dud was tight with Huey Cressmeyer's mom, Ruth Mildred. Ruthie was a licentious lez and defrocked physician. She worked at Columbia Pictures. She did all the film-goddess scrapes. She scraped Buzz's girlfriends, gratis.

Big fun, huh? Yeah—and Buzz figured **this:**

Dud would up and kill him. He'd frame some jigs for it and get away clean. He figured he should bide his time and kill Dud first.

Big fun, huh?

Elmer perched in Lyman's back room. Lunch was two highballs and three bennies. He was alone. The rest of the Crash Squad was gonesville. Buzz was occupied elsewhere.

They went by Huey C.'s bungalow and saw Dud's prowl car out front. They staked the crib and saw Dud lead Huey outside. Huey's face was glue-smeared.

Huey was glued to the planet Mars. Dud tossed him in his car and drove off.

Address-book duty loomed. Elmer had dropped Buzz at St. Vibiana's. His gig: brace Monsignor Joe Hayes. Elmer drove to Lyman's then. His gig: bone up on Jean Clarice Staley.

Jean bounced for maryjane, back in '36. He knew that already. It was old news. Lee Blanchard posted a background-check note. Jean Staley was allegedly an ex–Paramount starlet. She works as a carhop now. Blanchard attached a mug-shot strip. The Jeanstress wore glasses and still looked **goooooooood.** Blanchard closed out his note: "Additional file at Red Squad office/ Wilshire Station."

Ooooga-booga. That's food for thought.

The Red Squad was hush-hush. It was cloak-and-dagger and a one-man show. Lieutenant Carl Hull lock-and-keyed the files at the Wilshire DB. Hull was in the Navy now. Hull was an ardent anti-Red and pal of Whiskey Bill Parker. Hull hoarded one file set only:

The Communist Party (U.S.A.), its own self.

Parker greased the skids. The Crash Squad rated top access. He called Whiskey Bill. Whiskey Bill called Wilshire. The watch boss opened the office and found the file.

Some file. It ran **mucho** brief. Tortilla-thin meets threadbare.

Elmer sat at Carl Hull's desk and put his feet up. He

looted Hull's cigar and liquor stash and got comfy. He read through the file. There's our girl:

Staley, Jean Clarice. White female American. DOB: 1/28/09/Beaumont, Texas.

Jean graduates high school, 1926. Jean migrates to L.A. Jean's mom and dad kick in a dust storm, summer '32. Jean's got a kid brother. Robert Arthur Staley's a homo prostitute. He does a two-spot juvie bounce at Preston. Jean does that reefer bounce. Before that, there's **this:**

She's live-wire CP. She's in a cell with four other Reds. She carries the card. She toes the Red line and wears the Red beret. She's a part-time starlet and full-time Red reptile.

The cell boss is one Meyer Gelb. Jean's cellmates are a beaner named Jorge Villarreal-Caiz and two Commos—

Oops—

Named Lesnick.

Dr. Saul. Dr. Saul's daughter, Andrea.

It's old home week. Small world, huh? What goes around comes around. Life's one big circle jerk. It's who you know and who you blow.

Old Saul. Annie Staples' trick. Ed Satterlee's snitch. Psych doc of Orson Welles and Claire De Haven. Fuck-flop target of Sergeant E. V. Jackson.

Elmer skimmed file sheets. They ran threadbare. He ran dozy. An occurrence sheet jerked him awake.

October '33. That very hot month. The PD Arson Squad rousts the cellmates.

Per the Griffith Park fire. The blaze that scorched Wayne Frank. It's all Meyer Gelb's fault. He made "apocalyptic remarks." He predicted "big antifascist chaos."

The rousts went nowhere. Gelb retracted his remarks. The hullabaloo died out.

Kay Lake jive-talked this deal called the **Spiritus Mundi.** It's some eastern swami hoodoo. It's the place where all our shit coheres and our souls intersect.

Elmer got the heebie-jeebies. Kay just sold him on the **Spiritus Mundi. Woo-woo**—he's heading there now.

The carhops hopped on skates. They hopped cars-to-kitchen, round-trip. They wore red-and-white tunics and puffed-leg slacks. The girls looked good and hopped good. Jean Staley looked and hopped the best.

Simon's Drive-in stood across from Hollywood High. It was a streamline-moderne job. Cars circled a walkway ramp and an inside counter. Some bleached-blond cooze hopped Elmer. He popped her for whore vag in '39. She didn't recognize him.

Elmer sipped a pineapple malt. He spiked it with Old Crow and three bennies. Jean Staley hopped cars in his **perv**-view. He watched her sling burgers and glom tips.

She skated nice. She dipped her tray nice. She dipsy-doodled and drew wolf whistles and hoochie hoots. She was East Texas/barn dances/male kousins all Klanned up. Kay's **Spiritus Mundi.** He saw his shit and Jean's shit, entwined.

It perplexed him. He grabbed Tommy G.'s address book. Jean Staley's initials are in there. That Vice clerk got him her full name. He glommed her PD sheet last month and tumbled to her weed roust. He planted the address book to fuck with Dudley Smith. It's fake evidence in a real murder case. He planted names in the address book. Lin Chung and Doc Lesnick radiate Fifth Column. The klub**haus** is Fifth Column. Jean's revealed as Red now. Old Saul was her '33 cellmate. The cell got braced per the '33 fire.

Spiritus Mundi? Yeah, he gets that. Beyond that, there's just **this:**

Jean Staley. Barn-dance femme fatale. She sure can sling hash on skates.

54

(LOS ANGELES, 4:30 P.M., 2/3/42)

Ruth Mildred held court. She excelled at screwball comedy. Her office proved the point.

The dippy Deco furnishings. Props scrounged from **Dinner at Eight.** The cheesecake wall fotos. Ruth Mildred's nice-girls-in-a-jam.

Ruthie pointed to Joan Crawford. She said, "I scraped her. A coon trombone knocked her up."

Dudley roared. Juan Pimentel went **tut-tut.** Huey Cressmeyer snoozed on mama's couch.

Ruthie pointed to Katharine Hepburn. She said, "I scraped her. I sold locks of her snatch hair for a C-note a pop."

Lieutenant Juan grew a Hitler mustache. It sprang up dark and thick. He wore Statie blacks north of the border. He lived to cause fear, wherever he went.

Huey snored. He required resuscitation. Model-airplane glue laid him low. He built a Messerschmidt squadron and succumbed.

Ruthie pointed to Sylvia Sidney. She said, "I scraped her. I licked her bush while she was anesthetized."

Dudley yanked Ruthie's cord. "Regretfully, I must call for an intermission. I have questions for your grand boy before the lieutenant drives him south."

Ruthie dug out her dope spike and filled it. Nazi-issue amphetamine possessed pop. Harry Cohn swore by it. Ruthie injected his starlets. They toiled in grade-Z turkeys all day and Harry's private stag flicks all night.

"The Dudster's a killjoy. My baby needs his beauty sleep, and his mommy loves to strut her stuff."

Lieutenant Juan said, "Dr. Cressmeyer should re-settle in Tijuana. I would see to the reinstatement of her medical license. We are currently battling a VD epidemic. Our vivid nightclub acts have spawned this medical plague. Donkeys, you see. You never know where they've been and who they've been with."

Dudley roared. Ruthie roared big. She swabbed Huey's arm and tied him off. Huey snored. Ruthie tapped the spike and fed him the juice. She went **There, there** and held her baby's hand.

Lieutenant Juan timed the wake-up. His wrist-watch ticked off three minutes. Huey babbled and twitched.

Dudley shooed Ruthie and **El Fasco** out. He bolted the door and pulled a chair up to the couch. Huey twitched, babbled, twitched.

He slurred verses of the "Horst-Wessel-Lied" and "Lili Marlene." He babbled up the Deutsches Haus and its habitué, "Mitch." "Model-airplane man, model-airplane man." Huey made no sense.

Dudley lit a cigarette and blew smoke in Huey's face. Huey coughed. His eyes popped open, wide.

"I have questions, lad. Prompt compliance will earn you a pat on the head. Evasions will earn you a beating."

Huey pouted. "I want to go home. You've got me on some jaggedy hop, and I'm zorched to the gills. I want to mess with my pin map. I've got the Russian campaign all doped out."

Dudley twirled his ashtray. "You may have heard that two policemen and a Mex pal of theirs were mur-dered late last month. Your friend Tommy Glennon may have been involved. Wendell Rice, George

Kapek, Archie Archuleta. Do those names sound your chimes?"

Huey picked his nose and admired a loose nugget. Huey pulled out a paper clip and excavated his ears.

"I don't know no Archuleta. I've seen Rice and Kapek at the Deutsches Haus, but we just sling a few barbs at the kikes, and let it go at that. They're far right—but who ain't? If I'm lyin', I'm flyin'."

The Deutsches Haus. It appeared in Tommy's address book. The PD raided it in December. It was now Fed-infiltrated. That nixed an approach.

Rice and Kapek appeared in T.J. They wheeled a truck toward the border. He ran photo-device pix and saw them. Photo fuzz obscured the license plates.

Dudley chained cigarettes. "Far right to the extent that they'd run fugitive Japs?"

"No, that don't beat no tom-toms for me. But Rice used to brag that he was running wetbacks—if I'm lyin', I'm flyin'."

Dudley said, "Lad, how do you **know** this?"

Huey shrugged. "Fifth Column's Fifth Column. We all drink at the same trough and pick at the same fleas."

"On that note, then. Where's Tommy Glennon?"

"I ain't seen him since he left Quentin. That was back in November."

"Do any Japs habituate the Deutsches Haus? I'm thinking of a man named Kyoho Hanamaka."

Huey scratched his balls. "Japs on the loose, since

the Day of Infamy? Japs who ain't already in stir for the war's duration?"

"Can you connect Tommy G. to the Deutsches Haus, or Rice and Kapek?"

"**Nein**—'cause the Deutsches Haus didn't open up until sometime in '37, and Tommy was in Quentin then. As far as Rice and Kapek go, you've got Rice bragging that he ran wets, and Tommy used to run wets for Carlos Madrano. It's like the Fifth Column concept. Everybody knows everybody—if I'm lyin', I'm flyin'."

Dudley cracked his knuckles. "Let's talk about Tommy's address book."

"Okay."

"Let me run a few names by you. Lin Chung, Orson Welles, Dr. Saul Lesnick, Wallace N. Jamie. Can you relate these men to Tommy, or to anyone else that you might consider Fifth Column?"

Huey made the jack-off sign. Huey grabbed his crotch and went **Consider this.**

"Moving along, then. Monsignor Joe Hayes, a woman named Jean Staley, the hot-box phone by the **L.A. Herald** building, and fourteen pay phones in Baja, rumored to receive coded calls of a suspicious nature."

Huey squirmed. He was bored. The psycho thrill killer wants his diesel-dyke mommy.

"No, nix, **nein,** and **nyet,** Uncle Dud. All us fascist types use phone drops, but I don't know nothing about pay phones in Baja."

"Your name was in Tommy's address book."

"That ain't no large surprise. We used to correspond, from here to Quentin."

"He wrote 'Big Dick' beside your name. I'm wondering if you lads might have traveled the Hershey Highway at any time during your reform-school or on-the-loose sojourns."

Thrill-killer Huey. He kills Jews, kills jigs, kills Japs. He kills behind pique, ennui, and glue withdrawal. Now, he's **aghast.**

"It's a fucking lie! He ain't never seen my dick!"

Dudley flashed his photostat. There's that address-book page. Tommy extolls Huey's big dick.

"That ain't Tommy's printing! He used to write me! Tommy don't print that way!"

Huey was credible. He oozed indignation and righteous affront. He went Greek. Tommy went Greek. They sought the Greek grail—but not together.

The address book had been altered and planted at the klub**haus.** That seemed evident now. Who performed these misdeeds? Puerile Elmer Jackson comes to mind.

Dudley sat in Luke's Shanghai. It was Bill Parker's C-town haunt. Parker disdained the ritzier Kwan's. Uncle Ace vexed him no end.

Dudley sipped green tea. He'd dropped by Lyman's en route. The address-book pages were photostated and tacked to a bulletin board.

He studied the block printing. He saw hesitation marks. Huey's "Big Dick!!!!!" was a badly forged addition.

The botched New Year's stakeout. Tommy flees and drops the address book. Cretinous Elmer grabs it. The act spawns his series of inexplicable gaffes. That seems theoretically evident now.

Hideo called him at Lyman's. He found a burn-scar print in the book. It matched Kyoho Hanamaka's print card. Tommy was privy to Baja-based Fifth Column operations. That seems evident now. The print links Tommy to Hanamaka and his faked-death act.

Parker slid into the booth. He wore civvies and cradled a highball. He'd cut himself shaving. His belt piece weighed down his pants.

Dudley smiled. "It was good of you to meet me, sir."

Parker lit a cigarette. "I've told you before, we're both captains. This pertains to Jim Davis' admissions, and you're here as Jack Horrall's proxy. With that in mind, I'm listening."

"And, with that in mind, I'll open with a question. Have you seen the photostated pages from Tommy Glennon's address book posted at Lyman's?"

Parker said, "No, I have not."

Dudley said, "Names from the Watanabe job are crossing over to the klub**haus** job. Specifically, Lin Chung, Saul Lesnick, and the Deutsches Haus. We need to address this and limit the extent of Jim Davis' exposure, along with the risk of discrediting our arrest of Fujio Shudo, soon to be sentenced to death and executed."

Parker crossed himself and killed his drink. Beseech Kay and Joan, Bill. They round out the Trinity.

"We should set terms. Something that will appease Chief Horrall and satisfy both of us. Something we can both live with."

Dudley said, "Now, **I'm** listening."

"No frame on this job. No killing convenient suspects. Put Breuning and Carlisle on a tight leash."

"Agreed."

"Immunity for case-to-case witnesses who provide leads that clear the klub**haus** job. We've got a rubber-stamp grand jury installed now. We may as well put it to good use."

Dudley said, "Agreed—but within that, I must insert a codicil. Rice and Kapek were rogue cops of a most pernicious ilk. We must make every effort to suppress evidence of their malfeasance at trial, to limit general testimony, and to urge the presiding judge to issue a directed guilty verdict."

Parker said, "Agreed." A fresh highball appeared. Parker drained it double quick.

Dudley smiled. "Full disclosure, Captain. Rice and Kapek were spotted at the border, three nights before their deaths. They may have been running wets or fugitive Japs."

Parker shrugged. "You're Army SIS, Captain. Mexico is your jurisdiction. I don't care what you do there. Nor do I care if you judiciously abrogate the rule of law here in the States."

Dudley bowed. "I consider that a grand declaration and nod to informed latitude. It would please me to grant you a concession."

Parker lit a cigarette. His leaky Zippo whooshed.

"Put Jim Davis under pentothal. Take him to Terry Lux's farm and forcibly sequester him. Have at him there. We need to determine what he might know about the klub**haus** job."

Dudley said, "Agreed."

Parker said, "I cannot abide executing Shudo. Have Horrall brace the DA and hint at our impasse. We need a true bill from the grand jury, along with a decline-to-file DA's writ, buttressed by an insanity ruling submitted by a blue-ribbon panel of psychiatrists. We've got Shudo on multiple counts of kidnap and sodomy. He'll never get out."

Dudley offered his hand. Parker clasped it. The deal was **comme ci, comme ça.** The fucking Werewolf survives. Jack Horrall will fucking **SHIT.**

They made love straight off. They peeled their way to the bedroom and left the lights on. Joan held on his eyes.

She rolled under him and above him and moved him about. She got him just so and fixed on his eyes.

He tried to untie her hair. She swatted his hands

away and pinned them to the bed. She clamped his head and bent down to kiss him. She did not shut her eyes. He kept his eyes open. It sealed their spell.

They started that way and finished that way. Joan killed the lights then. She got them cozy. She said, I must tell you something. You must not interrupt.

She cinched narrative lines. The Rain, The Gold, The Fire. It's all one story, you see.

The charred box. The gold chip within. The dead man worked the gold heist. Wayne Frank Jackson died a short distance away. The elements have conspired in our favor. We owe this moment in the dark to The Rain.

The train journey south. The Griffith Park blaze. The gold bar stored in the locker. The gold bayonet. The burned fingerprint. Did Hanamaka singe his hands in the park that very hot day?

The Reverend Mimms bailed out the prime gold-heist suspect. The Reverend Mimms owns the klub**haus. It's all one story, you see.**

Fritz Eckelkamp escapes from the train. There's a partial bullet match to a robbery spree. Wayne Frank Jackson is detained and released. The spree precedes the fire. The fire occurs. Some Reds are detained and released. I met one of them at a party. **It's all one story, you see.**

Hideo Ashida put most of this together. He urged me to disclose it and to bring you in on the gold. It's yours as much as ours. Your skills surpass ours. I defer to Hideo in all matters that concern you. He's far less compromised in his affections. I will never be as exclusively in love with you.

I should be stitching sailors on a battleship somewhere. I attribute all of this to the war. Our convergence is a heady bit of wartime magic. Ask your friend the Wolf about that.

Have you felt him in your presence? He's determined to do his part in keeping you safe.

I wake up and see him at the foot of the bed.

Claire disdains the Wolf, you know. I find it endearing that a scientist should relinquish herself to this beast.

You're the beast I've relinquished myself to. I'll be decorous, and refrain from mentioning your littermate, Bill Parker.

I deserve such brusque mention. I shouldn't have brought up Claire.

I met her at that party I told you about. Did she tell you we'd met? It's the war again. The party couldn't have occurred at any other time.

She told me you were nude together, in a steam room. You and Orson Welles, no less. She didn't state your name, but I knew it was you. This very tall and brazen redhead, she said.

It was another magical convergence. Tell Claire that she's a fool not to believe.

I'm going to interview young Welles soon. His name turned up in Tommy Glennon's address book, as I'm sure you already know.

Tell him Red says hi.

I've been to the Maestro's house. Another party, some time ago. I may tell you the story one day.

You owe me a story, given the one I told you.

I wholeheartedly acknowledge my debt there.

I went to the party to observe Kay Lake. It should be a bitter rivalry, but we're becoming friends. She's got me keeping a diary.

Write of me frequently and fondly, dear.

My lips are sealed, but I may show you if the mood strikes me.

You have me reconsidering the notion of debts. It prompts me to say, How can I ever repay you?

Well, there's the gold, of course. And you might also find the man who killed my father. That would be nice of you.

55

(LOS ANGELES, 9:30 A.M., 2/4/42)

She hated him now. She conceded his brilliance and despised his effeminacy. She told him that Dudley was in and cut it off there. Ashida went smarmy and smirked.

Dr. Nort arrived. His presence muzzled her. She'd prepared jazzy ripostes. They spoofed Ashida's crush on Dudley. He was Renfield in **Dracula.** He intoned, "Master, I come."

Lyman's back room socked in heat. Joan cracked a window. Shrieks echoed upstairs. Mike Breuning phone-booked a snotty witness.

Dr. Nort said, "I matched the male pubic hairs to our victims. That leaves the female samples unknown. We've got one Latin, and one Caucasian."

Ashida said, "The semen stains. Were you able to—"

Dr. Nort cut in. "Rice and Kapek, most likely. O-positive is a very common type, and that's as far as I could classify the secretions. Archuleta was AB-neg. I got four differentiated ejaculate groups. Our boys plus two unknown males."

Joan lit a cigarette. "I examined the stains. There's no sign of cellular erosion, so I concluded that the stains were recent—perhaps as recent as the night of the homicides. Can we posit an orgy that went spontaneously bad? Do the unidentified ejaculates correspond to more than one killer? Say it's an orgy. Did our other men participate, abstain, or were the stains left at varying intervals?"

Dr. Nort sipped coffee. "We don't really know who secreted what. Beyond that, we've got no leads on the two women."

Ashida dunked a tea bag and blew on his cup.

The snotty witness screamed. The upstairs floor-boards shook.

"I have a theory. I think the killer led the victims downstairs, individually, with his ice pick pressed to their necks. All three are debilitated from their consumption of terpin hydrate. They stagger, flail, and knock those framed pictures off the right-hand side of the wall. There are a series of kick-mark indentations, low on that wall. They indicate a woman wearing pointed-toe shoes. The kick marks do not indicate any concentrated degree of force. It's as if she were observing the forced marches downstairs, and the kicks were her form of punctuation."

Joan mulled the theory. Dr. Nort shrugged and tapped his wristwatch. The snotty witness screamed. Dr. Nort went **eeek** and walked out.

Joan locked the door. She pointed to the corkboard and Jean Staley's green sheet.

"She's on Elmer Jackson and Buzz Meeks' interview list. We already know a few things that they don't. They may learn that she was in Meyer Gelb's cell, and that the members were questioned about the fire that killed Elmer's brother."

Ashida studied the green sheet. He scanned the text and tapped a routing stamp.

"She has a CP file. They keep all those files at Wilshire Station."

Joan pointed to the wall phone. Ashida walked up to it and dialed out. He spoke low and listened. He hung up and stamped one foot.

"Elmer saw the file yesterday. Captain Parker arranged it."

Joan said, "Here's what we're up against. Is Jean Staley germane to this case, or to the fire case, or to our other one? Will the fire be mentioned in the CP file? If so, how will Elmer react?"

"He's been alerted to a possible fire-case link. A gold-robbery link is most unlikely here."

Joan mulled it. Ashida slouched against the wall and twirled the phone cord.

"Miss Staley's name appeared in Tommy Glennon's address book. I find that book suspect in and of itself."

Joan leafed through the corkboard reports. She studied the book photostats. They were white on black and tacked straight across.

She saw what Ashida saw. Block-print forgeries. Hesitation marks and ruler marks. Four names were forged. The name Jean Staley was discernibly legit.

"You're right. Chung, Welles, Lesnick, and Jamie are forged."

The Teletype clattered. Joan tore off the sheet. Fourth Interceptor sent a communiqué. Lieutenant H. J. Ashida/you've been summoned south.

"This should please you, Hideo. Our handsome Irish friend has mischief in mind."

56

(TIJUANA, 5:30 P.M., 2/4/42)

It's dusk in teeming T.J. Soldier, beware. The ghastly ghouls are out.

The he-shes. The whores. The jarheads down from Dago. The zip-gun boys.

Ashida parked on Revolución. He gave a zip-gun boy ten centavos to watchdog his car. The boy was eight years old. He goofed Ashida's Army duds. Ashida mind-read him. **Usted es un Jap.**

Dudley shot him a note at the Biltmore. It said Jack Horrall kowtowed and pink-slipped his early release. The note critiqued probable address-book forgeries. The key suspect was one E. V. Jackson.

Ashida agreed. The why of it perplexed him. The note concluded: "Meet Lieutenant Juan Pimentel at the Blue Fox."

Strolling ghouls checked out Ashida. The sex-show barkers. The rat-meat taco vendors. The male prosties in bullfighter chaps. Ashida rigged his Man Camera and shuttered them out.

This is Mexico. Certain questions persist. Where's Kyoho Hanamaka? The fourteen Baja pay phones in Tommy's address book. **Qué es el** truth there?

Ashida strolled. There's the Blue Fox. It's licentious and lewd-legendary. Hoochie girls lured sailors inside. They wore blue fox masks and tails. They were otherwise nude and single-digit pubescent.

Ashida shut his eyes and pushed past them. He entered the Fox. Big noise hit him. He opened his eyes and saw **this:**

A bandstand. An androgynous trio. A tethered donkey sporting red devil horns. Tables packed with U.S. Marines.

The trio featured a sylph vocalist, trumpet, and sax. They whipped through the "Marines' Hymn" and segued to **this:**

"Mama's on welfare!!!"

"Papa's in jail!!!"

"Little sister's on the corner—yelling, pussy for sale!!!"

"Grandma's on white horse!!!"

"Grandpa's on glue!!!"

"Little brother's getting cornholed by some jigaboos!!!"

Ashida stood, stunned-o. Ghouls fluttered by. A girl tongued his neck. A boy grabbed his crotch. A he-she fondled his holster. He tried to move. He failed to move. The ghouls glued his feet to the floor.

He deployed Man Camera Left. Nude girls danced on a bartop. Seated sailors muff-munched them and jerked off. He deployed Man Camera Right. Fox-face girls table-hopped and fellated Marines.

He shut his eyes and shut it out. A schizy sound track rolled in the dark.

"There he is."

"You are very astute, Huey. Of course it is him. He is the only Japanese within view."

"Come on. You said you'd call me **'mein Führer.'** "

"If it pleases you—yes, of course."

"I think he's cute."

"He's Oriental cute, which is not my sort of indulgence."

"He won't open his eyes. This place must seem pretty raw to him."

"Come, Lieutenant Ashida. Captain Smith has a full night's work for you."

They took Ashida's car and hit the coast road south. Ashida drove. His ghoul colleagues lounged in the backseat. Pimentel sniffed cocaine. **Führer** Huey made kissy sounds. Pimentel reached over and played the radio. Father Coughlin proclaimed.

The drive protracted. Pimentel mimicked Jap Zeroes at Pearl. Huey mimicked bomb blasts and sailors fried alive.

They passed Ensenada and cut inland. They climbed scrub hills and found it: this weird A-frame chalet.

The lights were on. Dudley stood outside. He wore a kimono. He embraced Ashida and called him **"Ichiban."**

Pimentel and **Führer** Huey peeled off. They were bivouacked in the surveillance **haus** up the next hillside. Ashida unloaded his lab gear. Dudley assisted. Ashida Man Camera'd him.

He swayed here. He walked inimically straight in L.A. He's T. E. Lawrence West now. He's gone native. Call him Smith of Mexico. He overlords the brown hoi polloi.

His kimono swirled. Ashida studied the design. It was orange-and-black silk. Little Sinarquista snakes were inlaid.

They toured the hideaway. Dudley dubbed it the **"Wolfschanze."** He'd appropriated the chalet and planned to remodel it. Maestro Klemperer's L.A. spread inspired him. Claire had showed him jazzy snapshots.

Ashida viewed Hanamaka's hidey-hole. Dudley posed in Nazi tunics cut to fit him. Ashida read Hanamaka's journal. He trembled as he flipped pages. The lunatic Left and Right merge behind one banner. This war marks a prophecy fulfilled.

They sat down in the living room. Faded bloodstains covered one wall. Dudley served warm sake. A phonograph murmured **Parsifal,** low.

They discussed the gold and all events related. They time-machined back to May '31 and October '33. They stopped at the klub**haus** today.

They tracked police-file revelations. Fritz Eckelkamp and Wayne Frank Jackson. The liquorstore spree. Tommy Glennon's address book. Brother Elmer's forgeries.

Jean Staley. Elmer, poised to brace her. Miss Staley's

membership in Meyer Gelb's cell. Martin Luther Mimms. Dudley's plan to brace Chung, Jamie, and Welles.

The dialogue wound down. **Untersturmbannführer** Ashida remained attentive.

Dudley said, "Comb the place, top to bottom. See what you can find."

A midnight rainstorm came and went. Dudley drove back to Ensenada. Lieutenant Juan and **Führer** Huey stuck to the lookout **haus.** Ashida roamed the **Wolfschanze.** He'd inventoried his gear. It covered all contingencies.

Three microscopes. Three forensic hot plates. Print cards and print-lift tools. Evidence pouches/beakers/ Bunsen burners. Three forensic vacuums.

The task was confirm or refute. Try to match L.A.-to-Baja locations. The Hanamaka print linked the klub**haus** to the **Wolfschanze.** Try to link conversely here.

Prints first.

Ashida dusted the downstairs walls. He powdered wide swaths and naked-eyed them. He saw washcloth wipe marks overlaid with dust.

Thick dust. Hanamaka vanished on December 18. It was now February 5. The washcloth marks and dust overlay confirmed his departure date.

Ashida dusted downstairs furniture. He hit hard

surfaces only. They were all print-sustaining/all touch-and-grab.

He got wipe marks, smudges, and smears. It confirmed the professional wipe job. The smudges and smears overlaid the marks. That meant they were recent. The smudges and smears were surely Herr Dudley Smith's.

Ashida dusted the upstairs walls and furniture. He got the same results. The upstairs dust had settled in thick. Dudley kept the windows cracked wide.

Fibers next.

He installed vacuum bags and worked with flat and scooped nozzles. He vacuumed carpets, soft furniture, floor-to-wall points. He pulled up rug grit and dust and filled three bags.

He emptied the bags on Dudley's kitchen table. He naked-eyed the contents. It was all dust and rug grit.

Ashida switched nozzles. He installed a soft-bristled one. It caught buffed-surface particles best.

The one bathroom had been wall-and-fixture wiped. Washcloth swirls plainly showed. This was in-tight work. Get behind the toilet and under the sink.

Ashida worked on his knees. He swept the nozzle over flat surfaces and pushed it against sink pipes and wall planes. He got the sink, the bathtub, the toilet. No suction sounds reverberated. All fiber snags would run silent here.

Dawn broke clear and bright. His muscles throbbed. He smelled his own sweat.

He walked to the kitchen table. He donned his headlamp and looked into the bag. He naked-eyed toilet-paper scraps and one dark blue thread.

He plucked the thread and placed it on a microscope slide. He dialed close and saw the interior shaft. The weave indicated fine silk. The cross weave indicated cheap dye.

Maybe. Just possibly. This could be—

Ashida rigged a comparison scope. He removed the thread and placed it on the right-side mount. He dug in his evidence kit. He found his comparison thread.

He placed it on the left-side mount. He dialed both lenses tight. He looked left-right, left-right, left-right. He made this determination. It's an identical match.

Wendell Rice. His Hawaiian shirt. The shirt he died in. Wendell Rice was here at the **Wolfschanze.** Wendell Rice died at the klub**haus.**

Ashida went up-all-night woozy. He stumbled around the kitchen. He went weak-kneed. Flashes lit the one window. It startled him.

The flashes repeated. They hit once, twice, three times. A pattern repeated. Short, long, short. It was Morse code/dot, dash, dot.

Light hit the window. The same sequence repeated. Ashida knew Morse code. He deciphered it.

Dots and dashes. Dashes and dots. They spelled out "We love you."

The flashes hit windowpane glass. They hit downward. They flashed from somewhere outside and above.

Ashida brought binoculars. He grabbed them and

held them up to the window. He dialed in. He glanced up and out and saw **this:**

The lookout **haus.** A wide window there. Lieutenant Juan and **Führer** Huey. They're holding up a hand mirror. They're flashing "We Love You/ We Love You/We Love You."

Lieutenant Juan and **Führer** Huey. They're stark nude and entwined.

57

(LOS ANGELES, 10:00 A.M., 2/5/42)

The **Herald** headlined it. Tall type jumped out and slammed you. Sid Hudgens inked the piece.

WEREWOLF BEATS GAS CHAMBER!!! D.A. MANDATES LUNACY BOUNCE!!!

Elmer read the piece and reread it. He sat in his prowl sled. Simon's was packed. He read and **perv**-viewed Jean Staley, intermittent.

The Sidster's style packed panache. Chief Horrall was a "heartbroken humanist." He could not "abysmally abide" a "Werewolf barbecue." "Devoted-to-justice detectives" brokered a deal. NO GREEN ROOM TREK FOR WEREWOLF, D.A. BILL MC PHERSON SEZ.

Elmer tossed the paper and snarfed his breakfast.

He noshed nutritious today. His pineapple malt was infused with Old Crow. **Oooga-booga.** The Werewolf gets a skate. Sid fed him the inside dish back at Lyman's.

Bill Parker got all weepy. Poor Werewolf—boo-hoo, boo-hoo. He confabbed with El Dudster. Demands went down. It was a frame job, anyway. Fuck the fucking Watanabes. Who cares who killed them? The Werewolf rates a stroll.

Elmer scoped Jolting Jean. Her tortoiseshell glasses wowed him. She packed panache herself.

That same bleached-blond carhop hopped him today. That was good. He was saving Jungle Jean. He had to scurrilously scope her out first.

Her CP file hexed him. He got weepy for Wayne Frank. He recalled the good times. He ignored Wayne Frank's shitbird demeanor and Klan escapades.

Buzz hopped in the car. **Wham!**—this Okie cyclone.

"I ain't seen you in two days, but I thought I might find you here."

Elmer said, "I'm staking out a suspect."

Buzz wagged his eyebrows. "Yeah, I can see that."

"You feel like reporting? I ain't seen you in two days, either."

Buzz torched a cold cigar. "I braced that papist hump, Joe Hayes. He impressed me as a froufrou, but he didn't reveal no racy drift on Tommy. He said he was Tommy's confessor, and that was it."

Elmer made the jack-off sign. Buzz said, "I went

back to Lyman's then. Breuning and Carlisle had posted a note. It said Dud's coming back in. He's all set to brace Chung, Welles, and Jamie."

Elmer yocked. Buzz blew smoke in his face.

"Then I remembered that Huey Cressmeyer's mama works at Columbia, right by Huey's flop. So I drove over there, and the first thing I see is Dud's car, parked outside on Gower—with a Mex Statie sedan parked right behind it. I got the plate number, called the Ensenada barracks, and learned that that particular sled was checked out to some lieutenant named Juan Pimentel. This led me to believe that Dud and mama were baby-sitting Huey until Pimentel could get him down to Baja and hide his homo ass out."

Elmer whooped. "Because Huey's in Tommy's address book, and he's Dud's snitch, and he's jungled up with Dud in three thousand questionable ways—and we're set to pull him in for questioning."

Buzz rewagged his eyebrows. "So, I played a hunch on Pimentel. I called the Sheriff's Office here, plus Orange County and San Diego County. Get this. San Diego R & I has a green sheet on old Juan. He got popped in a fruit-bar raid in '37, but it got hushed up, because Juan's got juice with the Staties. **Then,** I go back to my stakeout at Columbia. I see Dudley, Huey, and some uniformed beaner who's got to be Pimentel walk out. Him and Huey wave bye-bye to Dud and take off in that Statie sedan. I tail them to the coast road southbound, and that's all the news that's unfit to print."

Elmer slurped his malt. He eyeballed Jean Staley. He mulled the Huey dish. Jean did this nifty tray dip.

Buzz said, "Are you going to brace her, or peep her for the rest of your life?"

Brace her, boss. You gots her under yo skin.

He swooped that night. He hit at 8:00 p.m. He bopped to her Beachwood Canyon hut. He wore his best chalk-stripe suit and new brogans. He primped and rang the bell.

She cracked the door. He saw one eyeball and badged her. She pulled the door wide.

She wore dungarees and a white tennis shirt. She'd pinned up her hair. She wore schoolmarm glasses. Her joy de viver undermined the dowdy effect.

"You're not the Sheriff's, because they've got that six-pointed thing. You're not the state AG, because they don't come around anymore. You're not the FBI, because Mr. Hoover goes for beefcake types, and that's not you."

Elmer smiled. She talked East Texas. She downplayed it. It still poked out some.

"If you're trying to tell me you've been around, you've succeeded."

"I'm not trying to tell you anything. I'm just wondering why you're letting me give you so much guff from jump street."

"Well, I did have some questions."

"All spiffed up, at this time of night?"

"Let me in, will you? It won't take that long."

Jean squinted. Her cheaters magnified her eyes. Jean the Defiant. Screw you—I still look good.

"You're stalling me. There's a whole lot of things I want to talk to you about, but I can't do it standing at your door."

She had buck teeth and sleek hair. Note the gray strands in with the brown.

"You've been frequenting Simon's. All the girls knew you were up to something."

Elmer said, "I popped that blond girl for pros vag a while back. She must have spread the word."

Jean went **Well, all right.** Elmer walked in. The front room featured Navajo rugs and green leather chairs. Stand-up ashtrays clinched it. Some men's club tossed a yard sale.

Elmer took a seat. Jean took a seat. Wind blew the door shut.

Jean said, "What's on your mind?"

"My name's Elmer Jackson, in case you were wondering."

"Is it Lieutenant?"

"It's Sergeant, and I'm lucky to have that."

"I'm not going to ask you what it's all about. Cops always get to it soon enough."

Elmer peeled a cigar. "Why was the state AG coming around?"

Jean crossed her legs and lit a cigarette. She hunkered in some.

"I was a Communist, back when lots of folks were.

A dumb hillbilly girl—that was me. And the CP was something I sure as you know what came to regret."

Elmer said, "You must have had a lot of visitors. Red Squad men, Feds, Racket Squad guys up the ying-yang."

Jean blew smoke rings. Elmer glimpsed her starlet side. She crouched inside herself and played to men.

"I was in a cell. All we did was rattle our own cages and listen to ourselves talk. We went to labor marches and carried banners. The Feds carried cameras and got pictures of us. We were real-live CP. We shot our mouths off, and you boys started coming around asking questions. That was enough for this little Red duck."

Elmer blew smoke rings. They came out all dispersed.

"Did you fink? You got disillusioned, it was the Depression, you realized the Party was all full of crap. I'm just thinking aloud now. Finking was a way out for most of you Commo types."

Jean crushed her cigarette. "There were five of us in the cell. I finked the guy I liked the least, and the one I figured would do the most harm in the long run."

"Who was the guy? Come on. His name's on six dozen lists somewhere."

Jean said, "Saul Lesnick. I finked him because he talked too much, and got people to convert to the Party just by wearing them down with the yak-yak. He was a Beverly Hills psychiatrist, if you can figure that."

Blackout sirens whooped. Elmer and Jean froze. The all-clear signal blew. They unfroze quick.

"Who else was in the cell?"

"A man named Meyer Gelb. He was the leader, and another big fatmouth. We had a brief wingding, which shows you how susceptible I was in those days. There was Dr. Saul's nutty daughter, Andrea, and a Mexican named Jorge Villareal-Caiz. He went back to Mexico and hooked up with his brother, Victor. They got embroiled in the plot to clip Leon Trotsky, then I heard they went fasco. If you want my opinion, the Party was no longer au courant, so in the end everybody just picked up their toys and went home."

Jungle Jean rats Old Saul. That was prime drift. Beyond that—**c'est la guerre.**

Jean said, "You look parched."

"Does it show that bad?"

"I'll whip us up mai tais. I used to barmaid at the Wan-Q."

"A mai tai and some peanuts. It sounds like supper to me."

Jean smiled. "Atlanta, Georgia?"

"Wisharts, North Carolina. Like Beaumont for you. It's this place you leave from."

"Leave for where?"

"The Marine Corps and Nicaragua. Then L.A., on a bet."

"That's your lifetime itinerary?"

"That's right. And it's all been prelude up to you."

Jean rolled her eyes and cut to the kitchen. Elmer

heard drawers scrape and slam. He scoped the front room. The crib played bohemian. The weird blankets induced eyestrain.

The Jeanstress returned. She dipped and posed, carhop-style. Elmer snatched a drink off her tray.

"Everybody's got an itinerary. I'd sure like to hear yours."

Jean sipped her drink and plopped her feet on a hassock. She said, "My name's in six dozen files you've read. You've got it down pat."

Elmer sipped his drink. "I'm just prolonging the interview. You'll say, 'What's this all about?' pretty damn soon, which will damn near break my heart."

Jean futzed with her tumbler. Ice cubes click-clicked.

"I'm dead bored, and you're not the only one prolonging. If you intended grief, you'd have dropped the punch line by now. It's Thursday night, and I've got tomorrow off. I've got nobody to stay up late with, and this is a swell diversion."

Elmer stretched his legs and plopped his feet on the hassock. Jean's feet bounced a half inch away.

"I've got a part-time girlfriend named Ellen Drew. She goes back to the '30's, at Paramount. Did you see **If I Were King**?"

"I knew Ellen. We used to schmooze at Lucy's El Adobe. She's still at Paramount, and she's on her second part-time husband. I also heard she turns tricks for Brenda Allen."

"Brenda's my other part-time girlfriend. I run that call service with her."

Jean lit a cigarette. "Your face just dropped down to your lap. Does running girls chagrin you?"

Elmer relit his cigar. The whore biz double-chagrined him. Jean had good sonar.

"Did you know a Paramount geek named Ralph D. Barr? He was some sort of stagehand or carpenter."

Jean said, "I knew Ralphie, but Meyer knew him better. Meyer had a cameraman gig at the studio, and he used to recruit for the Party there. He was running a one-man book on the side. He had his Commo aspect and his money-grubber aspect, and never the twain shall meet."

Ralph D. Barr. Arsonist and whipout man. Detained and released, 10/33.

"Barr was a firebug, wasn't he?"

"Coy doesn't suit you. You know from Ralphie. He set fires and pulled his pud until the fire engines came."

Elmer played somber. "My brother died in the Griffith Park fire. Remember? October '33?"

Jean played no-shit footsie. Her foot tapped his foot. She tapped with expertise.

"Here's something else that you know damn well, and I damn well remember. The cops rousted our cell. Because of that fire, because Meyer was making speeches, predicting fires and tidal waves and all sorts of CP hoo-ha, because capitalism was producing spontaneous combustion, so get ready for some god-awful thunderstorms and conflagrations. He was preaching that crap before the fire, so the cops came around, and then it all went blooey."

Blooey. That said it. Gasbag Gelb. Gasbag Lesnick. He gasbags to Annie Staples.

Jean said, "Meyer knew this fruity English poet. W. H. Auden, his name was. W.H. wrote a poem for one of his numerous boyfriends, and it had the words 'This Storm' in it. Meyer read the poem at his rallies, to work up the rubes. You know how this works. You provoke the rubes, and the cops come nosing around."

Elmer tapped Jean's foot. "Like yours truly."

Jean went **Yep.** Elmer said, "You and your comrades got leaned on, but it was just routine."

Jean went **Yep.** Elmer said, "What about the old gang? Do you still stay in touch?"

"Not much. Meyer loops through my life every so often. I saw him at a party a week or so back. Otto Klemperer's place. You know—that hotshot maestro who had the brain tumor. The Lesnicks were there, so we all said hi and bemoaned the Hitler-Stalin pact. It was typical CP horseshit."

Elmer heh-heh'd. Annie Staples was there. He'd hot-wired her.

Jean sighed. She'd had enough. **¿Qué es** this **jive, muchacho?**

Elmer came clean. "Your name turned up in a hoodlum's address book. Tommy Glennon. It all pertains to a case I'm on. The fire stuff is incidental. My brother died that day, and it's always mauled me."

Jean drained her drink. "My kid brother Bobby goes for boys. To each his own, okay? Bobby met

Tommy at some kind of Catholic youth event, because that's where those type of boys go to find chicken. Okay, they got something percolating. Bobby was staying with me then, and Tommy was calling him here. Bobby was crushed when Tommy got sent to San Quentin."

Elmer tapped Jean's foot. Jean tapped his foot back.

"Did Bobby know that Tommy raped women? That the evil little shit worshipped Hitler?"

Jean sighed. "Love is blind. Don't they say that?"

"I say we're both stir-crazy. I've got a fat roll yelling 'Spend me,' and I want to spend it on you."

Jean dressed up nice. She put on a floral-print dress and new glasses. A fox throw topped her off. For-real fox heads and fox paws stuck out. Elmer goo-goo'd the foxes. It coaxed Jean to laugh.

They played southern rubes on a date. They talked up Wisharts and Beaumont and all points between. He told Jean he hated the Klan. She loved that. She told him she hated the Reds now. He double-loved it.

They drove up to the Strip. It hopped sans marquee lights. The blackout created this ghost-town effect. Elmer played the big kahuna out to paint the town red.

He overtipped lavish. Waiters and barmen genuflected. They hit the Troc and the Mocambo. They danced fast and slow and worked up an appetite. Elmer waved to Charlie Barnet and Lena Horne.

He made like he knew them. Jean knew it was a shuck.

Dave's Blue Room was straight across Sunset. Brenda and him owned 10%. They made a big entrance. Kay Lake and Joan Conville waved from the bar. The standard Elmer Jackson hubbub ensued.

He's that bagman cop. He runs girls with Brenda A. Who's that cooze with the glasses? That fox throw's from hunger.

They noshed steak sandwiches and slurped Dave's renowned gin fizzes. They hashed out queer kid brothers and Klanned-up brothers roasted alive. A tipster cruised their table. He ratted a coon 211 gang. Elmer whipped a yard on him. The tipster salaamed. Jean said, "He was yanking your chain." Elmer said, "I'm out to spread the love tonight."

They ditched the Strip and levitated to browntown. Hear dem tom-toms? Let's get tantalized.

They cruised the Club Alabam. Elmer knew the hostesses and bar crew. He'd canvassed them on the klub**haus** job and treated them white. They treated him white right back.

High-yellow girls circled their table. They served illegal corn-liquor shots, on the house. Elmer and Jean downed three shots and toured the solar system. Elmer dispensed C-note tips. You gots to lay down dat love.

A bouncer played escort and dropped them at the Club Zombie. Elmer slid him two yards and sent him off loved. They entered the dark dinge dive. Elmer saw the tall jig he muscled with Lee Blanchard.

He soothed his tall ass. He genuflected his own self. He coaxed numerous smiles off of him. The tall jig poured two Baron Samedi cocktails. "One sip leaves you zombified."

Dat's no muthafuckin' shit, Daddy-O.

Four sips dive-bombed them. They side-draped themselves and weaved back to Elmer's sled. Elmer close-cleaved the middle lane and slow-crawled them up Central.

Per blackout regs. Under the speed limit. With cellophane taped to the headlights.

God got them to Lyman's, undead. The joint jumped with nite-owl cops and their consorts. A waiter read their zombified state and brought them coffee. Elmer crumbled bennies into their cups. The brew took hold **faaaaaast.** They went zombified to electrified.

They talked a lot. They drew stares. Elmer quick-sketched the barside gang. Buzz Meeks, Two-Gun Davis. Kay and Big Joan, reprised. Their talk drifted over. They spritzed heady concepts and big words.

Elmer talked. Jean talked. Elmer said he saved Two-Gun's life and got on the PD. Jean said she saw a colored man lynched in Beaumont. Elmer said him and Buzz were fucking with one very bad hombre.

It got late-late/early-early. The sky lit up gray-gray. They walked to Elmer's car in the rain.

Their electric charge waned. They both started yawning. Jean said, "Not right now, okay? I'm too bushed to be much use to either one of us."

Elmer said, "Okay."

The rain accelerated. Thunder boomed them up to Hollywood and Beachwood Canyon. Elmer parked outside Jean's place. They huddled up and ran inside. Jean's fox throw got soaked.

They kissed some. Elmer went dizzy. Joan ran her coil heater. They kicked off their shoes and fell asleep on the couch with their clothes on.

58

(LOS ANGELES, 10:00 A.M., 2/6/42)

The whiz kid. Fletch Bowron's shoofly. His swell apartment as fix-it shack.

The Bryson. Wilshire and Rampart. A swell spot with a high-window view. Blocked by workbenches. Crammed with disassembled radios and test tubes.

Wallace Jamie was portly and twenty-four years old. He lived to snoop and snitch. He'd keestered crooked cops in Saint Paul, Minnesota. Fletch hired him to rebuff the Feds and watchdog the PD. The move backfired. Indictments loomed.

They stood by the benches. Jamie issued halitosis and fondled dead tubes.

"This grand jury deal's a stifferoo. Everybody made suspect phone calls. You can't indict the whole world."

Dudley said, "I'm sure you're right, sir. This is strictly a routine inquiry, and I'll be out of your way in a very few minutes."

"I don't get this. You're an Army captain and a sergeant on the PD."

"Yes, and I have questions about a punk criminal named Tommy Glennon, whose dubious endeavors have aroused my interest in both of my professional guises. Your name appeared in his address book, you see."

Jamie shrugged. "Well, I'd like to help you out, but I don't know any Tommy Glennon. I've got a listed phone number, so maybe this chump got my name and address there."

Dudley said, "Yes, and you've been in the news lately."

Jamie smirked. "I get fan letters, sometimes. My uncle's Eliot Ness, and he's a well-known hotshot. I haven't gotten letters from any Tommy Glennon, though."

He evinced no hink whatsoever. He beamed forthcoming youth.

"I had a few technical questions, if you'd be so kind. You've convincingly cleared yourself in the matter of Tommy Glennon, and I'd like to move on."

"Well . . . sure."

"Let's take the hot-box phone outside the **L.A.**

Herald as our exemplar. It's a bookie-drop phone, which in no way concerns me. What does concern me are the implementations of Los Angeles-to-Baja pay-phone calls of a Fifth Column nature. Coded calls—pay phone to pay phone."

Jamie went bulb bright. His eyes popped. He almost drooled.

"Okay, this is what you might call intermediate spycraft. You'd have to have a dot-dot substitution code worked out in advance, and agreed upon by both the sending and receiving parties. It would have to be wire-recorded, and the sender would have to hold the device up to the pay-phone receiver. Code calls from regular phones to pay phones wouldn't work, because of the U.S.-to-Mexico relay systems involved."

Dudley said, "Please continue."

Jamie said, "It was canny of you to cite that hot-box phone as your exemplar, so I'll proceed in that vein. That hot-box phone is internally drilled to accept slugs, and you would need that type of drilling to gain access to the applicable Los Angeles-to-Baja relays, all of which have been rigged to feed into bookie rooms in T.J. and Ensenada. Slug calls to **outside** Baja pay phones would thus reach their terminus point **inside** those bookie rooms, **if** a subsidiary dot code were applied. American hoods developed this system in order to relay split-second information on fixed horse races to bookmakers operating in Mexico. **That's** the way it works. Your L.A. spy calls are intentionally made to terminate at the phone banks of bookie operations."

Such a bright lad. A swift autodidact. Pudgy and erudite.

"SIS has a tap on one specific Ensenada pay phone. That's how the coded calls have been picked up and decoded. There have been U.S. air-attack pronouncements, which seem fanciful to me."

Jamie said, "And I'm sure that that specific pay phone has been fruitlessly surveilled. Here's why that's the case. The code calls are retrieved from their bookie-room terminus. Your in-country spies work at that particular bookmaker's front."

He honey-trapped Lin Chung. Uncle Ace stoutly assisted.

Chung was a surefire traitor. Jim Davis revealed that. Chung bankrolled the first Baja sub deal. Chung deserved a good scare.

Dudley lounged upstairs at Lyman's. Ace promised Chung cocaine and white girls. He laced chloral hydrate in Chung's chop suey. Chung passed out in Kwan's Chinese Pagoda and woke up cuffed to a floor-bolted chair.

He rattled his cuff chain. He wiggled his chair. He grasped his I'm-in-the-shit dilemma.

The storeroom was window-taped and cloaked blackout black. Chung screamed and wet his pants. Dudley caught the telltale piss scent.

Ace phone-booked Chung. Dudley caught the telltale head thumps.

Chung screamed. Dudley said, "Why would your name appear in Tommy Glennon's address book, Doctor?"

Chung screamed. Ace rethumped him. Chung re-screamed and Chink-babbled. Ace said, "This cock-sucker speak English good as me."

Dudley roared. Chung rebabbled Chink. Dudley said, "As you wish, Doctor. But please allow my Chinese brother to translate before you continue."

Chung babbled Chink. Short bursts, long bursts, Chink gobbledy**gook.**

Ace said, "This cocksucker say Tommy don't have his address. Say he only know Tommy from eugenics study group at Four Families clubhouse."

He was credible. His name had been forged. That fact alone cleared him.

Dudley said, "What do you know about coded pay-phone calls from Los Angeles to Baja?"

Chung babbled polyglot. Dudley caught Spanish and French. The glot devolved to pure Chink.

Ace said, "I miss some of it. Gist is this cocksucker don't know shit."

Dudley said, "Two tangentially related events oc-curred in December, Doctor. A Japanese family was murdered in Highland Park, and a Jap sub came ashore on the coast, south of Ensenada. You were part of a plan to disguise Jap saboteurs as Chinese and hide them in and around Los Angeles. I would like you to admit your complicity, and give me your solemn promise that you will not engage in further sabotage aimed at the United States."

Chung babbled Chink. Ace said, "He can't speak no English back. He now in second childhood. We pour water on his brain."

Dudley laughed. "Please translate the Chinese idiom, my brother."

Ace said, "This cocksucker admit complicity. He blame crazy cop Bill Parker. Crazy Bill break up cabal and scare white partners away."

That was true. Jim Davis revealed that detail.

Chung babbled. Ace phone-booked him. He swung the fat main directory. He hurled good head-thwapping shots.

Chung gurgled now. He issued babble, down at a hush.

Ace said, "This cocksucker offer vow of fealty and eternal brotherhood. He say if you got daughter, he perform free nose job."

Dudley laughed and lit a cigarette. The sealed room sealed in heat. He cranked the wall heater off.

"There was a second sub incursion, early in January. What do you know about that?"

Chung blathered Chink. He slather-talked now. He oozed discombobulation.

Ace said, "This cocksucker say he don't know shit from shinola. It not his bund, 'cause his bund disband. He say one rumor heard. He say second sub fiasco copycat of first plan."

Ace phone-booked **El Chungo.** The hot seat shimmied. The floor hinges creaked.

Chung whimpered and snitch-babbled. Ace said, "I hear song on radio. This cocksucker 'popcorn kernel too pooped to pop.'"

Dudley laughed. "What did he just say?"

"He say he hear rumor. Jap Navy man hiding in L.A. plan second incursion. Man's name Kyoho Hanamaka. He don't know where man hide."

Bravos **pour** Le Chung. That's a swell lead.

Dudley said, "Wendell Rice, George Kapek, Archie Archuleta. Ask him what he knows."

Ace asked. Chung answered. He slurred his words one at a time.

Ace translated. "This cocksucker say he meet Rice and Kapek at Deutsches Haus. Very casual. They talk race science and go **Sieg Heil.** He say Archie C-town and J-town fool. Buy terp and pharmacy hop from illegal sources."

Chung rebabbled. Ace retranslated him.

"This cocksucker say he just waiting to see who win war. U.S. go postwar kaput. Nazis or Reds take over world then. Democracy for nancy boys and weak sisters. 'Comrade' or **'Kameraden.'** All same to this shitbird."

Dudley hit the lights. The storeroom went vivid bright. Lin Chung lolled in the hot seat. He's cuff-gouged down to the bone.

Ace ripped his shirt down the middle. Ace waved two glass jars. One jar of honey. One jar of big red ants.

Chung screamed.

Dudley said, "Restate the threat, my brother. No U.S. sabotage from this point on."

Chung caught the gist. He went **No, no, no, no, no, no, no.**

Ace applied the honey. Ace applied the ants. They were fat red fuckers. They verged on King Kong size. They were famished and deserved a tasty treat.

Lin Chung screamed. The Wolf materialized. He bayed. Dudley ruffled his fur and kissed his snout.

Chung plus Jamie. That meant two names down. One name remained. This lad deserved a rebuke.

Dudley took Los Feliz east. **Der Wunderkind** was **der Flash-in-der-Pan** and **L'Arriviste.** He rented a show-off shack in the hills. His type lived to soak up praise and impress.

Dudley went by the **Herald** first. He talked to Sid Hudgens and abridged his right of free speech. He laid down the law. I'm your new editor. I will edit all your klub**haus** reportage. Give me the final say-so. Let me peruse all your texts.

Sid agreed. Dudley jumped topics. Sid was a horse-race fanatic. Sid knew from hot-box phones and bookie rooms. Dudley pumped him for **this:**

Pay-phone relay bets. L.A. to Baja. Wallace Jamie's technical spiel. Sid, you dirt**meister.** What say ye to this?

Sid knew three relay spots in Ensenada. Two were

floating and unstable. Spot #3 stood upside the White Dog Klub.

El Dudster thanked El Sidster. And, by the way:

Mr. Hearst hates **Citizen Kane.** Orson Welles adroitly defamed him. Would he enjoy a spot of revenge?

Sid said, "In spades, Daddy." Dudley grabbed Sid's Leica then.

Der Fat Boy's house was two blocks up Berendo. Dudley caught the light and read curb plates. Spanish casas predominated. Fat Boy rented a posh Tudor job.

Dudley parked curbside and walked up the driveway. A gate stood ajar. He smelled swimming-pool chlorine and detoured on back.

Welles was alone. He lounged in a poolside lounge chair. He wore a terry-cloth lounge shirt and swim trunks. He skimmed a film script and oozed lounge ennui.

L'Auteur looked over. He clocked his visitor and gulped. There's a big man with a camera. He's got a badge and gun clipped to his belt.

Dudley walked up close. Welles said, "Hello there. Are you who I think you are?"

Dudley tapped the chair-back catch and put him flat on his back. Welles squealed. The film script flew. Dudley foot-stomped Fat Boy's neck and pinned him faceup.

"Do you know a man named Tommy Glennon?"
"Your name's in his address book."
"Are you a Communist?"

"Are you a Nazi?"

"When do you leave on your goodwill tour of Latin America?"

"Did you know that the OIACC is a Communist front?"

Welles croaked out answers. Straight nos eked out. His eyes bulged. His face flushed. **Die fahne hoch!!!** He endured the Hobnailed Boot.

Dudley hummed "Deutschland Über Alles." Dudley clicked his heels and slipped on sap gloves. Lead weights were stitched in.

He said, "No more steam-room encounters with Claire. I will not permit it."

Welles raised his hands and covered his face. Dudley kicked his hands away. Welles sissy-shrieked.

Dudley slammed him. Dudley aimed downward shots. He got Fat Boy's back, Fat Boy's gut, Fat Boy's legs. Fat Boy shrieked and chewed his shirt collar off.

"I'm building a network of informants, to be run out of Mexico. You are my first recruit. You will rat out leftists and outré rightists within the OIACC and your Hollywood circle. You will rat out the Jewish exiles who sponge off Maestro Klemperer. You will nod once to signal your compliance."

Welles squealed. Welles went **Yes/yes/yes/yes/yes/yes**—

Dudley kicked him in the balls and beat his face bloody. The camera contained color film. The blood red would predominate.

59

(LOS ANGELES, 9:30 A.M., 2/7/42)

Thad Brown said, "We're ten days in. Somebody say something to cheer me up."

Crash Squad briefing. All hands on deck. Torpor had set in. The klub**haus** job as snorefest. Lyman's back room as sleepwalkers' den.

Joan stood by the coffee urn. The klub**haus** job was the gold job. She fretted her gold cuff links and stayed wide-awake.

Mike Breuning mock-yawned. Dick Carlisle lolled his head. Lee Blanchard mimed a heroin nod-off. Buzz Meeks stretched out across three chairs and played dead.

Dr. Nort laughed. Her Dudley laughed. Her Bill looked nonplussed. Two-lover tension popped between them. Joan recalled the **Herald** headline. WEREWOLF BEATS GAS CHAMBER!!!

She sensed the story behind it. Jack Horrall had panicked. Dudley laid out Jim Davis' confession and caused a big uproar. Jack decreed a Smith-Parker summit. Bill seized the reins and forged a mercy deal.

Thad said, "Don't speak up all at once. I don't think I could take it."

Dudley said, "I cleared Lin Chung, Orson Welles, and Wallace Jamie."

Buzz said, "An ambulance took Chung to Queen of Angels. It seems that some hungry ants had themselves a nice lunch."

Dudley lit a cigarette. "Meeks, you are treading a thin line here."

Buzz hooted. The room hubbubed. Elmer Jackson played diplomat.

"I cleared Jean Staley. She was a Commo back in the '30s, but that's all she wrote."

Buzz said, "I cleared Monsignor Hayes. He's Tommy's priest, so his ass was in the book for a reason. I've been looking for Huey Cressmeyer, and I spotted him outside Columbia Pictures. He got into a Mexican Statie sedan, and I trailed him. I lost him on the coast road outside Balboa, and I'm betting he's in Mexico now."

Looks traveled. The whole squad clicked to Buzz. Huey was Dud's snitch. The whole squad knew it.

Thad Brown played diplomat. "You and Elmer head down to Baja and shake the trees for Huey. Consult the Staties first thing."

Elmer said, "Yeah, boss." Buzz winked at Dudley.

"I don't suppose you know where Huey is? I heard he calls you 'Uncle Dud,' which sure implies family to me."

Joan flinched and dropped her coffee cup. It doused her skirt. The room froze. Dudley went for his belt sap. He froze a split second on.

"That line is about to fray, Meeks."

Buzz grabbed his crotch. "Does it gall you that you

don't scare me? That you're just some Pope-sucking shitheel as far as I'm concerned?"

Dudley pulled the sap. Elmer stepped between him and Buzz.

Thad said, "Enough."

Bill Parker said, "This stops now."

Dr. Nort said, "Somebody else report."

Joan stepped in. "I dismantled the terp stills at the klub**haus.** I ran tests and determined that the terp in the feeder vats possessed the same molecular componentry as the terp from the still of a Japanese man named Donald Matsura. Hideo Ashida and I confiscated that still last month. Matsura committed suicide at the Lincoln Heights Jail."

Icebreaker. The floe snapped. The room thawed out some.

Lee Blanchard said, "I've recanvassed until I'm blue in the face. I got a lead that the klub**haus** fools filled up their own trash cans and started dumping their debris in their neighbors' cans. It was all booze bottles, used rubbers, musical-instrument reeds, and otherwise what you might expect. The neighbors said the **haus** was a hot-sheet spot, a jam-session joint, and a hobknob pit for whites, spooks, and beaners—which I think is what's behind these snuffs, not all this Sinarquista and Nazi jive. I've also got four eyeball-wit sightings of Rice and Kapek in the thick of it with colored whores that they obviously picked up on the jazz-club strip—even though them snatch-hair samples that Ashida found belonged to a white girl and a Mex girl. I realize that all of this contradicts Sid Hudgens' campaign to whitewash our dead pals, but then I'm not the one telling Sid what to write."

Mike Breuning coughed. "Dick and I have put together a list of the Japs that Rice and Kapek rousted while they worked the Alien Squad. We're doing divisional DB checks now, looking for cross-filed paperwork. Jack Horrall sealed their Narco files, so we've got no truck there. We're looking for file notes on Archuleta, but I think Jack foiled us there, too. He's trying to build a wall between our guys and Archie, because Archie's a low-life sack of shit."

Thad coughed. "Post the list and stand ready to roust the Japs who've managed to stay out of custody since the night of the homicides. Blanchard, you hit the jazz strip, get drunk or act drunk, and try to get a line on any whores or other women who might have frequented the **haus.**"

Joan said, "There's been no mail deliveries since two days before the homicides. I called the branch P.O. on Slauson and asked why. It seems that the route carrier's been off on a toot, and his mail's gone undelivered. He's out of the honor farm and back at work now. There should be a large stack of mail delivered later today."

Thad nodded. "Grab it, Joan. Read it, catalogue it, and compile a list of the senders."

Dr. Nort raised a hand. Thad went **Hold on, now.**

"I'm thinking of running a series of lineups. One for jazz-club types, one for suspect Japs, and one for

Mex political types. The Deutsches Haus keeps popping up, and I'm thinking of raiding it, even though
half of the habitués are Fed plants. Those Sinarquista
flags keep vexing me, so I got Sinarquista membership
lists from Treasury and the Feds' Subversive Detail.
We've got a whole battalion of those punks right here
in Boyle Heights."

Dudley cracked his knuckles. "I'm Spanish-fluent.
I'll make a stab at some interviews before I head back."

Thad nodded and yawned. He went **shoo.** Get out
of here/solve this fucking thing/don't scotch my fucking shot to be Chief.

The room evaporated. Dudley signaled Joan. It
meant **Tonight?** She signaled back. It meant **No, I've
got Bill.** Her Dudley chuckled. Her Bill caught the
exchange.

Joan pulled a klub**haus** shift. She worked, distracted.

Hideo Ashida booked to Baja and left tasks incomplete. It vexed her. The Dudley-Meeks tiff vexed
her. Her Dudley—baited and goaded. Her Dudley—
enraged past control.

Joan print-dusted. Ashida left her an undone-
surface list. Pipe fittings, radiators, phonograph legs.

She did the work. She powdered hard-to-reach
places and got bupkes. She worked, distracted.

The gold quest felt stillborn. Dudley nixed more
file checks. He believed they'd arouse suspicion. Don't
state undue interest or provoke it.

Ashida backstopped Dudley in Baja now. It juked his propensity to lust and deceive. Ashida tweaked Dudley's vanity perversely. Dudley viewed their compact as two geniuses entwined. Baja inspired corruption. It played to the venal and rewarded deceit. Ashida would seek to undermine Dudley. His lust was covetous and malignantly defined. He would conspire against her. His motive was jealousy. She had what he did not. He would attempt to steal her fair share of the gold.

Joan dusted phonograph tubes. She worked, distracted. Sid Hudgens had jammed her outside the **haus.** He flashed a sheaf of color snapshots.

It's Orson Welles. He's tear-streaked and bloody. There's poolside cushions soaked red.

Sid said, "Guess who?" It was easy. Welles saw her naked. He saw Claire De Haven, likewise. Actions spawn consequences. "Big Red" made this occur.

Joan dusted tubes. Large tubes and small tubes. It was tight brushwork. She got smudges, smears, and one latent print.

She applied tape and lifted it. She pressed it to stiff cardboard. She pulled her elimination-print file and ran comparison checks. She got no match.

She slipped on her headband light and reading glasses. She counted loops, whorls, and pocket dents. She numbered an unknown-print card.

The doorside mailbox clanged. There's the postman. He's back from his dry-out retreat.

Joan walked out to the porch. Two Newton blues

stood guard. One woofed her and waved. One said, "Hey, Red."

The mailbox was stuffed. Joan dislodged manila envelopes. Wendell Rice received four parcels. They were sent from Terminal Annex. All box mail was re-routed there. It bollixed mail traces up.

She opened a six-by-eight parcel. A small booklet was stuffed in. It was glossy-bound and cheaply printed. It comprised a gold-case lead.

The Back-to-Africa Manifesto. Authored by Martin Luther Mimms. The Rev bailed out Leander Frechette. Elmer and Buzz interviewed him.

Joan skimmed the text. It was plainly nuts. Nazi U-boats would escort Negro warships to the verdant Congo. Pilgrims would feast on barbecued Jews. Enslaved Congolese would guide the pilgrims downriver. Tame crocodiles would pull ten-ton canoes.

Joan slit the second envelope. It contained a sister tract.

AmeriKKKa for Whites!!! AfriKKKa for Blacks!!! (in support of the Reverend M. L. Mimms), by G. L. Rockwell.

The young Navy flyer. The Rev's white sidekick. Elmer and Buzz braced him.

Joan skimmed the text. It predicted racial apocalypse. The Learned Elders of Zion had annexed the **Jew**nited States. The Ku Klux Klan fought them back. Noble Negro legions rallied and joined their KKKause. The Jews sought to **Jew**nify the U.S. and

Russia. All noble Negroes must flee to AfriKKKa **NOW!!!!!**

Joan recalled pillow talk. Dudley riffed on Wendell Rice and George Kapek. One—they were batshit crazy. Two—Hideo Ashida's photo device snapped them in Tijuana. Three—they were probably running wetbacks and/or fugitive Japs.

Envelope #3. **The Red Swastika,** by Salvador Abascal. It's a catchy title. Pithy subtitles cover a full page.

A Polemic on the Potential Brotherhood of Dispossessed Totalitarians.

A Utopian Vision of Hoarded Monies and the Promulgation of a New Gold Standard to Assure the Solvency of Catholic Nationalists Worldwide.

Joan skimmed the text. Abascal was a devout papist and proponent of Sinarquismo. The tract extolled Nazis and defamed Jews. It extolled the Spanish Falange and defamed the Loyalist cause. It extolled Irish nationalism and defamed the British-Protestant oppressor. It was anti–U.S. imperialist. It was pro–Catholic workers worldwide.

Abascal veered hard right. He added hard-left hoo-ha and spiced up the brew. His first subtitle stated the theme. He described its first "radical implementation."

November 1940. A secret conference is held in Ensenada. The Hitler-Stalin pact flows in full bloom. Nazi and Soviet high-ups attend. They pooh-pooh their political divisions. They blare their antidemocratic ideals. They discuss fascism and communism. They define it as one philosophy, united. They acknowledge the curse of factionalism. They defame the divergent rhetoric that individuates and self-defines them. They redefine themselves as nonopposites. They are as one in their hatred of the democratic West.

Hitler will breach the pact. The Germans and Russians both know this. Hitler will invade Russia. The cost will be ghastly. America will enter the war. America will align with Russia and turn against Russia should the Allies win. How will **WE** survive such a catastrophe? How will **WE** surmount the horror of an Axis victory? What will **WE** do should **der Führer** decree Russia's annihilation?

The dialogue extends. Postwar strategies are discussed. What should **WE** do? **WE** must probe beneficial solutions. **WE** must assure totalitarian survival.

Joan caught the upscut. The all-caps **WE** said it. How do **WE** prepare for contingent postwar shitstorms? What do **WE** enlightened few do?

Abascal was crazy draconian. Rockwell and Mimms were race-baiting buffoons. They were collectively ridiculous. All three "Polemicists" were boobyhatch bait.

Joan slit envelope #4. She slipped out a tract. The title packed punch:

New Implementations of Air Attack in the Coming World Conflict, by Mitchell A. Kupp.

Bill talked a blue streak. Joan tuned him out. They lay in bed. She heard every third word he said.

Mitch Kupp. The airplane nut and Charles Lindbergh boon companion. Her father's death. Her personal vendetta. Kupp was her one hard suspect.

Kupp charters a plane in Duluth. He flies over Monroe County, Wisconsin. A blaze consumes Big Earle Conville that day.

There's a fuel spill nearby. She cannot prove that it caused the fire. She traces the fuel to the charter service. She cannot attribute motive. Mitch Kupp did not know Earle Conville. It all goes away.

She built her own arson file. She worked on it all through grad school. She moved to L.A. and neglected the file. Kupp's tract brought it all back.

Bill talked a blue streak. Joan heard every fourth word. She read the airplane pamphlet. It was not a hate tract or a political screed. It was scholarly and technically dense. Mitch Kupp believed that everyday Joes could fly model planes. He did not advocate race hate or seek to barbecue Jews. He advocated an armed civilian air corps. Airplanes could be built from prefabricated parts. Automotive drivetrains and rivet-forged wings would do the trick.

Bill talked a blue streak. It was all Dudley Smith and Werewolf Shudo and **Look what I did.** It was all **Don't you love me for it?**

She couldn't think. She was back at Big Earle's wake. She pried off the casket lid and viewed his charred corpse. She made herself look.

"You haven't been listening. I've been talking to the bedpost."

"I'm sorry. I know what you've been saying, though—and I admire what you did."

Bill flinched. "You don't act as if you feel that way. You act like you're somewhere else entirely."

She touched his face. "I'm here, and I'm with you. We're in bed, and we've just made love, and I don't know why you require more than that."

His eyes glazed up. He knuckled back some tears. "I know you're sleeping with Dudley. I figured it out today. You know what he is, and you still dishonor me in that way. I tell you that I saved a man's life that he tried to destroy, and you aren't even listening."

Joan brushed off his tears. "Don't ask me to love you for a self-absorbed grand gesture, when you make such gestures routinely. I won't let Dudley go, any more than I'd let you go. The difference between the two of you is that he wouldn't ask."

60

(ENSENADA, 11:00 A.M., 2/8/42)

Stakeout.

They perched on Avenida Floresta. They packed

zoom-lens cameras and box lunches. They sat in a surveillance sled and orbed the White Dog Klub.

Sid Hudgens supplied the lead. Wallace Jamie supplied the phone-relay perspective. Dudley supplied the '34 Ford. Ashida and Lieutenant Juan wore tattered civvies.

The bookie front worked out of a two-story row house. The house was bright peach stucco. Brisk foot traffic traipsed in and out.

Ashida had the front seat. Lieutenant Juan had the back. They raised their cameras and shot the basement entry.

Lieutenant Juan said, "It's supposedly a forty-man operation. I've seen these places. There might be as many as forty phones hooked to a relay board. Look how many men we have walking in."

Ashida shot sidewalk loiterers. He'd shot four rolls of film already. Lieutenant Juan ran his mouth. He was an invert. He was a pederast/**péde/maricón.** Ashida replayed the surveillance **haus** moment. "We Love You" tapped out in Morse code.

Men dawdled by the basement steps. El Lieutenant shot them.

"I've got thirty-odd scalps on my belt, you know. I burned up some saboteurs in a coastal cave. I saw loose teeth expelled. Their abdominal cavities burst."

Ashida reloaded his camera. Lieutenant Juan draped his arms off the seat back.

"I hope you enjoy gossip. You'll become bored with me if you don't."

A woman stood at an upstairs window. Ashida shot her. Lieutenant Juan made a face. Women—**ick.**

"Wendell Rice and George Kapek ran wets for Carlos Madrano. I'm not sure that Dudley knows that. They did a trial run for Captain Vasquez-Cruz, too. Dudley distrusts Captain José, because he thinks he has designs on his Claire. She injects morphine, in case you didn't know. I know the pharmacist who supplies her."

The window woman shifted. Her robe fell open. Ashida saw her breasts.

Lieutenant Juan went **Ick.** "Nice, if that's your sort of gambit."

Ashida shot the woman. A man appeared behind her. He slipped off her robe and kissed her neck. Lieutenant Juan sighed.

"Mexican men run teensy. You know that old joke? How can you tell a Mexican man in the dark? He's got a big belt buckle and a small pee-pee."

Ashida squirmed. La Juan's hands were too close.

"Salvy Abascal's seducing Dudley. Not in **that** way, of course. Salvy's killed a great many priest-killers, which I applaud him for. He's **muy guapo.** Don't you think he's got a big—"

Ashida muzzled him. "Dudley told me a story about a gold bayonet. It was inlaid with swastikas."

"Well, the swastikas sound like Dudley. He's gaga for fascist knickknacks. Don't get me going on **that.**"

"I thought he might have told you about the bayonet."

"Well, all I know is that there was supposed to have

been a secret Nazi and Russian meeting here, sometime in '40. All these alleged counteropposites got
cozy. They discussed melting some gold cache into
political artifacts, to save their keesters regardless
of who wins the war. Maybe it happened, maybe it
didn't. Dudley's bayonet story sounds rather like that.
The nice thing about gossip is that it doesn't matter
whether or not it's true."

SIS was Sunday dead. Ashida worked the squadroom,
solo. The Klein girl studied surveillance files and kept
to herself. Dudley gave her a kid task. It kept her busy
and supplied pocket change.

The gold cache. Melted artifacts. The Red-Nazi
confab. La Juan's gossip reverberates.

Ashida pushed it aside. He developed the bookie-
drop snapshots. It took three hours. He pulled SIS
sedition sheets. Mug-shot strips were attached.

It was drudge work. Cull the bookie-drop shots.
Cull the mug shots and compare faces. Confirm or
refute bookie-drop/Fifth Column malfeasance.

Ashida worked photo-to-photo. The Klein girl kept
to herself. Ashida eyeball-hopped. Bookie shots, mug
shots, repeat the process.

It was drudge work. He viewed right-wing and left-
wing fiends and traveled sedition-sheet byways.

With Redshirts and Goldshirts. With priest killers
and priest avengers. With Stalinists, Trotskyites, and
Sparticists. With the full idiot spectrum.

Ashida flipped photographs. The mug-shot stack dwindled. He yawned. He scratched. He chugged coffee. He rubbed his eyes and—

Hit **Santa Cruz, Luis Ramon. Born 4/19/11, Ensenada.**

Santa Cruz killed two **puto comunistas.** He beat them with a nail-studded plank and cut their dicks off. All misdemeanor charges were dropped.

Luis Santa Cruz:

Snapped outside the bookie front. Exalted Cyclops of the White Dog Bund.

Dudley decreed a raid. He said, "Go in with shotguns, lad. You and our chum Juan. The Wolf will walk point and provide for your safety."

It was a test. Ashida knew that. He must not disappoint.

They parked by the White Dog Klub. They'd discussed the play. They carried 12-gauge pumps. Dudley decreed lethal loads. **Oooh**—double-aught buckshot, rat poison–laced.

Lieutenant Juan ticked off numbers. On three, now. **Uno, dos, tres**—

They ran across the street. Pedestrians wigged out and scattered. They charged the basement door. It refused to give. Lieutenant Juan racked his shotgun and blew off the lock and jamb.

Ashida kicked the door in. The bookie room was

right there. Bookie dinks saw them and raised a raid ruckus. An alarm siren blew.

Fifty-some desks. Fifty-some men. Blaring telephones and stacks of flash paper. Wall-to-wall chalkboards, chalked with horse-race odds.

The dinks lit the flash paper. Bet slips ignited. Ashida saw a relay transmitter at the front of the room.

Lieutenant Juan triggered a spread. A chalkboard blew up. Men yelled **en español.** Smoke covered the room. Ashida triggered a spread and blew up a chalkboard. The recoil knocked him flat.

He hit the floor and crawled forward. Scrambling legs hit him. He crawled toward the transmitter. A man stopped to kick him. Ashida took four head shots. He jammed his shotgun up against the man's belly and blew his guts out.

His own scream outscreamed fifty-some screams. Blood spattered wide. Ashida crawled under the smoke line. He saw Luis Santa Cruz by the transmitter. Luis Santa Cruz flipped a switch.

The transmitter exploded. Santa Cruz vaporized. Legs ran over Ashida. Men fell on top of him. Flames shot up and out.

Ashida crawled and fired his shotgun. He hit legs and severed legs and brought down fleeing men. He killed them and crawled over them. He screamed in English and Japanese. He coughed out black smoke and crawled for the door.

61

(TIJUANA, 8:00 P.M., 2/8/42)

The boys are back—

Said boys crossed the border. Elmer wheeled his spiff '40 Buick. It featured wide whites and an 8-ball shifter. Buzz badged the turnstile goons. They salaamed to **los jefes.** Buzz dispensed dollar bills and contraband smut pix.

The goons cheered. They wore Nazified threads and went **Willkommen.** Buzz **Sieg Heil**'d them back. Elmer haw-hawed.

He peeled rubber southbound. We're here now. We're sanctioned. Let's find Huey C.

Elmer yodeled Old Crow. "We've got to bypass the Staties. It'll get back to Dud, **rápidamente.**"

Buzz snatched the jug. "I've been thinking about that hump, and I've come to some ripe conclusions."

"Such as?"

"Such as, he's a sissy. Such as, he's pussy-whipped. He's got his put-upon Irish wife and his bitch-in-heat Claire what's-her-name, and his umpteen daughters and that bastard girl Beth Short—and without them goo-goo talking him, he ain't shit. In my view, he ain't nothing but a charming lunatic who's got the world bamboozled. Moreover, he ain't as smart as Bill Parker—which just about kills him."

Elmer snatched the jug. "They've got each other dialed, that's for sure."

"You want the drumroll here? They're both poking the big redhead, which means they've got some juice that we don't."

Elmer brain-broiled the spiel. It got him torqued. He chronologized his own Dudster drift.

He don't gun down Tommy G. He finds char-broiled Eddie Leng. Eddie's Fifth Column, boocoo. He's Tommy's KA. Dud wants Tommy **muerto.** Sergeant E. V. Jackson's bored. He goes rogue behind feisty ennui.

Buzz gargled Old Crow. "We got to wrangle Huey someplace secluded and put the spurs to him. All these Fifth Column geeks are jungled up. Huey's got some answers that'll take us back to Kapek and Rice."

"Jack Horrall wants a clean solve on this one. Clean by his standards, I mean."

Buzz said, "Ditto yours truly. A clean solve puts it to Dud, not that I give a shimmering shit about those whipdick cops and how bad the PD looks."

They hit T.J. proper. Elmer slow-trawled Revolución. Buzz checked their backseat stash.

Brass knucks. Beavertail saps. Two sawed-off shot-guns. Leg restraints. Come-along chains. Thumb screws. Friction tape. Wadded-up socks. This cattle-prod gizmo.

Elmer slow-trawled. Buzz orbed multitudinous street whores. Elmer daydreamed.

He daydreamed Jean Staley. Their hot date

reverberated. He called Jean **mucho** times and got no answer. She didn't call him. He sent her flowers. No sweet thank-you call ensued.

He daydreamed Jean and Wayne Frank. Jean's Red cell ran adjunct to the Griffith Park fire. He sleep-dreamed Wayne Frank scorched alive and living flush on some island. Brown girls engulf him. He's melting gold bars into greenbacks.

They passed a **farmacia.** Buzz went **Whoa now** and jabbed him. Elmer idled the sled curbside. Buzz jumped out and ran in.

Kid beggars swarmed the car. Mangy muchachos all. They hawked religious medals and nudie pix of their mamas. They jabbered, "Joo want pussy?"

Elmer dispensed chump change and illustrated hate tracts. FDR with fangs and Jew beanie. Frau Eleanor blowing Joe Stalin. The kids whoop-whooped. Buzz hopped back in the sled. He waved a brown paper bag.

The kids waved adios. Elmer peeled out. Buzz dumped the bag in his lap. It contained **this:**

Liquid terp. Bennie rolls. 180-proof mescal. Diseased worms afloat in the brew.

They pulled into an alley and fortified. It juked their resolve. They jammed the knucks and saps in their waistbands. They ate two worms apiece.

Elmer said, "He's in T.J., if he's anywhere."

Buzz said, "He'll have some Statie watchdog. Dud won't let him go around unchaperoned."

Elmer said, "We've got to get him alone."

Buzz said, "**You** can chaperone me. Them worms got me seeing double and thinking evil thoughts."

T.J. by nite. It's this fucked-up phantasm. White man, beware. Hock your souls at your own risk.

They ditched the sled behind a church and paid two nuns to guard it. They scoured on foot. Buzz packed the flash roll. It was all **yanqui** five-spots. Elmer packed pidgin Spanish and bilingual savoir faire. They bopped loose and orbed for Hugh C.

Huey was a notable pervdog. He sniffed cocaine and model-airplane glue. He boffed boys and butch dykes like his mama. He was a Fifth Column shit-heel and smut-film conno**sewer.** T.J. offered all such deelites.

They scoured accordingly. They hit **farmacias** and flashed Huey mug shots. You see this fucker? He buy dope from you? No, señor—he don't.

The sky melted. The sidewalks weaved. Terp and mescal supplied the effect. The bennies supplied bounce. The terp supplied grip. The mescal sent sparks off their footsteps. Elmer saw his dead redneck kin in with all the nite-hopping spics.

They braced cat-meat taco vendors. They braced sailors down from Dago. They logged nada and no. They braced male prosties in Roman breastplates and padded jockstraps. They got ditto and nix. They hit the noxious nitespots next.

The Chicago Club. The Blue Fox. The Red Cat.

Donkey dives. Cunnilingus caves. Fellatio fiefdoms. Cocktail bars with built-in piss troughs. All-nude stage acts. Connie Lingus and her Cunt Corsairs. Some Cuban coon with a two-foot dick. Dig: he table-hops and dunks it in your drink!!!

They flashed Huey mug shots. Buzz dispensed five-spots. Elmer logged **¿Que?** and **Huh?** They weaved outside and over to Klub Falangisto. The motif celebrated boss man Franco. The walls featured atrocity shots from Guernica and Bilbao. Mex girls danced nude on tabletops. Marines match-singed their snatch hair and made them hop-hop.

Elmer and Buzz table-hopped. Buzz flashed the mug shots. Elmer gagged on burned-hair fumes. They got no, no, no, and one **yes.**

A fat corporal pointed upstairs. He said there's a camera club. He saw that Huey guy there. Look for a bare-chested Mex. He wears chaps. He's got bad acne. Huey keestered him while some slumming Shriners snapped pix.

Elmer and Buzz weaved over to a freight lift. An old guy in Sinarquista garb operated it. Buzz whipped a fivesky on him. The old guy ran them up. The doors slid open. They saw **this:**

One jumbo room. Blasting flashbulbs and wall-to-wall bedrolls. Ten thousand penetrations. Disembodied dicks and holes. Camera fiends jumping bedroll-to-bedroll. More flashbulb blips. "In The Mood" blasting from wall vents. Ten thousand fuck shrieks.

Elmer just stood there. Flashbulb pops made him

see quintuple. He saw five of everything. He **thought** he saw a guy in chaps. Buzz ran toward him or it.

He stumbled over bedrolls and kicked fuckers and fuckees elsewhere. He dumped camera fiends and sent cameras airborne. Elmer saw it all quintuple and lost it just as quick. He popped sweat. He almost lost his legs and his lunch. He shut his eyes and felt himself grabbed.

Buzz screamed upside his face. Elmer heard gibberish and "We got us a lead!"

Here's the drift:

The Mex in chaps turned tricks with El Huey. He poked Huey last night. Huey stole his trick stash. Huey's got a Statie bodyguard. His name's Juan. He goes Greek, too. Huey **ex**-capes from Juan and spawns trouble. Huey's HQ is the Klubb Satan. It's due east of T.J. He's bunked in at El Kasa 69. It's close by.

The boys are back in—

They scrammed. They retrieved Elmer's sled and tore eastbound. Buzz drove. Elmer mixed terp-and-bennie cocktails. Buzz made a purchase en route.

A roadside vendor sold scorpions in small cages. One sting and you're dead. They ate bugs and made dandy pets.

El Scorpio snoozed in his cage. Elmer prepped a kidnap kit. It featured one stuffed-sock muzzle/two brass-knuck persuaders/one come-along chain.

They tore east. They hit dirt roads and scrub hills. They topped a rise and caught this red neon blaze.

Buzz pulled up to it. There's Klubb Satan. It's perched on a packed-dirt flat.

The red blaze was El Diablo. He was two feet high. His dick was fifteen feet long. Said dick blinked, on and off. Note the pulsing pitchfork head.

The building was all cinder block. Sandbags formed the foundation. Locals porked in parked jalopies. Transaxles banged the dirt.

Buzz parked snout-out. Let's be prudent here. Let's boogie and **ex**-cape quick.

Elmer winked at Buzz. El Buzzo winked back. They slurped some mescal. Elmer noshed a toxic worm. They got out and stretched their legs. They hit the Klubb two abreast.

Loud noise/barnyard stink/tethered donkeys onstage. Wraparound booths and a strolling trio. They crooned into microphones. A Mex castrato warbled **this:**

"I've got a girl, her name's Roseanne, she uses a tortilla for a diaphragm!!!"

Elmer clocked the room. He went eyes left. Buzz clocked eyes right. Elmer clock-snared Huey—right there at ten o'clock high.

He's in this big booth. He's biting some boy's neck. Pervdog Huey. The boy was twelve, tops.

Buzz clocked left and caught it. He nudged Elmer. They slid on their knucks and threaded on over. They came off overt and covert.

They bopped up behind the booth. Buzz grabbed a fistful of Huey's hair and plain pulled. Huey flew up and out. He flailed his legs and shrieked soprano. His kiddie paramour shrieked. Elmer kicked Huey in the balls and stuffed a sock in his mouth. A big ruckus materialized.

Satanites craned their necks and peered over. They jumped up and out of their booths. They went **¿Qué?** and **¡Madre mio!** Buzz pulled his piece and popped two shots at the ceiling. The donkeys strained at their tethers and brayed.

Elmer slammed a knuck shot. Huey's rib cage deflated. Buzz **re**gripped Huey's hair and plain dragged him. Elmer ran up on the stage and untied the donkeys. They jumped off the stage and did some **goooood** Satanite trampling. Elmer pulled his piece and popped two shots at the ceiling. Buzz dragged Huey to the door and kicked it open.

The donkeys capsized tables and hoof-stomped revelers. Ten thousand Satanites screamed. The donkeys made for the door. Elmer held it open. The furry fuckers **ex**-caped into the night.

El Kasa 69 was out in the boonies. It was perched behind some hills and tucked out of sight. Buzz rifled Huey's pockets and plucked his room key. Elmer stashed his car in a scrub grove. He walked back to the room. Buzz had Huey double-cuffed.

El Kasa was a hot-sheet hellhole. Tar-paper huts.

Rafter rats. Mismatched wood-plank walls. Huey's room was a pus pit. Piss troughs and one bare mattress. Huey restrained thereupon.

He wore a Luftwaffe jumpsuit. He was wrist- and ankle-cuffed. He'd drooled up the sock in his mouth. Buzz dangled El Scorpio upside his head.

El Buggo malo y feo. He poked at his cage bars and issued evil intent. Huey fright-eyed him. He pissed his pants. The lap lake spread.

Elmer said, "It's about Dudley Smith. We want whatever you've got."

Buzz said, "That means all his current racket plans and everything he's got on Tommy Glennon and Fifth Column grief here in Baja. That also means whatever you've got on Wendell Rice, George Kapek, Archie Archuleta, and those homicides in L.A."

Elmer crouched by the mattress. Buzz scootched Huey's legs over and took a seat. Elmer plucked the sock gag. Huey whimper-screeched.

Words poked through. It was all **I-love-Uncle Dud** and **I-ain't-no-snitch.** Buzz sapped his legs. Elmer sapped his arms. Huey screeched and thrashed and went hoarse quick.

Buzz unlocked El Buggo's cage and poked him out on the mattress. El Buggo gravitated toward Huey. He crawled up Huey's legs and sniffed Huey's crotch. Huey screamed. Buzz positioned the cage on Huey's chest and lured El Buggo back in.

Elmer uncorked the mescal. Huey went **Gimme,**

gimme. Elmer bottle-fed him three good pops. Huey flushed roseate.

Buzz placed the cage next to his head. El Buggo stretched his legs through the bars. He got love-struck and tried to nuzzle Huey.

Elmer said, "Tick, tick, tick."

Buzz said, "That's the clock running out on your life."

Elmer said, "These fucking scorpions go straight for your dick. They inject their poison there."

Huey went **Okay, okay.** Elmer bottle-fed him. A worm dribbled out and hit Huey's chest. Buzz plucked him and dropped him in El Buggo's cage. El Buggo devoured him **faaaast.**

Huey coughed and drooled mescal. Huey evinced snitch fever. Huey tattled **this:**

"Uncle Dud's got these plans to run wetbacks and push horse to the niggers in L.A. He's got this sort-of partner, who runs the Baja Statie Constabulary. His name's José Vasquez-Cruz, and Uncle Dud don't really trust him. He glommed Carlos Madrano's dope stash, and Uncle Dud's got these dope-cadre guys in L.A., all ready to go."

Buzz said, "Where'd you get this?"

Huey said, "My pal Juan Pimentel. He's my body-guard here. He feeds me all this good dish."

Elmer sap-tickled Huey. "For instance?"

"For instance, this. Uncle Dud's got his wetback deal all brainstormed, but he's got to clear it with the

Baja governor first. The guy's name is Juan Lazaro-Schmidt, and he veers **mucho** right. There's got to be some kind of U.S.-Mexico 'guest worker' pact in place before Uncle Dud starts moving the wets north in big numbers. It's a combo deal. You pack the horse in the trucks hauling the wets, and kill two birds with one stone."

Elmer slurped mescal. Buzz snatched the jug. Elmer sap-tickled Huey. The shitbird resnitched.

"Okay, you've got a bunch of resident Japs all rounded up here in Baja. Okay, so Uncle Dud and this Vasquez-Cruz dink have got this piggyback plan cooked up, all abetted by Uncle Ace Kwan in L.A. The deal is, they'll move the Baja Japs north and jungle them up with the L.A. Japs, and hire them out as slave labor. Uncle Dud's already got the Ventura County Sheriff on board. Uncle Dud and Vasquez-Cruz also got plans to move horse up to L.A. in the trucks hauling all the Jap internees. Ace the K.'s got plans to pass off rich Japs as Chinks and hide them out in C-town while he bleeds their Tojo-loving asses dry."

Elmer and Buzz swapped looks. They conveyed **Vintage Dudster.** Huey went **Gimme.** Elmer bottle-fed him. Huey re-**re**snitched.

"There's been scuttlebutt disseminated at the Deutsches Haus. Uncle Dud don't credit all this, but I tend to. There's supposed to be a Jap air attack on L.A. later this month, with some sub shellings of these oil refineries north of Santa Barbara, coming before it. Uncle Dud holds the line at sabotage on U.S. soil. You got to give him that—he's a pro-U.S. white man. But this Vasquez-Cruz geek's allegedly bent on chaos. To top all this off, Uncle Dud's allegedly scared that this here klub**haus** job will bleed into the Watanabe job and deep-six the PD."

Elmer said, "Where'd you get this? The last part, I mean."

Huey went snitch smug. "I got it from Claire De Haven. I've been selling her morph on the sly, and she sure loves to talk. She's also screwing Vasquez-Cruz on the sly, and he tattles her things that she tattles me."

Buzz whooped. "Son, don't you stop there."

Huey coughed. "Claire loves Uncle Dud, but she thinks he's in over his head with all these racket gigs of his. Plus, she knows that Uncle Dud's putting the boots to some redhead in L.A., that Bill Parker's likewise poking. Claire says the redhead is just some 'incremental advance in the Parker-Smith exchange.'"

Elmer and Buzz swapped looks. They conveyed **More Vintage Dudster.** Huey yawned. Huey said, "I'm half in the bag."

Elmer fed him three bennies and one jolt of mescal. Buzz uncuffed him. Huey stretched and rubbed his ankles and wrists.

"You boys should visit the Deutsches Haus. There's this Mitch guy who frequents the place. He's from the Midwest—maybe Minnesota or Wisconsin. He's a brother model-airplane fiend. He knows all about air warfare, and he builds these real, flyable planes from prefabricated parts. I'm not jiving you, cousins. You can build your own airplane, and fly it. Mitch is always talking up this notion of Japs dropping flammable bombs and setting forest fires. He calls it 'chaos from the air.'"

Elmer mock-yawned. "What's this chump got to do with our shit at hand?"

Huey real-yawned. "Nothing."

Buzz jiggled El Buggo's cage. "What's with Dud and Tommy Glennon? He was Dud's snitch, but now Dud wants him clipped. I sense a lively tale there."

Huey went **harrumph.** "I never poked Tommy. Uncle Dud tried to lay that on me, but it was a humbug rap. Tommy's squeeze was this priest named Joe Hayes. Tommy likes his brown eye Irish and Catholic. He got turned out by priests, so he has to have it that way."

Elmer said, "Thank you for them unsolicited comments."

Buzz said, "Let's get back to Tommy and Dud."

Huey scratched his balls and picked his nose. He got this bennie-revved look.

"You want Tommy and Dudley? If you're sweet to me, I'll give you Tommy and Dudley like you've never had it before."

Buzz said, "Don't you get flirty or pouty with us. You do that, I let this centipede loose."

Elmer lit a cigar. "One bite and you're paralyzed. Two bites and you're dead."

Huey went **Oooh, I'm scared.** He put on an arch-fruit lisp.

"Okay, here's your Tommy and Dudley. It's the winter of '39, and there's a **very** posh costume party at a **very** swell mansion in Brentwood. North of Sunset, **daaaarlings**—pheasant under glass all the way."

Elmer said, "Don't string this out."

Huey tittered. "The party was **aaaall** about the Night of the Long Knives, which anybody who's **anybody** will tell you occurred in Germany in the summer of '34, when boss man Hitler had a beef with his Brownshirt **Sturmbannführer,** Ernst Röhm. Ernst liked boys, which anybody who's **anybody** does, but boss man Hitler just **couldn't** countenance that. So, he rounded up some hunky young **Black**shirts and sent them to this spa hotel in Munich, where Ernst and numerous like-minded **Brown**shirts were consorting, and the **Black**shirts found the **Brown**shirts all cozily entwined, and liquidated them presto-changeo."

Elmer said, "Don't stop now."

Buzz said, "Cut the travelogue and get to it."

Huey went butch baritone. "So, the party celebrated this noteworthy event, just for giggles. Everybody wore masks, the men wore Nazi uniforms, and the women wore these beautiful gowns. This highbrow opera music played on this Victrola. I was there, my mama was there, and Harry Cohn was there—even though he's a yid. Lots of Hollywood hotshots were there, Tommy G. was there, and this little Jap guy with burned fingers was there. He told people that he was there for the **real** Night of the Long Knives, but nobody believed him."

Elmer got goose bumps. He looked at Buzz. **He** had goose bumps. Huey sighed and strung out a **loooooooong** pause.

"**Well,** Dudley was **surely** there. He was **veeery** handsome in his SS uniform. He wore a sidearm and a bayonet on a black leather belt. Orson Welles was there. He wore a mask, but I **knew** it was him. He was chummy with this guy who owned the house— some music maestro. Welles always premiered his smut films at the house, and he showed a new one at the party. It was the dirty version of the Night of the Long Knives—and, **daaarlings,** it was a **hit.**"

Huey paused. Huey stage-sighed. Huey tossed his hair. This glue-sniffing psycho mimes Marlene Dietrich.

"Well, **meine Herren**—the **movie.** The killing was all faked, but the oooh-la-la was all real. It was men and women, women and women, men and men. The party quieted down when the movie ended, and the guests started fondling out in the open. They started peeling into the maestro's bedrooms. And, of **course**—Dudley had women **fighting** over him."

Huey paused. Huey stage-sighed. Huey threw his hair over one eye. The fruitcake loon mimes Veronica Lake.

"Uncle Dud kissed and petted with at **least** a dozen

women. The last woman was very tall and thin, and she led Uncle Dud outside and over to a pergola. Tommy and I were close by, but Uncle Dud couldn't see us. We were wearing Brownshirt uniforms, and we were cuddled up and collaborating with two cute **Black**shirt boys. Uncle Dud didn't know that we saw all of this, but Tommy spilled it to him when Uncle Dud visited him in Quentin last November."

Huey paused. Huey stage-sighed. Huey blew mock smoke rings. This Nazi shitheel mimes Bette Davis.

"Uncle Dud and the tall woman kissed passionately. Tommy and I watched. The woman knelt between Uncle Dud's legs. **Well,** her gown hiked, and Tommy and I saw those hairy gams. The moon passed over, and Uncle Dud saw them, too. The woman coughed, **meine Herren**—and it was **surely** a man's cough."

Elmer went dry-mouth. The room spun topsy-turvy. Huey turned female for real.

"**Well,** Uncle Dud screamed then. He pulled out his bayonet and stabbed the girl-boy in the face and the chest. He walked away, sobbing—and if you tell Uncle Dud that I told you all this, I'll be **very** peeved with you."

62

(LOS ANGELES, 9:30 A.M., 2/9/42)

Rain loomed. Low clouds hovered and seeped. Boyle Heights went garish to bleak.

It was Shitsville, both ways. Shack rows and strutting pachucos. Tripe-stew emporiums. Invasive food stench.

Dudley cruised Brooklyn Avenue. The cholos had subsumed the Jews, circa '35. The zoot suit reigned now. Frock coats and beanies, verboten.

Three interviews loomed. Thad Brown had cherry-picked a Fed subversive sheet. Local Sinarquista boys. Three, **todos.** Thad's curious. Did they frequent the klub**haus**?

It's a bind. He served two factions here. He had to plumb the extent of Wendell Rice and George Kapek's exposure. He served the PD there. He served Salvy Abascal and the Sinarquistas, most inimically.

He had to warn and exonerate. He wore Sinarquista green himself. He had to revamp the klub**haus** job and provide a credible solution.

To wit: kill a plausible suspect or suspects. To wit: spics, spooks, or treasonous swine. To wit: quash crossover leads to the Watanabe job. Nullify Bill Parker's Free-the-Werewolf extravaganza.

Dudley scanned curb plates. He was vexed. He felt

constrained. The fucking klub**haus** job consumed him. He should be back in Baja. He had nascent rackets to run. He had to revamp his search for the gold.

He's vexed. He's constrained. He's diverted.

There's dumb cracker Elmer Jackson and smart Okie Buzz Meeks. He's constrained there. He cannot dissolve their partnership. Jack Horrall straddles a fence. Clean solve, staged solve—he's ambivalent. Jackson and Meeks are in Baja now. They have not liaised with the Staties. They may or may not locate Huey. Juan Pimentel has the lad sequestered. Huey was staunch in his way. He would never blab to rogue cops.

He's vexed, he's constrained, he's diverted. He's buoyant, otherwise.

He has Joan. She exemplifies wartime passion and binds him to the gold. He has his brilliant Hideo.

The lad turned a single fiber. It placed Wendell Rice at chez Hanamaka. Hideo Ashida plumbed minutiae. He turned Hanamaka's print at the klub**haus.** A **triple** print check revealed it. He endured the raid at the White Dog Klub. The first Jap-internee transport is at the ready now. It will leave for Ventura County tomorrow. A load of "H" will be stashed on the bus. Hideo will debrief the captive Japs at the border.

He's vexed. He's constrained and diverted. He's more optimistic now.

He conducted his three interviews. They ran prosaically. The three boys attended LACC and bunked with their moms and dads. They eschewed zoot suits and went to Mass thrice weekly. They expressed their intent to avoid conscription and sit out this Jew-derived war.

They knew all about the klub**haus.** They had never set foot inside. They conceded a stern right-wing presence there. The presence of hopheads and jiga-boos negated that. The klub**haus** was inherently un-Catholic. **Está un sacrilegio.**

They offered up no names. They snitched off no klub**haus** klubmen. **¿Qué? ¿Qué? ¿Qué?** We don't know **mierda.**

Three convivial chats. A felicitous morning. Somewhat loosened constraints.

Rain loomed. Black clouds seeped and burst. Dudley drove west and hit his wiper blades. Pachucos ducked under awnings. Note their sodden zoot suits. No Sinarquistas, they.

A car nudged his back bumper. A horn went **toot-toot.** Dudley checked his rear-view mirror and grinned.

Well, now—it's Salvador Abascal.

They lunched at a taco tavern. Salvy knew all the good spots. They shared spicy platters and quaffed beer. Their back booth assured privacy. A waitress cleared their table. They lit cigarettes.

Dudley said, "I'm wondering how you knew where to find me."

"I called Major Melnick in Ensenada, and your

Lieutenant Brown here in Los Angeles. He passed me on to the impolitic Sergeant Breuning, who said, 'Oh, yeah—Dud told me about you.'"

Dudley smiled. "You mustn't consider me suspicious."

Salvy crushed his cigarette. "You have every right to be suspicious. I entered your life in quite the spectacular fashion. We surveil each other from afar and understand each other adroitly, even though we are but casual friends. We touch upon only the most obvious high points of our shared ideology, and rigorously avoid the specifics. This indicates mutual respect. We are not the type of men who indulge frivolous friendships. For men like us, there is no point in friendships that preclude a defining efficacy."

A grand lad. A mind reader and a seer. Father Coughlin thought the world of him. "He's an honorary mick, that one."

"I'm wondering how you came to save my life, and how you arrived at that man Trejo Caiz as my potential assassin."

Mariachi men strolled up. Salvy slipped them a dollar and shooed them off.

"Trejo Caiz was a Stalinist and a wheelman for the murder of Leon Trotsky. He had compiled a death list of fascist sympathizers, and you were on it. I learned of this in quite the roundabout way. Some three years ago, the late Carlos Madrano told me about you. He described you as a 'budding American fascist with profound law-enforcement credentials,' and a 'notable killer for Irish Republican causes.' I despised my boon acquaintance Madrano, and was overjoyed to learn that you had killed him and would soon join the SIS contingent in Ensenada. I have a superb intelligence network. They learned of Trejo Caiz's plan to kill you. I had both of you under surveillance up to the moment of your convergence."

Dudley roared. The Wolf appeared and lapped beer from the pitcher. Dudley reversed his coat lapel. Joan Klein's swastika map pin gleamed.

Salvy laughed. "Victor's brother lives on. Jorge Villareal-Caiz. A yet more pernicious **comunista.** There are no photographs of this evil **puto** extant. I see his face everywhere and nowhere, which confounds me. He is a priest-killer with many scalps to his credit. I have vowed to kill him."

The Wolf trusted Salvy. He was a discerning beast. He rarely bestowed approval.

"Let me indulge a hunch here. Did you and your stout **Kameraden** kill sixteen Jap submariners shortly after New Year's?"

Salvy smiled. "Yes. I received a tip that they were arriving, and carrying a great deal of money. Their plan was to impersonate Chinese men and perform sabotage in and around Los Angeles. We killed the men but did not find the money on the submarine."

Dudley winked. "Captain Vasquez-Cruz and I found the money and split it. My half was ten thousand dollars. I will acknowledge the sixteen scalps you took, and donate that amount to the Sinarquista war chest."

Salvy raised his glass. **"Meine Kameraden."**

Dudley raised his glass. "Do you have intelligence on a naval attaché named Kyoho Hanamaka?"

"No."

"Are you privy to plans for an air attack on L.A. later this month?"

"No."

Dudley said, "I pledge 15% of the profits from my admittedly criminal ventures to our shared cause."

Salvy said, "I am most humbly grateful, although I must risk your displeasure with two requests."

"Which are?"

"That you do not permit the sale of heroin to Mexicans, and that you quash all mentions of the appellation 'Sinarquista' as they might pertain to this scurrilous investigation of yours."

"I am in no way displeased, and I am happy to comply."

Salvy lit a cigarette. "These ventures of yours. Do they proceed apace?"

"Yes and no. I'll need to speak to Governor Lazaro-Schmidt soon. I require some assistance in the matter of exporting guest workers."

Salvy laughed. "You deftly omitted the word **wetback** in my presence."

Dudley laughed. "Lazaro-Schmidt. I'm assuming that you've met the man?"

"I have. He is **un hombre simpático,** if **un hombre** quite covetous and greedy. I find his relationship with his sister disturbing, though. She is a concert violist, and quite lovely. I must accede to decorum here and say no more."

Their waitress hovered. She poured tequila shots and hootchie-eyed **dos hombres guapos.**

Dudley downed his shot. He got that quick burn and glow. The Wolf licked his glass.

Salvy coughed. "If I were to tell you that I have plans to perform what might be termed 'cosmetic sabotage' on U.S. soil—gadfly gestures only—will you intercede and seek to expose me?"

Dudley leaned close. "You must solemnly promise that no American men, women, or children will be harmed."

Salvy leaned close. "Yes, you have my most solemn word."

Dudley sighed. "I'll profess vexation here. Gadfly gestures aside, I'm wondering what the world will be like when all of this is over."

Salvy twirled his shot glass. "Perhaps Europe and the East will realign. Perhaps the Hitler-Stalin pact will be reinstated as a hedge against chaos and the new American hegemony. I despise communism but quite often fail to see it as fascism's antithesis. A conference transpired in Ensenada, in the fall of '40. It was **comunista-fascista** and purportedly amiable. I have heard that numerous top dogs attended. It was the high-water point of the Nazi-Soviet Pact, and postwar escape strategies were discussed. It was reportedly proclaimed that the war would kill both Stalin and Hitler, along with all paper currencies, save the U.S. dollar. All those in attendance were urged to hoard gold."

Gold. Ever synchronous. The **Spiritus Mundi** speaks.

Dudley said, "My fascist brother."

Salvy said, "A Catholic hegemony. We must stake our loyalty there."

The Wolf jumped on the table. He cocked his head and howled his love for Salvador Abascal.

63

(LOS ANGELES, 1:00 P.M., 2/9/42)

The lab buzzed. Joan called it Jap**werk.** She worked Jap**werk** all day and all night.

Two chemists logged in radios. They scrawled serial numbers and searched for stashed contraband. Their gig was straight Jap internment. Joan's gig was Jap internment plus klub**haus** job.

She culled Rice and Kapek's Jap busts. She logged arrest and court dispositions. She wrote it all up and cross-referenced it. She determined custody status.

She noted habeas writs. She tagged current known whereabouts.

She pulled mug shots and clipped dispo bulletins. It was advance work. Thad Brown had ordered massive roundups. His goal was massive lineups. He'd subdivided the suspect types.

In-custody Japs. Released Japs. Known cholos. Jazz-club denizens. Perverted hepcats. Nazi-esque types.

We'll run lineups. We'll parade the above. 46th Street locals will orb them. Have you seen these dinks at or near the klub**haus**?

The job was twelve days in. They'd turned zero at-the-scene eyewits. Thad decreed one last shot at that.

Joan worked. Joan worked, distracted. It was drudge**werk** and scut**werk.** She worked, bored and gored.

That hate mail. The Back-to-Africa screed. Preacher Mimms, gold heist–linked. **The Red Swastika.** Salvador Abascal critiques the Ensenada conclave.

Fall 1940. Nazi and Russian hotshots meet. They discuss potential world-war outcomes and ponder potential means of ascent. She read the tract three times. The Nazis and Reds huddle and conclude **this:**

They must exploit a new postwar gold standard.

That tract gored her. Gold, gold, gold. Gold in the vox populi. Gold, omnipresent. Gold, subsuming her.

She read the Mitch Kupp tract. Her own past and dead father subsumed her. It wasn't a hate tract. It was scholarly and altogether nuts.

Joan worked. Joan worked, distracted.

Bill and Dudley. Bill's jealous outburst. Weepy Bill

and imperious Dudley. She wants Dudley more than Bill. She wants to talk gold with him. Dudley savaged Orson Welles. The **wunderkind** saw her naked. It drove Dudley to brutal rage. Bill would have sulked and hexed Welles from afar.

Joan **werk**ed. She logged evidence and ran circuits to the Alien Squad pen. She snagged file carbons and checked the Jap-arrest index. She ran into Lee Blanchard, outside the upstairs cot room. He stood by the file bank and flashed a shit-eating grin.

"We turned a habitué. Breuning and Carlisle grabbed him. They've got him in #3. Jack H. said you could watch."

"Who is he?"

"His name's Harold John Miciak. Breuning told me he's a lulu."

Joan stashed her carbons and walked to sweatbox row. #3 was spy-mirrored. A hall speaker spritzed sound. The hallway was SRO.

Jack Horrall. Sid Hudgens. Catbox Cal Lunceford. They played Mr. First Nighter and pressed their snouts up to the glass.

Joan joined them. Sid woo-woo'd her. Call-Me-Jack said, "Hi, Red."

The sweatbox ran standard. Twelve by twelve, cork-baffled walls, floor-bolted table and chairs. Miciak sat and feigned nonchalance. Breuning and Carlisle hovered. They phone-booked dipshit's shoulders and head.

The hall speaker spritzed. Breuning said, "Come

on, give." Carlisle said, "We can keep this up all day." Miciak sustained swats. His forehead and cheekbones grew welts.

He was too thin. He looked used up. He sported a hairnet conk and shaved whitewalls. He wore a gone jacket with wide-wing lapels.

He raised his hands. "Feel free to desist. I always like to absorb some hurt before I grovel and spill. It reestablishes my white-man credentials."

Breuning and Carlisle desisted. They hankie-wiped their brows. Breuning fed Miciak a cigarette. Carlisle lit it. Call-Me-Jack nudged Joan. **Some floor show, huh?**

Breuning straddled the spare chair. Carlisle sat on the table. Miciak blew smoke their way. Hudgens and Lunceford yukked.

Miciak cracked his knuckles. "You had some questions about that crib on 46th, right? You were seeking the lowdown from an informed perspective."

Breuning said, "Come on, give."

Carlisle said, "We'll give you a lunch chit for Kwan's Chinese Pagoda if you give good."

Miciak picked his nose. "That's a swell inducement."

Breuning said, "Give. We're not getting any younger here."

Miciak scratched his balls. "I would call the 46th Street spot an arsenal of democracy and a monument to free-thinking egalitarianism. It's what you might variously call a fuck joint, a blowhole, a jam-session crib, and a redoubt for thugs, goons, and the pro-Nazi crowd—but hep niggers, nigger jazz musicians, Mexicans, Mexicoons, and square-ass cops are welcome, too. Let me not tread lightly here. You've got jazz fiends, hopheads, boozehounds, terp men, bennie eaters, untold numbers of right-wing blowhards and Jew-haters, along with some name jazz guys. You've got coons like Wardell Gray, Dexter Gordon, and Charlie Parker—not to mention white cats like Stan Kenton, Art Pepper, and Bart Varsalona. You've got coon cops bringing in colored whores they popped for Pros-1 and fucking them upstairs. You've got mud-shark white girls who crave dark meat cavorting with shine smut-film actors with king-sized dicks, while the late Georgie Kapek takes pictures and peddles them for fifty cents apiece."

Miciak stopped flat. Miciak mugged at the mirror. Miciak performed a smut-film trick. He stuck out his tongue and stretched it up to his nose.

The hallway crowd slack-jawed it. Joan lit a cigarette. Call-Me-Jack popped digitalis. The Sidster sucked his pocket flask.

Breuning said, "Don't stop now."

Carlisle said, "We'll throw in free-drink coupons for Kwan's."

Miciak lit a cigarette. "Let us not euphemize or tread lightly here. You might call this exalted spot a lewd liaison lair. You've got divorced cops with no place to live paying the late Wendell Rice a buck a night to sleep on the floor. I would call the late Rice and Kapek the overlords of this hallowed joint.

They're selling confiscated Jap flags and crib sheets for the war-hire cop exams, not to mention confiscated Jap swords, daggers, and guns to these Mexican zoot punks out in Boyle Heights. The late **Sensei** Rice showed me a bayonet that must have been solid gold, all inlaid with this hammer-and-sickle design, made out of real rubies—"

Joan dropped her cigarette. It bounced off the mirror ledge and singed her skirt. She fretted her gold cuff links, and—

"—and you got this kid Link Rockwell. He's on leave from the Navy, and he's this jig preacher's pal. He sells tickets to these sex shows upstairs—and you got lots of pro-Nazi, pro-Jap, and pro-Sinarquista talk, and lots of **Sieg Heil,** and hate tracts being passed around, and traffic cops fixing tickets for a buck a pop, and auto-theft cops selling hot cars and counterfeit license plates, and—"

Joan lit a fresh cigarette. Her hands shook. She looped back to the gold bayonet. She fretted one gold cuff link clean off.

Jack H. grabbed her arm and steered her down the hall. He was I-need-a-drink trembly and pre-heart-attack flush.

"It's the guns, Red. It's all bad, and the guns are the worst of it. Check the Alien Squad's gun-confiscation roster and note all of Rice and Kapek's filings. Cross-check that against the lab's ballistics-comparison log, and pray that we're not too far exposed and deep in the hole. Do it now, and I'll owe you a very large favor."

Kay was late. Joan hogged their regular booth at Dave's Blue Room. She sipped her third scotch mist and chain-smoked. She respooled Jap**werk** and Jack**werk.** It comprised a six-hour sprint.

She logged 161 guns. They ran the gamut. Revolvers/automatics/rifles/shotguns. Rice and Kapek seized them all. They were all missing.

Gone meant **gone.** They're not in the lab vault. They're not in the Central Station and/or DB vault. There's no backup paper**werk.** They haven't been test-fired. There's no ballistics-comp sheets.

She did the **werk.** Lee Blanchard kibitzed. He laid out THIS BIG SNAFU and the upshot.

Breuning and Carlisle hard-nosed Miciak. They took him to the Lyman's sweat room and black-gloved him. He gave up relative bupkes. He refused to rat his other klub**haus** confreres. He said that Rice and Kapek bought off a slew of Newton Street blues, and quashed reports of klub**haus** misconduct. The **haus** thrived behind quasi-official approval. Local yokels ignored it. Preacher Mimms owned the property. He greased the yokels with fat Christmas baskets. They recruited saps for his back-to-Africa shuck. The klub**haus** was protected and sacrosanct.

Breuning and Carlisle beat Miciak half-dead. Thad Brown halted it. He drove Miciak to Queen of Angels and pledged a waltz on two 459 warrants. Miciak was half-dead and relieved.

She **werk**ed. She reported to Jack Horrall. Call-Me-Jack pledged his large favor. It floored her. She got floored twice in one day. Miciak blabs. Wendell Rice shows off this gold bayonet. Pinch me, I'm—

There's Kay. She's wearing her houndstooth-huntress ensemble. The black beret clashes. The saddle shoes are pure Kay.

Joan said, "You're late."

Kay slid into the booth. "Ask me why I'm late."

"Why are you late?"

"I'm late, because I ran into Jack Horrall. He told me the whole story three times, and to his credit, he never once mentioned your legs. I'm late, because I was looking for a certain item in sterling silver."

Joan laughed. "He served drinks in his office. He said, 'Don't you dare cry,' and 'Quit blushing, you've earned it.'"

Kay laced up their hands. "What's the first thing you thought of?"

"You know what it is."

"Tell me. Confirm how well I've come to know you."

Joan sipped scotch and bitters. The room went too warm. She reached over and reset Kay's beret. She'd seen Elmer J. do it. He always pulled up the stem.

"I've achieved rank parity with William H. Parker. It's the first thing that popped into my head."

Kay lobbed a small jewel box. Joan snagged it on the fly. She snuck a look and saw two captain's bars.

"Don't you cry, sister. Don't you dare blush, because you've earned it."

Joan wiped her eyes. "My academy class convenes in October. I'll ace the pistol range. I used to shoot rabid bats, back at home. I'd nail them from forty yards out."

Kay lit a cigarette and killed off Joan's cocktail. The jewel box glowed. The silver bars threw sparks.

"Go home and put some words on paper. Send one up for the ones you left behind. They don't have your grit, and they'll never have your luck."

She prayed for a blackout. Army searchlights strafed the sky, just so. She wanted to count moon craters. Empirical science meets God. Tell me what all this means.

No blackout. Easy come, easy go. It scotched her shot at cheap metaphysics. She took Kay's advice instead.

She scrawled up her diary. She described the Big Snafu and critiqued her antithetical lovers. She pondered the second gold bayonet. She wrote her name and rank twenty times.

The doorjamb creaked. She looked over. Bill Parker stood in the doorway. He's in uniform. He's half-gassed and grinning. He's cock-of-the-walk smug and proud.

Joan said, "You're just standing there. You usually walk straight up and kiss me."

"Don't look so disappointed. I pulled a coup at the grand jury today. I could have gone home and told my wife, but I came here instead."

Joan tossed him a breath mint. It hit his gun belt and fell to the floor.

"You could have told Kay Lake. Your wife ignores you, and Kay lusts for you. I don't really consider your wife much of a rival."

"You've got no beef with Kay. The two of you are friends now."

Joan tossed a breath mint. It hit his badge and fell to the floor.

"Tell me about your coup, and I'll tell you about mine."

Bill weaved and steadied himself. The doorway held him up.

"I nailed those Fed fuckers, and I nailed Jack Horrall. I pulled some wire mounts in December, when the probe was first announced. I gave up Jack H. and told the jury that he ordered it. They granted me full immunity. They were going to rubber-stamp no-bills. Now, they're going after Jack, Fletch Bowron, Ray Pinker, and the Jamie kid for real. I'll be the star witness, and I'll be sitting in Jack's chair inside six months."

Joan tossed a breath mint. It hit his necktie and fell to the floor.

"Bravo, Bill. Now, go tell Kay and Dudley. Then all the ones you care about will be up to speed."

"You've got a lot of goddamned nerve, bringing Dudley up to me."

Joan said, "I'll tell Dudley. It's what you really want. Everything you do is about you and Dudley, so why should I deny you that joy?"

64

(ENSENADA, 8:00 A.M., 2/10/42)

He returned to the charnel house. Dudley ordered a search. He picked through scorched cadavers and phone-line debris.

Forty-two bookies perished. Most were Fifth Column–adjunct. Their deaths served no purpose. No hard leads accrued.

Ashida sifted rubble. Juan Pimentel searched for lockboxes and safes. A.M. arc lights were up. Statie goons watchdogged the location.

It was the one Baja relay spot. It immolated in ten seconds flat.

Ashida sifted plaster dust. Blasted teeth jammed up his net. He relived the explosion. Fleeing bookies trampled him. He pumped his shotgun and blew their limbs off. He stumbled out the door.

He replayed it awake. He redreamed it asleep. He smelled it right now.

Ashida sifted dust. He snared wood husks and

scorched Bakelite chunks. Crazy Juan waved a skull and made kissy sounds. The plaster grit expelled gastric juices. Forty-two men burned alive.

A wedding band dropped from his sift net. It was pure gold.

Joan called him last night. She relayed the Miciak mess. She stressed Wendell Rice and **his** gold bayonet.

He told her he fiber-swept Hanamaka's hideaway. It paid off. He notched a fiber match to Rice himself. More threads converged. Dudley dubbed it the "Trifecta." The gold heist, Fifth Column grief, the klub**haus** job.

More evidence and more death. More open-air cadaver rot. More teeth in his sifting pan.

Ashida walked off. Crazy Juan yelled, "Come back, my love!"

Japs.

Japs, Japs, Japs. His ex–racial kin. His pre–Pearl Harbor brethren. His pre–Dudley Smith bund.

Ashida pulled up to the Statie barracks. Dudley shot him a last-second job. It was Jap-derived and Jap-defined. A Jap trial run was set to move north. Dudley and the Ventura County Sheriff colluded.

They moved precipitously. Captain Vasquez-Cruz cosigned the collusion. They bypassed Governor Lazaro-Schmidt.

Ashida parked and walked back to the loading

dock. The transport bus stood ready. Two Statie shits guarded it. They packed tommy guns.

Japs, Japs, Japs. Sixty men and women shackled. Japs, Japs, Japs. He employed the common vernacular now.

Dudley told him to interpret. Curry favor and seek last-minute rat-outs. Press on Japs still at large. Pledge snitch rewards. We'll feed you gourmet dog food and house you in de-luxe horse stalls.

Ashida hopped on the bus. He wore U.S. Army fatigues and jump boots. He carried his evidence kit and wore a holstered .45.

He counted sixty Japs. They were shackle-chained. Their arm and ankle cuffs scraped and drew blood. They were cinched up, seat back to seat back.

Ashida studied them. He stood by the gun guard's seat and let them notice him. It took a moment. They stopped talking, they looked up, they saw him.

He had them now. They fell quiet and studied him. He issued Dudley's snitch directive in Spanish and Japanese. A babble rose. He walked through the bus.

People hissed at him. People talked to him. He heard **traitor** in Spanish and Japanese. He ran the spit gauntlet. He caught globs on his fatigues and globs in his face.

He looked out the rear window. Two Staties stuffed bundles inside the wheel wells. It was uncut heroin.

The curses persisted. The driver and gun guard jumped on board. The driver kicked the ignition.

Ashida about-faced and walked toward the front of the bus. Hisses and curses overlapped. Spittle dripped off his chin. He threw out Spanish and Japanese. **Kyoho Hanamaka—do you know him?**

He walked seat row to seat row and repeated it. Spit bombs blurred his vision. An old man motioned him close.

Ashida leaned close. The old man spoke English. He said, "Hanamaka fascist. I valet for him. I help him mess up mountain house and pack. Two white policemen drive him over border."

Ashida opened his evidence kit. He flashed ID pix of Wendell Rice and George Kapek.

The old man nodded YES.

65

(SAN DIEGO, 12:00 P.M., 2/10/42)

The boys are—

They hauled north. Elmer drove. Buzz baby-talked his pet scorpion. They left El Huey naked, outside the Klubb Satan. Devil take the hindmost.

The coast road looked good. Eucalyptus trees and big wave swells. The klub**haus** job looked bad. Elmer masticated it.

They called Thad Brown from T.J. They said Huey was just plain nowhere. Thad laid out the Miciak mess. The looted guns were the gnarly nadir. Thad issued an APB on Link Rockwell. Flyboy Link staged klub**haus** sex shows and sold tix.

The klub**haus** job was Shit City. Buzz and him brain-waved it. There had to be an upside somewhere. Huey's Dudster tale, ditto. Dud attends a pervert hoedown and snuffs a he-she. That's blackmail bait. It could rescind Dud's hex on Buzz.

Elmer relit his cigar. A light drizzle hit. They passed Del Mar Racetrack. Buzz dropped bundles there on his days off.

They did one good deed already. He called Fourth Interceptor and played Mr. Anonymous. He tattled that so-called Jap sub attack. It retattled Huey's tattle. Sub attack planned!!! Japs target Santa Barbara refineries!!!

That was tattle #1. Tattle #2 was stale bread. Jap air attack!!! Late February, **banzai!!!** It was most likely vapors and bullshit.

El Scorpio snoozed in his cage. Buzz stuck a finger in and stroked his pincers. A pet store on Fairfax sold dead crickets. Buzz planned to stock up. Keep El Scorpio fat and sassy.

"Here's something I don't get. There's those fourteen Baja pay-phone listings in Tommy G.'s address book. My question's **Why?** Why's a psycho jerkoff like Tommy have those numbers? Is he **really** some hot-blood seditionist? On top of that, this English-language paper ran a story this morning. The Staties knocked over a pay-phone relay spot and disabled it. Does that mean them pay phones in Tommy's book are dead?"

Elmer said, "I got phone slugs in the trunk. We'll try to call those phones from that hot-box by the **Herald.** If we get dead air, we'll know something's cooking."

Buzz rogered him and yawned **wiiiiiide.** He tipped his hat low and snoozed off. Elmer chained cigars and daydreamed Jean Staley. He dressed her in Kay Lake threads. Kay had this black cashmere dress. He liked it best.

Full-on rain hit outside L.A. Elmer cut east on rinky-dink streets and north on Figueroa. The rain abated, the clouds dispersed, some sunshine poked through. Buzz yawned and stirred.

"Looks like home to me."

Elmer cut east on Pico and north on Broadway. There's the **Herald** building. There's the hot-box. There's Ed Satterlee, parked upside.

Elmer U-turned and pulled up behind him. He got out and unlocked his trunk. He kept his extralegal shit there. Throwdown guns, burglars' tools, mary-jane to plant on suspects. Pay-phone slugs. Crib notes per Tommy G.'s address book.

Buzz got out and stretched. They waved to Ed Satterlee. Ed the Fed waved back. They ducked into the phone booth. Elmer passed Buzz the address-book numbers and a handful of slugs.

El Buzzo spoke okay Spanish. He got the place-the-calls gig. The gambit was station-to-station. The L.A. operator hails the Baja operator. She shoots the actual calls.

Buzz went to work. Elmer moseyed up to Ed's sled and popped the passenger door. Ed nipped on a hip flask. Elmer slid in and went **Gimme that.**

Ed passed the flask. "Your boy Bill Parker pulled a fink play with the grand jury. Those halfhearted bills rigged to produce acquittals don't look so assured now."

Elmer sipped cheap brandy. "Bill Parker's right hand don't know what his left hand is doing."

Buzz lounged half outside the phone booth. Elmer eyeballed him. Buzz held up three fingers and pointed them down. That meant three disconnects.

Ed slurped cheap brandy. "What's Meeks doing?"

"We're tracking Baja pay phones. It pertains to the klub**haus** job."

"Are you working with Fourth Interceptor? They're chasing Baja pay phones."

Elmer went **nix.** "No, it's something else."

Ed the Fed shrugged. "As numerous wags have said, 'Fifth Column's Fifth Column.' We get lots of those Deutsches Haus creeps making calls from here."

Elmer orbed the phone booth. Buzz wagged nine fingers and pointed them down. That meant nine disconnects.

"How do you **know** this, sahib?"

Ed gargled cheap brandy. "We run photo surveillance.

We take pictures and match them to the plate numbers of the cars the creeps get back into. We get the registration details from the DMV and run the names against known-subversive files."

Buzz flashed fourteen fingers and pointed them down. That meant all disconnects.

Elmer said, "I don't suppose you've got any of those pictures on you?"

Ed reached under his seat. He snagged a stack of glossies and dropped them on Elmer's lap.

Elmer thumbed through. He saw a slew of unknown phone callers. He saw a far shot of Ensign Link Rockwell. **Oooh**—there's a tight shot. Dig that mean-looking Jap.

Jap on the loose. **Oooga-booga.** Why ain't this fucker detained?

"You got a name on him?"

Ed flipped the picture over. Scrawled on the back: **Kyoho Hanamaka.**

66

(LOS ANGELES, 7:00 A.M., 2/11/42)

Breakfast at Kwan's. Flapjacks and Bloody Marys. Jack Horrall, half-blitzed and dyspeptic.

"What you're saying in no way surprises me. Bill Parker rats to the Feds. It's on a par with 'dog bites man.'"

Dudley sipped coffee. He left Joan's bed for this bereavement. She finked Parker's fink play. She finked Wendell Rice's gold bayonet. La Bonne Joan—ever opportunistic.

"It ups the odds that the grand jury will issue binding indictments, sir. Forewarned is forearmed."

Jack dosed his morning jolt. He added Tabasco and Worcestershire. His highball glass glowed malignant.

"Parker's making his move. If I'm convicted at trial, he'll grab my job early. He'll work some voodoo on the City Council and push Thad Brown aside."

"Yes, sir."

"Talk to him. Horse trade. White man smoke heap big peace pipe. Tell that pious cocksucker that I'll pull my support of Thad if he recants his testimony extant."

Dudley scanned the room. The City Hall crowd noshed early. Fletch Bowron, Sheriff's brass, Jew lobbyists. They waved to Chief Jack and the big mick.

"I'll call Parker this morning, sir."

Jack salted his drink. His liver was shot. His pump was shot. His arteries bulged. His life span loomed as next week.

"You heard about that Miciak fuck? We've got Rice and Kapek selling Jap guns now."

"I was informed, sir. Mike Breuning called me."

"I'm starting to think I should countermand my clean-solve directive. Rice and Kapek's shit should never see the light of day. I've been giving this a great deal of thought. It's causing me to wax profound. I'm also shit-faced at seven-fucking-a.m."

Dudley grinned. "You've always been a lively man, sir."

"I'm also very enlightened, and not averse to enlisting jigaboos in our noble crusade. Which brings me to my pal Preacher Mimms."

Dudley lit a cigarette. Call-Me-Jack resalted his drink.

"Preacher Mimms owns the klub**haus.** That gives him a stake in this. He's also got his snout dunked in a great many poisoned streams."

Such as the gold heist. May '31. Mimms bails out Leander Frechette. Hideo and Joan uncovered it.

"You've piqued my interest, sir."

"Talk to Preacher Mimms. Ask him about his numerous enemies embroiled in perverted walks of life. Get a sense of the ones he'd like to see dead."

They shared rank now. Two uniformed captains/two august agencies. They drew stares at Kwan's.

Parker slouched. Dudley sat stiff straight. Joan would notch rank soon. Jack H. shot her an Academy slot. Captain J. W. Conville, Los Angeles PD.

Parker sipped coffee. His glasses were Scotch-taped. He'd chewed his nails raw.

"I read the posted summary at Lyman's. The stolen guns constitute a shitstorm."

Dudley lit a cigarette. "Yes, and a discomfiting and potentially scandalous one."

"Was that what you wished to discuss?"

"Among other matters, yes."

Kwan's buzzed. It was a lawyers' lair this a.m. Fletch B. and counsel. Ray Pinker and counsel. It refracted Whiskey Bill's snitch ploy. The Fed probe snarls and shows teeth.

Parker said, "I'm listening."

"Please restate your promise not to reveal Jim Davis, per a certain quadruple homicide."

"So stated, with a codicil. We still need to put him under pentothal, voluntarily or coerced. There's the currently pending matter of the klub**haus** job, and what he might know."

"I'll do it. Would you care to witness the interview?"

Parker nodded. Archbishop Cantwell walked in the door. He wore kelly green golf togs and drew delighted stares.

"Do I have your word that you will not seek to countermand my efforts in **l'affaire** klub**haus**?"

"End it. It's a lake of shit our police department will drown in."

"Thank you, Captain."

Parker lit a cigarette. "Let me anticipate your next salvo and nip it in the bud. No, I will not recant at the grand jury—even if Jack Horrall pulls his support of Thad Brown."

The Archbishop worked the room. He swapped jokes with Battling Gomez. He ogled Betty Grable and winked at Harry James.

Dudley said, "Would you reconsider if I offered to walk away from Joan?"

Parker said, "Emphatically no."

J. J. Cantwell sidled over and approached their table. He looked vividly elfin today.

"What are you two brilliant lads discussing so heatedly?"

Dudley said, "Women, Your Eminence."

Cantwell winked. "That's a topic I know nothing of, regardless of any rumors you may have heard."

The drive back protracted. There were flash storms and coast road tie-ups. The jaunt ran six hours, door-to-door.

He got a late start. A bayonet search postponed his departure. He badged the widows Rice and Kapek and tossed their houses, floor-to-floor. He searched two domiciles and two detached garages. The Widow Rice said two shitkicker cops had already been through.

No gold bayonet appeared. The widows knew nothing of it. They'd dumped Wendell's and Georgie's Nazi gear. Their loony husbands gored their goats. Goodbye to all that.

Alas.

Dudley parked and lugged his grip upstairs. Music

surged within his suite. It was dank and dissonant. Claire and Young Joan doted on Shostakovich.

He unlocked the door. Young Joan blasted the dour maestro. She sprawled on the couch. The Wolf sprawled beside her. Young Joan ruffled his coat.

Dudley doused the Victrola. Loud brass diminuendoed. Bass cellos swooped and died.

Young Joan said, "Hi, Uncle Dud." She patted a folder on her lap. The Wolf stirred and nuzzled her hand.

"I have something to show you."

Dudley smiled. "Perchance?"

"I found an L.A. Police intel file, in with some blank forms. It's good you came home when you did. Aunt Claire's out, and she wouldn't want you to see it."

The girl Mata Hari. His very own Hebraic offspring. She's always concocting intrigue.

Dudley dropped his grip and perched on the couch. Young Joan passed him the file.

"It's a CP cell, back in the '30s. I recognized one of the pictures."

Dudley opened the folder. It was standard Red Squad paper. A cover note prefaced it. Five suspect sheets and photographs were included. The note listed five CP members. The names stood out.

Saul Lesnick, M.D. Claire's psychiatrist and confidant. Her L.A. dope conduit. Plus Andrea Lesnick. Plus Meyer Gelb, plus Jean Staley and Jorge Villareal-Caiz.

It's **the** cell. Hideo and Joan uncovered the lead. The cell drew heat per the Griffith Park fire. Said heat cooled and died. It was stale news today.

Sicknik seditionists. Dr. Saul's schizy daughter. Florid cell boss Gelb. Red pawn Jean Staley. Priest-killer Villareal-Caiz. Reviled by the great Salvy Abascal.

Young Joan said, "Look at the pictures."

Dudley flipped through the suspect sheets. Four pix beamed, innocuous. Villareal-Caiz stood out.

As he well should. Here's the punch line. He's really José Vasquez-Cruz.

Claire found Vasquez-Cruz familiar. She'd "seen him somewhere, maybe a demonstration." She found him attractive. He concurrently repulsed her. Claire viewed all men that way.

Young Joan stroked the Wolf. He hated priest kill-ers and Communists. His hackles flared.

History. Munich, '34. The Night of the Long Knives. Brentwood, '39. A costume party replicates slaughter. Ensenada, now. History as fused circuit and final reprise.

Dudley brought the gold bayonet. He wore SS black. Salvy brought two stilettos. He wore Wehrmacht gray. They took Salvy's car. The Wolf lounged between them. He wore his spiked collar, swastika-pinned.

3:00 a.m. Calle Diamante. The priest-killer lives in

a bluffside casa. It's bleached-white adobe. There's a wide front lawn and eucalyptus trees.

Dudley knew the floor plan. Cruz-Caiz threw a party. Claire danced with **El Communisto.** He was **El Fascisto** then.

Salvy parked across the street. The Wolf growled and flashed his fangs. He told them to carry their weapons unsheathed.

They walked over. They veered toward the right-side front of the house. French doors marked the master bedroom. Gargoyle doorstops held them open. A breeze stirred sheer drapes.

Dudley heard snores and smelled stale perfume. It was Claire's scent.

They walked in. Salvy patted the side wall and tripped a light switch. The room went too bright too fast. The priest-killer sleeps, the priest-killer stirs.

He's wearing silk pajamas. The bedsheets are mussed. He's almost awake.

Dudley stepped up. He gripped the bayonet two-handed. The priest-killer opened his eyes. Dudley slammed the blade into his face.

It crushed his skull and tore one eye out. Blood exploded. It sprayed Dudley's tunic and drenched the pillows and sheets. The priest-killer gurgle-screamed. Dudley slammed the blade into his mouth.

It choked off all sound. Severed bridgework snagged the blade. Dudley yanked it free. He stabbed the priest-killer's face and smashed into his brains.

Salvy stabbed. He arced two knives, in and out. He stabbed one flailing arm and severed it. One knife blade broke off in his hand.

Dudley swung the bayonet crossways. He shattered the priest-killer's ribs and lanced through to his heart.

All that blood. **Comunista** red. All that offal and blood stink. Dudley smelled Claire through all of it.

67

(LOS ANGELES, 2/12–2/25/42)

I will take fate by the throat.

Beethoven said it. Dudley passed the maxim along. She repeated it to Kay. Diarist Kay loved epigraphs and thus lectured diarist Joan. She said, "It consecrates your opportunism. This war honors arrivistes. So does Los Angeles."

She should be in Wave training now. She should be field-dressing wounds and reading male VD charts. Fate intervened. A new set of should be's unfurled. She got drunk and caused four deaths. She should be in Tehachapi now. Elmer Jackson said, "You're the world's luckiest white woman, Red. You plowed some wetbacks hauling maryjane."

That's true. Luck and fate intertwine and spawn

opportunity. And opportunity carries a price. Consider this nightmare.

New Year's Eve through a booze veil. Blinding rain and the crash. The jail cell wake-up and policeman standing there. He's an opportunist, as well.

That dream bearably repeats. Repetition renders it banal. The dream sound track retains its verve. She hears young voices and pounding fists. They emanate from some enclosed space. The sound track horrifies.

Fate, thus defined. Cop life beckons her. She joins her fellow opportunists—wartime irregulars all.

Bill Parker and Dudley Smith. Hideo Ashida and Kay Lake. Thad Brown, Nort Layman, Call-Me-Jack Horrall. Elmer Jackson, Lee Blanchard, Buzz Meeks.

All task-assigned. All duty-driven. There for the body-in-the-box and the dead-cops caper. It's all one story, you see.

The story coheres in her diary. The supporting players recede and make room for the stars. She's as one with Dudley and Hideo. They all want the gold—and that's all that counts.

Fate. Opportunity. Misalliance. Fool's errand. Sacred quest. The gold heist and the fire. It's all one story, you—

She stands poised. Her forensic skills verge on genius. Hideo supersedes her in all things scientific. Dudley's fierce will supersedes all forensic application. It's their one story. It will culminate if and when they solve their intertwined cases. It will end if and when they get the gold.

It's Fate, prophesied. It's Opportunity, writ large. It's Luck, in the form of a boozed-up policeman and his college-girl crush.

I can help you, Lieutenant. Of course you can. I've always had my way with men. And you won't be the only man who finds me.

Her Bill. Her Dudley. A troika yet to resolve. She shared lust and gold fever with Dudley. She shared hurt and dashed faith with Bill. She holds her own with both of her lovers. She shares their stalemates. She shares their secrets. She knows things that no woman of her station should know.

Two-Gun Davis killed the four Watanabes. Werewolf Shudo was framed. Dudley did it. Bill plucked Shudo from death row. He did it to impress her and to wow God. He performed a penitential act to negate his adultery.

You do not cut deals with God. Protestants know this. Catholics do not. Bill snitched to the Fed grand jury. He did it with self-seeking aplomb. Dudley told her that he and Jack Horrall are scheming countermeasures. They will address Bill's grand-jury play and the ghastly klub**haus** case itself. Her lovers blur within their machinations. She's aswirl with their secrets. She's powerfully indebted to their conflict. The realization stuns her.

Dudley has pledged to solve her father's murder. It was not an idle boast. He added the caveat: "If a solution is there to be had." She told him about the air-warfare tract, mailed to the **haus.**

Mitch Kupp authored the tract. It was sent to Wendell Rice. That fact stunned Dudley. He held forth on fate and lunar tides. Dudley puts faith in talking animals and spirit worlds aligned. Bill cuts deals with God and weeps in shame. He comes to her nakedly revealed and blinded with desire. She will not give up either man.

Kay Lake mediates both men. She's the Bill-loves-Joan deus ex machina and piquantly critiques their affair. Schoolgirl intrigue is at play here. Kay is waiting out Bill's fatuous crush on the big redhead. Kay mediates Dudley Smith with bald malice.

She despises Dudley. She purports to see through to his cold, evil heart. She may or may not know that Dudley and Big Red share the sheets. Kay eavesdrops at Lyman's. She gleefully catalogues and passes on gossip. She should know the story. She's never said, "Are you or aren't you?" That seems odd in itself.

Kay collects rumors, Kay reveals rumors, Kay constellates rumors herself. One pithy rumor surfaces on occasion. Kay Lake shivved Dudley Smith late last year.

It was ridiculous. She didn't believe it. It exposed the fault lines of the Lyman's rumor mill. Cop work was inherently outré and given to extravagant expression. All provocative rumors have legs. The Kay-Dudley dish was pure fantasia.

Kay was triangle-happy. She observed troikas, and slid in and out of them. There's Joan/Dudley/Bill. There's Joan/Bill/Kay. There's Joan/Dudley/Claire

De Haven. Can she credit the war, or is it all just luck and lust, defined?

She's visited Otto Klemperer's spread on three more jazzy occasions. Kay and the Maestro play the piano together. The Maestro enjoys flirting with young women. He's hinted that his house holds a dark secret. Kay plays improvised piano chords. They're dark and secretly descriptive. There's an open secret swirling at chez Klemperer. Kay and the Maestro lead a cabal of New York leftists and their "Mexican friend." They're smuggling Shostakovich's new symphony out of Russia. The Maestro intends to conduct a preemptive performance. All proceeds will go to European war relief.

It's a benign secret. It dovetails with malign cop-world secrets. Kay told her that Dudley smokes opium. Kay said, "Don't tell anyone—it's a secret."

She hoards secrets as well as Kay does. She keeps a secret diary and performs secret deeds. She met Meyer Gelb at her first Maestro bash. He was Griffith Park fire–adjunct and thus adjunct to Karl Tullock and Wayne Frank Jackson. She checked statewide DMV records. There were no Meyer Gelbs listed. She ran nationwide records checks, with identical results. She attended her second Maestro bash. She prowled the Maestro's office and went through his Rolodex. There was no Meyer Gelb listed. She performed this secret deed sans compunction.

Jean Staley attended her maiden Maestro bash. She once belonged to Comrade Gelb's Commie cell.

Miss Staley was listed in the '38 L.A. White Pages. She lived in Beachwood Canyon. It mandated a covert approach.

Burglars' tools. Easily accessible. The crime lab kept an exemplar set.

She surveilled Jean Staley's bungalow. Miss Staley's car was missing. Miss Staley appeared to be missing herself. She let herself in to the bungalow. It was musty. The gas had been turned off. The walls bore print-eradication marks. The place had been deftly wiped.

Secret indications. Secrets, not yet revealed.

Claire De Haven attends the Maestro's parties. Kay calls her the "doomed poetess." Claire's morphine habit is a poorly kept secret. Guests see her coming and mime her deft touch with a spike. Claire remains a most stately dope fiend. She observed Claire and Orson Welles talking. Welles refused to go in the steam room with her. He saw both of Dudley Smith's women naked. Dudley issued commensurate warnings and a brutal rebuke. He probably possessed a secondary motive. She had no idea what. It was Dudley's secret—and she's not one to pry.

Terry Lux recut Orson's face. Orson recuperated in secret. Terry Lux is American First. Bill Parker spilled Terry's big secret. Terry was privy to the Watanabe snuffs.

Secrets.

Her secrets. The gold cabal's secrets. Cop secrets, above all else.

Navy blue to police blue. Fate, luck, and opportunity conjoined. Jack Horrall likes her legs and knows grit and brains when he sees them. She joins the ranks October 4. She'll be Captain J. W. Conville and the highest-ranking woman on the PD. Her precipitous commission will spawn cop resentment. She will rebuff it with imperious ease. Her serendipity mirrors that of Lieutenant Hideo Ashida. Fate, luck, opportunity. Cop noblesse oblige. Dudley Smith's largesse.

They both love him. They both know what he is. It's their dark secret, shared.

They talk, long-distance. Their mutual enmity has waned. They speak as fellow scientists and gold questers. She accepts his prissy deviance. He accepts her bedroom bond with the man he loves. They talk for hours. The U.S. Army pays for the calls. They discuss crossover leads in their three complex cases. They dissect every single lead and clue and possible connection. They do not covet the gold from an aggrieved perspective. They've both played this war for all it's worth and come out ahead.

She lucked out of Manslaughter One. He lucked out of the internment. Their war efforts run parallel to their personal ambition.

Hideo fights the Fifth Column in Mexico. His Jap-toady work repulses him. That's his only rub. It's her rub, as well. The internment is a disgrace. Wendell Rice and George Kapek exemplify the injustice. J-town stands decimated. The Manzanar camp opens next month. Hideo Ashida dodged that bullet. Great shame undermines his great luck.

Hideo works in Baja. Her L.A. workload has now doubled. It's all Jap**werk** and klub**haus** job. Thad Brown ran three lineups at Newton Station. Lineup #1 featured jazz-club patrons. #2 featured "political types." #3 featured uninterned Japs.

46th Street residents viewed fifty-odd men. No positive IDs resulted.

The Crash Squad meets daily at Lyman's back room. Their APB turned Link Rockwell. Ensign Rockwell was ensconced at a Navy flight school in Florida. Jack Horrall declined to extradite. Young Link and Call-Me-Jack were tight with Martin Luther Mimms.

Jack wants to bury the klub**haus** job. Dudley considers it insoluble. He wants to isolate klub**haus** leads that point to the gold and shitcan the rest. She and Hideo want the gold and a unified solve. Dudley is currently pondering klub**haus** countermeasures. Hideo told her that. The phone receiver froze in her hand.

Secret measures. Secret pleasures. Secret locales.

Dudley smoked opium. She asked Kay where. Kay said, "The basement at Kwan's."

She crashed the party there. Uncle Ace proved amenable. They'd met socially. Ace fed PD folks on the cuff.

He supplied the tar, the pipe, and the pallet. She joined twenty-odd Chinamen and DA McPherson's colored girlfriend. The pallet was too short for her. She smoked opium and flew off someplace. She traveled in a gold rocket ship. Gold dust dropped from the clouds.

68

(TIJUANA AND ENSENADA, 2/12–2/25/42)

He jumped rank. Major Melnick passed the word. He's now First Lieutenant Hideo Ashida.

Silver outranks gold in the U.S. Army. He traded gold bars for silver. The bookie-front fiasco secured his promotion. Juan Pimentel moved up to captain. He replaced the late José Vasquez-Cruz. Vasquez-Cruz **está muerto.** La Juan is the new Baja Statie boss.

Who killed Vasquez-Cruz? His first thought was rival wetback and/or dope runners. The Mexican papers set him straight. Vasquez-Cruz was really Jorge Villareal-Caiz.

The ex-Communist. Once installed in Meyer Gelb's cell. Linked to the Griffith Park fire. Linked to Dr. Saul Lesnick. Linked to Jean Staley. Linked to Tommy Glennon's address book.

Consider **this:**

It's January 8. Victor Trejo Caiz misbehaves. He's Jorge's

brother. He foolishly draws down on Dudley Smith. Salvy Abascal slays him right there.

Dudley Liam Smith—ever present. Dudley Liam Smith—**por vida.**

Dudley instigates his promotion. Dudley recommends and vets Juan Pimentel. Note the design. Pimentel is fearsome and most competent. He'll serve as Dudley's enforcer. Wetbacks/heroin/the Jap-prisoner dodge. Dudley has plans for La Juan.

Dudley—**por vida.** All circuits terminate there. Dudley rules his thoughts. La Juan flits in counterpoint. All alliances reign under Dudley Smith's command. Dudley indebts his underlings. Dudley corrupts and/or seduces. Ask Joan Conville. Ask Lieutenant Ashida himself.

They've been seduced and corrupted. They've become inexplicable friends. **Comrades** says it best. They're rogue scientists held spellbound by one man.

Phone calls sustain their new kinship. There's long stints of forensic and investigatory surmise. They interpret evidence across three case lines. They fondle gold objects as they talk.

They've reached conclusions. They agree. It's not a single conspiracy. It feels like three conspiracies and random events interlocked. The conspiracies are imperfectly contrived and erratically enjoined. The klub**haus** murders do not mark termination. All of it continues. The acquisition of the gold and the explication of all things past is the only permissible end.

He thinks that. Joan thinks that. They move from

gold heist to fire to klub**haus** to now—ceaselessly. They never-endingly probe evidence and indulge supposition. As per Tommy Glennon's address book. As per the Baja pay phones listed. They indicate a new and revised Tommy G.

He's more than Dudley's snitch and a pro-Axis blowhard. He's more than a rapist and wetback runner for Carlos Madrano. He's more sinister than that. Consider this fact. Kyoho Hanamaka touched Tommy's address book. He left a burn-scarred fingerprint.

The fourteen pay phones. Plus the coded slug calls. The bookie-front inferno blitzed that line of inquiry. No more code calls will be received. No more messages will pass through the front. They can't trace Hanamaka and Tommy G. that way.

Where are they? Hanamaka's a long-gone fugitive. Japs on the hoof draw heat. Tommy's a disordered psychopath. Such fiends leave traces. No one has visited Hanamaka's hideaway. Juan Pimentel continues to surveil it. No cars have tripped the photo-device wires. No license plates have been glimpsed. All this dizzies and confounds him.

He feels overmatched. Joan feels overmatched. The Jap and The Skirt. Sid Hudgens wrote them up that way.

He secured permission to visit L.A. and conduct field interviews. Dudley spoke to Major Melnick and got his okay. He'll drive up on his days off. Lee Blanchard will bodyguard him.

He's overmatched in L.A. and Baja. Dudley commands him in both locales. Dudley commands him domestically and commends him to voyeurize.

He lives in the Hotel del Norte. His suite adjoins Dudley and Claire's. He hears them make love. He rarely hears words and often gleans impressions. He senses chaos.

Claire now appears gaunt. She accosted him in the lobby one morning. She said, "Do you know what Dudley's capable of?"

He said, "Do you know the extent of my debt?"

Claire rarely speaks to him. The feral Joan Klein talks blue streaks. She spins teenage-girl tales. She's expecting an "important package from the East." Her comrades in New York will pass it on to her. She'll deliver it to "the Maestro in L.A."

Young Joan excels in puerile blather. One schoolgirl yarn stands out.

She's "spot-tailed" Aunt Claire. She got that term from one of Uncle Dud's soldiers. Aunt Claire had an affair with José Vasquez-Cruz. She saw them at it once. Vasquez-Cruz was really Villareal-Caiz. Somebody "slayed his greaser ass." She got that term from one of Uncle Dud's soldiers.

Spot-tails. Uncle Dud and Aunt Claire. Dudley Smith adopts and corrupts children.

Cruz-Caiz is dead. Dudley must have killed him. La Juan has replaced him. A second batch of Jap slaves will ship out on March 10. Manzanar opens its Jap-slave doors on March 25. Internment centers have sprung up regionwide. The Jap-slave diaspora now runs on overdrive.

His most pressing Army task is Jap-language translation. He gets Japs to rat other Japs. This Army task sickens him. His **secret task** thrills him. He tweaks Japs per gold-germane and three-case-germane topics.

Herr Hanamaka and Herr Rice. Gold political artifacts and the Nazi-Soviet meet. He's got zilch thus far. He logs sullen looks and spit globs. He now carries two handkerchiefs.

He's a traitor and a war profiteer. His fellow Japs sense that.

They're right. He's a gold bug. He wants to touch **THE** specific gold cache. It's alchemized gold. It's been molded into artifacts. It consecrates monstrous ideologies. It's his world war/I was there/I did my part souvenir.

He wants to earn the enhanced esteem of the monstrous Dudley Smith. He wants to pave a gold pathway through this war. He will see his racial countrymen slaughtered. He will see his native countrymen imprisoned in horse stalls. He wants to pave a gold pathway to a three-case solve. He wants to alchemize the riddles of that shithole backhouse on East 46th Street. He wants Dudley Smith to love him—because he's fought and endured.

He's heard Harold John Miciak's wire-recorded statement. It vividly explicates the cut-loose male id. The staggering range of misconduct. The mixed-race escapades at a fascist meeting spot. The booze- and dope-fueled obliviousness.

The klub**haus** commemorates nihilistic bonhomie. It's avant-garde in that way. The klub**haus** feels Fifth Column–tangential. The murders have begun to feel incidental. They are thus coincident to the '31 gold heist and the '33 Griffith Park fire. The crossover leads to those earlier cases are simply address-book and police-file names. The Hanamaka-to-Rice leads are all present-day. There's Rice's gold bayonet. There's Hanamaka's print in Tommy G.'s address book.

The klub**haus** caper. It feels like a sexual crime. It reads as coincident to Fifth Columnism and all preceding cases. Two women left pubic-hair exemplars upstairs. Said women play as prostitutes or jazz-club pickups and thus as non sequiturs. The klub**haus** job feels like a homosexual crime. It may possess roots within the wide range of klub**haus** misbehavior.

The bedroom sheet. Stained with feces and K-Y jelly. It's the sole forensic indicator. It complements his overarching instincts. The upstairs wall indentations. Low indentations. Surely made by a woman's right shoe. That indicates a two-person/three-victim crime. He postulates a homosexual man with a female accomplice.

Sexual crimes are lust and jealousy crimes. They are impetuously performed and irrational in nature. Sexual crimes are personal-animus crimes. They are directed at one victim only—even when two killers kill.

Wendell Rice.

George Kapek.

Archie Archuleta.

One man was the sole intended victim. He knows this. He knows this because he's a homosexual. He must solve this gaudy murder case and justify the admission.

69

(LOS ANGELES, 2/12–2/25/42)

Oooga-booga. Hear dem tom-toms? Dat hellhound's still on his trail.

He's jungled-up and fucked-up with Buzz Meeks now. Their T.J. swoop was hopped-up and shook-up and altogether nuts. The Huey Cressmeyer snatch was jacked-up and jumped-up and ill-advised. Buzz wants to kiss up and suck up to El Dudster or conversely slay him dead. Buzz wants to clip Tommy Glennon. Maybe Dud will make up with him then.

Maybe. Maybe not. Buzz is scared. **He's** scared. What if Huey blabs? It's katy-bar-the-door then.

They work the Big Case. It's Crash-Squad Apocalypse and Crash-Squad Abyss. They've canvassed from 46th Street to the planet Mars. Jack H. constrains them. He's sealed pertinent records. He's nixed further chats with Preacher Mimms. He's nixed a Newton Station approach. Rice and Kapek bought off the night-watch blues and the fucking Vice Squad en masse. There's no occurrence sheets extant. There's no loud-noise reports and D&D lists. Thad Brown's three lineups dry-humped the whole universe.

Harold John Miciak. That fat-mouthed bug-fucker. He monkey-wrenched the whole case. He ran his mouth and glued his mouth shut. **Get it?** He named no names. He ratted out the looted guns and Wendell Rice with some gold bayonet. He dick-teased the Crash Squad and the whole PD and zipped his trap shut.

Miciak's pitch could tank the PD. Jack H. and Dud know it. They've got to be brainstorming.

Figure this. They've formulated kill lists. Kill, kill, kill. Kill some right-wing spics. Kill some jazzhound jigs. Kill some white Nazi shits. Plant some evidence on them and **coon**vene a new grand jury. Nail post-mortem indictments.

It sounds **goooooood.** It might relieve overall tension. It might remove him and Buzz from the Dudster's gun sights. It floodlights his own mixed motives. He'd **loooooove** to file a clean solve. He'd **looooove** to end all this shuddering shit.

He'd love to gun-sight Jean Staley. Tough luck there. She flew the coop. She's off for Des Moines. She's driving **slooooooow** and sending him postcards. It's hinky. It gores his gonads. It dings his dick. It torques his tail raw. It's got him thinking.

Jean was ex-CP. That was back in '33. The Griffith Park fire occurs. Wayne Frank dies. Jean's cell catches heat. Call it coincidence. It was the Depression. The Red Beast got plain folks het up. Yeah, there's that. Then, there's **this:**

Wayne Frank was his brother. It could have been arson. He's supposed to be a detective. Jolting Jean jumped loose of their should-have-been love.

He B and E'd her crib and tossed it. Too much stuff was gone. The walls were all print-wiped. She left behind some lingerie. He sniffed it and went euphoric.

Jean weighs on him. He might call up some Arson Squad paper. Why'd she hink and boogaloo? It was just getting **gooooood.**

Dud weighs on him. **He's** the hellhound. Elmer J. gave the hellhound a hotfoot for kicks and suffered comeuppance. He's not the hotfoot type. That's strictly Bill Parker's MO.

Dud won't fuck with Whiskey Bill. Parker's too far up the PD's ass to mess with. Joan Conville laid some lowdown on Kay Lake. La Kay relaid it to him. Dig: Parker sold the PD out to the Fed grand jury.

He could do something similar. He had the grit to survive and thrive. He could shadowbox Dud the Impaler and Jack H. himself. Elmer V. was no Whiskey Bill. He lacked Parker's stature and juice. He had some backwoods skills, nonetheless.

He should do the PD a big favor. It would buy him love from Dudley and Jack. It would offset the chance that Dud would clip him and Buzz. The favor should pertain to the klub**haus** job or Parker's Fed-probe play.

He gave it one shot so far. Thad Brown refused to raid the Deutsches Haus. The December raid went bust. So Sergeant E. V. Jackson donned disguise and worked his way back in.

He bought some two-tone loafer jackets and Tyrolean porkpies. He laced venom into his Carolina drawl and played Klansman adrift. He tossed barbs at the Jews and ballyhooed the L.A. Reich. He drank German beer. He jumped three fat fräuleins. He pulled **this** out of his hat:

He's **Herr Doktor** Vengeance. His brother fried in the Griffith Park fire. He's out to vaporize the Commie cell that started the blaze. **Herr Doktor** Vengeance knows some names.

Meyer Gelb. Jean Staley. Dr. Saul Lesnick. Andrea Lesnick. Jorge Villareal-Caiz. Who's got the scarified skinny? **Herr Doktor** Vengeance pays cold cash for hot drift.

Die Krautniks went **Vass**? They were ditzy dilettantes. They were juvenile jerkoffs hooked on hate and the "Horst-Wessel-Lied." **Herr Doktor** Vengeance dropped more names.

Wendell Rice. George Kapek. Archie Archuleta. You know these guys? John Harold Miciak. You know him? You dig the Sinarquistas? You like nigger jazz? You been to this hot spot on East 46th?

Nobody bit. **Herr Doktor** Vengeance hunkered in and observed. He attended a eugenics lecture. A three-hundred-pound porker extolled the master race. He attended a lecture on postwar reconciliation.

The Nazis and Russkis kiss and make up. They've got some mysterious gold cache. They hatched a plan in Mexico. Let bygones be bygones. The real foe is democracy.

Herr Doktor yawned through the lecture. His luck fizzled then. Some just-out jailbird busted him.

This Klan fool's a cop. I saw him last month. He's on the Alien Squad. I was locked up in Lincoln Heights. He was hauling in Japs.

Deutsches Haus—auf Wiedersehen. Fat fräuleins, adios.

He misses Jean Staley. He sleeps with Brenda and thinks about her. He sleeps with Ellen and thinks about her. He sleeps with Annie Staples and thinks about her.

He thinks about Dudley Smith. He got terped at Ellen's place and woke up on the floor. A speckled bug started talking to him.

The bug rebuked his promiscuous ways. The bug said shit like "You're scared—but somebody's got to take that mick booger down."

The bug egged him on. He started tapping the piggyback mounts at Brenda's trick spot. He's been playing the recordings of Annie S. and Saul Lesnick. He heard gasbag Saul gasbag **this:**

His analysand Claire De Haven's been running distraught. She's miffed at her lover man, Dudley. She thinks he killed a passing fling of hers. The man was a Mexican State Police captain. His name was José Vasquez-Cruz. That name played out pseudonymous. He was really a Commo named Jorge Villareal-Caiz.

Old Saul found this flabbergasting. He said, "I knew Jorge! He was in my CP cell with Meyer Gelb! Remember? I introduced you to Meyer at Otto Klemperer's party!"

Annie remembered it good. **He** remembered it good. He planted Annie at that party. He hot-wired her. He heard that introduction as it transpired. He thought nothing of it then.

Old Saul regasbagged. Annie reran her gee-whiz shtick. Old Saul resnitched his analysand.

Claire told him that Dudley beat up Orson Welles. Lover man added insult to injury. Dudley made Orson his informant. Orson told her all of this. He's now finking leftists on his OIACC tour. Dudley forbids Claire to see Orson. She sees him anyway. Fuck lover man. He's screwing a red-haired tart in L.A.

Old Saul re-**re**gassbagged. He dropped the kicker then.

"Claire was very agitated. She kvetched throughout the whole session. She said, 'Kay Lake will surely be at Otto's next party. I'm going to make up to her and talk to her about Dudley. The girl is a seasoned gossip. I'm sure she knows things about Dudley that I don't.'"

The recording spritzed out. He spent three full days restitching **this:**

Klemperer's party. **In Brentwood.** Huey's Night

of the Long Knives party. **In Brentwood.** "North of Sunset, **daaarlings.**" Orson Welles was there. "He was pals with the guy who owned the house—some music maestro."

He let it sit for a week. He rehashed it with Buzz Meeks. They grabbed a reverse directory and looked up Klemperer's address. Yep—it's Brentwood, north of Sunset.

They brainstormed their next move. Eyewits didn't apply here. All the Long Knife party guests wore masks. Huey and Tommy G. saw it. Their "dates," ditto. Dudley pulls his bayonet and chops the he-she.

Huey and Tommy. Call them hostile eyewits. Huey wouldn't **re**blab. Tommy wouldn't blab at all. Their dates were unknown. It was a perv bash. There'd be no formal guest list.

They checked dead-body reports. West L.A. Division. Winter '39. Up near Brentwood. North of Sunset Boulevard. Up in that **très** posh turf.

They snagged a dumped-body decomp. It was up in Mandeville Canyon. It was out in some woodsy preserve. A male stiff got chomped by coyotes. The critters ate his feet and his dick. The dump site was half a mile from Klemperer's crib.

The DB report was dated 3/5/39. The stiff was roughly two weeks DOA. The cops ID'd him. The coroner tagged cause of death. The hump died from stab-wound trauma.

He's Cedric Francis Inge. Age twenty-seven. White

male/6'3"/135. Sixteen sodomy beefs. Drag-revue performer. "Gene the Queen" Harlow to his-her friends.

So far, so **goooood.** Here's the next angle. Dudley Smith's got his nuts in a vise. Who would he call? Who else? He'd call Mike Breuning and Dick Carlisle.

Buzz and him checked old duty rosters. Breuning and Carlisle worked the Bunco night watch then. There it is—2/19/39.

Breuning and Carlisle clock out. It's "personal business." They vamoose at 11:20 p.m.

Buzz and him hashed it out **gooooood.** He said, "Do you really want to blackmail Dudley Smith?"

Buzz gulped and popped sweat. Buzz said, "Not right yet, I don't."

They let it sit for a week. He called Annie Staples then. She met him at Scrivner's Drive-in on 6th and Vermont. They slurped pineapple malts and discussed Annie's crush on Orson Welles.

He said, "I foresee a date at Brenda's trick spot. I'll be in the camera hole. Notable woof-woof may well ensue."

Annie said, "Orson needs to lose weight."

He said, "I'll slide you a grand."

Annie said, "Let me guess. You want me to pump him for certain information."

He said, "Winter '39. A party at Otto Klemperer's place, and a movie he screened. Put the spurs to him. I want to see how he reacts."

70

(LOS ANGELES AND BAJA, 2/12–2/25/42)

The Wolf licked the blood off his gold bayonet. It consecrated his conversion.

He's a reborn apostate. He mimed History and reprised the Night of the Long Knives. It erased his wretched moment at Herr Klemperer's house. He's a fascist now. He's more specifically a Sinarquista.

The Wolf decreed a commemorative rampage. He enlisted Salvy and Juan Pimentel and issued the Wolf's directive. They staged a raid and stole Cruz-Caiz's heroin stash. He killed **El Communisto**'s key henchmen. Sinarquista Greenshirts cut up the bodies and buried the offal. He kept Hideo out of it. Hideo would have had qualms.

The rampage continued. Salvy had kill-listed eight former Redshirts. They were torturers and nun-rapers of the Calles regime. They lived in seclusion throughout Baja. El Dudster and Plucky Salvador slaughtered them. Stout Juan fed their guts and limbs to greedy ocean sharks.

Traitors and rapists, all. Thirteen deaths in all. He filed thirteen notches on his bayonet. The Wolf drank thirteen drafts of blood.

Reprise and revision. Munich, '34. Brentwood, '39. The lakeside spa and Herr Klemperer's house.

The Brentwood bash spawned chaos. Mike and Dick salvaged him. Tommy Glennon forced him to relive the nightmare. San Quentin, last November. Tommy's smirky blackmail pass. He'll find Tommy and kill him. He'll nullify all impediments. He'll kill Buzz Meeks and Elmer Jackson as whim dictates.

He told Salvy about the gold. He omitted nothing. He pledged 15% of all gold profits to the Sinarquista cause. Salvy joined the gold-questing band. He'll tell Hideo and Joan in due time.

Said band is egalitarian. There's an Irishman, a Japanese, a woman. A Mexican lawyer and rightist firebrand now join them. **Está la nueva familia** and cause to exult.

Hideo and Joan talk long-distance. Their one topic is gold. They remain his L.A. family. They supplant the wife and daughters he never sees. Favored daughter Beth Short lives up near San Francisco. She promises visits but repeatedly renegs. Beth is boy crazy. She may be spreading herself thin.

His Mexican family sports fractures. Young Joan Klein first detected the schism. She'd tailed Claire to liaisons with **El Puto** Cruz-Caiz. It explains Claire's recent sobbing fits and bedroom retreat. Young Joan remains secretive and obstreperous. It befits a fifteen-year-old girl born on Halloween. She speaks in riddles and hints at her "package from the East." He deadpans these salvos. The girl has a fantastical penchant for left-wing intrigue.

His own intrigues consume him. The klub**haus** job

remains in acute disarray. Jack Horrall has granted him sanction. He's free to plumb more immediate paths to a solve.

He schmoozed up Sid Hudgens. He told him to plant three pithy items in the **Herald.**

Hot item!!! PD stalwarts pursue Fifth Column suspects!!! Klubhaus solve at hand?

Hot item!!! PD stalwarts pursue Mexican suspects!!! Klubhaus solve at hand?

Hot item!!! PD stalwarts pursue Negro suspects!!! Klubhaus solve at hand?

Martin Luther Mimms will supply suitable suspects. Call-Me-Jack is convinced of that. Preacher Mimms is out of town now. He's recruiting for his back-to-Africa shuck. Herr Mimms gleefully bilks his own people. A Smith-Mimms summit must be penciled in. They'll eat soul food and drink corn liquor. They'll trip the dark fantastic.

The klub**haus** job is all taxing tangents. Huey Cressmeyer escaped from Juan Pimentel and remained at large for three days. Huey revealed that two cornpone cops snatched him. The crazed crackers roughhoused Huey. He rebuffed their hurt. Huey said he snitched Tommy G. and Wendell Rice, **los dos.** He stuck to this tale.

Thad Brown said Redneck Elmer worked a Deutsches Haus incursion and learned less than zilch. Cretin Elmer and Cagey Buzz may be harboring leads. He should kill them both. Now might be good. Why wait for Armistice Day?

Taxing tangents. Jackson and Meeks. Likewise, James Edgar Davis.

He's cultivated Two-Gun. He's coddled and cajoled him. He's endured a slew of boozy dinners at Kwan's. Jim will not submit to pentothal. "I spilled my guts on the Watanabe job, Dud. You and Bill Parker know, you sure as shit told Jack Horrall, and Bill must have told the latest college girl he's perved on. That's status quo for me, and I'm sticking to it."

Two-Gun Jim remains balky. He radiates intransigence. His sclerotic face pulses and beams **Fuck You.** This may necessitate force.

Like his Orson Welles approach. Fat Boy in blood-soaked lounge garb. That was a crackerjack play.

Orson passed through Ensenada. El Porko was on his goodwill tour. They enjoyed a beachside dinner. Orson waxed acquiescent. He exemplified the if-you-can't-beat-'em-join-'em school of cowed informants. He tattled numerous tinseltown Reds.

As in his own psychiatrist. **There's** a red reptile. Saul Lesnick, M.D.

He was Claire's headshrink. The gold-quest gang knew all about him. Lesnick snitched Reds to Ed Satterlee. Lesnick tooled for Meyer Gelb. Orson met Gelb at Otto Klemperer's place. Orson showed up at the '39 **Walpurgisnacht.** They crossed paths in costumes and masks and never knew it. Orson screened his Long Knives smut film. He dressed as a Red Guardsman and rolled film. Leni Riefenstahl mocked him and tossed a drink in his face.

Psychic recurrence. Confounding convergence. Chez Klemperer as star-crossed place. The cosmos sends a message. Hark—the gold is yours.

The cosmos speaks to the Wolf. The Wolf drinks the blood of his master's victims and licks the gold bayonet clean. The Wolf sniffs out strategic imperative and reports back to him. Governor Juan Lazaro-Schmidt appeared at the Hotel del Norte. His sister Constanza played with a middling string quartet. They performed a recital at the del Norte. Beethoven and Hindemith. The Wolf scared up a ticket and arranged a chance meet with Governor Juan.

The **Führer** and Herr Goebbels detest Hindemith. They are hidebound in that regard. The sonata was lovely. It was properly dissonant and no more. The Wolf hopped onstage and curled up at Constanza Lazaro-Schmidt's feet. She played achingly well. She paused to let the violins and cello ascend. She stroked the Wolf then.

Stunning creature. Dark hair and eyes. Long legs and almost too broad shoulders. She bit her lips as she played. Her white gown bunched at the hips. She kicked off her shoes for the "Grosse Fugue" and dug in barefoot.

The Wolf approved of Constanza. Her scene enticed. The Wolf escorted him to the lobby at intermission. Hark—there's the governor. The Wolf introduced them and trotted off.

He was a slight man. He was elegant and smaller than his sister. They wore identical lapel pins. The pin clasps faced outward. The gold swastikas were tucked out of sight.

They chatted up the war and made nice-nice. He brought up the U.S. crop-worker conundrum and requested a chance to discuss it. They made plans to meet in a fortnight.

The recital concluded. Beethoven 131 went out in a rush. The Wolf led him back to the artists' dressing rooms. He saw Constanza unhook her gown and adjust her brassiere. The fabric was sheer. She had lovely dark nipples.

J. Lazaro-Schmidt and sister. Salvy distrusted their relationship. Salvy urged him to hold that thought.

Late February brought rain. Pacific storms hit the coast. Wave swells lashed Santa Barbara. A Jap sub lobbed shells north of there. Sea wolves aimed at the Ellsworth Oil Depot. The shells fell short. The sea wolves turned tail. Fourth Interceptor imposed a press blackout. The attack was kept mum.

He bennie-laced his a.m. coffee. The brew complemented his rainy mornings and spiked his ability to read and assess. He read Jap residential files and scoured for leads on K. Hanamaka. He brainstormed and cinched a few things up.

Sea attack. Air attack. Those prefab airplane parts he saw in the shore cove. Left-behind parts. Flame-charred to disguise them. Nazi and Soviet insignia.

Psychic recurrence. Confounding convergence. Something Huey Cressmeyer said. "Mitch," the model-airplane man. A Deutsches Haus regular. Mitchell A.

Kupp. Madcap aviator-inventor. Joan's #1 father-snuff suspect. He charters a plane in Duluth. Earle Conville burns to death in western Wisconsin.

Joan tracks a fuel spill back to him. She suspects but cannot prove malfeasance. A scholarly tract arrives at the klub**haus.** Mitch Kupp authored it. He critiques firebomb warfare and proposes funded research. Everyday Joes can fly build-ur-self planes. He's prefabbed kits himself.

It all dovetailed. Joan subscribed to notions of psychic recurrence and star-crossed place. She **made** stars cross. She summoned Mitch Kupp to her very own constellation.

He ran nationwide file checks and cross-checked subversive membership lists. Kupp was pegged as America First. He had no police record. He had a California driver's license and lived in San Berdoo.

Psychic recurrence. Confounding convergence. Star-crossed place.

He surveilled Mitch Kupp. Herr Kupp lived in a small house with a detached garage. Madcap Mitch. He worked in the garage and kept the door open.

See the airplane parts. See the prefab rivets. See the Nazi and Soviet stencils. See the workbench and bottled arson accelerants. See Madcap Mitch sniff paint thinner.

Madcap Mitch. He'll stay put for now. Instinct is proof. Due process is a shuck. He's fairly sure that Joan will want to kill him.

71

(LOS ANGELES, 2:15 A.M., 2/25/42)

Sirens kicked on and whooped. They invaded her dream. She was hunting ring-neck birds. She was back in Tomah some—

Joan opened her eyes. Bill stirred. The whoop-whoop hit overdrive. Bill grabbed his glasses. Searchlights swooped. They invaded the bedroom. Blackout drapes went translucent.

Bill got up. The drapes backlit him naked. The alarm felt inadvertent. A bogus one went down last night. Full blackout/false alarm/7:00 to 10:00. One large pain in the ass.

Joan said, "Shit."

Bill peeled back the wall drapes. Searchlights crisscrossed. The bedroom soaked up light. The phone rang. Oh shit/**no** shit—three short and shrill bursts.

It was PD code. It meant This Is Real. It meant Report for Duty **NOW.**

Joan got goose bumps. She stepped into her shoes and threw on last night's clothes. Bill tripped into his trousers and fell back on the bed. Courtyard doors banged. Rubes jumped out on their porches to gab and watch the show.

Joan buttoned her blouse. Bill tied his shoes and

looped his gun belt. Joan tossed him his shirt and necktie. They tripped into each other and ran outside.

A drunk neighbor wolf-whistled. Bill was untucked and disheveled. Joan's blouse tail drooped. They made the sidewalk. Bill's prowl sled was haphazardly parked and nosed south.

They slid on damp asphalt. They banged their knees getting in. Sirens whooped loud. Searchlights glared bright.

Joan said, "Shit."

Bill said, "Shit."

He kicked the ignition. He pulled out and cut east on 1st. Searchlights flutter-lit the street. Fools stood outside and gawked. Joan dug in Bill's pants pockets and pulled out his cigarettes.

They tore through Bunker Hill. They hit a rise at Figueroa and got a wide downtown view. They saw it and heard it simultaneous.

Artillery fire. Flak bursts. The antiaircraft guns outside City Hall.

Joan fumbled her cigarette. Bill fumbled his. He fishtailed downhill and bumped the curb upside Central Station. Joan squeezed his leg. Bill touched her hair. She got out and ran inside.

Bluesuits jammed the entrance hall. They wore tin hats and riot gear. They shouted. Two words overlapped.

It's Real/It's Real/It's Real.

Joan heard machine-gun fire. She pegged it northeast. City Hall again. Those .30-caliber BARs with hundred-round belts.

Ceiling lights burned dim. Joan ran down to the basement and hit the generator switch. It juiced up real light. She ran back upstairs. The armory door stood open. The watch sergeant passed out tommy guns.

A bluesuit lobbed a roll of tinfoil. Somebody yelled, "Windows!" Joan snagged the roll and ran upstairs to the lab.

She tore off strips with her teeth. She foil-crimped curtain-windowpane junctures and cut off escaped light. She looked out a window crack. Flak bursts glowed pink. The goddamn sirens and searchlights persisted. She thought she saw an airplane wing.

The phone rang. She snatched the receiver and said her name. Flak noise drowned out her voice. She thought she heard a voice. It was long-distance faint. The flak noise subsided. The voice said, "Joan, is it you?"

Hideo Ashida. Filtered through party-line jabber. She heard Mexican voices. It was switchboard gobbledygook.

Joan talked loud. Mex jabber smothered her voice. She cupped her free ear. Flak noise came and went. Hideo got fractured words out.

It's real. I'm with Dudley. We've seen aircraft heading north. Coastal artillery. We're coming up. You won't believe what we've—

She lost him. Two minutes passed. She clutched the receiver. She bit her lips and chipped a tooth.

Hideo came back on. The switchboard screech

resumed. She caught crazy chatter and fractured-sentence talk.

Alien Squad.
Red Alert roundup list.
Uninterned Japanese.
Stand by.
Take photographs.
Suspects.
Klubhaus job.
Work confiscations.

More jabber-screech. More cacophany. Then profane **español.** Then a blare disconnect.

Joan dropped the phone and ran down the hallway. She hit the Alien Squad pen at full sprint. The boys were garbed up and armed for **JAP.**

They wore tin hats and bandoliers. They slid .45 dumdums into tommy-gun drums. Lew Collier dispensed pickup lists and divvied up partners. Lee Blanchard got Robby Moss. Elmer Jackson got Cal Lunceford. Catbox Cal wore gloves. He dipped his dumdums in a jar of liquid strychnine and hand-fed his tommy gun.

Joan opened the supply closet. She pulled three mug-shot cameras off a shelf and quick-loaded film. She affixed flashbulb strips and boxed up everything. Thad Brown spotted her and walked straight over.

He said, "Holy shit, Red."

She said, "Holy shit, Thad."

He passed her a canvass list. "Call these people and get them over here. Promise them whatever you have to. Tell them we're being attacked, so do your god-damn duty, and we'll shitcan extant warrants, or we'll tap our slush fund and pay you twenty bucks apiece. They're our 46th Street locals and jazz-club people—off our first canvass. We've got Red Alert Japs coming in, and I want to run lineups. We could get lucky here. This is fresh lineup meat, and I want to see if any of these yokels can make positive IDs. Most of these people won't have cars or will be too scared to drive, so arrange your pickups with Newton Patrol, and get on it."

Joan flashed the V sign. Thad said something. Antiaircraft bursts drowned him out. He flashed the V sign and popped in earplugs. Joan laughed and shooed him off.

She walked back to the squad pen and pulled a desk phone over. She yanked the cord taut and barricaded herself in the closet. It was half-ass quiet and claustrophobe-cramped. She began stiffing calls.

She got hang-ups and no-answers. She got fearful yelps and **It's just like Pearl Harbor!** She talked nice to folks and harsh to folks and promised police escorts. She shamed folks. She pledged slush-fund gelt and dinner chits for Kwan's. She worked two hours straight and smoked herself hoarse. She logged **I'm not going out in this** calls. She logged **shit yes** calls. She called canvass names and Newton Patrol, contrapuntal. She hooked nine stout souls up with the Newton switchboard.

She'd sweated through her clothes. She stepped back out of the closet and into the blare.

The artillery. The flak. The BARs. The station was sealed tight. The windows were blackout-crimped. The generator lights cut in and out. The blare ate its way inside her head.

Joan lugged her cameras down to the jail. Fourteen Red Alert Japs crammed up the main holding cell. They were beat to shit and ratchet-cuffed behind their backs. They dripped blood on the floor. They saw the big white cooze and spit at her through the bars.

Werewolf Shudo's cell was straight across the catwalk. He dick-flashed the Red Alert Japs. They dick-flashed him right back.

Joan dodged spit blobs and pressed close to the bars. She deployed all three cameras and snapped photos. The Japs blinked back flashbulb glare. They crowded up to the bars and mugged. They hopped around. They yelled pro-Emperor slogans and stuck out their tongues.

She shot all fourteen men. She unloaded the film and scooped up the spent flashbulbs. She lugged her camera box up to the lab and dropped it off.

The lab windows faced north. City Hall was two blocks off. The trifecta blared: artillery, BARs, flak.

Joan caught her breath. She wrote a cover note and dropped it in the box.

"4:30 a.m., 2/25/42. Corroborative photos. Current per this date. Mug-shot comparison/14 male Japanese."

It was cold. The generator lights usurped the pipe

heat. Her blouse stuck to her back. Her wet stockings had stretched.

She walked to the lineup room. Thad Brown chatted up the eyewits.

Four squarejohn whites. Three colored hepcats. Two Mexican boys in aloha shirts and slit-bottomed khakis.

Thad winked and handed her his clipboard. Fourteen rap sheets and mug-shot strips were clipped in.

The hepcats and Mex boys ogled her. She walked to the lineup stage and studied the clips.

Fourteen righteous criminals. No known Fifth Column ties. Uninterned for that reason. Red Alert for that reason. All uninterned Japs posed a threat.

All young men. All ex-cons. 459/211/502 PC. 390 sex deviate. Sodomy/stat rape.

Joan studied the mug shots. All fourteen men wore neck boards. The photos were dated 8/38 to now. All fourteen men had aged. They were all frayed-cum-raggedy ass.

The lineup stage was harsh-lit and one-way glass-fronted. Height strips lined the back wall. Fluorescent lights bore down. Potential eyewits faced the stage and grabbed look-sees.

Joan walked back and milled with the eyewits. Thad Brown passed out dinner chits and sawbucks. The white folks took it stoic. The hepcats and Mex boys yipped. One hepcat said, "Remember Pearl Harbor." A Mex boy said, **"Banzai."**

Thad laughed. "You know how this works. We've

got fourteen suspects. They'll be wearing neck boards numbered one to fourteen. You study the men and decide for yourselves, without conferring with anyone else. Raise your hand if you're certain, and talk to Miss Conville."

A buzzer buzzed. A wall light pulsed. Mike Breuning popped through the stage-right door. The shackle gang dogged him. Their cinch chains dragged on the floor.

They were kicked to shit. Black eyes, cuts, contusions. One half-detached ear. Sap damage. Beavertail saps with rough-stitch edges. Cops armed for **JAP.**

Breuning positioned the men. They stood behind raised number plates and blinked back bright light. The eyewits eyeballed them. Thad said, "Take your time, folks."

They grabbed good look-sees. Joan watched their eyes click. She ticked seconds on her wristwatch. Two full minutes passed.

A white lady looked over and held up five fingers. A hepcat looked over and flashed five more. Joan flashed five fingers. Thad caught it and flashed the stage. Joan checked the clipboard. There's suspect #5.

Hiroshi NMI Yamura. Age 34. Grand Theft Auto/Peeping Tom/Stat Rape.

The white lady said, "I saw him go in and out of that horrible clubhouse. He was always inebriated."

The hepcat said, "I used to see him at Mumar's Mosque and Happytime Liquor. He used to shoot craps outside the clubhouse, but after Pearl Harbor he dropped out of sight."

Breuning detached Yamura. He unlocked his cuffs and shackle chain and threw on a headlock. The stage was soundproof. It went down hush-hush. Yamura thrashed his arms and went dead-legged. Breuning clamped his neck and dragged him off, stage right.

The white lady crossed herself. The hepcat shrugged. A Mex boy said, "Screw his mama sideways. My brother-in-law got it at Pearl."

The lineup room adjoined sweatbox row. Joan passed Thad his clipboard and took the stage-right door. She heard shrieks and thumps and followed them. Two short hallways intersected. She saw Breuning drag Yamura, and Dick Carlisle kick him from behind.

They dragged him and kicked him. Breuning popped the #3 door and hauled him inside. Carlisle slammed the door. It squelched a loud screech.

Joan walked over. She goosed the wall speaker and peeped the mirror wall. Breuning and Carlisle proned out Yamura. Carlisle kicked his head and back. Breuning rifled his pockets and plucked his wallet and keys. Yamura screamed. Carlisle slid on sap gloves. Breuning went through the wallet sleeves.

He saw something. You could tell that. Joan read him plain. He faced the mirror wall and waved the wallet. He knew somebody's peeping. Somebody always peeps.

Breuning yelled at the wall mikes. "He's got a driver's license in another name. There's an address on 46th. It's right by the klub**haus.**"

Yamura flailed. He kicked Carlisle off of him. Carlisle tripped and hit the back wall. Yamura reached into his right shoe and pulled something out. He put the something in his mouth and bit down hard.

He **Fuck You**–fingered the mirror. His legs twitched, his arms twitched, his back arched off the floor. He belched foam and went spastic jerky. The foam was half blood. Dick Carlisle saw it and screamed.

72

(ORANGE COUNTY, 5:00 A.M., 2/25/42)

They cut inland. Coastal roadblocks stalled their progress north. Artillery jolts deafened them. Tracer rounds blurred their sight. Beach guns fired at airplane wisps and plain shadows.

Ashida drove. Dudley commandeered Major Melnick's staff car. It was full-boat SIS. Big V-8/two-way radio/ammo-packed trunk. They blasted out of Ensenada and went AWOL.

Sirens blared at 3:00 a.m. The Baja alert aped the L.A. alert. Some Statie coastal goon saw Zeros and tripped the alarm. He radioed beach batteries north to San Diego. Full artillery launched at 3:10.

It spread. Whatever this was spread exponential. Jack Horrall patch-called Dudley and ordered them up.

Whatever this was hit Baja and L.A. The City Hall guns blasted Jap Zeros or Jap wisps. The Alien Squad mobilized and roused Red Alert Japs.

Coastal guns blazed. Spotters spotted whatever it was. Juan Pimentel sicced the Baja Staties. They patrolled beachfronts. They ran floodlights and strafed wave lines north to T.J. They shot at Jap subs or Jap wisps or whatever it was.

No Jap subs blew up. No Jap Zeros exploded. Something was up there and/or down there. Somebody saw something and punched the trigger. Chain reaction. Jap fever. Some L.A. somebody. Some Baja somebody. Something was up there and/or down there.

Prophets prophesied that something. Code-call intelligence accrued. Fourth Interceptor logged it. SIS ignored it. Possible airfields in San Berdoo County. Late February attack.

The bookie-front raid backfired. The transmitter exploded. It blitzed a code-call approach. Now hear this: the fucking prophecy's fulfilled.

Ashida drove blackout-blind. Eastbound streets blurred. He heard ack-ack and siren screech. Predawn lit the sky. A plane passed overhead. He thought he saw wing rivets and a hammer and scythe. Something's up there. He knew he saw something.

Dudley chain-smoked. He wore his I'm-brooding-don't-talk-to-me look. He rolled down his window. Ashida smelled cordite and spilled gasoline.

The two-way radio beeped. Dudley flipped switches and plugged in his headset. He said, "Yes, Thad." He listened. He said, "Yes, Thad," and unplugged.

"We may have a klub**haus** lead. A man named Yamura or Nunakawa killed himself in custody. His driver's license listed his address as 682 East 46th. That's the klub**haus** block, and Thad wants us there. He's dispatching Lunceford and Jackson, as well."

Ashida gunned it. He drove eighty-plus, blackout-blind. They crossed the L.A. County line. Sirens whooped and sputtered. He pushed it to ninety. He hit Gardena and caught Western Avenue. The sky cleared some. He took Imperial Highway east and hooked onto Central north.

Low-rent L.A. at dawn. Gun chatter somewhere. No plane-crash debris. No foot traffic. Locked-tight business fronts.

78th Street. 77th Street. 76, 75, 74. Ashida saw smoke. Two prowl cars sped past them. Their cherry lights whirled.

Ashida floored it. He fishtailed and blew a string of red lights. Dudley unholstered his sidearm and winked.

Smoke roiled up dark and thick. Ashida got it now. He hit the siren and unholstered. He steered the car with his knees and jacked a shell into the breech.

Full dawn hit. 51, 50, 49. Black smoke plumed.

Parked cars issued flames. Here's your something. It's for sure. There's a Negro Riot on the Jazz-Club Strip.

They drove into it. Dudley cracked his windwing. Negroes rock-shattered windows and hauled off whiskey crates. 48, 47. Negroes bashed down the doors of the Club Zamboanga and Port Afrique. They swung two-by-four bashing rams. They smashed parked-car windows and hurled wine-bottle bombs. Car seats ignited, car windows blew.

Ashida downshifted and pulled right. Somebody somewhere yelled, "It's a Jap!"

Shots hit the car. The windshield exploded. Shots dinged the trunk and pierced the rear doors. Dudley grabbed the wheel and pulled it hard right. The car banged the curb and stalled flat.

Dudley got out. Ashida got out a split second on. Dudley braced his arm on the car-top and fired into the mob.

Three Negroes fell. A man's chest blew up. Dudley fired hollow points. He shot one man in the neck and blew a man's arm off.

The mob issued one big scream. Ashida aimed and fired straight at it. He shot two men in the back. They careened and crashed and bumped heads.

Dudley ran toward 46th Street. Ashida ran after him and caught up. They turned the corner. They saw the klub**haus,** ablaze.

Flames scorched the top floor. The air stung. Negroes hauled swag out the front door. Furniture, radios, trombones. Sinarquista tapestries.

Ten Negroes. Twenty Negroes. Negroes in gang silks and zoot suits. Negroes slurping muscatel. Negroes waving Nazi flags on sticks.

Somebody somewhere yelled, "Dig the Jap!"

Dudley walked toward them. Ashida followed him. The Negroes made buzzing-airplane sounds and turned their arms into wings.

Dudley aimed and fired. Two zoot suiters fell. The mob screeched and dispersed all whichways.

A kid stumbled to the sidewalk. He cradled a big saxophone and peeled toward the avenue. Ashida saw his coffee skin and almond eyes. Tokyo meets the Congo.

Ashida aimed at his face. He squeezed the trigger and saw it break red. The sax pitched backward with him. The kid death-cradled it.

73

(LOS ANGELES, 6:00 A.M., 2/25/42)

The tin hat mussed his hair. The tommy gun weighed ten tons. He gots dem Red Alert Blues.

Cal Lunceford wrote dem blues. Catbox Cal. A hate dog to rival Wayne Frank. Wayne Frank hated up dem jigs and dem Jews. Sergeant E. V. Jackson disapproves. He gots dem Red Alert Blues.

Elmer breezed into Central Station. Catbox Cal lagged back. They steered a six-man shackle chain down to the jail. Joan Conville was there. She circled the holding pens and snapped photographs.

The Jap attack or big scare or plain fuckup fizzled out. It was all for Jap naught and **OOPS** writ large. Fletch B. scheduled a press confab. He'd dish the gist later today.

The jail overflowed. Werewolf Shudo waved his pecker at his Red Alert pals. Elmer unshackled the new fish and got them penned up. Catbox Cal sulked.

Thad Brown walked over. He looked spookified.

"You and Lunceford roll back out. We've got a riot at 46th and Central. The klub**haus** has been torched. Dudley and Ashida put down some shines."

Elmer gulped. Catbox Cal giggled. Thad snatched a cigar from Elmer's coat pocket.

"Check this address. 682 East 46th. It's right by the klub**haus.** We took it off a DL on one of our suspect Japs. He killed himself with a cyanide pill, which I don't like the looks of. Get over there. Dud and Ashida are busy with the fire department."

Lunceford snatched a cigar. "How many shines did they bag?"

Thad said, "Eight."

Lunceford said, "There's hope for this world. I wouldn't have thought Ashida had it in him."

———

L.A. was deadsville. It's **The War of the Worlds,** redux. Orson Welles did that radio show. Flying saucers and zombies. Folks thought it was real. Folks wigged out, resultant.

Elmer drove. Catbox Cal resulked. They ran Code 3/ lights and siren. They ignored traffic signs and laid tracks.

They hauled south and east. There's the jazz-club strip. It's been manhandled. Note the scorched cars. Note the smashed windows. Note the kicked-in doors. Note the soot-filtered air. Note the blues holding spectators back.

Elmer cut left on 46th. Sayonara, klub**haus.**

It was torched toast. The upstairs had smooshed the downstairs. Hose steam hissed. Beams wiggled and collapsed. Rubble mounds sizzled.

Note the two fire trucks. Note the three morgue wagons. Note the eight sheet-draped gurneys. The Dudster posed for pictures. Firemen aimed box cameras. Ashida looked shell-shocked.

Lunceford said, "Coon hunt."

Elmer said, "Son, you are wearing me thin."

Lunceford shut up. Elmer shot east. He checked curb plates and read addresses. 674, 676, 678. There's no 680. There's 682—

It's a small wood-frame job. It's one-story and dilapidated. Dig that porch rat. He's big and black and scaly-tailed. He exemplifies beady-eyed evil.

Elmer parked at the curb. They got out and walked up the steps. The soul rat skittered off. The dump radiated quietude.

Lunceford pulled his roscoe. Elmer eared the door and got all-quiet squared. He nudged the door. It slid open easy.

Lunceford squeezed in ahead of him. The front room was musty. Thin curtains let in light. Pizza-pie boxes were stacked on a table. Elmer smelled stale cheese and mold.

All quiet. **Oooga-booga.** Where de peoples at?

Lunceford walked ahead. He cut through the front room and eased toward a back hallway. Elmer slow-orbed the front room.

He caught stale food and stale air. His hackles jumped. The joint felt quick-vacated. That proclaimed **Hideout.**

He eased toward the hallway. He thought he heard footfalls. Wood planks squeaked. The squeaks overlapped. He thought he heard footfalls—two sets.

He thought he heard whispers. He froze right there. His ears perked. He thought he heard **"Run."**

He crouched and stared down the hallway. Something moved. He thought he heard something. He caught a shutter-click glimpse.

It's a Jap. He's going for the back door. Shutter click. There's that surveillance pic. Shutter click. Ed the Fed showed it to—

It's Kyoho Hanamaka, that evil little—

There's **"Run"** again. There's footsteps heading

back this way. There's a stumble sound and Lunceford in the hallway. He's quick-walking straight for—

Elmer hit the floor. Lunceford pulled his gun. Elmer pulled his ankle piece and aimed straight up.

He squeezed slow. He got Lunceford in the legs and the gut. Lunceford lost his legs and dropped his gun and flew ass-backward. Elmer squeezed slow. He got the cocksucker in the chin and took his fucking face off.

74

(LOS ANGELES, 10:30 A.M., 2/25/42)

Flashbulbs popped. Newshounds swarmed and scrawled notes. Mayor Fletch blathered. He lived to jive the Fourth Estate.

City Hall was Jap Attack and Fed Indictment HQ. The briefing room overflowed. Dudley stood at the back. Sid Hudgens sidled up to him. He flashed the a.m. **Herald.** The attack claimed ten-point headlines. The backup piece ran under the fold.

INDICTMENTS ISSUED IN PHONE-TAP PROBE!!! PROMINENT ANGELENOS J'ACCUSED!!!!

Fletch B. himself. Chief Clemence "Jack" Horrall.

Hotshot PI Wallace Jamie. Police chemist Ray Pinker. Lesser-known legal beagles galore.

Sid said, "I never thought the Japs were up there. Pearl taught us they come in fast and low."

Dudley winked. "There was a grand scuffle at 46th and Central. Let's see if Fletch deigns to mention it."

Fletch drooped off the lectern and mauled the microphone. He lived to grandstand and distort.

"For those of you who remain unconvinced, let me repeat. There was no air attack, Jap or otherwise. There **were** shells dropped, but we don't know by who, and they failed to detonate. Several folks throughout the city were struck by falling debris, but there were no serious injuries and no fatalities."

Dudley grinned. Credit a madcap inventor. Build-ur-self airplanes aloft.

Fletch coughed and hankie-wiped the microphone. He thrived on deceit.

"The only fatalities resulted from a Negro riot, in the vicinity of 46th Street and Central Avenue. Negroes looted numerous liquor stores and jazz clubs. A score of Negroes were fatally wounded by other Negroes, who have not yet been identified."

Sid whistled shrill. "I hope they didn't torch Minnie Roberts' Casbah. The DA gets his ugambo there."

Laffs rocked the room. Sid lived to offend and provoke. Fletch undid his necktie and buffed the microphone.

"On a more dour note. The Negroes set fire to

a clubhouse under police investigation. And, in an unrelated incident, Officer Calvin S. Lunceford was shot and killed by a Jap seditionist, who has not yet been identified, and who remains at large."

Catbox Cal. A jailbait-jumper and a sloven at best. The world will not mourn.

The room rumbled. Dead cops goosed circulation. The Hearst rags would pounce and exploit.

Fletch said, "It would have been impossible for any unlogged airplanes to have taken off or landed unseen in L.A. County or any adjoining county. Those shells were most likely unintentionally dropped by U.S. Army scouting craft, sent up in the wake of the preceding yellow-alert blackout."

Sid whistled shrill. "There's been reports of coded calls from here to Baja. They supposedly mentioned secret air bases in San Berdoo County, and inquiring minds want to know if Jap planes could have departed and returned there."

Fletch said, "Poppycock. Inquiring minds should inquire about the rising tide of Negro crime in Los Angeles."

Sid despised Fletch. Mr. Mayor picked his pockets bare at PD pokerfests.

"How does it feel to be under Federal indictment, boss?"

Fletch said, "The truth shall set me free."

———

San Berdoo was sixty miles out. It was a tank town. Farmhands and low-rank Army. Package stores and whorehouses. Shitkicker cops up for grabs.

Dudley dawdled en route. He called Joan and gave her the address. He pledged a grand surprise. He side-stepped discussion of the fool air attack and declined to ascribe blame.

He'd spotted a kit plane, down in Orange County. The car-engine hum alerted him. The hammer and sickle gave it away. He got the picture then.

It was cloudless and midmorning cool. He'd changed into civvies. The riot left his uniform soot-streaked. Hideo impressed him. He followed his **Führer**'s lead and shot quick and true. He'd ride out conscience pangs in due course.

The Lunceford item troubled him. Catbox Cal dies. Elmer J. survives. An alleged Jap slayer remains at large. Elmer's proximity was worrisome. The lad magnetized trouble and/or caused it himself.

He hit San Berdoo proper and drove straight to the address. The garage door stood open. He parked across the street and walked over.

A breeze kicked in. Solvent fumes blew down the driveway. Dudley scanned the garage. He saw blueprints for build-yourself torpedoes. He saw tin snips and hand-cut propellers.

Drivetrains and flywheels. A box of clutch pedals. Spark plugs, rivet guns, Messerschmitt stencils. Bottled arson accelerants. A snap-in-place airplane control board.

Dudley walked around to the back. Tarpaulins dotted the yard. They covered irregular mounds. Fuselage panels stuck out.

A back door was propped open. He saw a kitchen crammed with boxes. He smelled glue and saw legs jammed under a table.

He walked in and skirted the boxes. Madcap Mitch glued up a toy Stuka. He was forty-five or so. He sported a goatee and a soil-crusted smock.

Dudley said, "Hello, sir."

Mad Mitch looked up. He had quick blue eyes.

"Cop, huh?"

"That's right."

"Federal?"

"No, city."

Mad Mitch went **You got me.** "I'll admit I dropped those bombs. They were deliberate duds, and nobody got hurt. I didn't drop any gas or set any fires, which I damn well could have done."

Dudley smiled. "I'm not accusing you of anything, sir. I'm here to compliment you on your work."

Mad Mitch picked up the Stuka and zoomed it. The great Charles Lindbergh admired this man. He had deft hands and nativist chutzpah.

"I picked up rumors of an air attack and alerted the kids in my squadron. We decided to launch an armada and do some joyriding."

"Your kids, sir? Your squadron?"

Mad Mitch scratched his arms. They were solvent-scarred and overlaid with ripe sores.

"Frat boys, mostly. Engineering students. They build my kits and go hog wild. You can't keep good kids down on the ground when they want to be up in the air."

Dudley smiled. "You sell your kits through the mail, do you?"

Mad Mitch smiled. "Blueprints and parts. U.S. and Mexico. The spics are my best customers. **Yo habla español,** daddy?"

Dudley heard footsteps behind him. Stacked-heel footsteps. A tall woman's gait.

"Are you a saboteur or a spy, sir? Are you a Fifth Columnist?"

"Nix to all three. I'm just a card-carrying white man, and I'm proud to attend the beerfests at the convivial Deutsches Haus."

Dudley heard short breaths behind him. She stood out of sight. She was sight-and-sound close.

"I read your air-warfare tract, sir. I'm wondering if you ever considered the setting of forest fires as an implementation."

Mad Mitch slapped his knees. The table jolted. The toy Stuka jumped.

"I most certainly have, and I've already done the research. April 9, 1938. I took a joyride and dropped a torch bomb near Tomah, Wisconsin. I got up a sweet bar-bq."

Joan stepped up. She wore a tweed skirt and a green cashmere sweater. Mad Mitch said, "Hello there, sweetie."

Dudley felt her hand at his belt line. She pulled out his piece and shot off the full clip. She bull's-eyed Mad Mitch. Muzzle flare scorched his face. His teeth exploded. His hair caught fire.

75

(LOS ANGELES, 4:00 P.M., 2/25/42)

Time blurred. She dropped things. **Shock** failed to explain it. **Numb** missed the point.

They left him there. Dudley swatted out the fire and jacked the pipe heat. It would speed decomposition and foil time of death. Dudley knew the San Berdoo Sheriff. They'd schemed together. They'd schemed per wetbacks and captive Japs.

Time blurred. She dropped things. She saw rural Wisconsin sans through line. The fuel spill. Big Earle's wake. She hunts quail off Lake Mendota. She shoots rabid bats. She visits the Little Bohemia Lodge. Dillinger escaped from there. It was April '34. She'd just turned nineteen.

Vindication distorted it. **Barrel through** said it best. It's the Conville code. She said she'd do it and did it. Dudley made it happen. Men always indulged her.

Central Station supplied distraction. It remained

chaotic. The air-raid snafu and the riot. The klub**haus** blaze and Cal Lunceford's death. Last night and this morning blurred. She thrived on police disorder. She threw herself into it. She superimposed her father's killer. Muzzle-flare sparks flame.

She developed her booking photographs and file-clipped them. The station teemed. She saw new cop faces. War-hire rookies came by to help. They talked up the Fed-probe indictments and Bill Parker's role. She kept hearing **Bill.** It registered as incantation. The same with **Dudley.** War-hire babble. This **Dudley** guy waxed some shines.

Bill and Dudley. One of them would call her. She'd sleep with one of them tonight.

Joan walked down to the jail. She pulled log-in duty. The jail was SRO. Red Alert Japs, held for transfer. Mexican illegals—INS transfer bait.

Wetbacks. They exploited the air raid and border grief and broke for L.A. The PD snagged three truck-loads. That meant work. Log property. Fumigate ragged apparel. Call the INS.

Joan worked in the property office. It adjoined the main catwalk and holding pens. The jail was wall-to-wall shouts and jeers.

Packed pens. Trilingual ruckus. War hires baited the inmates and cracked jokes.

The babble distracted her. She dumped confiscated satchels and searched for contraband. She logged zip guns and hair pomade. She logged **fotografías de niños** and Spanish fly.

Two war hires lounged by her door. They dropped double entendres and defamed the wets. Come-san-chin, the Chinese cocksucker. This cholo I popped worked at the Blue Fox. He said the donkey poked Eleanor Roosevelt. I'd pay to see **that.**

Joan half-heard it. She logged contraband and fixed on her task. Brass knuckles. Matchbooks and swizzle sticks. A .45 ACP clip.

"The goddamn wets. Listen to that racket. It's like New Year's Eve. Remember that rainstorm? They were swarming over the border fences and clouting cars. They thought we'd have our guard down, on account of the rain."

"They were right about that. We were stretched, 'cause all the drunks and the rain had us hopping."

"They sent me out to Venice. Some Navy woman blitzed a jalopy with four beaners up front. She's dead drunk, and she dispatches all four. Then we find two dead kids in the trunk. Cute little kids—a boy and a girl."

"Oh shit. That's a rough go."

" 'Rough go' don't say it. They were breathing through airholes on the ride up from T.J., but the trunk got crushed and they smothered to death."

"A six-down 502. Tell me that ain't a world record, and tell me the Navy skirt didn't draw twelve to life, wets or no wets."

"Nix to that. The drift is Bill Parker put the fix in. He had it bad for that cooze, and he got her a skate."

Shock failed to say it. **Numb** missed the point. It explained recurrent nightmares. Thumps and muffled shrieks.

She bolted. The war hires went **Say what?** She swerved and bumped her way out to the sidewalk. DT shakes developed. Her hands trembled. She tried to light cigarettes and gave up.

She swerve-walked to City Hall and elevatored to the DB. She stared at the floor and cringed at hellos. Ringing telephones scared her. Door slams turned to thumps. Soft voices turned to shrieks.

Dudley was out. Bill was gone. She looked everywhere and gave up. She locked herself in the women's washroom. It was somebody else in the mirror. She hid from the thumps and the shrieks. They blasted her through the locked door.

She killed Mitch Kupp. She did it to break the impasse of Dudley and Bill. She sided with Dudley there. Dudley gave her sex and danger and recast her as himself. She coveted his mastery. She murdered and gave him the power to destroy her. Bill covered up the children. She gave him the power to destroy her before they'd formally met.

Indictments. True bills. No gold and no captaincy. Justice carries a price.

Joan swerve-walked to her car and drove to the Strip. She knocked on Kay's door and got no answer. She sat on the steps and considered true bills and justice. She drove back downtown and conjured the means.

Central Station. Still vividly chaotic. Don't fuck with America. The thought startled her and moved her.

She cleaned out her locker. She placed her microscope in Hideo's locker and removed her gold cuff links. She placed them face-out on his desk.

Central Station. Big Earle would have loved it. She memorized every face she saw and sent up appropriate prayers.

Forgive this theft, Lord.

She broke the clasp on the evidence locker. She stole fourteen terpin hydrate vials and stashed them in her purse.

Nursing school in Oak Park. That hot Chicago night. Sirens like last night. Prowl cars and morgue sedans. The Feds got Dillinger outside the Biograph. Crowds formed. She saw his hearse on Lincoln Avenue. Woman waved handkerchiefs, men doffed their hats. Vendors sold ice-cream bars.

Joan looked out her bedroom window. Dusk came on pink-gray.

She bundled up her diary pages and boxed them. She postage-stamped the box and addressed it to Miss Katherine Lake. She placed it outside for the postman.

Rain hit. Her next-door neighbor spun disks. Joan heard "Moonlight Serenade" and "Tuxedo Junction."

She drank the terp. It burned going down and stayed down. She prayed for her police friends and all the people she'd gone through. She asked God to punish her for her vile and reckless actions and her sinful misconduct with men.

Forgive my proud follies.

Forgive my fatuous dream of the gold.

Forgive my lifelong arrogance.

Forgive my regret without remorse.

Forgive my remorse without repentance.

Forgive this final heedless act and condemn not this expiation.

Shapes and colors took hold. She stretched out on the couch and kicked her shoes off. She saw Dudley's wolf. The Maestro's steam room appeared.

There's Orson Welles and Claire De Haven. Orson's a Wisconsin boy. He hails from Kenosha. She shouldn't be naked with a wraith socialite and a movie star.

The steam turned all different colors. Rainbows drifted by.

Orson said, "So long, Red."

Claire said, "Good-bye, Joan. See you in church."

Part Three
SINARQUISMO

(February 28–
March 25, 1942)

76

(LOS ANGELES, 9:00 A.M., 2/28/42)

The rental pastor substituted Housman for Scripture. He had quite obviously compiled notes as to who this woman was and opted for lilting elegy. She was cut off in her prime; she had everything this life offers to look forward to; her seat at the banquet was very much assured.

Hardly, sir. Joan Woodard Conville killed herself. She had gorged herself at your banquet already. Stop reciting "To an Athlete Dying Young." Let me offer up a more suitable graveside selection.

"This storm, this savaging disaster."

It's from Auden, sir. Joan quoted it repeatedly and never ascribed a specific source. Auden's lines summarize Joan's life since New Year's Eve. Catastrophic events subsumed her; she fell into the police demimonde that has threatened to subsume me. Her proud grit and resourcefulness took her only so far. Ask the man standing next to me. He was Joan's lover, and should have been mine. When this service concludes, I will reach into his left pants pocket and pull out his cigarettes. He's a feckless and erratic man, which serves to blunt his great ambition and yet more spectacular gifts. He'll flinch when I touch him, and know that I've restated my claim.

The PD bounced for the service. A twelve-car cortege traveled out the Arroyo Seco to this hillside memorial park. The service commemorated Joan's brief transit in Los Angeles, to the exclusion of her Wisconsin years and her nursing school and university stints in Chicago. The mourning corps was all PD, with two exceptions. Joan loved official garb and regalia; I first saw her in her Navy lieutenant's blues. She would have loved this mourners' conclave, because she loved a certain breed of man.

Captain Bill Parker wore dress blues; Captain Dudley Smith and Lieutenant Hideo Ashida wore Army olive drab. Jack Horrall, Elmer Jackson, and Buzz Meeks wore dress blues, along with Thad Brown and my cohabiting friend, Lee Blanchard. Nort Layman and Ray Pinker wore black suits; Brenda Allen wore a charcoal gray ensemble. I wore a black cashmere dress, because I look good in it, and because I pander to men as shamelessly as Joan did.

Two men stood apart from the graveside gang. Sid Hudgens eulogized Joan in the **Herald.** The piece was entitled, "Adios, Big Red," and bore Sid's trademark low wit and leer. The subhead read "Girl Forensic Whiz a Suicide. Worked Baffling Cop-Killing Case."

Adios, Big Red failed to address Joan's crowded love life and the New Year's Eve misadventure that brought her to us and to here. Orson Welles stood behind Sid. Joan met him briefly at Otto Klemperer's. She told me that Dudley savagely beat him and turned him out as an informant. Dudley was Joan's other lover. I never told her that I knew.

"'Eyes the shady night has shut/Cannot see the record cut,/And silence sounds no worse than cheers/After earth has stopped the ears.'"

The pastor droned on. His delivery stank. Spoken poetry requires snap and verve. Elegies should inform rather than soliloquize. Big Red packed a wallop. She was a brilliant forensic biologist and consort of brilliant rogue cops. All men wanted to sleep with her. Don't mess with Big Red. A drunken Indian groped her. She blew his left foot off with a 10-gauge shotgun. Lee was there for Joan's New Year's Eve mishap, and told me the full story last night. Joan's sodden drive up from San Diego claimed six lives, rather than four. Two of them were children. Bill Parker withheld that fact from her.

The burial crew placed Joan in the ground. I recalled a song I heard at a colored dive in Sioux Falls. "Ashes to ashes and dust to dust, stormy weather cause your pump to rust." I laughed as Joan's casket went thunk. The pastor glared at me. I'm a cutup, as Joan was. We're both prairie Protestant girls, and we both believe.

That was it. Adios, Big Red. The wake's on the PD. Scrambled eggs and booze at Kwan's await.

I stuck my hand in Bill's pants pocket and pulled out his cigarettes. Don't look so shocked, Captain—I loved her just as much as you did.

The wake was boozy and predictably weepy. I sat with Elmer and heard his account of the Negro riot and Catbox Cal Lunceford's death. Elmer said he'd been scanning mug books, in an attempt to ID the Jap gunman. He was nervous about something but refused to tell me what.

Uncle Ace Kwan served Ming Dynasty Eggs and his world-famous mai tais. He is a remorseless psychopath, known crime partner of Dudley Smith, and Jack Horrall's Chinatown enforcer. I sipped a single mai tai and chain-smoked my way through the wake. The liquored-up testimonies bored me; I indulged my sport of imputing motive as I watched people interact. Only two mourner-celebrants held my interest today. Of course: Bill Parker and Dudley Smith.

They are both devoutly Catholic and bound by faith and enmity; I share a recent history with both men. Pearl Harbor storm-tossed our lives and revealed startling opportunities. Joan succumbed to them in the romantic form of Dudley and Bill. I was more circumspect and possessed the presence of mind to avoid Dudley at all costs. Our one clash was brief and remains unacknowledged by the police world and by Dudley himself. I very simply love Bill and want him for my own. Joan gave herself to both men; it was a stunning act of idiot courage and self-abnegation.

Both men stood at the bar; they eyed each other sidelong and retained a decorous distance. They were brusquely civil in all their dealings and only met to negotiate. Bill respected and despised Dudley. Dudley respected Bill and glibly concealed his hatred. Each was astonishingly aware of the other's presence. I saw it now. I watched them drink, smoke, and talk to others as they remained in psychic sync. Ace Kwan walked up and whispered to Dudley; Bill caught every nuance of the approach.

Elmer drifted off to talk to Buzz Meeks. I threw a bold stare at Dudley Smith. I knew he'd turn around and see me at some point. Ever bemused and bent on seduction, he'd smile and wink.

Brilliant girl. It took some fifteen minutes, but the evil bastard did just that.

I went home and practiced. Otto has been teaching me Medtner's "Sonata Reminiscenza," and the shifts in tempo continue to perplex me. This was my moment to play the entire piece through, in honor of Joan. I was determined to do it, regardless of gaffes and flubbed notes. The piece depicts the passage of time as both temporal and eternal. I arranged the sheet music on the stand and commenced.

I possess the ability to play and actively daydream

in concurrence, and it laid waste my interpretation here. I thought of Otto and his part in smuggling the Shostakovich symphony out of Russia, a convoluted journey with numerous stops scheduled along the way. My impromptu performance was meant to honor Joan, but snapshots of my late friend undercut my concentration. I flubbed a great many notes and scotched my narrative momentum. Otto had received a V-mail letter from Maestro Shostakovich. It contained note sketches meant to portray German tanks approaching Leningrad. I started hitting those notes, and begged Joan's forgiveness. I played those notes to the point of exhaustion.

The doorbell rang. I got up and walked out to the porch. The postman had left a good-sized package.

It was addressed to me. I noted Joan's handwriting and return address.

77

(LOS ANGELES, 4:00 P.M., 2/28/42)

The wake protracted. Joan, we hardly knew ye.

She left him her microscope and gold cuff links. It was symbolic. It meant **Follow my lead and carry the torch.**

The PD owned Kwan's today. Jack Horrall deposed Uncle Ace and reigned as potentate. The main dining room was all PD. Cops juiced and table-hopped.

Ashida watched. He sipped tea, cold sober. Cops deferred to him now. He held Army rank and carried a gun. He soared at the riot. Close-range dumdums inflicted brutal damage. He felt no remorse. That could change. Kill now, pay later. Hold for probable nightmares.

Jack H. worked the bar. He rolled dice with Thad Brown and chomped rumaki sticks. Breuning and Carlisle snoozed in their booth. Lee Blanchard arm-wrestled Lew Collier. Buzz Meeks showed off his pet scorpion. Elmer Jackson fed the beast chop suey tidbits.

Ashida eye-tracked Elmer. Cal Lunceford's death stank. Elmer's part felt schizy and all wrong. Jack Horrall dumped the Lunceford snuff. Catbox Cal knew Rice and Kapek and veered hard right. Screw Cal, over and out. Thad Brown debriefed Elmer and took a threadbare statement. Thad bought the "unknown" Jap suspect. Sayonara—that's it.

Elmer caught his eye and table-hopped over. He maneuvered a highball and a plate of egg rolls. He plopped down and stroked his broken heart.

"I'm grieving for Red. I should have stolen her away from them shitheels Parker and Smith. She was too much woman for them. I would have tamed her rangy ass with my warm redneck love. We would have bred some good-looking kids."

Ashida smiled. "Kay's your woman. If you have to love from afar, she's the one."

Elmer belched. "You're on target today. Dead-eye Hideo. You take some scalps, and it goes to your head."

"Kay called me. She said Joan sent her a package, and she wants to meet with us to discuss it."

"**Us?** Yours truly, E.V. Jackson? I never say no to a hobknob with Kay, but you've got me scratching my head."

Joan kept a diary. They'd discussed the contents. The diary described **everything.** The gold. Elmer's gold-crazed brother. The three-case confluence. Kay Lake hates Dudley Smith. She demands an audience, now. It must pertain to the diary. What fresh hell awaits?

Ashida sipped tea. "I read the statement you gave Thad. There were spatial discrepancies in your account of the shooting and the Japanese man's escape. You've worn a spare .38-snubnose in an ankle holster the whole time I've known you, but suddenly it's gone. Lunceford was felled by a .38 Special two-inch. I ran the ballistics myself. You killed him, Elmer. I'll give you a skate if you'll tell me why."

Elmer killed his drink and lit a cigar. He brushed ash off his coat and blew smoke rings.

"Cal was in with a Japanese guy, and he warned him out of the hideout. I caught a glimpse of him, and Cal came at me. I pulled my throwdown piece and dropped him. That's all you need to know, and all I'm going to say."

Ashida twirled his teacup. "Did you recognize the Japanese man?"

"Ed Satterlee showed Buzz and me a surveillance pic. It was that Navy guy you and Dud were looking around J-town for."

"Kyoho Hanamaka?"

Elmer said, "That selfsame hump."

78

(LOS ANGELES, 10:00 P.M., 2/28/42)

Uncle Ace pulled the plug. He said, "Time to go. I got business to run. Mourn dead girl enough."

He pried Breuning and Carlisle off bar stools. He shook Buzz awake. Buzz jiggled El Scorpio's cage and hexed him. El Dudster and Whiskey Bill were long gone. Ditto Kay and Brenda. The wake veered to stag night. Call-Me-Jack slept it off in his limo. Nort Layman snoozed with him. Thad Brown and Lee Blanchard single-filed out.

Ace said, "Elmer, you go. Chop, chop, you cocksucker. You perpetual thorn in my ass."

Elmer hit the road. He wolfed bennies and Old Crow and got eroticized. He drove to Brenda's place and promoted some woof-woof.

It was perfunctory. The postlude went ten seconds. Brenda said, "Shoo. Don't think you're spending the night. You've got Joan and who knows who else on the noggin. Let me sleep in peace."

Elmer hit the road. He drove down to the Strip and pay-phoned Ellen. She said, "Okay, sure. But make it a quick one. The baby's got the flu."

That dick-wilted him. He went over anyway. It was perfunctory. The postlude stretched. Ellen war-talked him into a coma. Wake Island this. The Solomons that. "Go back in the Marines, you dippy cracker. My husband's older than you. You've got no right to sit this one out."

Elmer hit the road. He was wide awake and still libidoized. He cut down to La Brea and pay-phoned Annie. She invited him over and said she was hungry. She told him to snag a pizza pie.

Annie lived on Hi-Point off Pico. Elmer found a pizza pit on San Vicente and turned a quick loop. Annie snarfed half the pie and plopped him down on the couch.

She said, "You're scared. You've got the jimjams like I've never seen."

He said, "I'm in the shit like I've never seen, and it's not like the shit and I ain't acquainted."

"Is this police-type shit that you aren't inclined to discuss?"

Elmer rolled his eyes and went **Yep.** Annie stretched out on the couch and plunked her head in his lap. She yawned and stretched. She pat-patted her mouth.

"Wake me if you get lonely. We'll play the radio or hit the sack."

Rain drummed the windows. Annie dozed. Elmer percolated. He lied to Thad Brown. He said he scanned mug books and ID'd Catbox Cal's killer. It was a dink named Kyoho Hanamaka. He's the fiend at large.

He covered his tracks there. Hideo **un**covered them. Hideo won't blab. He was **re**-covered there. Add on Dudley, Buzz, and the Huey snatch. Yeah, sweetie—I'm **scared.**

Annie started snoring. Elmer hit the road. He drove to Hollywood and B and E'd Jean Staley's place. It was you're-way-deep-in-the-shit dark.

He sniffed her lingerie and got transported. He time-traveled Jolting Jean's life. Beaumont, Texas. The dust bowl. Jean goes west and goes Red. Meyer Gelb's cell. The Griffith Park fire and Jean's queer brother. The whole deal induced hink.

Elmer hit the road. It was 3:14 a.m. He knew she'd be there. She'd be wearing the black cashmere dress and sipping the bright red Manhattan. She had permanent back-room access. She was just that jungled up.

Elmer drove to Lyman's. He's the mystic maharajah. He nailed it just that tight.

The dress. The cocktail. Kay at Crash Squad HQ. She's snooping. She's reading the file carbons tacked to the board.

She said, "I knew you'd show up."

He said, "I had a hunch you'd be here."

Kay lit a cigarette. "Something's frightening you."

Elmer lit a cigar. "Women keep telling me that."

"Joan sent me her diary. There's some things you should know."

Elmer dug on her dress. It head-bopped him, periodic. There's only her. There's no one else.

"You shivved Dudley. It had to be you."

Kay said, "Yes, it was."

79

(LOS ANGELES, 9:00 A.M., 3/1/42)

There's Beth. She's almost eighteen. She's stunningly lovely and most stunningly refracts him.

Her small eyes. Her set jaw. Her dark hair. She'll see him and run to him. This Army captain's her dad.

Dudley lounged outside Union Station. Porters wheeled luggage carts. Cabs clogged the breezeway. Parked cars stretched up to Alameda. Beth stood on her tiptoes and shielded her eyes.

She'd called him, impromptu. She was up in Vallejo with her cuckold dad. El Cornudo stifled her joie de vivre and made her keep house. It mandated a Baja retreat.

She had blue eyes. He had brown eyes. He was tall, she was petite. They were otherwise of the same—

She saw him and beelined. Her standard gambit was sprint and collide. She knocked him up against his staff car. She dropped her grip and burrowed in.

He said, "My dear girl."

She said, "I've never seen you so handsome."

They stepped back and squared off. There's that full view. Beth wore Claire's Christmas gifts. Twill slacks and a dark red sweater. The ensemble complemented and jazzed up his ODs.

"I'm here. It's twice in three months, so it must mean that I love you."

Dudley laughed. "You're a Boston provincial no longer. You've seen Los Angeles, and now you must brace yourself for Mexico."

They talked themselves hoarse. Beth's faux dad and half-blood sisters. His rocky road with Claire. Claire's faux child, Joan Klein. His split L.A. and Baja duties. Compliant Major Melnick cuts him travel slack. Her day-to-day crushes. Cute boys off to war. Navy pen pals, Point Loma to Pearl.

They fell quiet. Beth played the civilian-band radio. She scootched close and laced up his free hand. Swing broadcasts whooshed them south.

They crossed the border and cut through T.J. Beth went agog. His sheltered lass viewed raucous Revolución. She orbed the nude barkers outside the Blue Fox. The famed **negrito** waved his two-foot dick and drew stellar crowds.

Dudley swung south on the coast road. Half-assed beauty washed out the T.J. stink. High cliffs and sea swells. Fishing craft and Statie speedboats. Full-scale Jap cove alert.

He's meeting Juan Lazaro-Schmidt in La Paz today. Juan Pimentel's flying him down. El Governor wants to talk turkey. He wants El Dudster to attend a moving wingding. His cable included a postscript. "You will see through it, of course."

He misses Hideo. Hideo's his brilliant son, in with all his daughters. Major Melnick signed a dual-duty chit. Hideo has been assigned to probe spy mischief in L.A. He convinced Melnick that Baja fiends lurked there. "Hideo's our man, sir. I strongly recommend him."

It's a white lie. Hideo will hit L.A. and work the klub**haus** job. Lee Blanchard will watchdog him. Field interviews loom.

The case slogged on. They were thirty-two days in. Jack H. fretted the gun angle. Rice and Kapek glommed Jap weapons, wholesale. A great many were likely sold to Boyle Heights pachucos. Thad Brown proposed an East L.A. youth sweep. Roust local cholos. Stress the gun angle. Note this downside:

Some Sinarquista lads might draw heat. That's discomfiting.

Beth said, "Mexico is hard to fathom. I can't quite believe everything that I'm seeing."

"Ensenada is a bit more genteel. I have to fly down

to La Paz, but Claire and Young Joan will give you a proper first look."

"You say 'Young Joan' like you're not sure you should trust her."

"She's sui generis, that one. She lacks your grace, but she's possessed of grit in abundance. I can't imagine how she'll turn out."

Beth smiled. "You take guff from women that you'd never take from men."

Dudley smiled. "It's my Achilles' heel—but don't tell anyone."

La Paz.

Off the south Baja coast. Swell Pacific and inland gulf views. Tuna boats and shack shanties. Grand white houses and yet-more-grand churches. Thick foliage and gargantuan insects. All quintessentially Mex.

Captain Juan dropped him at the Statie airfield. They discussed their plans on the flight down. Wetbacks and heroin. Jap slaves, to boot. Captain Juan urged caution. Lazaro-Schmidt was no **pendejo.**

He'd dropped Beth off at the del Norte. Claire swarmed her and laid on the love. Young Joan was less effusive. Ever watchful, that one.

Dudley cabbed to El Governor's casa. It was sunny and gulf warm. He wore a tropical-weight suit and a belt piece. Flaunt your allegiance. He wore his swastika lapel pin, face-out.

The casa was built up a hillside. Lazaro-Schmidt knew from flaunt. It was double-deck, peach-pink adobe. The pitched roof was inlaid with hand-painted tiles. Big-name artists' work on glazed cement. Picassos, Klees, and Kandinskys overlapped. Squiggles and doodles baked in the sun. The effect was modernist chaos.

The front door was flush with the street. Dudley walked up and rang the bell. It sparked shrieks from Strauss' **Elektra.** The door clicked open, full automatic.

Dudley stepped inside. The front room dipped below sea level. Four steps took him down. The room was done up fasco moderne.

Thronelike chairs. All brown leather. Ebony tables and settees. Hammered-bronze lamps and Axis-flag-motif carpets. Mussolini's lair meets **Better Homes & Gardens.**

Recessed wall paintings. Lit by pink neon tubes. More Picassos, Klees, and Kandinskys. **Der Führer** and Red Beast Stalin would frown. It was decadent art.

"Franco's men sacked a train passing through the Pyrenees. These paintings and my roof tiles were to be sold to raise funds for the Loyalist cause. The general and I are old friends. I appreciate art in a way he does not, which explains his most generous bequest."

Dudley whecled. The thick carpet threw sparks. There's Lazaro-Schmidt. Note his cashmere lounge suit. It befits Hermann Goering at play. His swastika pin beams, face-out.

"I'm impressed, sir. Your lovely home expresses a grand theme."

Lazaro-Schmidt plopped into a throne. Buffed leather engulfed him.

"Which would be?"

"These times we live in. Art as the sole voice that will transcend the clash."

" 'This savaging disaster.' A friend of mine exhorts crowds with those words."

Dudley plopped into a throne. He faced Lazaro-Schmidt head-on. The fasco motif disfavored his host. El Governor ran elfin. He lacked **Il Duce**'s notable heft.

"You may recall our brief chat at the recital, sir. I have schemes to propose and resources to pledge. I can vouch your immediate profits, and all I require is your promise of protection and a wave of your official pen."

Lazaro-Schmidt smiled. "Wetbacks. We must not euphemize here. I am set to sign the guest-worker pact with California's Governor Olson in August. It will effectively legalize the temporary immigration of Mexican **braceros,** who will pick crops in the verdant San Joaquin and Imperial valleys. You wish to move wets north more urgently. All that the traffic will bear. You are prepared to offer me a price per head, and I am prepared to consider offers."

Dudley smiled. "Yes, but that's just one operation I have to propose."

El Governor plucked lint off his lounge suit. He was dainty. He lacked **Il Duce**'s feral depth.

"Let me anticipate your other proposals. You wish to defray the cost of the Baja internment by housing our resident Japanese in U.S. internment camps and municipal-police road camps for the war's duration. You have a plan to hide wealthy Japanese in Los Angeles, under the protection of Hop Sing and Uncle Ace Kwan. You plan to implement the heroin racket you took over from José Vasquez-Cruz, belatedly revealed to be Jorge Villareal-Caiz. My official signatures will provide the unrestricted travel visas that you require. They will free you to move wets, Japs, and dope north, free of scrutiny."

Dudley flicked lint off his trousers. Monkey see, monkey do.

"You know my plans in advance of my comradely pledges and supplications, sir. Have you had me surveilled?"

Lazaro-Schmidt said, "Yes, and I am aware of the purging of Cruz-Caiz's men that you and Salvy Abascal performed in the wake of **El Capitán**'s death. I know that you killed Carlos Madrano, in advance of your army posting here in Baja. I have assessed you through secondhand sources, and have largely extrapolated your designs. I am ready to do business with you, should we come to felicitous terms."

Dudley scanned the room. He saw gold statuettes on a wall ledge. Tigers, panthers, jaguars. Perhaps solid gold.

"I'm chastened, sir. I thought I'd walk in here and knock you off your feet."

Lazaro-Schmidt laughed. "I am not easily dislodged."

"Nor am I easily chastened, sir."

"I will add that I know you are quite concerned with the whereabouts of my friend Kyoho Hanamaka, and further add that I did not facilitate his exit from Mexico, nor do I know where he is now. I know that you have discovered Kyoho's hideaway, and are spending considerable time there."

Dudley said, "Yes, and I discovered a gold bayonet in a cache hole. It was swastika-adorned, and I've come to learn that there's a companion piece, adorned with a hammer and sickle."

It was a curveball. El Governor deflected it.

"I would call Kyoho ambidextrous. He plays the totalitarian field, and he does not know which beast will prevail in the end."

Dudley said, "The Red Beast, I fear."

"Yes, the Red Postwar Beast, who will turn on the Allied nations that buttressed its dubious triumph to begin with. This poses a challenge to the more far-sighted members of the German high command. They must sow the seeds of their postwar redemption now, while the outcome of the war remains in doubt. They must prove themselves palatable and potentially valuable to the postwar West, and see to the hoarding of monies for their ultimate relocation."

Dudley fondled his lapel pin. "I've heard that there was quite the confab in Ensenada. November of '40, it was. The Russians and the **Kameraden** got down to brass tacks. The Hitler-Stalin pact won't last. One of us must lose this war. How will civilized and enlightened men like us survive in such a predicament?"

Lazaro-Schmidt fondled his lapel pin. "I attended the conference. I told both factions that Mexico might well prove to be a gateway for the establishment of gainful resettlement throughout Latin America, with proper guarantors of safety provided by U.S. Intelligence services based in Mexico herself."

Dudley said, "I would be loath to hide godless Reds."

"You won't have to. Germany will lose the war— and a newly reformed civilized world will require Nazi brainpower to help keep the Red Beast in check."

Dudley slapped his knees. "Will all unruly Nazi acts be forgiven?"

"Of course. The concept of realpolitik holds sway here. Seeds of reconciliation have already been planted. Humanistically inclined Nazis have begun a process of atonement with world Jewry. You will see a moving example at the ceremony I've invited you to. It is realpolitik at its bald-faced best."

Dudley scanned the wall ledge. He caught a boffo photograph. Abwehr boss Canaris. NKVD boss Beria. A festive cantina backdrop.

"Is that your conclave there?"

Lazaro-Schmidt twinkled. "Indeed. As subtext, I'll add that Canaris has been leaking German secrets to British Intelligence since '37, during the same time frame that Beria has been sending parcels to Churchill himself. As further subtext, I'll add that both men were quite anxious to visit the legendary Blue Fox."

Dudley roared. The Wolf appeared. He pointed to a photograph on a bookshelf. Dudley studied it. Constanza Lazaro-Schmidt attacked her viola.

El Governor plucked the photograph and passed it over. Constanza bore down **bellísima.** Her bow threw sparks. She'd snapped a string. Her white gown dipped off one breast.

"My frenzied sister. She was Kyoho Hanamaka's lover, some time ago."

The Statie airfield had been prettified. It was a rush job. The theme was Welcome Exiles!!!

WILLKOMMEN signs lined the runway. Statie goons rolled out a red carpet. An old lady distributed pamphlets. They were quasi–symphony programs. A Spanish-language text ballyhooed the virtuosi.

Four uprooted souls. All first-chair musicians. Late of the Dresden Staatskappelle and Hitler's death camps. Miklos and Magda Koenig. Sandor Abromowitz. Ruth Szigeti. **Mittel** European Jewry. Austro-Hungarian, all.

Their flight was due. Dudley stood behind a rope line and mingled. The welcome crowd ran forty, tops. They were all Mex and ran to type. Oldster **kultur** hounds. **Konzert**goers in this heathen land.

A small airplane swooped toward the runway. A baggage cart rolled into view. The **kultur** hounds applauded. A Statie sergeant wheeled the Lazaro-Schmidts. They waved Hungarian flags on sticks.

Governor Juan wore a seersucker suit and white bucks. He eschewed his swastika lapel pin. Constanza wore a pink summer dress and spectator pumps. The Wolf strained at the rope line. He plainly desired her.

The Lazaro-Schmidts hopped off the cart and stood by the red carpet. A Statie corporal carried out a long-cord microphone. Dudley leafed through his program and checked the photographs.

The overfed Koenigs. The aged Abromowitz. The thin-sculpted Ruth Szigeti. They wore symphony black and held stringed instruments. **Das Vaterland** was good to them then.

The airplane dipped and landed. The pilot fishtailed up to the carpet. The **kultur** rubes cheered. The Wolf cocked his head and pawed the ground. **What is this shit?**

The Statie corporal pushed steps up to the airplane. The door swung open. The four refugees filed out.

The men wore overcoats and winter-wool suits. The women wore long dresses and fur wraps. The gulf heat smacked them. They looked like they'd pass out.

They weaved onto the carpet. Lazaro-Schmidt and fair Constanza dispensed **abrazos** and handshakes. The refugees looked gaunt and all beat-to-hell.

They broiled in their winter ensembles. Old man Abromowitz grabbed Ruth Szigeti's arm for support.

The rubes lapped it up. They tossed bravos. An old girl dipped into a paper sack and tossed rose petals. The Koenigs glared at the crowd. Old Abromowitz reeled. The Szigeti woman waved.

Lazaro-Schmidt braced the microphone. He spoke high-end Spanish and cut straight to the Big Theme Gist. He hit Expiation, Redemption, Reconciliation. He hit Forgiveness and Asylum. Our **hermanos y hermanas** were spared certain execution. Honor knows no national or ideological boundaries. German men of conscience saw to the rescue of these four gifted people. They are dedicated to the overthrow of Adolf Hitler and determined to create a better tomorrow for all citizens of the world. Our four new friends will be resettled into the exile community in Los Angeles. They will resume their musical careers as this storm of catastrophic war rages around us.

Applause blitzed the wrap-up. Constanza grabbed the mike and announced a reception. "My home, tonight. There will be music."

The refugees reeled. Sing for your supper. Ruth Szigeti fumed and peeled off her fur coat.

Her arms were bare. Dudley saw torture scars and an SS tattoo.

The Wolf pre-prowled the wingding. Dudley walked the beach outside the house and peeped windows.

Said house was classic Spanish. It ran inimical to El Governor's modernist spread. A night breeze stirred sand. The Wolf loped back and reported.

The refugees greeted Los Beaners. Well-wishers engulfed them. It was **mucho** enlightened and disingenuous. El Governor played host. Juan Pimentel wore Statie black and clicked his heels, Nazi-esque. The refugees avoided him. The **kultur** hounds swilled free champagne and snarfed free hors d'oeuvres.

Constanza circulated. Her dress straps kept slipping down her shoulders. She had short hair and wore no makeup. She went barefoot. Open windows stirred that beach breeze. Her pink dress swirled.

She'd coupled with Kyoho Hanamaka. It was "some time ago." That mandated thought.

The Wolf curled up on a beachfront chaise. Dudley peeped a picture window. A valet laid out folding chairs. The refugees unpacked their instruments and sat down. Ruth Szigeti wore a black cocktail dress. She rolled up the sleeves and revealed half her tattoo.

They ripped into baleful Bartók. The room went **kultur**-hushed. Dudley slipped inside and skirted the crowd. He walked toward the back of the house.

Bisecting hallways. Brushed-adobe walls. Hardwood floors and silk tapestry rugs. Garish oil paintings. An all-jungle motif. Green foliage and predator cats.

Dudley opened doors and flipped light switches. He saw servants' quarters and storage rooms and a closet jammed with skeet guns and horse-riding tack. He opened the adjacent door and caught Constanza's scent.

She wore sandalwood perfume. He'd smelled it at the del Norte recital and the airfield. He flipped a wall switch. Floor lamps popped on and cast light.

The room ran fifteen-by-fifteen. It featured rough wood walls and floors. Phonograph records, a Victrola, a desk. Ornament shelves and framed wall photographs.

Dudley walked wall-to-wall. The shelves held small gold statuettes. Constanza's wolf pack glared at him. Male wolves snarled. Mother wolves suckled their cubs. It refracted her brother's menagerie. It refracted his own wolf worship. He hefted a wolf cub. It was solid gold. Gold plagued him and followed him, everywhere.

He studied the photographs. Constanza feeds jackals large slabs of meat. She's wearing a bush jacket and safari hat. There's Constanza kissing a jaguar. She's wearing a summer dress tossed above her knees.

Constanza feeds wolves. She's wearing lederhosen and a loden coat. Rhine maiden Constanza. Constanza, the Black Forest nymph.

The German motif extends. Constanza stands with pianist Wilhelm Kempff and conductor Karl Böhm. Wehrmacht officers huddle behind them. It's a symphony bash. Constanza's laughing and blowing smoke in the air.

More photographs. Constanza with Pierre Fournier and Alfred Cortot. Both men welcomed the **Boche** to France. Constanza wears a slit-legged gown. That's Paris by night behind her.

We return to Deutschland now. Consider this

photograph. Constanza warmly greets Adolf Hitler. **Musik Maestra** and furious **Führer.** Both evince delight.

Dudley stood by the desk. He noted the swastika paperweight. It was solid gold. He noted the blue leather diary.

It was locked. The clasp and keyhole were solid gold. The front cover was gold swastika–embossed.

Women as diarists. Intimate thoughts and deeds recorded. He recalled the late Joan Conville. She kept a diary.

He touched Constanza's diary. He kissed the gold swastika and caught Constanza's scent.

80

(LOS ANGELES, 9:00 A.M., 3/2/42)

"The rain, the gold, the fire. It's all one story, you see."

I knew Joan's diary now. I had studied it to the point of memorization. She repeated that annunciatory phrase many times. She said the words to Dudley Smith on the first occasion. They had just made love, and Joan had settled in to tell her most complex and harrowing tale. She succumbed to evil in that moment. She recounted her rogue investigation with Hideo Ashida; she stitched the evidential links, from the discovery of Karl Tullock's body up to a series of forensic crossovers to the Rice-Kapek murders. Her summary circumcribes a state of shock and awe, and depicts her immersion in the police world that has consumed me since 1939 and my collision with Lee Blanchard. Joan's diary spotlights her analytic skills and her surpassing ability to plumb evidence and assess motive. Self-analysis eludes her. She cannot frame and assume a moral stance as to Dudley Smith. Her capitulation is wholly erotic and steeped in her overweening pride and ambition. Dudley Smith's hold over women derives from the hold that women have over him. He projects a casual mastery over any and all perils. Joan found that irresistible. She was a woman determined to conquer a man's world. She wanted Dudley Smith's mastery more than she wanted the gold and a clean Rice-Kapek solve. Her efforts to countermand Dudley's hold by the means of her concurrent affair with Bill Parker proved fruitless. She misjudged the two men as antagonists and failed to see them as complicitous and cravenly needy in all their strategic designs. I love Bill Parker unto the death and hate Dudley Smith just as passionately. I must take Joan's account of her last six weeks and deploy it to a broad moral advantage. I must break the usurious bond between Bill Parker and Dudley Smith and see to Dudley's most severe censure.

I'm writing these words on the upper-floor terrace of my house above the Sunset Strip. Yet more rain seems to be brewing. This house symbolizes my own capitulation to the police world that so consumed Joan. Lee Blanchard bought this house with bribe money. He tanked his boxing career because he knew he'd always be good and never great. Lee gave a wayward South Dakota girl a home; it's a place where I muse, ponder, study, and cultivate opportunity with a ruthless will very much like Joan's. I now possess the sum of Joan's criminal knowledge. I have a grasp of Dudley's racketeering plans. I know that Two-Gun Davis killed the Watanabe family and that he confessed to Bill Parker and Dudley Smith. Bill cut deals and saw to the dismissal of Werewolf Shudo's death decree. I know all about Joan's mission to avenge her father's death and her suspicions of one Mitchell Kupp. I know that Dudley promised to look into him. I read yesterday's Sunday **Herald** and spotted a page-eight piece. Mitch Kupp's decomposed body was found at his house in San Bernardino. He had been shot dead at point-blank range. I sense a Dudley-and-Joan-at-their-most-crazed symbiosis here.

Hideo Ashida lives in Joan's diary. He lives triangulated with Joan and Dudley, ever indebted to Dudley, ever corrupted, ever lustful and unfulfilled. Joan admired him, came to despise him, and developed a fond regard for him during the fevered merging of the gold quest and the klub**haus** job. Hideo and Joan coveted the gold and coveted a clean murder-case solve just as furiously. Hideo's desire to push through to a proper case solution jumped out at me. I had initially planned to meet Hideo and Elmer Jackson together. I put out feelers toward that end as soon as I'd read the diary. I reconsidered the approach almost immediately.

Joan's diary was evidence. I trusted Elmer and did not trust Hideo. I wanted to present the evidence of Joan's diary to them individually and gauge their individual reactions. I met them at Dave's Blue Room yesterday. I reported the contents of Joan's diary—but withheld a certain piece of information from both men.

Elmer evinced shocked outrage. He had brushed up against the events that Joan had described since New Year's. His brother died in the Griffith Park fire and was surely involved with Karl Tullock and the summer '33 robbery spree. Elmer had been cuckolded. His friends Hideo and Joan told him nothing. They ran their rogue investigation and brought in Dudley Smith. Elmer was enraged. Two purported friends had betrayed him. Elmer feared and hated Dudley Smith. Dudley had facilitated Joan Conville's and Hideo Ashida's lies and omissions. Elmer's hatred now burned that much more fearfully and recklessly bright. Sweet Elmer, combustible Elmer. Now dangerously close with Buzz Meeks—who hated Dudley and did not fear him at all.

Elmer guzzled gin fizzes and chain-smoked cigars. I watched him flail at all of it as he fought back tears. I had omitted that key diary thread. It was a soundly reasoned omission.

Hideo, Joan, and Dudley had formed a pact to get the gold. I withheld that fact from Elmer. I withheld my perception that they were every bit as gold-crazed as Karl Tullock and Wayne Frank Jackson. I withheld this fact because I had to withhold it from Hideo Ashida. Elmer was volatile. He might go for Hideo's throat—with Hideo's gold greed as the spark that lit his fuse.

My dear friend Elmer. Pie-eyed from six gin fizzes. A silent moment passed between us. Telepathic sparks flew. We had engaged a deadly and foolhardy agenda. We will take down Dudley Smith.

Elmer weaved out of Dave's Blue Room; Hideo Ashida timorously walked in. He wore his Army uniform, replete with sidearm, and caused jaded heads to turn. He sipped coffee in lieu of gin fizzes and heard me out impassively.

I presented Joan's diary as evidence and cited my purely academic interest. I knew that Hideo underestimated women and saw me as an idiot child. Hideo held Joan in the same low regard, until she became his gold-quest accomplice. I excised Joan's gold-quest narrative; I worked around it in the same manner as I had with Elmer. I further omitted Joan's withering critique of Ashida's homosexuality and fawning allegiance to Dudley Smith. I wanted to stun Hideo with what I knew and sustain his idiot-child assessment. This idiot child was now armed with damning facts but possessed no formal agenda. Hideo sat through my recitation, implacably. His eyes flickered when I told him that Jim Davis killed the four Watanabes. It was his only notable reaction.

I want Hideo to seize on Joan's reluctance to describe and analyze the gold quest. I want Hideo to feel safe here. I'm banking on the threads of reluctant decency that Joan and I have both glimpsed in him. What will you do now, Hideo? Which way will your tortured conscience lead you? Will you tell Dudley that I've seen the diary or will you omit?

Bill Parker's tortured conscience rivals Hideo's. Joan watched him falter and ascend in near-direct proportion. Bill keeps mum on Two-Gun Davis and the Watanabe frame; Bill diverts the Werewolf's gas-chamber trek. Bill cosigns an expedient solution to the klub**haus** job and boldly sells the PD out to the Federal grand jury. Bill falters and ascends; Bill pratfalls, dusts himself off, and stumbles toward his next moral encounter. He caroms between God and Old Crow bonded bourbon in the hope that the former will obviate the need for the latter. He fears the loss of Dudley Smith more than he fears Dudley Smith himself, and clings to the bereft notion that Dudley Smith's brutal élan facilitates the fortunes of his beloved police department. He stops short of condemning Dudley Smith as monstrous—because to do so would reduce him to the role of most meek collaborator.

I had to bank on Hideo Ashida's few decent instincts. I had to hope that Bill Parker would pray or drink himself through to the truth of Dudley Smith's malevolence.

Joan excelled at portraiture. She nailed William H. Parker and went on to nail the Dudley–Claire De Haven misalliance. Dudley and Claire exemplify a barely contained madness. Dudley hoards Nazi regalia and hints at a fascist conversion. Claire defends the Moscow show trials and waves the Red flag with aplomb. Dudley dallies with opium and Benzedrine. Claire boots morphine. A U.S. Army posting buttresses Dudley's Baja racket schemes. They adopt a fifteen-year-old red diaper baby. Dudley brutally beats Orson Welles and suborns him as an informant. Claire fellates Welles in Otto Klemperer's steam room.

Claire is a man-trap woman. She holds sway over men in the manner that Dudley holds sway over women. Claire is horrified at the power she's granted him and aghast at the erosion of her so-precious self. Claire fears that Dudley killed her lover, José Vasquez-Cruz. Vasquez-Cruz was really Jorge Villareal-Caiz. Villareal-Caiz stood foursquare in Meyer Gelb's Red cell. As Joan Conville said, "It's all one story, you see."

And it's my story now. I'm a bit-player-in-waiting. Claire suspects that a "South Dakota slattern" shanked

Dudley last December. Dudley pooh-poohed the assertion and passed it along to Joan. Claire added this: "Maybe I'll confront the slattern at one of Otto Klemperer's parties. She's like the bad penny, always showing up at them."

Claire, I'd **love** to gab. I know we'd have things to discuss.

Those looming storm clouds burst; I gathered up my diary pages and carried them inside. I placed Joan's diary pages in a good-sized cardboard box and addressed it to William H. Parker. It was 11:25 now. The postman always arrives around noon.

81

(LOS ANGELES, 11:30 A.M., 3/2/42)

He lied to Dudley. He omitted and withheld. It was split-second instinctive.

Ashida drove through Bunker Hill. He replayed the phone call. The Biltmore switchboard had patched him through to La Paz. Dudley issued klub**haus** directives. His chance to rat Kay fizzled out.

They met at Dave's Blue Room, yesterday. Kay described the contents of Joan Conville's diary. Joan willed her the pages. Joan candidly described her post–New Year's life and spilled leads on their intertwined cases. Joan laid out her liaisons with Dudley and Bill Parker. Kay talked for two hours straight.

He braced himself for The Bomb. The Bomb did not exist—or Kay declined to drop it.

Joan detailed the gold heist and its current re-emergence. Joan omitted the subsequent gold quest altogether.

Or Kay abridged her account. She played editor and expurgated at will. She excised Joan's pages and recounted only what she wanted him to know.

Rain clouds unzipped. Ashida ran his wiper blades. He crossed Loma and looked north to Belmont High. He replayed Kay's key remarks.

"Here's something you should know, Hideo. Jim Davis killed the Watanabes. He initially confessed to Bill Parker, and to Dudley more recently. From the look on your face, I can tell that Dudley failed to inform you."

Kay provoked him. Kay taunted him and scolded him. "You should have told Elmer everything. His brother died in that fire." Kay provokes, Kay scolds, Kay taunts and dares.

"I know everything that I've told you. I will leave you guessing as to what I might have withheld. You will tell Dudley whatever you decide to tell him. I will seek to expose any and all false solutions to the klub**haus** case."

Kay closed with that. The moment felt telepathic. Kay wanted a clean solve. He wanted a clean solve. Joan might have expressed his desire. Kay might have read him just right.

Telepathy begets telepathy. He talked to Dudley a second time this morning. Dudley said, "Our late friend Joan kept a diary, lad. She'd mentioned it to me several times. Will you go by her bungalow and do a toss and forensic? She may have tattled a few of our secrets that we don't want commonly known."

Ashida cut west on 1st Street and north on Carondelet. Central Property kicked loose the door key. The idea came to him then.

He parked beside the courtyard and walked back. He lugged his evidence kit. Nobody saw him or stopped him. Nobody slack-jawed the Army-togged Jap.

He unlocked the door and locked himself back in. He turned on all the room lights. Joan's bungalow remained unrented and appeared to be intact. It was a suicide scene. The PD and morgue men had come and gone last week.

Ashida checked the kitchen. He looked under the sink and saw a wastebasket. It contained booze empties and coffee grounds. They were piled halfway up. He checked the sink drain and ran some cold water. The drain trap worked well. That was good. It enhanced forensic detail.

He tossed the bungalow.

He went through the closets, the one dresser, the front-room shelves. He went through Joan's desk drawers. There was no typewriter. That was good. He found pens and writing paper in the bottom-left drawer.

A soft blotter covered the desktop. Ashida popped his evidence kit and filled an atomizer. He utilized deionized water and liquid dioxide. He sprayed the blotter and watched pen indentations rise.

Joan had block-printed and applied hard strokes. "Dudley" and "Bill" crisscrossed the blotter. He saw "despite his best intentions" and "confiscated gun lists."

The "Dudley" and "Bill" impressions were instructive. They sparked a secondary notion. It would tweak Dudley's vanity and densify this construction.

He took a hundred sheets of writing paper and dumped them in the kitchen sink. He spritzed them with diluted kerosene and dropped a match. The pages burned. He counted off ten seconds. He doused the flames with tap water and created a wet mess.

He turned off the water and cleaned up the mess. He dumped the bulk of the wet paper in a grocery bag. He placed the bag in his evidence kit and performed his obfuscation tasks.

They were **extra** precautionary. Dudley trusted him. He relied on that fact.

Ashida unscrewed the sink drain. He smeared sodden paper to the inside walls of the pipe. He tweezed paper fragments and affixed them to the drain holes. He screwed the drain trap back on.

He scooped wet paper and smeared the inside of the wastebasket. He covered all contingencies. The ruse stood complete.

Joan's telephone worked. The landlord forgot to

kill her service. Ashida roused a local operator and placed a long-distance call. Person-to-person. La Paz, Baja. Hotel Los Pescados/Captain Dudley Smith.

The operator said she'd place the call and ring him back. Ashida hung up and prowled the bungalow. He caught Joan's tobacco and lilac soap scent. He examined her Navy uniforms. He saw red hairs caught in a fine-bristled brush.

The phone rang. Ashida grabbed it.

Dudley said, "Hello, lad. You're calling from Joan's apartment, I take it."

Ashida coughed. He white-knuckled the receiver. The phone cord went taut.

"There's no diary. She burned the pages in the kitchen sink, and left unmistakable traces. The cops who came through missed them. I raised a few indentations off her desk blotter. I saw partial sentences, along with your name and Captain Parker's."

Dudley laughed. "I'm sure she wrote my name a great many more times than his, and wrote it with far greater passion."

Ashida forced a laugh. "I'm sure she did. And I'm sure a trained graphologist would confirm it."

"Lad, you delight me. Such wit on such short notice. Go forth and do your duty now. Put your grand mind to work on the klub**haus** mess, before Major Melnick calls you back."

Ashida forced a joke. "I'll call you if I find the gold."

Dudley said, "Yes, lad—you do that."

The line went dead. Ashida replaced the receiver. He'd committed treason. His motive revealed itself.

You'll never love me as I love you. I cannot place Kay Lake in jeopardy. This ruse punishes you.

82

(LOS ANGELES, 3:30 P.M., 3/2/42)

WAYNE FRANK JACKSON. 1907–1933. BELOVED BROTHER AND SON.

The headstone read thus. No 211 Man. No Gold-Heist Goon. No Embroiled with Communists. No Fifth Column–Adjunct.

Elmer stood graveside. He was half-tanked. He flagellated his dumb cracker ass and hexed Hideo Ashida.

Ashida broke his heart. Ashida should have told him the whole story. Joan wrote it all out. Kay regurgitated it. The bad news hurtled, here to Hell.

The Dudster, Joan, and Hideo. They harbored leads. They knew he planted the address book at the klub**haus.** Two-Gun Davis iced the Watanabes. Joan writes it out. Kay regurgitates it. Here's the part he don't get:

Kay says Joan told all. Thus, Kay told all. But—one thing don't conform to type.

Dud, Joan, and Hideo. Three covetous cookies.

Wouldn't they go for the gold? Where's their big fat doughnut? Did Joan fail to write that down or did Kay fail to mention it?

Inglewood Cemetery. Wayne Frank's wobbly stone. It didn't read Klan Klown. It didn't read Kid Brother Elmer's Got de Hellhound on His Trail.

The furry fucker's name is Fear. Buzz and him thumped Huey C. Did Dud find out? Dud snuffed a fruit at a Nazi bash and waltzed on it. Does Dud know that he knows?

Nobody knows de trouble I'se seen, nobody knows my redneck sorrow—

Elmer scrammed. He sprinkled flask booze on Wayne Frank's grave and hit the road. Three bennies detoured his hooch load. He drove home and fed his tropical fish.

The mailman was due. Jean Staley owes him a nice postcard. Elmer J. digs Jean S. Sister, why'd you run out on me?

Elmer sat on his porch. He lit a cigar and watched storm clouds brew. The mailman showed. He dropped off the light bill and a card, postmarked St. Louis.

The front displayed the churning Mississippi. Jolting Jean scribbled up the back.

Dear Elmer (You Sweet Dog),
    My eastward trek continues. I'm looking forward to a party with some old friends in Albuquerque. Wish you were escorting me.
XOXOXO, Jean.

Tilt. His shit detector clicked on. Something ain't right here.

The card was postmarked St. Louis. St. Louis is way northeast of Albuquerque. Jean's headed for Des Moines. Des Moines is north**west** of St. Louis. Jean's not taking no regular route. Here's the capper here:

He got a Texas-postmark card, two days back. Jean's hot to hit that Albuquerque wingding. Texas is east of New Mexico. It's all fucked-up geography.

The mailman stuffed mailboxes. Elmer ducked into his flop and grabbed the stack of cards Jean sent.

He studied them. He tracked postmarks and skimmed Jean's scrawl. **Ooops,** there's—

The Kansas City card preceded the Denver card. KC's east of Denver and should have come first. Here's one he missed. The Lubbock card extolls the Rocky Mountains. That don't fit. Jean ain't seen those mountains yet.

The cards are all checkmarked. **Oooga-booga.** There's all these different shades of ink.

Elmer goosed the mailman. "Lou, what's with these cards? They're coming all out of sequence, like this girl's trying to put one over on me. And what's with all these checkmarks?"

Lou studied the cards and tapped them on his teeth. Lou shiteater grinned.

"It looks like these cards got routed through a mail-drop system and sent on to you from a drop here in L.A. You know from mail drops, right? They're these services that gigolos and call prosties use, all over the country. It's like a relay pipeline for people on the run and on the lam, who want certain folks to think they're somewhere else. Mail comes in, and the drop employees log it in or out and charge your account. These places are all over the U.S., so mail gets forwarded, and that way you can get whatever postmark you want. You get a lot of smut books and hate tracts sent that way. It's like a cheating-wife-and-husband parlay. You can't be in two places at the same time— but sometimes you'd like to convince folks that you are."

Elmer snatched the cards and fanned them out. He fanned a spray and pointed to the checkmarks.

"What's with these here marks, boss?"

Lou went **oooh-la-la.** "I know those marks. Look— they're half cross, half **X** mark. That's Bev's Switchboard. It's out in West Hollywood. Blow Job Bev Shoftel runs the place. She's one for the record books."

Nite-owl stakeout. 1:00 a.m.—Fountain and Crescent Heights.

Bev's Switchboard was county turf. It was a rinky-dink storefront upside a swish bar. Elmer brought his B and E tools. He parked his sled across the street and got up some gall.

He ran a routine check first. He went by the West Hollywood Sheriff's Station and braced the Vice boss. The boss confirmed Lou the mailman.

Blow Job Bev turned out the twelve-year-old sons

of the L.A. elite. She devirginized movie-biz scions and the offspring of Hancock Park swells. Bev's Switchboard was a racket drop. It serviced smut merchants, hate-tract purveyors, and filmland shitheels. Plus homo prosties, dirty-picture girls, dubious "actors" and "musicians." The service passed on phone messages and forwarded mail. The service rented on-site mailboxes. Sometimes the mail just jumped box-to-box. Bev's been popped for smut and indecent exposure. She flashed her snatch at some dowagers at the Wilshire Country Club.

Bev's got a pedigree. Bev snitches for Sheriff Biscailuz. Bev's Switchboard is Sheriff's-protected. Yeah, and there's **this:**

The Feds are homed in on Bev's. Sheriff Gene just quashed a premises search warrant.

Elmer said, "What were they looking for?"

The Vice boss said, "They were looking for incoming mail sent from mail drops in Phoenix, Albuquerque, Salt Lake City, Denver, Kansas City, and St. Louis."

That meant pay dirt. Jolting Jean sent **him** cards from those cities. Jolting Jean allegedly passed through them.

The Vice boss said, "The requesting agent was this nosebleed Ed Satterlee. He's purportedly tonged up and on the grift."

They wrapped up at 5:00 p.m. Elmer split West Hollywood Station and went shopping then. He bought a miniature camera, film, and some flash-bulbs. He popped bennies and brainstormed names.

Three-case names. Crisscrossed through three case lines:

Wendell Rice, George Kapek, Archie Archuleta. More names: Fritz Eckelkamp, Eddie Leng, Donald Matsura. Still more names: Martin Luther Mimms, Leander Frechette, George Lincoln Rockwell. Yet more names: Harold John Miciak, Cedric Francis Inge, Catbox Cal Lunceford. Boocoo names: Meyer Gelb, Jean Staley, Dr. Saul and Andrea Lesnick. **Mucho** names: Jorge Villareal-Caiz, Kyoho Hanamaka, Lin Chung, Tommy Glennon. Bent-cop names. Fifth-Column names. Commo names. Nazi names. Jap names, Chink names, Mex names—

Elmer checked his watch. It was 1:19 a.m. The fruit bar roiled. The jukebox blared and supplied noise cover. Do it now, son.

He'd packed his B and E and camera shit in a gym bag. He grabbed it and crossed the street, fast. Traffic was scarce. Bev's Switchboard was flat brick. A door awning covered him. The door was push lock/one keyhole.

Elmer got out a #4 pick. He probed said keyhole. The booger failed to fit. He got out a #6. That booger probed deep. He twisted it left/right, left/right. The mechanism snapped, the doorjamb shimmied and popped.

He stepped inside and threw the reverse bolt. The joint was deep dark. He pulled his flashlight and got his eyeballs adjusted. He beam-strafed the whole premises. He saw **this:**

The back wall was rigged with pullout mail slots. The east wall was lined with file cabinets. A desk and chair faced the front window. The west wall was foto-festooned. Film-biz schleppers mugged. For sure: part-time talent/full-time gigolos and whores.

Elmer walked to the back wall. He yanked a dozen mail-slot pulls and got no give. They were locked crab's-ass tight. He kept his beam low and walked to the east wall. The cabinets ran alphabetical. Little letter plates were stuck to the drawers. He slid over to the **S**-for-Staley drawer and gave it a tug.

He hit pay dirt. **Woo-woo!**—the booger's unlocked.

The drawer was jammed with file folders. Elmer maneuvered his flashlight and lit the name tags. He finger-walked from Sadler and Samuelson on. He saw the odd name Szigeti, Ruth. Two non-**S** files were clipped to it. Koenig, Miklos & Magda, Abromowitz, Sandor.

Elmer finger-walked. No familiar names mauled him. He hit Sperling, Phil and Sroloff, Ralph. **Bam!**—he hit Staley, Jean.

He pulled the file. It contained one sheet only. "Recent transactions" was typed at the top. Plus notes on "postcards received & forwarded/out-of-town postmarks assured."

Postcards forwarded. To one geek only. A lunk-head named E. V. Jackson. Postcards from Phoenix, Albuquerque, Salt Lake City. Postcards from Denver, Kansas City, St. Louis. That means **this:** Jean sure as shit sandbagged him.

Elmer got out his camera shit and foto-snapped the page. The flashbulb popped bright. Elmer extracted it and dropped it in the gym bag.

Names. Names. Names. Take your pick. Open file drawers await you. It hit him, quick. Jean's Commo cell. Villareal-Caiz, the Lesnicks, Meyer Gelb.

Elmer file-jumped. He pulled the **V** drawer and finger-walked. **Bam!**—there's no Villareal-Caiz. He pulled the **L** drawer and finger-walked. **Bam!**—no Saul or Andrea Lesnick. He pulled the **G** drawer and finger-walked. **Bam!**—there's Meyer Gelb.

The file contained one sealed envelope. It was addressed to "MG 226/CO Bev's Switchboard." That was plain dumb code. 226 was Gelb's box number. Note the return address: "PO Box 1823/ La Paz, Baja."

Elmer slid to the front desk and rifled the drawers. Shit—there's no envelope steamer. He slid back to the **G** drawer. Fuck it. He ripped the letter open with his teeth.

For what? There's just this blank sheet of paper. It's a head-scratcher. What's that there? It looks like a dried stain.

Elmer head-scratched it. He worked his dim brain every which way. It hit him, belated.

Blotter paper. Microdots. Fourth Interceptor issued a bulletin. "Report all such/A-Level evidence."

He nicked the envelope. He brain-broiled. He ran more names and pulled more file drawers. He pulled the **H** drawer and got zilch for Kyoho Hanamaka.

He repulled the **L** drawer and got **nyet** on Catbox Cal Lunceford. He repulled the **G** drawer and finger-sprinted.

He hit Gainford, Garfield, Gersh, Gifford. He hit Glennon, Thomas Malcolm. **That's** some pay dirt.

Elmer skimmed the transaction sheet. There were no mail-outs scrawled. Tommy's PO box number was scrawled in. Box 7669/La Jolla, California.

La Jolla. A swank enclave down by San Diego. It's close to the Baja border. It's a hot lead. More circles loop and constrict.

Elmer went through Tommy's file. It contained one fat envelope. Elmer ripped it open and yanked the contents.

Tracts. Little hate pamphlets. Hate, hate, hate. Kill, kill, kill. Recipes for Jap fricassee and Chinaman stew. Kill the jigs, kill the Jews, kill the British Protestant oppressor!!!

Elmer dumped the tracts in his gym bag. He broiled more names. He hit the **A** drawer and trawled for Archie Archuleta. He got **nein** there. He hit the **C** drawer and trawled for Lin Chung. Tuff luck—there's no Chinaman Chung.

He went light-headed. He weaved. This was all some wild-ass shit. He got his feet under him. He pulled the **R** drawer and trawled for George Lincoln Rockwell.

He finger-walked. Rehnquist, Rillard, Roberts, Robertson—Rockwell, George Lincoln. No transaction sheet. One fat envelope stuffed in the file.

Note the note clipped to it. "Forward to T. M. Glennon, Box 7669/La Jolla."

Elmer slit the envelope. He banked on more hate tracts. He got smut pix instead.

Fuck, fuck, fuck. Suck, suck, suck. All black-and-white glossies. Pokey-pokey shots. In the mouth, up the love trail, up the dirt road. Two men and two women. The men wear leather masks. One man wears a Nazi uniform. One man wears Red Guard threads. The women wear zero. One woman's white, one woman's Mex.

Circles constrict. **Oooga-booga.** Circles meld and overlap.

The pubic-hair samples. Ashida found them. Doc Layman typed them. Two samples are female. One sample's white, one sample's Mex. Note the foto backdrop. Fuck, fuck, fuck. Suck, suck, suck. It's there in all the pix.

It's the upstairs bedroom at the klub**haus.**

83

(LA PAZ, 8:00 P.M., 3/3/42)

Seduction.
He knew it. She knew it. Her coy act at the exile

bash proclaimed it. The Wolf caught her scent and proclaimed her lust.

Constanza recorded the Wieniawski **Légende.** She played the soaring violin part. A randy Pole composed the piece. The motif was explicitly Latin. Recurrent themes depicted star-crossed lovers aswirl.

Dudley sat in a harborside cantina. His booth overlooked the east-facing gulf. He sent Constanza a mash note-cum-invitation and got no response. He purchased her phonograph record and slipped it to the maître d'. A fat bribe assured steady play.

There's Constanza's solo now. Love subsumes conflict, conflict subsumes love. She'll walk in soon. She'll wear a white dress. One strap will slip off her bare shoulder. She'll hitch it up repeatedly. She's perfected the move.

Dudley chain-smoked. He wore his summer uniform and brown gun belt. Harbor craft bobbed a few feet away. A sea breeze hit open windows and cooled the place off.

Constanza walked up. She wore the white dress. He stood and bowed. Constanza laughed.

"I heard my third recapitulation, all the way out on the dock. I will reinterpret the composer's intent if I record the piece again."

Dudley smiled. "Don't spoil my interpretation. The piece infatuated me."

"You succumb to infatuation, as long as it serves you. It's a ruthless trait that I admire in men."

A waiter snapped to. He brought Cointreau on ice

and Dudley's third scotch. Cointreau was her drink. The Wolf told him so. Constanza tucked her dress pleats and slid into the booth. Dudley sat across from her. Constanza sipped Cointreau and lit a cigarette.

"My impolitic maid warned me about you. She said, 'There's a strange man prowling the house, and looking at things that he shouldn't see.'"

"I saw you posed with beautiful animals and quite notable men. I was smitten at the airfield, and conquered when I saw you with the jaguar and your German friends."

Constanza twirled her ashtray. A dress strap slipped off her shoulder. She hitched it back up.

"My brother forewarned me. He said, 'Captain Smith is a voyeur who misses nothing. Poor boys confronted with affluence always love to look and touch. If there's anything you don't want him to see, you should hide it in advance of your party.'"

"And what did you hide?"

Constanza said, "I hid nothing."

Dudley lit a cigarette and twirled his ashtray. Their fingers brushed.

"You brother intercedes in your life in a manner that some might find unseemly. My friend Salvy Abascal told me that."

"Did Salvy tell you that I am his occasional lover? He has his child bride, who will supply him with children, and the women he ruts with and talks to."

The cantina was built on a barge. Waves tapped loose pilings. Constanza swayed in time with them.

"It's the war, you see. You are the U.S. Army captain and certified foreign devil. My brother only trusts people who want things from him, once he has vetted their most pressing common concerns. He has had you surveilled and knows of the British soldiers you killed in your homeland. He knows of your rich **puta** lover Claire, and her odious beliefs. He knows of Claire's young charge Joan Klein, and has verified her outré stories of leftist intrigue. Would it surprise you to know that Joan's New York comrades are acquainted with the Koenigs, Ruth Szigeti, and Sandor Abromowitz? My brother interceded for me because he distrusts wartime alliances and knows more than I do. He considers you to be a voyeur and quite the rank amateur. He intercedes and looks out for me by accommodating my own voyeuristic impulse."

Dudley crushed his cigarette. "It's all alliance, is it not? Once again, we come back to the war and those we might learn to trust or distrust."

Constanza crushed her cigarette. "Alliances overlap. That is because spheres of interest and influence are ever mutating. In wartime, the only true common interests are profit and ultimate survival. Take the musical underground. In it, the musical Left and Right clash and just as often collude. It is all toward the end of profit and survival assured."

Dudley said, "I saw that at your party. Your photographs of Herr Kempff and Herr Böhm, and your exiles so bravely and disingenuously repatriated."

Constanza said, "You are perceptive. However

amateurish, you compel me to report what my brother reports to me. There are mock traitors in the **Führer**'s high command, you see. They are strategically saving volubly articulate Jews from extermination. It is all part of an exoneration ruse, to be put into effect should Germany lose the war. An identical plan has been implemented in Russia. The Russians fear that the U.S. will invade their country should Germany lose the war. It is all about establishing moral credentials now, and paving the way for the appearance of redemption in what will surely be a bitter and rancorous postwar era. It also asserts the need for a mutual accommodation of Communist and fascist beliefs in the present, so that both sides will be couched to prove themselves indispensible to the ultimate victors."

Dudley stirred his drink. Constanza's strap slipped down her arm. He reached over and pulled it up. Constanza touched his hand.

"Let's see if I can extrapolate off the point you just made. I would guess that our current exile friends and all others that may follow will be put to use as informants. They've served the cause of Communist-fascist amity. But their efficacy should not stop there."

Constanza said, "My brother allows that you are quick. You confirm it by keeping up with me."

"You keep bringing up your brother's intercessions. His influence daunts me. I've begun to think of him as a rival and romantic impediment."

Constanza smiled. "We will get to the topic of the two of us in good time."

"Pray forgive my great haste."

Constanza smiled and lit a cigarette. Her hair was brown more than black. She was pale more than tan. She wore a man's wristwatch.

"My brother knows a **comunista** named Meyer Gelb. Comrade Gelb is working on the Russian end of the exoneration scheme I described to you. Russian émigrés, badly used by Stalin, will be approached by my brother and suborned as informants, wherever they are resettled. Meyer will approach the Koenigs, Mr. Abromowitz, and Miss Szigeti in Los Angeles."

Red Meyer. The Griffith Park Fire. Gelb's '33 cell. Brother and sister know Kyoho Hanamaka. The intersections failed to surprise him.

"Let me extrapolate. Your brother knows high-ups in the Fatherland. Comrade Gelb knows high-ups in Mother Russia. You're describing a blackmail racket."

Strolling musicians dipped by. They jiggled jangly maracas. Constanza went **Shoo.**

"Yes, and I should add that Comrade Gelb has marvelous dirt on the Koenigs, old Abromowitz, and Miss Szigeti. They sold three hundred Jewish musicians into the **Führer**'s death camps in order to save their own skins."

Dudley lit a cigarette. "You are telling me quite a great deal. I find it as disconcerting as your brother's unseen presence at our table."

Constanza laughed outright. She covered her mouth, double quick. She had pronounced buck teeth.

"I was Kyoho Hanamaka's lover. He showed me the gold bayonet you later found at his hideaway. Like you, I had heard of a companion piece, adorned with Soviet symbols."

"I mentioned the Communist bayonet to your brother. Let me hazard a guess here. You had his living room bugged."

"Yes. Again, I'll state that you are very perceptive."

Their hands were close. Dudley touched her fingers.

"Again, I'll state that you are telling me quite a great deal."

Constanza squeezed his hand. "You want the gold. Men like you deem such treasures irresistible. I share your desire, body and soul."

The barge lurched. Dudley lurched. The room went double hot. He saw gold bars that weren't really there.

"Do you know where it is, or who has it? As much as it pains me to ask, does your brother know?"

Constanza said, "I don't know, nor does my brother. Kyoho most likely knows—but he is hiding somewhere undisclosed in the U.S."

The room went triple hot. Dudley fluffed his napkin and wiped his face. Constanza leaned in and undid his necktie.

"Much of this dates back to a fire in Los Angeles. Kyoho and Comrade Gelb were burned there. Gelb lays the source of his wounds on the Spanish Civil War, which is rubbish. Kyoho tells a similarly self-serving lie. My brother and I know all of this—but no more."

"And you don't know who has the gold now?"

"The alliance that I have described to you has many layers of buffering. The top few men surely know the status of the gold. My brother is just a minor cog, who tells me things. I am a woman, and no cog at all."

Dudley cracked their window and roused some gulf air. Constanza opened her clutch and removed a vial of perfume. She daubed her left wrist and held out her arm. Dudley took her hand and kissed the scented spot.

"And the **Kameraden**'s ultimate plans for the gold?"

"The establishment and implementation of a strategy of escape, resettlement, and credible exoneration. Select members of the world's great totalitarian regimes, collaborating toward that end. Beyond that end, I know only of plans to hoard the gold and invest in U.S. defense industries, to further induce gratitude in our presumed conquerors, and to increase the likelihood that the new identities of our comrades will not be revealed."

Dudley said, "Darling, you are recklessly impolitic. However much your revelations excite me."

Constanza said, "I know something about you. The gold would be incomplete for you without a woman."

Dawn broke bright and warm. Ensenada looked drab. La Paz creamed it, hands down. Ensenada was T.J. South. La Paz was Saint-Tropez for Irish arrivistes.

Dudley elevatored up to his suite. He was dead bushed. He closed that harborside haunt with Constanza and caught a late Army flight back.

He yawned and saw fatigue spots. He unlocked the door and saw Beth asleep on the couch.

The bedroom door stood ajar. Overhead lights snapped on. He heard radio hum.

He walked in. The fatigue spots made him blink. Claire threw herself at him.

She hit his chest and spit in his face.

She clawed at his mouth.

She ripped the buttons off his coat and tore the captain's bars off his shoulders.

She beat at his face.

She defamed his redheaded whore and hexed her in Hell.

She called him a "fascist insect."

She called him a "cowardly killer."

She hurled herself up at him and bit off a piece of one ear.

It's Dublin again. It's 1919. He's out sniping British soldiers. He comes home to Maidred Conroy Smith. She wields her razor strop.

84

(LOS ANGELES, 9:00 A.M., 3/4/42)

I waited on my front porch. I was to be Otto's goodwill ambassadress and accompany him to Union Station. We would greet four Austro-Hungarian string players, late of Nazi concentration camps. A cryptically defined relief organization had secured their release and brought them here via steamship, transport airline, and overnight train trek from Baja. The extravagantly generous Maestro had secured them courtyard apartments in Santa Monica. My contribution was good cheer and a grocery bag stuffed with two-dollar champagne and paper cups.

The day was bright and cool; I glanced across the street and down to the Strip. A PD prowl car was parked at the curb, just above Sunset. I had no doubts as to the occupant. This is what Captain Bill Parker does. He perches outside the homes of provocative young women and plots his next move. He intrudes, he entraps, he blunderingly seduces. Ask yours truly and the late Joan Conville.

Bill had something on his mind now. Provocation abets provocation. I had sent Joan's diary special delivery. He'd received it, read it, and wanted to talk.

Otto's big Chrysler turned left on Wetherly and headed up to me; the chauffeur wheeled a clumsy U-turn and bumped the curb in front of my house. I walked over and hopped in the back. The Maestro kissed my cheek and wrangled me in. We passed the prowl car, southbound. Bill slept behind the wheel. Incident recalls incident. Joan returned home from a party at the Maestro Manse and found Bill parked outside. She wrote her first diary pages with Bill passed out on her bed.

It was a half-hour drive downtown, and Otto wanted to yak. I positioned myself on his good side and played to his vanity. The brain tumor had constricted his facial muscles and marred his fierce good looks. It made conversation difficult and frustrated a man born to yak at great length. Otto is six-foot-seven and disposed to yak and command. When Otto yaks, one listens.

We lit cigarettes. Otto settled in to run discourse. Dr. Saul Lesnick had diagnosed the tumor. Otto credited Dr. Saul with saving his life; I credited Dr. Saul with the array of damning mischief exposed in Joan's diary.

The Maestro held forth. He was composing a nightmare tone poem in the Richard Strauss–**Elektra** mode. The piece would depict events that had occurred in his own haunted house. Declining chords would portray a murderous occurrence in Nazi Germany's past and sequentially link it to a rumored reenactment in his own home. The orchestral part would subside to a hush then. Low-register piano chords would announce the first of his brain-tumor blackouts.

The Maestro yakked orchestral structure, and paused only to light cigarettes. I squeezed in a few questions about our goodwill mission and how our exile chums had escaped Europe. Otto cited vague rumors. Exoneration-minded Nazis had bounced for their repatriation. They were moved out on a trans-port flight to Mexico; the airplane was loaded up with precious mercury ore for the return flight. Our exiles comprised a first refugee wave. Otto said it seemed like a ruse to him; exoneration-minded Russians were purportedly releasing prisoners to establish their own humanitarian credentials.

The blithe hypocrisy stunned me. I asked Otto where he picked up the "vague rumors." He said, "A chatty Communist named Meyer Gelb told me. The man impressed as fraudulent, so perhaps the rumors themselves are just propaganda or idle schmooze of some sort."

Meyer Gelb appeared in Joan's diary. Joan met him at the Maestro Manse. His Communist cellmates Jean Staley and Saul and Andrea Lesnick attended the same party. The cell was scrutinized in the Griffith Park fire inquiry. Joan considered the cell germane to the welter of cases that had so consumed her and Hideo Ashida. I asked Otto how he came to meet Meyer Gelb. Otto said, "He's Saul Lesnick's analy-sand. Saul invites him to my parties."

We found our chums by the taxi stand outside Union Station. They stood by a large mound of luggage and stringed-instrument cases. It was an up-to-the-moment Ellis Island snapshot. They weren't quite the huddled masses. They looked exhausted and apprehensive and exhibited not one ounce of relief.

Sandor Abromowitz fell into Otto's arms; they were former comrades from the Berlin Opera. The Koenigs were heavyset, frail, and proud. I carried their luggage, but they refused to take my arm for support. Magda Koenig gave me the stink eye. She figured me for a party-crashing dilettante and Otto's young whore. Ruth Szigeti was thin and wobbled on brand-new high heels. She took my arm and wasted no time bumming a cigarette. Her flat, straight hair and hollow cheeks were straight out of Brecht and the horror musicales of Weimar Berlin. She had schizophrenic gray-green eyes and warmed to the notion of brushing against me. I pegged her as a lezbo or at least an avant-garde creature who veered any and all ways.

The gang piled into Otto's imperial-sized auto. The chauffeur pulled down the jump seat, but we were still strapped for room. The Maestro yanked fat Abromowitz up on his lap; the frail Koenigs scrunched in side by side. The jump seat was narrow and built for one only. I staked my claim and hopped onto it. Ruth Szigeti staked her claim and hopped onto my lap. She said, "Do you mind, **Liebchen**?" I said, "Given your ordeal, how could I?"

The chauffeur pointed us westbound on Wilshire Boulevard. Otto played host and served up my bargain-basement champagne. War and music talk bubbled in English, French, and German. There was no talk of death camps or the oppression of Jews in Hitler's Germany. An implicit pact rendered the topic verboten. I stifled my curiosity and kept my mouth shut.

Otto was throwing a party tonight. He announced it and leaned back to read reactions. Mr. Abromowitz and the Koenigs went stone-faced. Ruth Szigeti said, "Will you be there, **Liebchen**?" I assured her that I would be and summoned up my own ideal guest list.

Claire De Haven and Meyer Gelb. **There's** two party cards. I'd love to meet Communist carhop Jean Staley. What about Dr. Saul and Andrea Lesnick? I went back to Bill Parker's incursion with them and would **adore** a chance to get reacquainted. Don't forget Orson Welles, Dudley's newly cowed informant. He might be in the market for a new steam room pal.

Magda Koenig gagged on cigarette smoke and rolled down a window. I looked out and saw that a PD prowl car was providing an escort. Mike Breuning and Dick Carlisle sat in the front seat; a man in Mexican Statie garb sat in the back. Breuning looked over and saw me. I waved; he waved back. Carlisle yelled, "Hey there, Kay!"

Mrs. Koenig rolled up her window and cut off the exchange. I got chills in an overheated limo. Ruth Szigeti jiggled into me and draped an arm around my neck.

Joan's diary. Dudley Smith's orbit. The ubiquity of a single rogue policeman.

We journeyed through Beverly Hills and West L.A. A sea breeze welcomed us to Santa Monica. The chauffeur turned north on 4th Street and pulled up in front of a palm-lined courtyard. Our exile chums got out and surveyed their new home. Ruth Szigeti reluctantly undraped me. Her left blouse sleeve had rolled up; I saw knife scars and an ominous tattoo.

I got out last. I smelled salt air and watched the prowl car park behind us. The chauffeur unloaded the luggage and instruments; Otto escorted the gang to their new digs. The Maestro owned numerous beachside properties, the Seabreeze Court among them. He was forfeiting rental income from three bohemian bungalows. Otto Klemperer defined noblesse oblige.

I lagged back and strolled over to the prowl car. Breuning and Carlisle were piling gift baskets on the hood of the sled. The baskets featured withered fruit and cheese of the hold-your-nose ilk.

The Statie introduced himself. He was Captain Juan Pimentel. The captain was an emissary of Governor Juan Lazaro-Schmidt and the governor's friend Dudley Smith. The baskets denoted the governor's warm **bienvenidos** to our immigrant pals.

Pimentel impressed me as a vicious little shit. His spiel indicted the repatriation plan as a shuck. Meyer Gelb had uttered "vague rumors." That was suspect in itself.

Pimentel clicked his heels. "Your new Americans are the first wave of the governor's humanitarian effort to rescue persecuted Jews from the horrors of fascist Germany."

I pointed to his SS-style hat. His spit-shined jackboots and flap-holstered Luger were just as snazzy. I said, "I'm all for the rescue of persecuted Jews, but I must note that you dress fasco yourself."

Pimentel clicked his heels. It expressed disdain and moral confusion. He clicked his heels again. It gave him something to do and suppressed his urge to kill infidel women.

Breuning and Carlisle cracked grins. **That Kay Lake's a sketch.** I'd belted a few with Sid Hudgens at the PD's New Year's bash. The Sidster plied his crazy craft. He called Mike and Dick "maladroit mastiffs on a mission to maul for their master." And, **who's** their master?

Who else but?

Rain drove the party indoors. That was okay by me. Joan described the Maestro Manse as a lodestone for the Meyer Gelb–Saul Lesnick set. I came to perch and observe. Sid Hudgens had attended numerous Klemperer soirées. He called them "bilious bacchanals and Baedekers of early-wartime indulgence." Sid was right about that. The Klemperer crowd came to harangue, gesticulate, bloviate, and dubiously critique. **I** was there to worry the Griffith Park fire and the proximity of Meyer Gelb's cell.

I stationed myself on the second-floor landing and looked down on the huge main room. I had been home to change clothes and see if Bill Parker was still poised to pounce. He wasn't. He'd be back, though. He'd have Joan's diary memorized and worried down to page pulp.

The party swirled below me. Mr. Abromowitz and the Koenigs beat back admirers; Ruth Szigeti drifted off with Barbara "Butch" Stanwyck. Party delirium had set in. Folks harangued, gesticulated, bloviated, and dubiously critiqued. Cigarette smoke obscured faces. Saul Lesnick arrived with a zaftig young woman. I recognized her. It was Annie Staples, Elmer and Brenda's college-girl vixen. Elmer told me she was jobbing Dr. Saul for the Feds. Elmer had worked the camera at Brenda's Miracle Mile trick spot, and had caught Annie's act.

Orson Welles arrived. I noticed his plastic-surgery scars straight off. The Sidster told me that Terry Lux did the plastic job. It smoothed out the obvious signs of the Dudster's thumping. Claire arrived, with two young girls in tow. The older girl was Beth Something. She was Dudley's reputed spawn. I made the younger girl as Joan Something. She was Dudley and Claire's **enfant sauvage.** Joan Conville's diary supplied explication. Joan Something perplexed Dudley. He found her otherworldly and considered her a counterpart to his fantasy wolf. Claire was haggard, ever the doomed poetess. I knew her MO. She'd seek out Dr. Saul and hit him up for a fix.

The party would run late. Otto's parties always did. I had time for an interregnum before I hit the main floor. I ducked into the conservatory and sat down at the piano. "Sonata Reminiscenza" was embedded within me and fully memorized. I decided to play it all the way through.

The piece demands a meditative approach. It is both pictorial and diffuse. The piece depicts recollection and portrays the sweet heartbreak of time lost and recalled. I always mark the moment as I sit down to practice it. Today is March 4, 1942. I am twenty-two years old and have knocked around a bit. A late and dear friend of mine willed me some words she wrote. The words comprise a debt I must repay and punitive measures I must enact. This is for Joan Woodard Conville.

So, I played. I hit notes too soft, too hard, and just right. I veered off the established score and hit notes to the words "This storm, this savaging disaster." I veered back to the score and lost myself in shifting tempos. Someone entered the room behind me; I heard rudely loud footsteps in approach.

"You're playing Nikolai Medtner. I hate him, because he hates the Bolsheviks."

I stopped playing and looked up. Joan Something

stood to the right of the bench. She wore a red party dress I'd seen Claire in. A tailor had altered the sleeves and hemline to fit someone much smaller. Joan Something was fifteen or sixteen and discernably otherworldly. She wore dark-framed glasses; her black hair bore gray streaks.

"I'm sorry, but I don't know your name."

"Sure, you do. My aunt Claire says you know everything. I'm Comrade Joan, and you're Comrade Kay, but you're really not much of a comrade if you like Medtner."

I said, "Rachmaninoff hates the Bolsheviks. Scriabin hated them, as well. I'd say that puts Medtner in good company."

"You think you're clever, but you're really just glib. Rachmaninoff and Scriabin are yesterday's news. Comrade Shostakovich is au courant. I'm part of the collective that's smuggling in his new symphony, in case you think I'm just a silly young girl who has no business being in Comrade Otto's house."

She spoke Brooklynese. She had Dudley Smith's small brown eyes. She flexed her jaw while she spoke and glared more than looked at you. Her part in the smuggling effort surprised me. I felt confluences merge.

"It was nice of you to come up for this party, Comrade. I'm sure Comrade Otto appreciates it."

Comrade Joan lowered her voice. She leaned against the piano and dropped into stage-whisper range.

"I've gone undercover down in Mexico. My fake dad's an Army officer in Ensenada. My aunt Claire's his lover, but I don't think for much longer. My mock dad's a fascist, but he's nice to women, even though he cheats on Aunt Claire. He's got a wife and five real daughters, and his illegitimate daughter is nice, but she's stupid and boy crazy."

I said, "You're very perceptive, Comrade."

The girl swooped over to the low-register keys. She sat down at the bench and banged the first four notes of Beethoven's Fifth. She did it one time, two times, three times—each time harder and faster. I looked over my shoulder and saw Claire De Haven standing in the doorway.

We stared at each other and nodded in sync. Comrade Joan hopped off the bench and ran to her mock mom. They disappeared down the hallway.

So much for Comrade Medtner. Comrade Claire and Comrade Joan had excised him for now. I walked back to my observation perch and looked down at the party floor.

The Koenigs and Mr. Abromowitz remained bombarded and beleaguered. Partygoers continued to harangue, gesticulate, bloviate, and dubiously critique. I scanned the room for new faces and spotted Meyer Gelb.

He'd been pointed out to me at a previous party. There he was now—tall, florid, heavyset. Joan had run nationwide records checks on him. They turned up negative; he had no listed address and no driver's license issued within the forty-eight states. He came to Otto's parties in cabs. Joan had noted his burn-scarred hands and had surmised the source as the Griffith Park fire. Gelb was waving his hands in Magda Koenig's face at this very moment.

I scanned the room again. Faces popped in and out of smoke clouds. I saw Ruth Szigeti necking with Butch Stanwyck's husband, Robert Taylor. Butch herself watched and delightedly grinned. Someone called out "Jean!" A woman turned and walked toward the voice.

Jean, as in Staley. Slender, dark-haired, stylish glasses. It had to be her—she fit Joan's precise description. She entered my line of sight from the back of the house; her hair was noticeably wet. I wondered where she had just come from.

I walked downstairs and through the big room. It was all war-talk cacophony and gesticulation. Dr. Saul held court for daughter Andrea and Miklos Koenig; I noticed Andrea notice me. She had buzz-sawed me at a Claire De Haven party in mid-December. Andrea lived to harangue, gesticulate, and **dish.** Party guests were her **very** favorite victims. She tended to **find** people. I walked out the terrace, to let her find me.

I sat in a deck chair and looked out at the rain. Wind buckled the awning above me. I counted days backward to the Rice-Kapek murders. January 29 to March 4. That made thirty-five.

The investigation had gone fallow since the catastrophic blackout and Joan's suicide. Hideo split his duty time between L.A. and Baja; Dudley rarely attended briefings. The Crash Squad continued to meet and hash out go-nowhere leads. Lee reported an over-arching sense of futility. His drunk act on the jazz-club strip had gleaned no leads; the Negro riot had turned jazz-club regulars that much more truculent. Thad Brown teethed on the bootjacked guns. He was planning to run an East L.A. youth sweep. Rice and Kapek had purportedly sold a good many firearms to Mexican hoodlums.

"Hello, Miss Lake. I haven't seen you in a dog's age. I chewed your ear off at one of Claire's dos, remember?"

I pulled a chair up beside me; Andrea slumped down and kicked off her shoes. She wore a man's greatcoat over her party dress. The left breast pocket was pinned with Spanish Civil War medals. Meyer Gelb had worn that coat just a few minutes back.

Andrea's hands were a mess. Her nails were chewed bloody; her fingers were nicotine-stained. I lit two cigarettes and passed her one. Let's dish, Andrea. How about Meyer Gelb as a topic?

"I like that coat you're wearing, Andrea. It's not yours, is it? It's much too big for you."

Andrea jiggled the breast-pocket medals. She said, "To hear Meyer tell it, he killed more fas-cists than the Red Guard at Leningrad. I think he bought them from an old lefty down on his luck, and passed them off as his own."

"He must have whole rooms full of that sort of junk at his house."

"If he has a house. If he doesn't sleep in a coffin like

Dracula, and come out only at night. If he doesn't just appear at Mr. Klemperer's parties to grandstand and schmooze up his old comrades."

"You're saying that nobody knows where he lives?"

Andrea flicked her cigarette out in the rain. She'd smoked it in ten seconds flat.

" 'Kay Lake's nosy. She's a fascist chippy and keeps her ear to the ground.' Claire De Haven told me that."

" 'Andrea Lesnick loves to tattle.' A little birdie told me that."

Andrea giggled and made bird sounds. " 'Miss Lake's a hoot.' That's my grand pronouncement, and I figured it out for myself."

"Yes, and what have you figured out about Comrade Gelb?"

"What's to figure? Meyer's Meyer. My daddy and I were in his cell back in the early '30s, and Meyer went off to the Spanish Civil War, and he became this big hero and got his hands burned in a pitched battle with Franco's Falange. Or, there's the persistent rumor that Meyer and some Jap Navy man were doing acid dips on their fingerprints way back."

Or, he burned his hands in the Griffith Park fire.

"Was the Navy man's name Kyoho Hanamaka?"

"I don't know. Rumors are rumors. All I know is that it was just some loopy Jap."

"Jean Staley was in your cell, wasn't she? She's here at the party now."

Andrea snatched my cigarettes. She lit one up and

dropped the pack in her purse. The awning dripped rain just a few feet away.

"Meyer's Meyer and Jean's Jean. Everybody made her for a snitch way back when. The CP was full of snitches then, and everybody made Jean for a secret right-winger, because she was such a conniver and a square. She's a carhop, but she sucks up to rich people in the arts. She bunks in their guesthouses, like she's hiding out and on the lam, even though she's got a nice little place in Hollywood. My daddy says Jean's a piece of work. She plans theme parties for rich people and hides out like the bogeyman's on her case. She's holed up in Mr. Klemperer's guesthouse right now, and she leaves the curtains down all the time. My daddy says she's a nympho and an exhibitionist. He said she blew Clark Gable at a party, while all the other guests watched."

Andrea paused to catch her breath and chain cigarettes. I mulled the Jean Staley dish. Jean's name appeared in Tommy Glennon's address book. Kyoho Hanamaka touched the book and left a burn-scarred fingerprint. Jean Staley was on Elmer Jackson and Buzz Meeks' interview list. Jean was bunked up across the backyard. That fact explained her wet hair.

Andrea stood up and slipped her shoes on; Meyer Gelb's greatcoat brushed the ground. She said, "'Miss Lake's not as smart as she thinks she is.' My daddy told me that. 'Miss Lake's a stooge for the L.A. cops.' That's another good one you can chalk up for Claire."

I stood up and extended my hand. I almost said,

"Thanks for the dish, kid." Andrea swatted my hand and skipped back inside the house.

It was midnight. The party was approaching its gesticulating and fawning nadir, and the guesthouse lights were still on. I walked to the door of the main house and peered in. Jean Staley was ardently occupied with Mr. Abromowitz and the Koenigs. Mr. Abromowitz snoozed while Jean gesticulated and fawned.

I took off my shoes and ran across wet grass to the guesthouse; rain plastered my dress and soaked me down to my skin. The shades were up and wind had blown the door all the way open. Careless Jean. Exhibitionist Jean. Sloppy Jean, ditto.

The front room was a jumble of tossed clothes and dumped cosmetics. I walked into the bedroom and left squished-stocking footprints. Jean would know there had been an intruder. An open suitcase sat on the bed. A stack of picture postcards was arrayed atop a pile of lingerie.

The cards displayed the Mississippi River and the low skyline of Des Moines. I turned the top card over and whooped audibly. It was addressed to Elmer V. Jackson. Elmer's address was scrawled below.

Jean plied Sergeant Elmer with schmaltzy greetings from the American Midwest. The postmark caught my eye and stopped me cold.

It was postmarked Des Moines. But it wasn't a **canceled** postmark. It was dated March 9. Today's date was March 4.

I checked the rest of the cards. All four featured

Des Moines pictorials and breezy greetings to Elmer; all four featured uncanceled Des Moines postmarks. The postmarks ran a full week ahead of today's actual date. That meant the postal cancellations and forwarding would be accomplished in L.A.; that meant Comrade Jean was jobbing and/or sleeping with horndog Elmer. It meant that Elmer had become entangled with a material witness in his own brother's probable arson death.

I left everything where it was and squished back across the wet grass to the party. I ignored the bloviators and gesticulators and squished upstairs to the conservatory. Otto kept spare blankets in a closet there. I grabbed one and swaddled myself. The couch by the piano supplied a cozy roost. I stretched out to think and/or doze.

Goofball Elmer and **What Is This?** fought the tug of my late-night exhaustion. My next-door neighbor's cat jumped on the couch, but I knew he didn't really. I saw picture postcards of Des Moines and heard Joan's casket go **thunk.** A woman said, "Katherine?"

I opened my eyes. Claire De Haven was perched on the edge of the couch. Claire, the doomed poetess. Edna St. Vincent Millay for the poor.

Who had aged since the first time I saw her. Who had given herself to Dudley Smith. Who held a rosary and prayed for Dudley to survive my knife wounds. Who survived the idiot onslaught of Bill Parker and my dilettante self.

Her fingers were as tobacco-stained as Andrea

Lesnick's. I said the first thing that came to me. It was, "Oh shit. I'm sorry."

Her voice was raw. "It's not enough."

"It has to be."

"You gained my trust and betrayed me. It's not within me to forgive you."

"Ask Monsignor Hayes about forgiveness. Ask Bill Parker the next time you see him at Mass."

"He's a man. I expect less from them. I expect women of your caliber to behave more gallantly."

I said, "Word travels, Claire. I'm a prairie slattern and a switchblade assailant, or so you believe. How could I behave gallantly?"

She said, "I admire your sense of risk, even as I despise you."

I said, "I admire your ability to withstand Dudley Smith, even as your love for him confounds me."

A single tear ran down her cheek. I reached up and brushed it away.

"Will you continue to crash the party, Katherine? Will you continue to bombard people who've done you no harm?"

"You threw the party, and I crashed it. You instilled the sense of risk that you see in me. I'll repay the debt and nullify my meager apology."

Claire took my hand and placed it back on her cheek. She kissed the palm and placed my fingers in her mouth. Her eyes flickered between hard and soft. She placed my hand on her breast. The nipple pebbled up at my touch.

"Sweet girl, you don't know who you are."
"Dear lady, you don't know my resolve."

Bill's prowl sled was parked in front of my house. He tapped his headlights as I swung into the driveway; I got out of my car and got into his.

Joan's diary was there on the seat. Bill turned on the roof light and illuminated the pages. I leafed through the stack. Bill had marked the full manuscript in red ink.

He handed me his flask; I took a sip and passed it back. Bill killed the roof light. Late-night shadows fell over us; light rain tapped the windshield.

"You've been to a party, and your dress took a beating."

"I would have asked you to escort me, but I thought your wife might disapprove."

Bill said, "Don't get catty. We have things to discuss."

I squared off the manuscript between us. The numbered pages ran to 324. Joan wrote them in one month's time.

"You should hear this injunction first. I'll expose any and all manufactured resolutions to the klub**haus** case, regardless of how it affects the craven deals you've cut with Dudley Smith."

Bill nipped on his flask and mumbled in Latin. He started to cross himself; I reached out and pinned his hand to the seat.

"Send one up for Joan, before you even think of

the plight you're in. Think of what your sweaty crush got her."

Bill sighed. It was too dark to see his face. I pictured him rolling his eyes and thinking, **For the love of God, WOMEN.**

I hit him. I swung around and punched his face and knocked his glasses into the backseat. Bill wiped his mouth and reached for the flask; I grabbed it first and tossed it out my window.

"You killed her. Don't put it off on Dudley for one instant. She killed six people in a drunken stupor worthy of you, and you robbed her of the dignity of paying a just price for her actions. You wanted her, and that was all that mattered. You swooped down on her and used her, and she couldn't resist Dudley, because he was so unlike you in all the easy ways and so like you in his soul. You used her, and Dudley used her, and you didn't have the kindness or decency to pull her out of this crazy world you forced her into."

Bill said, "Yes. But I'm the one you trusted with her diary."

85

(LOS ANGELES, 9:00 A.M., 3/5/42)

Thad Brown said, "We're thirty-six days in. This job commenced back when Hitler was a corporal. It you're as bored as I am, raise your hand."

Ashida polled the room. Breuning and Carlisle raised their hands. Buzz Meeks raised his hand. Lee Blanchard raised two hands. Ray Pinker had assumed Joan's lab slot. He **Sieg Heil**'d Thad and roused some laughs.

Captain Parker looked hungover. He disdained Crash Squad shtick and kept his hands down. His lip was split, like somebody had smacked him. Elmer J. was AWOL. Dudley was down in La Paz.

The back room looked worn-out and threadbare. The food and booze inducement felt thin. The blackboard hung loose. The bulletin board drooped. The tacked reports wilted.

Ashida sipped coffee. He wore his winter Class As and gun belt. He scrolled back to Joan's place every half second. He'd betrayed Dudley there.

Thad said, "We've got collateral cases up the wazoo now. We've got the Lunceford snuff and that Hanamaka guy that Elmer ID'd. We've got the klub**haus** arson, and the presence of that hideout crib down the block. And don't tell me the proximity is a coincidence."

Ray Pinker said, "I've forensic'd the place three times. It was repeatedly vacuumed, so there's no trace elements worth a shit. I can't turn a latent print to save my life. There's rubber-glove prints on all the room surfaces and cooking utensils, so I'd bet the inhabitants were gloved up at all times."

Thad leaned into the blackboard. "What about the klub**haus** torch?"

Pinker kicked his chair back. "It was deliberately set. I found powdered-accelerant traces on a downstairs floorboard. The first floor ignited, and the rioters caught arson fever and started chucking bottle bombs."

Breuning said, "Monkey see, monkey do. The firebug lays down the accelerant and drops a match. He's got the blackout and all the air-raid grief for cover. The jigs go all copycat and get up a bonfire."

Thad cracked his knuckles. "We're coming up against that Miciak shitheel's statement. There's the sheer bulk of all the criminal and PD-implicated shit that transpired at the klub**haus.** We've got to work the confiscated guns that Rice and Kapek were selling. I want to run a sweep out of Hollenbeck Station. We'll raise some hell, rattle some cages, and see if we can tie some beaners to our homicides."

The room rumbled. **That's** policework. The boys foot-stomped the floor. Ashida went **aw-OH.**

Blanchard said, "My so-called drunk act on the jazz strip is going nowhere. I'm a well-known cop, and the coons have got all closemouthed since the riot."

Carlisle smirked. "Mr. Celebrity. 'The Southland's good but not great white hope.' He spawns fear and envy wherever he goes."

Blanchard kicked Carlisle's chair. Carlisle cringed and **un**smirked. Fight fever peaked and fizzled, fast.

Thad pitched Blanchard. "You and Lieutenant Ashida work a Mutt and Jeff and comb the strip again. We've got to ID the women who left those pubic-hair samples."

Blanchard said, "We should try to ID the other cops who habituated the klub**haus.** We might pull some leads there."

Thad went **nix.** "Chief Horrall says no. He thinks it'll open a whole can of worms."

The Teletype clacked and unfurled paper. Parker walked up and tore out the sheet.

He read it. He rubbed his split lip. He glanced at Ashida.

"They're moving the Werewolf back to Atascadero today. I thought you'd want to know."

Ashida watched the move-out. Sayonara, Werewolf— thanks for the memories.

Two male nurses plucked him out of his cell. They wrestled him to the catwalk floor and shot him up with jungle juice. The Werewolf flailed and bared his fangs. He bayed at some nutso moon and went loosed-limb floaty.

Ashida stood close by. The nurses fish-eyed him.

He's a Jap. He's Army brass. Who gave him that .45? The Werewolf's his daddy.

They cuffed and shackled the Werewolf. They straitjacket-wrapped him. They grabbed his arms and wrangled him upstairs and outside. Ashida followed them out.

Newshounds sent a cheer up. Sid Hudgens and Jack Webb led the pack. The hounds howled and pawed the sidewalk outside Central Station. Flashbulbs pop-pop-popped.

Ashida blinked back bulb glare. Monster Matinee. He saw passing papas hold their toddlers up to watch.

Mike Breuning and Dick Carlisle lounged on the steps. Breuning flicked his cigarette butt and hit the Werewolf's back. A little girl tossed her ice-cream cone and missed the Werewolf by inches. The Sidster scribbled up a scratch pad.

A nuthouse wagon idled curbside. The driver slid out a gurney on casters. The nurses hoisted the Werewolf and triple-wrapped him in. More flash-bulbs popped.

The nurses hopped in the back. The driver fishtailed eastbound on 1st Street. News fotogs snapped Ashida. He's this Jap stoic. He's all dolled up, Army style.

Ashida rubbed his eyes. That bulb glare had him seeing double. He saw two Elmer Jacksons, straight across the street. Two Elmers bolted the Moonglow Lounge and booze-weaved toward the station.

Ashida blinked and got back his eyesight. He saw one Elmer now. Elmer stumbled over the curb and made straight for him. He got up in booze-breath range and cut loose.

You little Jap shit/you should have told me/my brother died in that fire/you fuckers wanted the gold/I watchdogged your ass when the Japs bombed Pearl/you should have told me/you little Jap shit, you—

Mike Breuning stepped in. He grabbed Elmer's coat collar and jerked him half off his feet. Elmer wheeled and sucker punched him. His Marine Corps ring gouged Breuning's cheek down to the bone. Breuning yelped and threw sissy punches. Elmer moved close and slammed elbows. He smashed Breuning's nose, Breuning's teeth, Breuning's dumb jug head overall. He put Breuning down on the ground and kicked one jug ear half off.

86

(LOS ANGELES, 11:00 A.M., 3/5/42)

His elbow hurt. He was skunk drunk. Breuning's snaggle teeth snagged up his suit coat. He snagged Dumb Cracker of All Time honors. They foretold his futile fate. Dudley Smith would fuck him up the dirt road.

Elmer lurched through City Hall. He lurched toward the Vice squadroom and his cozy cubicle. He lurched by sweatbox row. He thought he saw Buzz Meeks in box #2. He lurched past box #3 and hit the home stret—

Something bushwhacked him. Two geeks snatched him and shoved him into box #4. He hit the bolted-down table and plopped into the bolted-down chair.

Bill Parker kicked the door shut. Thad Brown thunked a thermos down on the table. Parker unscrewed the top and poured out hot coffee.

Elmer took a test sip. It burned his tongue and stung his teeth. Parker and Brown pulled up chairs. Parker said, "We talked to Buzz Meeks. He told us you forged up Tommy Glennon's address book and placed it at the klub**haus.** He also mentioned that the two of you put the boots to Huey Cressmeyer, down in T.J. Huey purportedly snitched off Dudley Smith's racket schemes, up here and in Baja."

Elmer sipped too-hot coffee. His hands shook. He scoped Parker's fat lip and willed savoir faire.

"Who smacked you, Bill? Was it Kay, or some other swift college girl?"

Brown chortled. "My money's on Kay."

Parker deadpanned the shtick. "We don't know if Meeks gave us the whole drift on you two and Huey, and it doesn't really matter. The spatials on the Lunceford shooting are off, and you've quite noticeably ditched your ankle piece. That doesn't matter, either. You fired it on a liquor-store stakeout in October of '40, and a spent-ballistics file exists. Guess what, dipshit? We got a match to the pills you pumped into Catbox Cal."

The green room looms. The last mile beckons. Your ass is grass, son.

"So, I'm fucked."

Brown shook his head. "No, you're not. Lunceford was Fifth Column, and he was in with that Jap hump, Hanamaka. You're getting a waltz on Manslaughter One. We consider the shooting kosher, and this room is as far as it goes."

Parker said, "Thad and I have read Joan Conville's diary, and I've discussed the text with Kay Lake. I know that Miss Lake has discussed that text with you and Hideo Ashida, but I'll add that she omitted one key narrative thread."

No green room. The coffee had cooled down. Elmer took a big gulp.

"I already figured that out. The Dudster, Joan, and that little shit Ashida were out for the gold from the git-go. I sensed that Kay was fibbing on that. She didn't tell me, because she thought I'd go berserk on account of my brother. She didn't tell Ashida, because he's Dudley's lapdog, and he's a participant in this whole crazy gold hunt anyways."

Brown smiled. "Elmer's not as dumb as most folks think he is."

Parker said, "Let's not get carried away."

Elmer yukked. The coffee diffused the booze. Son, you're in the catbird seat.

"Okay, then. We got our three big cases, going back to '31. You two, me, Buzz, Kay, and maybe Ashida want a pure solve on the klub**haus** job—but Jack H. and the Dudster want to put the onus off on some shines. And you two are all ditzed, because Bill clean-solved the Watanabe job and kept mum on it, and our pal Jim Davis killed them Watanabes, and you don't want that leaking out, and Dud told Joan Conville that he intends to pentothal Jim D. to see if he spills any crossover leads to the klub**haus** caper. One of you's our next chief. Jack Horrall's afraid of Bill, because his grand-jury plays served to get the Werewolf sprung, and Jack can't retaliate. You want my opinion on that?"

Parker sighed. "Give us your esteemed opinion, Sergeant."

Elmer stood up and kicked blood back in his legs. He scratched his balls and worked up some brain juice.

"Judge and jury will sure as shit acquit Fletch B., Call-Me-Jack, Ray Pinker, and the Jamie kid, along with all them others. That's for-sure gospel—regardless of Bill's testimony. While I've got you here, I'll tell you why. J. Edgar Hoover don't want bad blood between the Feds and the PD, not when we got this here Jap internment to deal with. You got a spell of time to make hay on the klub**haus** job, before the acquittals come down, and Jack H. figures he can pull the plug on the job and give Dud his marching orders, and then it's good-bye, jigaboos."

Parker sighed anew. "You're right, Thad. He's not as dumb as folks think."

Elmer hoot-hooted. Brown said, "Meeks told us that Ed Satterlee offered you a shot to listen to the Fed's phone and bug recordings and delete your own voice. I'd like you to provide that same service for Captain Parker and me."

Elmer plunked back down in his chair. He hooked his thumbs in his suspenders and put his feet up on the desk.

"In exchange for what?"

Parker said, "In exchange for let bygones be bygones. That means any and all illegal and questionable shit that you've pulled since New Year's. That stated, I'll add that we're easing Breuning and Carlisle off the job. We're keeping you and Meeks, Ashida and Blanchard on. Dudley's permitting Ashida to do field interviews, and Thad and I are convinced that Ashida wants a clean solve, regardless of his relationship with Dudley. I'm not going to tell Dudley that Kay revealed the contents of Joan's diary to you and Ashida, and the only attendant risk here is what Ashida might tell Dudley himself."

Brown lit his pipe and shook out the match. He raised his feet and nudged Elmer's feet off the desk.

"That leaves Blanchard and Ashida, you and Meeks as our line detectives. Ashida's driving back to Baja tonight. We're swearing him in as a war hire when he returns. The four of you will have carte blanche. We'll ride out interference from Jack Horrall, if and when it occurs."

Elmer snagged the full gist. "You're freezing Dudley out. You're driving him to make some dumb play that will put his dick in the wringer."

Parker lit a cigarette. "Don't say it, Thad. 'He's not as dumb as most folks think.' "

Brown said, "Our biggest concern is the guns. I rebraced Harold John Miciak last night, and bought him out of a GTA bounce in Fresno. He fleshed out the statement he gave Breuning and Carlisle, as it pertained to the guns. He told me that Rice and Kapek sold all the guns to pachuco right-wingers. We're compiling a roust list off the Feds' subversive files. You're the first man on the Crash Squad we've shared this lead with. It's a bigger deal than I let on at the briefing this morning. We're going in with shotguns and sedition-stamped grand-jury subpoenas. There'll be three two-man flanks. That's Captain Parker and me, you and Meeks, Blanchard and Ashida."

Elmer wolf-whistled. "You are taking a very dicey risk with Ashida. You are risking him spilling everything we get to the Dudster."

Parker gulped. Brown gulped. Their throat doo-hickeys bobbed.

Brown passed Elmer a snapshot. It was a niteclub-type deal. The backdrop denoted Club Alabam. A jolly trio mugged in a booth. Dig said trio:

Meyer Gelb, Jean Staley, Tommy Glennon.

Elmer wolf-whistled, **loooooooooow.** Brown said, "It was in with Miciak's property, up in Fresno. It's date-stamped February 27, which makes it one week ago. Miciak refused to comment on the picture. I had some hayseed cops hard-nose him, to no fucking avail."

Elmer brain-strained it. Jean's allegedly back east. Jean's mail-drop play via Bev's Switchboard. Smut pix with klub**haus** backdrops. Tommy G.'s La Jolla PO box.

Parker crushed his cigarette. "Here's the big question. What's a Nazi like Glennon doing with two Communists like Staley and Gelb?"

Elmer lit a cigar. "I think I know where Tommy is."

Brown said, "Then go find him and arrest him."

Elmer scrammed. He booked out of box #4 and cut back to box #2. Bad Buzz still sat there. He looked un-Buzz-like forlorn.

"I know where Tommy the G. is. Let's go get him."

87

(ENSENADA, 4:00 P.M., 3/6/42)

Silver bars to gold oak leaves. The SIS command. We mustn't mince words here. Juan Lazaro-Schmidt pulled strings.

Ralph Melnick jumped to lieutenant colonel. Fourth Interceptor promoted him and called him back stateside. It occurred abruptly. Colonel Ralph threw a party.

At Major Smith's new office. It was Colonel Ralph's ex-office. It was twice as large and twice as grand. Mess orderlies served cake and champagne. Dudley invited guests.

Hideo Ashida and Juan Pimentel. Claire, Beth, and Young Joan. Salvy Abascal. The two Lazaro-Schmidts.

Dudley circulated. He tossed the FDR portrait out the window and drew scattered applause. Captain Juan raised a toast. "To outgoing despots and incoming **Sturmbannführers.**"

The right-flankers loved it. Claire and Young Joan scowled. Colonel Melnick giggled. He loathed Double-Cross Rosenfeld.

Beth looked perplexed. She did not comprehend repartee or lovers' passion. She'd witnessed his tiff with Claire. Both parties raised welts and drew blood. He belt-lashed Claire. His severed ear required stitches.

The moment drew nigh. Colonel Melnick called for order. The guests moved in close. Dudley clicked his heels. Constanza removed his silver shoulder bars and pinned on his gold oak leaves.

Major Dudley Liam Smith. The bluff Irish lad ascends.

Constanza kissed him, full on the lips. Beth gasped. Young Joan smirked. Claire wheeled and walked off through the squadroom. Dudley heard glass break. Dudley smelled sprayed champagne.

The orderlies made haste. They moved out with towels and whisk brooms. Claire's display of pique upstaged him. Constanza hooked two fingers through his belt loops and tugged. They bumped hips and kissed again. It restated her claim.

The guests dispersed. They shuffled and formed war-chat cliques. Hideo caught his eye. Dudley gestured toward the squadroom. Hideo filed out first.

Dudley joined him. He smelled Dom Pérignon '29. The orderlies whisked up glass shards. Hideo sat at the duty sergeant's desk. Dudley pulled a chair up.

"Is something troubling you, lad? I doubt that it's the trifling domestic scene you just witnessed."

Ashida said, "The klub**haus** aspect of our cases troubles me. I think there's a very simple solution at the heart of it. I would like your consent to explore all possibilities in my field interviews, before Chief Horrall orders you to implement a more expedient solution."

Dudley smiled. "You have my consent. I will add that you know a great deal about my business dealings here in Baja, and I would ask that you steer clear of them as they might pertain to your investigation."

"Yes, I agree."

Dudley fondled his oak leaves. They were solid gold.

"I would advise caution on a second front, as well. Dick Carlisle called me and described your contretemps with Elmer Jackson, including the vile comments he made to you and the beating he inflicted on our friend Mike. Dick said that Elmer made a garbled reference to gold, which I find discomfiting. Please be careful there. Beyond that, I would like you to draft an extensively detailed report on our three cases, for my exclusive review. Requisition any and all files you need, under your SIS sanction and my signature as your new commanding officer. Interpret all the evidence and theorize as to how the three cases cohere. Have the report to me in one week's time."

El Rancho de Narcóticos was ten miles east of T.J. Carlos Madrano built it. Dudley and José Vasquez-Cruz usurped it. Juan Pimentel now sub-**Führer**'d the ranch.

Dudley and Captain Juan dropped in. Sinarquista goons straw-bossed the operation. Statie noncoms patrolled the perimeter. They packed tommy guns and Brazilian mastiffs on short tethers. The dogs hunted feral cats and mauled dope-worker slaves on command.

The conversion lab was up-to-date and unhygienic.

Four chemists brewed Mexican poppies into Big "H." Low-peso peons packaged the shit. A slave barracks adjoined the lab. The slaves worked sixteen-hour shifts and got Sunday mornings off. A local priest performed Mass. He was hooked on Big "H."

Dudley toured the grounds. Captain Juan played tour guide. Governor Lazaro-Schmidt had joined the cabal. He'd requested a progress report.

Four large trucks and three large buses stood by the barracks. Their big-scoop wheelwells would move the shit north. Interned Japs would ride the buses. Legally vetted wetbacks would crowd up the trucks. Hideo Ashida would watchdog future border crossings. He'd speak Jap to the Japs. He'd tally confiscated gelt and secure property lists.

Wets, Japs, dope. A trenchant trifecta. El Governor would vouch the three fronts. He'd grease the skids with the U.S. Relocation brass. Their Jap jails would overflow. He'd sign on California farm bosses. He'd exploit his office and sell them cut-rate wets.

Dudley spot-checked vehicles. He kicked tires, popped hoods, tightened loose spark plugs. Juan Pimentel watched. He said, "You haven't told me the governor's percentage."

Dudley swung a wrench and cinched up wobbly lug nuts. Slack tires just wouldn't do.

"15% of our combined ventures. He provides the official sanctions, while we provide the work."

"Do you not find the governor's relationship with his sister quite strange?"

Dudley winked. "I would call it outré, and perhaps perverse."

They dined at Neptune's Locker. It was a driftwood and barnacle barn on Avenida Costeño. Native swells and U.S. stiffs loved the place.

Their table overlooked the yacht pier. Film moguls cruised down from L.A. and went slumming. Nude starlets baked on warm teakwood. The governor openly stared.

He wore a trim-cut navy blazer and white ducks tonight. The London Shop dressed him. He shopped in Beverly Hills once a month.

They drank absinthe frappés. Constanza wore a yellow sundress. Dudley wore his ODs. He felt dowdy beside these two.

They toasted Dudley's precipitous promotion. They toasted their business deal and a certain German **jefe.** Constanza hummed the "Horst-Wessel-Lied." The table was set with mock-gold flatwear. Lazaro-Schmidt raised a mock-gold fork.

"To new friends and acquisition. To that precious commodity we seek."

They tapped forks over the table. The absinthe had Dudley light-headed. Constanza ran a hand up his leg.

"Tell the major about Kyoho, Juan. He's quite naturally curious, and I need to gauge whether or not he's the jealous type."

Lazaro-Schmidt laughed. He lit a cigarette and shot his shirtcuffs.

"It may dismay my sister, but I think of Kyoho as a conspirator more than I think of him as her lover. As a conspirator, I would surmise that he was the most adroit and politically savvy of all those in the left-right cartel. He was always tight-lipped, especially as it pertained to the gold. He was here for the conference in November of '40, and I recall that he seemed to be very much within himself, amid the few instances of camaraderie that I witnessed."

Constanza lit a cigarette. "Juan was there for the opening ceremony and the departures only. He was not there for the formal meetings where the strategies pertaining to the gold itself were discussed."

Dudley said, "Do minutes for the conference exist?"

Lazaro-Schmidt said, "Yes, but they are not to be found. They would be a priceless discovery, of course."

Constanza dipped a hand under the table. Dudley threaded their fingers up.

"It would delight me to have you drop some names, Governor. The conference has me starstruck."

Lazaro-Schmidt waved the gold fork. "The Russians were without significant style or substance. Molotov, Beria, a few elevated apparatchiks. They were there to betray Butcher Stalin and the Communist International, and I credit them only with their ardent belief that informed leftists and rightists must unite to survive a certain postwar apocalypse. Our

Nazi **Kameraden** were quite another barrel of fish. They shared the revelation with comparable urgency and comported themselves with inestimable class. Wilhelm Canaris was most cultured and gracious. Ernst Kaltenbrunner was thin, gorgeously attired, and six and a half feet tall. My acquaintance Meyer Gelb drove the German contingent around Ensenada, without their ever once suspecting that he was a Jew."

Red Meyer, redux. Dudley pondered it.

"Gelb attended the conference?"

"I'm sure he was there as a rogue Stalinist, and the tool of an enlightened faction within the Comintern. He served as a chauffeur, but was not privy to the conference itself."

"But minutes of the conference do exist?"

"Yes. An American man took them with him at the end of the conference. I know nothing about this man, but I saw him leave for the airfield with a briefcase cuffed to his wrist."

Dudley said, "Please describe the man."

Lazaro-Schmidt said, "He was tall, and he had a southern accent."

Constanza booked a suite at the del Norte. It was insolently close to his suite and Claire. They walked through the lobby, entwined. Beth and Young Joan sat in lounge chairs and saw them. Beth scowled. Young Joan scrutinized.

His body revved, his mind raced. They'd sniffed cocaine in the cab. The seditious siblings, the gold, some elliptical gap. They hadn't discussed the heist/ the fire/the gold's full origins. They assumed each other's lust for possession and possessive intent. The sibs went back with Kyoho Hanamaka. Governor Juan attended the confab and knew Meyer Gelb. His body revved, his mind raced. **Tell me everything.** He almost shrieked it.

They elevatored up to the suite. Constanza pushed him into the back wall and held him there with her mouth. She kissed his eyes and his neck. The doors slid open. She grabbed his waistband and pulled him down the hall. He fumbled the key out of her clutch and unlocked the suite.

The front room was all dark shapes and shadows. He kicked the door shut and pushed Constanza into a chair. He dropped to his knees and held her there with his mouth.

He threw her dress up and pulled down her stockings and underwear. Constanza drew back and hooked her legs over the width of the chair. He caught her scent. She grabbed his hair and pulled him into it.

He wanted that. He knew she knew it. He stretched her legs. He found the wet and the fit and the place. Constanza fell into Spanish. She went **Sí, sí, sí, sí, sí.**

She made different sounds. He learned her tones and her tastes all together. Her breath raced. She pushed up. She pitched and buckled off one drawn-out **Sí.**

She held him there with her legs then. He'd hoped that she would.

It rained all night. They made love all night. They talked in between. It reprised his first night with Joan.

Pious you. You kill people and sense God as an innocent. You see the abrogation of all moral law in my relationship with my brother.

Yes. I disapprove and am concurrently titillated.

I disapprove of La Comunista. She is strident and indecorous. You must confirm or refute that you killed her Red lover. My brother believes that you did. He believes that my occasional lover Salvy may have assisted you.

I'll confirm or refute when I know you better. Forgive my circumspection until then.

I have never been circumspect. I despise your Red whore. She is La Comunista Estúpida. I find your young charges compelling, however. They are both of you, regardless of their blood. Young Joan possesses your ferocity, and young Beth possesses your hunger.

Your perceptions honor me, darling.

You are tall and urbane. One rarely sees that in Mexican men. My brother is urbane, but he is a shrimp.

Your brother is urbane, but not quite as perceptive as you. I rather enjoyed his perceptions of Meyer Gelb, though.

Meyer Gelb is a puto, a parasite, and an extortionist. He is an evil Stalinist, and he hates Trotskyites more than he hates fascists such as you and me. He will extort the very life's blood from our Jewish exile friends.

Betray me not, mi corazon. It would surely devastate me.

Do not tell me that. It will assure my betrayal.

Caustic you. So determined to take my measure in the course of a first-night's encounter.

One takes a lover's measure immediately or not at all. You need women to record your triumphs. You need to capitulate to women in a manner that many would find unseemly.

I commune with a wolf I met on the British moors, in 1921. He will sleep with us tonight, and he is very astute about women. He has told me that your designs are entirely felicitous, and has recently informed me that I underestimate a reckless young woman in Los Angeles. He's close to convincing me that the silly girl intends me great harm.

88

(LOS ANGELES, 7:00 A.M., 3/7/42)

I was still woozy from Otto's party, three nights ago. It wasn't a liquor hangover or a case of party-behavior regret. I barely touched booze; I abstained from flirtatiousness and cutup antics. I felt the undertow of Otto's provocative guest list. It was a nexus of criminal-case suspects, present and past.

Meyer Gelb. Jean Staley and her postcard ruse, geared to deceive my pal Elmer. Gelb's tenuous connection to the four exiled musicians. Gelb, Staley, the Lesnicks. Communist comrades in '33; party guests nine years on. Jorge Villareal-Caiz did not attend the party. Dudley Smith allegedly killed him. Claire De Haven told me that. She told me that with my hand on her breast.

I'm seated at a folding table in my backyard now; I'm ten feet from the incinerator that I use to burn rubbish. I put the incinerator to hasty use late last December; I burned the clothes I wore during my impetuous attempt to take Dudley Smith's life. Canny Claire made me for this crime. Elmer picked that nugget up during a hot-sheet surveillance. A call girl named Annie Staples was servicing Saul Lesnick.

The Claire-Dudley liaison is imploding. Claire went to Mexico with a murderous madman and now pays the price. Claire told me this herself. She told me with my hand on her breast.

Bill called me an hour ago; he bluntly stated that he and Thad Brown are now colluding. They are pushing Mike Breuning and Dick Carlisle off the klub**haus** case, while they retain my Lee Blanchard, partnered up with Hideo Ashida. Bill has characterized Hideo as a young man who perpetually "falls from shit to clover." Hideo is surely the luckiest Japanese in these parts. He has whizzed through the internment push and has secured a U.S. Army commission. Bill told me that he will soon be doubly credentialed. Double-Trouble Hideo will also serve as a war-hire policeman. He is down in Baja now, but will soon be returning. He will cut his teeth in an upcoming "pachuco sweep."

Bill Parker, fired with holy purpose and fixed upon task. Joan Conville's diary chastened and dismayed him. I'm glad I hit him in the mouth. It served to wake him up.

Bill told me that he will abet my pledge to expose false solutions to the klub**haus** case and will publicly excoriate the slaying of any and all bogus suspects. This is a direct contravention of his pledges to Dudley Smith. I have concluded that Hideo has not revealed the existence of Joan's diary or the fact that I hold possession. Hideo pines for a clean klub**haus** solve. He was robbed of a clean solve on the Watanabe case and harbors guilt for his part in the frame-up of Werewolf Shudo. I know this. Hideo's desire for a clean solve supersedes his lust for the gold and his kid crush on Dudley Smith. I know this. Hideo's desire for a clean solve transcends his bond with Dudley and Joan Conville, and cuts through all their criminal and romantic circumlocutions. I know this.

I pondered romantic triangles within a triangulated case structure. I pondered triangles in general. I thought of Brenda Allen, Elmer Jackson, and Annie Staples. A brainstorm hit. I ran inside to the phone.

Brenda's preferred meeting spot was Dave's Blue Room. She and Elmer owned a sizable percentage. Brenda's preferred pose was midmorning gin fizzes; her preferred conversational style was the full-speed monologue. One buckled in for these.

Our back booth assured privacy. The waiter brought a full pitcher of fizzes and left us alone. Brenda revved up on the war, FDR's tax bill, and her monthly bribe cut to Sheriff's Vice. She laid on the prelude and arrived at her preferred topic: her call-biz partner and part-time lover, Sergeant E. V. Jackson.

". . . and I'm thinking of calling the Missing Persons Squad about this boy, Citizen. I don't care that he's got Ellen Drew on the side, or whatever else he's got going—but we're running thirty-four girls, and it's an around-the-clock enterprise that he's been neglecting while he's been working that klub**haus** job down in darktown, him all partnered up with Buzz Meeks, who I know for a fact has gunned down numerous colored and Mexican gents under dubious circumstances."

So far, so good. I arranged the klatch to get a bead on Elmer's recent actions. I sipped midmorning gin and egg whites and formulated a question. Brenda relaunched her monologue and cut straight to Jack Horrall.

"As you well know, I've got my weekly date with Call-Me-Jack, which involves perfunctory woof-woof in the missionary manner, and always on the floor, and I've got the long-standing rug burns to attest to this long-standing arrangement. Well, Jack don't take very long, and he always segues to his long-standing spiel about the woes of the big-city police chief, and this morning it's all about how your chum Whiskey Bill Parker showed up at his office last night and summarily announced that he would oppose and expose any bogus solving of the klub**haus** job, despite Jack and the Dudster's wishes, and it left Jack in a veritable tizzy, because Citizen Jack is now under Federal indictment, and vulnerable in about six trillion ways."

Bill fulfilled his pledge to me. My heart swelled. My well-aimed smack in the mouth surely did it. Brenda drained her third gin fizz and lit a cigarette; I jumped at my chance to ask a question.

"Brenda, what's going on with Elmer and Annie Staples?"

Brenda tittered and formed a circle with her left forefinger and thumb. She poked her right forefinger through the middle of the circle. It was international sign language for fuckee-fuckee.

"Well, Citizen, to begin with, Annie likes it more than she should, given that she repeatedly does it for money. Second, I told Ed Satterlee that he could use my Miracle Mile wall peek to get some footage on Annie in the kip with some Commie psychiatrist, and I heard a rumor that Elmer got embroiled in that play. I confronted him, but he refused to blab. Annie's always been too smart for her own good, which don't sit right for a line girl. To top it off, I saw Annie in Hollywood last week. She was hobknobbing with Sid Hudgens at Breneman's Ham 'n' Eggs, all huddled up thick as thieves."

89

(ENSENADA, 10:00 P.M., 3/7/42)

The walls were thin. His suite adjoined theirs. The walls were sound sieves. He sat at his desk and worked through the tiff.

Ashida read photostats. He'd submitted stat requests

and gotten fast replies. Treasury and Alameda PD kicked loose. LAFD Arson stats had been pledged.

He read. He took notes. He sat up against a sieve wall. The two suites ran contiguous. He worked and eavesdropped.

1927. Fritz Eckelkamp's heist spree. Liquor-store jobs. Cash on hand, always. The quick in-and-out. Alameda PD snags Fritz. He falls behind multiple counts.

Claire shrieked. She defamed the Redheaded Succubus and the Nazi Half-Breed Whore. Dudley shrieked. **She** was the whore. She was a Dope-Addict Shrew and a Mex- and Nigger-Fucker. She fucked that Putrid Puto Jorge and that Nigger Welterweight in L.A.

Ashida read stat pages. Alameda PD supplied a background sheet. He traveled back to Weimar Berlin. **Willkommen, Herr Jap.**

Claire shrieked. Dudley shrieked. They traded **You're** the Dope Fiend barbs. Claire defamed Ace Kwan. Dudley demeaned the Jew Maestro. Claire went singsong. **Somebody-stabbed-you/somebody-stabbed you/I-think-it-was-a-girl.**

Fritz was a Sparticist. He fought Brownshirt thugs and swung a nail-studded plank. He robbed diamond merchants at gunpoint. He firebombed a **bierhaus** and fried two Brownshirts to a crisp.

Ashida wrote, "FE precedes all criminal cases and all intrigues. FE as precipitating agent? FE escapes from gold train, 5/18/31. Catalytic moment of all cases combined?"

Claire called Dudley Pussy-Whipped and Shanty Irish Scum. Dudley called Claire a Round-Heeled Poseur. A silent gap stretched. Then they laughed, then they moaned, then bedsprings creaked.

Ashida ran from it. He sat in the lobby bar and nursed a dry sherry. It was late. The lights were dim. He was the sole patron. Joan Klein messed around at the piano.

She possessed some skill. Her forte was hybrid improvisation. She melded Chopin and Gershwin tonight. Ashida caught strains of a jumpy mazurka and Concerto in F.

Young Joan. She's Dudley's and Claire's odd creature. The hotel management indulges her. She's become Spanish-fluent in record time. The head barkeep pays her a pittance to play show tunes. She wows patrons with her oddball transcriptions.

She wrapped up Chopin Meets Gershwin. She hit two sour notes and went out with a bang. Ashida applauded. Young Joan walked over and sat down with him.

She sipped his sherry, uninvited. She cleaned her glasses with his napkin. People recognized it. She had Dudley Smith's eyes.

"Comrade Chopin drank patent compounds and went insane. Comrade Gershwin died from a brain tumor. The fascist patriarchy stifles the creative class and drives them nuts."

Ashida smiled. "Comrade Stalin's agrarian purges have left four million dead. Consider that the next time you start fomenting."

Young Joan waved faux wolfsbane. "Uncle Hideo's a square, but he's not a fascist, like a certain party I could name. The jury's out on Uncle Hideo, in more ways than one."

Ashida waved faux wolfsbane. "Stop being cryptic and uncanny. Stop making with the non sequiturs and comrade talk. Nobody knows what you're talking about half the time."

Young Joan replaced her glasses. Her small eyes magnified.

"Aunt Claire took Cousin Beth and me to this swift party. Everybody talked in non sequiturs. I met Bertolt Brecht and Orson Welles. Comrade Welles squeezed my knee and called me 'cutie.' I met some swell string players from the Dresden Staatskapelle, and I drank absinthe and had visions."

Ashida grinned. He indulged the girl more than he should.

"What did you see, specifically?"

"I saw this violinist named Ruth Szigeti making the beast with two backs with Robert Taylor, while Miss Barbara Stanwyck herself watched. Then I saw this man named Comrade Meyer Gelb hit Comrade Ruth up for a blow job, and try to get her to snitch out Trotskyites in this studio orchestra."

Meyer Gelb. From the mouths of babes. This loopy child source.

"What else did you see?"

"Nothing. Visions are visions, and I'm not going to tell you I saw something I didn't. I'm not going to lie just to entertain you, when you think I'm just a silly girl playing Mata Hari."

Ashida went **Stop it.** "Don't misunderstand me. I don't think that at all."

"Don't underestimate me, Uncle. If I'm just this silly girl, then why does Juan Pimentel pay me to get next to you and pump you for information?"

Pimentel was an invert. **Maricón en español.** Pimentel possessed sonar and radar. Pimentel sensed inversion in him.

RHIP. Ashida had master keys. They unlocked the SIS squadroom and all the file banks. He was Dudley's exec now. It covered him. Boss, I was just working late.

Pimentel perved on him. Pimentel had no shame. Pimentel corrupted a mere child and sicced her his way.

Ashida unlocked the squadroom door and hit the fluorescents. Bright tube light bore down. SIS kept intel files on all the Baja Staties. They were deemed corruption-prone.

Statie folders filled up two file banks. **N** to **Q** filled a full drawer. Green sheets detailed suspect history. Addendums listed "Possibly Related Intel."

Ashida unlocked the drawer. The Pimentel file was stuffed between Pecheco and Pizzaro. One green sheet poked out the top. Ashida plucked it and skimmed it. The sheet revealed **this:**

Pimentel, Juan Ramon. DOB 5/26/11. Suspect Personal History. One derogatory report.

"Arrested in raid on homosexual nightclub. 2/19/37. San Diego PD."

Ashida flipped the green sheet. Three intel notes were typed on the back.

"Subject Pimentel alleged to be highly skilled in area of telephone (pay-phone) technology."

"Subject Pimentel holds graduate degrees from Mexican Polytechnical Institute, Guadalajara. Purportedly attended technical institute in Germany. Purportedly knowledgeable in microdot technology."

"Subject Pimentel purportedly attended assumed subversive conference/Ensenada, mid-11/40. Conference purportedly brought together high-ranking Soviet and Nazi intelligence officers. Subject Pimentel purportedly assigned chauffeur duties & was spotted with Abwehr Commandant Wilhelm Canaris & Gestapo chieftain Ernst Kaltenbrunner."

90

(SAN DIEGO, 11:00 A.M., 3/8/42)

The boys are back in town.

At this lice-lair motel. On the PD's dime. Staking Tommy G.'s PO box. To no fucking good avail.

The Seaglade Motel. Off the main drag in Dago. A hot-sheet hut for sailors and jarheads. All-nite whore traffic. One big VD stain.

Buzz read a Donald Duck comic book. He gassed on Donald's rage and perved on Daisy Duck. Elmer gabbed with Thad Brown, long-distance.

He spilled his break-in at Bev's Switchboard. Thad went **Yikes.** Elmer steamrolled the reaction and ran down the mail-forward scam. Link Rockwell held a box at Bev's and sent smut pix to Tommy's box in La Jolla. The pix featured klub**haus** backdrops. A white girl and Mex girl frolicked with masked men. The girls fit Ashida's snatch-hair prognostications.

Thad went **Yikes.** Elmer relaunched his spiel.

The post office stakeout bore no ripe fruit. Fruitcake Tommy hasn't showed. Elmer ran down the envelope in Meyer Gelb's box. It featured a La Paz PO box return address and no return name. The envelope contained blotter paper and maybe microdots.

Thad went **Yikes.** He told Elmer to ring Ashida— chop, chop. Tell him to check the La Paz box and apply his brain to microdots. Beyond that—chop, chop. You and Meeks go find that Tommy fuck.

Elmer went **Yeah, boss.** Buzz read his comic book. Thad laid out some hot PD dish.

Whiskey Bill keestered Jack Horrall. **Ouch!**—straight up the shit chute. Bill pulled Breuning and Carlisle off of the klub**haus** job. Bill told Jack he'd quash a bogus-suspect solve. **Ouch!**—Bill keestered Dudley Smith.

Elmer went **Yikes.** Buzz tapped his wristwatch—wrap this shit up. Thad motor-mouthed. He said Parker's wrangling a material-witness writ. Link Rockwell's at some Navy flight school in Florida. Parker wants to extradite him. Jack Horrall's dragging his heels.

Elmer went **Yikes.** Thad went **Chop, chop, you dumb hayseeds.** Thad went **Quit jerking off and go to work.**

They restaked the post office. The posh hamlet cocooned them. La Jolla was swanksville. Cypress trees and golf courses. Nice stores with candy-cane awnings. A nifty beach close by.

The stakeout was yawnsville. They pondered a more direct approach. Brace the Postal Inspection Service. Have the postal cops dump Tommy's PO box.

They discussed it. They nixed it. This was a strong-arm job. The postal cops would demur. They had to snatch Tommy. They had to hurl some hurt on him before they dumped him on Thad.

Swanksville. Yawnsville. They sat in Elmer's civilian sled and evinced ennui.

Buzz said, "Maybe Tommy ducked down to T.J. He's bored, so he's thinking he'll go catch the donkey show and see his pal Huey. I say we go down there and stir up some shit."

Elmer said, "We overstirred the shit the last time we went down there. I say we check with SDPD Burglary. We're brother officers looking for a hot-prowl man. They might have some fresh cases and some leads they could share."

SDPD was close by the Seaglade. That greased the skids. They drove over and parked in a visitor's slot. The building was whitewashed adobe and two stories high. They walked up to the DB. Dago was a turkey town. Burglary Division was one fat-slob cop.

The dink sat in a gnat-sized office. His desk plate read SGT. LEW SARNI. They walked in, deliberate. The dink shook himself awake.

"L.A., right? You've got that look. You're down here on a job, and you need a hand."

The dink dwarfed his dink-sized desk. Elmer and Buzz straddled chairs and faced him. They lit up cigars. Elmer tossed the dink a one-dollar Cuban. It bounced on his desk.

"We're looking for a hot-prowl geek named Tommy Glennon. He's a homo, but he rapes women. He's got a postal box in La Jolla, and we thought you might have made him for some incidents down here."

Buzz slid the dink a mug-shot strip. The dink lit the cigar and studied the fotos.

"We've got a series of 459/rapes, and your guy matches the suspect's description. The victims are all Navy women, working out of Point Loma. Navy CID's handling it, because they make the rape-o for a sailor. The guy's vicious, and he's pulled six jobs so far, but the whole thing's going nowhere."

Elmer said, "That's it?"

The dink savored his cigar. He flicked ash and went **Yum-yum.**

"No, that isn't it. A Wave officer called us and reported a man following her and skulking around her apartment house. He matches your guy's and our suspect's description, but CID and the DB here can't spare a stakeout team or a woman cop to play decoy."

Buzz whipped out his flash roll. He peeled off two yards and dropped them on the desk.

"Let us handle it. What CID don't know won't hurt them."

The dink coughed cigar smoke. "Well . . . uh . . . I like to accommodate the L.A. boys whenever I can."

Elmer said, "Give us the Wave's statistics. We'll take it from there."

Ensign Margaret May Mewshaw. An Omaha transplant. Ensign Meg lived in Pacific Beach. She lived alone and had no boyfriend. She lived in a second-floor/ street-facing crib. It was a two-crib stucco building. Outside stairs led up to her door.

They waited for dusk. They hunkered in and car-sat across the street. Ensign Meg was home alone. They brought a short dog of 151 rum. It got them lubricated and motivized.

It was late-winter warm. Ensign Meg kept her front window cracked and the shades up. She played the radio. Bucky Beaver shilled Ipana toothpaste. Charlie Barnet played "Cherokee."

Ensign Meg schlepped around in her slip. She was a big blonde. She had that Annie Staples scope and je ne sais quoi. Elmer got erotified. Tommy G. was a leg man. Ensign Meg had legs from Dago to Detroit.

Elmer said, "I don't get it. Tommy's a fruit, but he rapes women."

Buzz said, "Sex is powerful juju."

"Moonlight Serenade" drifted over. Elmer yawned. That tune and 151 put him dozy. He wisped off somewhere. He saw Wayne Frank in a limousine packed with gold bars. He saw Dudley in the green room at San Quentin. Buzz went **Ssshhh** and el-bowed him awake.

"Hush now. We got a prowler."

Elmer rubbed his eyes and looked out his window. This jamoke stood by the stairs. He's wearing gloves. He's holding a tool pouch. He's pivoting to creep up-ward. Hold the phone, mama. It's Tommy Glennon.

They bolted the sled and ran over. They crouched

low at the foot of the stairs. Tommy stood outside Ensign Meg's door. He brandished a lock pick and blew on it for luck. Buzz kicked a tin can, accidental. Tommy heard it and glanced down the stairs.

He saw the boys. He was trapped-rat confined. He dropped the pick and pulled a shiv and charged down the stairs.

Elmer charged up. He pulled his belt sap and crashed Tommy low. Tommy stabbed down and snagged his sport coat. Elmer sap-slammed a nut shot and cartwheeled him. Tommy screeched and tumbled ass over elbows.

He hit the ground, all bruised and splayed. Buzz rabbit-punched him and bashed his head on a stair ledge. Elmer tripped down the stairs and cuffed his hands behind his back.

They cuff-dragged him across the street. They made the sled in one split second. Elmer unlocked the trunk. They dumped Tommy in and slammed the trunk shut. Ensign Meg looked out her window. **What's all this ruckus?** Elmer blew her a kiss.

Tommy thunked around in the trunk. Buzz jumped in the car. Elmer got behind the wheel and burned tread. They had a spot all picked out. The caustic-sewage dump behind the Point Loma base.

Elmer wheeled them there, rapid. The spot adjoined an air-artillery range. The dump was barb-wired up. Caustic gack bubbled and gurgled. Evil swamp creatures gamboled within.

Elmer brodied up to the fence. He got out and unlocked the trunk. Buzz got out and jerked Tommy
up on his feet. Tommy was beat-on and green at the
gills. Buzz tossed him in the backseat and scooched
him toward the middle. Elmer got in and sandwich-
jobbed him on the other side.

Tommy huffed and squirmed. Elmer tapped the
roof light and halo-lit him. Buzz pulled his throw-
down piece. He popped the cylinder and flashed the
six-bullet load.

Elmer said, "We got some questions."

Tommy quiver-quaked. Buzz dumped five bullets and spun the cylinder. He snapped it shut and
winked at Tommy. He put the muzzle to his head
and pulled the trigger twice.

The hammer hit empty chambers. Tommy wriggled
and squealed. Elmer said, "We got some questions."

Buzz held up his piece. He spun the cylinder and
snapped it shut. He winked at Tommy.

Tommy said, "Fuck your mother."

Buzz put the muzzle to his head and pulled the trigger.
The hammer hit an empty chamber. Tommy wriggled
and squealed. Elmer said, "We got some questions."

Tommy wriggled and squealed. Tommy bleated
and squealed. Tommy said, "Okay, okay, okay."

Elmer said, "You dropped your address book New
Year's Eve. I guess you figured that out."

Buzz said, "There's some names we were curious about."

Elmer relit a cigar. "Let's start with Eddie Leng. The number to his slop chute was right there in your book."

Tommy coughed. He was bruised and contused. He talked, squeaky-frail.

"Eddie was an old pal of mine. He was a terp man. He was all tonged up, and he got snuffed in C-town on New Year's Eve. You're climbing the wrong tree if you think I did it. It was this Jap, Don Matsura. He had a terp still at his place in J-town, and he peddled terp to the Japs and the Chinks. He hung himself in the Lincoln Heights Jail, but Ace Kwan might have helped him."

Buzz said, "You're in the know, son."

Elmer fed Tommy a jolt of 151. Tommy gulped and coughed out residue. Elmer caught a residual spritz.

"What else you got on Eddie and Don Matsura? You got any KAs for them?"

Tommy coughed. "How's Cal Lunceford sound? He was this shitheel cop on the Alien Squad, but he's dead now. It was in the papers. Some ex-caped Jap shot him. Cal was Fifth Column, and he was in with Eddie and Don Matsura, plus a whole lot of other shitheels. Before you ask, I ain't got no proper names."

Elmer fed Tommy a jolt of 151. Tommy sucked it in and kept it down.

Buzz said, "St. Vibiana's. What's going on there? What's with you and Monsignor Joe Hayes?"

Tommy said, "Come on, don't make me say it."

Buzz said, "I'll say it for you. You and the monsignor travel the dirt road together. You're both Coughlinites and Jew-haters. Let me hazard a guess here. Being tight with priests got you juice with Dudley Smith."

The roof light haloed Tommy. He got this caged-mick look.

"I snitched for Dud. I'm pals with Dud's boy Huey Cressmeyer. I ran wets for Carlos Madrano, so you could say I been around and know some people you might be interested in. Dud visited me in Quentin, last November. I put the squeeze on him, which I shouldn't have done. Dud put your cracker pal, Mike the B., and Dick the C. on me, but I got away, because your cracker pal here didn't have the stones to shoot me."

Elmer brain-strained it. Tommy extorts Dudley. Let's call his shakedown wedge **this:**

Winter '39. That Nazi costume bash. Tommy gets a **biiiiiiiiiiig** eyeful. Dud slays that he-she bitch.

Buzz pat-patted Tommy. Good snitch dog. Let's give him a treat.

He snatched the 151 and fed him two jolts. Tommy coughed and joy-kicked the front seat.

Buzz said, "Let's get back to the address book. What's with that hot-box phone, by the **Herald.**"

Tommy said, "I was relaying gibberish calls. It was all dot-dash-dot, dog-cat-pig, code shit that means something if you know how to decode it. My call scripts got patched through to a bookie drop in Ensenada, and I got the scripts at my mail drop in L.A. It was all through what you call cutouts, so I never knew who was writing the scripts or giving the orders.

I got this sort-of tip from a Mex bookie who was forwarding the messages. He told me they were going to
this political guy and his sister in La Paz, but then he
clammed up."

Elmer said, "Come on, there's got to be more there."

Tommy coughed. "Okay, okay, okay. The bookie
guy zipped it, but I extrapolated some shit, because
Fifth Column's Fifth Column, and it's all one big
sort-of-happy family, which sure loves to talk. I know
Deutsches Haus guys, guys with the Mex Staties, and
guys from that nutso 46th Street place. I know **things**
just as good as I know all these guys. I know Dud
killed Carlos Madrano, I know there were some sub-
berth killings in Baja, and it was all part of a play to
pass Japs off as Chinks, and—"

Elmer cut in. "Eddie Leng was tight with a
Chinatown doctor named Lin Chung. You're a guy
who knows guys, so I'm wondering if you know him."

Tommy smirked. "I know Lin. Everybody knows
Lin, including a notable dead guy named Eddie Leng,
who don't know him no more."

Buzz poked him. "Don't string this out. Finish
whatever it is that you got to say."

Tommy resmirked. "Okay, okay, okay. Eddie was
tight with Lin, and Lin was tight with these rich
white guys who were behind that first sub landing.
Eddie introduced me to Lin, and Lin said the **second**
landing was the work of a left-wing/right-wing alliance, and they were setting up some kind of postwar

reconciliation deal. They're pulling all sorts of evil shit in the here and now, but they intend to make themselves look good by exposing it after this war is over."

Elmer brain-braced it. "Was Dud embroiled in any of this?"

Tommy laughed. "**Nein** to that. Dud leans Fifth Column, but it's just a cocktease. He loves Nazi threads and regalia, but he ain't no saboteur. He's just some kind of fetishist."

Buzz said, "Let's revisit the klub**haus.**"

Tommy said, "Goody. That sounds like kicks."

Elmer said, "Link Rockwell. Them smut pix he planned to send from his mail drop to yours."

Buzz flashed the key pix. Elmer shot good camera dupes. You've got two women. One's white, one's Mex. There's that klub**haus** backdrop.

Tommy shrugged. "If you're asking me who the two janes are, I don't know. They're just jazz-club chippies out for distraction."

Elmer said, "We're here, and we're all ears. Give us some more on the klub**haus.**"

Tommy said, "I'm parched. Give me another nip first."

Buzz grabbed his hair and pulled his head back. It stretched his mouth wide. Buzz juked in the juice.

Tommy gargled it and kept it down. Buzz wiped his hand pomade-free. Tommy's mouth snapped shut. He went electrizied. He looked sloshed, slammed, and slathered to shit.

"I like this stuff you're slipping me. It makes me want to hot-prowl and commit some swell misdeeds."

Elmer said, "The klub**haus.** Let's get back to that."

Tommy squirmed. He was cuffed tight. Steel ratchets gouged his wrists. The evil punk bloodied up the backseat.

"The smut pix were just some Link Rockwell deal. Beyond that, the klub**haus** was just this place where anything goes."

Elmer gnawed his cigar. "Our lab guy found jizz stains and fecal matter on an upstairs bed. That reads 'queer shit' to me."

Tommy went **C'est la vie.** "I hid out at the klub**haus** for a week, after you blew that stakeout on me. Okay, I knew Wendell Rice and Georgie Kapek, but just to say hi to. I knew they were cops, and I knew they were Fifth Column, but then so's everybody else in the exalted Thomas Malcolm Glennon's world."

Buzz sighed. "The 'queer shit,' Tommy."

Elmer sighed. "Chop, chop, you pervert. It'd delight me to put some hurt on you."

Tommy yawned. It was I'm-so-bored stagy. Elmer bitch-slapped him. Tommy licked blood off his lips and rebounded quick.

"Okay, 'queer shit,' a topic dear to my heart. I didn't really **know** Rice and Kapek, but I knew they were afraid of this queer kid who hung out on the jazz strip and brought boys to the klub**haus** for some pokey-pokey. He was a blondie kid, sort of tall, maybe some kind of musician, and he was pals with a crazy

Jap that Rice and Kapek busted, but the Jap made habeas and got himself sprung. Now, Mr. Jap was a sword man. Rice and Kapek popped him with this big blood-caked sword, and after he waltzed, he became a sure-as-shit klub**haus** regular. He used to kill chickens for all these slop chutes in J-town, and he licked the blood off the swords that he used."

Elmer brained-snagged it. He witnessed that log-in. Rice and Kapek/the blood-flecked sword. This could be good. Paperwork might still exist.

Buzz said, "The **haus,** Tommy. Keep going there."

"What's to tell? It was too crazy for me, so I vamoosed."

Elmer said, "What did you squeeze Dudley with?"

Tommy said, "Brace yourself, daddy. Dud snuffed a drag boy at a party. Huey C. and I witnessed the whole thing. I'll give you my long-held opinion on that, for what it's worth. Dud knew that she was really a he, and he was **looooving** the encounter until something flipped his switch."

Elmer looked at Buzz. Buzz looked at Elmer. They both orbed Tommy G.

Buzz said, "Kyoho Hanamaka? Ring a bell?"

Tommy said, "Nix."

Elmer said, "José Vasquez-Cruz. His aka's Jorge Villareal-Caiz."

Tommy said, "Ixnay."

Buzz said, "Archie Archuleta?"

Tommy said, "I knew that **pendejo.** I used to see him at the klub**haus,** and from what I heard, he was a notable J-town and C-town crawler. He was cinched up with more strange-o's than you can count, and he veered Fifth Column right. He knew Mex girls who'd pose for smut pictures, and he knew Sinarquista heist guys and set them up with Rice and Kapek, to buy these guns they'd confiscated from these Japs they'd tossed in the clink. RIP, Archie. He was a white man, as much as any Mex can be."

Elmer soft-lobbed it. "This Commie girl, Jean Staley. How come she's in your book?"

Tommy drop-jawed that one. He's gone on 151. He's all stage ham now.

"Jean's been known to **play** Red, but she's been a Federal snitch since the ice age. She was in a CP cell back in the '30s, while she was meanwhile tattling to her handler and running shakedowns on movie people and her fellow Reds with this yid, Meyer Gelb. Meyer's a ganef and a penguin-fucker from way back. There's nothing he ain't done or considered doing. He got Jean shaking down these Trotskyites he hates, because he's a Stalinist, and these Red-faction humps hate other Red-faction humps more than they hate confirmed fascistos like yours truly."

Elmer digested it. Tommy credentialed it. Jean, baby—say it ain't so.

Buzz wiggled the 151. "Bottoms up, Tommy."

Stage Ham Tommy. He goes all rubber-faced.

"I've heard **that** one before, but I have to add that I'm the brunser, more than the punk."

Elmer cringed. Buzz bottle-fed Tommy. The stage

ham smacked his lips. The backseat socked in heat. Elmer rolled down his window and breathed deep.

"What's Meyer got Jean doing now? There's a picture of you three at the Club Alabam, just last week."

"Souvenir pictures are the blahs, hoss. They send girl photographers around, and Meyer always succumbs."

"I asked you a question, fucker."

"Okay, okay, okay. The answer is shakedowns. That's the Jean and Meyer bailiwick. This time, they're putting it to these left-wing musicians that got so-called rescued from **der Führer**'s clutches, to make the so-called rescuers look good when Uncle Sambo wins the war. You sound me, muchacho? Meyer's setting Jean up to extort them and recruit them as informants."

One more time. Jean, darling—say it ain't so.

"How dirty is she?"

"She's a mud hen from way back, hoss. She goes back to that Kraut hump, Fritz Eckelkamp. Does **that** name ring a bell? He ex-caped from that gold train that got robbed back when I was still in pigtails. Jean got around and **gets** around, and she sure plays Jezebel in the process. She was married to a pathetic geek named Ralph D. Barr. Ralphie set fires and yanked his crank when the fire engines showed up. He was a suspect for that big Griffith Park fire, but he was a small-blaze specialist and got absolved. Jean told me he was hung microscopic."

Elmer looked at Buzz. Buzz looked at Elmer. They both orbed Tommy G.

Buzz said, " 'Fifth Column's Fifth Column.' We get that. Past that, have you got a specific source for what you been feeding us?"

Tommy made horn-call sounds. Tommy blew a **loooooong** fanfare.

"Hold your hats, race fans. We're at Del Mar, and my #1 nag is at the gate. He's my #1 source for Fifth Column scuttlebutt, and he's none other than your ex-chief, James Edgar Davis."

Buzz looked at Elmer. Elmer looked at Buzz. They both orbed Tommy G.

Buzz sighed. "It's getting late. Tell us something we don't know."

Tommy blew a long fanfare. He wet his pants for such shtick.

"All in all, I've raped twenty-three women. I killed two bags in Frisco and a thin cooze at a truck stop in Visalia. I killed an old Jew lady in South Beach and did a necrophile job on her. I made like Dracula and drank her blood, and I yanked out all her gold teeth."

Buzz grabbed a loose seat cushion. He clamped it over Tommy's head and pulled his belt piece. He pumped a full clip into Tommy's face. Blood and cushion stuffing exploded. Shots tore out the trunk ledge and ricocheted. A skull chunk hit Elmer's cheek.

Buzz said, "I got me an old granny who's one-sixty-fourth Jewish. I don't condone that sort of grief."

91

(SANTO TOMAS, 12:00 P.M., 3/9/42)

The Wolf growled and paced. This bluffside spot vexed him. Swooping gulls and salt spray. A dirt parking lot. Tables perched close to a cliff.

Dudley sat outside. The spot induced vertigo. He'd called the meet. Salvy suggested this cantina. They served Baja's best **mariscos.**

Mucho carros jammed up the lot. The Mex Army favored El Dumpo. It was their place. They ignored the rats clustered by the kitchen. The cantina was subramshackle. Army staff cars brodied on loose dirt. Dudley ate exhaust fumes.

He sipped lukewarm beer. His table overlooked the lot and a hundred-foot drop. Mex soldiers chortled all around him.

He was furious. He conceded Fear. Bill Parker enlisted Thad Brown and applied a vise squeeze. Parker levied his no-false-solution decree and sandbagged Jack Horrall. He violated the Smith-Parker truce. He slammed Jack H. and offered up an irresistible concession. Parker said he'd erase every bug and tap recording now in Fed custody. This action would spark courtroom acquittals for Jack and his gang. Fletch Bowron, Ray Pinker, the Jamie kid. All the lesser defendants. **Poof!**—all would go free.

Parker pulled Mike and Dick off the klub**haus**
job. Pinker stymied Jack H. there. Elmer Jackson
put Mike in Queen of Angels. Call-Me-Jack nixed
reprisals. Parker has adroitly nullified one Dudley
Liam Smith.

Salvy was late. Dudley chain-smoked. He conceded
Fear. Parker's machinations depleted his ranks. They
left him with Hideo Ashida, **todos.**

Hideo was newly war-hired. He was partnered up
with lackluster Lee Blanchard. Jackson and Meeks
were off to hell and gone. Their partnership spelled
chaos. Hideo came through and supplied hope.

Brilliant lad. He turned up an old Arson Squad accelerant swatch. It derived from the Griffith Park fire.
He compared it to a klub**haus**-blaze swatch and got
a match. The match linked two crimes spaced nearly
nine years apart.

Dudley chain-smoked. He conceded Fear. The Wolf
bodyguarded him. Constanza returned to La Paz.
He missed her. His union with Claire had imploded.
Beth was poised in retreat. The promotion-party incident unhinged her. Claire was up in L.A. She was
prowling for new lovers there. He **knew** that.

Salvy was late. More Mex **soldaten** arrived. They
drove custom-fitted U.S. confiscations. Special tail-
pipes. Hood-mounted BARs. Bleeding-saint and
snarling-panther paint jobs.

They stomped three abreast. They entered the cantina and commandeered outside tables. They pinched

waitresses and demanded fast service. "Neutral" Mexico. Soon to be Allied-allied. Axis in temperament and aesthetic.

Salvy showed. A car appeared, he appeared, **el carro** peeled off. Salvy employed Greenshirt flunkies. They chauffeured him and groomed him. He appeared more than arrived.

Dudley stood up. They exchanged **abrazos.** Hail-fellows-well-met. Men's men, **por vida.** Two damn good backslappers.

"My dear comrade."

"**Mi** mayor. Will you be content to stop there, or do you wish to rise to four-star general?"

Dudley laughed. "I'm a police sergeant in my heart and soul, lad. I was one when this war started, and I'll be one when this war ends."

Salvy laughed. "You are an entrepreneur, a strategist, and a treasure seeker. I am humbled and gratified by your generous pledge to our shared cause."

Dudley poured two beers. They clicked tankards and sat down at the table. The Wolf trembled. That cliffside drop loomed.

Dudley lit a cigarette. "I bear discomfiting news from Los Angeles. My errant police colleagues are determined to round up a large number of young Mexican men, who they believe may have frequented that damnable klub**haus.** I'm afraid that quite a few stout Sinarquista lads may fall into this melee. My colleagues are looking for guns, sold out of the klub**haus.** You had assured me our East L.A. lads were not klub**haus** affiliates, but I need you to convincingly reassure me now."

Salvy lit a cigarette. "Yes, of course. I am grateful to have been informed of this, and you have my most sincere reassurance."

Dudley sipped beer. It was warm. The Wolf prowled adjacent tables. He sniffed raucous Mex soldiers and growled.

"I require another assurance, as well. I proffer this request couched in my utmost respect for you as a comrade and a man. I have become involved with Constanza Lazaro-Schmidt, and I have been informed that you are her occasional lover. I request that you terminate this relationship, and that you sever all contact with Constanza immediately."

Salvy blinked once. Dudley blinked once. Salvy stubbed out his cigarette. His veins pulsed.

"You have my assurance, but I will issue a warning along with it. Constanza and her brother are shamefully as one, and they are more utilitarian than ideologically fascist. I have given you my pledge and additional caveat, and we need not mention this matter again. I commend you for not threatening me and blowing this trivial request out of proportion."

The Wolf growled. He smelled Salvy's rage. He saw his pulsing veins and incipient tremors. Salvy checked his wristwatch. He went **uno, dos, tres**— and winked.

The cantina exploded. It went up, just like that. It's

a fireball. There's blasted-out glass and wood shrapnel. There's smoke, flames, and palm trees ignited. Detonation equals earthquake.

The outside **soldaten** ran for their cars. They trampled civilians and kicked over tables and chairs. They tumbled into their taco wagons and slammed bumpers, en masse. It was straight from the Keystone Kops.

The inside **soldaten** ran outside. They stumbled over scorched timber and screamed. Twelve men, **todos.** They pitched crazy-spastic, in flames.

Salvy said, "Priest-killers and nun-rapers. Redshirts of the Calles regime."

A car pulled off the coast road and skidded into the lot. Four Greenshirts piled out. They held sawed-off shotguns. They dodged flying debris and ran up to the burning men.

They pumped buckshot into them. They severed limbs on fire. A burning man staggered and knocked over tables. Dudley pulled his piece and fumbled it. The burning man got close. Salvy pulled his piece and shot him dead.

92

(LOS ANGELES, 2:00 P.M., 3/9/42)

Annie Staples arrived in her work clothes. That meant tartan skirt, crewneck sweater, and saddle shoes. She was Elmer and Brenda's college girl, and pitched her charms to men thrice her age. Brenda set up the lunch and urged Annie to be forthcoming. We met at Jack's Drive-in on the Strip.

Annie was blond. She was tall, leggy, and busty, and hailed from Coeur d'Alene, Idaho. We dined in my car. Monarch burgers and pineapple malts. I understood Annie's allure. She was all college girl. Bill Parker would flip for her.

We made small talk during our lunch; Annie guilelessly dished on her tricks and told me she once spent a cozy weekend with the allegedly straitlaced Thad Brown. She tricked with Wendell Willkie during the '40 campaign, and said he was a sweetheart. Our carhop skated by and removed our trays; we lit cigarettes and settled down to business.

I said, "Brenda saw you with Sid Hudgens at Tom Breneman's. I sense a story there."

Annie blew smoke rings. "Well, I'd call it a complicated story."

"Those are my favorite kind."

"Brenda told me you know some of it already, because you know about her trick spots, and you're such good friends with Elmer Jackson. She said you know Sid, and you've met Ed Satterlee, and they're part of the story, too."

I said, "L.A.'s a small town for a big town, and I've been ensnared with the PD for a good three years. You tend to run into men like that, in the course of things."

Annie thought that was a hoot. She doused her cigarette in her coffee cup and chuckled a bit. She had changeling's eyes. One veered blue, one veered green.

"You tend to run into men like that, and I tend to sleep with them. You could say I ran a parlay with Elmer, Sid, and Ed, and Ed was the one who put me to good use, beyond the old you know what."

Elmer and I gabbed at Hideo Ashida's swearing-in party. He spilled the beans. I told Annie that I was up to speed on her shakedown gig with Ed the Fed. The mark was Dr. Saul Lesnick. Elmer filled in for Ed behind the camera one night. He caught wind of Annie pumping Dr. Saul. It got him thinking—and Elmer thinks impulsively, at best.

Annie said, "Well, sister, you've got most of it."

"Ed was interested in sexual and political dirt, wasn't he? Mr. Hoover gets his jollies that way, and you never know when dirt like that can be useful."

"Yep. That's the gist of it."

"Confirm this, will you? That first night Elmer ran

the camera. Dr. Saul was discussing his patient Claire De Haven."

"That's right. Claire, the rich-girl Communist. Her and her cop lover, down in Mexico. Claire said you tried to kill the lover, but old Saul didn't believe it. The upshot is that Elmer heard all this, and he offered me money to wear a microphone and go to Otto Klemperer's parties, and ratchet up my pump job on old Saul."

I said, "Because Elmer wanted to keep tabs on Dr. Saul, and Claire always attended those parties, and Elmer was curious about what she might say regarding Dudley Smith."

Annie smiled. She was truly big-girl lovely. Call her Ingrid Bergman, with ten thousand chromosomes askew.

"Elmer was very curious about Mr. Smith, and I think he's got some kind of vendetta going against him. I told Elmer a little tale that old Saul told me, where Mr. Smith beat up Orson Welles, because he had a sort-of deal going with Claire. Elmer said he'd like to wire me up to pump Mr. Welles, which I'd do for free, if Mr. Welles lost some weight."

Brenda called Elmer "shakedown happy." This jibed with something I knew about him. He was a canny judge of character and voyeuristically inclined.

Annie ordered a second malt. Brenda thought she looked best on the sturdy-milkmaid side. I asked her how Sid Hudgens played into all this. She told me

Sid was shakedown happy, all on his own, apart from Elmer and Ed. Join the crowd, Sid. Annie Staples knows from shakedowns.

Sid wanted dirt on film folk and politicians. He was putting out a sub-rosa scandal sheet and wanted dirt too hot for the **Herald.** He tried to recruit Annie as his very own Venus flytrap. She was still considering his pitch.

Annie's second malt arrived; she dunked her straw and siphoned the goo in a wink. Annie played a cameo role in Joan Conville's diary. Joan observed her futzing with her microphone outside Otto Klemperer's guesthouse. I teethed on the nexus of the whole three-case megillah. It was Meyer Gelb's cell and how the four surviving members still hovered in plain sight. The Cell. What old Saul might know and might have written down.

And Annie Staples was sitting right beside me. She's a one-woman nexus. In the market for a shakedown shill? Annie's the tops.

She had malted-milk residue on her upper lip. She's about five-foot-ten and built like a discus queen. I grabbed my napkin and daubed the goo off her lip. Annie likes people to touch her.

"I know that old Saul is a Federal informant, and that he reports to Ed Satterlee. Do you know if his informant duty went back to the early '30s, when he was in a Communist cell?"

"No, I don't think so. I think he signed on with Ed

more recently than that, because his daughter was in prison for vehicular manslaughter, and Ed used that as a wedge to turn Saul out as his fink."

I lit a cigarette and thought about Elmer. He'd gone AWOL from Crash Squad briefings; Lee told me this.

Annie said, "Penny for your thoughts."

I said, "I was thinking about Elmer."

"What's there to think about? I'm in love with him, and he's in love with you."

I laughed. Elmer and his dead brother, Elmer and his shakedown girl. Early wartime L.A. The pursuit of the big main chance.

Annie jiggled the charms on her charm bracelet. Little dogs, doghouses, arrows piercing hearts.

"But Ed did have a snitch in Saul's cell back then, and Saul and Andrea didn't know it. It was this woman named Jean, and she was no kind of Red. Ed dished her to me. He said she's still in cahoots with this Meyer guy who ran the cell, even though the cell's dissolved. Jean used to be married to some crazy firebug. This Meyer guy's going to get her to shake down these exile musicians."

I said, "I'll pay you a thousand dollars to make wax impressions of all the keys that Dr. Saul carries."

Annie detached a little dog charm. She placed it in my hand and gave me a squeeze. She said, "For luck, sweetie. Because where you're going with all this, you're sure going to need it."

"Annie, will you—"

"Sure, sweetie. It's not like I've never caught him with his trousers off."

93

(LOS ANGELES, 3:00 P.M., 3/10/42)

Army brass. War-hire cop now. His luck holds. He's serendipitous and fuckstruck.

The Hollenbeck muster room was cluttered and cramped. The reduced Crash Squad was all ears.

The boys straddled chairs and faced Thad Brown. Ashida, Elmer Jackson, Buzz Meeks. Lee Blanchard and Bill Parker. Cigarette and cigar smoke/one big iron lung.

Ashida side-eyed Elmer J. Elmer's outburst still rankled. Jap, Jap, Jap. Elmer stooped to **that.**

Thad said, "We've got nine male Mexicans on our roust list. We need to determine whether or not Rice and Kapek sold them Japanese-confiscated guns. They filed no gun-confiscation paperwork, so we've got no comparison sheets to check against any guns we bag tonight. What we **do** have is the threat of illegal possession of firearms and possibly related armed robberies, to use as a wedge to extract information on our homicides."

Blanchard said, "Say it, boss. 211 pops will make us look good, if this whole job dips south."

Elmer said, "Blanchard's a pessimist."

Buzz said, "Blanchard's a Bolshevik."

Thad rolled his eyes. "We've got three squads tonight. There's Captain Parker and me, Jackson and Meeks, Blanchard and Ashida. On a related topic, that Navy chump Link Rockwell's in custody down in Florida. A naval district judge should be issuing an extradition ruling soon."

Elmer said, "Anchors away, whipdick."

Buzz said, "Link's tight as ticks with the Reverend Mimms. They're the world's foremost salt-and-pepper act."

Parker said, "We're going out tonight, and we muster here at 1930 hours. Shotguns, riot gear, and one paddy wagon per squad. Go home and sack out. We'll be stretching these humps all night."

Buzz whistled. Blanchard whooped. They dogged Parker and Brown out to the hallway. Elmer kicked the door shut. Ashida gulped. Elmer pulled his chair up close.

"I'm sorry, Hideo. I shouldn't have said what I said. It was plain wrong of me, and I apologize."

Ashida stuck his hand out. Elmer bone-crushed it. Ashida mock-winced.

"I understand. You've been seething since you met with Kay, and I more than warranted your outburst."

Elmer displayed an envelope. He waved it and pulled out a sheet of soft-bond paper. Ashida saw faint spots. They resembled pinpricks dipped in soluble oil.

"Where did you get this?"

"At Bev's Switchboard. You know, that loopy mail drop in West Hollywood. It was in Meyer Gelb's mail-holding file, and it was addressed to a PO box in La Paz, down in Baja."

Ashida touched the sheet. It was high-rag content and top-grade absorbent.

"It's microdots. We'll need a microdot camera to bring up the text."

Elmer whooped. "I knew that was it. I saw a piece about that shit in **Reader's Digest.**"

Mail drops. Meyer Gelb. The dicey Lazaro-Schmidts hailed from La Paz.

"Hideo's in a trance. He's hanging out the 'Genius at Work' sign."

Ashida laughed. "We can't bring up the text without that camera."

"What about a plain old microscope? Could that get us in close?"

Ashida said, "Meet me at the lab. I'll see what I can do."

They two-carred over and hooked up at six. The day-shift chemists had clocked out. Ashida locked them in. Elmer jammed a chair under the doorknob.

Ashida scissor-cut the paper and shaped three equal strips. Elmer watchdogged the process. Ashida rigged a microscope and slide-clamped swatch #1. He dialed down to maximum range. Faint ink blurs appeared.

He ran swatch #2 and swatch #3. He got eight more ink blurs.

Ashida shook his head. Elmer went **Shit.** Ashida placed the strips back in the envelope and resealed it.

"There's something you should know, Elmer."

"Let me guess. You can't withhold this here lead from Dudley, like you withheld Kay's spiel on Joan Conville's diary."

Ashida balled his fists and fumed. He despised that mannerism. It made him look eff—

Elmer woofed him. "You're on the fence about Dud now, aren't you? I'm not all that surprised. Kay wouldn't have clued you in if she thought you'd tattle to him. And here's something you might want to consider. Maybe Kay's smarter than you are, and maybe she's cooking up something good."

Ashida stomped one foot. Elmer haw-hawed. Ashida walked to the mail slot and dropped the envelope in.

"It's out of our hands now. I might be on the fence, and I might not be. You've got the box number in La Paz as a lead, and that's it."

Elmer stomped one foot. He did good impersonations. He mimed effete rage, **c'est bon.**

"You're trumping me, Hideo. I'm coming out second-best here."

Ashida walked to his locker. He turned away from

Elmer and unlocked it. He grabbed the gold bar off the top shelf.

Robbery swag. Thirty-three pounds plus. Worth twenty grand, U.S.

He turned and faced Elmer. Come, let us adore it. He held it out, worship me–style.

Elmer trembled and dropped his cigar. He lurched and bumped a glassware shelf. A glass beaker toppled and shattered on the floor.

Ashida said, "Take it. Your brother died for this, and I don't want it anymore."

Elmer picked up his cigar. He looked electrified. He dredged half a voice.

"What do you want?"

"A clean solve on the klub**haus** job."

Elmer kicked glass under a work desk. He brushed ash off his suit coat and went **Nyet.** Ashida placed the bar back in his locker. He tossed a lab rag over it. Gold as holy sacrament. Men died for this.

"Tell me how you turned the lead on Bev's Switchboard."

Elmer said, "It commenced with Jean Staley. I braced her, and she jobbed me out of my socks. We had a nifty first date, and then she plain vanished. I started getting postcards from U.S. 66, but Jean was really here in L.A. Bev's Switchboard was stiffing the cards and jobbing up the postal cancellations."

D. L. Smith on E. V. Jackson. He's half smart here and there. He trips on his dick otherwise.

"I need those cards. They may contain microdots, inserted between the inside and outside pieces of cardboard. I'll take them back to Ensenada with me. I might be able to locate a microdot camera there."

Elmer said, "Okay, boss."

Ashida said, "I'll try to work out a truce for you and Buzz. Keep the bar. I'm sure Dudley will accept that concession."

"All I want is a fair shot at whoever killed my brother. It has to be a plain murder. The gold's just a way in to figure all that out."

Ashida bowed. "I lost my taste for the gold when Joan died. All I want is a shot at a solve."

Elmer relit his cigar. Lab fumes and hot ash. Ignition, combustion, explos—

"I got no beef with that. You're Dud's boy, so you handle everything pertaining to that fucker."

"That's fine, but he'll want to know how you know whatever you know, and we have to keep Kay and Joan's diary out of it."

Elmer said, "You're right, boss."

Ashida said, "You should know something. You should know that I'll reveal whatever I learn at the sweep tonight to Dudley."

Elmer said, "You should know that fence-sitters tend to teeter and fall. You should also know that Buzz and me did Dud quite the solid. You know our missing chum, Tommy Glennon? Buzz and me braced him and killed him."

Ashida teetered. The fence wobbled. The floor dipped.

"What did he tell you?"

"My lips are sealed, boss."

94

(LOS ANGELES, 8:30 P.M., 3/10/42)

The boys are back in town.

El Towno said it best. Boyle Heights was T.J. North. It was tacofied territory. It was one big beaner bin.

Hola, fuckers. Here comes trouble. All you wicked Juans and dirty Diegos gonna get shit-kicked tonight.

Elmer and Buzz comprised Two Squad. They wore tin hats and lugged cut-down shotguns. They packed grand-jury subpoenas. Said paperwork was stamped "Alien Sedition Act."

A paddy wagon trailed them. Two Squad worked the flats upside Lincoln Heights. One Squad and Three Squad were off elsewhere. Three squads, three turf quadrants, three righteous roust lists.

Three three-man rousts. That standardized the sweep. Elmer and Buzz caught three doozies. Chuy **"El Perro"** Mendez. Frankie **"El Cabrón"** Carbajal. Carlos **"El Cucaracha"** Calderon. The Dog, the

Fucker, the Cockroach. Suspected 211 men and right-wing nuts. The flats **gots** to swing tonight.

Two Squad worked north-northeast. Los cholos lived in a tight radius. Elmer and Buzz walked. The paddy wagon chugged in low gear. Elmer was fitfully fucked-up and dizzy distracted.

It was Ashida. It was Ashida's microdot play. It was Ashida's gold bar. It was Ashida's implied double-cross of one Dudley Smith. It was Tommy Glennon, to boot.

Buzz snuffed Tommy, impromptu. That didn't faze him. They dumped Tommy in the waste dump and let the swamp beasts eat him up. That was likewise okay. But Tommy bleated a klub**haus** lead in his pickled prelude to death.

This Jap. Rice and Kapek popped him. He was a "sword man." He had this queer white-boy pal. The white boy might be a musician. The white boy frequented the jazz strip and poked boys at the **haus.** The Jap sword-sliced chickens at J-town slop chutes. The Jap licked blood off the swords that he used. The Jap made habeas and was on the loose somewhere.

Elmer teethed the lead. He was fungooed and fucked-up. He was ditzy and diverted. The shotgun weighed ten tons. The tin hat banged his head. He walked the flats, distracted.

He'd witnessed a property log-in. It was late January. Kapek and Rice talked up a sword man. The sword man licked blood off his swords. It disgusted Kapek and Rice.

He checked Alien Squad roust sheets last night. Guess what? No fucking sword man was listed. Guess what? No Jap swords were property-logged during that time span. Guess what? No chicken-killing sword lickers were tagged in the MO file.

He'd read the initial log-in report. He recalled that much. He had the sword man's name tucked someplace unconscious. Rice and Kapek pulled his paperwork. That had to be it.

The sword man. Hideo Ashida. Cause for ditzy distraction.

He got Jean Staley's postcards to Ashida. Army SIS just might possess a microdot camera. Him and Ashida worked out a cover story. It explained how he knew all this three-case hullabaloo. It served to cloak his ass with Dudley Smith.

Dig **this:**

He was at Joan Conville's place. He was hot to pour Big Joan the pork. Joan was terped up. She was burbling, out of her gourd. She kept mumbling shit about the gold and her diary. He found the diary and read it. He learned everything. He put the diary back where he found it. He bid Joan adieu and waltzed off, unlaid.

The story played **goooooood.** It jibed with Ashida's lie to Dudley. Joan burned the diary. She was suicide-fevered. Ashida found that burned-page mess.

The rousts proceeded. The Cockroach went easy. Papa Roach fumed. Mama Roach wrung rosary beads and went **Aaay, caramba.** The Cockroach submitted to cuffing and shackling. Elmer gave him a cigar. They hoisted him into the paddy wagon and split for **El Casa de Perro.**

The Dog went easy. Mama and Papa Dog whimpered and retreated. El Perro wore a Sir Guy shirt and slit-bottom khakis. He submitted to cuffing and shackling. Buzz gave him a cigar. They hoisted him into the paddy wagon and hit **El Casa de Cabrón.**

The Fucker went rough. He tried to run and tripped over a lamp stand. Buzz grabbed his hair and smashed his face on the floor. Elmer cuffed him. Buzz shackled him. Mama and Papa Fucker evinced boredom. They were blitzed on white port and lemon juice.

The extraction went rough. The Fucker flailed and kicked. They tossed him in the paddy wagon. Elmer sat on his legs. Buzz sat on his head. The Dog and Cockroach haw-hawed. The driver cop hauled for Hollenbeck Station.

Four bluesuits met them. They grappled the punks through the jail door and got them ensconced. The Dog and the Cockroach went in the drunk tank. One Squad's and Three Squad's geeks were already there. That made eight geeks, all in all. They whooped and demanded their rights. A colored trusty slapped them around.

The blues dumped the Fucker in sweatbox #2.

Buzz recuffed him to a chair. **Oooh**—what's that on his right hand?

It's a coiled-snake tattoo. It's **El Symbol** of Sinarquismo. This mandates some thought.

Elmer ducked down to the file room. He tapped the **C** cabinet and pulled Frankie Carbajal's sheet. **Aaay, caramba.** Frankie peddled maryjane, Frankie 211'd bodegas, Frankie whipped his **chorizo** out on women.

That was it. Just one file sheet. No Fed routing stamps. No subversive rebop noted. No KA list attached.

Elmer walked back to the sweatbox. Frankie was trussed to that chair. Buzz rode a matching chair and skunk-eyed him. Elmer pulled a chair close and relit a cigar.

Buzz lit a cigar. He got it going good. The sweatbox fumed up. Frankie cough-coughed.

"You guys are sadistic. I've got asthma. Those cigars aren't doing me any good."

Buzz said, "Did you catch Frankie's tattoo?"

Elmer nodded. "We got that to consider, along with the fact that Frankie's a whipout man."

Buzz said, "I'll bet he habituates schoolyards and whips it out on little kids."

Frankie said, "I whipped it out on Eleanor Roosevelt. She was serving cookies and punch at some crippled kid's gig in the Heights."

Elmer said, "A whipout man's a whipout man. I don't see no distinction between kids and our swell First Lady."

Frankie squirmed in his chair. He looked consumptive. He sported a hairnet conk. His zoot pants rode up to his sternum.

"I whipped it out on Ann Sheridan and the Liltin' Martha Tilton. They were at this war-bond drive on Hollywood Boulevard. I escaped into the crowd and whipped it out on a B-girl at the Firefly Lounge."

Elmer sighed. Buzz sighed. Elmer uncuffed and unshackled Frankie. Buzz slipped on sap gloves.

"Your whipout escapades don't interest us. Your tattoo interests us. There's some names we'd like to run by you. There's a certain spot on East 46th Street that we'd sure like to discuss. Fifth Column shit's a hot topic these days, and we'd sure like to hear your thoughts about that."

Frankie rubbed his wrists and ankles. Frankie said, **"Viva Sinarquismo. Chinga tu madre."**

Buzz roundhoused him. One slap/ten-ounce palm weights/see Frankie fly. El Whipout Man whipped off the chair and hit the floor flat on his back. Buzz stepped on his neck and pinned him supine. Elmer read him the riot act.

"Here's where you determine your fate, son. Prompt answers get you a cozy cell and a shot at a kickout. Horseshit and jive gets you a bunk in the fruit tank at Lincoln Heights. Gene 'the Mean Queen' Kefalvian's in custody there. He goes for Mexican shrimps like you."

Buzz released his foot. Frankie coughed and rubbed his neck. Elmer helped him up and sat him back in his chair. Buzz slipped off his sap gloves and pat-patted him on the head.

"I'll take the cozy cell and the shot at a kick-out. I saw Gene the Queen fight Chuco Ortiz at the Olympic. He put a drubbing on him."

Buzz said, "Señor Carbajal's no dummy."

Elmer said, "Señor Carbajal's on the Fed's subversive list, or he wouldn't have been on our roust list. He's got no routing tags on his green sheet here, so I'm guessing that all the Feds have got on him is his membership in them goofy Sinarquistas."

Buzz cracked his knuckles. "Let's see what Señor Carbajal has to say about that."

Frankie flashed three fingers downward. It was Klan kode. It meant KKK. This beat-on beaner aped redneck rubes.

"I say '¡**Viva Sinarquismo!**' I say, '¡**Sinarquismo por vida!**'"

Buzz relit his cigar. "Let's note Frankie's point, and get to them names."

Elmer said, "Let's start with Archie Archuleta. He's Mex, and he hails from Frankie's neck of the woods."

Frankie snapped his suspenders. "I knew Archie. He's dead now, and he got snuffed along with two cops—which is sure as shit what all this is about."

Buzz said, "Frankie's quick on the uptake."

Elmer said, "Don't stop there, Frankie."

Frankie fluffed out his conk. It glistened with Lucky Tiger pomade.

"Archie recruited Mexican boys for **La Causa.** He

pulled them out of the CYO at St. Vibiana's. This priest named Joe Hayes ran the St. Vib's chapter. He was a Coughlinite and a big Sinarquista contributor, not to mention a big sissy. He was poking this crazy Tommy Glennon guy up the **culo.** I didn't know Tommy too good. He was just a face in the right-flank crowd."

Elmer said, "The klub**haus.** 46th, just east of Central. Wendell Rice, George Kapek, and a cop named Cal Lunceford."

Frankie shrugged. "I dropped in for visits. A bunch of my fellow Greenshirts did, and so what? I won't give up no active shirts, but I'll tell you I hardly knew Rice and Kapek, and Lunceford didn't show up there all that much. He was a keep-to-himself sort of guy. They all took the blood oath and joined **La Causa,** but they're dead now, so who cares?"

Elmer said, "Let's get this out of the way. We all know a Jap spy killed Lunceford, and you've got no goddamn idea who killed Rice, Kapek, and Archuleta."

Frankie said, **"Sí. Es la verdad, muchacho."**

Buzz slipped on his sap gloves. "Son, I don't like you telling us who or what you won't give up, and you trying to set the terms of this herc interrogation."

Frankie flashed the Klan sign. Frankie flexed his coiled-snake tattoo.

"I curse your syphilitic mama, Tex. I curse your white Protestant-oppressor ancestors going back six generations, and—"

Buzz roundhoused him. Teeth and gold bridgework flew. Ditto blood. Ditto gum flaps. Ditto a slice of his tongue.

Frankie pitched backward. The chair jerked loose of its struts. Frankie crashed into the wall. The chair toppled. Buzz balled his fists and cocked big left-rights.

Elmer jumped up and held him back. Elmer bear-hugged him and ran **Whoa now**'s. Buzz went limp and dropped his hands. Elmer hug-walked him out of the sweatbox and dumped him in the hall.

He slammed the door and threw the lock. Frankie gurgled blood and quaked abject. Elmer pulled off his suit coat and squatted beside him. He wadded the coat and passed it to Frankie. The little hump blotted his face.

Elmer hit the wall switch. The sweatbox went all dark. He got up close to Frankie. He touched him soft and whispered **this:**

You've got to talk/you've got to talk/you've got to talk. I won't let that Okie hurt you, if you talk to me.

Frankie gurgled and spit blood. His breath went asthmatic. Elmer baby-talked him. The sweatbox went eerie dark. Frankie caught some asthma breath and snitched **this:**

The Greenshirts fingered a sub attack. It was last month. The Japs lobbed the Ellsworth Oil Refinery. The shells went adios and pfft. Rice and

Kapek were muy Fifth Column. Catbox Cal, just as much. They sold Jap guns to the Greenshirts. The shirts got plans to commit 211s. La Causa needs the gelt. Catholic dinero fuels los Sinarquistas. They've got this initiation rite. You got to kill three priest-killers.

Salvy Abascal's El Führer. He's got kill lists of priest-killers and Reds. El Führer's got this Irish fool eating out of his hand. The fool's an Army major and an L.A. cop. They're smuggling "H" and wets. They're selling Baja Japs as slaves. The Irish guy's got his head up his ass. He don't know shit from shinola. Salvy's put Greenshirt plants in with the wets. Them fake wets are set to escape and pull sabotage.

It came out in stutters and gasps. The sweatbox was blackout dark and reeked of slobber and blood. Elmer cleaved close to Frankie. The little hump bled on him. The little hump gasped for breath and gasped **this:**

Archie the A. Call him "El Pimpo." He brought girls to the haus. There was this queer boy. He went to all the jazz clubs. He orchestrated the pervo shit at the haus. He had this Jap friend. The Perv of All Pervs. He sold curios. He ate raw chicken flesh. He sucked blood off samurai swords.

95

(LOS ANGELES, 11:00 P.M., 3/10/42)

Salvy said, "You seem fretful, Comrade."

Dudley lit a cigarette. He'd chained the whole pack in nothing flat.

"I could say the same about you, lad."

"Yes, but I am more high-strung to begin with. I have never possessed your most serene composure."

They slouched in Dudley's prowl sled. They'd parked up from Hollenbeck Station. They had a clear front-door view.

The sweep stood complete. They'd observed the haul-ins. Nine fish were now jailed. Salvy tagged three Sinarquistas. Miguel Santarolo, Frankie Carbajal, Mondo Díaz. Hard boys all. Salvy said they'd never roll and bleat.

Dudley chain-smoked. His throat felt raw. His nerves ran raw, besides. Hideo called him, pre-sweep. Hideo tattled an odd chat with Elmer Jackson.

Elmer tumbled to the three-case convergence. He wouldn't say how. He knew about the gold and fixated on the fire. A three-case principal must have killed his brother. Elmer believed it. Elmer vowed revenge.

It was unsettling. Hideo's punch line troubled him.

Elmer and Buzz Meeks killed Tommy Glennon. The act redeemed Elmer's New Year's Eve fuckup. The act proclaimed a vow of fealty to one D. L. Smith. Hideo foisted his gold bar on Elmer. Hideo urged him to confess to Father D. L. Smith. The gold gift seems justified. How Elmer tumbled remains perplexing.

Salvy lit a cigarette. "You needn't concern yourself as to what my boys might reveal about our plans. They know very little, and I'll secure them a lawyer and post bail in the morning. This klub**haus** mess will subside and resolve at some point, and I'll keep my boys sequestered until then."

Elmer Jackson showed. He walked out of the station. He lit a cigar and stretched loose some kinks. He looked disheveled. He was coatless and sported a badly stained white shirt.

Dudley beeped the horn and flashed his high beams. Elmer looked over. Dudley got out and stood on the sidewalk. Elmer ambled on up.

He leaned against a streetlamp. It backlit him nicely. The stains were wet blood.

Elmer said, "Forgive my appearance, Dud. A suspect got between me and Buzz."

"Turner Meeks is a vivid interlocutor. He's been known to lose patience with rowdy Mexicans. Might you tell me the suspect's name?"

"Frankie Carbajal."

"I'm assuming that he rolled in the end."

"Such as it was, boss. He said the Sinarquistas are planning some 211s, and they plan to use some guns that Rice and Kapek sold them. Archie Archuleta brought girls to the **haus,** which don't surprise me at all. Frankie was hipped on some queer jazz-club geek and some Jap with a sword fetish."

Bland revelations. Ho-hum. Nothing cata-strophic there.

Elmer pointed to the car. "Who's the cholo?"

Dudley smiled. "He hardly concerns you."

Elmer smiled. "Tommy Glennon concerns both of us. Buzz and me clipped him, in case you didn't get that from Hideo already. I don't expect an attaboy on it, but I'd sure like you to acknowledge the favor we did."

Dudley said, "Muted bravos, Elmer."

"Don't you want to know what he spilled?"

"I was getting to that, yes."

Elmer blew smoke rings. "He laid out some old news. You and Carlos Madrano ran wets, and Joe Hayes was his bun boy. He tried to squeeze you when you saw him up at Quentin last year, but he didn't say what with."

Dudley lit a cigarette. It was a gaffe. His hand trembled. Elmer caught it.

"I had quite the chat with Hideo. He told me that you've put some things together since the last time we spoke. I'm wondering how you came upon what you learned."

Elmer stretched and rubbed his back against the streetlamp. He was milking this. **You overreaching bumpkin, I will kill—**

"I was over at Joan Conville's place about a week before she died. I was putting some moves on her, but it wasn't going my way. Joanie was terped, and she was mumbling about the gold heist and the fire. She kept fading in and out, and she talked up a diary before she passed out for real. I tossed the place, found it, and read it. It was mostly woo-woo about you and Bill Parker, but she wrote up her forensic shit with Hideo pretty good. I put some threads together, and figured the three of you were out for the gold. I put the diary back where I found it, kissed Joanie good night, and scrammed."

Vivid verismo. Elmer Jackson in quintessence. Woman-crazed and self-seeking. Less than half smart.

"Sally forth, lad. Keep the gold bar. Kill your brother's killer with my most fond regards."

96

(LOS ANGELES, 11:30 P.M., 3/10/42)

I watched the Maestro compose. We sat at his piano; Otto picked out low-register chords and jotted notes on a scratch pad. He was working on the nightmare tone poem we had discussed several times. Otto encouraged me to improvise at the moments his imagination faltered. I filled in with passages from the three Bartók concerti; I was undermining Otto's more foreboding motifs. My mission was therapeutic more than anything else. I was seeking to derail the Maestro's darkly foreboding moods and loosen the hold of his formal therapist: the darkly corrupt Saul Lesnick.

Otto hit chords as I smoked and sipped brandy. Once again, I studied the piece of paper secured by the sheet-music stand. Words by Meyer Gelb and W. H. Auden. Once again, I came up against Comrade Gelb's old Communist cell.

This storm, this savaging disaster.

Otto tapped the music stand and smiled at me. He said, "When I compose, I must always immerse myself in the mood the music attempts to express. Here, we have the chaos of my brain tumor and the muted light of my recovery, with recapitulative passages depicting the ongoing slog of the war."

I hit a series of random chords, up and down the keyboard. They were meant to represent the overlapping jabber of the too-rude and too-voluble guests at Otto's all-too-frequent parties. The chords covertly announced my intention to pump the Maestro for information on Jean Staley.

Otto said, "Tell me what that earsplitting passage represents, and perhaps I shall tell you a compatible tale."

"Your parties," I said. "Nesting grounds for parasites, all given to one doctrinaire view. All belligerent and convinced of their own uniqueness."

Otto laughed and clasped my left hand; he poised

it over the keyboard and banged a run of similarly unpleasant chords. I pulled my hand free and laughed with him.

Otto said, "Call it a crude parody of the German tanks approaching Leningrad in Comrade Dimitri's new symphony, and anoint it the expression of my own loneliness and need to smother it with the company of idiots."

I laughed and got to the point. "Jean Staley comes to mind there. She seems to have colonized your guesthouse permanently. One might call her 'the woman who came to dinner.'"

Otto found this uproarious. I failed to add "while she's been dodging a major police inquiry and perpetrating a bewildering mail ruse."

"Jean has colonized my guesthouse before, and will colonize it again. She is a Communist, you see. She purports to despise private property, even as she appropriates it. She sublets the homes of the rich to suit the whims of the decadent Right, which I find delightfully hilarious."

I banged right-hand chords up and down the keyboard. "I sense a provocative story, **Liebchen.**"

"Aaah, Katherine Ann Lake in her vamp mode, and ever the rival of other provocative women."

"I'm hardly Mata Hari, **Liebchen.**"

"No, but you are the consort of inquisitive policemen, and I know when I'm being pumped."

I laughed and covered my mouth. I was once again a conniving schoolgirl in Sioux Falls, South Dakota.

Otto sipped brandy and lit a cigarette. "I wasn't there for the party that Jean midwifed, but I had given her my consent to sublet the house, and to do with it as she saw fit. Saul Lesnick had diagnosed my tumor, and I was taking a rest cure prior to my operation. So, I'm afraid my story lacks the level of detail that might give it a corresponding punch."

Once again, Saul Lesnick. Once again, Meyer Gelb's cell. Annie Staples called me early this evening; she told me that she had secured wax impressions of Dr. Saul's office keys.

"I've never minded incomplete stories."

"I know that about you, dear. You're quite capable of ascribing your own endings."

"Otto, you're taunting me—"

"It was early in '39. Jean sublet my home for a party she described as having a 'pro-fascist theme.' I left the sanitarium and returned here. I immediately felt that something evil had happened in my absence, but I was debilitated, and disinclined to confront Jean as to what might have occurred. I was stuporous from headaches and the medicine that was prescribed to alleviate the pain, so I don't know where I was or who the other person was when the following occurred."

The Maestro taunted and teased me. I almost blurted "Don't string this out."

Otto hit the tanks-approaching chords from the **Leningrad** Symphony. They were ever dark and foreboding. The Maestro knew how to build suspense.

"The conclusion, dear Katherine. A man approached

me and berated me for living in a haunted house. I beat that man to death."

I shut my eyes. Otto hit the ominous chords again. I barely heard my own voice.

"And then?"

"And then, I told Dr. Lesnick. And Saul told me he knew an FBI man who could make it all go away, for a goodly amount of money."

"Was the FBI man Ed Satterlee?"

"Yes."

"Was Jean Staley the conduit for the financial transaction?"

The Maestro said, "Yes, she was."

This/storm/this/savaging/disaster/the rain/the gold/the fire/it's all/one story/you see.

I drove home and sat down at my own piano; I picked out those notes and tried to will a single three-case solution. The gold robbery as genesis; the fire as corresponding catastrophe; the Communist cell as point of constellation. Meyer Gelb, Jean Staley, Saul Lesnick. Ed Satterlee as snitch-recruiter. Otto Klemperer kills a man; Lesnick and Satterlee quash public exposure. The Maestro Manse as a current constellation point. Gelb's current plan to recruit four exiled musicians and turn them as informants.

Lee was off at Hollenbeck Station; he'd told me the East L.A. sweep should run through the night. The house echoed those twenty-odd notes. My thoughts went nowhere constructive. I thought of Joan through it all.

The doorbell rang; I knew who it was; who else perched and pounced this late?

I got up and opened the door. Bill walked straight past me and beelined to the liquor shelf. I allotted him time to guzzle a tumbler of scotch. I knew all his brusque movements and modes of peremptory address.

He'll turn to face me. He'll reveal unsettling moments from the East L.A. sweep. He'll take me in because I'm the woman he loves, and I hit him in the face ten days ago. I'll notice the coffee stain on his wilted white shirt.

Bill did just that; the stain was off to the side of his necktie. He stood ten feet away from me and made no move to close the gap. He said, "Thad and I braced a dink named Miguel Santarolo. He said Rice and Kapek sold the Greenshirts a large quantity of Jap guns. He laid out some planned 211s and snitched off Salvy Abascal's Irish-cop **hermano.** I'm sure you won't be surprised to learn that Dudley has been murdering priest-killers down in Baja, or that he's now a slavering fascist convert."

I sat down on the couch; Bill sat down beside me. I took off his hat and sailed it across the room. It hit the piano and landed on the adjoining carpet. Bill shut his eyes. I put my hand on his chest and felt his heart race.

"Annie made those wax impressions. We've got access to Lesnick's office now."

"Have Ashida toss it. He's primed to betray Dudley. There's a glimmer of decency in him that we can exploit."

I unbuttoned his shirt and ran my hand over his chest. Bill said, "Oh Jesus, Kay." He fumbled at my legs and snapped one garter strap. I went dizzy. He kept his hand there and kept his eyes shut.

It was who kisses who now. I pulled off Bill's shoes and unclipped his holster. He clamped his hand on my hand and held it to his heart. I threw my free hand back and hit the light switch by the couch. It was who kisses who in the dark now.

Bill surprised me there. He pulled me close and touched me under my sweater. We bumped noses and scraped teeth as we kissed in the dark.

97

(LOS ANGELES, 8:00 A.M., 3/11/42)

Mondo **"El Tigre"** Díaz. He defines intractable. Sweatbox #4's his new habitat. Ashida played good guy. Blanchard played bad guy. They were ten hours in. They eschewed rough stuff. They fed **El Tigre** doughnuts and coffee. They plied him with booze and contraband weed.

El Tigre revealed zero. They stressed the Sinarquistas and his Peeping Tom busts. **El Tigre** came off bemused. He wore a sharkskin zoot suit and a coiled-snake pendant. He sported snarling-tiger tattoos.

Blanchard yawned. Ashida yawned. **El Tigre** told stale jokes. A lion is fucking a zebra. If a nigger and a Mexican jump off the Taft Building, who hits the ground first? Come-San-Chin, the Chinese cocksucker. That old chestnut.

El Tigre was twenty-nine. He graduated Lincoln High and LAJC. That was enticing. Ashida dispatched the Hollenbeck watch boss. **El Tigre** came off educated. See what you can find out.

Díaz lit a cigarette. He'd smoked all of his and half of Blanchard's. He was bright-eyed and bushy-tailed.

"You guys have been good to me. I'll concede that. You've read me pretty well, too. You know a tough nut to crack when you see one. I got popped for 459, back in '38. It was a humbug roust. Two jamokes named Dougie Waldner and Fritzie Vogel leaned on me. They were rough boys. I withstood their grief, so you can bet your bottom dollar I'll withstand yours."

Blanchard yawned. "That Fritzie's a mean one. He's never learned the art of waiting your suspect out."

Díaz said, "I'm the intransigent type. The day you wait me out will be the twelfth of never."

Blanchard rolled his eyes. He ruffled the phone book on the table. The '41 White Pages. Heavy and fat. The classic tell-me-now tool.

Ashida said, "You're well-spoken, Mondo."

"For a beaner. That's what you're saying."

"No, I'm saying you're well-spoken, by any and all standards."

"Don't butter me up, Charlie Chan. I've been buttered up by experts."

Blanchard yawned. "Charlie Chan's a Chink. You're confusing him with Mr. Moto. Peter Lorre plays him in the movies. I popped that little twerp for possession of morphine. Some studio bulls put the skids to it."

Ashida yawned. Díaz mock-yawned. Peter Lorre—snoresville. The room buzzer buzzed. Ashida got up and cracked the door.

A bluesuit passed him a folder. "That educational stuff you asked for. LAJC requisitioned it from the U.S. Passport Office. Your pal here did some traveling and raised some eyebrows."

Ashida nodded. The bluesuit took off. Ashida shut the door and skimmed file pages.

Díaz had a Passport Office green sheet. He'd matriculated in Germany, circa '35. He attended Dresden Polytechnic. He had a graduate chem degree. He'd joined the Nazi **and** left-wing Sparticist parties. He built bombs for Franco's Falange and blew up Loyalists in the Spanish Civil War.

Díaz said, "Mr. Moto's in a trance. He's conniving something. He's the inscrutable yellow man of the East."

Blanchard said, "What gives?"

Ashida dropped the file and grabbed the phone book. He applied a two-hand grip and a baseball swing and smashed Díaz in the head. He heard his nose snap and watched blood burst. He reversed himself and slammed downward. Díaz whiplashed and jackknifed and bounced off the chair.

Blanchard jumped up and stood back. Díaz burrowed into the chair legs and covered his head. Ashida pounded his back. He made like Mr. Moto. He talked pidgin singsong.

"Dresden Polytechnic."

"Your chem degree."

"Your conflicting memberships."

"Fascist or Communist. I'll hit you until you roll."

Díaz scrunched down and covered up. Ashida phone-booked him. He hit Díaz in the back, Díaz in the legs, Díaz in the head. He caught side shots of drop-jawed Lee Blanchard. He heard Díaz singsong-yell:

"Fuck Salvy."

"Fuck his puto Greenshirts."

"I'm playing the left-right field."

"I'm in with the real Kameraden."

"We've got cutouts and mail drops and microdots."

"We've got rebop straight from Buck Rogers."

"We're running shakedowns and we'll have spaceships before this war is through."

"We're invisible."

"We're everywhere."

"We'll rule the postwar world."

"Ask my cutout, Two-Gun Davis. Ask sub-Führer Meyer Gelb. We're invisible and we're everywhere."

98

(LOS ANGELES, 11:00 A.M., 3/11/42)

Crash Squad confab. The big postmortem. Let's kick loose leads to death.

The squad ran underweight now. Ashida split for Baja and pressing Army shit. The roster ran Elmer, Buzz, and Lee Blanchard. Plus Bill Parker and Thad Brown.

They hogged the Hollenbeck muster room. Thad brought a jug. They yawned and stretched and crapped out at one long table.

Elmer was bennie-bopped. Ashida's absence jazzed him and gored him. Ashida grabbed Jean Staley's postcards. They might contain microdots. That was all good. Ashida foxed him otherwise. He dumped that microdot letter in the mail slot. It would shoot to La Paz. He'd probably snitch the PO box number to Dudley. Ashida was playing Dud ad hoc. Betray him/rat **to** him/betray him. Ashida ran this treadmill to The Big Where?

The Big Where? was everywhere. Him and Buzz were half-ass estranged now. Buzz overthumped Frankie Carbajal. They half-ass made up, in the wake. They agreed to withhold certain shit that Frankie revealed.

Like Frankie's sabotage rat-out. Like Abascal's double-cross on Dud. Like Abascal's plan to work wetback saboteurs and plant bombs on U.S. soil. The withhold felt dicey and clammy. The withhold felt good. Him and Buzz were running pure rogue now.

Dud vetted the Tommy Glennon snuff and told him to keep the gold bar. Dud vetted his shot at Wayne Frank's killer. It all felt dicey-clammy and good. This new Crash Squad had formed. It was him, Kay, Thad, and Bill Parker. Ashida half-ass cosigned their main gig.

Cornhole Dudley Smith. Nullify his evil shit. Notch a clean klub**haus** solve. Ashida was a wild card. Buzz was wild card #2. Buzz was running hurt-crazed and kill-crazed. He laid Joan's diary scoop on him. The scoop gave Buzz this big hotfoot. Yeah—but toward what goddamn end?

Everybody yawned. Everybody stretched. Crash Squad vexation meets Crash Squad exhaustion. The jug went around. Elmer abstained. Booze defused his bennie drift. Thad B. intoned some bad news.

"This Greenshirt fuck Abascal fucked us. He got

a lawyer to get Díaz, Santarolo, and Carbajal moved into Federal custody. Hollenbeck Patrol raided their domiciles and turned sixteen revolvers and automatics that Rice and Kapek sold them. The Feds are holding those little Nazi shits under Alien-Sedition Act provisions. My guess is they'll be in stir awhile, and then get deported to Mexico."

The room rippled. Abascal be wicked whammy. Elmer caught a whiff of Ed the Fed Satterlee here.

Buzz yawned. "This priest Joe Hayes is Tommy Glennon's bun boy."

Parker said, "**Ouch**—he's my confessor."

That roused some yuks. The jug went around. Elmer abstained. Buzz lit a big cigar.

"Archie Archuleta recruited out of the CYO at St. Vibiana's. You got lots of rich-ass Catholic laymen contributing to the cause. Who knows how many 211s those dinks have pulled so far."

The room rerippled. Buzz stifled a big yawn.

"Here's something that may shock the more naïve among you. The Dudster's hatching racket schemes down in Baja. I don't see no dropped jaws on that one, so I'll add that he's partnered up with Salvy Abascal on that front, which makes him a second- or thirdhand accomplice to all of Salvy's seditious shit."

The room triple-rippled. Elmer slapped the table and focused eyes his way.

"Look, Dud's covered as long as Jack Horrall serves as Chief. We've got our next chief right here in this room, and it's either Brother Bill or Brother Thad.

We all know how bent the Dudster is, but we've got ourselves a homicide job right now. The next chief can put the hurt to Dud—but we should only talk up real case leads."

Thad said, "Hear, hear."

Parker said, "Elmer's right. And all our Dudley Smith accusations are second- and thirdhand supposition."

Buzz said, "I hate that mick cocksucker."

Blanchard said, "**That's** hot off the ticker tape. Roll the presses on that one."

More yuks ensued. Elmer slapped the table. He was bennified out to the planet Pluto.

"I got a lead, but I can't reveal my source on the first part of it. It's a no-shit, somebody-killed-those-guys-at-the-klub**haus** lead."

Thad said, "We're listening."

Blanchard said, "Elmer tends to draw things out."

Elmer laughed. "My source told me a crazy Jap and a queer white kid frequented the klub**haus.** The Jap was a nutty sword man who killed chickens and licked blood off the swords he used, and the fruit kid was a jazz-club habitué. Rice and Kapek popped a Jap like that in January, and I witnessed the property log-in, but all the paperwork and property has gone missing, and I can't remember this Jap's name."

Thad said, "Okay, that's the first part, and you've still got our attention."

Elmer said, "You've got the gist right there, which Frankie Carbajal confirmed last night. But he added that the Jap sold curios for a living, which narrows down a possible make on him. There was queer action going on in the upstairs bedroom, and any Jap sucking blood off samurai swords looks like a real lead to me."

Buzz grabbed his crotch. "I got your real lead, throbbing twelve inches."

That roused yuks and yawns. Blanchard nipped on the jug and stubbed out his cigarette.

"Here's your real lead, but I'm not sure how it pertains to the klub**haus** job. First, there's this. Ashida broke Mondo Díaz, but he took off and split back to Baja—which I don't like, given what he is to Dudley. It turns out that Díaz is a chemistry whiz, and he went to college in Germany, and he knows something called 'microdot technology,' and he betrayed Salvy what's-his-name and threw in with some left- and right-wing guys he calls the **'Kameraden.'** They're out to profit off the war, they're running a shakedown racket, they've got mail drops and intermediaries, so nobody knows nothing they're not supposed to. It's all one big fucked-up megillah, and Mondo's personal high-up was a certain ex-chief of ours named James Edgar Davis."

Oooga-booga. Nobody's yawning now. Elmer recalled Joan's diary. Joan laid out good Davis dish.

Thad slapped the table. The room simmered down quick.

"We've got to act on this. For the PD's sake, if nothing else."

Parker said, "I happen to know that Dudley has plans to pentothal Davis. We need to get to him first."

Sweep fever resumed. They went Mex sweep to Chink sweep in a hot tick. Two squads formed. One Squad: L. Blanchard, T. Brown. Two Squad: B. Parker, E. Jackson, B. Meeks.

We rendezvous at Kwan's, 1300. Chink-o-phile Davis haunts C-town nonstop. He's Chink-fluent and Chink-defined. He's got a rumored C-town pied-à-terre.

The sweep could wait. Elmer detoured first. He racked his brain and snagged that log-in Jap's name. There it is. It's Robert "Banzai Bob" Yoshida.

He dipped by Central Station and combed the Alien Squad files. He found what he missed the first time.

Banzai Bob's log-in sheet. 1/24/42. No habeas tab. The klub**haus** job occurred 1/29. Banzai Bob was a railroad clerk. Banzai Bob was **not** a curio dealer.

Elmer called the Lincoln Heights Jail and talked to the watch boss. The boss checked detention records and came back on the line. He said Banzai Bob had been in stir, 1/24 to now. That nixed him as a klub**haus**-job suspect. Elmer told the boss to plant Bob in a sweatbox. He'd be right there.

He bopped to Lincoln Heights. Banzai Bob spoke good English. Bob was native-born. He voted for FDR three times. This internment drive's the shits.

He'll be on the bus for Manzanar, 3/25. It's like Pharaoh and the Jews. **Let my people go!!!**

Elmer commiserated. Elmer slipped Bob a ten-spot and a stack of girlie mags. Bob was delighted. Bob revealed **this:**

He didn't know no queer white boy. He didn't know no klub**haus** or jazz-club crawlers. He didn't know no curio men. His daddy bequeathed him his samurai swords and nail-studded dick sheaths. Who knows where Daddy got them. Daddy was bughouse crazy. Daddy committed seppuku on 10/8/39. Sayonara, Daddy.

Banzai Bob conceded **this:**

Yeah, he sword-slaughtered chickens. So what? He was a part-time Buddhist priest. It was like them Jew rabbis. They kosherized food. He decapitated it.

Sayonara, Bob. You've been exonerated. Elmer laid tracks for Kwan's.

Two Squad was set to go. Buzz supplied beavertail saps. Bill Parker supplied rock salt–packed shotguns. He cautioned Elmer and Buzz. The PD was Hop Sing–allied. Ace Kwan was Jack Horrall's lapdog. Go easy on Hop Sing storefronts.

They fortified on mai tais and pork fried rice. Ace Kwan served them. Ace professed ignorance. **Don't know Jim Davis' hideaway!!!** Ace lied like a rug.

They lit out on North Broadway. It brought back New Year's Eve and french-fried Eddie Leng and the start of all this multitudinous shit. They lit out three abreast. Elmer gassed on their mission. **Oooga-booga.** They packed pump guns and walked tall.

They bypassed Hop Sing fronts. They leveled rival tong fronts. They blew out plate-glass windows. They raided chop suey pits and bookie joints. They dumped the fly-specked produce in open-air stalls. They prowled Chink-smut theaters on East College Street. They saw surreptitious Chinamen slam their underhung ham.

They ran field interviews. They got **Don't know where Chief Davis live!!!** ten million times. They tore through "O" dens. They dumped hopheads off dope pallets and got ditto. They knocked over the late Eddie Leng's Kowloon. Elmer spotted a Four Families warlord. Buzz dunked his face in a bowl of wor-wonton soup. The warlord revealed **this:**

I see Dudley Smith and Lin Chung!!! They wrestle Davis into car!!! Don't hurt me, don't hurt me!!! Parking lot on North Hill!!! Broad-daylight abduction!!!

That was lead #1. A B-girl at Moo-Shoo's Mandarin disgorged lead #2.

Jim Davis live above garage off Alameda and Ord. He fly Hop Sing and Don't Tread on Me door flags. He keep sewer rats as pets.

Two Squad hotfooted on over. They kicked down said door. Jim Davis was gone. The ex-chief lived in a rodent resort. Note the swastika wall flags. Note the beaver pix taped beside them. Sewer rats ate out of dog dishes. A box of hand grenades sat by the bed.

They tossed the place. Buzz snatched the beaver pix. No further leads surfaced. Bill Parker decreed a breather. They schlepped back to Kwan's and revitalized.

Uncle Ace served lunch-crowd leftovers and Singapore Slings. He told Elmer Miss Lake called and said to call her back. Elmer ducked over to the pay phone and slug-dialed Kay's number. He got two rings. Kay came on the line. She said, "Elmer, is that you?"

"It's me, for sure. I'm at Kwan's, and Ace told me you wanted to gab."

Kay said, "Lee called me from Chinatown. He told me about Mondo Díaz and what he said about Jim Davis and the **'Kameraden.'** Díaz said they were running shakedowns, and Annie Staples told me some things that got me thinking."

Elmer yukked. "Well, shit, then. When you think, I listen."

"All right. Annie told me that Jean Staley wasn't really a Red, and that she and Meyer Gelb planned to extort a group of Jewish refugees that Otto Klemperer has befriended. Otto shares a minor history with your friend Jean, and she's been staying in his guesthouse while she's been sending you postcards from her automobile trip."

Elmer went **woooo.** "I can tell you found out some things that I didn't tell you."

Kay said, "I've got that knack—which is why you love me so much."

Elmer said, "Hold that thought. A notion just smacked me, and I'll let you know if it pans out."

Brentwood was swank. Lots of leafy streets and big Spanish houses. Brentwood north of Sunset was woodsy swank. You had deep-set yards and cribs more like estates.

Elmer surveilled the Maestro Manse. He hunkered low in his sled. Dusk came and went. He settled in for a **loooooong** eyeball stint.

He parked behind Jean Staley's '35 Ford. He got her DMV stats and ID'd her car. He went by Central Station, en route to here. He burgled Hideo Ashida's locker and stole a priceless something. He laid said something on the front seat of Jolting Jean's car.

The Maestro Manse was done up modernistic. Elmer perched across the street and got the **looooooong** eyeball view. He pissed in a cardboard coffee cup and smoked cigars. He scratched his balls and brain-strained Jean Clarice Staley.

Jean, the carhop. Jean, the ex-starlet. Jean, the faux Red and Fed fink. Jean, the ritzy-house sub-letter. Jean's jungled up with Meyer Gelb. Red Meyer extorted movie stars and Commos. That was back in the '30s. Meyer and Jean got current blackmail plans. There's these hebe exiles swapped out of Krautland. Meyer's got designs on them.

Jean, baby—say it ain't so.

Tommy G. tattled her good. Jean went back with

Fritz Eckelkamp. That cinched her to the gold heist. Jean was hitched to an arson dog named Ralph D. Barr. That cinched her to the fire. Tommy G. revealed all this. Tommy G. dubbed Jim Davis his spy conduit. Mondo Díaz tapped Chief Jim, likewise.

Elmer lit a fresh cigar. Elmer pissed in his piss cup and tossed the piss out the window. Elmer scoped the Maestro Manse and heard a door slam.

Then a cough. Then high-heel taps. Then Jean herself. She made for her car. Moonglow lit her up. She wore a tight skirt and a camel-hair coat. She wore nifty tortoiseshell glasses.

Elmer hunkered extra low. Jean crossed the street and went for her sled. She opened the driver's door. The roof light flashed. She saw you know what and fucking **SHRIEKED.**

Elmer jumped out and swooped down on her. Jean dumbstruck'd the gold. She was bug-eyed and all trancelike. She sensed nothing else on planet Earth.

She touched the bar. She traced the mint marks. She caressed the bar and all but drooled. She fondled the contours. It's the Fatted Calf. Come, let us adore—

Elmer swooped and clamped her mouth shut. Elmer said, "You can keep it, if you tell me some things."

Santa Monica was close. They car-o-vanned to the Goody Goody Drive-in. They sat in Elmer's car. Elmer ordered coffee and spiked it with 151.

It was cold and clear. The beach was close. Cars whirred by on Wilshire. Jean snuggled close to him.

Elmer nudged her back. Ixnay, sister. Don't you vamp me tonight.

"Tommy Glennon's my source on most of this. Some police-file dirt fills out the rest."

Jean said, "How is Tommy? I haven't seen him in a coon's age."

"Tommy's off for parts unknown. Sort of like you, with that fake-postcard shuck you were running on me."

The gold bar sat on the floorboard. Jean kicked off her shoes and foot-fondled it. Her nylon stockings went **screee.**

"You're telling me you sussed out the drop at Bev's Switchboard, and you know what's going on there."

Elmer sipped spiked coffee. "Let's start with Tommy. He was making what he called 'gibberish calls' to some sort of relay phone down in Baja. He got his so-called scripts for the calls at Bev's. All of this here shit is specifically spy shit, and you've got to have some sort of knowledge of it, because everybody knows everybody in this tight little world of yours, and all this shit is rolled up in a tight little ball."

Jean lit a cigarette. "You've got to be more specific than that. I don't know anything about Tommy making 'gibberish calls,' and I don't know anything about spies in Baja or elsewhere. I was in the CP back in the '30s, back when it was the thing to do. I met some questionable folks, but I'm not part of any spy ring run by the Comintern or the domestic CP, or any-body else. Get it? I renounced Communism, and you know what I am in my heart?"

Elmer smiled. "You're a shakedown girl."

Jean smiled. "Give Sergeant E. V. Jackson a gold star, because he hit it right on the head."

Elmer respiked their coffee. "Let's get back to Tommy for a second. All that code-call stuff got decoded and sent to a brother and sister in La Paz, way south in Baja. There's some hotshot left-wing/right-wing cabal looking to make hay with whoever wins this here war. Does any of this make sense to you?"

Jean said, "No. But I've been around CP guys and their pals for a long time, so I can tell you that the far Left and the far Right share a lot of spit, because what they really hate is the square white man's U.S."

Elmer sipped coffee. The 151 subverted the ben-nies and had him seeing wisps.

"There's a klub**haus** off of 46th and Central. Two cops named Wendell Rice and George Kapek got snuffed there. They had a Mex pal named Archie Archuleta. He got snuffed, too."

Jean shrugged. "If you're asking me if I know any-thing about all this, the answer is no."

"Frankie Carbajal, Miguel Santarolo, Mondo Díaz, and Salvador Abascal."

"No. It sounds like a cavalcade of cholos to me, and I don't play the Latin-lover field."

Elmer smirked. "What about Two-Gun Davis? He's the ex–L.A. police chief."

Jean tossed her cigarette. "Strictly from hunger. He's a fellow traveler all over the spectrum, but he sways distinctly right. We talked about Meyer Gelb that first time we met, and Meyer and Jim Davis go back a ways. Jim's also tight with Saul Lesnick, for what that's worth."

Elmer teethed on it. Elmer flashed the klub**haus** smut pix. Jean squinted at them and went **nein.**

"If you're asking me who the two skirts are, I've got no idea."

"Sex shows at the klub**haus**? Queer stuff at the klub**haus**? A nutty Jap who licks blood off swords, and his homo companion?"

"Elmer, I know nothing about that clubhouse, so why would I know something about the strange-o types who congregate there?"

Elmer teethed Jean overall. "Tommy said you knew Fritz Eckelkamp. That takes you back to '31, Eckelkamp's escape, and the gold robbery later that same day. You're tight with Meyer Gelb, so that takes you back to '33 and the fire that killed my brother. Them first two events are all hooked together, and don't tell me they're not. They're both a ways back, and now we got the klub**haus** job tethered in, and the same names keep popping up. There's some kind of story here, and you're the only one I got to tell it to me."

Jean sipped spiked coffee. She took little sips. 151 was hoodoo hooch.

"I'll tell you what I know. I'll start at the start, and you can fill in whatever blanks you can."

"That's what I need to hear."

"You haven't issued any kind of threats yet. I haven't heard you say 'Give me this' and 'Roll over on this guy, or I'll run you in.'"

Elmer shook his head. "I don't know where I can go with any of this, without it causing a big upscut and getting shot down, because it's all too damn embarrassing for everybody concerned, and the smart thing to do is make it all vanish. I'd like to find out the whole story on my brother and get a clean klub**haus** solve, and running you in wouldn't help me any there."

Jean said, "Okay, then. I'm fifteen years old and crapping out in a Jesuit college dorm in San Francisco. I meet Fritzie Eckelkamp, who likes his stuff underage, and one thing leads to another. It's '27 now, and Fritzie goes down behind his robbery string in Alameda. He's up in Quentin now, and we correspond and keep in touch. Fritzie wangles a retrial in L.A. and gets on that train that's all loaded up with gold. Before you ask, I don't know if Fritzie got hipped on the gold before or after he escaped from the train, or if he had anything to do with the heist. All I know is that he sure got hipped on it in good time, and this gold bar you promised me didn't come from nowhere."

Elmer sipped spiked coffee. Jean sipped spiked coffee. She scooched her legs and surefire vamped him.

"Don't stop there, now."

Jean caught some breath. "Fritzie told me there might be a crash-out, and he said to wait by the phone. I did, and I sure as hell got the call. I was twenty-two then, and I dressed all high school girl. I stole a car in Sacramento and picked Fritzie up in San Luis Obispo. There were roadblocks all the way southbound on the 101, but the cops bought my schoolgirl act and neglected to check the trunk. The roadblocks were lifted, north of Malibu and this swanky nuthouse. I got Fritzie into L.A. and dropped him at a fleabag hotel in Echo Park. That's when I met Meyer Gelb, and that's when Fritzie stopped being the so-called man in my life, and Meyer took over the job."

She'd played kosher so far. The last part felt rehearsed. Her Fritzie-Meyer spiel played too pat.

"Keep going. You're doing good in my book."

Jean said, "Some time passed. I'd been selling maryjane in Sacramento and moving it through Tulare County, into Nevada. That made it a Federal bounce. A Fed named Edmund J. Satterlee popped me, and I gave up Meyer as a Commo to buy my way out. Ed fed me a diet of Communist tracts, and I faked a conversion and joined Meyer's CP cell in L.A. Ed got me a screen test at Paramount, because he was chums with the studio cops, and that's when I entered my silly-starlet phase. The deal was, Ed learned that

Meyer recruited for the Party at Paramount, and that he ran a handbook there, and he wanted me to keep tabs on him. That's how I became a so-called movie actress."

Elmer tossed a tweaker. "What's Fritzie doing while all this is going on?"

Jean rebuffed it. "I told you. Fritzie walked out, Meyer walked in."

It still played hinky. It still played too pat.

Elmer said, "Keep going. You've got me tantalizized."

Jean removed her glasses and buffed them on her skirt. She was buck-toothed and half cross-eyed. She was still a hot dish.

"So, I met a prop man at Paramount and married him. Ralph D. Barr. I lied the first time we talked. I was afraid you'd roust me if you knew I was hitched up with this big arsonist and Griffith Park fire suspect. Of course, Meyer and Ralphie were two peas in a pod, and they both loved fires, floods, cataclysms, and storms. Ralphie was an active firebug, but Meyer was just a fire talker and a gasbag. He was preaching apocalypse before the big fire, working up the rubes at garment workers' marches and the like. Then the fire occurred, and Meyer and me and the other fools in the cell got leaned on, and it all went away until you knocked on my door."

Elmer sighed. "So that's it, then?"

Jean sighed. "That's it."

"Wayne Frank Jackson, Karl Frederick Tullock, Kyoho Hanamaka. Ring any bells for you?"

"Well, Wayne Frank's your brother, who I didn't know from Adam—and you still haven't told me why you thought he was murdered and not just burned up by accident. I don't know the second guy, and Kyoho was pals with Meyer, but I hardly knew him. Meyer said he swung right **and** left, and that he was some big-deal spy for the Jap Navy."

Elmer brain-drained it. "Gelb and Hanamaka have got these allegedly burn-scarred fingers. I'm wondering if they got them in the Griffith Park fire."

Jean shook her head. "Meyer was with me the day of the fire. Him and Kyoho were strange-o types of the first order, and they burned their fingers doing print-eradication dips, if you can feature that kind of action."

Elmer beagle-eyed Jean Clarice Staley. She read 96.6% kosher overall.

"Let's get back to Gelb, Tommy the G., and that spy shit we discussed."

Jean squirmed. She was hot to grab the gold and scram.

"Like I said, I'm strictly from shakedown. I pulled jobs with Tommy, mostly on political types, but I just sent incriminating photos and wire recordings through intermediaries, so I never knew who the marks were. I'm really just a courier and an informant. I finked Saul Lesnick to Ed Satterlee, years before Ed exploited his daughter's vehicular-manslaughter beef and turned Saul as his own snitch. All **I've** done spywise is forward mail for Meyer through Bev's

Switchboard, which is the Grand Central Station of spy mail, because it's 1942, and everybody and his spotted dog is Fifth Column and thinks this new world war is the gateway to untold riches. Also, Bev's is in L.A., and L.A.'s close to Mexico. Meyer says the alleged **el jefe** of this alleged right-left conspiracy is a Mex, but I think it's all fantasia, because I think Mexico's a repository for all of Meyer's nutty get-rich-quick schemes and political notions. Bev's is Sheriff's-protected, and—"

Elmer cut in. "Why'd you send me them postcards? Why'd you pretend to be traveling?"

Jean turned on her baby browns. Jean laid on the **oooh, baby** and soft-soaped him.

"You're a cop, Elmer. I sure go for you, but that's what you are. I told Meyer you were nosing around, and he told me to scram for a while. I had a bunch of microdot postcards I was supposed to forward, so I decided to send them through you, because I knew you'd save them, and then I could retrieve them. Also, Bev Shoftel was starting to think that Sheriff Biscailuz was souring on their protection deal, so sending the cards to you seemed safer, because then I could resend them through Bev, if her biz was still protected."

Jean, baby. Say it ain't so. You exploited my redneck ass and ran me in circles.

"Ed Satterlee requested a search warrant for Bev's. How does that snatch you?"

"It doesn't snatch me at all. Ed's business is Ed's business, and thanks for the tip."

"Where's Meyer live? Nobody can pin an address on him."

"Nobody knows where Meyer lives. He's just that secretive. We communicate through Bev's."

"What's Fritzie doing now?"

"I told you. Fritzie walked out, Meyer walked in. Fritzie's out in the vapors."

"You arranged a party at Otto Klemperer's place in the winter of '39. Tell me about that."

Jean foot-stroked the gold bar. Her nylon stockings went **screee.**

"I know the Maestro through Meyer. He contributed to Meyer's Free Spain funds, which were all scams to begin with. The Maestro was holed up at Terry Lux's dry-out farm in Malibu, because he'd been suffering from these bad headaches. Some America First guy, a priest from a wealthy family, came to me through Tommy Glennon, who I already told you was my kid brother Robby's squeeze. The priest laid out the theme of the party. It was supposed to be all about some event in Nazi Germany four or five years before. There was supposed to be costumes and masks, and it all sounded strange-o to me. That's it. I set the party up, but I didn't attend it. I heard rumors that something went very bad—but everyone I knew who was there held their mud about what all happened."

Elmer brain-strained it. "Was the priest a man named Joe Hayes?"

"Yes."

"Do you know a man named Dudley Smith?"

"No, but I've heard of him. He's supposed to be a hatchet man for the L.A. Chief of Police. People are afraid of him."

"Klemperer and Meyer Gelb. Give me some more there."

"What's to give? Otto throws parties, and Meyer attends."

"You attend, too. Here's my guess there. You've got these music and movie hotshots passing through, and Meyer trawls for his marks."

Jean said, "Bingo."

Elmer said, "Bingo how?"

Jean said, "Meyer's always trawling for marks, and he's got no conscience in that regard."

Elmer smiled. "Rat him, then give me something I can use, in case this whipdick and I ever meet."

Jean lit a cigarette. "Otto's befriending these refugees. They're all Jewish musicians, let out of Germany. Meyer's set to run a squeeze on them. He says it's all hooked into some mysterious cabal, but I think he's just in it for the gelt."

Kay knew those folks. They were okay by her. They'd endured too much grief as it was.

Elmer said, "No soap. No shakedown, no extortion. That's straight from me. Tell Meyer I'm looking to hurt him. Tell him I'll put him in the shit if he goes ahead."

Jean said, "Okay, sweetie. I'll pass it along."

Elmer kissed his fingers and brushed back Jean's hair. La Jean swooned a bit. It felt half real/half fake.

"Take the gold and go someplace safe. This whole deal could blow up in our face."

Jean dumped the bar in her purse. She dropped a wet one on him and booked triple quick. The bar was triple fat and heavy. Her purse sagged down to her feet.

99

(LOS ANGELES, 1:00 A.M., 3/12/42)

The mad eugenicist. The butcher plastic surgeon and tong affiliate. Your host, Lin Chung.

Slumlord Lin. The crazy sawbones owned half of Montebello. He packed Chink refugees into gimcrack cribs and charged usurious rent. An opium den flanked his office. "O" fiends test-trialed Lin's "Youth Forever" blends. Lin and Dr. Saul Lesnick synthesized them. Let's build a hophead master race.

Lin's office was **Führer** bunker–sized and all knottypined. Physical-culture posters drooped off the walls. Norse vixens performed calisthenics. It refracted Leni Riefenstahl and **Triumph of the Will.**

Dudley watched **Herr Doktor** work. Lin jacked a spike with sodium pentothal and geezed up Jim Davis. Chief Jim was strapped to a gurney. He's a suckling pig at a luau. A sock is stuck in his mouth.

Chief Jim went loosey-goosey. He was prone to run his mouth and blab impolitic. In truth serum, **veritas.** Let's see what results.

Lin bowed and left the office. Chief Jim looked knocked-down euphoric. Dudley lit a cigarette and blew smoke in his face.

Hideo called him, postsweep. It spurred the abduction. Mondo Díaz snitched Davis as his spy-ring conduit. Lee Blanchard observed the snitch. Blanchard will likely resnitch it to Bill Parker. Hideo further revealed **this:**

Elmer Jackson showed him a microdot letter. Hideo ran first-round tests and failed to raise the text. Elmer refused to forfeit the letter. Hideo grabbed it and dropped it in the crime lab mail slot. It was addressed to a Baja PO box. La Paz/box 1823.

Elmer snagged the letter at Bev's Switchboard. Bev's stood self-indicted now. It's a seditionist mail drop. Dudley called the La Paz post office. He spoke Spanish and came off Army-SIS brusque. He picked up a ripe tidbit. Miss Constanza Lazaro-Schmidt rented box 1823.

Chief Jim looked ripe to pluck. Dudley pulled his gag. Jim coughed and gurgled euphoric. Jim looked gaga guileless and eager to please.

"I'm anxious to hear your thoughts about several

events and the numerous people who may have attended them, Chief. We have a celebrated gold robbery in 1931, the celebrated Griffith Park fire of 1933, the recently celebrated klub**haus** murders, microdot communiqués, the Sinarquistas, and individuals named Tommy Glennon, Meyer Gelb, Jean Staley, Fritz Eckelkamp, Wendell Rice, George Kapek, Archie Archuleta, Karl Frederick Tullock, Martin Luther Mimms, Leander Frechette, George Lincoln Rockwell, Kyoho Hanamaka, Eddie Leng, Donald Matsura, Mondo Díaz, Miguel Santarolo, Frankie Carbajal, Juan Lazaro-Schmidt, and his sister, Constanza."

Chief Jim deadpanned the names. He said his pet rat Lucifer fucked his pet rat Brünnhilde. Dr. Saul fed them eugenics potions and imbued them with eternal youth. He planned to name their ratlings Hitler, Stalin, and Saul Junior.

Dudley said, "You're veering off a bit, Chief."

Davis said, "Lucifer raised money for some far-right boys. Meyer Gelb's a kosher cowboy. He's right-left and who knows what else. Meyer gave a speech at this Mexican confab. Vodka and schnitzel. The 'Horst-Wessel-Lied' and the 'Internationale.' Meyer's a goldbug. He wants the gold, but who doesn't? There's good colored trim at the klub**haus,** but I like fourteen-year-old white girls myself. There ought to be a law—and, frankly, there is. Preacher Mimms preaches the new gold standard. Meyer's a kosher extortionist. Kyoho refueled Jap planes at the Blue Fox on the Day of

Infamy. He took Ernst Kaltenbrunner and some apparatchiks to the Fox his own self. Lucifer's a muff-diver. That's a rare trait in rats. Is this the DTs, Dud? I've had the DTs before."

The confab. Goldbugs. Blathering nuts and realpolitik. Oddball egalitarianism. **Aus der Neuen Welt.**

"I wonder if I might ask you a few more specific questions, Chief."

Davis said, "No. I won't let you. They're my DTs and my pretty pictures I'm seeing. I fucked Theda Bara and Vilma Bánky, and you didn't. I fucked your Irish mama. Lucifer fucked Marlene Dietrich in Dresden. There were these white boys and spic boys in this college there. Wallace Jamie, Joe Hayes. Juan Pimentel and Mondo Díaz. You want microdots and phone relays? They've got them. Jamie's America First. Father Joe blows Father Coughlin. They own a drop in West Hollywood, but Blow Job Bev's got her name on the deed. This Juan spic was there at the confab. Talk about your spy brain."

Aus der Neuen Welt. Realpolitik. Lucid instants couched in dross.

Postwar-strategy talks at a donkey club. We all want the gold. That means you. We're all goldbugs. We're all in this together. It's all one story, you see.

100

(LOS ANGELES, 2:30 A.M., 3/12/42)

My émigré friends lived in adjoining bungalows. They were night owls to begin with; they required no urging to stay up late, socialize, and make music. Elmer called me at home an hour ago and told me that he had braced Jean Staley. He said we should discuss the fruits of the interview, and told me I should pass a message to "those refugee chums of yours."

"Jean was in on some shakedown deal with Meyer Gelb," Elmer said. "And I figured out he had an eye on your chums. Tell them to breathe easy. I paid Jean off and sent her back on the lam again. She's indispensable to that shitbird Gelb, so he won't be squeezing your chums, no way at all."

I called the Koenigs and relayed the good news. Hence this impromptu celebration. My refugee chums had learned one aspect of the L.A. gestalt very quickly. When in doubt, throw a party.

Magda Koenig whipped up a pot of goulash; Ruth Szigeti journeyed out to a liquor store and stocked up on booze and mixer. I called Elmer back and told him he'd be a fool not to attend. He said, "We both know I'm a fool, but I'll be there anyway."

Bill called me a few minutes later. He relayed the latest sweep leads and closed with "For what it's worth, I love you." He hung up, just as I started to swoon.

The party was running full steam now. Ruth had invited four of her most recently acquired lovers, two of each sex. There was an usherette from the Aero Theatre and Miss Barbara Stanwyck. There was Brenda Allen's sought-after male prostitute, "Ten-Inch" Tony Mangano. There was sepia songster Billy Eckstine, hot off a record-breaking engagement at the southside Congo Club.

The goulash was spicy and tasty; Miklos Koenig made mean rye-whiskey Manhattans. Ruth shared brief bedroom intervals with Babs and Tony, and returned from them both looking pooped. The disparate batch of folks seemed to get along swell. Ruth played Paganini's 24th violin caprice; Billy Eckstine held pace with her and warbled an a cappella "Ebb Tide." Elmer the J. walked in the door and withstood a refugee stampede.

Miklos Koenig and Mr. Abramowitz pumped his hand and pounded his back; Magda demurely kissed both his cheeks. Elmer and Ruth shared a look that might best be described as lustful and opportunistic. Miklos force-fed Elmer a bowl of goulash; Elmer told him it was savory, but ain't this the sort of grub the Communists eat? Babs asked him to fix a slew of her unpaid traffic tickets—which Elmer graciously agreed to do. Elmer addressed Billy Eckstine as

"Sir." He apologized for the Vice Squad raid on the Harlem Hutch in August '38. Sir Billy impulsively embraced him.

Elmer and Ruth fell into each other's gravitational pull. I eavesdropped on their screwball conversation. Elmer said things like "You're Jewish, right?" and "I'll bet Hitler's boys were right on your tail." Ruth asked Elmer how many Negroes he'd lynched and if his mom and dad bullwhipped their slaves. Elmer told Ruth she had green panther eyes. Ruth told Elmer he had beady eyes and said that she preferred circumcised men.

Dawn came up. I played hesitant Liszt on Miklos Koenig's piano while Magda Koenig scrambled two dozen eggs. It was a very fine party. I looked out the front-door window and spotted a Ruth-meets-Elmer vignette. They leaned up against a wilted palm tree. I watched the not-too-dumb cracker and the Jewish refugee kiss.

101

(ENSENADA, 7:00 A.M., 3/12/42)

He worked all night. SIS maintained a small crime lab. Their photographic gear excelled. He examined the Jean Staley/Elmer Jackson postcards. He found microdots on two out of six.

The cards were two-ply pasteboard. He separated the pieces and got microscopically close. The dots looked like pinpricks. He dialed down and exposed them at maximum power. They remained dots. No text was revealed.

Ashida swigged coffee. He pondered ways and means and got an idea. He walked to the photo room. He pulled a Minox Riga camera and loaded it with high-resolve film. He shot twenty-four exposures. He photo-snapped the postcard pieces and developed the film.

The darkroom was well stocked. Ashida did the cut-and-dunks inside four hours. He hang-dried the prints. He got all cardboard grain. No microdots were exposed.

He found a paint atomizer. He sprayed a large piece of posterboard black. He taped the twenty-four photographs to sheer sheets of paper and placed them on an easel stand. He placed the posterboard on its own easel. Both stands were frame-only and hollow-backed.

He poked pinholes in the posterboard and placed the two stands close together. He rigged the posterboard easel in front of the photo easel. He aligned the stands just so.

He squinted through the pinholes. He saw the taped photographs just so. He dragged a forensic arc light up into position. He hit the juice and illuminated the back-easel sheets from behind.

It was very sheer paper. Ashida naked-eyed the flaws in the bond. He reloaded his camera and cut the overhead lights.

Black room, blinding arc light. He placed the camera lens up to the pinholes and snapped shots into the flare. The pinholes limited his photographic field and homed it in on the invisible dots.

He shot twenty-four exposures.

He developed the film.

Microdots appeared.

They were naked-eye visible. The text appeared as a blur.

Ashida microscoped all twenty-four prints. He dialed deep and brought up bursts of visible text. It wasn't coded. It was Spanish language. The sentences ran out of sequence. He poked his pinholes randomly and photographed the dots that way. He juggled prints and microscope slides and rigged up a first-draft sequence.

He quick-translated to English. He scanned words and cribbed up a text. Said text was all **LISTS.**

Of U.S. defense manufacturers.

Of pro-Communist and pro-Axis comrades/ **Kameraden** within.

Of gold prices now.

Of gold prices predicted, up through '44.

Of sub berths on the Baja coast.

Of secret airstrips geared for takeoffs and landings. All situated north of L.A. All in the San Joaquin Valley. All near agricultural-crop properties.

This admonition. Typed in boldface:

"EYES ONLY. DO NOT REVEAL TO JLS & CLS UNDER ANY CIRCS."

JLS, CLS. Surely the Lazaro-Schmidt siblings.

Ashida jumped microscopes and rigged up fresh slides. He dialed down to maximum power. He brought up more text. It was all numbers and single letters.

The import hit him. It was Bible code. He'd learned the rudiments in grad school. Chapter and verse listings. King James page listings. Substitutions to transpositions to coherent text.

Ashida combed the lab and squadroom. He found a KJV Bible in the watch sergeant's desk. He worked with scratch pad, pen, and microscope.

He jumped Bible-to-scope. He fought eyestrain. He jumped Genesis-to-Revelation and covered all sixty-six books. Numbers-letters, numbers-letters. Chapters and verses. Sacred text to microdot text.

He worked for five hours straight. The translated text read thus:

"My trusted Comrade, or should I say **Reichsführer,** second only to me. We have veered left and right as this storm rages. Tovarich and **Kamerad** mean the same to us now. The NKVD and Gestapo are as one. 'Hail' or **heil,** makes no difference. I say both to you—Captain Juan Pimentel."

Ashida pulled up to chez Hanamaka. Genesis to Revelation. A recent memory perks. Cause and effect perk, in retrospect.

The bookie-drop raid. The phone-relay system identified and destroyed. Forty-odd men burned alive. Pimentel acts boldly. He incinerates evidence and kills co-conspirators. Comrade, **Kamerad,** tovarich. The perverse brotherhood survives.

Plus, something Dudley told him. A cove cave south of Ensenada. Pimentel acts boldly. He flame-throwers saboteurs. Comrade, **Kamerad,** tovarich. The perverse brotherhood survives.

Ashida parked in the carport. He'd called Pimentel and suggested a meet. Pimentel suggested this place.

Ashida arrived early. He wanted to reconnoiter. He wanted to check his photo device.

He got out and examined it. The trip wire stretched the full carport width. The photo housing was dust-streaked. It appeared operational. He pressed levers and heard car-tire thuds. The picture tube showed three rear license plates.

Two Baja diplomatic plates. One U.S./state of California plate.

Ashida memorized the numbers. He walked up to the house and unlocked the door. He had his own keys. Dudley trusted him.

The front room was breezy cool. Dudley kept the

windows open. The telephone still worked. Dudley saw to that.

Pimentel was late. Ashida left the door cracked. He'd hear **Kamerad** #1 arrive.

Ashida dialed the Mexican Motor Vehicle Bureau. A male clerk took the call. Ashida cited his Army rank and serial number. He stiffed the plate request and stressed **diplomatic.**

The clerk went **Un momento.** Ashida eyed the door. The clerk came back on the line. He kicked loose the name and address stats.

Juan Lazaro-Schmidt. Constanza Lazaro-Schmidt. Two La Paz addresses.

Ashida hung up and dialed the Ensenada operator. He asked her for a stateside hookup. The main DMV in Los Angeles. Person-to-person. The head clerk, **por favor.**

The operator **Sí, sí**'d him. Ashida hung up and eyed the door. Pimentel was late-late now. The phone rang inside three minutes. Ashida jumped on the call.

He laid out his Army credentials. He recited the plate number. The clerk had him hold the line.

He held. He watched the door. The clerk came back on the line. She kicked loose the name and address stats.

Claire Katherine De Haven. A 1910 DOB. A Beverly Hills address.

Ashida hung up. The room warmed up. He walked to the back window and took some deep breaths.

He counted lies, omissions, distortions. What he'd

told Dudley. What he hadn't told Dudley. Joan's diary. The East L.A. sweep. His end run with Elmer Jackson. His microdot findings. What he learned about Juan Piment—

"Alone at last. However you might judge me, you can't say that I haven't been patient."

Ashida wheeled. Pimentel wore Statie black. His tunic was custom-tailored. Silver daggers marked the Waffen-SS. Braided shoulder boards marked the Red Guard.

Ashida said, "Should I call you **Reichsführer**? I don't know the equivalent rank in the Russian Army."

Pimentel blew a kiss. "You'll call me sweetie pie in just a few minutes, once you've seen what I have to show you."

Ashida backed away. He bumped a window sash and froze. Pimentel crooked one finger and walked past him. He turned down a short hallway.

He sashayed. He rolled his hips. He did mambo steps and went **Tra-la-la.** Ashida followed him. The hallway dead-ended ten feet ahead. Brushed-oak panels. No doors inset. A tight cul-de-sac.

Pimentel tapped a wall plank. A panel slid back. Ashida saw pulleys and hinges. A dark space opened up.

Pimentel said, "Kyoho was quite the pack rat. Dudley never discovered **this** little cache."

Ashida caught up. Pimentel pulled a light cord. Presto—cul-de-sac, cubbyhole, closet.

It's six feet wide and deep. It holds period costumes. They're all nineteenth century and displayed on wall pegs. Pastel silk gowns. Cossack cavalry wear. German Navy kit. Imperial couture. The czarist era. The reign of Otto von Bismarck.

Pimentel giggled. "Does it make you feel special? There's really just a very few of us who know."

"Like the Lazaro-Schmidts? Like Claire De Haven?"

Pimentel went **tsk, tsk.** "The disapproving American. Ever so judgmental. He can't see through to the roots of what we have here. It's like your national treasure, the motel. Couples dress up to meet in sordid little places. We have this snazzy dressing room, and a surfeit of bedrooms upstairs."

Ashida said, "Couples?"

Pimentel touched his coat sleeve. Ashida pulled away. Pimentel went **tsk, tsk.**

"Well, the Lazaro-Schmidts are a couple, however much you might disapprove. And Claire met José Vasquez-Cruz here, up to the point that he was revealed to be a Communist priest-killer, and our gorgeous comrade Dudley killed him. People come here to don costumes, and who can blame them? We all want to be something more beautiful and gilded than what we really are."

Ashida shuddered. "What costume will you wear? Are you a comrade or a **Reichsführer** at this moment?"

"That's hardly the question. The question is what you'll wear."

Ashida froze. Pimentel leaned close and kissed him. Ashida grasped his arms and opened his mouth. He felt Pimentel's tongue. He felt Pimentel's hand between his legs.

He kissed back. He smelled mothballs and old wool. He shut his eyes and saw Bucky and Dudley. He opened his eyes and saw the moles on Pimentel's eyelids. He smelled talc and cheap aftershave.

He stifled a screech. He shut his eyes. He clamped down and bit Pimentel's tongue off. Blood burst into his mouth. Pimentel screeched. Ashida pulled his piece and emptied the clip.

Pimentel pitched and flailed. He took down a row of hatboxes. He smashed into mothball sachets and gold brocade gowns.

102

(LOS ANGELES, 3/12–3/25/42)

This kiss.

His first kiss with Ruth. It started something. Kay told him she peeped the event and saw worlds implode. He hasn't forsaken Brenda, Ellen, or hot-damn Annie Staples. Ruth hasn't forsaken her hot-damn yen for both girls and boys. Kay told him about this other kiss. That kiss got him all brain-broiled.

Kay visited Hideo Ashida. He was plunked in the Army stockade outside T.J. Dudley extracted him from the Statie jail. The beaner cops popped him and held him there. He snuffed that Juan Pimentel cat. Hideo Ashida, tagged for Murder One.

The Mex cops tortured Hideo. They beat him and attached electrodes to his balls. They installed hungry rats in his cell. The Dudster wangled a writ and secured him a stockade berth. Kay saw him there. Hideo was woozed up on morphine. The Army docs prescribed it for his thumped-upon head. Kay asked him why he juked Pimentel. Hideo babbled, "This kiss."

"This Kiss" tweaked him. It cinched him up to "This Case" and all the attendant queer shit. Queer Tommy Glennon. Queer Joe Hayes. Queer Huey Cressmeyer and queer klub**haus** traffic. Pimentel got snared in a queer-bar raid. San Diego, '37. That cinch-up cinched numerous threads.

He goosed Thad Brown. Thad record-checked Captain Juan, back to his bassinette. He glommed El Juan's Statie file and some adjunct paperwork. Pithy dish was revealed.

Pimentel studied in Krautland. He attended Dresden Polytechnic, circa '35. Class lists came with the paperwork. Wallace Jamie, Mondo Díaz, and Padre Joe Hayes were Dresden alums. Pimentel studied relay-telephone techniques. That cinched him up to a slew of pay-phone snafus. Pimentel studied microdot technology. Pimentel hobknobbed with

Nazis and Reds at that Baja shindig. That cinched him to this whole shit-shrouded conspiracy.

Hideo killed him at Kyoho Hanamaka's place. He called the Staties and surrendered right there. Pimentel—microdot whiz. Hideo—forensic whiz. Microdot postcards. The Staley-Jackson snafu. Hideo's pledge to decode them postcards.

The overall dish strained his brain waves. He dished it straight back to Kay. She dished Bill Parker. Whiskey Bill dished Thad Brown. They held an All-Dish Summit at Lyman's. Buzz Meeks joined them. They made no progress toward a three-case solve.

Ace Kwan dished some dish. Ace said Dudley pentothaled Jim Davis. Chief Jim revealed gibberish. Dud ensconced him at the Terry Lux nut farm. Jim's got congestive heart disease. Jim's going through the DTs. Jim's tick-tight with Mondo Díaz. Jim's cinched to the left-right combine. **Sieg Heil,** you fat sack of shit.

Jim's stuck in stir. That's one witness down. Link Rockwell's witness #2. He's in the Navy brig in Sarasota, Florida. The Navy won't permit extradition. Whiskey Bill's preparing a hot question list. A Navy lawyer pledged cooperation. He said they'd film the interview and send it along. Witness #2's scratched for now.

Witness #3 crapped out. Adios, Ralph D. Barr. He was Jean Staley's ex-hubby and a Meyer Gelb KA. Ralphie: Paramount stagehand/firebug/noted whipout man.

He got popped in Detroit. The Motor City bulls nailed him for Red agitation. It was summer, 1940. He firebombed the love shack of a high-up Ford man. The cops hard-nosed him. He snitched Gelb and ex-frau Jean. He said they recruited him for the CP. Ralphie torched his cell in the Detroit City Jail. Ralphie self-fried in true firebug fashion. Scratch witness #3.

Scratch three more witnesses. Díaz, Carbajal, Santarolo. Salvy Abascal interceded on their behalf. He called in Catholic fat-cat favors. Papist lawyers sprung the trio from PD custody. They're now in Fed custody.

Bill Parker requested further interviews. The U.S. attorney rebuffed him. Parker was a Federal bar–licensed lawyer. He called Fey Edgar Hoover personally. Fey Edgar rebuffed him. Parker requested a sitdown with Ed Satterlee. Fey Edgar rebuffed that request. Ed the Fed had been placed under house arrest.

Scratch seven witnesses. Scratch the Parker-Jackson shot to erase the Fed-probe recordings. Scratch that avenue to secure acquittals for Jack H. and Fletch Bowron. Ed the Fed was their conduit. Ed the Fed was set to unlock the evidence vault.

Lawyers will fuck you when no one else will. Salvy Abascal is a lawyer. He's an overall shitheel to rival Dudley Smith. Yeah—and him and Buzz have got a hole card to lay Salvy's ass low.

Frankie Carbajal's key revelation. This delirious dish:

Abascal is jobbing his Irish **Kamerad.** Abascal is planning sabotage behind El Dudster's back. Abascal has piggybacked Dud's run-wetbacks racket and has infiltrated saboteurs in with the wets. The saboteurs are set to bolt their San Joaquin Valley huts. They're fruit-pickers **and** bomb-tossers. **That's** a hot new one.

Him and Buzz got advance warning. They've withheld the word. It bought time. He bought them time with Dudley. He told him they slayed Tommy Glennon. He got the green light to slay Wayne Frank's slayer in return. Dud cares naught for the klub**haus** job. All Dud wants is the gold. Yeah—but it's all a lot bigger than that.

Strategies. Plays, plots, ploys, plans. His overworked brain's overheated and pitched to a boil.

He's prowled the jazz-club strip. He's trawled for the Jap sword man and his queer white companion. He's notched no solid leads. He's likewise trawled for the two skirts in the klub**haus** smut pix. You get lucky sometimes. He spotted them at the Congo Club. They were full-fucked forthcoming.

We've been to the klubhaus. Link Rockwell and Archie Archuleta drew us in. We posed for the pix. Our male costars wore masks. Link worked the camera. We never met Wendell Rice and George Kapek. We don't know who snuffed them. We don't know no Jap sword man and no queer white boy. You sound us, Daddy-O?

Sí, yo comprendo. Vaya con Dios, you slovenly sluts.

He jumped locales then. He jumped darktown-to-J-town and trawled for the sword man. He'd eliminated Banzai Bob Yoshida. Sword man was allegedly a curio dealer. He pounded J-town under shit conditions. The bulk of the Jap populace was now stuck in stir. The remaining Japs fish-eyed him and played it sullen. Sword man? Queer friend? Eat shit and die, White Oppressor!!!

The klub**haus** job was thus dead-stalled. He worked around it. He finally finagled an Annie Staples–Orson Welles tryst. Brenda put it together. Welles tricked out of the service and gassed on big blondes. The fuck-fest transpired at the Miracle Mile love nest. Sergeant E. V. Jackson voyeurizized.

Annie seemed to enjoy it. **Der Wunderkind** surely did. Annie steered Fats to some pillow talk per Major Dudley Smith. Welles described the savage beating Dud put on him. Welles described Terry Lux's plastic job and his snitch recruitment. Welles went on a goodwill tour conceived by FDR. Dud wanted rat-outs on Commies and other such scum. Welles was Claire De Haven's part-time lover. Dud was jealousy-jammed. Welles considered the Dudster insane. **I'll tell you this, Annie. He's dropping into some hellish abyss.**

Annie excelled at the Welles tryst. Kay paid her to make wax impressions of Saul Lesnick's keys. Annie delivered there, ditto. Who's set to raid his office? Him and Buzz are good bets.

Yeah—but all bets are off on the gold now. Joan's dead. Hideo Ashida's imprisoned. Dud's the sole gold quester still extant. The gold to the fire. That's your '31 to '33 parlay. Jean Staley dished there. It felt incomplete. What if nobody killed Wayne Frank? What if he fried of his own dumb volition? What if kid brother Elmer's got nobody to clip for revenge?

His brain's overheated. He's overworked. He's running bag for Jack Horrall and Fletch Bowron. Gold-star contributors are dumping gelt on their defense fund. They fear Fed-probe convictions and expulsion from office. He's siphoning cold cash to their lawyers. Bagman Elmer rides again.

He's overworked. His brain's overheated. His body and soul's overtaxed. Temptress—thy name art Ruth Klarfeld Szigeti.

She's from Budapest. He's from Wisharts, North Carolina. She's forty-three. He's twenty-nine. She's Jewish. He's a Scottish preacher's kid out of some unholy bog. Her dad conducted the Hungarian National Opera. His dad peddled Klan kode books. He's seen some whopping bad grief in his day. She's seen the Nazis machine-gun three hundred Jews and dump them in a ditch.

The Nazis made her watch. The Koenigs and Sandor Abromowitz stood beside her. They didn't get blasted themselves. Here's the big why of that.

The Jews were Commies and big anti-Nazis. Ruth and friends snitched them out for asylum. Their life savings bought them tickets to Mexico and the U.S. The dead three hundred were musicians and college profs. The death-squad Nazis were distantly allied with Meyer Gelb. The slaughter warned Comrade Gelb. His postwar scheme was a distant jerk-off dream at this moment. It could go blooey at any point.

Ruth was braced in advance of the slaughter. You will survive. You will emigrate and inform. You will facilitate extortion. You will fink at Comrade Gelb's behest.

Comrade Gelb. Comrade Jean Staley's shakedown boss. Comrade Elmer bought Comrade Jean off and scared her out of L.A. Comrade Elmer derailed Comrade Gelb's current shakedown play. Comrade Elmer's a big hero to Ruth Szigeti and friends.

The Koenigs and old man Abromowitz have crowned him their king. Ruth throws herself at him in bed. Ruth's omnivorous. She throws herself at cocktail waitresses and pizza-delivery boys. It doesn't faze him. Her big hurt fazes him. He plays the fool to quash the hurt and make her laugh.

Ruth runs abrupt. She whips him the woof-woof and hops out of bed to practice her violin. He lives to jolly her and eradicate her grief for a while. She flaunts her death-camp tattoo. He tickles it and makes her howl. He tells her Marine Corps and cop stories and lays on the laffs.

They're both treading quicksand. He'll escape his patch or he won't. She's got it worse than him. Her quicksand is all in her memory—and it sure as shit won't go away.

103

(LOS ANGELES AND BAJA, 3/12–3/25/42)

Fractures.
Fissures.
Absences.
Checkmates.
Stalemates.
Abandonments.
Banishments.
Rifts.
Claire left him. Young Joan left him. Beth left him. His Mexican family has cut him adrift. Juan Pimentel is dead. Hideo Ashida has been imprisoned. Salvy Abascal is off, preoccupied. He's running their biz ventures sans Salvy's aid and Greenshirt collaboration. He's neglecting his Army duties and his triple-murder case. The gold quest lies dormant. Army doctors have diagnosed Hideo's "advanced fugue state."

Hideo masterminded the gold quest and their three-case inquiries. Mike Breuning and Dick Carlisle have been removed from the klub**haus** job. A hostile faction runs that investigation now. Elmer Jackson and Buzz Meeks are running rogue. Elmer read Joan's diary. The rogue redneck knows the gold heist and fire jobs intimately.

He misses Claire. He misses Young Joan. He misses Beth. His wife and daughters have booked passage to Ireland. He misses Hideo most poignantly.

Hideo killed Juan Pimentel. A lust motive glimmers there. A hidden closet was revealed at chez Hanamaka. It was packed with garish costumes. Captain Juan's severed tongue was found on the floor. Responding Staties noted Hideo's blood-smeared lips.

Hideo has withheld from him. He senses that. His hideous omissions feel paradoxically defined. Juan Pimentel's death plays non sequitur. He interfered in some vexatious manner and caused Hideo to react. Hideo was doing microdot work at the SIS lab. Singed cardboard and misplaced equipment suggest it. The microdot work revealed something. Hideo is near catatonic and in no shape to tell him what.

He had requisitioned a full range of three-case paperwork. A range of newly discovered files was cached within it. He gave the paperwork to Hideo to study and analyze. He searched Hideo's quarters in Ensenada and L.A. The paperwork has gone missing. Hideo remains his sole hope for a three-case solution and shot at the gold.

Missing paperwork. Three-case principals, missing in action.

Link Rockwell—in Navy custody. Díaz, Carbajal, Santarolo—in Fed custody. James Edgar Davis— exiled to Terry Lux's retreat.

Count Joe Hayes missing. He called the Archbishop and requested a formal chat with Monsignor Joe. His Eminence brusquely refused. Count Orson Welles missing. He's off carousing and moviemaking. He's an unproven snitch, so far.

Impasses.

Stalemates.

Checkmates.

Credit Bill Parker's strategic aplomb.

Jack Horrall has not returned his phone calls. Parker's Fed maneuvers have put Jack squarely in his debt. Thad Brown has fallen under Parker's pious spell. The two great rivals for postwar Chief of Police. Now allied against Dudley L. Smith.

He's made moves to restore a counterbalance. He's requisitioned a second set of three-case paperwork. He's saving it for Hideo's hopeful return to health.

Hideo haunts him. He pulled strings with U.S. Army courts and secured binding writs. Hideo will not stand trial for the murder of Juan Pimentel. He will not rot in Leavenworth or a Mexican prison. Hideo will be interned at a U.S. relocation center later this month.

Three-case paperwork will await him. The U.S. Army is building him his own crime lab. Hideo will waltz the day that fascist Japan surrenders.

Countermeasures.

Logical applications.

Counterbalancing tasks.

Kyoho Hanamaka haunts him. He's the crux of all explication. He's the secret sharer. The gold heist and fire precede his tour of fascist-Communist hot spots. His friendship with Meyer Gelb precedes. His German-Russian schooling sets the course of hellish events to come. The gold is hoarded and left to snowball in value. World war looms as inevitable. Hanamaka envisions a postwar brotherhood. The gold will finance the survival of totalitarian rogues in extremis. A conspiracy is born. Murderous pratfalls occur. Personal agendas surface. 1942 marks a chaotic nexus. He must exploit it.

Countermeasures.

He's issued a second APB on Kyoho Hanamaka. He's tapped police agencies, jails, hospitals. Plus relocation centers and travel hubs. He's blanketed Mexico and the U.S. Kyoho Hanamaka—arrest and detain.

Countermeasures.

Makework.

Tasks to tether him.

He's adrift. He's not demoralized. Constanza tethers him. They thrive as one imagination. Constanza loves the Wolf and trusts in his powers. They envision the gold and lust for it as one shared dream. Brother Juan lusts for the gold—but lacks their imagination. Brother Juan attended the '40 conference. He knows things he might not have revealed. Constanza was

Herr Hanamaka's lover. She rutted with the one man who knows the whole story. Her body consecrates their dream quest.

Constanza withholds from him. He's yet to brace her. He needs to know the mail-drop secrets of box 1823. He falters with women, on occasion. It's his Achilles' heel.

Constanza's passion exceeds Claire's. Terry Lux told him that Claire is kicking morphine at his retreat. Kay Lake urged the treatment and visits Claire daily. The Wolf views Kay Lake suspiciously and considers her a deadly proposition. His own opinion vacillates and finally rests at disbelief. The Lake girl is grandiose and heedless to her core. Claire has always overestimated her and vilified her to a fault. Kay Lake and Claire De Haven now live in rapprochement. They are casualties of early-wartime L.A. Only the war could have spawned such a fatuous misalliance.

He found Claire's morphine stash in their hotel suite. He injects the drug periodically. He drifts off on a cloud where no woman ever beats or betrays him.

104

(LOS ANGELES AND BAJA, 3/12–3/25/42)

We were fated, Bill and I. He knocked on my door last December 6; he'd concocted an injudicious plan to entrap Communists and recruited me on the day before Pearl Harbor. He instilled my bitter loathing of Dudley Smith and introduced me to Claire De Haven. I was sucker bait for the heady series of events that have followed. I was at loose ends, in the Joan Conville manner. Bill hopped from crush to crush and ensnared us both. He pointed Joan on her way to self-immolation and allowed me to glimpse a blithe evil that I cannot turn my back on. The late diarist has provided the current diarist with the means to rectify her botched knife assault. I shouldn't have done it; I could not have taken a human life and lived with the consequences. And why kill when one can facilitate a self-immolation of the sort that consumed my dear friend?

Joan's words indicted Dudley. I will draft a freshly revised indictment. It will take various epistolary forms. I will create scripts for the Catholic Bill and Claire to perform for their confessor, Joe Hayes. The scripts will contain innuendo and misinformation calculated to push Dudley to blunder. Dudley is blunder-prone now. Elmer told me that Salvy Abascal has monumentally betrayed him, and has hinted at possible deadly ramifications. Dudley collects protégés. Witness Mike Breuning, Dick Carlisle, and—most auspiciously—Hideo Ashida. I encountered Breuning at Lyman's a week back. He was in his cups and mourning the loss of some essential Dudley Smith. He told me that Dudley's women are leaving him, one by one. Dudley's corps of able and compliant men must be made to follow. This is the basic design of my malicious levy of words.

Hideo's current gambit is no words. I have visited him at the Army stockade and am convinced that he is feigning a catatonic state. He is doing this in order to circumvent confrontation and capitulation in all matters pertaining to Dudley Smith. Dudley Smith and Hideo Ashida love each other deeply. Dudley's love is fraternal. It's the love of a brutalized Irish boy who saw British soldiers murder his brother, leaving him alone to suffer the whims of a sodden and vicious mother. Dudley holds Hideo Ashida to be James Conroy Smith, reborn. Dudley worships brilliance and mastery and possesses the generous gift of acknowledging it in all manner of people. He sees Hideo as his fascist-utilitarian kin. Hideo's love for Dudley is wholly lustful and at odds with his fulsome knowledge of Dudley's evil.

Hideo has omitted and withheld from Dudley. Dudley will not crack unless Hideo cracks first.

Dudley sees the Smith-Ashida alliance as a perfect wartime union. Hideo sees it as a vouchsafe of his wartime survival and fugitive sexual urge.

I will rob Hideo of his early-wartime love. I will covertly engage and collaborate with early-wartime fury and racial animus. I will rip Hideo free of Dudley Smith—so help me God.

I am possessed of a ghastly agency here. The war facilitates me; I consider the war to be a dear friend. I worship catastrophe in the manner of the nineteenth-century romantics. Chaos vitalizes me and assigns me tasks. I accede to the fact that this is my personal madness.

The war gave me the great Otto Klemperer and his nightmare story of beating a man to death. The war gave me a small part in the American passage of Shostakovich's new symphony. The war gave me a brief colloquy with an imbecilic monster.

I've been visiting Claire during her dope cure at Terry Lux's clinic. Jim Davis is now enrolled there. Two male nurses were walking him back from the infirmary. He recognized me from various PD functions and said hi.

I asked him how it felt to betray your country and side with fascist and Communist killers. I asked him why he molested underaged girls. I asked him how it felt to disembowel four human beings and let an innocent man take the rap.

Davis didn't seem to understand me. Terry most likely had him doped up.

Claire and Chief Jim head the sick list; numerous three-case witnesses top the custody list. Hideo Ashida remains in stir. The internment push has leveled Japanese communities throughout Los Angeles County. City jails, work farms, and barracks shantytowns overflow with imprisoned Japanese. They'll soon be scoured Jap-free. The exodus to permanent relocation centers will kick into high gear. Hideo Ashida will head northeast to the Owens Valley. Dudley Smith will surely enhance his accommodations. I might run into the Dudster some fine visitors' day.

Part Four
MANZANAR

(March 25–
April 2, 1942)

105

Exodus, 7:14. "And the Lord said unto Moses, Pharaoh's heart is hardened; he refuses to let the people go."

He watched. He pointed his binoculars east and tracked the migration. He'd spent his last free night at the Biltmore Hotel. A high terrace supplied the view.

Whole families trudged. They pulled handcarts piled with luggage and folded overcoats. Prowl cars trailed them. FBI men walked alongside. The pickup spot was north-northeast. Army buses revved their engines there.

Ashida watched. He stood by himself. His mother and brother had already been interned. They were sequestered at Heart Mountain. He was Manzanar-bound. The Owens Valley. Up in the Sierras. A two-temperature zone. Broiling heat, freezing cold.

He got off lucky. There would be no Mexican jail

or U.S. prison. He sidestepped death by torture and brutal mistreatment. All praise to Dudley Smith.

Manzanar would suit him. Preferential treatment had been arranged. Dudley assured him of that. He canned his **I'm catatonic** act. They had a nice chat.

He detailed the text of the microdot postcards. He laid out Juan Pimentel's spy-ring complicity. He did not snitch off the two Lazaro-Schmidts.

Dudley was Constanza's lover. She was spy-ring complicit. Dudley would or would not determine this for himself.

He played God with Dudley. It was a jilted-lover move. He employed need-to-know tactics with Dudleyesque aplomb. He apologized for killing Pimentel. It left Dudley's "business fronts" understaffed.

Dudley took it all in. There were no accusations. There were no probes or digs per the murder and no displays of pique.

They embraced. They vowed to retain close contact. Ashida pledged his loyalty.

I'll remain assiduous. I'll study any and all files you provide. I'll press for a three-case solution and shot at the gold.

Dudley said, "Chin up, lad. We'll both survive and prevail." Dudley evinced psychopathic good cheer.

That was last night. He trained up from Baja then. He packed one suitcase and ordered a last room-service meal. He slept on the living room couch. Early sunlight roused him.

Ashida walked out. He affixed his blinders and

took the back service stairs down. He cut through the lobby and walked north on Olive. The migration was due east. He looped in west of the swarm.

He cut east on 1st Street and passed Central Station. He took a last look up at the crime lab. The pickup spot was dead ahead.

He dawdled over. Two hundred Japanese huddled at 1st and Los Angeles. They pushed off the sidewalk and covered the street. Four buses were double-parked.

Army noncoms cinched luggage to above-the-bus racks. They unloaded handcarts and checked names off clipboard lists. Men, women, children. Knots of four, five, and six. Name tags pinned to overcoats. Families in tight little cliques.

Ashida scanned faces. The Japanese suck it up. The kids stuck close to mom and dad. He saw flat eyes and no spilled tears.

He jostled into the throng. He removed his blinders and donned his Man Camera. He picked out details. People recognized him.

Little girls clutching dolls. Who's that man there? Little boys clutching toy trucks. It's Running Dog Ashida.

Name tags pinned to coat lapels. More eyes pinned his way. Old men with canes. Running Dog Traitor. Luggage lashed to bus racks, piled skyscraper high.

He dialed his Man Camera close. He saw men hiss. He saw women dodge his lens. A fat man mimed spitting. A high school boy mimed **FUCK YOU.**

The boarding commenced. The noncoms herded

people onto buses. Ashida stood his ground. Men elbowed and jostled him on purpose. Spit globs hit his coat. He heard Shudo/Werewolf/Watanabe. The crowd thinned a bit. He Man Camera'd the sidewalk and saw them.

Bill Parker. Elmer Jackson. Kay Lake.

They smiled at him. They waved at him. They made no moves to screw it up with words. His eyes clouded over. Tears doused his camera lens.

Two noncoms approached him. They called him Dr. Ashida. They said something about Major Smith and sitting up front.

Ashida waved to his friends. Elmer Jackson bayed like a hound dog. Kay Lake blew him a kiss.

The driver and gun guard gabbed. It was all baseball and promiscuous Wacs. They'd rigged up a jump seat. Ashida sat between them. Wire mesh closed off the hoi polloi Japs.

They looked forlorn and apprehensive. They played it stoic. They saw Ashida up front with the round eyes. Ashida supplied thought balloons. Race traitor/white man's tool/running dog.

The bus rolled through L.A. and San Berdoo counties. Ashida's bus took the pole spot. Three buses trailed it. The gun guard yakked Ashida up.

Manzanar ain't too bad. The weather bites Chihuahua dicks. Families get housed all together. The mess halls are done up homey. You can plant

your own garden. There's Christian and Shinto chapels. There's work assignments. Kids go to school.

That Major Smith's a sketch. That's some brogue he's got. He's got swell quarters set up for you.

The journey slogged. The driver and gun guard shot the shit and yakked over engine throb. The buses refueled at a filling station outside Visalia. The guards passed out sandwiches and declared a piss stop. The Sierras loomed off to the east.

The stop consumed an hour. The captive Japs hogged both rest rooms and pissed the local yokels off. Hooligans went **Banzai** and made like the Zeros at Pearl. The gun guards pulled their billy clubs and moved them along.

The slog resumed. The temperature dropped. The caravan chugged through steep mountains. Ashida shivered. The gun guard passed him a blanket.

They hit the Owens Valley. It was wide, flat, and bleak. Tall mountains bordered it. The air was dry and cold. Snow covered the peaks and iced up the ground.

There it is. Manzanar War Relocation Center. It's all the way off by itself.

There's all these claptrap buildings and all this barbed wire. The family huts extend a mile out. It's perfectly symmetrical. It's all jerry-rigged.

There's all these wide streets. They're unpaved and squared off. The crisscross goes on forever. It's cold today. There's nobody out and about.

Fifty-odd buses were parked by the guard gate.

MP's in hooded greatcoats smoked and chewed the fat. A first lieutenant stood off by himself. Ashida recognized him.

Al Wilhite. Ex-Burglary hardnose. Known Dudley Smith toady and apologist.

The new buses pulled up to the bus line. Wilhite approached the lead-bus door. The gun guard kicked it open. Ashida walked out first.

Wilhite saluted him. "Welcome to Manzanar, sir. Major Smith has requested that I show you to your quarters."

They were jailhouse de-luxe. Dudley Smith vouched good hotels. The Biltmore in L.A. The del Norte in Baja. This three-room Manzanar suite.

A bedroom. A well-equipped lab. A workroom with built-in shelves and a large desk. A fresh set of three-case paperwork, all neatly stacked.

Plus a kitchenette. Plus an Army scrambler phone. He could make and receive his own calls.

His suite was detached. He had stormproof windows and a Mount Whitney view. Central ducts supplied heat. He had privacy. The shack rows stood a full hundred yards off.

Al Wilhite pointed to the paperwork. "That's your job, for as long as it takes you. And, there's a man at the Lone Pine Hospital. Major Smith would like you to interview him. He's being treated for severe burns there."

———

Dusk settled in. A mountain gale stirred loose snow. It swirled high and obscured rooflines. Manzanar went arctic cold. Steam heat warmed the suite.

Ashida dozed. Al Wilhite brought him his dinner. The MP's mess hall employed local cooks. Those guys knew their stuff. The jailbirds rated Army cooks. They got substandard fare.

The meal was good. It included French champagne. Relentless Dudley. Ever the Dudleyesque touch.

Ashida heard voices outside. He checked his front-room window. Three young men stood by the steps. They wore Belmont High letter jackets and held whomping sticks. Go, Mighty Sentinels. Green-and-black, 4-ever.

He walked outside.

He said, "As you wish."

He motioned them forward to beat him.

They came at him low and knocked him flat on a snowdrift. They arced their sticks and brought them down hard. They thumped his arms and legs. Swirling snow covered their faces.

106

(LOS ANGELES, 9:30 P.M., 3/25/42)

Ruth kicked him out. Lazy love gave her the frets. She cited her violin and an audition. You have other women, **Liebchen.** Go, pester them for a while.

Elmer hoofed it. Ruth dispensed good advice. Make the rounds. Visit the girls. Ask those questions you should have asked before this.

He hopped east. He split Santa Monica and cut back to L.A. proper. The SaMo PD ran shoreline blackouts. That meant doused traffic lights and house lights. He drove out of it and lit a cigar.

He passed the SaMo-city border. He went from no lights to muted lights and cellophane-dim stop-lights. Folks drove faster. Wilshire opened up.

A light rain kicked in. He cut north to Laurel Canyon. He caught Brenda in her robe and up for a chat. She drew the line there. No transitory woof-woof tonight.

They sipped Cointreau and noshed salted peanuts. They discussed their hot-sheet biz. Elmer snagged his chance and steered the talk.

"Bev's Switchboard keeps popping up in the klub**haus** job. I was wondering if you knew who actually owns the place."

Brenda blew smoke rings. "This priest Joe Hayes

has a small percentage, but the Ness family's got more of a percentage on the books. You know—that racket buster Eliot Ness, and his nephew, Wallace Jamie. That twerp who's in the shit on the phone-tap probe."

That hitches up. Jamie and Hayes. It bespeaks Fifth Column calumny. Thad Brown turned bonus paper on Mondo Díaz. The INS compiled it. Dig: Hayes and Jamie attended Dresden Polytechnic. Likewise, Mondo Díaz and Juan Pimentel. **Sieg Heil**—it's Deutschland '35.

"Bev's is Sheriff's-protected, right? Gene Biscailuz is taking a few points there."

Brenda said, "Eight points, Citizen. One more than we're paying Jack Horrall. That doesn't mean that Gene don't have misgivings. The rumor is that he's been rethinking the protection, because Bev's is so damn flat-out crooked."

Elmer sipped Cointreau. "That's some tasty dish. It's funny how these things drop on you out of the blue."

Brenda laughed. "You came here to pump me, Citizen. And I'm not talking about in the sack."

Ellen kept late hours. The baby bawled nonstop and shitcanned her sleep. She was shooting some back-lot oater. Her hubby was off with the Air Corps. He might catch her bored and eager to yak.

Elmer cut to Hollyweird. He parked outside the Green Gables and elevatored up. He peeped the fire-escape window. The lights were on. Ellen wore a shorty nightgown. Ellen paced and smoked.

He climbed back inside and door-knocked her. Ellen opened up and went **Ssshhh.** He knew the drill. The baby's sleeping, you dipshit.

They sat around and tipped Lucky Lager. Ellen cited a migraine. It quashed a stint in the kip.

They kept their voices low. The baby had keen ears and lived to disrupt. Elmer steered talk to Jean Staley.

This job I'm on. It's strictly routine. Her name popped up. You two were fellow starlets, huh? Right here on the Paramount lot.

Ellen inveighed. Insomniacs ran talkative. Ellen lived to dissect and rehash.

"Jean was a strange-o. She fell into her actress gig, but I always made her for a grifter at heart. She had a strange-o kid brother. His name was Robby, and he wanted to be an actor, but he couldn't get his foot in the door. He was a swish, and I think he was in with some swish boys who rolled pathetic old queens for kicks."

Elmer cinched it. Robby was Tommy Glennon's ex-squeeze. Jean told him that. He lashed up loose strands. The queer white boy, the Jap sword man's pal.

"Was Robby tall? I'm working off witness descriptions of some fruit kid I've never seen."

Ellen lit a cigarette. "Robby was short. He was a shrimp in the mode of Alan Ladd, but without the charm and good looks."

Elmer said, "Jean and men. There's got to be a story there."

Ellen said, "Sure, if you don't mind Communist no-goodniks and firebugs."

"Shit, don't stop now."

"Who's stopping?"

"Ellen, come on. Don't—"

"Jean had this strange-o lover named Meyer Gelb. He recruited for the CP at Paramount, and he was hawking a pro-Red script titled 'This Storm,' which Jean told me was strictly from hunger. Meyer exerted a sick-o power over Jean. He made her marry a sick-o grip named Ralph D. Barr, who set fires and whipped his pecker out on the girls at Le Conte Junior High. Ralphie used to rig explosives and set contained fires for the cheap-o westerns the studio used to shoot out in the Valley. This was strange—because Meyer had these burn scars on his hands, and the rumor was that Terry Lux and some Chink plastic surgeon did skin grafts on him."

Ellen dished good dish. It confirmed prior dish. It cinched up Staley/Gelb/Barr/Lux/Chink-o Chung et al.

"Sergeant Elmer's in a trance. Don't tell me this is 'strictly routine.' You've got your jaws locked on something."

Elmer yukked. "All right. We've got all these strange-o types. What about other friends and known associates?"

Ellen crushed her cigarette. "There was this tall southern guy. He impressed me as a grifter, and he had a drawl sort of like yours."

Cinch knots unraveled. Elmer pulled out his wallet and fanned the photo sleeves. He flashed his Wayne Frank picture. Ellen orbed in on it.

"Yeah, that's the guy. And I hate to say it, but that Klan sheet looks pretty good on him."

Surprise didn't cut it. **Shock** missed the point. **Spiritus Mundi** said it best.

Kay's shtick. We share one soul and one fate. Our shit's all interlocked. We're as one and fucked-up by life's follies. We swirl as our foolish fate plays itself out.

Annie was bright-eyed and bushy-tailed. She looked 1:00 a.m. in-her-robe **goooood.** She scoped his dizzy demeanor and fixed him a quadruple scotch. He guzzled it.

The couch dipped. He saw the six-eyed beasts in the Book of Revelation. Wayne Frank grew six eyes and burned a Klan cross. Tommy Glennon levitated. Gold dust rained down on L.A. Joan Conville resurrected. Revelations ripped his way.

Mondo Díaz. Frankie Carbajal. The Dresden boys. Joan said it's all one story. Kay said she'd marry him if he sussed it all out.

Annie said, "Penny for your thoughts."

Elmer opened his eyes. The couch resettled. The Revelation gang waved good-bye.

"Ed Satterlee. You've spent time in the sack with him. Tell me something I don't know."

Annie furrowed up. "I think he's a secret Red, but nobody knows it. He's always saying we'll win the war with Germany but lose the war with Russia, which wouldn't be such a bad thing. He says we should be prepared for that, because the Reds are the wave of the future."

Ruth said, "Have you ever killed anyone, Elmer? You have heard my own horrible story, and I must insist that you respond in kind and answer me candidly."

The bed sagged. They'd sweated up the sheets. The bedroom was cold. A sea breeze ruffled the curtains and induced goose bumps.

"I clipped a political fanatic in Nicaragua. He was trying to kill the police chief we had here in L.A. then. Jim Davis was grateful, and that's how I got on the PD."

Ruth finger-walked up his rib cage. She did deliberate things like that. Her panther eyes gleamed.

"You are a bloodthirsty type. I would have thought you would have more scalps on your belt."

Book of Revelation. Six-eyed beasts. Tommy Glennon and Catbox Cal Lunceford. Additional scalps on his belt.

"That's as far as it goes. I've never had the misfortune of passing through Nazi Germany, and I've never come up against the likes of Meyer Gelb."

"You say Comrade Gelb's name casually, as if you know this man in a personal way."

"I'm working an investigation. His name keeps coming up."

Ruth shrugged. "There is not much one can say about Comrade Gelb. He is a Communist, so he is both enlightened and deluded. He is also an extortionist, which has earned him my enmity. I owe my American passage to Herr Comrade, but many good people died as a result. My friends and I will not be impressed into informant duty, and we ardently applaud your coercive efforts with Miss Staley. Maestro Otto has passed along rumors as to Comrade Gelb and his left-right bund, but they impress me as nebulous poppycock."

Elmer shrugged. "That's all you've got on Meyer the G., huh?"

Ruth grabbed his hair and pulled their heads close. She did abrupt things like that.

"I formally met Gelb only once. It was in Munich, in '36 or '37. We met at a reception for Wilhelm Furtwängler. We were two Jews, and we briefly discussed our prospects for leaving Germany alive. Gelb bore an odd resemblance to a Sparticist hoodlum I knew in Berlin in the '20s. His name was Fritz Eckelkamp, and he was quite the mad boy. I mentioned this to Herr Gelb, and noted that my rather bland comment disturbed him."

Revelation. **Spiritus Mundi.** Six-eyed somethings. Ellen Drew's dish. Jean Staley's drift.

Ellen's dish enticed. Terry Lux and a Chink plastic man grafted up Gelb's hands. Jean's drift gored and perplexed.

The train escape and gold heist. Jean finagles Fritz Eckelkamp through southbound roadblocks. The roadblocks stop north of Malibu. "Near this ritzy nuthouse." It's the Terry Lux clinic, for sure.

"Elmer, where are you? You are certainly not listening to me."

Elmer fought off chills. His goose bumps grew goose bumps.

"I'm sorry. What were you saying?"

"I was commenting on Comrade Gelb, and I was saying that when the four of us were flown to La Paz, the airplane stopped in Juarez to refuel. An FBI man boarded the plane and queried us on Comrade Gelb. He wanted to know about Herr Gelb's plans to relocate refugees, but it occurred to me that he already knew the answers, and that perhaps he and Herr Gelb were in league. He added that we should mind our p's and q's, or risk expulsion from America."

Elmer tingled. "Was the FBI man's name Ed Satterlee?"

Ruth said, "Yes, it was."

107

(TIJUANA, 9:00 A.M., 3/26/42)

The T.J. Express. Two trucks and two buses. Perched at the border. Japs and wets set to roll.

To internment camps. To PD road gangs. To San Joaquin Valley farms. **Arriba, Japos y braceros.** You're plain old slaves now.

Salvy was late. Dudley briefed the Statie drivers and gun guards. They resented him. Juan Pimentel was their immediate boss and sub-**Führer.** El Dudley mollycoddled his killer. **El Puto** Ashida got a soft stateside berth. It pissed the slave crew off.

Salvy was late. It pissed **him** off. Salvy was set to ride north with the slaves. He was charged to glad-hand farm and road-gang **jefes** and dispense bonus cash. Salvy excelled at such tasks. Salvy possessed the gift of gab and the PR-man touch.

Salvy was late. Dudley was double-pissed. Al Wilhite called him last night. He reported Hideo Ashida's first day in camp.

Hideo praised his accommodations. Youthful thugs beat him up. That was most regrettable. Hideo had pressing tasks. He had file work to assess and a french-fried Jap to debrief.

Kazio Hiroki. Note the suspect initials. Wilhite snagged him off the Hanamaka APB. Hiroki is bilingual. Hideo will brace him in English and Japanese.

Salvy was late. Dudley fumed and performed roll-out tasks. He head-counted slaves. He stashed heroin in engine compartments. He teethed on Constanza, nonstop.

He saw her naked. He saw her clothed. He dressed her in fascist garb. She wore brown jackboots and carried a riding crop. She surveyed Waffen-SS troops and found them unkempt. She lashed them and drew blood.

Salvy was late. Dudley teethed on Constanza. He loved her. He did not fully trust her. He'd run intermittent stakeouts on the La Paz post office. Hideo snatched and mailed Elmer J.'s microdot letter. Constanza must have received it.

His stakeouts continue. He wants to nail her at the location. Tell me why I should trust you. Declare your loyalty and lead me to the gold.

Salvy was late. Dudley teethed on Constanza. He saw her in white gowns. Her shoulder straps kept slipping. He saw her in Brownshirt riot gear. She raised her riding crop and whipped Marxist thugs.

"**Mi hermano,** I apologize for my tardiness. Greenshirt business has kept me occupied."

There he was. Salvy snuck up on you. He was Latin decorous and ever deferential. Dudley raised a hand to slap him. Dudley hugged him instead.

"Your tardiness is confounding, but I trust and revere you, regardless."

Salvy laid on back slaps. He had that Latin love-tap touch. Salvy beamed. Latins lived to ingratiate.

Dudley pointed to the lead bus. The driver goosed the gas. The engine purred. The gun guard jacked shells in his piece. The shackled slaves pitched boo-hoo.

"Bon voyage, lad. Call me from Fresno or Bakersfield. I'll be staying with Constanza in La Paz."

Salvy shook his head. "I cannot accompany the convoy, Dudley. **La Causa** needs me here. I have urgent duties in Ensenada, and at the encampment. There will be many other convoys, but I cannot go with this one."

Dudley saw red. He flushed and felt his veins swell. Salvy love-tapped him. **Poquito** cuffs.

"Do not be angry, brother. I see that you are disappointed, and your anger hurts me. The Staties will perform my duties, and I will accompany the very next convoy. I promise you that."

Dudley flushed, warm to hot. He stepped close and almost threw elbows. Salvy love-tapped him. Dudley almost screamed.

The box rows flanked a service counter. The boxes were pullout, shelf-parcel size. They were numbered off-kilter. 1823 adjoined 901.

Dudley stood by the stamp machines. The PO resembled a pint-sized Alamo. He'd caught an Army flight down. He wore civvies and a belt piece.

Constanza called him in Ensenada. She suggested

a tryst and come-hithered him. He said, **"Sí, mi corazon."** She said, "My place at six."

It was 3:20 now. Constanza said she had afternoon errands. She mentioned the grocery store and the post office. She decreed this surveillance herself.

It was stand-around/blend-in surveillance. That's the most boring type. Dudley read postal circulars and wanted bulletins. The bulletins tagged U.S. fugitives and deserters. Dudley yawned and stayed awake.

3:40, 4:00, 4:20. Dudley got impatient. His thoughts boomeranged.

Salvy had mollified him. He should have hit him and cowed him right back. Constanza had a darkroom. She developed her wildlife photos there. She might possess her own microdot camera.

The Wolf appeared. He enjoyed La Paz. He hunted wharf rats and peeped Mexican women. Constanza loved the Wolf. He slept between them most nights.

4:40, 5:00, 5:10. Constanza walked in and strolled to box 1823.

Dudley peeped her. She unlocked the box and pulled out four envelopes. She sifted through them. The last one tweaked her. She evinced surprise.

She slit the envelope. Dudley stepped close. She examined the contents. Dudley got **muy** close. He saw a soft-blotter page.

Constanza looked up and saw him. She smiled, Latin stylish.

She said, "My alert darling."

He said, "I'll need to read it, of course."

The process consumed her. He watched her work. The darkroom cast pulsing red light.

She placed the page flat on a workbench. It was magnification glass–topped. A small arc lamp beamed light from below it. The light was bright-bright.

She sprayed saline water on the page surface. It brought up collodion and aniline dye. The page glowed purple now.

Constanza donned magnification-lens goggles. She loaded her camera and placed the lens up against the page. She moved the lens left to right and snapped photos. She shot twenty-four exposures per quadrant. Her photographic field covered the full page.

She unloaded the film and cut it into ninety-six strips. She placed them in a developing pan. She sprayed on emulsifier. It brought up ninety-six small prints.

Spanish words appeared. Constanza kept her goggles on and skimmed the out-of-order texts. She took a white grease pencil and numbered the prints from 1 to 96. She clipped them to three clotheslines.

The prints dried in an hour. Dudley donned the goggles. Constanza turned on a fluorescent arc light. She positioned Dudley beside print #1 and had him read left to right.

Message #1 was a variant. Hideo described the postcard texts. This was more of that.

Lists:

U.S. defense installations. Leftist and rightist

plants there employed. Established gold prices now. Gold prices predicted, up to '44. Jap sub berths upside Baja. Secret airfields. All upside San Joaquin Valley farms.

Message #1 dittoed postcard information. Message #2 was all new. It revealed **this:**

A list labeled "Defense Contacts." Lists labeled "Farmers," "Ordnance Makers," "Airfield Supervisors." San Joaquin Valley locations, listed below.

One ellipsis loomed large. There was no closing salute. Plus, no admiring nod to Juan Pimentel. Plus, no admonition: "Do not reveal to JLS & CLS."

Dudley tracked the logic. The postcards were sent to Pimentel himself. Elmer Jackson intercepted them and shot them to Hideo Ashida. The postcard dots expressed exclusion. They nixed the two Lazaro-Schmidts. Said dots nailed them as submembers of a factionalized cabal. The postcard sender distrusted the two Lazaro-Schmidts. This dot sender trusted them fine.

One cabal. Stratified and well buffered. Factions within factions. The intelligent, the resourceful, the superbly self-protective. To wit: Pimentel and the Lazaro-Schmidts. To wit: Meyer Gelb and Kyoho Hanamaka. Allied with the reckless and near insane. To wit: Jim Davis, Saul Lesnick, Lin Chung. To wit: Tommy Glennon and Catbox Cal Lunceford. To wit: dead cops Wendell Rice and George Kapek.

Dudley removed the goggles. Constanza ran her hands through his hair.

"You see how many layers there are, and how little most of us in the middle range know."

"I knew you and your brother were part of it. You all but told me some weeks ago. You wouldn't have known what you know about the gold if you were fully on the outside."

They stepped out of the darkroom. The normal light burned Dudley's eyes. Constanza placed her hands over them.

"I have not betrayed you. I simply omitted what you had already surmised. I assumed that you already suspected Juan Pimentel."

Dudley nuzzled her hands. "You forward dot mail sent to you. The various forwarding levels are buffered past comprehension. Pimentel was one step up from you and your brother. Beyond that, you have no idea who's who."

Constanza stroked his cheek. "I have never doubted your ability to assess and extrapolate."

Dudley said, "I have a certain matter to discuss with your brother."

Governor Juan's office. It was a big-cheese refuge and spot to receive and anoint. Note the pedestal desk and throne chair. Short beaners sit tall here.

Dudley walked in. Constanza followed him. She shut the door and bolted it. Governor Juan looked up.

His chair sat on risers. His desk sat waist-high. Goldbug Juan. All these gold figures on shelves.

His perfect suit. Gray wool with flecked gold high-lights. His gold collar pin and burnt-gold necktie.

Dudley walked up to him. Constanza sat beside the desk. She lit a cigarette. Juan's desk lighter flamed.

Juan sensed intent. He slid his chair back. It bumped a window ledge. Dudley picked him up and threw him. He crashed into a bookshelf and fell to the floor. Gold-etched volumes fell on his head.

Dudley kicked him. The books scattered. Dudley kicked his face and split his nose. Dudley sliced a new harelip. Juan bit his coat sleeve and muzzled shrieks.

"I read a dot letter that Constanza received. It convinced me that I should issue a stern warning. There will be no sabotage on U.S. soil. Your cabal or clique or junta may not kill Americans."

Juan whimpered. Dudley kicked his balls and kicked his legs. He pulled his Arkansas toad-stabber. It brought back '28. He shot a 459 man and took a souvenir.

Juan whimpered. Dudley leaned over him. He grabbed his hair and carved a Jew star on his forehead.

Juan screamed. Constanza crossed her legs and blew smoke rings.

The Wolf watched them sniff cocaine and make love. They steamed up Constanza's bedroom. Dudley held a hand out. The Wolf licked white powder off his fingertips.

They lay three abed. The Wolf purred and dozed. Constanza stroked him.

"The scar will never heal. You've marked him for life. He'll look in the mirror and know that I've told you everything. He'll recall that he raped me on my tenth birthday, and he'll never touch me or tell me who to sleep with again."

Dudley burrowed into her. He felt schizy. His heart raced. He fought chills. He saw three of everything. Constanza, the Wolf, the bed.

Constanza stroked the Wolf. Constanza stroked him. His pulse ratcheted down some. She gave him her breasts.

"We can use him, my darling. We can use him as he has used me. We can find the gold by ourselves, and keep all of it. These rumored comrades would not dare to trifle with a fearsome man such as you."

The Wolf warmed him. Constanza warmed him. She threw a leg over them both.

"You must know something, my love. I consider it definitive. I will never be able to fully give myself to a man as long as my brother draws breath."

He caught a midnight flight back. He still felt schizy. His pulse still raced. He ran too hot or too cold.

He smelled Constanza all over him. He held his hands out and shared her scent with the Wolf. He cabbed home to the del Norte. He unlocked the door and turned on the lights.

The Wolf hopped on his favorite chair and dozed off. Dudley smelled something familiar. Perfumed stationery. The envelope on the floor. He knew that—

The L.A. postmark, her handwriting, her now-banal scent.

He opened the letter. It ran six full pages. Claire cut loose on him.

His Irish pomp and bonhomie. People laugh behind his back. Her dope cure and how it purges his fowl touch and stink. His infantile brag. His groveling need for women. His puerile rule over weak men. His shanty mick cultivation of all things high-class. His jejune grandiosity. His vile regard for God's law. The precise moments that Beth Short and Joan Klein saw through him. His rage cloaked in pitiful terror. His shallowness. His abject neediness. His idiot criminal schemes that all run aground. His sheer fraudulence. His effete eye for callow young men. His remorseless cruelty. His repugnant selfishness. His trifling life passed unmourned and casually unremembered.

He dropped the letter and weaved into the bedroom. His heart raced. He saw three of everything. He saw three nightstands on Claire's side of the bed. He pulled open the top drawer. He saw three syringes and dope spikes and vials of morphine sulfate.

He grew three arms. He ripped off his coat and fashioned a sleeve tourniquet. His three hands shook. He saw three syringes, three spikes, three vials. He rigged the kit and punctured the stopper. It took three tries. His third try hit the vein. He went slack and fell back on the bed.

108

(LOS ANGELES, 8:00 P.M., 3/27/42)

The PD kept a suite at the Ambassador Hotel. It was used to stash important witnesses and entertain politicos that Jack Horrall sought to impress. The Cocoanut Grove was three floors below; the Tommy Dorsey Orchestra was headlining tonight. "Song of India" drifted upstairs. It made me want to jump out of bed, grab Bill, and dance.

But we were naked, Bill wasn't the dancing type, and he was occupied with my typed draft of Claire's handwritten letter to Dudley. We were both anxious and apprehensive. Dudley should have received the letter by now.

Bill said, "You're presuming a small kernel of self-knowledge in the man. One that he won't be able to shake."

"Yes, but not conscience," I said. "I expressed Claire's sentiments in my own words, and inferred that a great number of people see through him. He's immune to remorse, and he has no germ of probity to appeal to. He has to be made to question his hold over those he commands and seeks to intimidate."

Bill smiled and cleaned his glasses on a pillowcase. We sat with our backs on the headboard and sipped room-service bourbon. We were lovers and hotel co-habiters now; Bill's marriage cohabited his conscience more than mine. Lee Blanchard didn't care what I did with men. We were cohabiters in name only. Bill understood the arrangement more than I first thought he would.

He said, "I've got your script memorized, and I'll be seeing Monsignor Hayes soon. I'll lay out your version of Dudley and the klub**haus** job, and make the monsignor fear for his own safety."

"Claire's recuperating. She'll go to confession a few days after you. She'll spear Dudley from oblique angles."

Bill kissed me and pulled the sheet below my breasts. Seeing me nude always underlined exactly what this was and that I wasn't his wife. I knew he'd say something dispiriting next.

"We cannot maneuver Dudley into criminal indictment without bringing down the PD. We cannot strategically circumvent him to any sure advantage. He's simply too well situated, and too many powerful men owe him and need him."

"He's inviolate as long as he's perceived as sane," I said. "And the best way to unnerve him is through his women."

Bill said, "He has to lose his shot at the gold. A three-case solve has to explode in his face. We have to hope that Hideo Ashida values a clean solve more than he values his loyalty to that shitheel."

109

(MANZANAR, 9:00 A.M., 3/28/42)

The file stacks. Newly compiled and exhaustively comprehensive. A full three-case brief.

He'd lost his Ensenada set. Post-Pimentel chaos had engulfed him. Dudley had supplied this replacement. It contained all-new paperwork.

Newspaper clips. Custody files and visitors' logs. Bertillon charts. Detailed background briefs and summary reports.

Ashida worked at his desk. His beating-injury pain had subsided. He'd self-treated his wounds. He'd rested. He'd applied alcohol rubs and ice packs. He felt better now.

He'd scrambler-phoned Elmer and Kay this morning. He'd bug-checked the phone and tagged it pristine. Elmer and Kay updated him. They laid out the faux Claire letter. Faux daughter letters would follow. Plus, faux Claire and Bill Parker confessions to

Joe Hayes. They laid out the Jamie and Ness family ownership of Bev's Switchboard. Plus, the Hayes family-money cut. Plus, the L.A. Sheriff's protection clause. Plus, Jean Staley as Ed Satterlee's snitch. Jean drives Fritz Eckelkamp southbound, post–gold heist. Wayne Frank Jackson as Meyer Gelb's KA.

Terry Lux and Lin Chung. They plastic-cut Meyer's hands. Ruth Szigeti. She knew Eckelkamp in Berlin, circa '20s. Circles constrict and overlap, circles remain in ellipses.

He updated Elmer and Kay. He laid out the microdot revelations. He pitched the left-right cabal, then to now. He stressed the Dresden Poly convergence. He told them everything Dudley had told him. Elmer and Kay stood up-to-date. They'd repitch Parker and Thad Brown. **He** stood up-to-date. He was set to push forward, **now.**

Ashida stacked the files. He worked chronologically. He jumped back to '27. He read the Eckelkamp arrest reports and background sheets.

Alameda. A small East Bay burg. It's couched between Oakland and Berkeley. Alameda's the county seat. Their rinky-dink Sheriff's force roams countywide. Fritz Eckelkamp pulls countywide 211s. County bulls pop him at his eleventh heist. He admits his prior robberies. It's tacitly confirmed. His confession was coerced.

It's old news, so far. The background brief's got more snap.

Eckelkamp riffs on Weimar Berlin. The street

skirmishes. The Nazi-thug-versus-Marxist-thug riots. Nazi thugs and Marxist thugs allied in blackmail schemes. A Nazi-Sparticist kidnapping ring.

Deutschland, '26. Evidence of right-left alliance. Ensenada, '40. The **formal** alliance meets. It pervades three case lines: '31, '33, '42.

More background facts. Fritz Eckelkamp is born Protestant. He's orphaned early. He's raised by a Jewish family. He's Yiddish-fluent.

Ashida cut back to Alameda. Fritzie is tried, convicted, slammed for twenty-five years. He's sent to San Quentin. He studies law texts and petitions for a retrial. It's now 2/31. His application is granted. The trial is scheduled for Los Angeles District Court.

Three newspaper stories were clipped to the file. They were perfunctory. Clip #1 announced eight convict retrials. Judicial errors had been determined. The retrials would take place in L.A. They would begin in mid-May, '31. Clip #2 announced the gold-train run. It was set for May 18. There it is—San Francisco to L.A. Clip #3 announced a rail workers' strike. It would cripple but not halt operations. The San Francisco train yards have endured labor strife. The strike would hit 4/25. That meant **this:**

Certain train runs would be combined.

U.S. government runs. California state runs. That meant **the** run. Ashida surmised **this:**

The convict-retrial run and gold-train run were **secretly** combined. Fritz Eckelkamp learned this. He had leftist contacts at the Frisco train yards. He planned the mass escape. He escaped for good. The other convicts were gunned down. Fritzie worked solo. He cut his fellow convicts loose, impromptu. He planned the derailed-track snafu. The escape went down. Chaos reigned. It suited Fritzie's designs. Marxist realpolitik. Expendable convicts are killed. Only his freedom counts.

Ashida backtracked. He pulled the Alameda custody file and skimmed it. He caught a hot file note.

Fritzie met Leander Frechette in '27. They were county-jail inmates then. Frechette. He's these three things. He's Negro/mentally dim/big and inhumanely strong. He's the chief gold-heist suspect. He's the bête noire of the Santa Barbara Sheriff's and Deputy Karl Tullock. Frechette was a trainman and rail-yard worker. He'd been jailed for Assault One. He took part in a Frisco labor brawl. An obscure file note sizzled. A guard boss caught the odd friendship. Here's this Kraut armed robber and dim colored youth.

Ashida surmised:

Frechette is not dim. He feigns insolvency. It complements his labor-thug pose. He conspires with Fritz Eckelkamp. He tells Fritz that he works gold-run jobs on occasion. The heist is theoretically planned. It's a jailhouse-bullshit concoction. It's conceived in advance of Fritzie's San Quentin jolt. It's all shuck and jive at that stage.

Ashida backtracked. He pulled Fritzie's jail visitors' log and skimmed it. He caught a hot file note.

Martin Luther Mimms visited Fritzie. There's

Mimms, in Alameda County. He's a corrupt preacher/slumlord/race racketeer. He owned the 46th Street klub**haus.** He's tight with ranking L.A. cops. Jump—'27 to '31. Mimms springs Leander Frechette from the Santa Barbara jail. Mimms halts the beatings of Deputy Karl Tullock.

Mimms. He's L.A.-based. He's tight with high-up L.A. cops. Who's **the** boss L.A. cop in 1931? It's James Edgar "Two-Gun" Davis.

Names. Dates. Guesses. Extrapolation. Surmise.

Frechette creates the initial train-track diversion. He employs his fearsome strength and bare hands. The escape occurs. The train journeys south. There's a second track snafu. It's Frechette's work, as well. Frechette off-loads the gold bars on his person. He hands them off to—

?????

Jean Staley facilitates Fritzie's escape. She's Fritzie's lover. They haul southbound. They dodge road-blocks. Jim Davis aids the escape. He clues Fritzie and Jean in to roadblock deployment. Said roadblocks are pulled on U.S. 101 south. Right before this ritzy nut farm. It's Terry Lux's nut farm. This is all informed guesswork.

Elmer Jackson chats up Ruth Szigeti. She cites Eckelkamp's resemblance to Meyer Gelb. Her statement startles Elmer. He almost blurts **his** big guess on the scrambler-phone call.

Ashida surmised. Let's confirm or refute. This investigation is all about **that.**

Meyer Gelb has burn-seared fingers. They're covered by graft marks. Meyer Gelb was hauled in and braced per the Griffith Park fire. His scarred fingers tweaked the Arson Squad cops. That has to be true. Gelb's fingerprint ID has been compromised. What's their next step? What would the Arson cops do?

They'd order up a Bertillon measurement chart. They'd establish a certified Meyer Gelb ID. That raises this question:

Was Fritz Eckelkamp Bertillon-charted? Did Alameda County or the San Quentin lab chart his measurements?

Ashida prowled file paper. He jumped '27 to '28 and Fritzie's Quentin jolt. There it is. The Quentin lab charted him, 1/12/29. That's one comparison point.

It takes two to make this work. Ashida jumped— Eckelkamp to Gelb. He jumped '29 to '33 and the Griffith Park fire. He thumbed Arson Squad and Red Squad reports. Comrade Gelb's cell is hotly scrutinized. Comrade Gelb is hard-nosed. What's with your fingers, Jewboy? Let's Bertillon-chart this kike.

There it is. 10/18/33. The PD crime lab charts Meyer Gelb. Ray Pinker measures him.

Ashida studied the two charts. Ashida dripped sweat on the pages. He compared the height and limb-length numbers. He compared the finger spans. He compared twenty-three separate phrenological marks. Every single mark matched identically. This is no extrapolation. Fritz Eckelkamp is Meyer Gelb.

Now, we extrapolate.

Jean Staley lied to Elmer Jackson. She omitted a key fact. The roadblocks are pulled just north of Terry Lux's clinic. Jean takes Fritzie there. Dr. Terry and Lin Chung perform plastic surgery. They make Eckelkamp Gelb. Jean Staley knows this, full well. Fresh-cut Gelb joins the CP and forms his own cell. Jean S., the Lesnicks, and Jorge Villareal-Caiz join up. **Sieg Heil**—they raise the Red flag.

Cut to summer '33. It's two months before the Griffith Park blaze. A rash of liquor store 211s plague the L.A. cops. Liquor-store jobs are Fritz Eckelkamp's meat. Eyewits ID a man who resembles Wayne Frank Jackson. Let's posit a two-man heist squad. Strange bedfellows. Faux Jew/face-cut Meyer Gelb and Klan klown Wayne Frank Jackson. Let's posit that prefire Gelb/Wayne Frank bond.

Ellen Drew has already confirmed it. She has **not** confirmed a Gelb/Wayne Frank **chronological** point of convergence. Ellen Drew was a **mid-'30s** Paramount starlet. She met Gelb-who's-really-Eckelkamp **then.** She met Wayne Frank Jackson **then.** Wayne Frank was alive **then.** She ID'd Elmer's wallet pic. That cinched her identification.

Ergo:

Wayne Frank did not die in the Griffith Park fire. Ergo: somebody else did. Ergo: somebody snatched Wayne Frank's dental chart from the office of his cut-rate dentist. Ergo: somebody planted the real dead man's chart under Wayne Frank's name. Ergo: those efforts confirmed Wayne Frank's death. Ergo: Wayne

Frank's perceived death was deemed essential—but to who and to what criminal end?

Ashida surmised. Ashida tossed conclusions. Ashida linked three-case players, flesh-to-flesh. Eckelkamp-Gelb to Jean Staley to Leander Frechette. Leander to Martin Luther Mimms. Toss in the late Ralph D. Barr. Toss in Ed Satterlee. He suborned Jean Staley. He ordered her to fink out fresh-cut Meyer's cell.

Saul Lesnick's in that cell. Satterlee makes him his snitch. Kay Lake has duplicate keys to Lesnick's office.

Ashida caressed the file stacks. He'd dripped sweat all over them.

It's all one story. I will not be denied the full truth of it.

Kazio Hiroki. The same initials. It must be him. Al Wilhite has implied it. Who else could he be?

A waiting room adjoined the burn ward. Ashida sat alone. Wilhite drove him from Manzanar to Lone Pine. The interview had been prearranged. The subject requested Dr. Ashida. Dr. Ashida was his preferred interlocutor.

Hiroki was bilingual. They could chat in English or Japanese. Wilhite issued strict orders. "You will take no notes. You will write nothing down. You will report to Major Smith, verbally."

Wilhite sat downstairs. He'd worked off Dudley's APB. Hiroki hid in plain sight. His cover was interned Jap, vouched by forged papers. He'd journeyed north-northeast. Baja to L.A. L.A. to Manzanar. He had a cot in "C" row, bachelor barracks 3.

Hiroki was clearly insane. He torched his barracks and scorched himself, severely. A doctor noted preexisting burn scars. The doctor told Hiroki that some Army cops wanted to brace him. Hiroki said, "Dr. Ashida, one hopes."

A nurse walked in. Ashida stood up. The nurse walked him to the ward proper. It was three rooms off a hallway crammed with drip gizmos. Ashida smelled medicinal salve and charred flesh.

The nurse opened the door and about-faced. The room was small. There was a crank-up bed and guest chair. Air vents diffused salve and burn stink.

Hiroki was bandage-mummified and cranked up to face guests. An intravenous bag fed him pain juice. His face was uncovered. It was him. It's all one story, you—

Ashida pulled the chair up. He said, "芦田先生."

Hanamaka said, "花丸司令官."

His voice was firm. His neck was unbandaged. His vocal chords were most surely intact.

Hanamaka shut his eyes. Ashida unscrewed the fluid bag. He pulled out an envelope and poured in three crumbled Benzedrine. Get your man perked up and loose-lipped. Dudley taught him the trick.

They traded pleasantries. Hanamaka alternated English and Japanese. **So happy to meet you** and

あなたの最近の人生に興味を持ってきました. 渡辺事件. 警察 署の仕事.
Juan Pimentel and のメールドロップニュース.

Ashida quick-translated. **I've followed your recent
life with interest. The Watanabe case. Your police
department work. Mail-drop news from Juan
Pimentel.**

"I would say that I'm notorious, more than justifi-
ably famous."

Hanamaka switched to English. "I'm sure that you
and Major Smith know a great deal about my endeavors, going back some years."

Ashida sat down. "Yes, but I'm sure you can fill in
a few gaps."

The stimulant took hold. Hanamaka's carotid vein
pulsed. His hands twitched. He spoke more rapidly.

"I should tell you that I love fire, and that the small
barracks blaze was merely an experiment. I wanted
to see if I could eradicate the burn scars the Griffith
Park fire inflicted, along with the print-eradication
scars that Meyer Gelb and I so foolishly marked ourselves with."

Ashida said, "Meyer Gelb is really Fritz Eckelkamp.
Terry Lux and Lin Chung cut him a new face shortly
after his escape from the gold train."

Hanamaka smiled. "The American Jew is the
German Gentile, and quite the covert anti-Semite.
The leftist firebrand is really an armed robber."

"That statement tells me a great deal about this
politically diffuse cabal of yours."

Hanamaka said, "I'll quote Meyer here. 'This

storm, this savaging disaster.' The disaster is History, and the cabal was formed as a means to survive it."

Ashida smiled. "I'll quote the Book of Proverbs. 'Envy thou not the oppressor, and choose none of his ways.'"

Hanamaka sipped water. Benzedrine spawned dehydration. He held a small canteen. He sipped through a glass straw.

"Bible to Bible, Dr. Ashida. I read the Los Angeles papers on New Year's Day. A rainstorm of biblical proportions had unearthed a man's body in a wooden box. I knew that a reckoning of biblical proportions was about to occur."

Ashida tingled. "Yes?"

"Yes, and I had been thinking about Karl Tullock for some time already. Two months earlier, I had read a locally distributed golf magazine, published in San Diego. An article described a driving range, soon to be built on the exact spot where Tullock reposed. I'm sure you've heard the complaint 'It's hard to find good help these days.' That complaint proved itself especially true in the world of the domestic Fifth Column. I dispatched Wendell Rice and George Kapek to find the box and dispose of it before the excavation crews began work. Rice and Kapek bungled the job, because a reckoning was preordained."

Ashida coughed. The burn stink stifled him.

"Who set the Griffith Park fire?"

Hanamaka said, "Ralph Barr, on Red Meyer's orders. Meyer wanted to create an apocalypse that would take the lives of many oppressed workingmen, which would be a Marxist-fascist ruse to rival the temerity of the Reichstag fire. Meyer also knew that Karl Tullock had found a spot on the CCC crew, and was closing in on Wayne Frank Jackson as a gold-robbery suspect. Meyer wanted Tullock dead and Wayne Frank believed to be dead. When weather reports predicted one-hundred-degree heat and strong winds that day, he put Ralph to work creating a very subtle accelerant."

Ashida inched his chair back. Hanamaka oozed contagion. The Mummy escapes his crypt. His wrapping suppurates.

"Wayne Frank was suspected of a string of liquor-store heists in the summer of '33. It was shortly before the fire, and liquor-store jobs were Fritz Eckelkamp's well-established pattern. Was Eckelkamp-Gelb Wayne Frank's partner on those jobs? The gold heist occurred two years and three months previously, so I would assume that Wayne Frank met Gelb before May of '31, or am I mistaken here? Were those robberies a means of Wayne Frank's introduction to Gelb and your cabal et al.?"

Hanamaka shook his head yes. Hanamaka shook his head no. He was fully Benzedrined. His eyeballs glowed.

"You must realize that the Comintern and their kindred fascist counterparts are criminals first and foremost, over and above whatever ideologies they might express. You should not be surprised to see armed robbery as a recurring motif in this account of political misdeeds. On that note, yes. Gelb was Wayne Frank's partner in those robberies. Yes, Karl Tullock suspected Wayne Frank of complicity in the gold heist. Tullock had, in fact, been shadowing Wayne Frank—but Wayne Frank's presence on the CCC work crew was at first largely coincidental. Wayne Frank had been scouting potential targets for Meyer's 'workingman's apocalypse,' and the work crew seemed like a good candidate. But then he saw Tullock's name on a hire sheet, and told Meyer. That was when Meyer truly conceived his notion of workingmen burned alive."

Ashida coughed. "**Sensei,** when did Meyer Gelb and Wayne Frank Jackson meet?"

Hanamaka said, "Wayne Frank met Meyer in his Fritz Eckelkamp incarnation. They met in the Alameda County Jail in 1928, before Fritz was sent to San Quentin. Wayne Frank was serving time for plain drunk and vagrancy, and Fritz Eckelkamp was plain Fritz. That jail became a point of convergence for the gold heist—Fritz, Wayne Frank, and Leander Frechette. That was the genesis of the robbery. That was the moment that Fritz inculcated Wayne Frank with Marxist rhetoric and converted him. It was culminatingly the moment when Fritz and Wayne Frank saved Leander from a gang of race-baiting jailhouse thugs, and ensured that the robbery would actually occur."

Wayne Frank Jackson. Elmer's Klansman brother. Revealed as a Comintern dupe.

"Something troubles me, **Sensei.** It's Wayne Frank's statements pertaining to the robbery. His brother Elmer speaks of Wayne Frank as no more than a sad fantasist."

Hanamaka smiled. "You are quick to note that, **Sensei.** Let me add that Wayne Frank was then a man of intemperate appetite, and is now a man of strict circumspection. He went on a bender shortly after the robbery, and awoke one morning in an opium den in San Francisco. A nosy Chinese man told him he had been mumbling about the robbery while in his opiate haze. Wayne Frank was already a seasoned treasure dreamer, albeit one who had now transcended his sad origins. That moment in the opium den shocked him. He incorporated the gold robbery into the repertoire of his once-obsessive persona. He used it as a means to publicly express 'I could not have done this.'"

Explication. Revelation. Ashida had clenched himself numb.

"You torched the klub**haus,** didn't you? You were holed up down the block. You used the same accelerant that Ralph Barr used in Griffith Park."

Hanamaka said, "Yes, and those were taxing days for me. Some unknown person killed Rice, Kapek, and their friend Archuleta, and the puerile Cal Lunceford was chaperoning me. They were all manipulated and given tasks via mail drop, and the murders felt like yet another preordained catalyst. I felt you, Major Smith, and the other policemen converging. I took advantage of the Negro riot and burned the klub**haus.** I wanted to divert your investigation and create a new level of chaos, and the angry Negroes proved themselves to be convenient scapegoats."

Ashida said, "Whose body stood in for Wayne Frank's? A dental-plate substitution must have been worked."

Hanamaka smiled. He was **Sensei** Death. He was Mr. Death's-Head.

"Wayne Frank's assignment was to kill Karl Tullock during the fire, and then disappear. We were afraid that Tullock had informed other Santa Barbara policemen of his suspicions, so Wayne Frank's disappearance was deemed a necessity. Wayne Frank decided to kill a second man during the fire, and pass that man off as himself. Wallace Jamie was quite young then, but he was already acquainted with another comrade named Joe Hayes. Wallace and Father Joe were fellow travelers on the Right, and dabbled on the Left. They would reunite a few years later, at a German technical college. Wallace had a meddlesome younger brother named George. Wayne Frank got George a job on the CCC work crew. George ran a German-American Bund cell, and began recruiting at the work site. George was also about Wayne Frank's size and build. Wayne Frank decided to kill him and disguise it as his own death. George only came to work occasionally, and was never carried in any sort of official CCC log."

Gears snapped in place. Ashida heard clicks. He'd guessed abstract parts of it.

"And then?"

"Then Meyer had Terry Lux build prosthetic dental work off of Wayne Frank's actual teeth. Then the fire occurred. Then Wayne Frank beat George to death, knocked out all his teeth, and inserted the prosthesis. Meyer preinserted forged dental records for Wayne Frank at a downtown L.A. dentist. It facilitated the coroner's decree. Wayne Frank died in the fire. Then Wayne Frank deftly disappeared."

Ashida said, "Leander Frechette?"

"Last seen in San Francisco, some years ago."

"And the gold? Where is it now?"

Hanamaka went **C'est la guerre.** "Meyer entrusted it to a Mexican Stalinist. I think he was a money conduit for the assassination of Leon Trotsky. The gold was transported to Mexico, to be deployed for political purposes, with one bar left in a Los Angeles storage facility, to cover pertinent expenses. Meyer has hoarded the gold, and now it is pledged to the cause of postwar resettlement. Only Meyer and the Mexican Stalinist know where it is. Meyer trusts the Stalinist, because he made him endure a rigorous initiation. Meyer had him butcher forty Trotskyite priest-killers, and make it look like fascists did it. The man fawningly complied."

Ashida watched the fluid bag drain. The mixture was down to mere drips.

"Where is Meyer Gelb hiding?"

"No one knows that."

"Let's return to the gold."

Hanamaka shrugged. "It has lain fallow, and has exponentially increased in value. A good deal of time has passed. A convergence in Dresden brought about an enlargement of our original band of **Kameraden.** Wallace Jamie brought Joe Hayes, Mondo Díaz, and Juan Pimentel in. You killed Pimentel, and I'm sure you know of the other men."

Ashida checked the fluid bag. It had drained dry.

"Would you call Meyer Gelb the key architect of the gold robbery?"

"No. It was Wayne Frank."

"Where is he now?"

"I have no idea."

"Are the **Kameraden** really Communist or fascist?"

Hanamaka said, "At this point, who can tell?"

110

(LOS ANGELES, 9:00 P.M., 3/28/42)

Oooga-booga. The DTs, dead sober. It's like this gag song. I gots jitters like Jell-O in an earthquake.

Ashida called him and Kay. He relayed his talk with Kyoho Hanamaka. Wayne Frank masterminded the gold heist. Wayne Frank was sure as shit alive.

Elmer boozed and noshed at Linny's Delicatessen. His table fluttered. The pickle jar leaped. The walls talked back to him. He is Risen, He is Alive.

Buzz was three blocks over, on Bedford. They were set to 459 Saul Lesnick's office. Buzz brought cans of paint and brushes. Buzz brought pistol silencers. The rendezvous time was 9:30.

Elmer snarfed Old Crow and pastrami. Him and Buzz had spent the day at Kay Lake's place. Kay dished Buzz her version of the whole story. It put Buzz up to speed with him, Kay, Whiskey Bill, and Thad Brown. Buzz buzzed straight to Meyer Gelb. He vowed to find that whipdick.

Whiskey Bill showed up. He brought subpoenaed phone bills for Ed Satterlee and Doc Lesnick. He wrote a quickie writ and ran it by a PD-lapdog judge. PC Bell kicked loose bills going back six months.

They divvied up the bills and worked at Kay's dining room table. The bills listed the callees' names and phone numbers. The tally job took four hours. It revealed **this:**

Doc Lesnick and Ed the Fed called each other boocoo times. They were snitch and snitch runner. There was no surprise there. Ed called Bev's Switchboard nineteen times. **Woo-woo**—it's a spy mail drop. Ed called Padre Joe Hayes fourteen times. Hot potato—El Padre went **waaaaay** back with the spy-ring boys and owned points in Bev's.

Here's a scorcher. Doc Saul and Ed the Fed called the Baja phone-relay number fifty-nine times, all in all. Up till Ashida and Pimentel torched the relay room. Those calls indict both callers up the ying-yang.

Satterlee called Tommy Glennon's L.A. hotel room. Satterlee called Tommy's La Jolla crib. Mark that forty-two times, total. Satterlee and Lesnick called Jean Staley's Hollywood place. Mark that twenty-three calls.

Here's an El Scorcho. Ed the Fed called Baja's governor, Juan Lazaro-Schmidt. Mark that fourteen calls. Hideo said El Juan was jungled up with El Dudster's rackets. El Dud was bonking Juan's sizzling sister. Hideo said the seditious sibs were spy-ring complicit.

Doc Saul and Ed the Fed called AX-4869. It's a darktown exchange. They called the number twenty-four times, total. Dig: it's the hideout-house number. Kyoho Hanamaka holed up there. Cal Lunceford died there. The klub**haus** was just up the street.

Ed the Fed called Martin Luther Mimms. Twice

at his crib, thrice at the Congregation of the Congo. Mimms was deeply gold heist—embroiled. Ed and Doc Saul called Wallace Jamie—fourteen and nineteen times apiece. Both gents placed umpteen calls to Drs. Terry Lux and Lin Chung. Both gents called the C-town flop of James Edgar Davis.

A final head-scratcher scratched. Ed the Fed placed a recent spate of late-nite calls. He called all-nite eateries and cop spots. As in Lyman's and Kwan's. He called them interchangeable. Who you lookin' fo, Brutha Ed?

Elmer paid the bill. He schlepped over to 416 Bedford and donned his B and E wig. Buzz was parked curbside. Elmer got in and tossed him a french-dip sandwich. Buzz snarked it.

Beverly Hills. The psych-doctor district. Pitch your woes to Doc Saul. He'll fuck you up worse than you are.

416 was a mock-château job. Lobby, elevator, stairs. Offices above. Kay made keys off Annie Staples' wax mounts. It was a walk-in caper.

Buzz said, "The building's empty. Everybody up and left two hours ago."

Elmer grabbed their tool kit. It was two grocery sacks, double-wrapped. Buzz jiggled the keys. They choked back B and E giggles and charged.

They crossed the sidewalk. Elmer lugged the bags. Buzz held the keys. The lobby door opened easy. They checked the directory. Saul Lesnick, M.D.: suite 216.

They took the stairs. The second-floor hall was pitch-dark. Elmer flashed his flashlight and read door plates. There's 216.

Buzz unlocked the door. They stepped in and locked themselves in. Elmer hit the lights.

The waiting room featured agitprop art. Workers Unite!!! Beefcake boys waving scythes. Elmer made the jack-off sign. Buzz unlocked the inner-office door.

Elmer hit the lights. There's the psychee's couch. There's the psych doc's desk. There's file cabinets. There's more Commo wall art. Tanks rolled through Red Square. Butcher Stalin screamed. The Russki alphabet resembled DT hieroglyphs.

Buzz yanked at the file drawers. They were locked. Elmer dug into his bag. He pulled out the two silencers and tossed one to Buzz.

They tap-screwed their roscoes and stood back. They aimed in unison and blasted the drawers. The silencers went **pfffft.** Bullets pierced the file locks and ricocheted through the drawers. The office got all gunsmoked up.

They slid the file drawers open. They both went **wooooooo.** They thought they'd find patient folders. Nix to that. They found wire-recording spools.

Elmer grabbed all of them. He dumped them in the bags. Buzz hit Old Saul's desk. The drawers were locked. Buzz aimed tight and blasted them open. Gunsmoke smoked the whole room now.

Elmer dug through the drawers. Old Saul stashed his jerk-off books there. It was Nazi shit. Hopped-up

Hildegards in black tunics whipped terrified Jews. The Hildas wore jackboots and had tits out to here. The Jews wore skullcaps with propellers on top. Full-page ads hawked dick-size enhancers and eugenics brews.

Elmer tossed all the drawers. He thought he'd find correspondence and an address book. Nix to that. He found more Nazi shit and a jack-off suction device.

Buzz flashlight-flashed the walls. He said, "Looky here." Elmer tracked the beam.

He saw wires spackled to wainscot strips. He saw wires stuck to wall junctures and tucked under rugs. He saw painted-over wires stuck to lamp stands.

"He's bugging his patients. I don't see no other explanation."

Buzz said, "Let's fuck that fucker up."

They pulled the wall wires. They unspooled the rug wires. They dumped the lamps and yanked the microphones. They got out their paint and brushes and refestooned the walls.

Buzz painted swastikas and hammer and sickles. Elmer painted **X** marks over them. Buzz painted "Death to Traitors!!!" Elmer painted "America Forever!!!"

111

(LA PAZ, 10:00 A.M., 3/29/42)

Cocaine and cigarettes. Their standard breakfast. Rut
and talk. Their standard MO.

They stuck to Constanza's bedroom. Peons put-
tered, just outside. Constanza motormouthed. She
plumbed two topics. Her brother and the gold.

Dudley played attentive lover. His thoughts ran
afield. Al Wilhite found Kyoho Hanamaka. Hideo
was debriefing him. Hideo had failed to report.

The bed sagged and grazed the floor. It succumbed
to overuse. They banged the headboard loose
last night.

Constanza said, "I was thinking of the brand you
stamped upon my brother. I would imagine he'll employ Terry Lux to prettify the damage you did."

Dudley sniffed cocaine off a bread plate. He shivered. He got the chill, the numb teeth, the whoosh.

"Terry's the best at what he does. I could hardly
begrudge your brother his services. I'm dining with
Orson Welles in Ensenada tonight. He utilized
Terry recently. Terry deftly allayed some damage
I inflicted."

Constanza lit a cigarette. "Fierce you. Such utility.
Such brutal agency."

Dudley kissed her breasts. Constanza and cocaine.

His morning bifecta. She seized his body. His mind whooshed elsewhere.

The microdot letter. The planned sabotage. He'd warned off brother Juan. He did not report possible attacks to Fourth Interceptor. Kyoho Hanamaka. Constanza's former lover. He'd described Kyoho's self-torch job. Constanza said he saw too much in Deutschland and Russia. It was his time to die. He simply gave up.

"You haven't mentioned the gold in at least three minutes, darling. Are you relinquishing your grasp?"

Constanza primped him. She wiped his face with a bedsheet. The whoosh raised a sweat.

"Allow me to gloat over my brother. You enacted a long-overdue revenge."

Dudley lit a cigarette. "I pentothaled a rather sodden **Kamerad.** He described a convergence at a German technical college. The late Juan Pimentel, and young men named Díaz and Jamie. Joe Hayes, whom I've mentioned before, was a member of their bund. The mid-'30s, I think. I'm wondering if the overall cabal was formed then."

Constanza said, "No. I believe it all began to germinate before the fire. I would call the meeting of Kyoho and Meyer Gelb the point of germination. Meyer was recruiting for the Comintern at the Paramount Studio. People fell under his sway. The Kommisariat was Meyer's idea. He predicted the world conflict, as we see it today. His prophecy preceded Kyoho's sojourn in Germany and Russia."

The Wolf cocked his head. Constanza's scent aroused him. He probed Constanza's mind. She disclosed just so much. This vexed the Wolf.

Constanza said, "I have a lead on the minutes for the Baja conference. What would you pay for them?"

Welles was late. Film folk ran breezy and tardy. He knew that beast inside and out.

He'd extorted them. Harry Cohn paid him well. They misbehaved. He snapped furtive photographs. They starred in Columbia cheapies, resultant.

Johnny Weissmuller jumps jailbait. Tallulah Bankhead snarfs muff at lezbo hot spots. Duke Ellington sires Kate Hepburn's mulatto love child.

Welles was late. Like Salvy was late in T.J. Salvy refused to chaperone the Japs and the wets. The Wolf teethed on it.

Dudley ordered a private room. The del Norte staff salaamed and obliged. Welles drew flocks of autograph hounds. This room would hold them off. Orson called and requested the audience himself. It was a snitch and snitch-runner confab. It mandated privacy.

Dudley drummed the table. He felt fluttery. The flight back induced jitters. Cocaine exacted a price. He missed Constanza more than he should.

Dudley Liam Smith. Such a schoolboy crush. How unsound of you.

The door swung open. Such élan. Orson Welles **entered** rooms. He walked to the table. He was six-three and porcine. He exuded bonhomie and snitch fear.

Dudley stood up. They shook hands. Fat Boy's clasp was damp and weak. Dudley wiped his hand on the tablecloth. He made a blunt show of it.

They sat down. Dudley poured champagne. It was one-dollar swill. **L'auteur, le gourmand.** He'll gag on it.

"It's good to see you, Dudley."

"You're looking sleek, lad. Would you consider me brusque if I asked what brings you to Ensenada?"

Welles sipped champagne. He almost but not quite pulled a face.

"It's quite the ad-lib proposition. Howard Hughes flew us down. Dolores del Rio's sister needed a blind date."

Dudley went **Tu salud.** "Allow me to chart your train of thought, lad. You have information for me, and you thought you'd kill two birds with one stone."

Welles guffawed. Note the coward's cringe within.

"That's Dudley Smith for you. He cuts to the third act, and forswears the amenities."

"On that note, lad. You're not here to waste my time, and who am I to deny Miss del Rio's comely sister your presence?"

Welles coughed. "Well, I've been making

appearances for the OIACC, as you well know. I've been traveling with a small jazz combo, and I've put together a few incidental things I thought might interest you."

Dudley sipped rotgut champagne. He pulled a face and gagged it down.

"I'll set the scene, lad. You're traveling throughout Latin America. The combo plays inoffensive music during the cocktail receptions that precede your dinner talks."

Welles said, "Right you are. And one of the musicians was a froufrou kid I first met at an admittedly bent party at Otto Klemperer's place in '39. Otto was holed up in a sanitarium then, and—"

Dudley clamped his champagne flute. The stem snapped. Fat Boy missed it. Dudley dropped the shards on the floor.

"—and the kid told me he was there at the party, which chagrined me quite a bit. He went on to tell me a rather outrageous story about the America Firsters he met—"

Dudley cut in. "Describe the party, lad. Set the scene for me."

"Well, it was what you might call a masked ball, and the theme ran decidedly right of center. People wore Nazi costumes, and I screened an admittedly risqué film that I'd shot. I wore a mask, but the fruit kid recognized my voice from my radio broadcasts, although I'm reasonably sure that no one else did."

I was there. You wore a Red Guard costume. I saw parts of your film. It repulsed me.

"Please continue, lad. You've piqued my interest, quite adroitly."

Welles smiled. Mere hints of praise induced simpers.

"Well, the kid told me that he'd seen some real-life Nazis, whom he'd seen in newsreels, there at the party. They were talking out on the porte cochere, and they'd removed their masks. It was about dawn, and there had already been quite a ruckus. Some comatose woman was carried away, on the Q.T., which was—"

The She was a He. Dead is not comatose. Do you know who you're talk—

"Here's where it gets intriguing, if a bit outlandish. The kid told me the real-life Nazis were discussing the 'Führer's ultimately futile war' and some sort of 'future exoneration scheme.' One man said they should assassinate Hitler, or deliberately fail at it, but publicize the failure. Another man said their 'Red **Kameraden**' should do the same thing with Stalin. There was some talk of potential postwar escape routes to Latin America, specifically pro-fascist or pro-Communist countries."

Dudley said, "Please continue. It's like your **War of the Worlds** broadcast. You've got me on the edge of my seat."

Welles beamed. "Well, the kid sounded sincere about all this, and I'll admit to having a soft spot for good stories. This was one story I couldn't quite shake, and I tossed out hints to a few left-wing and right-wing types I met at various functions. I got a lot of murky responses, and heard rumors that this so-called plot derived from Mexico."

Dudley lit a cigarette. "I'm tipping off the edge of my seat. Please continue."

Welles laughed. "All right. Here's the conclusion, and we jump from the winter of '39 up to the present day. The kid told me a man named Wallace Jamie was at the party. He saw him unmasked, and he just recently put together who the man actually is. He recognized Jamie from newspaper photographs, a few weeks ago. That's because Jamie's in Dutch on that big Federal probe. The kid also said he recognized two other men who'd been at the party. Their pictures were in the papers, because they'd been murdered. I'm talking about Wendell Rice and George Kapek. They didn't actually attend the party. They wore chauffeur's garb and stood outside, on the porte cochere."

Autopsy pix. The dead cops. Gasping mouths. Ice-pick punctures. Single hand-span bruises.

"It's a small world, eh? Then the kid tells me that he knows another fruit kid, who's also a jazz musician, up in L.A. He didn't know the other kid's name, but he said that when those murders were all the rage in the papers, the other kid told him he'd been to jam sessions at the clubhouse where the bodies were found. He bragged that he and a so-called 'Red-fasco woman' killed Rice, Kapek, and a Mexican friend of theirs. I'm telling you all this because Claire told me you were involved in the police investigation."

112

(LOS ANGELES, 9:00 A.M., 3/30/42)

Sheriff Eugene Biscailuz. "Clean Gene" to his supporters. "Last Seen Gene" to his detractors. Frequently glimpsed at the Saints and Sinners Drag Ball.

We met the Sheriff at Kwan's Chinese Pagoda; Uncle Ace set a table for four in the Chiang Kai-shek Conference Room. Hop Sing goons peddled trinkets out of the room, twenty-four hours daily. REMEMBER PEARL HARBOR!!! signs and I AM NOT A JAP!!! T-shirts were current hot sellers. Ace also sold Jap shrunken heads. They were purportedly harvested by Chinese death squads, in retaliation for the Rape of Nanking. Elmer gave me the true lowdown. Chinese kids at Nightingale Junior High were the culprits. They robbed recently planted graves in Japanese graveyards. Dr. Lin Chung performed the decapitations and supervised the shrinking process.

Thus, breakfast with Sheriff Gene. Bloody Marys, hangtown fry, and Emperor Tso's flapjacks. Elmer, Bill, and I sat across from the Sheriff; he was three morning cocktails in and emitted a glow. His eyes clicked: Bill to Elmer to me. He already knew Bill and knew Elmer through Brenda—but what's this young cooze doing here?

Bill kicked things off. He'd sent the note requesting the sit-down and had braced Biscailuz in advance. Brusque Bill: the meeting pertains to Bev's Switchboard.

"We know you've got points in Bev's, Sheriff. We'd be going the search-warrant route if that weren't the case."

Biscailuz said, "I can read tea leaves. You're talking about a raid."

Elmer butted in. "Nobody's judging you for those points, boss. Everybody's got operating costs. You know damn well that Brenda and me are letting Jack H. dip his beak."

Biscailuz winked at me. "Miss Lake's got judgment written all over her. I know girl Bolsheviks when I see them."

I laughed and lit a cigarette. Bill lit up out of my pack.

"There's a great deal of seditious drop mail passing through Bev's. I want to raid the premises and seize it. Wallace Jamie and the Ness family hold the deed to Bev's, and a priest named Joe Hayes has a profit percentage. We're not looking for publicity, and we're not looking to turn this into indictments. We only want to depose Wallace Jamie, in order to turn leads on the klub**haus** job and two related cases from '31 and '33."

Elmer butted in again. "I know you know Ed Satterlee, boss. A little birdie told me Ed was looking to hang a search subpoena on Bev's, but you kiboshed it. Ed's Fifth Column up the wazoo, to the extent that Mr. Hoover's got him under house arrest. That's the sort of shitheel who sends drop mail through Bev's. We figure these here traitors are beset by factionalism, and Ed was looking to gain some sort of advantage with that subpoena plan."

The Sheriff drained his third cocktail. "Let's see if I'm reading you right. This 'we' you keep mentioning is you two policemen and Miss Lake. You're not proxies for the PD, which means you're open to a little horse trading. Which means you'll throw Uncle Clean Gene a bone."

Bill fumed. I kicked his leg under the table. My message was **Concede. We need him more than he needs us.**

"Ed Satterlee told Elmer that he'd accord him the opportunity to erase his own name on any Fed-probe recordings currently held in custody. I've been charged to erase recordings that might implicate Chief Horrall. With Satterlee suspended from duty, a new strategy to enter the evidence vault will have to be conceived and executed. If such a plan can be implemented, I'd enter the vault myself, and erase every single wire-recorded mention of your name."

Biscailuz winked at me. The novelty of a woman in the room floored him. Brenda wasn't sure which way he bounced. He ordered girls out of the girl book. He kept a copy of the boy book handy.

"That's okay for starters, Bill. It takes care of **me,** but it doesn't take care of **mine.** For what it's worth, I like Wallace Jamie, and if he's Fifth Column, I'm a Hottentot. Moreover, his Uncle Eliot will be mayor of Cleveland soon, and I want **him** to owe me. So, I **won't** permit you to depose Wallace, but I **will** permit you to seize anything and everything on-site at Bev's."

Elmer butted back in. "You ain't said what you mean by 'mine.'"

"'Mine' means 'me and all my deputies.' 'Mine' means 'erase every spool in Fed custody, to make damn sure me and mine don't get smeared.'"

Bill said, "It's a deal." Clean Gene dropped his eyeglass case and ducked below the table to retrieve it. He wanted to look up my skirt. I'd have to tell Brenda: the Sheriff veers toward girls.

Bill and I tucked in at the Ambassador. We discussed the Lesnick burglary first thing.

Doctor Saul hadn't reported it. That much was sure. Bill threw feelers out at Beverly Hills PD. Elmer and Buzz robbed his office and desecrated it.

Their wall artwork defamed the **Kameraden.** Saul Lesnick—**j'accuse.** We're onto you and yours.

"We," "We're," "Us." Sheriff Gene picked up on it and parlayed it to his tactical advantage. I extended "We" to include Annie Staples, and described our phone chat early this morning. Annie called me. She said she was servicing Saul Lesnick tomorrow night; the assignation would take place at Brenda's Miracle Mile trick spot. This was to our benefit. Doctor Saul unburdened himself to Annie and would most likely whine about the burglary-desecration. And Elmer would be there to film it.

Room service delivered club sandwiches and coffee; Bill and I lunched on the bed. Assignation, rendez-vous, shack job. Bill crossed himself every time I said the words.

"The phone records," he said. "What's the first thing that comes to mind? Where do they most conclusively point?"

I said, "To collusion and conspiracy. And, given what we know about the principals, a conspiracy that must be judged as politically and socially diffuse."

"And what string of calls plays most out of sync with the rest?"

"Ed Satterlee's late-night calls to Lyman's and Kwan's. Two all-night PD watering holes. The calls serve to pose the question: 'Who was Ed the Fed looking for?'"

Bill snagged his trousers off the floor. He dug through the pockets and pulled out three mimeographed sheets of paper. The cheapo typeface and multiple exclamation points screamed **Sid Hudgens!** I breezed through the text; it was the Sidster's privately circulated subscription scandal sheet.

The inimitable Sidster. Ever alert for watchful postal inspectors. He laid out the lurid lowdown—but stopped short of pure pornography. He used initials in lieu of real names. He gave you the tantalizing tattle and dystopian dish. Celebrity abortions, miscegenist liaisons, lezbo love nests. Alluring alliteration. Muff-munching matrons at the Lincoln Heights Jail. Doped racehorses and fixed fights. Draconian drag queens. A regular "Police Blotter" feature. Perennial poop. Filmland fellators and cunning linguists, caught "in flat-footed flagrante."

I laughed out loud. Bill said, "We shake down Sid for his subscriber list. We lay out Dudley and all the known **Kameraden.** You write the text, and insert the appropriate initials. We wallpaper Dudley, the comrades, and every conceivable man jack that might be inclined to do the Dudster dirt."

D.S.: that hellhound Hibernian. Malevolent Mexicans. S.L.: that sicknik psychiatrist and shitbird shrink. Feckless Fascists and riotous Reds. Waterlogged wetbacks. Pustulant policemen and jungle-bred Japs.

I fell off the bed, laughing. I'd never laughed so hard. I thought my roars would never stop.

113

(LONE PINE, 2:00 P.M., 3/30/42)

They reset the stage. The burn-ward room, the bed, the chair. Benzedrine in the fluid bag. The burn salve and charred-flesh stink.

The Mummy and Mr. Moto. Their second encounter. A vitalized Hanamaka. Ashida, poised to interrogate.

"Tell me about the klub**haus, Sensei.** You might begin by giving me your overall impressions."

Hanamaka plucked at his bedsheets. He was **drug**-vitalized. His mind sped. His limbs spastic-twitched.

"Egalitarian and degenerate. Those two words define the klub**haus.** Mr. Hudgens of the **Herald** is quite the cheeky man. The German spelling of house. A touch first bestowed by policemen, there on the scene. One can be certain of that."

Ashida said, "The sexual activity. The use of narcotics. The seemingly at odds political views."

Hanamaka grinned. **Sensei** Death rides again. His breath was foul. His teeth rattled. He oozed putresence.

"'At odds' aptly describes the atmosphere. 'Fugitives from normalcy' might best describe the klub**haus** clientele. There were no racial or political barriers to hinder conversation. The constant jazz music served to alleviate tension. There was a single consensus among the fugitives. 'The most discordant jazz is our voice.'"

Ashida prickled. The queer white boy. A jazz player. His Jap sword man pal. Elmer J. shared the lead.

"Jam sessions. Phonograph music. The proximity of the jazz strip. Diverse characters passing through."

Hanamaka jiggled his water cup. "You're leading me, Dr. Ashida. You want me to identify a specific denizen, and you're disingenuously setting the scene before you ask."

Ashida coughed. "A white youth. Blond and tall. Most often accompanied by a Japanese man given to licking blood off samurai swords. That was the Japanese man's parlor trick. I'm assuming he performed it at the klub**haus.** The white youth was homosexual. Forensic evidence indicates homosexual activity upstairs."

Hanamaka shrugged and shook his head. **Sensei** Death emits deceit.

"No. I did not encounter such men at the klub**haus.** I disdain homosexuals and Japanese who perform parlor tricks. Such individuals would most certainly catch my eye and rouse my indignation."

Ashida jumped tracks. "Let's discuss the gold. I want to conclusively determine the chain of possession."

"The chain began with Leander Frechette and the Reverend Mimms. Meyer considered Leander reliable, because they dated back to Meyer's previous incarnation, as Fritz Eckelkamp, and Leander was there for the conception of the robbery, along with

Wayne Frank Jackson. Meyer trusted Leander, and, by extension, the Reverend Mimms. Meyer put great stock in Negroes, and held them to be avant-garde. The Reverend Mimms' buffoonish black nationalism delighted him no end."

Ashida undid his necktie. "Please continue, **Sensei.**"

"Leander had been exonerated by the Santa Barbara Sheriff's. He had withstood the brutal ministrations of Deputy Karl Tullock, and had prevailed. The Reverend Mimms bailed Leander out of custody, and was a noted friend of Chief Jim Davis, a nativist huckster known to have close friends on the Left. He later became a comrade–**Kamerad,** as you must know."

Ashida said, "The gold. Let's continue with the chain of possession."

Hanamaka sipped water. He'd cracked his glass straw. Blood dripped off his lips.

"You must realize that unforeseen events intervened, along with fortuitous circumstances. Dresden Polytechnic, for example. The serendipitous convergence of Hayes, Díaz, Pimentel, and Jamie. The Spanish Civil War converged. Meyer earned his share of battle stripes there."

Ashida shook his head. "You're repeating yourself, **Sensei.** Let's return to the chain of possession. I'm trying to establish a chronology."

Hanamaka shrugged. "Frechette and Mimms returned the gold to Meyer at some point. I don't know where it was stashed during what I would call an 'intervening period.' Juan Pimentel took possession of the gold after the Baja conference, at Meyer's directive. It has since gone to the Stalinist priest-killer. I mentioned him to you in the course of our first interview."

Ashida said, "Wayne Frank Jackson. Where was he during this interim period?"

"He was in periodic touch with Meyer, but beyond that, I have no idea."

The room broiled. Steam heat jacked the burn stink. Ashida removed his suit coat.

"Frechette and Mimms returned the gold at some point, and Meyer once again took possession. Were Frechette and Mimms reluctant to relinquish it? Did a disagreement occur? Was force employed?"

"I was surprised at how easily they forfeited the gold. It shocked me at the time. Meyer gloated over the ease of the transaction. He held Negroes to be the most malleable of beasts. He considered them exalted, prone to whimsy, and subservient at their core. When one exalts, one is compelled to demean."

Ashida coughed into his handkerchief. The burn stink and salve stink accreted.

"Let's return to the klub**haus.** I find it illuminating that you decided to nest there, in a hotbed of degenerate behavior and impolitic discourse. Were you sent there? Were you told to observe, inform, or attempt to impose order?"

Hanamaka licked his lips. The blood had congealed.

He looked worse today. The give-and-take taxed him more.

"José Vasquez-Cruz sent me in. I knew him from Meyer's cell, when he was Jorge Villareal-Caiz. He was a **Kamerad,** in both his guises, and in the latter he was a captain in the Mexican State Police. He smuggled me out of Baja in the wake of Pearl Harbor, at the behest of Governor Lazaro-Schmidt. So, yes, **El Capitán** installed me in the house down the street. As you state, I was told to visit the klub**haus** and 'observe and inform.' Most preposterously, I was also told to attempt to restore order."

The room went ice-cold. Ashida glanced out the window. Snowflakes brushed the screen.

"The klub**haus** offended you. You discontinued your visits. I'm wondering if you were told to investigate the murders of Rice, Kapek, and Archuleta, on your own. The comrades must have feared the police investigation. We had drawn very close to a number of your people. Were you told to investigate? Did you arrive at a suspect or suspects?"

The Mummy cranked his bed up two notches. The Mummy pushed himself off his pillows and bowed at the waist.

"I prevaricated on the topic of your white youth and his Japanese friend. I cannot tell you whether or not the youth was homosexual, but he was surely tall and blond. He played the saxophone, and he worshipped the Negro jazz greats most exaltedly.

A woman frequently accompanied him to the **haus.**
She was frizzy-haired and roughly thirty years of age.
And, yes, the white youth had a Japanese friend, who
was plainly psychopathic."

Man Camera. Time Machine. The klub**haus** job
now stands some sixty days in. We're back in the upstairs hallway. There's dent marks on the wall facing
the bedroom. There's his working hypothesis.

Two killers. One male, one female. Rice, Kapek,
and Archuleta—terped to the gills. The man and
woman lead them downstairs. The woman stands
to the right of the victims. She sways. She punctuates
the death march. She kicks out at the wall and leaves
shoe-mark indentations. There's his overarching con-
viction. The crime was organically homosexual and
homosexually spawned.

"The blond youth, the woman, and the sword man.
Did you hold them to be murder suspects?"

"Instinctively, yes. They stood out as unique in a
most unique milieu."

"Once again, **Sensei.** Who possesses the gold at
this moment?"

Hanamaka said, "Once again, the Stalinist Mexican.
The most exalted slayer of priest-killers is our **Führer**
and most exalted comrade. I would give you his name,
but I don't know it."

114

(LOS ANGELES, 9:00 A.M., 3/31/42)

They huddled at Kay's place. Bill Parker snagged four wire players and four earmuff sets. Four socket plugs supplied juice.

They worked at the dining room table. Elmer divvied up the spools. Lesnick had scrawled analysand names on the boxes. They stuck to Claire De Haven, Orson Welles, Otto Klemperer.

Those three adjoined the whole megillah. No **Kameraden** wires existed. That meant no Meyer Gelb.

Kay distributed coffee and ashtrays. Buzz plugged in the cords. El Buzzo crowed a bit. He'd triple-checked their subpoenaed phone bills and snagged a doozy.

Ed the Fed Satterlee. 2/14/42. He calls a bail bondsman, up in San Fran. Buzz calls the bondsman and hits pay dirt.

Here's the pitch. Leander Frechette's been jailed for a soft-prowl 459. Ed the Fed bails him out.

Attaboy, Buzz. You pin-mapped Big Leander. Now, what about **these** calls?

Ed's late-night calls. All to Lyman's and Kwan's. Interchangeable calls. All to pay phones there. Who you looking for, Ed?

Everybody set up and lit up. The room got smoke-ified. Everybody pushed buttons. Wire spools spun.

Elmer heard static and line fritz. It cleared inside six seconds. Doc Saul and Orson Welles schmoozed the big Leningrad siege. They exhausted that topic. Welles bemoaned his weight. Doc Saul said he'd prescribe pharmaceutical cocaine.

It got boring then. Welles pitched boo-hoo. He was a genius. Boo-hoo. America was a philistine encampment. Boo-hoo. "I get more ass than a toilet seat, Saul. How come I'm so damn unfulfilled?"

Boo-hoo. The government should subsidize his movies and pay him a hundred Gs per. Boo-hoo. "I should lose weight. A hatcheck girl at the Trocadero blew me. We steamed up the hatcheck booth."

Kay pulled off her earmuffs. It cued the whole gang. Elmer dumped his earmuffs. Buzz and Whiskey Bill followed suit.

Kay said, "Claire's weeping. Dudley takes his pleasure, and then ignores her. He spends hours tending to his clothes. A cobbler custom-fitted him for jackboots."

Buzz said, "That's a good one. All I've got is your maestro chum haranguing the doc about Beethoven. The late quartets are some shitfire 'Apotheosis.' Lesnick told him Beethoven's got certified coon blood, which accounts for his rhythmic stance. He read it in some eugenics journal. Herr Goering is going to exhume the body and take bone samples. They've got some Nazi breeding farm in Norway.

Kraut wenches and Norse-god men screw all day. The wenches pop frogs for the Fatherland."

Elmer said, "Count me in."

Kay laughed. Whiskey Bill rolled his eyes. They re-donned their earmuffs and went back to work.

Boo-hoo, boo-hoo. Orson Welles talked drivel. Elmer listened in. Boo-hoo. The plight of the artist. Boo-hoo. The burden of social consciousness. "I drilled Norma Shearer, Saul. That old girl shtups with the best."

Elmer switched spools. He swapped Welles for Claire De Haven. Claire defamed El Dudster and Joan Conville. "Really, Saul. She's beyond Amazonian. She's something out of the **National Geographic.**"

Parker pulled off his earmuffs. It cued the whole gang. Elmer dumped his earmuffs. Kay and Buzz followed suit.

Parker said, "Klemperer's telling Lesnick about the headaches that he diagnosed as a brain tumor, and he's fawning over Lesnick for saving his life. Then there's a gap, where the two discuss the war, and then it gets good. Klemperer begins talking in fragments. He says that a man was 'hectoring' him and ragging on him as a Jew and a leftist, and the man says that he knows 'Meyer's girl Jean.' Klemperer tells Lesnick that this man is taunting him, and he 'plays horn' in Negro jazz clubs. Klemperer repeats the phrase 'He's taunting me' at least a dozen times. Then he states that he beats the man to death. Then he begins fawning over Lesnick again. Then he states, 'And you took care of it, Doctor—you and your FBI friend.'"

Elmer went **wooo.** "The FBI friend's sure as shit Ed Satterlee."

Kay said, "Otto told me that story. He confirmed that Satterlee was the FBI man, but the story itself was fragmented to the point of incomprehension."

Buzz said, "The part about this guy being a horn player gores me. For one, it takes us back to the jazz strip again, and we all know our current klub**haus** suspect is a queer and a jazzman."

Parker shook his head. "Our homicides occurred on January 29. This Klemperer-Lesnick session occurred the week after Pearl Harbor. That exonerates this particular jazzman, and it's not like he's the only jazzman in captivity, queer or otherwise."

Buzz shook his head. "Yeah, but this guy tells the Maestro he knows Meyer's girl Jean. That's fucking significant, and it takes us back to the klub**haus** job and the whole shooting match again."

Kay lit a cigarette. "Yes, and I'm not convinced that Otto killed anyone, which means that this particular jazzman could be our jazzman, who's good for the klub**haus** job and possibly a whole lot more."

Parker shook his head. "Jazzmen are jazzmen. There's millions of them. Gelb and Staley aside, I don't consider this any sort of real lead."

Elmer said, "We've got Hideo deposing Kyoho Hanamaka now. He's our key source. Somebody should talk to Hideo and see what Hanamaka spilled on the klub**haus** angle, and if any of it pertains to our queer jazzman and his Jap playmate."

Buzz lit a cigar. "Meyer Gelb. This whole deal comes down to him. He's Fritzie Eckelkamp cut into Gelb, which takes him back to '31 and the gold job. He's all over this whole thing, and I am currently doing everything within my power as a member of this white man's police department to find him and have a long chat with him."

Parker sighed and redonned his earmuffs. It cued the gang. Talk gets us nowhere. Let's get back to work.

Elmer redonned his earmuffs. Kay and Buzz followed suit. Elmer fish-eyed Buzz. El Buzzo radiated the lynch mob gestalt. Buzz had Meyer Gelb on the brain. Ditto El Dudster. Buzz figured Dud would kill him soon. Buzz figured he should kill Dud first.

Elmer switched spools and spun spools and smoked himself hoarse. He played the analysand field. Orson Welles boo-hoo'd and bragged up his conquests. Claire De Haven boo-hoo'd and skewered Dudley Smith. The Maestro extolled the Bruckner symphonies and the upcoming "exile migration." Elmer perked up and took note.

Well, shit. There's Meyer Gelb, again.

Elmer pulled off his earmuffs. It cued the whole gang. Kay dumped her earmuffs. Parker and Buzz followed suit.

Elmer said, "Here's the Maestro. He's talking up his comrades Ruth Szigeti, the Koenigs, and old man

Abromowitz. They're being repatriated to L.A., and he wants to help out. Lesnick talks the Maestro into getting them jobs as movie-studio musicians, then says to have them keep their snouts down and report to Comrade Gelb."

Buzz cracked his knuckles. "I intend to have words with that whipdick."

Kay said, "That entails finding him first."

Parker four-eyed Elmer. He tapped his wristwatch. **We've got pressing biz downtown.**

They reconvened outside the Fed Building. Elmer lapel-pinned his badge. Parker displayed his search warrant.

"A Fed district judge signed it. He's an old law school classmate, and he hates Fey Edgar like death itself."

Elmer skimmed the legalese. Limited premises/custody vault only/all wire recordings on-site. On-site listening consent granted/one day only.

"We've got to erase the whole kit and caboodle. That's the only sure way to cover ourselves and Sheriff Gene's guys. It's a whole shitload of work, with the Fed squadroom right down the hall."

Parker pinned up his badge. "The judge called ahead. We're covered there. We've got the means to scotch the whole probe, but they'll know it was us. We'll have to ride out whatever shit hits the fan."

Elmer gulped. "Fey Edgar will wet his pink-lace undies. He'll be on the horn to the U.S. attorney inside half a second."

Parker winked. It fell flat. He possessed no savoir faire. He lacked Dudsteresque panache.

They breezed in and breezed up the side stairs. The Bureau owned the full third floor. A desk agent manned the lobby. They walked up. He looked up. Parker passed him the paperwork.

He read the full writ. He said, "The vault, huh? You fellows must be turncoats. A whole lot of PD guys are going to burn in this deal."

Parker said, "We've been detached to the grand jury. We're on your side as far as this one goes."

The agent yawned and stretched. He passed the paperwork back. This rebop left him nonplussed.

"Judge Leffler called ahead. You know the rules, right? You can listen to whatever you want, but nothing leaves the room. You know how to use the machines?"

Parker nodded. Elmer broke a sweat. The desk man led the way back.

Elmer stared straight ahead. They passed boocoo doorways. Elmer heard squadroom bustle and counted his footsteps. He hit eighty-nine. The desk man turned right and unlocked a door.

Some vault. Just this dumb room crammed with boxes. Note the wire spools sticking out. Two player contraptions. Two earmuff sets. One beat-up desk and two chairs. A wire log clamped to a clipboard.

The desk man said, "I leave you to it."

Parker saluted him. Elmer feigned nonchalance. The desk man vamoosed. Parker locked the door.

Elmer went **wheeewww.** Parker picked up the log

and skimmed it. You had twenty-some pages. Maybe eight hundred calls and taps.

Parker scanned pages. Elmer dumped his coat and undid his necktie. He futzed with the gizmos. He plugged in the earmuffs and ID'd the erase switch. Parker got all bug-eyed.

He crossed himself. He waved wolfsbane. He did all this papist shit.

"The Feds bugged the pay phone at Kwan's. We've got EX-4991 calling MA-2668. PC Bell tagged the call at 3:14 a.m., on March 6. It's a West L.A.-to-downtown toll call, and it runs sixteen minutes."

EX-4991. That's Ed Satterlee's home number. Holy heart attack—

The wire log listed box 56. They tore through four box stacks and found it. Two spools were stuffed in one envelope.

Elmer rigged the two gizmos. The wires spooled up tight. Parker passed him his flask. They traded pops and tamped down their wigs. Parker kicked the chairs back. They sat side by side. They donned the ear-muffs and replayed the call.

The phone rang. Static and line fuzz bled into **this:**

"There you are. I figured I'd get you sooner or later, and 3:00 a.m. in a Chinatown slop chute doesn't surprise me at all."

Ed Satterlee speaks. He's crusty, per always.

"Ed, I've been wanting to talk to you."

Mike Breuning speaks. He's servile, per always. Elmer and Parker swapped looks.

Satterlee said, "I gathered that. You called the Bureau nine goddamn times. You're lucky I'm a night owl, or I wouldn't have caught you at all. I'm just hoping you aren't jerking my chain."

Breuning said, "It's Dudley, Ed. He's gone bat-shit. You wouldn't believe some of the stunts he's been pulling."

Satterlee said, "I'd believe anything you might want to tell me about Dudley Liam Smith, which is one damn good reason why I do my best to avoid him and stay on his good side."

Breuning said, "I've got to get out from under him, Ed. He's gone off the deep end, and I thought maybe you could help."

Breuning speaks, frazzled. He's caught the snitch virus. **Oooga-booga.** Snitch fever permeates the call.

Satterlee whistled. The phone line hissed.

"If you're asking for help, you've got to pay for that help. If you're offering me an up-to-date derogatory profile on Dudley, I'd be inclined to help you, if and when the time is right."

Breuning said, "That's awful damn equivocal."

Satterlee said, "Lay it out for me. And it better be a little spicier than Dud's framing a few jigaboos for the Rice-Kapek job."

Breuning speaks. He's delirious now. Dat snitch voodoo's gone to his head.

"He's hooked on Benzedrine and opium. He's gee-zing morphine, but he thinks nobody knows. Bill Parker's checkmating him. He's gone full-fledged

Nazi. He parades around in Nazi uniforms and preens like a fruit. He's running heroin and wetbacks. He's selling Japs off as slave labor. He's in with this Sinarquista hump Salvy Abascal, who's playing him like he's the village idiot. He was in with Joan Conville and Hideo Ashida on some gold angle, but Joan's dead and Ashida will be heading to Manzanar, and now he's flapping in the wind all by himself. He told me he found the guy who killed Joan's dad and made Joan kill him. He killed a drag boy at a pervert party in '39, and Dick Carlisle and me cleaned it up. He's murdering Reds in Mexico. He killed a Statie captain who was screwing his Commie girlfriend. The Baja governor's sister has got him pussy-whipped, and Abascal's got him hoodwinked. I'm way far exposed, Ed. I've run point for Dud for eleven goddamn years. I need a safe-haven deal with an outside agency. He's a Nazi and a traitor, and he's chopping the heads off these Redshirt guys who kill priests. I'll depose, Ed. I'll give Dudley up. He's a feather in your cap, Ed. He's the biggest scalp you'll ever take. Ed, you've got to help—"

The line fritzed. The call died. It cut off Mike Breuning's sobs.

Doc Saul slogged it. His gourd was elsewhere. That was evident. Boolah, boolah. Annie gave it the college-girl try.

Elmer and Parker watched. Elmer ran the camera.

They were dead bushed. They'd erased all the Fed vault wires. It took ten hours. They heard Mike Breuning's sobs the whole time.

They discussed the Breuning-Satterlee call. They caught Breuning's snitch virus. Ed the Fed was house-arrested. He posed no threat to Dudley Smith. They stole the Breuning-Satterlee wires. They could ditz Dud with them. They could pass the virus on.

The crawl space was tight-cramped. Elmer and Parker smoked it out. Smoke hazed the see-thru mirror. Elmer placed the camera lens flat on the glass. Their sound gear caught pillow talk.

Saul waved off the woof-woof. He was abstracted and limp-noodled. Two-minute Saul. He'd rather talk anyway.

Grave Saul. Distracted Saul. He suffers from de white man's burden. De chickens be comin' home to roost.

Annie said, "What is it, sugar? What happened to my stallion of the sack?"

Elmer yukked. Parker oozed pious censure. Annie smoothed out the bedsheets. Saul assumed a crucifixion pose. Nobody knows de trouble he's seen.

Annie goo-goo-eyed him. Annie tickled his ribs and got bupkes.

"You're remote tonight, baby. You're wearing that crown of thorns, as my preacher daddy used to say."

Saul said, "You wouldn't understand. I can't blame you for what you don't know. You're game, but you're not enlightened."

Elmer yukked. Annie winked at the see-thru. Old Saul sighed.

"Hoodlums laid waste to my office. They stole valuable recordings and smeared jingoistic slogans on the walls. I can't go to the Beverly Hills Police or the FBI, and I certainly can't go to my friend Ed Satter—"

Saul stopped cold. Annie tweaked on **Satterlee.** Old Saul tweaked her tweak. Elmer tweaked both tweaks.

Parker said, "He nailed her reaction."

Elmer went **Yep.** Old Saul eyeballed Annie. He pushed off his pillow and zoom-lensed her.

"Do you **know** Ed?"

Annie shrugged. What's with this Ed? I don't know this Ed whoever.

"I tricked with Eddie Cantor once. It was after this Save the Jews wingding. He's the only Ed I know."

Parker said, "She's not convincing."

Elmer went **Yep.**

Old Saul jumped out of bed. He was stooped and chicken-chested. His cashew dick flop-flopped.

He orbed the walls. He patted the walls. He poked at wall junctures. He's an old CP hand. He knows from wall bugs and honey traps.

He poked wall moldings. He pulled a spackled wire off a baseboard and yanked it out from under a rug. Annie jumped out of bed. She faced the see-thru, buck naked. She flashed this fetching **Oh shit** look.

Old Saul caught it. He dropped the wire and went for Annie. Elmer and Parker jumped.

They tore out of the crawl space. They tumbled into the bedroom and dog-piled old Saul. They floor-pinned him. He sissy-kicked and flailed. Annie snagged the sap in Elmer's waistband.

She applied a good grip. She whipped shots at old Saul's genitalia. Old Saul screamed. Elmer gassed the floor show. Annie yelled **"You Fucking Traitor"** roughly ten zillion times.

115

(ENSENADA, 8:00 P.M., 4/1/42)

Fat Boy unfurled a portable screen and set up his projector. Dudley cut the lights. His suite subbed for Grauman's Chinese.

Fats boomeranged. He returned to L.A. and shot straight back to Ensenada. He supplied that klub**haus** lead. He'd retrieved a memory. It spurred this return visit.

Orson met a fruit kid on his goodwill tour. The kid attended the **Walpurgisnacht** party. He was a jazz musician. He knew another fruit kid. **That** kid attended klub**haus** jam sessions. **That** kid was a jazzman. **That** kid bragged up the klub**haus** snuffs. **That** kid and "some Red-fasco woman" snuffed Rice, Kapek, and Archuleta.

It was secondhand drift. It comprised a hot lead, regardless. It supplanted prior leads. It confirmed the queer white boy and Jap sword man.

Here's Orson's memory. Orson met that other kid. The kid appeared in the **Walpurgisnacht** smut film. He'd bragged up his Jap sword-licker friend and some darktown clubhouse. It had to be him.

Hence, Orson returns. Hence, this home movie. Roll it, Fats.

Dudley pulled a chair up. El Gordo adjusted the film spools. He wore Bermuda shorts and a loud Hawaiian shirt.

"Your man's the clarinet player. When the camera pans to the woodwind quintet, you'll see him."

Dudley cued Welles. Lights, camera, action. Wagner hit the sound track. Trumpets and low strings. It's **Götterdämmerung.** Dig the bleak intercessional strains.

A title card: "Berlin, '29." It denotes bleak atop bleak. Here's Alban Berg's **Lulu** and grainy stock footage.

It's a street riot. It's Reds versus Brownshirts. There's Marxist banners and swastikas ablaze. Bullyboys wield two-by-fours. The Brownshirts outnumber the Reds. It's a rout. Blood flows in crisp black-&-white.

There's a quick cut. Weill and Brecht replace Berg. There's **"Mackie Messer."** Lotte Lenya warbles it.

Bam!—there's a new title card. "Near Munich, 6-30-34." **Bam!**—we're outside a country inn. There's a dumb paper moon. The inn looks one-dimensional. We're on a cheap studio set.

Four black-clad SS men approach the door. Two men are Negro. Two men look Samoan. Fat Boy Welles provides surreal laffs.

Schubert usurps **The Threepenny Opera.** It's a woodwind quintet. We're inside the inn. There's a Nazi-garbed ensemble. Three string men and one oboe. The queer boy's on clarinet. It's his skin flute in lieu of hard flesh.

Welles said, "That's him."

"Him." Their triple-snuff suspect. He's blond. He's innocuous. He's lanky, and seems to be tall.

A quick cut. **Auf Wiedersehen,** Schubert. "Mack the Knife" returns.

We're in a small bedroom. We're peeping an all-boy bacchanal. It's a daisy chain. The lads wear Brownshirts and nothing else. They're cinched groin-to-buttocks. They pump and gesticulate. There's pelvic thrusts twenty boys long.

The SS men enter the room and shoot them. They employ toy Lugers. Cap-gun pops hit the sound track. The daisy chain collapses. The bugger boys disengage.

Dudley studied the film. He'd seen stray cuts at the party. He recalled none of it now. He was gone on hop then. He was flat sober now.

The screen blurs. **"Mackie Messer"** goes garbled.

Wagner rides again. It's **Das Rheingold.** More trumpets and more low strings.

The screen unblurs. The daisy chain replicates. It's men and women now. They're linked groin-to-mouth.

The camera cuts away. Walter Pidgeon appears and struts as Adolf Hitler. He's Homerically hung. He rubs his toothbrush mustache. Claire De Haven kneels and gobbles his **schvantz.**

116

(LOS ANGELES, 7:00 A.M., 4/2/42)

I'm writing a letter to Hideo Ashida now. I will hand-deliver it to Manzanar. I will include a wire recording of Ed Satterlee's phone chat with Mike Breuning. I may send the second recording to Dudley Smith.

It's beginning to cohere. Joan's "all one story" is careening toward final explication. Hideo recounted his first interview with Kyoho Hanamaka; second and third interviews may well have occurred. My letter will urge Hideo to move beyond mere dissembling and omission. I will demand that he repudiate and fully betray his dear Dudley.

I'm exhausted. I visited Claire at Terry Lux's retreat last night; we gabbed until dawn and had steak and eggs in the lounge. Jim Davis sat a few tables over; a male nurse attended him. Comrade Jim is faltering. He had trouble lifting his fork.

Claire's morphine cure is proceeding. She talks and smokes incessantly and rails against her once-dear Dudley. She reads the Bible and obscure prayer books and often coils a rosary around one hand and forms that hand into a fist. Dear Claire. She showed me letters that Beth Short and Joan Klein have sent her. I studied the girls' cursive styles and unformed sentence structures. Dudley has seven daughters; these two are his favorites. Their expressed condemnation would dismay and perhaps bitterly wound him. I would, of course, craft both texts.

Elmer and Bill leaned on Sid Hudgens. They imposed a gag order on Sid's scandal-sheet machinations and secured his subscriber list. I will write the text that Sid's 461 paid subscribers will read. The sheet will be sent to key SIS personnel and ranking officers in the Mexican State Police. Every known comrade/**Kamerad** will receive the sheet; it will go out to Jack Horrall, notable Feds, Archbishop Cantwell and L.A.'s papal high brass. It will go out to Dudley himself. I will smear Dudley Smith in the Salacious Sidster's trademark style. I will instigate insidious ink. Everything that I write will be true.

Hatred fuels me now. It fuels this letter I'm writing. I now pass my hatred along to Hideo Ashida.

I described the Saul Lesnick–Annie Staples misadventure. Bill and Elmer tossed Doctor Saul in the Lincoln Heights drunk tank and let him stew for six long hours. They hauled him to the City Hall DB then. I observed the interrogation through a wall mirror; a wall-mounted speaker served up sound. Lesnick vividly confirmed the **Kameraden**'s postwar strategy and stoutly defended the grand ideals of enlightened dictatorship. Bill and Elmer let him blather. Lesnick laid out no less than the world as he saw it. It was one creepy credo. Sid Hudgens would label it "dippy dialectic" and a "miasmic manifesto." It featured the doctor's eugenic rationale for slaughtering infants. It ballyhooed Hitler's Norse breeding camps. It included a stirring defense of the Moscow show trials and Stalin's mass execution of deviationists and perceived traitors. Stalin's agrarian purges and Hitler's assault on the Warsaw Ghetto Jews were plain poppycock. Doctor Saul voiced an intense distaste for one Sergeant E. V. Jackson. He told Elmer that he'd be castrated and sold into slave labor once the comrades took over the world. Elmer turned to the mirror and winked at me.

Doctor Saul talked himself out; Bill got the interrogation down to brass tacks. He asked the questions. Elmer hovered and tapped a phone book on the sweatbox table. Lesnick gulped and credibly snitched.

He'd heard rumors about the gold but possessed no specific information. He was conversant with the **Kameraden**'s mail drop and microdot shenanigans.

He did not know who the prior **Führers** were and did not know who the current **Führer** is. He knew Meyer Gelb and Jean Staley. He did not know that Gelb was once Fritz Eckelkamp and did not know where Gelb hid out. He described Ed Satterlee as an apostolic theoretical Trotskyite and committed Marxist. Ed was the **Kameraden**'s fix-it man. Lesnick professed ignorance of the klub**haus.** He had never been to the klub**haus.** He did not know Kyoho Hanamaka. He had never met Wendell Rice, George Kapek, and Archie Archuleta.

Bill released Lesnick. Go, shitbird. Twist in the wind. Describe your ordeal to your comrades. I watched Lesnick weave through the City Hall lobby. He bumped into an old friend on his way out the door.

The man was the L.A. **Bürgermeister** of the Negro Nazi League, and was known to pimp colored girls to DA Bill McPherson. The long-lost soulmates embraced. I overheard their conversation. Lesnick suggested lunch; the **Bürgermeister** suggested Kwan's. He went way back with Ace. Ace owned a sweatshop that enslaved eight-year-old kids. The kids stitched the League's banners and armbands.

The Fifth Column is everyone. Hideo Ashida told me that. It was New Year's Eve. Hideo had just returned from Venice. Joan Conville plowed a car full of wetbacks and left six dead. Bill Parker put the fix in. He had the hots for the big redhead. It's all one story, you—

We know most of it now, Hideo. There's a good deal

still to be learned. It entails your betrayal of Dudley Smith. I command your loyalty in this moment. You know what he is. You know this is true.

Bill and Elmer are set to raid Bev's Switchboard. Do you recall the speech I gave two weeks after Pearl Harbor? Pershing Square was packed. I decried the Japanese internment. You were beaten for being there and being a Jap. I baited the crowd. I told them their options were do everything or do nothing. I'm telling you that now.

117

(LONE PINE, 4:00 P.M., 4/2/42)

Sensei Hanamaka, aka "The Mummy" and "Dr. Death." He's faltering. He's entered an implosive state.

His grin's stretching wider. His fangs protrude more. He's caving in. He'll die soon. He'll become a Jap Shrunken Head.

Interview #3. It reprised 1 and 2. The salve and burn stink. The visitor's chair and the hospital bed.

Ashida said, "I'd like to hear your impressions of Wendell Rice and George Kapek."

Sensei coughed. His fluid bag drained. Sledgehammer dope hit his veins.

"They were second-generation rightist. Rice's father was in the Silver Shirts. Kapek's father is a gauleiter in rural Czechoslovakia. I saw them the first time in the winter of 1939. They were chauffeuring America Firsters to a Nazi-themed party in Brentwood. They served well in the manner of henchmen, as evinced by their minor roles in moving illegals under the aegis of Carlos Madrano. Such employment continued into the era of José Vasquez-Cruz, abutting the era of your mentor, Dudley Smith."

Ashida flinched. He hasn't called Dudley. He's put it off repeatedly. Three crucial interviews. What to tell/ what to omit/what to obfuscate.

"Again, were they homosexual? The crime seems to be homosexual in its origins."

"I would not call them homosexual. I would call them fetishistic. Their fetishism was fueled by dope and liquor, along with the trinkets that Archie Archuleta procured for them in Little Tokyo. What would you pay for a slaughter sword deployed at the Rape of Nanking? Your mentor, Dudley Smith, might well be described as a fetishist. Juan Pimentel considered him such."

Dudley was. Dudley **is.** Kay's faux Claire missive. Fetishism implies the lavender look. Dudley's "effete eye for callow young men."

Slaughter swords. The Jap sword man. His queer white boy friend. Confirmations accrue and overlap.

"You appear to be deep in thought, Dr. Ashida. I consider it peculiar that you are not taking notes. Did

Major Smith tell you not to? I could see where he might want to avoid a public record of our talks."

Ashida bristled. Don't torque me, Tojo. He'd heard Elmer J. tell a Jap suspect that.

"Major Smith is a close friend, and my former commanding officer. I consider all his suggestions, but do not consider them commands."

Hanamaka leered. Opportunist Ashida. Race traitor Ashida. The white man's lapdog. He heels at Major Smith's command.

"Let's return to the trinkets. What were the other types that Archuleta procured, in addition to the swords you mentioned?"

Hanamaka said, "Torture devices. Vile ones. Suits of armor in the shape of Japanese soldiers, fitted with interior spikes meant to inflict horrible death on the wearer. I would call devices such as these militaristically homosexual. Archuleta brought a sampling of them by the klub**haus** one day while I was there. He said he was the middleman for a 'fruit' who sold them to 'strange-o types' he encountered on the jazz strip, although the 'fruit' did his primary business through the U.S. mail. Archuleta mentioned the 'fruit's' sister very briefly. She was the purported brains of this mail-order business. The sister visited the klub**haus** one night. I recall her vividly."

Elmer on Jean Staley. Jean and her "froufrou" kid brother. Robby, ex-jailbird and would-be actor. Not a musician.

We're up against prior descriptions. The would-be

killer's tall and blond. Jean Staley is short and dark-haired. A tall blond brother seems unlikely. Archuleta's fruit and the queer-white-boy killer? Probably separate men.

Hanamaka coughed. Blood dripped down his chin. Ashida cracked his evidence kit and pulled his Jean Staley mug shot.

He flashed it. Hanamaka nodded yes. His ID was conclusive. It tied Robby Staley to the Jap sword man. It tied Robby to the queer white boy, once-removed.

Hanamaka yawned and shuddered. The dope jolt had depleted him. Metamorphosis. Here comes your Jap Shrunken Head.

"I think I know you now, Dr. Ashida. One thing continues to perplex me, though. Do you consider yourself Japanese or American?"

Ashida said, "You don't know me at all. I'm as American as you're not."

The main-gate guard left him a package. It contained one letter and one wire spool. An MP sergeant lent him a player and listening earmuffs.

It snowed. Manzanar was socked in tight. Hold for the mid-April thaw. You freeze or broil here. Manzanar's a two-climate zone.

Ashida holed up. The heating vents hummed. He read the letter four times. He played the wire recording twice.

He paced his suite. He looked out at the snow. A

mess corporal brought him his dinner. The burn-ward doctor called. Kyoho Hanamaka died at 8:29 p.m.

The letter rankled. Kay was nothing but Kay-like. She was imperious, didactic, jejune. Kommisar Kay. Categorical and Manichean. There is no way but my way. If I believe it, it's true.

Your options are do everything or do nothing.

The wire call revealed Dudley in extremis. Mike Breuning levied a multicount indictment. Mike closed with sobs.

Ashida sat in the dark. He sipped champagne and willed the Baja-to-Manzanar call. The MP's mess hall served chilled champagne nightly. He'd come to expect and enjoy it.

He thought about Kay. She tried to seduce him last December. Kay's faux Claire letter. Dudley's effete eye for callow young men.

The phone rang. Ashida grabbed the receiver. Static cut off his "Hello?" Dudley was Dudleyesque. His blunt approach channeled Kommisar Kay.

"You've been among the missing, lad. I've gotten secondhand reports, from Al Wilhite, but I haven't heard from you."

Ashida cleared his throat. "I wanted to conclude my interviews before I reported. I'm sorry if it inconvenienced you."

"Hanamaka's dead, lad. Lieutenant Wilhite just called me. You won't be seeing our fair Kyoho again."

Man Camera. Let's frame this moment. There's the

dark room. There's his window view. It's all snow and prison-camp searchlights.

"He gave up nothing of note. He was incoherent most of the time, and he gave up nothing we hadn't already learned."

Dudley sighed. "The gold? The cabal's chain of command?"

Ashida said, "No. The decadent behavior at the klub**haus** amused him, and he provided me with a great many anecdotes. We spoke at length three times. It was very frustrating."

Dudley sighed. "Soldier on, lad. Study the files I sent you. Put that grand brain of yours to the task."

Ashida said, "I'm sorry, Dudley."

Dudley said, "I know you are. I hear it in your voice."

The line went dead. Ashida stifled a sob. Kommisar Kay had it right. There's no alternative. It's everything or nothing.

Part Five
REALPOLITIK

(April 3–28, 1942)

The El Lay Lowdown. Volume I, issue 4. Our motto? "All the news that's **un**fit to print." April 3, 1942 issue. Surreptitiously circulated since November 1941. Our serpentine circulation: 461 paid subscribers, and climbing via vile word of mouth. Dedicated to the proposition that **YOU WANT THE DISH.** All items written by Party Peeper 69. Subscription rate: $20.00 per year. Direct all inquiries to PO Box 69, Terminal Annex, Los Angeles.

Peeper 69 last left you in Nazi-nullified Paris, France. There was no need for insinuating initials in my climactic close-out piece. The frazzled frogs can't lasso me with libel suits from across the U-boat-undulating Atlantic. I joltingly **j'accused** piano putz **ALFRED CORTOT** of hunkering down with the Huns. I ditzed divaesque **DANIELLE DARRIEUX** for bedding down with the Boche. Cello cheese **PIERRE FOURNIER?** Shacked between the sheets with fetching filmstress **LENI RIEFENSTAHL.**

A barrage of bilious letters urged me to can the travelogues. If it ain't happening in El Lay, it ain't happening. Peeper 69 aims to please his rapacious readers. This issue repugnantly returns us to loopy Los Angeles—but with a twitchy twist.

The El Lay Lowdown speciously specializes in Hollywood dirt. Plus pulsing political scandals and the annihilating antics of El Lay socialites. Our regular "Police Blotter" feature features yet more Tinseltown tattle. And this issue turgidly turns its spotlight on the El Lay Police Department's most sinfully sinister and snaggled snafu.

Hear those surging saxophones and cloying clarinets? They announce the boogie beat of a big southside murder case. Dead men tell no tales—but we've got three stagnant stiffs grousing from the grave. Bent cops W.R. & G.K. demand justice; their Mex **muchacho** A.A. shrieks in **español.** Carrion cops case the corpses and lick their lips. This job's a maximum moneymaker and a shot to unseat J.H. as Chief.

W.H.P. Don't trust this guy. He'll sell his soul for the pomp of power and college cooze. Don't trust H.A. He's a Mr. Moto manqué and a jittery Jap. Don't trust pustulant policeman M.B. He's in league with furtive Fed E.S. There's a tapped telephone at a Chinatown eatery habituated by hellhound cops. M.B. and E.S. conspire via wire. Mr. B. rats out his maladroit mentor, that hellbound Hibernian hatchet man—D.S. himself.

D.S. is the duped deus ex machina of our dreary drama. Fifth Column finagling defines the big murder case. Caustic Commies M.G. and J.S. frame the fray. Feckless fascists W.J. and J.H. have joined them. Sicknik Sinarquista S.A. is playing D.S. for the fool. We've got riotous Reds and nutty Nazis galore. We've got **farshtinkener** factions out to glom gorgeous garlands of gold. Greed and graft, kats and kittens. Peeper 69's put his paws on the pulse of this story. He knows **alllllllll** about that perv party at the Maestro's manse in the winter of '39. **She** was really a **He,** and who can blame D.S. for taking ultimate umbrage? Thank heaven M.B & fellow cop D.C. cleaned up the mess.

It's hurtling to a head, dear readers. E.S. is under house arrest; H.A.'s joined the Jap diaspora and has been shipped out to Manzanar. Seditionist psychiatrist S.L. has been pounded by the police. Ex-Chief J.E.D. mutters murderous murmurs at a swank beachside retreat. Quo vadis, D.S.? You're the creepy crux of our drama. You've been spread cruciform, and demons of your own devising are coming for you.

118

(LOS ANGELES, 2:00 P.M., 4/4/42)

Double play. This raid and the scandal-rag blast. The rags went out, first-class mail. They should bull's-eye today.

And there's Bev's. It's straight across Fountain. It's transmitting Raid Me rays.

Elmer watched the door. Bill Parker watched the door. They sat in Bill's civilian sled. They brought shotguns and pry bars. It's a smash-and-seize job.

Parker smelled like Kay. That musky scent she wore. Elmer got all flustered and jealous. He teethed on them as bedmates. It hurt **baaaaaad.** He teethed on Wayne Frank Alive for relief.

Wayne Frank Alive hurt. He teethed on Ruth in the Kip. She'll call when she calls. That was her artiste's way. He teethed on Doc Lesnick. Thad Brown got a tip. Doc Saul ensconced himself at Terry Lux's place. He had company there. As in Claire De Haven and gaga Jim Davis.

Salvador Abascal. Teethe on that dink. He sprung Díaz, Carbajal, and Santarolo. He got them habeas. They waltzed out of Fed custody and rewaltzed back to Baja. That was **baaaaad** grapevine. Here's the **gooooood** grapevine. Fletch B. got preemptive acquitted. The grand jury pulled their true bills.

All charges were dropped. Mass acquittals were predicted. Guess who jump-started **that** shit.

Parker said, "I'm getting antsy."

Elmer said, "What's wrong with right now?"

They grabbed their gear. Riot guns and hefty pry bars. They ditched the sled and jaywalked. The front door stood open. They walked right in.

Raid Me rays?—**shit.** Here's what they got:

Mail-Drop Holocaust. Mail-Drop Inferno. Mail-Drop Mud Slide. All the mail slots were spread wide. There was no mail stuffed inside.

Elmer orbed the walls. Whiskey Bill, ditto. They saw open file drawers and no files visible. Plus open desk drawers in plain sight.

Plus Blow Job Bev and Wallace Jamie, perched in deck chairs. Looking smug. You can't seize vapors. You can't raid stale air.

Parker said, "You were tipped."

Jamie said, "People talk. Word travels. Fellow travelers travel, too." Bev giggled and flipped them the bird.

Parker went for Jamie. He kicked his chair over and smashed his head on the floor. Jamie bitch-yelped. Parker kicked him in the balls and cuffed his hands behind his back. Bev jumped up and whore-yelped. Her deck chair capsized.

Elmer scoped the room. He saw juncture cracks behind the file banks. He dropped his pump gun and ran to the east wall. He jammed his pry bar behind the **A** to **D** bank and pulled.

Metal screeched against linoleum. The file bank

slid out. No paper scraps or mail debris got revealed. Elmer yanked out the **E** to **J** bank. Lice eggs got revealed. Elmer yanked out the **K** to **R** bank. A mousetrap and stale cheese got revealed.

Metal screeched against linoleum. Jamie and Bev screeched Fascist Assault! Elmer pulled out the **S** to **Z** bank. He saw boocoo mail debris.

Glossy stuff. Spilled catalogues. Jammed upside the walls. In there with mouse turds and soot.

Elmer knelt down and pored through it. **S** to **Z** skank got revealed.

Sally's Sexy Lingerie. Crotchless Panties Our Specialty. Fat models with full beavers exposed. Silver Shirt closeout. Lo prices on bullwhips and nigger knockers. The Best in the West. Tasty Tessie. Hairpie deluxe. Pubic locks 4-sale. Your choice of blond, brunette, or red bush. Write to Tasty Tessie 2-day!!!

Vivid Violet. Certified nympho. Frat parties welcome. Special college-boy rates. Call Sharon, 24 hours. Your place or mine? No Negroes, Mexicans, or sailors. Call for introductory rate. Boys, Boys, Boys!!! Wicked Willie's got 'em!!! See fotos in May '41 issue of **Hung Magazine**!!!

Parker stomped the premises. Blow Job Bev pitched a fit. Jamie yelped for Uncle Eliot Ness. Elmer snagged a crumpled catalogue.

Johnny Shinura Curios. Exotic & Erotic Items. The Mysterious Orient Lives! 482 East 2nd Street, Los Angeles.

Ooooooh, what's—

East 2nd Street. J-town. The Jap sword man. He's a curio dealer. 482's not a storefront. The Crash Squad would have nailed it already. It's some warehouse stash hole. It has to be that. The sword man, the blood licker, the queer white boy's—

Elmer thumbed the catalogue. Check this out. You've got iron maidens and swastika branding irons. There's SS tunics for your dog. You've got a Jap soldier suit of arms. It features sharp spikes inside. It's now available in four sizes!!! It's guaranteed to cause **EXCRUTIATING DEATH!!!**

119

(ENSENADA, 5:00 P.M., 4/4/42)

The watch sergeant called in sick. It was SOP. He was an all-time goldbrick. He habituated the Blue Fox and White Dog Klub. His work went undone.

Dudley filled in. Major D. L. Smith, among the squadroom pogues. He worked at the sergeant's desk. He filled out the duty roster and sorted the mail.

The squadroom buzzed. SIS ran full Saturday shifts. Dudley buzzed. He had Benzedrine for breakfast and lunch. The Wolf was down in La Paz. Constanza doted on him.

Dudley slit envelopes. The mail was SOP-plus. Fourth Interceptor demands Jap head counts. The Staties demand liaison meets. There's Jap sub alerts. There's Redshirt rallies east of Piedra Rojas. Please infiltrate.

Plus a plain envelope. Addressed direct to him. An L.A. postmark and no return address.

Dudley slit the envelope. Three mimeo sheets were stuffed in. The cheap ink bled. The cheap paper wilted. Say what? It's Sid Hudgens' private rag.

The El Lay Lowdown. Sid's standard fare, free of restraints. 461 subscribers. William Randolph Hearst, take note.

Dudley skimmed through it. He skimmed through Holly**weird** tattle, couched in Sid's standard style. Men's room hijinks and gang bangs. Sid's standard fare. He skimmed to "big southside murder case." He hit "pustulant policeman M.B." He quick-skimmed to "D.S. himself." He went hot/cold/hot and skimmed the full text.

He made this noise. Code clerks glanced over. He threw an arm across the desk and dumped a file box. He made a worse noise. It just seeped out. More clerks looked over. He dumped his coffee cup and smashed a typewriter into the floor.

He made a worse noise. It was screechy effete. The whole squadroom watched.

Opium.

The tar, the match, the pipe.

Stopover, Dublin. He views James Conroy Smith's resurrection. A brotherly reunion turns sanguine. They go on the hunt together. Protty militiamen fall. The Wolf hunts with them. Bloodthirsty beast. He slays and eats his prey.

Stopover, Rome. Salvy's confession and papal audience. I did not betray Dudley Smith, Your Holiness. He is my **Führer** as thou art God's sole worldly lord.

Stopover, L.A. Meyer Gelb assumes a supplicant's pose. He bows. He bestows the gold. He explains everything.

Stopover, New York. Maestro Klemperer conducts at Carnegie Hall. It's the Shostakovich symphony. He's proud of Young Joan. She did her part. Uncanny child. Gray hair at fifteen. She's surely the spawn of the Wolf.

The bedroom door slid open. The Wolf followed Constanza in. He called her, or thinks he did. The night's been a blur. He thinks he described the letter. She must have sensed his duress.

The Wolf jumped on the bed. Constanza sat on the edge. She took his hands. Her voice was soft.

I journeyed up to love you and assuage your fear. It is all hearsay. It's a smear tactic employed by my brother, allied with Meyer Gelb. They are creating

dissension among the Kameraden, because they fear you so. They possess the gold or know where it is. They fear that we will take it from them. We ourselves will live in fear as long as my brother remains alive.

I cannot believe that Salvy would betray me. You were his lover. Please refute the assertion and tell me that it isn't true.

You collect acolytes and younger brothers. It is not a trait I admire in you.

Harsh you. Your stern words wound me.

You have never been wounded as I have. Consider the horror my brother inflicted, as you permit him to draw breath.

You were approached and offered the minutes for the Baja conference. Has a sum been mentioned? Was the approach credible?

The approach was tendered through my mail drop in Los Angeles. The note was block-printed with a ruler, which bespeaks spycraft to me. The sender failed to explain himself further. The sum mentioned was ten thousand dollars.

120

(LOS ANGELES, 1:00 P.M., 4/5/42)

Chez Lux. Health retreat, dry-out farm, divorce hideaway. Sid Hudgens has dubbed it the "Nose Job Notre Dame." Jack Horrall and Gene Biscailuz boil the booze out under Terry's supervision. Fritz Eckelkamp was cut into Meyer Gelb here. The guest bungalows are enclosed by high hedgerows and pepper trees. The medical buildings resemble a Bauhaus college campus. There are tennis courts, putting greens, a first-run movie house. Noted comrades skulk in residence. Saul Lesnick, Two-Gun Davis. Lin Chung concocts eugenics potions in Terry's lab. Orson Welles will soon engage Terry's weight-loss regime. Steam baths and cocaine do the trick.

Claire and I sipped coffee on her terrace. Our own comrades were otherwise deployed. Buzz was chasing Meyer Gelb; Elmer was chasing J-town leads in the wake of the Bev's Switchboard raid. Bill assigned my own Lee Blanchard to bodyguard Sid Hudgens. The mock scandal sheet had been widely received; the Sidster feared Dudster reprisals.

The setting was lovely. Claire and I sat side by

side; Claire kept a hand on my knee. It was companionable, more than seductive. Ten years separated us; the war enthused us equally; my enthusiasm was girlish and ghoulish when compared to hers. Claire saw the war as the culmination of her long leftist immersion. The current worldwide horror was the horror of her failed attempts to spark revolution. She failed to grasp the horror of her own profligacy and could not acknowledge its self-perpetuation. She viewed her personal life and the war as one inextricable struggle. I viewed my personal life and the war as an opportunity. I put my hand on Claire's hand on my knee. I thought of Edna St. Vincent Millay as I did this. "Through my mother's hand. / I saw the web grow, / And the pattern expand."

Claire said, "I'm not going to issue a false confession to Monsignor Hayes. I've read your script a dozen times, and I've decided that I cannot and will not do it. I called Captain Parker this morning. We discussed the matter, and he told me that he has arrived at the same resolve. He said the monsignor has consented to a formal police interview. Your scandal mock-up must have frightened him, dear."

I squeezed Claire's hand. "You called Bill Parker. I must say I've heard everything now."

"God despises half-assed apostates. I can't justify that scripturally, but I know it to be true."

We lit cigarettes and blew smoke at the sky. The

retreat caught sea breezes; cloud patterns expanded and swirled. I released my enclosing hand and let it fall free; Claire laced up our fingers.

"I did something you should know about."

"Yes?"

"It began back in Ensenada. It was shortly after I realized that Dudley had become involved with the Lazaro-Schmidt woman. I heard them talking on the phone, and eavesdropped. He was discussing a Nazi-Soviet conference with this creature, and I picked up quite a few details. The conference occurred in Ensenada, in the fall of '40. Dudley said he'd pay dearly to acquire any typed minutes that might exist."

I squeezed Claire's hand. "I know about that conference," I said. "It was all over Joan's diary."

Claire placed my hand on her knee. Mature woman, young woman. Edna St. Vincent Millay and early-wartime flirtation. Pinch me—I'm a South Dakota farm girl.

"I did something precipitous, Katherine. I recalled what you told me about Bev's Switchboard and mail drops, and I ruler-printed a note to the Lazaro-Schmidt woman. I told her I had the minutes, and I'd be willing to sell them to her for ten thousand dollars."

Claire, the bold apostate. Claire, the vengeful lover. Precipitous, indeed.

"Did you tell her where to contact you?"

"No. I wrote that I'd contact her again."

I said, "We can't overdo it here. We sent your letter to Dudley, as well as the scandal sheet. I was going to send notes from Beth Short and Joan Klein, but it may be altogether too much, and alert him."

Claire smiled. "I should mention that Joan has moved into Otto's guesthouse. She's become a yet-younger version of your still-young version of Mata Hari. If the Shostakovich symphony ever arrives in this country, it will be due to that rather outré child's efforts."

Jean Staley vacates the guesthouse; Young Joan Klein moves in. Otto Klemperer's Home for Wayward Women.

"Otto told me a horrible story, Claire. It goes back to the time of his blackouts, and it has the feel of a blackout itself. A man was making 'vile comments' to him, and he beat the man to death. He told Saul Lesnick about it. Lesnick and Ed Satterlee exploited the situation and hushed it up. Otto paid them a good deal of money, of course."

Claire said, "Otto killed no one, dear. Saul was drunk one night, and explained it all to me. The man was Japanese. He sold rather horrific curios, and he rented a few items to Orson Welles, to use as props in a smut film he was making—one that I appeared in, as a lark. The film was debuted at what I've been told was a rather decadent party at Otto's house, while Otto was here at Terry's place, taking a rest cure. Otto met the Japanese man at some point after that party.

He beat the man, but not badly. He was insensate from the pain medicine that Saul had prescribed, and convinced himself that he'd committed murder. Saul and Ed Satterlee were more than willing to exploit this addled belief."

The drive to Manzanar consumed eight full hours. I journeyed from springtime Los Angeles to a bleak outpost of the California Sierras. Bill secured me a visitor's pass and warned me that an MP lieutenant named Al Wilhite was a Dudley Smith toady and had likely been assigned to watchdog Hideo Ashida.

Hideo was expecting me. Bill called him on his scrambler phone and arranged the rendezvous. Dudley might well learn of it; I didn't care; my visit was contrived to place Hideo in a state of moral jeopardy from which he could not run.

I drove into snow country; the temperature dropped at dusk; mountain winds slammed my car as icy blacktop skewed the traction. I concentrated on driving and nothing else. I learned to drive on winter prairie roads; this was more of that; I hit a flat plane right before Manzanar and slalomed just as I did in rural South Dakota.

Road signs announced the camp; I saw perimeter lights a half mile ahead and slid the last hundred yards up to the gate. I saw cabin rows, bisecting paths, barbed wire, and pivoting floodlights. The gate guard issued me a parking pass and gave me directions to the canteen. Visiting hours were over, he said. But they made exceptions for Dr. Ashida—he was a star boarder here.

I could have visited Hideo in the plush suite that Dudley had secured for him—but Hideo nixed that idea. He knew I was coming to further recruit and suborn him. He wanted me to feel ill at ease within a public context of his own people.

I parked and began my trek uphill. Mountain gusts pushed me forward, back, from side to side. The canteen was three paths up and three paths over. I trudged a good mile and a half; the family huts stretched just that far and wide. They were dimly lit and shuttered; no faces peered out at anomalous me.

I found the canteen. It was dim bulb–lit and hung with frayed Japanese lanterns. The interior walls were rough pine-planked and joined at severe right angles. One small room, rough wood furniture, wall photographs of majestic Mount Fuji.

Hideo sat off by himself. Four older men sat in a group. The canteen was a Japanese bachelors' club, prison camp–style.

I sat down across from Hideo. He said, "No outrage, please. It's spartan, but it's not the Warsaw Ghetto or the Lubyanka."

He'd lost weight. He wore gray flannels and a brown anorak. He warmed his hands on a thermos and poured me a cup of hot tea.

I took off my gloves and sipped at it. I played cutup

and waved to the old men; they looked down and made me feel like a farceur and wretch. Hideo said, "At least you tried. I'd have thought you'd become someone else if you hadn't."

I smiled. "I subjected you to that wiretap," I said. "You're subjecting me to your fellow bachelors and this spartan accommodation."

"You didn't subject me to anything I didn't already know about Dudley. You tend to overplay your hand, Kay. Your subtext was 'he's finished,' but I'm not sure I agree with that."

Touché, Hideo. We're here to bargain, and I know you'll set boundaries. You fear implacable women. I know that about you.

"I spoke to Claire today. She told me Otto Klemperer crossed paths with our Japanese sword man. It confirms his presence in our suspect pool."

Hideo said, "I consider him tangential. The homosexual youth may or may not be an actual suspect. Kyoho Hanamaka placed him with a white woman, about thirty. It confirms my key thesis. Without actual names and evidence, these confirmations are no more than supposition."

I said, "You're a killjoy. You're like those old men over there."

"Since you're fishing for compliments, I'll provide one. Your epistolary approach is inspired. You surely got Dudley's attention with the scandal sheet, but I wish you hadn't sent it to the Staties."

"It lured Monsignor Hayes. He's coming in, with a lawyer. Bill's set to interview him."

Hideo sighed and stomped one foot. He was impatient. Tell me what you expect of me. You're a woman. I'm bored already.

"Tell me what you want. I'll say yes or no immediately."

"I want you to forge a document. Minutes for the Baja conference in '40."

"To be sent to whom, and under what cover?"

"Constanza Lazaro-Schmidt," I said. "It should be crafted to induce greed for the gold, and I want it sent anonymously."

Hideo drummed the table. "Quid pro quo? There's two specific concessions I require."

I said, "Tell me what you want. I'll say yes or no immediately."

The riposte sailed right by him. He said, "I want to conduct the interviews with Leander Frechette and Martin Luther Mimms."

"And, second?"

"I do not want Dudley Smith harmed. You may expose him and seek to contravene his designs. You may not kill him, physically harm him, or seek to imprison him. Tell your vindictive lover Bill Parker that. Tell your volatile friend Elmer Jackson that. Tell the trigger-happy Buzz Meeks that. All four of you must know that I will not permit Dudley Smith to be harmed in those specific fashions."

Touché. You trumped me. This girl knows when she's ceded the high ground, and when she's licked.

"I've never seen you this passionate."

Hideo said, "I love him. He gave me the world, and it was not an insignificant gift."

121

(LONE PINE, 10:00 A.M., 4/6/42)

You're a Jap.

The main drag bustled. The spring thaw hit all at once. It engendered foot traffic. Folks stormed the grocery store and the hardware store. Who's that big goon cuffed to that Jap?

The goon wore civvies. He was an MP PFC. Ashida wore civvies. The cuff chain dangled in plain sight.

You're a Jap.

Folks saw them. Folks passed comment. It was snide but civilized. Manzanar was close by. It juiced local business. The war had its upside. Why's this Jap on the loose?

Because he's Manzanar's star boarder. Because he's out shopping. Because he's buying forgery gear.

The MP mapped the excursion. They hit a stationery store and a bookstore. It created a mild upscut. Biz was biz, though.

Ashida purchased four reams of quality bond paper

and four fountain pens. He bought corresponding bottles of ink and German- and Russian-language study texts.

They hit the hardware store. Ashida bought a rubber-stamp kit and three hobbyist's knives. Ranch locals cruised him. He bought a bottle of gum arabic. A ranch boy sidled close. He pulled his eyes into Jap slits and giggled. The MP moved him along.

His lab was well stocked and equipped. All praise to you know who. The shopping jaunt bypassed Al Wilhite. Subterfuge and spycraft. He slid the MP fifty scoots and made him pledge silence. You know who taught him well.

Ashida skimmed the usage books. He gained German and Russian vocabulary and enhanced his syntactical grasp. He was Spanish-fluent. He possessed one typewriter. It was a '36 Underwood. Verisimilitude. The concept buttressed his Baja '40 construction.

The minutes were composed and typed **at** the conference. The German and Russian factions shared this one machine. It was a late-vintage U.S. import. Verisimilitude. Staff flunkies typed in Ensenada hotel rooms. It was a rush job. Be sure to flub and overscore words.

Ashida composed at his desk. He typed off his hand-scrawled notes. He kept the German text lofty and ambiguous. The **Kameraden** fear committed words on paper. The Russian comrades are less circumspect.

Man Camera. Time Machine. Spring '42 as the fall of '40. Retrospective verisimilitude. You must express ridicule and contempt. It must wound Dudley Smith in the present tense.

Ashida assumed a Russian voice. He's a high-up apparatchik. He castigates the Dresden Poly boys. Díaz, Jamie, Hayes, Pimentel. They are all rightist refuseniks and deviationists. They cannot comprehend the grand ideal of left-right amity.

Ashida played a hunch. He recalled Joan's diary. She described a tract sent to the klub**haus.** Salvy Abascal wrote it. The tract critiqued the Baja conference and the postwar utopian dream promulgated there. The tract suggested Abascal's presence at the confab. Call him a right-wing stooge at the prom and no more.

Here's the hunch. He cruised through Dresden Poly. He knew the boys there. He withheld this from Dudley. He's a longtime outlier in the left-right cabal.

That's the hunch. Here's the fictive reinterpretation.

Abascal is no more than a stooge racketeer. He's out to grab the gold for himself. The apparatchik has heard rumors. Abascal's militant Catholic stance is a ruse. He's a Brit-loving monarchist. The Irish are subhuman pigs.

Salvador has hoodwinked Dudley. That's confirmed evidence now. It should be retroactively advanced. The apparatchik should express it. Abascal's goal has always been racket appropriation. He's been looking for a U.S. sugar daddy. His goal foreshadows **this:**

He found his sugar daddy. Dudley Smith's muddleheaded when it comes to wild young men. Exploit the Dudley-Salvador fissure. Render it a chasm. Grant Meyer Gelb retrospective **Führer** status.

Ashida wrote Russian text. The apparatchik defamed Salvador at great length. Meyer Gelb was conversely lauded. Ashida overscored and flubbed words deliberately. The German and Russian texts stood complete. He forged varying ink signatures.

The textual work took eight hours. He aged his paper next. He boiled a hydroxide solution and laced it with tap water. He filled an atomizer and sprayed his pages. He fan-dried them. It created a frayed yellow effect. He repeated the process four times. Verisimilitude. Quadruple-aged paper. He worked through the night and into the next day.

He built the stamp. He devised one symbol for one cause united. He cut rubber and sawed wood and glued ink pads tight. He worked through that next day. He forgot to eat.

Die Fahne hoch!!! Beastly ideology, one savage beast. He's half Nazi eagle, half Russian bear. He's a lumbering creature with wings. His claws drip blood. His contorted beak screams. Crossed hammers offset the swastika. The four points are sharp workers' scythes.

122

(LOS ANGELES, 4:00 P.M., 4/7/42)

Papal slugfest. Bill Parker versus Padre Joe Hayes and some dioscean shyster.

They hogged a DB sweatbox. Parker wore civvies. Hayes wore his penguin suit. The lawyer wore a blue blazer with a Loyola crest. Elmer peeped the see-thru. He goosed the hall speaker up high.

Parker and Hayes indulged blah-blah. Elmer tuned it out. He gassed with Kay yesterday. She passed on Hideo's report. Kyoho Hanamaka was dead now. He supplied good drift, premortem.

It confirmed the Jap sword man and the queer white boy. The white boy had a white girl pal. Archie Archuleta peddled the sword man's trinkets. Jean Staley masterminded the mail-order biz. Fruit brother Robby helped out.

Padre Hayes told stale jokes. The prelude protracted. Elmer brain-revved. The sword man had to

be Johnny Shinura. That Bev's Switchboard catalogue spelled it out plain. Shinura had no green sheet.
Shinura was uninterned and out on the hoof. Shinura
peddled his shit out of a J-town loft. The Feds seized
the building a month ago. It was government-sealed.
Where's Sword Man Johnny now?

The prelude deprotracted. Joe Hayes lit a cigarette.
Shyster McBride lit a cigar. Parker pushed an ashtray
across the table.

"The Sinarquistas, Monsignor. Their leader,
Salvador Abascal. They're going on the Feds' 1-A subversive list next month."

Hayes said, "I wouldn't call them subversive. A
great many Catholics support them, morally and fi-
nancially, and I'm proud to stand among them. We're
not subversives—we're just concerned Catholics,
like you."

Parker said, "Like Dudley Smith?"

"Yes, like Dudley."

McBride said, "Captain Parker's a nonpracticing
lawyer. I've got a hunch he's about to introduce
People's Exhibit A."

Parker popped his briefcase. He pulled out a wire-
player gizmo and plugged it into the wall. He tapped
two switches. Hold tight, fuckers. Dud's in the hot
seat now.

Mike Breuning and Ed Satterlee gabbed. Elmer
gassed on the replay. Breuning finked El Dudster.
Hayes got the scandal sheet already. This tapped call
doubled it down.

Wetbacks. Heroin. Jap slaves. Nazi fucks and Red fucks and a lost gold cache. Dud's priest-killer snuffs.

Hayes went pale. McBride went all flushed. Parker turned the gizmo off.

"There are a few issues I'd like to discuss, Monsignor. Chiefly, your partial ownership of Bev's Switchboard, and your Dresden Polytechnic alliance with Wallace Jamie, Mondo Díaz, and Juan Pimentel."

McBride shook his head. "Monsignor Hayes declines to answer."

Parker lit a cigarette. "Continuing, then. Bev's Switchboard as a confirmed seditionist mail drop. Your own mail-drop collaborations, coded phone calls to a relay station in Ensenada, and the general range of your far-right, and/or far-left, alliances."

McBride said, "Monsignor Hayes declines to answer."

Hayes squirmed. He quick-lit a cigarette and fumbled the match. Elmer gassed on the show.

Parker said, "Continuing, then. Mr. Abascal as a possible saboteur and/or seeker and hoarder of a gold cache stolen from a U.S. Mint train in 1931."

Elmer squirmed. That saboteur query ditzed him. Frankie Carbajal blabs at the sweep. El Salvy plans sabotage in the San Joaquin Valley. Him and Buzz held back the lead. It's their fallback card. It's insurance against all forms of censorious shit.

Hayes and McBride huddled. They pressed heads. Whisper, whisper. Parker cleaned his glasses on his necktie. He looked devil-dog pissed.

McBride said, "Monsignor Hayes will issue a blanket statement that addresses your last few points. No rebuttals, Captain. This is a police interview, not a courtroom proceeding."

Hayes said, "I would never condone sabotage. I seriously doubt that the Sinarquistas would ever perform it or even consider performing it. I have heard vague rumors as to a cache of gold, including the rumor that Salvy took possession of it, and somehow all of this pertains to a leftist-rightist cabal out to establish their postwar credentials, regardless of which side wins. Concludingly, let me state that these rumors impressed me as poppycock, and the Salvy I know would never collaborate with anyone on the Left."

Elmer relit a cigar. Fuck you, Father Joe. You speak with forked tongue.

Parker said, "Continuing, then. A clubhouse on 46th Street, east of Central Avenue. Homosexual activity, on the premises. One Thomas Malcolm Glennon, one Robert Clinton Staley, a homosexual jazz musician and his known associate—a Japanese purveyor of fetishistic curios."

Hayes and McBride huddled. Whisper, whisper. They pressed heads again. McBride snapped his suspenders and kicked his chair back.

"The Monsignor admits to intimate relationships with Tommy Glennon and Robby Staley. Should you be fishing for leads on the murders of Wendell Rice, George Kapek, and Arturo Archuleta, I'll state that the monsignor has a beaut, and it's yours for across-the-board immunity."

Parker went all Donald Duck. Steam hissed out his ears. His eyeballs popped in rage. His glasses fogged up.

"DA McPherson has authorized me in that regard. I'm listening, Monsignor."

Hayes said, "I know of the musician, but I don't know his name. His Japanese friend is named Johnny Shinura, and his curio business is located on East 2nd Street. The musician has a friend. She's a high-strung woman, about twenty-eight years of age. I don't know her name, either. Rice, Kapek, and Archuleta purportedly raped a woman at the klub**haus.** I credit the rumor, but I don't know the victim's name. One might call rape a good motive for a triple homicide, although I've never seen the allure."

Elmer brain-drained the lead. It played good and backstopped Hideo Ashida. Hideo theorized a male-female deal.

A Vice bull walked up a desk phone. He looked bored. The phone cord was stretched taut.

"It's Meeks. He sounds agitated."

Elmer snatched the receiver. "Yeah, boss."

Buzz said, "I found Meyer Gelb."

123

AWOL. "Absent without official leave." Abdication, flight, retreat.

He trashed the squadroom four days back. He abandoned his command. SIS men witnessed his tantrum. He holed up with Constanza. They made love and sniffed cocaine. They donned Nazi uniforms and fondled his gold bayonet.

He told her he killed Cruz-Caiz with it. She told him to kill her brother with it. She reprised haughty words.

"I cannot truly give myself to a man as long as my brother remains alive."

Dudley drove the coast road north. Constanza left this morning. She flew back to La Paz. She has a chamber recital tonight. Call him the widower, adrift.

Adrift, untethered, bereft.

He assigned himself tasks. Make phone calls. Shore up the home front. Visit the dope ranch. Issue command directives. Visit the Jap holding pens. Hold sway over your peons. Return to duty, starched and pressed.

Dudley cut inland. His phone task had backfired. He called Claire's house in Beverly Hills. A maid brushed him off. He called Mike Breuning and Dick Carlisle at home and got no answer. He called Beth at her real dad's place in Vallejo. She hung up on him.

He'd lost weight. His trousers hung slack. He stood two days awake. He'd brought Claire's stash kit with him. He could geez and rest up at the ranch.

Constanza called him an hour ago. She told him that Bev's Switchboard had contacted her. Bev said she'd received a letter. He told Constanza to read it to him.

She did. The note was ruler-block-printed. It restated a prior note she'd received.

"I've got the minutes. I want ten thousand dollars. I'm tired of waiting. I'll write again soon."

Dudley cut through scrub hills and desert patches. A warm wind kicked in. Tumbleweeds hit the car and caromed off. He ran a tumbleweed gauntlet. Tumbleweeds scraped the windshield and rendered him blind. He floored the gas and plowed past them. He got scared and went **whee!** and laughed.

It hurt to laugh. He sounded shrill. Wisps passed in front of his eyes. The wind lulled and died. He saw the ranch up ahead. He saw cars he knew and cars he didn't recognize.

He pulled up and parked outside the lab hut. He saw the foreman's car and the head chemist's car. He saw no straw-boss jalopies. He saw a low-chopped '40 Ford and a '38 Packard. He smelled high-test gasoline fumes.

He got out and stretched his legs. He unholstered his piece. He weaved and saw wisps, wisps, and wisps.

The lab door flew open. The sound echoed loud. Three Blackshirt Staties walked toward him. He smelled burnt-almond fumes.

Boots scuffed gravel behind him. The Wolf growled, out of nowhere. A wet rag smothered him and scoured out the wisps.

Stench. Mildew and urine. Words—off to what we call left. Cognizance. Brain function. Spanish words. What we call language. Crackle sounds. What we call radio.

"Bombing attacks."

"Suspected sabotage."

"Crop-farm acreage."

"San Joaquin Valley."

Cognizance. Scent. Of blood and entrails, of rancid fur. His face burned. Burnt almonds means a chloroform tincture. That's brain function. It's the will to forge thought and isolate sensation. It's the ability to link sensation to thought.

Dudley Liam Smith, you've been sandbagged. Dudley Liam Smith—you took a nap.

He opened his eyes. He saw four squashed rats and his own bloody hands. Entrails and fur. Bite marks on his wrists. He'd squashed them himself.

The Wolf licked his face. It revived him. The Wolf supplied a travelogue.

We're in the Statie barracks jail. Blackshirts commandeered your biz fronts. Japs, dope, wetbacks. You've been usurped.

He kissed the Wolf and thanked him. The Wolf told him to torture and kill Meyer Gelb. Herr Gelb has the gold. **Es la verdad.** Kill Juan Lazaro-Schmidt. Constanza will leave us if you don't.

Cognizance. Brain function. They stole his gun, his watch, his money. He's on a bare cement floor. Cognizance. Language. "Sabotage," "San Joaquin Valley." Brain function. The ability to extrapolate.

You're still exhausted. You remain impaired. Let the Wolf explicate here.

Sid Hudgens spoke **la verdad.** Salvy Abascal has betrayed you. He smuggled saboteurs in with that last batch of wets. It's why he refused to ride north. **Salvy es El Grand Jefe de los Kameraden.** You are a dupe of your own sentimentality. Trust wolves before you trust dashing and fawning young men.

124

(LOS ANGELES, 7:00 P.M., 4/8/42)

The Crash Squad HQ stood abandoned. Daily briefings had been discontinued; the report boards drooped off the walls. The once-hot cop murder job now ran parallel to cases going back eleven years. Attrition and factionalism had decimated the squad proper. Mike Lyman's back room returned to what it once was: a rendezvous spot for married cops and their girlfriends.

Like Bill Parker and me, drinking highballs and dining on cheese puffs. Meeting in cop-assigned places. Utilizing them as love shacks and hole-ups, where we hashed out **What the hell is all this?**

Elmer was off somewhere; Buzz notched an address for Meyer Gelb and was staking out the location. He talked to that bail bondsman in San Francisco; the man kicked loose Leander Frechette's address. The DA granted Joe Hayes immunity. The Japanese sword man was ID'd as Johnny Shinura. The invert white boy had a gal pal. Hideo Ashida considered them viable klub**haus** suspects. Kyoho Hanamaka was dead. Hideo lied to Dudley. **Sensei**

Death told me nothing. Hideo crossed the line over to God's side.

It might all be breaking. It might dwindle down to dashed leads and misinformation. None of us knew.

We had the back room to ourselves. I wanted to head to our Ambassador spot and make love. Bill wanted to hash out **What the hell is all this?**

I said, "Hideo wants to interview Frechette. It's part and parcel of his forged-document deal."

Bill said, "We'll have Lee bodyguard him. He can't go to San Francisco alone."

"Hideo called me this morning. He's completed the minutes, and he'll be sending them along to the Lazaro-Schmidt woman."

Bill just nodded. I dug through his pants pockets and pulled out his cigarettes. It was a regular routine of ours; Bill always gasped.

"Say something, please. It's a nice breezy night, and I'm antsy."

Bill smiled. "Here's two observations. First, you know how to get a man's attention. Second, I need to have a talk with Buzz Meeks. He most certainly intends to kill Dudley, and I have to dissuade him, before he goes off half-cocked."

I laughed. The Teletype clacked and rolled paper; Bill got up and detached the sheet. He read through it and crossed himself.

"It's from Fourth Interceptor. They're reporting

multiple incidents of sabotage, up near Bakersfield. There's three dead at a private-plane hangar. A garage filled with bomb materiel was blown up in Taft, with two more dead there. Maricopa's got a Bund hall, arsoned. It was packed with illegal ordnance, and was torched to the ground."

I crossed myself. "It's truck-farm country. Dudley's running illegals up there."

Bill ran the full distance Code 3, lights and siren; we made the night trek to Kern County in probable record time. Bill called ahead and spoke to a Sheriff's captain. The man said his Subversive Squad had raided the Bund hall on Pearl Harbor Day. The ordnance had remained on the premises; the county and the Feds were embroiled in a big jurisdictional brouhaha. The man closed with "If you've got questions, I might have some answers by the time you get up here. And there might be an L.A. angle on this thing."

Kern County was low, wide, and flat; U.S. 99 north cut straight through it. It was farm and oil country. Pump derricks stood tall; they framed the low-lying terrain. We crossed the Maricopa city limits and saw lights beamed up a half mile ahead. It had to be arc lamps at the arson scene. Bill sighted in on the glow and drove straight to it.

Forty-odd lamps threw light on a half block

torched to a husk. Rubble mounds stood ten feet high. Firemen probed them with axes and shovels. Bill parked beside a perimeter rope closing off a slew of fire trucks and prowl cars. The mounds hissed and spat embers. Uniformed deputies lounged around and watched.

We got out and walked over to them; a tall man noticed us and ambled up. He said, "Captain Parker and Miss Lake, right? Who else could it be at this time of night?"

Bill flashed his badge; the captain introduced himself as Bob Boyd and passed us calling cards and BIG BOB BOYD FOR SHERIFF campaign buttons. I pinned on my button; Big Bob all but swooned.

He said, "Here's what we've got, and here's the consensus. We've got eight dead at three sites, with three holed-up winos fried in this Bund hall. We think some ex-caped wetbacks from some farms south of here are good for all three jobs. They took off just preceding the blasts, so that has to be it. We tossed out a dragnet right quick, and we snagged a hinky Mex named Mondo Díaz at the Bakersfield bus depot. We ran a subversive-sheet check on him, and damned if he didn't get nailed by your police department just recently. He bailed into Federal custody, hightailed to Mexico, then made his way back here. He's not a righteous wet—but we think he's the ringleader of these bomb-tossing sacks of shit. We leaned on him at the county jail, and he admitted as much. He's in with some Nazi beaners called the Sinarquistas, so why they'd want to up and bomb a Bund hall, I'll never know."

Bill said, "Plant Mr. Díaz in a sweatbox, Captain. I'd like to have a few words with him."

The All-Star PD hits Kern County. Big Bob Boyd proves himself a most gracious host.

The Sheriff's Detective Bureau hopped at midnight. Off-duty deputies showed up for the show. They brought their wives and girlfriends; they were all Big Bob supporters and inclined to think I was swell. The incumbent Sheriff, "Kickback" Kit Denkins, was a notorious no-goodnik. He took bribes from crooked building contractors and solicited high school girls for their soiled underwear. Big Bob was running an insurgent campaign against him. He called up a group of his partisans and suggested a hoedown. The bite was a dollar a head. All the proceeds went to his campaign pot. Big Bob provided corn liquor and potato chips. Plus a gallery peek at the Bill Parker–Mondo Díaz tiff.

The gang convened in sweatbox #2. A see-thru mirror framed booth #1. I dropped a ten-spot in the kitty and drew a round of applause. It was an SRO crowd: eighteen deputies and their dates. Big Bob joined his fans. He jacked up the volume on the wall speaker and supplied us with swell front-row seats.

Bill and Mondo Díaz sat at the #1 table. Why mince words? Díaz looked beat to shit. The gang tossed back corn-liquor shots. A preperformance hush enveloped us. We crowded up to the see-thru and watched.

Bill dispensed commiseration. Those hayseed cops sure thumped you. I don't feature that, myself. Mondo, you're looking at a gas-chamber bounce. We've got you for eight counts of Murder One, easy. Plus capital-charge sedition and treason. You'll suck gas inside six months.

The gang cheered. "Suck gas" spurred the ovation.

Díaz said, "Your mama sucks Chihuahua dicks."

The gang booed. "Chihuahua dicks" spurred the response.

Bill pulled out his pocket flask and urged Díaz to take a few pops. The gang rumbled; they admired the ploy; the city-slicker cop knew his stuff.

Díaz chugalugged Old Crow. Bill spoon-fed him. Things look grim, Mondo. I won't lie to you there. One hand washes the other. There's a few things I'd like to know about Salvy Abascal and the Sinarquistas. If you'll provide a few answers, I'll see what I can do for you.

Díaz said, "Okay, **pendejo.** Ask me something simple first, so I don't get all gun-shy talking to you."

Bill slid his cigarettes across the table. He smiled as Díaz lit up.

So, **Mondo.** Tell me this, **Mondo.** Why would a right-wing cabal like the Sinarquistas blow up a Bund hall? I'm perplexed, **Mondo.** I'm out of my depth here. Call me a **pendejo**—but you're taking me beyond my ken.

Díaz killed off the flask. Entranced cops pressed up to the see-thru and left nose prints on the glass.

"Here's your primer on the new dialectic, **pendejo.** Sinarquismo's left as much as it's right. Suppose I told you **La Causa**'s financed by the NKVD, out of Moscow? Suppose I told you the Hitler boys contribute to the Redshirt Brigade in Ensenada? Suppose I quote this Greek guy, Aristophanes? He said, 'Whirl is king.'"

A fat deputy said, "What's 'dialectic'?"

Big Bob said, "This guy's the guy talking Greek, not that Aristo-whoever guy."

Mrs. Big Bob said, "This is wearing me thin. Bob, you get in there and phone-book that creep."

I said, "Hush, now. You don't get a show like this every day."

Bill enacted deep befuddlement. I can't piece this together, **Mondo.** I know you went to this German technical college. You're educated, so you know all about the Greeks and all this other highbrow shit. I've read your green sheet, **Mondo.** You can't be a Red and a Nazi at the same time. Any fool with a high-school education knows that much.

Üntermensch Bill baited the hook. **Übermensch** Mondo snapped up the bait.

"Here's the thing about History, **pendejo.** Every

so often someone comes around and explains that what's what ain't what. This is by way of saying that Salvy Abascal gave a talk at Dresden Poly. It was pro-Nazi, which wowed my little clique. He had this Jewish pal named Meyer Gelb, which conversely ticked us off. He explained the rudiments of total-itarianism, which allowed us to see that the Reds saw things the same way we did. He pointed out that Jew Hatred and Workers Unite was all the same shuck. Do you know what 'prescience' is, **pendejo**? It's when you predict the future and it comes true, against all empirical evidence. Which is by way of saying that Salvy predicted this war we're in, along with a U.S. and Russian victory, which necessitates the need for a potently inclusive new totalitarian alliance to surmount the inevitable postwar chaos and monkey-wrench the world's new idiot taste for democracy."

Bill said, "I read a Federal subversive summary. It described a conference, along the lines of what you just described. I'm wondering if you were there."

"Of course I was there. I was there when they signed the Magna Carta and when Moses parted the Red Sea. I was there when your **puto** forefathers signed the Declaration of Interdependence. You're wearing this look I've seen before, **pendejo.** You just figured out that what's what ain't what, and I'm not just some dumb pachuco."

Bill said, "Do minutes for the conference exist?"

Díaz laughed. "They're a myth. They're like **Das Kapital** and the **Protocols of the Learned Elders of Zion.** They're some jive that the great unwashed thinks is real."

"The gold, Mondo? What about that? Is that just a pipe dream, too?"

"It's all a pipe dream. It's a nightmare, and nobody knows where the goddamn gold is. Ask Salvy and that cracker pal of his. For all I know, they cashed it in for S & H Green Stamps."

Big Bob said, "Miss Lake's right. You don't get a show like this every day."

125

(SAN FRANCISCO, 10:00 A.M., 4/9/42)

Blanchard crowed and groused. The Fed-probe acquittals. His domestic woes. He blew steam from Manzanar to Golden Gate Park.

"Whiskey Bill and Elmer J. That's the word. They pulled some mischief in the Fed vault. Nobody doubts that Bill Parker's smart. But he's out in the open with Kay now, and that ticks me off."

Ashida ignored him. They sat outside Kezar Stadium. Leander Frechette picked the spot. Leander will walk up. He'll ask how things stand. They'll trek memory lane.

The Alameda County Jail. Remember, Leander? You, Fritz Eckelkamp, and Wayne Frank Jackson. Your screwball alliance. You conceived a daring gold heist.

Blanchard arranged the meet. He called Frechette last night. Leander was affable. Blanchard assured him—this ain't a roust.

It's a waltz. He'll know that. His criminal actions preceded all legal cutoff dates. How's this shit stand now? That's easy. Chaos has intervened.

Blanchard said, "Parker's a pervdog. I respect him, but I don't like him. He's out to set the white man's world record for entrapping college girls. First Kay, then Big Joan. The war put a bug up his ass. His libido's overheated. He's been running roughshod since Pearl."

Ashida ignored him. Chaos has intervened. He sent the forged minutes out. Constanza Lazaro-Schmidt will receive them. Dudley Smith will read them. Dudley might note a grievous narrative lapse.

Elmer called him this morning. Elmer sobbed and begged forgiveness. He'd just heard a radio broadcast.

Eight dead in Kern County. Three sabotage attacks. Farmworker saboteurs. Mondo Díaz, in custody. Díaz, the ringleader. Wetbacks for the drudge work.

The report stunned Ashida. He'd interviewed Díaz at Hollenbeck Station. Elmer sobbed. He said he'd withheld crucial drift. The East L.A. sweep. Elmer and Buzz Meeks squeeze Frankie Carbajal. Frankie reveals the sabotage plan. He reveals the plan under duress.

Escaped wetbacks. All torch men. Salvador A. was behind it. Dud S. didn't know shit. Elmer and Buzz withheld the lead. They'd gone rogue. The lead was their hole card. It's their redneck mea culpa now. Eight people got blown up.

Elmer sobbed and hung up the phone. Kay called a few minutes later. She'd been up to Kern. Bill Parker braced Mondo Díaz. Mondo riffed dialectic and finked the deal out.

The **Kameraden** pulled the sabotage. Salvador A. ordered it. He's Comrade Number One. That **puto** Irishman didn't know shit.

Chaos intervenes. It's hubris ascendant. Comrade Ashida perpetrates it. He plays a hunch based on a specious assumption. Salvador is not **El Grande Jefe.** Meyer Gelb is. The faux minutes proceed off that hunch. Comrade Ashida writes as **Herr Apparatchik.**

Herr Apparatchik defames Abascal. He's a cholo chump out for the gold. **Herr Apparatchik** ignores Comrade Hanamaka's lead. Hanamaka said the big boss is a "Mexican Stalinist." Here's a revised hunch. Abascal **is** that Stalinist.

The minutes go out. They are geared to spark two confrontations. Dudley versus Abascal, Dudley versus Gelb. Chaos intervenes. Dudley reads the minutes. They contradict breaking news. **His** wetbacks as saboteurs? **Unknown** to him? He might sense Salvador's hand. He might sense Salvador as El Boss **Führer.** He might sense the document had been faked.

Chaos intervenes. Statie goons pop Dudley at his dope ranch. Dick Carlisle shot that dizzy dish to Lee Blanchard. Dudley called Jack Horrall. Chief Jack pulled strings and got him released. Dudley's on the loose now. He's a gone-rogue Army major. He'll probably run to Constanza. He'll be with her when the minutes arrive.

Herr Apparatchik. Née Comrade Ashida. He sent the minutes out precipitously. He demanded no money. He disregarded consequences. He's culpable here.

Elmer's culpable. Buzz is culpable. They should have reported the sabotage lead. Kay's the most culpable. She's their **La Jefa** and queen bee. She bends men who want to fuck her to her impervious will. She assessed him as a man who declines to fuck women and adroitly massaged his love for Dudley Smith. The minutes have gone out. Dudley will know that Comrade Ashida forged them. He has the skill. No one else does. Dudley will know that he betrayed him.

Chaos intervenes. They're closing in on the klub**haus** killer. It seems like small recompense. Jean Staley and brother Robby. Johnny Shinura, curio broker. Johnny's the Jap sword man. Who's the queer jazzman? Who's the woman who got raped?

A clean solve looms. The details remain uncertain. Chaos may subsume all resolution. Winner take nothing—if he forfeits Dudley Smith's love.

Nannies pushed strollers by. Vendors pushed food carts. Storm clouds whooshed overhead.

Blanchard nudged him. "You got tears in your eyes, Hideo."

"I thought I could have something both ways, but I forgot to consider the price."

"Welcome to the world, son. Our friend Kay taught me that selfsame thing, quite a while back."

They walked and talked. Kezar to the rose garden, Stanyan Street to Fell. Ladies pushing strollers gawked them. It was relative size more than race.

Ashida was small and slight. Leander loomed high and blocked out the sun. Folks called him "Skyscraper" and the "One-Man Eclipse."

He confirmed Dr. Death's chronology. He confirmed the cabal's chain of command. Salvy was the Stalinist and Top Dog Comrade. Meyer Gelb deferred to him.

Leander was affable. He worked as a longshoreman. He eschewed agitation and indulged a yen for 459 PC. He had a wife and kid here in Frisco and a wife and three kids in L.A. He kept in mail-drop touch with select comrades. He refused to name names.

They bought ice-cream bars and lounged on the

grass. Blanchard lounged twenty yards back. He was the bodyguard. Ashida ran the Q & A.

"Hanamaka told me the gold has lain fallow for some time. Gelb and Abascal are the only ones who know where it is."

Leander shook his head. "I've never known Comrade Kyoho to be mistaken about anything, but I think he's wrong here. I think Wayne Frank and the Reverend Mimms might be able to give you a more recent accounting."

"Why?"

"The Rev wanted to repo the gold, and I can't say that I blame him. I'd call him the first man among us who wised up to the way life plain old is. He'd come to see the **Kameraden** as a bunch of treacherous shitbirds who'd blow the whole world up if they got half a chance. All that 1931 idealism and commitment got to be ancient history, and the Rev wanted his fair share of the gold, just like any other properly self-interested man in your run-of-the-mill democracy. He heard that the Sinarquistas and some of their satellite thugs were looking for a clubhouse rental, so he had Link Rockwell rent them the 46th Street place. Link stayed on and did some infiltration. The Rev figured Link might get some leads on the gold there, which he sure as hell did. He heard Salvy and Wayne Frank took hold of the gold, not Comrade Gelb. That's as far as the Rev takes the story, because he always busts out laughing then."

Ashida said, "That's all you know? They took possession of the gold, and that's it?"

Leander winked. "The Rev's got the storytelling prowess. He can surely tell you more."

Ashida let it go. Leander ran intractable. He held his hole cards tight.

"Jean Staley. Her brother, Robby. A Japanese curio peddler named Johnny Shinura. A purportedly homosexual jazz musician. He's tall and blond, and he has a female companion, purportedly very nervous and roughly thirty years of age. The three klub**haus** victims purportedly raped her."

Leander tossed his ice-cream stick and wiped his hands on the grass. A stroller lady strolled by. She gawked the jig and the Jap.

"Jean's brother was a homo, for what that's worth. Johnny S. was bughouse crazy, but you must already know that. I don't know any woman who got raped, but the jazz quiff has got to be Chuckie Duquesne."

126

(LOS ANGELES, 9:00 A.M., 4/10/42)

Ruth practiced. She played Sibelius and lit the whole courtyard. He recognized composers now. He heard concerto strains out here on the street.

Elmer fought the jimjams. He'd had the sweats and frets since he got the word. Eight Kern County dead. Him and Buzz could have stopped it. They held it back and covered their backsides.

He sobbed to Kay and Hideo. He sobbed to Buzz. He sobbed himself into these frets. He sat in his sled and waited out Sibelius. Don't interrupt Ruth. She'll bite your head off. She's caught the muse.

She fed her lovers cues. Morning practice meant Get Out. Elmer sat in his sled. He had a clear courtyard view. Some geek will exit her bungalow. Ruth sustained heavy bed traffic. Kay called her "relentless" and "egalitarian."

Elmer fought the frets. He fretted up the Kern County dead and Meyer Gelb. Buzz found Comrade Meyer. Buzz conceived a bold approach and pin-mapped that shitheel.

The hump lived in L.A. The hump had to. The hump attended Otto Klemperer's parties. He always arrived alone. Joan's diary stated that. How'd Gelb get to the parties? Let's try taxicabs.

Buzz called the Maestro. He laid out a line of officious shit and coaxed a list of party dates. He canvassed cab dispatchers then. He had the party dates and the Maestro's address. He checked evening pickup logs for dates going back to Pearl Harbor. He checked sixteen cab companies. Company seventeen—**tilt.**

He tagged seven parties and seven pickups in Beverly Hills. The Simon's Drive-in at Wilshire and Linden. It's a neutral pickup spot. Comrade Gelb's cautious. Comrade Gelb must live nearby.

Buzz tagged seven pickups. Buzz tagged the same hackie three of those times. Buzz braced the cat and lubed him. The hackie had good recollection. He remembered this guy. The guy had burn-scarred hands.

Buzz pounded pavement then. He made Gelb for an apartment-house dweller. The blocks south of Charleville were all house blocks. That restricted his range. He schlepped Wilshire to Charleville, Charleville to Beverly Drive. He entered apartment-house foyers. He scanned mailbox slots. He got no Meyer Gelbs and no hinky M.G.s. That approach tapped out. He ran block-to-block stakeouts then.

He car-perched and peeped doorways on Linden. He saw Gelb on stakeout night #3.

We got him pin-mapped. What's next? That's obvious. We kidnap him and turn on the heat.

Elmer eyeballed Ruth's bungalow. He had peeper tendencies. He liked to perch and watch. He saw nifty shit that way.

Sibelius diminuendoed. Babs Stanwyck breezed

out Ruth's door. Note her wet hair and love-struck demeanor. **Woo-woo!** Round Heel Ruth rides both ways!

Babs breezed to her boss Packard coupe and peeled northbound. Elmer breezed into the courtyard. Ruth sat on her steps. She looked flustered and distractified.

"Sergeant Elmer has once again been lurking. It is a leitmotif with him. He lurks to allay his restlessness and to sate his curiosities. Sergeant Elmer is a voyeur. He should move to Berlin and join the Gestapo."

Elmer yukked. Ruth had that mordant streak. It played off-kilter now. She still played distractified.

"I liked the Sibelius."

"There was nothing to like. You are an undiscerning listener. Barn-dance music is more your métier."

Elmer sat down beside her. Their arms brushed. He felt tremors. Round Heel Ruth, electrizized.

"You seem shook up, sweetie. You'd think a sleepover with Babs would have you all pacified."

Ruth lit a cigarette. "I was at the Musicians' Local on Vine Street all night. I filled in for an absent first violin and recorded the third Bartók Quartet. Babs came by to pick up a book I'd borrowed, and to wash her hair. She enjoys my shampoo, more than she appreciates my prowess. You are ever the policeman, Elmer. You attribute motive in a most paranoic way."

Elmer laughed. "Let's hit the hay. It's been too long, and I've missed you."

Ruth X-ray-eyed him. "You've been crying. Your face is flushed and mottled, and your beady eyes are bloodshot. Am I the source of your tears? I would think a man as promiscuous as you would engage a woman such as I with more distanced affections."

Elmer teared up. Not that much. He was done in and sobbed out.

"I withheld a confession. Eight people died. I'm in some shit I can't step out of, in more ways than I can count."

Ruth flicked her cigarette. It hit a wet grass strip and fizzled.

"**Scheiss,** eh? Are you in the **scheiss** as the Koenigs, Sandor, and I seem to be? We are facing a Federal deportation order, my callow friend. The lawyer Otto secured for us explained the motive behind it, so I will explain it to you. Your Mr. Hoover is perturbed, because our names were mentioned in a memorandum pertaining to extortion and an FBI agent under house arrest. Expulsion from the United States. Does not my **scheiss** exceed your **scheiss, mein herr**?"

Extortion. House arrest. That meant Ed the Fed Satterlee.

"I didn't come here to brawl with you, love. I didn't show up to compare notes on who's got it worse, either."

Ruth said, "You have blood on your hands. Allow me to commiserate, and add that it is not Jewish blood, and not the blood of three hundred."

"Are we going for volume here? Is Jewish blood any better than plain old white and Mexican blood?"

Ruth wheeled and slapped him. She knocked off his hat. Her nails raked his cheek and drew blood.

Buzz said, "I'm going to kill him. Dudley Liam Smith, **muerto.** It's the only way this deal makes any sense."

Elmer relit a cigar. "This deal has never made sense, and it never will. There's too much to it, and it goes back too far. It's not supposed to make sense. Kay told me that, and if Kay says something, it's true."

Daylight stakeout. Elmer's sled. Four eyes on 562 South Linden. This four-flat apartment house. This pink mock château. Gelb had the upstairs-left spot.

Buzz relit a cigar. "I rented a motel room, up the Ridge Route. Nice and secluded. We'll put the blocks to El Comrade there."

Elmer said, "Bring your pet scorpion. One look at him, and Gelb'll shit his britches."

Buzz scoped Elmer's cheek. "Ellen clawed you, right? I've seen a couple of her pictures. She's got that caged-tigress thing going."

Elmer tiger-growled. "Girlfriend #4 scraped me. **She's** your jungle cat."

Buzz said, "I mixed a terp and chloral hydrate cocktail. We'll sedate Gelb and toss him in the trunk."

Elmer blew smoke rings. "You don't seem too upset about those dead folks up in Kern."

Buzz said, "Easy come, easy go. It's not like losing your own near and dear."

Elmer dozed. He dipped to some torrid locale. Jungle Cat Ruth scratched him. Jungle Cat Annie loved him. Jungle Cats Brenda and Ellen tossed him out in the rain. Jungle Cat Kay took him home to her glade.

Some stray cat nudged him. Elmer blinked and opened his eyes.

Buzz went **Looky, looky.** He pointed across the street and up. Frankie Carbajal ambled toward Comrade Gelb's place. He wore a Sir Guy shirt and loose flannels. Note the creepy-crawler tennis shoes and gun bulge.

Elmer rubbed his eyes. It's no mirage. Frankie's out of custody and up from Mexico. El Whipout Man de Sinarquismo. He's loose in Beverly Hills.

Buzz said, "We'll give him five minutes. If he comes out with Gelb, we'll grab them from behind."

Elmer said, "We'll work singles otherwise. I'll flip you for who takes Gelb."

Frankie jogged up to Gelb's door. He knocked. The door stayed shut. Frankie whipped out a set of lock picks. He had fast hands. He picked the lock and crept in. The door slammed shut.

Buzz dug out a quarter and flipped it. Elmer called heads. The quarter hit tails. Elmer went **Shit.**

They timed Frankie's visit. Elmer orbed his wrist-watch. It ticked off two minutes flat. The door popped open. Frankie stumble-walked back out. He looked all of a sudden fright-wigged and racked with the frets.

He stumble-walked down the stairs and weaved back toward Wilshire. Elmer and Buzz piled out and foot-dogged him. They closed the gap. They closed too fast. Frankie looked back and saw them.

Buzz pulled his roscoe. Elmer pulled, likewise. Frankie pulled his waistband piece. They all got their bearings. They all dug in and aimed straight and threw shots all at once.

Frankie stood his ground. He popped two rounds. They hit parked cars and zinged wide. Elmer and Buzz ran up, shooting. Buzz cracked this Chevy's windshield and tore up the ragtop. Elmer nailed Frankie, waist-high. Frankie pitched ass over elbows and popped shots at the sky.

Elmer and Buzz ran up. Frankie sprawled, supine. Elmer kicked his gun hand. Frankie spit blood and dropped the piece. Looky-loos craned out their windows. What's this big noise about?

Buzz looked around. Frankie bit his lips and pawed at his hip wound. Elmer went **Aw-oh.** An old lady across the street screamed.

Elmer reholstered. Buzz grabbed Frankie's neck scruff and dragged him down the Wilshire-flank alley. Frankie wailed and flailed. Buzz looked around. Parked cars and hedgerows covered him. He shot Frankie three times in the head.

Muzzle job. Frankie spilled the sabotage lead. Dead men tell no—

Elmer wheeled and ran. He ran to the mock château and stumble-tripped up the stairs. He kicked the door off the hinge plates. It caved in and crashed upside Meyer Gelb's legs.

He's flat on his back. He's been tortured. There's congealed cuts on his arms and his neck. There's a bullet hole in his forehead. It's small caliber. The blood's dried maroon.

Elmer prowled the room. The walls were plastered with pix of Boss Man Hitler and Butcher Stalin. Note the scrawled-up margins. It's all weird shit about fires and storms.

127

(LA PAZ, 9:00 A.M., 4/11/42)

The plaza newsstand hawked the L.A. papers. The **Herald** headlined the Fed-probe acquittals. They ran the snuff piece, page two.

BEVERLY HILLS SHOOT-OUT! POLICE KILL SUBVERSIVE! MAN SLAYS COMMUNIST BOSS!

Dudley stood by Constanza's PO box. He read the snuff piece three times. Sid Hudgens inked it.

899

Jackson and Meeks blew up Frankie Carbajal. Frankie torture-slashed and shot Meyer Gelb. "'Gelb snuff open and shut,' B.H. cops state."

Constanza was late. Like Salvy was late. Like Welles was late. People stood him up now. People sandbagged him and jailed him. People ignored his phone calls.

Hideo was nowhere. He was AWOL himself. He'd bolted the squadroom and relinquished his command. Jack Horrall bailed him out. The Staties seized his biz fronts. Jack told him to lay low in Baja. "We're holding your job for you, Dud. The PD's your home, and always will be. Poke some señoritas, and work on your tan."

Constanza was late. She said she'd meet him at 9:00. She was expecting a package. From Russia, no less.

From a "Comrade Dimitri." A package of "grave import." Constanza spoke in riddles now. She ignored him in bed. His squadroom outburst and jail stint provoked the retreat. She patronized him. She urged him to buck up and fly right.

Dudley chain-smoked. He reread the **Herald** piece. Sid Hudgens, ubiquitous. Sid's scandal rag slandered him. It was true drift, regardless. He called Sid and left a message with the copy chief. Sid ignored his call.

Constanza showed. She ran a sorry-I'm-late number and kissed him on the cheek. **Put some oomph in it, you chola whore. I'm still Dudley Smith.**

She unlocked her box. Two packages were crammed in. One rolled package. One flat package. The rolled package was V-mail-stickered and Russian-postage-stamped. It was addressed to Comrade C. Lazaro-Schmidt.

The flat package was ruler-marked. Straight edges, right angles, no cursive exposed. It was sent from Bev's Switchboard. It's the minutes, dear Lord.

They read in Constanza's bedroom. The text was Russian and German. Constanza was fluent in both. The paper looked authentic. The seal looked authentic. The Nazi eagle and Russian bear were conjoined as one beast. The Wolf disapproved.

Constanza read him through the text. Inconsistencies accrued. Dudley considered them. Constanza read him through again. Dudley nailed a basic falsehood.

The text read wrong, overall. It stooped to defamation. It defamed Salvy Abascal as it exalted Meyer Gelb. It plainly stated Salvy's presence at the confab. That was patently untrue. Dudley plumbed connective threads and nailed the source.

Joan Conville. She reads a tract Salvy wrote. It was sent to the klub**haus.** It critiqued more than praised the Baja confab. The minutes ridiculed Salvy. He loved the British monarchy. He hated the Irish. He despised Catholicism. He wished to appropriate the Baja rackets. He needed a ruthless American front man for this.

Joan reads the tract. She tells him about it. She tells

Hideo Ashida. The basic falsehoods of these minutes germinate there.

The minutes have been forged. They were retroactively composed and geared to provoke confrontation. Salvy is underestimated. The forger lays out divisive fodder. He seeks to spark a Smith-Abascal war. His duplicitous design reveals itself here:

The sabotage incursion. It violates D. L. Smith's no-sabotage decree. Salvy declines to ride north with the wetback saboteurs. It underlines D. L. Smith's jailhouse revelation. Salvy is Comrade #1.

He is locked-in fucking certain of it. These minutes were composed and sent before the attacks. They exposit a preattack assertion.

Meyer Gelb is Comrade #1. He believes it. Hideo Ashida believes it. A second confrontation is provoked here. It's D. L. Smith versus Comrade Gelb. The forger cannot foresee the attacks or Comrade Gelb's death. Genius is one thing. Prescience is another. The minutes are brilliantly conceived and executed. The technical skill. The boldness and glibness. Hideo Ashida forged the minutes. Hideo Ashida betrayed him and trashed his deep love.

Dudley said, "They're a fake. It's Hideo Ashida's work. He's the only one capable of it."

Constanza said, "Betrayal does not occur in a vacuum. Ashida had to have help. You will notice that my brother is not mentioned in this document. The omission is deliberate. Ashida wants to protect Juan.

First he rapes me and pimps me to his **Kameraden.**
Now he attempts to rape you. Dry your wet eyes, my
frail darling. Kill Juan in my name. Kill him before I
cease to love you."

El Governor always worked late. Constanza told him
that. He worked at home and at the Baja Government
Palace. Go by the palace. Look for a fourth-floor light
burning. He might be there. He might be at home.

Dudley drove by the palace. No fourth-floor light
burned. He brought his gold bayonet. Constanza decreed death by blade.

They'd sniffed cocaine and made love. She encouraged him. She urged him to seek her favor and atone
for his recent sloth. She bundled him off with the Wolf.

Dudley drove by the house. Juan's office light
burned. A winding footpath led to a backdoor. Juan
kept it unlocked. Constanza told him that.

He parked streetside. He consulted the Wolf. They
discussed political and romantic alliance. Constanza
had coupled with Salvy and Kyoho Hanamaka. She
admitted the liaisons. She did not withhold love affairs past. Lovers past withheld from her. They withheld the truth of the gold. She knew no more than he
did. The Wolf told him that.

Dudley left the car unlocked. The Wolf walked
point. He sniffed the footpath and low-growled. They
hooked around to the back door. Dudley swung the
bayonet and mauled rosebushes and shrubs.

The door stood ajar. They entered the house. Turn right and then left. Constanza told him that. "Juan never shuts his office door. He'll look up from his desk and see you. I know him as a sister and lover does."

They followed her dictates. They stepped into the office. Constanza failed them here. The office was lit bright. There was no Juan.

Dudley dropped the bayonet. The Wolf cocked his head. Dudley walked to Juan's desk. A note had been placed on the blotter. Juan employed an elegant cursive. It covered a single sheet.

April 11, 1942

Dear Major Smith,
   She will convince you to kill me sooner or later. Having no wish to die, I have resigned my governor's position and have flown to Havana. I will remain there for the war's duration. You have mutilated me, but I will not let you kill me.
   Terry Lux has allayed the marks of your mutilation, and we had quite the chat about you. I brought up your union with Constanza; Terry found the notion perturbing.
   "Those two only love efficaciously," he said. "Dudley must be after more than Constanza's favors. Don't tell me. He's heard about the gold, and has fixed upon your luscious sister as integral to the prize."

We laughed ourselves silly. I won't shilly-shally here—Terry's a long-standing **Kamerad.** He's heard about the gold. He's coveted it, and dismissed it as so much piffle in much the same manner as the rest of us have. Terry turned serious at this point. He said, "What was Constanza after? She's as jaded on the gold front as you and I."

I said, "She wants Dudley to kill me." Terry replied, "Go somewhere safe, Juan. Dud will go to outrageous lengths to appease women. He's quite the child in that regard."

I'll close now, and head to the airfield. Has Constanza told you that I raped her and took her as my incestuous child bride? The truth is altogether more subtly complicitous than that.

All best,
J. Lazaro-Schmidt

128

(LOS ANGELES, 8:00 A.M., 4/12/42)

Claire was off at Mass. She intended to pick Joan Klein up at Otto's place and bring her back here for a visit. Young Joan had a surprise for us; it entailed the piano in Claire's suite. I had joyous notions about that surprise—but the swirl of what I now call All of It ruled my thoughts.

I enjoyed the view from Claire's terrace. The setting was lovely; the passing parade was provocative. Terry Lux walked Saul Lesnick by a few minutes ago; a doddering Jim Davis had preceded them. All of It. Supporting cast glimpses. Joan Conville's All One Story.

Elmer, Hideo, and I conferred on the phone, at least once a day. I was kept up to speed on All of It and shared the information with Bill. Meyer Gelb, once Fritz Eckelkamp, had been murdered. Elmer and Buzz shot and killed the fleeing Frankie Carbajal. The Beverly Hills PD made Frankie for the homicide. Elmer saw the body and thinks otherwise.

The corpse was stiff-cold. The torture cuts had congealed. Elmer talked to Dr. Nort Layman. Dr. Nort had performed the postmortem; he tagged the time of death as 2:00 a.m. Elmer found the body at 11:30. Dr. Nort removed a .25-caliber bullet. The cause of death: one small-bore gunshot wound to the head. The postmortem exonerated Frankie Carbajal. The Beverly Hills cops liked him, regardless. A Mex fascist kills a Communist. Cops slay the slayer. It played nicely open-and-shut.

The Carbajal shooting troubled Elmer. It came on the heels of the sabotage revelations. Frankie had pretipped Elmer and Buzz. They sat on the lead. Then Frankie appears and enlivens their stakeout. Elmer may confirm my hunch or play it mum. Buzz killed Frankie in cold blood. It silenced Frankie. He could not snitch the held-back lead now. His death bought Elmer and Buzz a skate.

What they hath wrought. What we have all precipitated.

The forged minutes have gone out. Constanza Lazaro-Schmidt must have received them; Dudley must have read them. How will he react? The minutes pushed him toward Meyer Gelb and Salvador Abascal. Dudley could not have killed Gelb. He was ensconced in Baja and did not know where to find him. Gelb was killed by a small-bore weapon. Dudley employed big-bore weaponry.

Thad Brown passed Bill a tip. Jack Horrall had issued an ultimatum. Dudley has one week to turn himself in or suffer PD-sanctioned reprisals. Call-Me-Jack has sought outside-agency help here. A

Federal posse stands on call. Postal inspectors and Treasury agents. Ex–Texas Rangers. The hard boys who took down the Ma Barker mob, along with Bonnie and Clyde.

What fate hath wrought. What we have all precipitated.

Dudley might go after Salvador. Dudley might deem the minutes a ruse and comport circumspectly. Dudley might surmise that Hideo Ashida forged the minutes. What Hideo hath wrought, in the name of love. What early-wartime L.A. has done to us all.

I heard voices out on the walkway. Young Joan sounded gleeful; Claire kept going **Ssshhh, people sleep late on Sunday.** The terrace door swung open; Joan saw me and crashed into me and waved a poster tube.

I noted the V-mail sticker and Russian postage stamps; I saw that the tube had been resent by Constanza Lazaro-Schmidt. Confluence. Comrade Shostakovich to a fascist seductress to Maestro Klemperer. What this war hath wrought. Otto could now upstage Maestro Toscanini and stage his benefit show.

We ran inside. We crash-landed the piano and pulled out the score. I sight-read my way through it and isolated the best three-handed part. It was the tanks-approaching-Leningrad passage that Otto had already played for me. Claire arrayed the appropriate sheets on the music stand; Joan sat down at the bench between us. We were the just-formed Dry-out Farm

Trio. We poised our hands over the keys. Claire gave the downbeat.

Boom, boom, boom. Nazi tanks circle Leningrad. It was bluntly ominous music that made us all roar. We hit true notes and flubbed notes and laughed through it all. **Boom, boom, boom.** What life hath wrought. How did I get this pigshit lucky? I'm a rogue prairie girl from Sioux Falls.

129

(LOS ANGELES, 1:00 P.M., 4/12/42)

Coffee klatch. Crash Squad alumni, at loose ends. Lyman's back room, now moribund.

The alums kicked their chairs back and got cozy. Ashida, Lee Blanchard, Buzz Meeks.

Buzz sipped coffee. "BHPD likes Carbajal for the Gelb job. Elmer and me are breathing a big sigh of relief."

Blanchard sipped coffee. "Dr. Nort disagrees."

Ashida sipped coffee. "I gave Elmer Frechette's lead on Chuckie Duquesne. He's on his way up to the Musicians' Local right now."

Buzz said, "Elmer's a busy bee. He told me he went by Johnny Shinura's building and did some shinnying up a drainpipe. Johnny's roost had been cleaned out, but he found two bedrolls on the third floor. He figures Johnny and Chuckie were hiding out there, up until the Feds seized the place."

Blanchard lit a cigarette. "If Chuckie's our queer white boy, then who's the woman who got raped? Joe Hayes says that's our motive, right there."

The back room oozed sloth. Ashida tidied up. He straightened the report boards and emptied ashtrays. He tossed stale cold cuts. He dumped booze empties.

Buzz lit a cigar. "I caught Jack Horrall and Brenda A. going at it here. The '36 Olympics were on the radio. Jack's a floor man from way back."

Blanchard said, "Hideo's due back at Manzanar. I'm driving him up."

Buzz tossed a paper sack. Ashida snagged it on the fly. Buzz said, "I almost forgot. Elmer snatched this from Shinura's place. He wanted Hideo to see it."

Ashida emptied the sack. Leather strangling gloves fell out.

Black leather. Fetishistic. A Weimar Berlin and red-light Tokyo item. Palm-weighted. One size fits all.

Buzz whistled. Blanchard went **oooh-la-la.** Ashida held the gloves up.

"They explain the single-hand-span bruises on the victims' necks. All the killer had to do was apply moderate pressure. The palm weights would do the rest."

Buzz said, "Hideo's theorizing here."

Blanchard said, "As theories go, I like it. It fits

Hideo's man-woman theory. The man holds the ice pick and keeps our guys immobilized, while the woman applies the elbow grease."

Buzz waved his cigar. "I'll bite. But who is this crazy ginch?"

The Teletype tapped-tapped and furled paper. Blanchard tore it off the spool.

"M. L. Mimms is back from his rouse-the-natives tour. Two airport cops saw him get off the late New York flight. The Navy JA's kicked Link Rockwell loose. He was on the same flight as the Rev."

He saw Dudley everywhere. **Cri de coeur.** He saw him conjured and unbidden. All men looked like him. No man looked like him. **Je m'excuse, pour ma trahison.**

Ashida cabbed southbound. The hackie **You're a Jap**'d him. Ashida shut his eyes and saw Dudley. The cab passed through darktown. **Je ne te verrai pas blessé.**

Kay pledged him the Mimms interview. It secured their forgery deal. She stipulated a co-interviewer and suggested Elmer. He tried to find Elmer. He called the DB and Brenda's house. Elmer was out. He called Kay's place and got no answer. He tried the Musicians' Local. He asked if a Sergeant Jackson had been by. Sergeant Jackson was looking for a horn man named Chuckie Duquesne.

The clerk said, "No, but that's an odd coincidence. An Army major named Smith called and asked for Chuckie's address, which I sure don't have. This major was some mick with a brogue. He told me a nutso story about how he identified Chuckie from some smut film that Orson Welles showed him. I told him Chuckie's a clandestine sort of guy, but he'll be gigging at the Taj Mahal tonight. Orson Welles himself. Don't that take all?"

The hackie cruised Central Avenue. They hit a midday traffic lull. Ashida steered him by the klub**haus.** It was a flat vacant lot now. Jordan High footballers scrimmaged. They were colored. The white coach looked like Dudley Smith.

The hackie U-turned back to Central. There's the jazz strip. Club Alabam, Port Afrique, Club Zombie. The façades have been refitted. Rioters had torched cars and business fronts. He killed two of them. Dudley Smith killed many more.

The cab dropped him at 48th Street. The Congregation of the Congo hogged half a block. A wide storefront with wide picture windows. Easel-propped window art.

Colored pilgrims in Africa. They rode lions and zebras and boiled white folks alive. The Rev offered steerage and deluxe passage rates. The USS **Negro** sailed monthly.

Ashida walked in. White janitors dusted the pews and swept the aisles. The Rev and Link Rockwell stood by the pulpit. Link wore Navy khakis. Both men smoked corncob pipes.

They saw Ashida. Looks flew, bilateral. **He's that Jap cop.**

Ashida walked up. Both men grinned. Both men proffered handshakes. Both men jut-jawed their pipes.

Rockwell said, "Leander told us you might drop by."

The Rev said, "Dr. Ashida's hipped on the gold. I don't think I'm being precipitous by stating that. Will you give him a gander, Link?"

Rockwell went **After you.** Ashida trudged a short hallway. The Rev trailed him. Rockwell opened a closet door and pulled a light cord.

Hosanna. At long last. Come let us adore it. Behold the sacred vault. It's a good-sized closet. Gold bars are stacked floor to chest-high.

The Rev chortled. "Too bad it's not real. If you've got a moment, Link will elaborate."

Rockwell said, "As Leander told you, the Rev had me infiltrate the klub**haus.** I made friends with the late Frankie Carbajal, who had developed quite a dislike for his onetime **hermano,** Salvador Abascal, along with his close friend, Wayne Frank Jackson. Frankie coveted the gold, which was then believed to be in the possession of the late Meyer Gelb and Señor Abascal. The late Frankie put together some leads and learned that the gold was stashed in a bank safe-deposit vault in San Diego. The Rev and I brought in Ed Satterlee then. Ed secured a seizure writ that allowed him to secure the gold and sequester it in a nearby warehouse.

I flew the gold up to L.A., and the Rev brought in a metallurgist to weigh the bars and calculate their value. He was the one who determined that they were all fake."

The Rev kicked at the bars. The Rev jabbed his pipe at Ashida.

"Cast iron, and thick-gold-plated. Formed to exactly resemble and weigh the same as solid-gold bars. Even the mint markings match, down to a tee. The bars were designed to fool the naked eye, and no more than that."

Ashida grabbed a bar and hefted it. He'd held a real bar. The fake bar was indistinguishable.

"The robbery itself. The chain of possession and levels of dispersal. Did factionalism occur? The robbery preceded all known accounts of the forming of the **Kameraden.** I have a well-developed theory, and I'm wondering if you'll confirm or refute it."

The Rev winked. Link Rockwell winked. Mr. Moto's got the floor. Both men jut-jawed their pipes.

"Leander walked the bars off the train. He portrayed the dumb Negro kid. The Reverend Mimms portrayed a colored sleeping-car porter. Kyoho Hanamaka portrayed a Japanese chauffeur, and Wayne Frank Jackson portrayed a white swell, perched in a limousine. Salvador portrayed a Mexican youth, hovering in the background. Skin color as disguise. Racial prejudice as a means of obfuscation. The switch was accomplished in that manner."

The Rev bowed. "You left out Eddie Leng and

Don Matsura. They were in on the job. They played Oriental train-yard workers. They also helped out with the escapes and the track-switch snafus."

Rockwell said, "Otherwise, you're right with Eversharp."

Ashida said, "The initial cadre of **Kameraden** was formed at Dresden Polytechnic. Kyoho Hanamaka underplayed its importance to me. Abascal gave a speech, and Carbajal, Pimentel, Jamie, and Hayes heard the message. The Spanish Civil War loomed. The big war loomed, and Salvador saw it as a fait accompli. He prophesied the Hitler-Stalin pact and Hitler's ultimate abrogation. The idea of a left-right postwar alliance took hold and flourished intellectually. The initial heist conspirators—Eckelkamp-Gelb, Wayne Frank, Leander, Salvador, Hanamaka, the Reverend Mimms, Leng, and Matsura—were watching gold prices escalate and waiting out the statute of limitations on the robbery. The statute clock stopped on May 18, 1940. The original conspirators were caught up in the crazy politics of upcoming war, but not to the extent of the Dresden Poly boys. The boys had been to Spain, the Fatherland, and Russia. Kyoho and Salvador had spent time there, and forged connections. High-level Nazis and Soviets knew the war would go bad for them, as early as the late '30s. Salvador and Kyoho exploited their fear, and proposed the Baja conference of November '40. The gold lured the bigwigs in. They capitulated to Abascal's vision of postwar alliance, but the gold cinched the deal."

The Rev bowed. Rockwell said, "Right with Eversharp."

Ashida said, "You were perpetrating a shell game. The gold achieved the status of an open secret and a wet dream. Your informal alliance grew as the war loomed that much more palpably close. Kyoho and Meyer Gelb went back to the heist and the fire. They were Communists and arsonists and God knows what else together. Saul Lesnick signed on from the Left. He was in Gelb's CP cell. Ed Satterlee played tangential to the heist. He signed on in a fix-it man capacity. Jim Davis signed on from the Right. Salvador killed priest-killers at Meyer's behest. It all blew chaotically out of proportion. Idiot ideologues shot their mouths off, and rumors spread. Terry Lux, Lin Chung, Wendell Rice, and George Kapek. The Lazaro-Schmidts, Villareal-Caiz, crazy Bundists, Reds, and Sinarquistas. Come, one and all. We'll survive this war or we won't. The bigwigs were over in Russia and Germany, engaged in a fight for their everyday survival. They had no idea that the original conspirators had no intention of sharing the gold with them, after postwar gold prices had skyrocketed. Factionalism and personal rivalries raged within the original robbery band. Rancor fell short of fatality. The chain of possession shifted along those lines as gold prices and war catastrophe escalated. Salvador Abascal succeeded Meyer Gelb as the **Kameraden**'s top dog. The title is surely meaningless, if illustrative of how deep this self-deluded madness goes.

Salvador got the job because he was in the original robbery band and because he recruited the Dresden Poly boys. The Nazi bigwigs loved him because they thought he was a fascist. The Soviet bigwigs loved him because they considered him a Red, and because he'd slaughtered Trotskyites. The Rev's got his back-to-Africa con. Gelb was extorting Jewish refugees that the **Kamerad**-Nazis had cut loose. You're all criminals first, and ideologues a distant second. You'll split the gold on Armistice Day, and you'll sell out the comrades overseas to the highest intelligence-agency bidder."

The Rev went **whew.** Rockwell wiped his face with a handkerchief.

Ashida wiped his face. "Here's a prudent guess. Wayne Frank shipped the real gold to Switzerland, right after the Baja wingding."

The Rev said, "Mr. and Mrs. Ashida didn't raise any dumb kids."

Rockwell said, "I met some real hot dogs at the wingding. I got Ernst Kaltenbrunner and Anastas Mikoyan's autographs."

The Rev jabbed his pipe. "Take a bar with you, Doctor. Makes a swell paperweight."

130

(LOS ANGELES, 4:00 P.M., 4/12/42)

Peep job. Girlfriend #4 evinced hinky behavior. That mandates brainwork and eyeball scrutiny.

Elmer peeped Ruth's courtyard. He car-lounged. He popped bennies and gargled Old Crow. 1 plus 1 equals 2. He pondered a quick-toss B and E.

He'd gone by the Musicians' Local. A clerk fed him a hot lead on Chuckie Duquesne. Chuckie, aka "Kid Lightning." He was gigging at the Taj Mahal tonight.

The Taj. A **coon**verted garage at 28th and Budlong. He schmoozed the clerk and got her phone number. She just **loooooved** policemen. He brought up his friend Ruth Szigeti. She played the violin. She recorded a Bartók piece, here at the Local. That was three nights back. The quartet worked dusk to dawn.

The clerk went **nix.** She worked the late shift that night. No such quartet passed through.

That's 0 plus 1 equals 1. Add this to that:

Ruth lied to him. Ruth came off flustered that last time they gassed. He talked to Nort Layman. Dr. Nort autopsied Meyer Gelb. Dr. Nort confirmed his I Was There/I Saw The Stiff call.

Gelb was cold. Frankie Carbajal didn't snuff him. Nort fixed the TOD as 2:00 a.m. The torture cuts were inflicted postmurder. Said cuts were all fussy. It felt like a squeamish-woman job. The small-bore gun, the cuts, the prissy gestalt. **Cherchez la fucking femme.**

1 plus 1 equals 2. 2 plus 2 equals 4. Gelb was a shakedown man. He extorted Ruth and her refugee chums. He victimized Ruth. La Ruth brooked no shit from man or beast. That's 4 plus 4 equals 8. 8 equals confirm or refute.

Bennies and booze equals pins and needles and juiced-up intent. Elmer got out and breezed through the courtyard. It was pin-drop quiet. Ruth's door was locked.

He got out his pick set. He pulled a thin-edge pick and jabbed the keyhole. He pushed deep and rode the door in.

He shut the door. The front room looked okay. No hink details jabbed him. He walked through the kitchen. It smelled like fried eggs. Ruth left her breakfast dishes out. No hink details jabbed him.

He shinnied through the bedroom and checked out the porch. A taut clothesline ran through it. Damp clothes were pinned on.

Two brassieres. One camisole. One pinned-up white blouse. Spots down the front of it. Almost removed. Blood red fades to pale pink.

Elmer cut back to the bedroom. He'd slept with Ruth here. He knew the layout. He went straight for the one chest of drawers.

The top drawer featured underwear. He ran a hand

through it. The middle drawer featured scarves and folded skirts. He ran a hand through it. His hand hit metal. He pulled a small revolver out.

A purse gun. .25-caliber. A five-shot cylinder. 1 plus 1 equals 2.

Elmer sniffed the barrel. He caught cordite fumes. He broke the cylinder. He saw one shell gone.

The front door jiggled. Stacked heels tapped the floor. He caught cigarette smoke and bath scent.

She walked straight to the bedroom. He gave her a heartbeat to see him. She stopped short. He turned around.

She wore a flower-print dress and a mousy cardigan. He held up the gun. She grabbed an ashtray off the bookcase and crushed her cigarette.

"So?"

"So, why?"

"So, what can one more death mean to me now?"

Elmer shook his head. "You'll have to do better than that. I don't want to hear 'the war made me do it.'"

Ruth said, "He called me and ordered me to his apartment. He ordered me to lure Otto Klemperer into my bed and make him admit his Communist Party allegiance. I told him that he had created enough chaos, and condemned him for the idiotic ideals his idiotic alliance had foisted upon us. I was enraged in that moment. I demanded the gold that I had heard so many rumors of. I told him that I would use it to ransom Jews out of Germany. He said, 'Why should

I care about Jews?' I knew he was Fritz Eckelkamp then, and that was when I shot him."

She was touch-me close. He smelled her breath and counted her gray hairs.

"It's a gas-chamber job. You'd do better with a jealous-lover plea."

"What will you do?"

Elmer said, "I don't know."

The Taj was unlicensed and nouveau-swank. It was couched behind a house row. Four garages got bull-dozed and comprised one cabaret. The refurb job was par excellent.

You had booths, tables, and a raised bandstand. There's an ebony bar and blue-flocked wallpaper. It's a boss swami's playpen.

You had standard booze and bootleg booze. There's absinthe and Everclear. You've got colored waitresses in saris. The Taj welcomes a race-mixed clientele.

Elmer and Buzz showed early. They grabbed a prime wallside booth. They figured they'd take Chuckie backstage. Chuckie foxed them there. He was onstage with his sidemen already. Chuckie played bass sax. A white dink played trombone. A black hepcat played fluegelhorn.

Chuckie was tall and blond. He ran six-two and 140, tops. He sported a ducks-ass haircut. He wore zoot pants and a plaid Sir Guy shirt.

Buzz craved results. Let's move now. Elmer nixed it.

Let's wait. Johnny Shinura might show. A Chuckie's gal-pal type might materialize.

The Taj filled up. A good crowd filtered in. They snatched the wallside booths and floor tables. They swarmed the bar. They flirted and gassed. They craved Le Jazz Hot and distraction.

Elmer and Buzz drank Green Lizards. Their swell waitress made them as cops. Green Lizards were 151 rum and crème de menthe. Buzz was half-tanked. Elmer was benzified out of his gourd. Killer Ruth ruled his thoughts.

The combo tuned up. Kid Lightning and his Bolts from the Blue. They honked and blatted. The blue motif prevailed. Blue spotlights lit them up.

The low ceiling trapped cigarette smoke. Elmer and Buzz orbed the premises. Where's Sword Man Johnny? Where's the Gal Pal? Elmer watched the door. **Oooga-booga.** Dudley Smith walked in.

Elmer nudged Buzz and pointed over. Looky, looky. Dud wore civvies and looked whippet thin.

Buzz clenched up. Dud walked to the bar. He ordered a drink and glanced around. Elmer and Buzz were perched off aways. Dud didn't see them. Dud eyed the bandstand and Chuckie D.

The Bolts tuned up. Chuckie's king-sized sax weighed him down. Elmer watched the door. Race-mix cliques filed in. Hideo Ashida followed them.

Elmer nudged Buzz and pointed over. Looky, looky. Buzz saw Ashida. Hideo stood barside. He saw Dudley. Elmer and Buzz caught that, plain. Dud was preoccupied. He missed Ashida and eyeballed Chuckie D.

The music wasn't music. It was fucking noise stew. Elmer killed his drink and watched the door. Where's the gal pal? What does she look like? Fuck—Johnny Shinura walked in.

Elmer saw him. Buzz saw him. They swapped **oooga-booga** looks. Ashida saw Johnny. Elmer caught that. Dud missed Johnny altogether. He sipped his drink and eye-drilled Chuckie D.

Ashida stood upside the pay phone. He eye-clicked Dud to Johnny. Jap Johnny stood tiptoed and waved his arms at the bandstand. Chuckie caught it and un-strapped his sax.

Chuckie tromped Johnny's way. Dud caught it. He unbuttoned his coat and touched his belt piece. **Oooga-booga.** A colored doorman braced Johnny. Hit the road, Tojo. We don't seat no Japs.

Ashida crouched by the pay phone. The doorman missed him. Johnny pitched a fit. I'm an American, Sambo. You're just some nigger to me.

Folks looked over. Folks hubbubbed. Johnny pitched that **loud** fit. The doorman pulled a waist-band sap and swung it. Johnny pulled a hip piece.

He drilled the doorman. Two shots echoed. The door-man collapsed and convulsed. Folks started screaming.

Chuckie flinched. Chuckie did this big double take. Chuckie made the big man at the bar.

Dud caught it. They drew down simultaneous and

fired point-blank. Chuckie blew out a shelf of booze bottles. Dud shot muzzle-tight. Chuckie's face blew up, muzzle-burned. His hair shot flames.

Buzz froze and unfroze. Elmer froze and unfroze. They stood up and unholstered late-late. Ashida stumbled toward Dudley. Elmer and Buzz aimed and let fly.

More bottles exploded. Elmer shot high and off left. Buzz nailed Johnny. Sword man pitched back and shot back. His shots hit high and off right.

Elmer braced his gun hand and aimed real careful now. He triggered in on Dudley Smith and squeezed off two perfect shots. He caught a blur simultaneous. He saw Ashida's suit coat. He blew Ashida up against Dudley. They toppled bar stools and crashed to the floor, all tangled up.

Elmer screamed. Buzz crashed tables and ran to the bar. Johnny slumped up against it. He'd dropped his piece. He was gut-shot and woozed. Buzz shot him straight in the face.

The whole room screamed. Elmer screamed over it. He kicked screamers out of the way and pushed to the bar. Ashida's suit coat was powder-scorched and tattered. He'd bled up the floor. Dudley sobbed and held him tight.

L.A. **Herald Express.** Monday, April 13, 1942.
Page-two feature. Byline: Sid Hudgens.

FOUR DEAD IN NITECLUB BLASTOUT!!!!!

Hero Cops Prevail in Juice-Joint Holocaust!!!!!

An ill wind blew the blues last nite, at the noxious near-southside nitespot, the Taj Mahal. It's unlicensed; it's unsanitary; it serves bilious booze and jittery jazz out of season. It caters to caustic cats and kittens, and a catastrophic convergence has caused it to close its doors for good.

Police Sergeants Elmer V. Jackson and Turner "Buzz" Meeks appeared, hot on the trail of jazz jackal Charles "Chuckie" Duquesne, and his jackalesque Jap henchman, John Kimoji Shinura—suspects in the baffling "klub**haus**" slayings of January 29. Policemen Wendell Rice and George Kapek were killed, along with their savvy Sancho Panza, Arturo "Archie" Archuleta. Sergeants Jackson and Meeks tracked Duquesne and Shinura to the tempestuous Taj, where four fearsome fates fatally intervened.

Enter legendary Police Sergeant Dudley L. Smith, currently on leave to serve with the

Army's crack Secret Intelligence Service. Enter Hideo Ashida, the PD's crack forensic chemist and sly sleuth, who puts Charlie Chan and Mr. Moto to shame. They were on the Jackal and Johnny the Jap's trail, as well. Enter the Taj Mahal's tipsy doorman, Willis "Big Daddy" Gordean. Shots shattered the smoke-smacked air as the Bolts from the Blue blasted onstage. The police contingent made their move, and Duquesne, Shinura, Ashida, and Gordean lay dead. Colored canary Loretta McKee caught the two killers' dying declarations and last words. "They were in awful bad shape, and on their way out," she said. "But I managed to hear what they were mumbling."

And, what's that, our sepia songbird?

"Chuckie said, 'I am the klub**haus** killer,' and 'Man, what a gas.' Johnny said, 'Viva Hirohito' and 'Pearl Harbor was cool.'"

Infamous last words, dear reader. But here's our heroic happy ending. Police Chief C. B. "Jack" Horrall has stamped the coruscating klub**haus** job "Case Closed." Mayor Fletch Bowron will bestow the Los Angeles Civic Service Award on Hideo Ashida, posthumously. Elmer Jackson and Buzz Meeks will be feted with the Los Angeles Police Department's Medal of Valor. Citing nervous exhaustion, Sergeant Dudley Smith has resigned his Army commission and is now recuperating at a swank beachside retreat.

131

(LOS ANGELES, 4/14–4/26/42)

Niteclub Blastout to wartime exile. Official forfeiture and unofficial censure. Malibu is rarely intemperate. He goes back with Terry Lux. The Wolf carries news from the outside world.

Deals were struck. Jack Horrall brokered them. The Staties commandeered his biz fronts. He resigned his Army commission and will not be court-martialed. He will not be prosecuted for his misjudged stateside misconduct. Here's a cheeky footnote: "Sepia Songbird" Loretta McKee is DA Bill McPherson's girlfriend.

The Baja authorities will not seek indictments. Terry's dry-out farm is not Folsom or San Quentin. He enjoys a grand suite of rooms. They remain locked at all times, and thus constitute custody. Two-man guard teams police him. He's permitted late-night strolls around the property. His guards eavesdrop on his chats with the Wolf. They consider him whimsically insane.

Meyer Gelb is dead. The true killer remains unknown. El Salvy remains at large. Jack H. has implied that he will be sternly rebuked. Mexican cops have been charged to infiltrate the Sinarquistas and disrupt them from within. Ed Satterlee remains under house arrest and has cut immunity deals. Monsignor Joe Hayes has been granted immunity. Wallace Jamie has divested his financial interest in Bev's Switchboard and has pledged to leave L.A. The klub**haus** job has been officially stamped a clean solve. Chuckie Duquesne's woman friend remains unidentified.

Jim Davis and Saul Lesnick also bunk at Terry's farm. Lesnick resides in a locked ward and is prone to screaming fits. The gold remains unfound. Postal inspectors grabbed Bev Shoftel and arrested her on eighty-four counts of felony mail fraud. Treasury agents raided mail drops in twelve U.S. cities. The comrades-**Kameraden** have been nullified to the point of extinction. Jack H. was blunt here. Bill Parker told him the whole story. A ragtag band of opposed comrades engineered the coup. Parker, Elmer Jackson, Buzz Meeks. Kay Lake—most spectacularly.

Claire has kicked morphine. She'll leave the farm soon. Constanza joined her brother in Havana. She plays in a string quartet there. Terry said they've received a recording contract with RCA Victor.

Resourceful Constanza. She's taken Cuban strong-man Prío Socarrás as her inaugural lover.

He spends his time reading and contemplating his ultimate release. He'll remain a policeman as long as Jack Horrall remains Chief. He plays the Bruckner symphonies. Otto Klemperer's interpretations hold him spellbound. He plays **Tristan und Isolde** most obsessively. Kirsten Flagstad sings the latter part. He listens and transmogrifies her to Kay Lake.

He sips mint juleps with Jim Davis. Chief Jim is lucid on one topic only. The Fifth Column is everywhere but rarely achieves coherence. It's no more than an amalgam of mischief-minded souls hooked on current dangerous ideas. Jim mentioned a pervert party, back in '39. Salvy noticed you then, Dud. He was there, but he was costumed and masked up. He had plans for you from that time on. He's not really a fascist. He's a Stalinist. He killed those priest-killers because they were Trotskyites. It's a wild and fucked-up world, ain't it?

Yes, it certainly is. And he must absent himself for a spell.

He needs rest. He's earned this interval of meditative renewal. He's a privileged dry-out-farm inmate. Kwan's Chinese Pagoda caters his meals. Special chop suey cartons conceal opium. Uncle Ace visits him often. They guardedly discuss their postwar plans.

The Wolf sleeps at the foot of his bed. Their

dialogue takes in the world and the cosmos. They mourn their most dear Hideo Ashida.

He misses Hideo. He snipped a lock of his hair in the ambulance that transported him to the morgue. Hideo's betrayal does not trouble him one whit. The great gift of Hideo himself renders it small.

Hideo was put to rest at Manzanar. He wires graveside flowers each week. He sent condolence notes to his mother and brother and got thank-you notes back. He keeps the lock of hair in a Japanese lacquered box.

His bedroom window overlooks a tree-lined walkway. He keeps vigilant watch for Kay Lake. She wears cashmere dresses and heather-toned skirts. Her eyes are so dark brown that they're black.

Stunning girl, I can't begin to imagine your fate.

132

KAY LAKE'S DIARY

(LOS ANGELES, 8:00 A.M., 4/27/42)

A certain **Kamerad** was due. I expected her to be prompt and to be candidly forthcoming. It took a great deal of effort to ascertain her identity and determine her whereabouts at the time of the klub**haus** killings.

I sat on a walkway bench near Claire's bungalow. I was within view of Dudley's locked domicile. Extensive records checks and cross-checks brought me here. I began pulling paper in the wake of the Niteclub Blastout. The Blastout was a local sensation. Elmer Jackson was its most auspicious surviving casualty. His stray shots killed Hideo Ashida. He aimed at Dudley Smith, fully intending to kill him. He told me this and told no one else. The papers pinned the blame on the conveniently dead Big Daddy Gordean and Johnny Shinura. My dear Elmer. Volatile and impetuous. Sweet-natured and tolerant for a cop. Guilt-racked now. Done in by internal sabotage and Hideo Ashida's death. The man who reminded me that Hideo had sussed it all out. A woman attended the klub**haus** deaths and may have helped commit them. We owed Hideo his clean solve. Elmer said, "Maybe there's some records checks you can run."

I was at loose ends; Elmer was at loose ends, verging on shell shock. He was estranged from Ruth; Annie was visiting her ailing dad in rural Idaho. Ellen was off with her husband and son; Brenda was tending to their call-service business. The Blastout remained hot news. Loretta McKee replaced Lena Horne as Charlie Barnet's colored canary. Mrs. Big Daddy sued Los Angeles County.

Duke Ellington was busy composing his "Niteclub Blastout Suite." A land baron purchased the Taj Mahal, with plans to refurbish and reopen it as the Klub Blastout. Jo Stafford and the Pied Pipers will play the gala opening.

This blithe exploitation enraged Elmer. He raged against himself and the **Kameraden** and his long-gone brother, who started the whole thing. He told me to run directory and phone-call checks on Chuckie Duquesne. "You might turn something there."

Bill swore me in as a PD clerk-typist. He assigned me a cubicle with a desk and a telephone. I ran jail checks first. I learned that Johnny Shinura was in Lincoln Heights on the night of the murders. Chuckie Duquesne had never been arrested. Johnny and Chuckie were bunked in at the East 2nd Street warehouse then. That was their collective last known address. They squatted there after the Federal seizure and Johnny's formal eviction. Chuckie lived somewhere before that. He had to have had a formal address. I ran DMV checks and turned up an address in Echo Park.

Chuckie rented a house there, and had a telephone installed. I called PC Bell and secured his phone bills from October '39 up through last year. One suggestive female name repeatedly popped up.

I recalled Hideo's theory. The case was definitively homosexual. It derived from two-person animus.

The foot scuffs on the upstairs hallway wall had been made by a woman.

I ran DMV checks. I learned that Chuckie did not own a registered automobile. I secured car stats for Chuckie's female friend. I spent many hours in the former Crash Squad command post. I studied the master file; I studied the initial canvassing sheets in particular. I noted the north/south/east/west canvassing perimeters. The crime occurred on a Wednesday night into Thursday morning. The proximity of the jazz strip troubled me. I walked the strip and saw that most of the clubs possessed no parking lots or assigned parking spaces. The strip hopped on weeknights; patrons had to park their cars somewhere; the somewhere within the canvass perimeters would be packed with club hoppers' cars. The klub**haus** killer or killers would have had to park outside those perimeters and walk to the **haus.**

I drove to 46th and Central and walked my own expanded perimeter. I noted NO NIGHTTIME PARKING signs in all directions. That's when I knew I had a chance to solve it; that's when I knew that the debt to Hideo might be repaid.

It took one more phone call. I buzzed the PD's Traffic Bureau and requested a list of parking tickets issued on the night in question. Her name was on it. She had parked on 41st Street, east of Hooper. It was three blocks past the northeast perimeter.

I placed my cigarettes and matches on the bench beside me. I'd met the woman twice before; she bummed out of my pack on both occasions. She smoked too much and talked too much and divulged inappropriately. I beckoned her here. I wrote to her and told her I knew. She had my full consent to divulge inappropriately.

Andrea Lesnick walked up. She sat down and went straight for the cigarettes. Her fingers were nicotine-stained; her nails were bitten down to the quick.

She said, "Miss Lake knows my secret. She figured out what the dumb cops couldn't."

"You parked in a red zone. They missed the citation you were issued."

"They raped me."

"I know."

"I've been to Tehachapi. San Quentin can't be any worse. 'Vengeance is mine, saith the Lord.' I'll enter the green room with my head held high. I've groveled enough in my lifetime. Chuckie convinced me of that."

I lit a cigarette. "I was wondering how you met him."

Andrea said, "I met him at a party at Otto's place. Everybody who was anybody was there, but we all wore masks. Chuckie was gigging there. Wendell and George were there, but they were chauffeuring some America Firsters, so they had to stay outside. Archie stayed outside, too. The car-park boys were Mex, so Archie spoke Mex to them, and Jewed them for half of their tips."

"I've heard of this party, Andrea. People wore Nazi costumes. Orson Welles screened a pornographic movie."

Andrea shook her head. No, no, **no.** Let me tell it **my** way.

"Miss Lake's a C.T., and a provocateur. She's a snitch, and she's in with the cops. It's my story, and I don't have to let her prompt me or tell me how I should confess."

I touched Andrea's arm. She pulled away and chained cigarettes.

"Wendell and I got stoked on each other, and we necked in this limousine he was driving. We petted, but he wanted more than I wanted to give him, so I said, 'Whoa, son.' Wendell got ticked off, because the party was very libertine, and he told me I should give him what everybody else was getting, but I left him high and dry instead. Chuckie and a boy Robby Staley set him up with were necking, outside by a pergola. They witnessed some horrible thing that gave Chuckie nightmares for the rest of his life, but he never told me what it was."

I glanced out at Dudley's jail suite. Andrea poked me and brought my gaze back to her. Look at me, look at me. It's **my** story I'm telling you.

"Wendell was hateful and spiteful. He started sending me letters and snapshots of him and his wife, doing you know what in the you know where. It went on for a year and a half or so, then it stopped, and some time passed. Then my daddy sent me to the klub**haus** to pick up a eugenics book he'd lent this boy Link Rockwell. Wendell, Georgie, and Archie were there, alone. That was when they raped me."

She'd dribbled ash on her blouse and sweater. Both garments were burn-marked already. Her fingers were gnawed. She gnashed her hands when she wasn't smoking. She was unbearable to behold. She condemned me as glib. She commanded my prayers for the rest of my life.

" 'Vengeance is mine,' saith You Know Who. Which is just what Chuckie and I started planning. It was a double-dip. I got keestered, and he got nightmares from that party. We started frequenting the klub**haus,** and Chuckie poked boys upstairs. I told Wendell, Georgie, and Archie that I wanted to do it again with them, while Chuckie watched. That's how we got them alone at the **haus.**"

Her hair. She curled strands around her fingers and twisted them taut. She maimed herself. She left bald spots. Self-inflicted stigmata. Collaborator women shaved bald.

"We lured them upstairs. Chuckie gave them terp cigarettes laced with poison. They smoked them and became woozy, and we led them back downstairs. Chuckie sat them down on the couch. He was left-handed, so I had to scooch around him just so. He held an ice pick to their necks, and I put on these strangling gloves that Johnny Shinura gave me, and I strangled them right there."

I looked in her eyes. One was blue, one was gray. Her eugenicist daddy. I suspected experiments gone awry. She sat on her hands so she wouldn't gnash or pull her hair out. What would Hideo Ashida do? It came down to that. I said, "I wish you safety," and walked away.

133

(LOS ANGELES, 8:00 A.M., 4/28/42)

Union Station. The Welcome Wagon awaits. They're packing brass knucks and belt saps. **Bienvenidos, señor.**

Jack Horrall dispatched them. His orders ran succinct. Beat the fuck half dead. Tell him no sabotage. Return to Mexico. Come back, we kill your spic ass.

Elmer and Buzz lurked outside the station. Cars clogged the front lot. The breezeway hopped. Porters schlepped suitcases. Tourists hailed taxicabs. The Baja train was past due.

Elmer and Buzz lurked. They got their orders.

They got their reward. They were acknowledged whizbang detectives. Jack H. shot them two Homicide slots.

El Salvy walked outside. He scanned the front lot. Cars zigzagged through. Elmer and Buzz swooped.

They grabbed him and hustled him. They pinned his arms. He went along, peaceful. They worked the two-man accordion press.

Salvy complied. They waltzed him off to the side of the building. Elmer grabbed his hair and elbowed him in the windpipe. Salvy gasped and squeaked. Buzz pinned him against the wall. Elmer stuffed a sock in his mouth. They unhooked their knucks and saps and let fly.

Octopus job. They worked him, four-fisted. Elmer smashed his ribs. Bones crunched and snapped. Buzz squatted low and ripped uppercuts at his balls. Elmer punched his teeth out. The sock trapped loose choppers and sopped up blood.

Buzz hurled sap shots. They sliced Salvy's ears half off. Buzz intoned the edict. Elmer hummed the "Marine's Hymn." He checked the parking lot. He saw this man upside a Cadillac. He thought, Maybe, maybe not.

He dropped his hurt kit and walked over. Well now—and amen. It was good old good-looking Wayne Frank.

He sported some gray hair. He wore wingtip shoes and a swell chalk-stripe suit.

He said, "Try not to kill Salvy. Him and me share a history."

Elmer said, "I like your car. Life's been good to you."

Wayne Frank spit tobacco juice. "I've got a wife and two kids in New Orleans, and a wife and three kids in Atlanta. If I can avoid this here futile war, I'll have it made in the shade."

Elmer smiled. "You always believed in the Resurrection. It was your favorite Bible story. You always said you might die young, but you'd just as likely return."

Wayne Frank smiled. "I visited Wisharts last year. Sue Bailey asked about you. She's with the TVA now. She had herself a damn fine job with the Willkie campaign."

Sue B. was a six-foot blonde. She justified the climb. Him and Wayne Frank fought over her. He kicked Wayne Frank's ass good.

"Those New Year's rainstorms stirred up some grief, didn't they?"

"Let's not talk about that."

"New Year's is New Year's. Remember? We always listened to Cliffie Stone's **Hometown Jamboree.**"

Wayne Frank spritzed tobacco juice. "You look pretty good, for a man who's just seen a ghost."

"I've learned a few things since New Year's. I've had a good spell to prepare."

Wayne Frank said, "I always told you I'd make something of myself."

Ghosts. Apparitions. Warlocks, poltergeists, ghouls. Wayne Frank's alive. Hideo Ashida's dead.

Elmer drove out to Santa Monica. He hadn't seen Ruth in a coon's age. He should put her at ease. You never know. She might throw him some woof-woof.

Wilshire was bright and breezy. The beach air felt sweet. He parked outside Ruth's courtyard. Longhair music wafted over. Ruthie sat on her porch. She played her radio full blast.

Elmer got out and walked over. Ruthie saw him. She primped and turned off the radio. She looked grim—per always, these days.

"I've been reading about you. The widow Big Daddy Gordean asserts that you are trigger-happy."

Elmer dittoed Wayne Frank. "Let's not talk about that."

"Shall we discuss Brahms? That was the Double Concerto I was enjoying."

Elmer relit a cigar. "Let's discuss what's eating you. Maybe I can help you out."

Ruth said, "You have not the cachet. A deportation order has been issued against me. I am held to be a seditious alien, and I have no means of redress."

She had green panther eyes. He had beady eyes. They discussed it their first night. Elmer slalomed in and dialed their eyes tight.

"You can't deport the wife of a U.S. citizen.

Husbands can't fink out their wives for Murder One."

Ruth turned on the radio. A violin and cello tangled chords and fought. She kept the volume low.

"Might we have a Jewish wedding?"

Elmer said, "Don't press your luck."

Part Six
KAMERADEN

(April 29–
May 8, 1942)

134

(LOS ANGELES, 4/29–5/8/42)

Early-wartime L.A. The blackouts, the attendant car wrecks, the impromptu race riots spurred by enveloping dark. The grinding shame of the Japanese internment. The revelry of fearful folks disinclined to step outside. The unexpected pregnancies and great volume of kids expected in the fall of '42.

The muzzle flash of Pearl Harbor burned bright through the spring, as the phenomenon of the war was subsumed by the war as our refuge and justification. Early-wartime L.A. was a time of great crimes and witheringly ambiguous solutions. It was a time to celebrate the shit-kicking American spirit and our mass resolve to see this thing through. Early-wartime L.A. The booze and the muzzle-flash love affairs. There was no better time to howl and throw parties.

Jack Horrall hosted an acquittal bash at Kwan's Chinese Pagoda. It celebrated Bill Parker's and Elmer

Jackson's bold move to squelch the Fed probe. The PD and City Hall crowd showed up in force. The acquittals formally justified the soirée. I held it to be a wrap party for the span of events preannounced by a New Year's Eve rainstorm. The gang was there. **We** were there. Comrades and adversaries crammed into Ace Kwan's back room. Bill, Elmer, Buzz, Brenda. Thad Brown and Nort Layman. Mike Breuning and Dick Carlisle. Ray Pinker, Fletch Bowron, my beleaguered Lee Blanchard. DA Bill McPherson, with Loretta McKee in tow. Reconciliation overwhelmed rancor. Something big had ended as the war progressed. I chatted with Mike Breuning. He said, "**Whew,** Kay." I said, "**Whew,** Mike" right back. Our conversation fizzled then. There was no need to say anything else.

We were there. Provocateurs and profiteers. Bill Parker danced and drank with Claire De Haven. They argued the Baltimore catechism and defamed my most revered Martin Luther. Then something extraordinary happened.

Jack Horrall gave a speech. He blew raspberries at the Feds and crowed over the mass acquittals. He praised the diligent detectives who solved the klub**haus** job and notably omitted Dudley Smith. He broke down and wept as he lionized the "late and surely great" Hideo Ashida.

Elmer married Ruth Szigeti two weeks later. There had to be a hidden story there—but Elmer refused to divulge it. The Protestant service dismayed Ruth. The wedding party vacated the church and reconvened in Mike Lyman's front room. Fake gold bars served as dinner-table settings. The Reverend M. L. Mimms supplied them.

Buzz brought his pet scorpion. He slid steak tidbits into his cage and dared people to stick a finger in and pet him. The acquittal-bash crowd celebrated the Jackson-Szigeti nuptials. Otto Klemperer and Joan Klein joined us, along with the Koenigs and Sandor Abromowitz. Barbara Stanwyck and Robert Taylor dropped by and heckled Ruth. We've lost you to a cop bumpkin. Say it ain't so. You've lost nothing, **Liebchens.** My husband understands me as I understand him.

Indeed. Brenda Allen, Ellen Drew, and Annie Staples had served as Ruth's maids of honor. Ellen hawked her new Paramount oater; Annie told Elmer not to lose her phone number. Bob Taylor took Brenda aside. He slid her a roll of bills and told her to set Babs up with "Ten-Inch" Tony Mangano.

I sat with Elmer and Ruth at the head table and overheard their conversation. Ruth thanked Elmer for his great generosity. Elmer said, "Hush, now. It's not like I'm suffering, and it's not like I don't like you."

Early-wartime L.A. Profiteers and privateers. My most valued **Kameraden.**

Otto debuted Shostakovich's **Leningrad** Symphony the following week. The performance was not billed as such. The five-hundred-dollar-a-pop tickets were sold via hushed word of mouth. Otto was preempting Maestro Toscanini's formal premiere of the work. He had put together an orchestra of relocated exiles and film-studio musicians. Ruth Szigeti was the first-chair violin; the Koenigs and Sandor Abromowitz played alongside her. The occasion was strictly black-tie. The Wilshire Ebell Theatre held roughly one thousand seats. The proceeds were earmarked for European war relief. Every woo-woo movie star and local hotshot of the day was there. I squeezed Bill Parker's hands as Otto raised his baton and went **Now.**

The symphony was brutal, at the expense of majestic and elegiac. It was an hourlong disruption of my most dear hopes and my most conceited dreams. I rode with the shock of it. Foreshortened crescendos dashed my sense of savagery as beauty and the beauty of art itself. Human love will not sustain us in this time of horror. Comrade Dimitri mocked the assumption. He sought only to instill a brutalized survivors' resolve.

So be it, then.

The antithesis of resolve is relinquishment. It's wartime L.A., and I am a brilliant and passionate young woman with stories to tell. Circumstance is destiny. I may never live as boldly and adroitly as I live now. This is my war and my country. Do not mock the love that I hold for both. I willed thunderstorms as a child in Sioux Falls, South Dakota. I must do that here and now. **Reminiscenza,** this storm, this savaging disaster. My options are do everything or do nothing. My hot date with History continues. It is now May 8, 1942. These final strains of the **Leningrad** Symphony mark my refusal to die.

DRAMATIS PERSONAE

This Storm is the second volume of the Second L.A. Quartet. The first volume, **Perfidia,** covers December 6 through December 29, 1941. The L.A. Quartet—**The Black Dahlia, The Big Nowhere, L.A. Confidential,** and **White Jazz**—covers the years 1946 to 1958 in Los Angeles. The Underworld U.S.A. Trilogy—**American Tabloid, The Cold Six Thousand,** and **Blood's A Rover**—covers 1958 to 1972, on a national scale.

The Second L.A. Quartet places real-life and fictional characters from the first two bodies of work in Los Angeles, during World War II, as significantly younger people. These three series span thirty-one years and will stand as one novelistic history. The following list notes the previous appearances of characters in **This Storm.**

DRAMATIS PERSONAE

SALVADOR ABASCAL. A real-life Mexican fascist.

SANDOR ABROMOWITZ. An exiled Hungarian musician.

BRENDA ALLEN. The real-life Allen appears in **The Big Nowhere** and **Perfidia.**

ARCHIE ARCHULETA. This character is a dope fiend and rowdy Fifth Columnist.

AKIRA ASHIDA. The brother of police/U.S. Army chemist Hideo Ashida. Mr. Ashida appears in **Perfidia.**

HIDEO ASHIDA, Los Angeles Police Department/ Army SIS. Ashida appears in **Perfidia.**

MARIKO ASHIDA. The mother of police/U.S. Army chemist Hideo Ashida. Mrs. Ashida appears in **Perfidia.**

EUGENE BISCAILUZ. The real-life Sheriff of Los Angeles County. Biscailuz appears in **Perfidia.**

OFFICER LEE BLANCHARD, Los Angeles Police Department. Blanchard appears in **The Black Dahlia** and **Perfidia.**

FLETCH BOWRON. Mayor of the City of Los Angeles. Mayor Bowron appears in **Perfidia.**

"BIG BOB" BOYD. Captain, Kern County Sheriff's Department.

SERGEANT MIKE BREUNING, Los Angeles Police Department. Breuning appears in **The Big Nowhere, L.A. Confidential, White Jazz,** and **Perfidia.**

LIEUTENANT THAD BROWN, Los Angeles Police Department. The real-life Brown appears in **Perfidia.**

VICTOR TREJO CAIZ. Fifth Column assassin.

ARCHBISHOP J. J. CANTWELL. The real-life boss of the L.A. Archdiocese. Archbishop Cantwell appears in **Perfidia.**

FRANKIE **"EL CABRÓN"** CARBAJAL. Hoodlum and raucous Fifth Columnist.

SERGEANT DICK CARLISLE, Los Angeles Police Department. Carlisle appears in **The Big Nowhere, L.A. Confidential, White Jazz,** and **Perfidia.**

DR. LIN CHUNG. A plastic surgeon and proponent of eugenics. Dr. Chung appears in **Perfidia.**

LIEUTENANT LEW COLLIER, Los Angeles Police Department. Collier heads up the PD's Alien Squad.

JOAN CONVILLE, Los Angeles Police Department. Miss Conville appears in **Perfidia.**

FATHER CHARLES COUGHLIN. The real-life radio priest and nativist blowhard.

HUEY CRESSMEYER. Glue sniffer, psychopathic killer, and Fifth Column traitor. Mr. Cressmeyer appears in **American Tabloid** and **Perfidia.**

DR. RUTH MILDRED CRESSMEYER. Dr. Cressmeyer is Huey's mom, and a film-studio abortionist. She appears in **American Tabloid** and **Perfidia.**

DRAMATIS PERSONAE

EX-CHIEF JAMES EDGAR "TWO-GUN" DAVIS. The real-life Davis appears in **Perfidia.**

CLAIRE DE HAVEN. Dope addict and shrill left-winger. Miss De Haven appears in **The Big Nowhere** and **Perfidia.**

ELLEN DREW. The real-life film actress. Miss Drew appears in **Perfidia.**

MONDO **"EL TIGRE"** DÍAZ. Hoodlum and raucous Fifth Columnist.

CHUCKIE DUQUESNE. Jazz musician and psycho killer.

FRITZ ECKELKAMP. Armed robber and Marxist-fascist extortionist.

BILLY ECKSTINE. Real-life singer and bandleader.

SERGEANT COLIN FORBES, Los Angeles Police Department. The real-life Forbes works out of the PD's Hollywood Station.

LEANDER FRECHETTE. Labor goon and heist man.

MEYER GELB. Armed robber and Marxist-fascist extortionist.

TOMMY GLENNON. Hot-prowl rapist and Nazi shitheel.

SERGEANT AL GOOSSEN, Los Angeles Police Department. The real-life Goossen works out of the PD's Hollywood Station.

WILLIS "BIG DADDY" GORDEAN. A bouncer at the Taj Mahal Klub.

KYOHO HANAMAKA. Japanese naval attaché and Fifth Column mastermind.

MONSIGNOR JOE HAYES. Morally dubious priest with the L.A. Archdiocese.

CHIEF C. B. "CALL-ME-JACK" HORRALL, Los Angeles Police Department. The real-life Horrall appears in **Perfidia.**

SID HUDGENS. Newspaper scribe and scandal-monger. Hudgens appears in **L.A. Confidential** and **Perfidia.**

SERGEANT ELMER JACKSON, Los Angeles Police Department. The real-life Jackson appears in **Perfidia.**

WAYNE FRANK JACKSON. Drifter, armed robber, Fifth Columnist. Brother of Sergeant Elmer Jackson.

WALLACE N. JAMIE. Real-life private eye.

OFFICER GEORGE KAPEK, Los Angeles Police Department. Shitbird cop on the Alien Squad.

JOAN ROSEN KLEIN. Fifteen-year-old girl, on the loose in Mexico. Miss Klein appears in **Blood's A Rover.**

OTTO KLEMPERER. The real-life conductor and composer.

MAGDA KOENIG. An exiled Hungarian musician.

DRAMATIS PERSONAE

MIKLOS KOENIG. An exiled Hungarian musician.

UNCLE ACE KWAN. Tong warlord and restauranteur. Uncle Ace appears in **L.A. Confidential** and **Perfidia.**

KAY LAKE. Miss Lake appears in **The Black Dahlia** and **Perfidia.**

DR. NORT LAYMAN. A Los Angeles County deputy coroner. Dr. Nort appears in **The Big Nowhere, L.A. Confidential,** and **Perfidia.**

CONSTANZA LAZARO-SCHMIDT. Concert violist and fascist femme fatale.

JUAN LAZARO-SCHMIDT. Governor of Baja, California, and Marxist-fascist tool.

EDDIE LENG. Restauranteur, tong man, Fifth Columnist.

ANDREA LESNICK. Ex-Communist and lunatic about town. Miss Lesnick appears in **The Big Nowhere** and **Perfidia.**

DR. SAUL LESNICK. Red tool and headshrinker to the stars. Dr. Lesnick appears in **The Big Nowhere** and **Perfidia.**

OFFICER "CATBOX" CAL LUNCEFORD, Los Angeles Police Department. Shitbird cop on the Alien Squad.

DR. TERRY LUX. Hotshot plastic surgeon and closet nativist. Dr. Lux appears in **The Big Nowhere** and **Perfidia.**

"TEN-INCH" TONY MANGANO. Call boy and fruit hustler.

DONALD MATSURA. Dope peddler and skeevy Fifth Columnist.

JAMES J. McBRIDE. Lawyer for the L.A. Archdiocese.

LORETTA McKEE. Vocalist at the Taj Mahal Klub.

BILL McPHERSON. The L.A. district attorney. McPherson appears in **L.A. Confidential** and **Perfidia.**

SERGEANT TURNER "BUZZ" MEEKS, Los Angeles Police Department. Corrupt cop, on the prowl. Meeks appears in **The Big Nowhere, L.A. Confidential,** and **Perfidia.**

MAJOR RALPH D. MELNICK, Army SIS. The boss of the SIS contingent in Baja.

HAROLD JOHN MICIAK. Psychopathic flotsam. Miciak appears in **White Jazz.**

THE REVEREND MARTIN LUTHER MIMMS. Slumlord and race racketeer.

HECTOR OBREGON-HODAKA. Jazz aficionado and Fifth Columnist.

CAPTAIN WILLIAM H. PARKER, Los Angeles Police Department. The real-life Parker appears in **L.A. Confidential, White Jazz,** and **Perfidia.**

CAPTAIN JUAN PIMENTEL, Mexican State Police. Fifth Column mastermind.

DRAMATIS PERSONAE

RAY PINKER, Los Angeles Police Department. The real-life forensic chemist appears in **L.A. Confidential, White Jazz,** and **Perfidia.**

OFFICER WENDELL RICE, Los Angeles Police Department. Shitbird cop on the Alien Squad.

GEORGE LINCOLN ROCKWELL. The real-life race baiter and provocateur.

SERGEANT LEW SARNI, San Diego Police Department. Fat-slob Burglary cop.

EDMUND J. "ED THE FED" SATTERLEE. Dubious FBI agent. Satterlee appears in **The Big Nowhere** and **Perfidia.**

JOHNNY SHINURA. Jazz hound and broker of fetishistic curios.

"BLOW JOB" BEV SHOFTEL. Hooker and proprietress of a notorious mail drop. Miss Shoftel appears in **Blood's A Rover.**

ELIZABETH SHORT. The illegitimate daughter of Dudley Smith. Miss Short appears in **The Black Dahlia** and **Perfidia.**

FUJIO "THE WEREWOLF" SHUDO. Sex psycho and scapegoat for a quadruple homicide. Shudo appears in **Perfidia.**

SERGEANT DUDLEY SMITH, Los Angeles Police Department/Army SIS. Smith appears in **The Big Nowhere, L.A. Confidential, White Jazz,** and **Perfidia.**

JEAN STALEY. Carhop and Commie seductress.

BARBARA "BUTCH" STANWYCK. The real-life film actress.

ANNIE STAPLES. Call girl and shakedown artist.

RUTH SZIGETI. An exiled Hungarian musician.

ROBERT TAYLOR. The real-life film actor.

ELLEN TULLOCK. Deputy Karl Tullock's querulous widow.

KARL TULLOCK, Santa Barbara County Sheriff's Department. Thuggish cop, on the prowl.

CAPTAIN JOSÉ VASQUEZ-CRUZ, Mexican State Police. Politically ambiguous war profiteer.

JORGÉ VILLAREAL-CAIZ. Communist tool.

ORSON WELLES. The real-life film auteur.

AL WILHITE. MP lieutenant at the Manzanar internment camp.

ROBERT "BANZAI BOB" YOSHIDA. Part-time Buddhist priest and samurai-sword peddler.

A Note About the Author

James Ellroy was born in Los Angeles in 1948. He is widely considered to be the greatest living crime novelist and a major literary figure, genre designations aside. His L.A. Quartet and Underworld U.S.A. Trilogy novels have won numerous awards, were international best-sellers, and are now available in Everyman's Library editions. **This Storm** is the second volume of Mr. Ellroy's Second L.A. Quartet. The first volume, **Perfidia,** was much honored, and achieved international best-seller status. The Second L.A. Quartet places real-life and fictional characters from Mr. Ellroy's first two bodies of work in Los Angeles, during World War II, as significantly younger people. The design is monumentally ambitious.

Mr. Ellroy currently lives in Denver, Colorado.